Buffy

the Vampire Slayer™

OMNIBUS

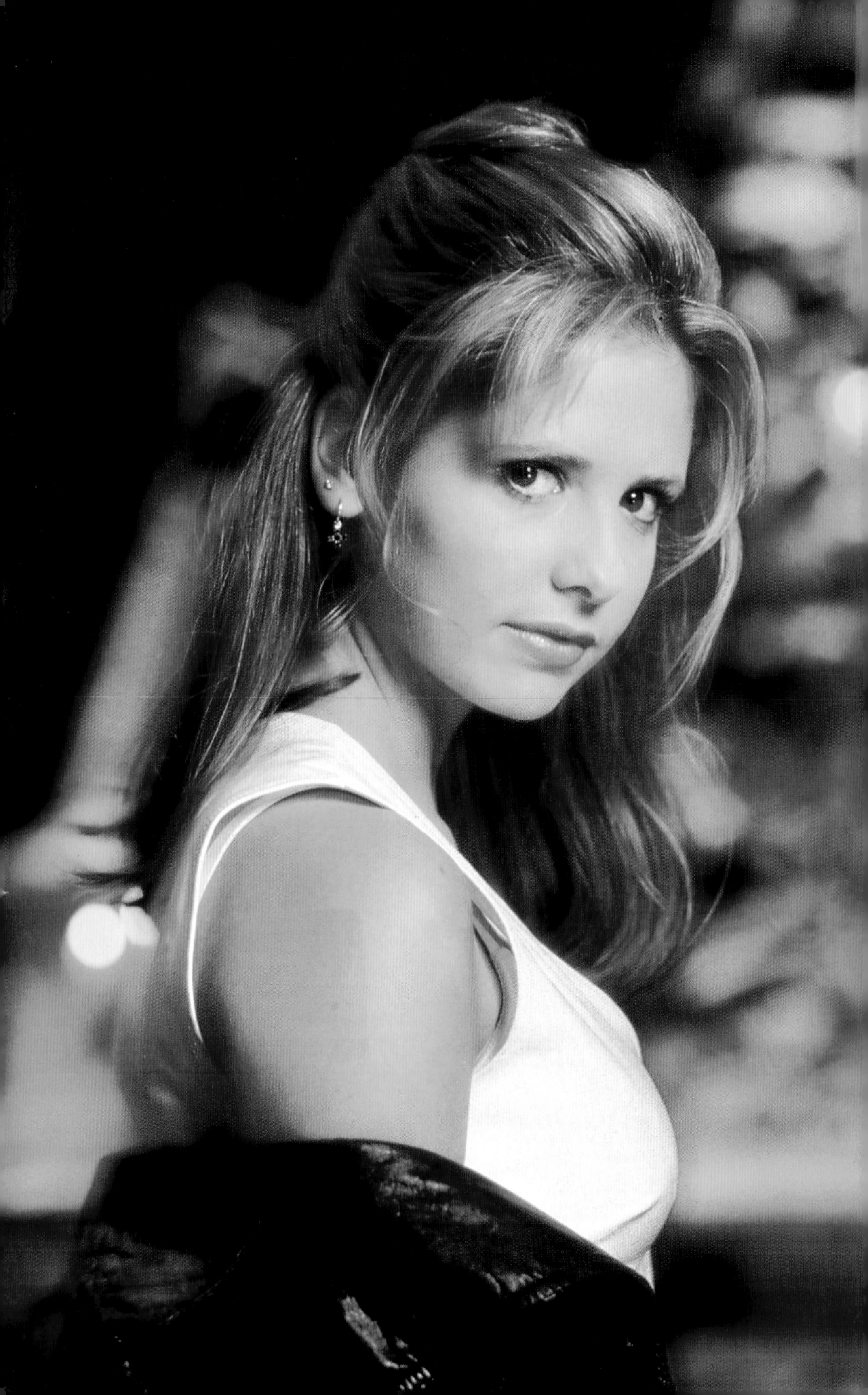

Buffy the Vampire Slayer™

OMNIBUS

VOLUME 1

JOSS WHEDON
JOE BENNETT
DAN BRERETON
CHRISTOPHER GOLDEN
HECTOR GOMEZ
PAUL LEE
SCOTT LOBDELL
FABIAN NICIEZA
ERIC POWELL
CLIFF RICHARDS

Based on the television series created by Joss Whedon.

These stories take place before Buffy the Vampire Slayer's *first season.*

DARK HORSE BOOKS®

Publisher MIKE RICHARDSON
Editor SCOTT ALLIE
Assistant Editor KATIE MOODY
Assistant Editors on Original Series ADAM GALLARDO, BEN ABERNATHY & MATT DRYER
Collection Designers LIA RIBACCHI & HEIDI FAINZA
Cover Illustration PAUL LEE & BRIAN HORTON, from *Buffy the Vampire Slayer* #51

Special thanks to Debbie Olshan at Twentieth Century Fox, David Campiti at Glass House Graphics, and Michael Boretz, Caroline Kallas, and George Snyder.

BUFFY THE VAMPIRE SLAYER™: OMNIBUS VOLUME ONE

This volume reprints
Buffy the Vampire Slayer: Spike & Dru #3, originally published December 2000;
Buffy the Vampire Slayer: The Origin #1-3, originally published January through March 1999; and
Buffy the Vampire Slayer #51-59, originally published November 2002 through July 2003;
all from Dark Horse Comics.

Published by Dark Horse Books
A division of Dark Horse Comics, Inc.
10956 SE Main Street
Milwaukie, OR 97222

darkhorse.com

To find a comics shop in your area, call the Comic Shop Locator Service toll-free at (888) 266-4226.

First edition: July 2007
ISBN-10: 1-59307-784-X
ISBN-13: 978-1-59307-784-6

10 9 8 7 6 5 4 3
Printed in China

INTRODUCTION

It's nearly ten years since I started editing *Buffy* comics, an assignment I accepted without having seen the show. The first story to see print was a short in the *Dark Horse Presents* 1998 annual, which hit the streets that August. Although we'd begun work on *Buffy* much earlier, the first issue of the monthly book came a month later; the series lasted over five years, slightly past the end of the television series.

I've edited every Buffy comic to see print, and as we begin Buffy's Season Eight—Joss Whedon's relaunch of the comic, continuing the official story of the character—the *Buffy Omnibus* series begins a complete chronological reprint of the earlier stories, which were done with little or no involvement from Joss.

The old *Buffy the Vampire Slayer* #1, and that story in *DHP*, are not in this volume. When we started work in early 1998, we set the first stories in the then-current Season Two. *These* stories, set at the very start of Buffy's career, came later. A few months into our initial run, Buffy novelist Chris Golden suggested adapting Joss's original film script—a *faithful* adaptation, as opposed to the tongue-in-cheek 1992 film. This led to *Buffy: The Origin*, reprinted here. Soon afterward, Golden proposed a Spike and Dru comic, co-written with James Marsters, who (of course) played Spike on the show. There were two follow-up comics written out of chronological order, so this volume reprints the *last* of them, set long before Spike and Dru had ever heard of Sunnydale.

Toward the end of the original series—of both the show and the comics—Scott Lobdell was writing the comic. He proposed a sort of *Buffy: Year One* story. For those of you who didn't grow up on comics, Year One is a term that, like so many things, we owe to Frank Miller. It's not so much an origin story as a story set at the beginning of a character's career—in this case, between the burning of Buffy's L.A. high school and her arrival in Sunnydale. Joss's plans for Season Seven, the final season of the show, were so tight it was impossible for us to set stories parallel to those episodes. So we looked to Buffy's past. There were the loose ends with Pike, her boyfriend from the film; a trip to Vegas; and her time in an institution, referred to in the 2002 TV episode "Normal Again." The Year One stories form the majority of this book, and will conclude in Volume Two.

One creative choice that I made here was to include Dawn. It met with some criticism from fans. Dawn wasn't *really* there during these events, but as the show had explored, and we explored in a series called *False Memories*, Buffy would *remember* her having been there. I always liked Dawn as a character, and so Lobdell and I—and Fabian Nicieza, who came on to co-write—decided to keep her. And thank god; otherwise we never could have done "Dawn and Hoopy the Bear."

The stories in this volume take place before Buffy Summers ever reached Sunnydale. They were written and drawn over a stretch of five years. During that time, my approach changed a lot. When I agreed to edit *Buffy*, I'd never seen the show, and neither I nor anyone else at Dark Horse had direct access to Joss. That changed, as I began working with the show's writers, and eventually Joss himself—leading to his own series, *Fray* (2001), and the projects he oversaw and co-wrote, *Tales of the Slayers* (2002) and *Tales of the Vampires* (2003). These won't be reprinted in the omnibus series, as I consider them more of a lead-in to Joss's reign on Season Eight than a part of my earlier series. But working with him on *Fray* and the *Tales of* books helped me bring the original series closer to his vision. This book is an interesting case study in that evolution. I hope you enjoy it.

Scott Allie

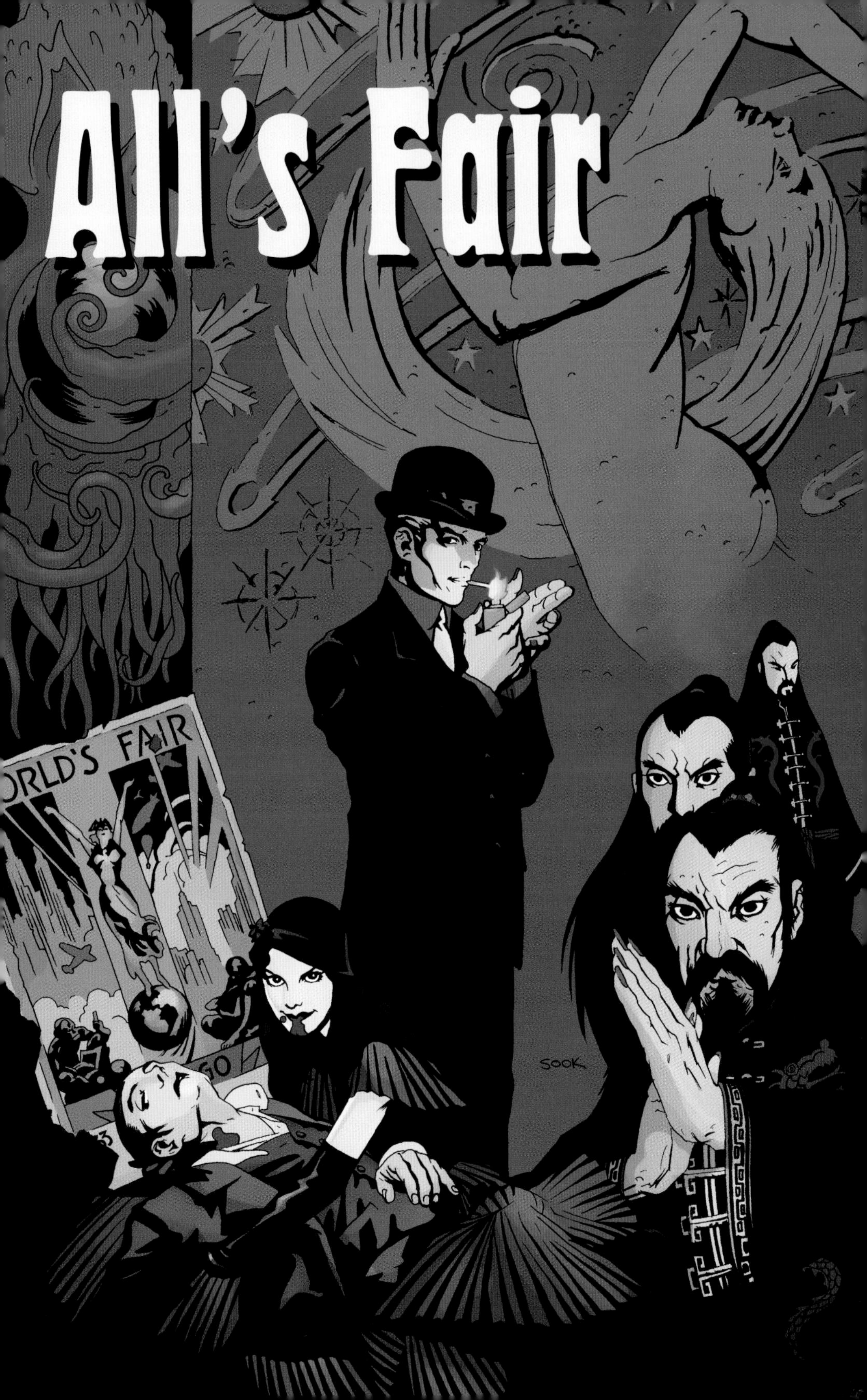
All's Fair
ORLD'S FAIR
SOOK

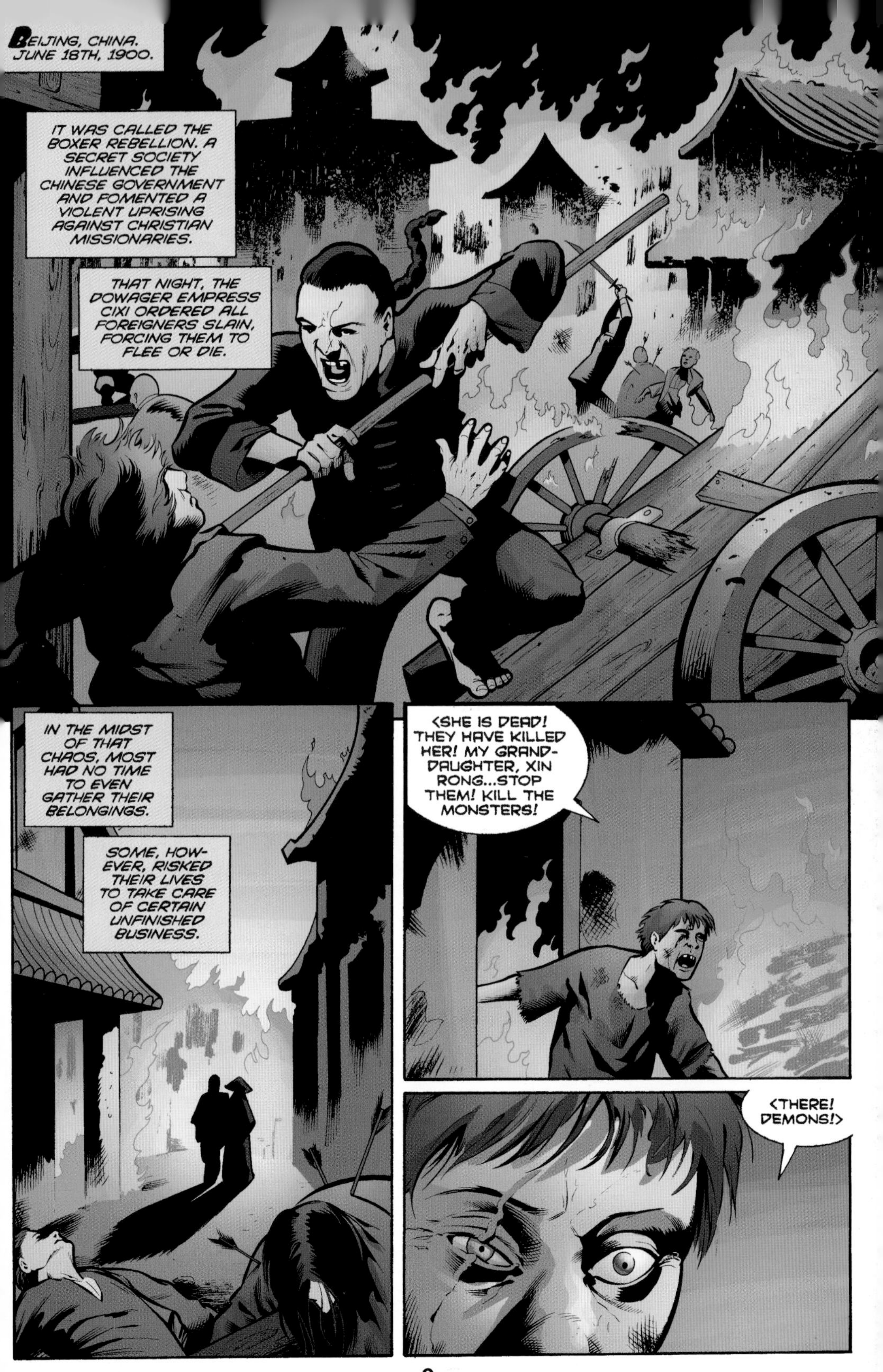
BEIJING, CHINA. JUNE 18TH, 1900.
IT WAS CALLED THE BOXER REBELLION. A SECRET SOCIETY INFLUENCED THE CHINESE GOVERNMENT AND FOMENTED A VIOLENT UPRISING AGAINST CHRISTIAN MISSIONARIES.
THAT NIGHT, THE DOWAGER EMPRESS CIXI ORDERED ALL FOREIGNERS SLAIN, FORCING THEM TO FLEE OR DIE.
IN THE MIDST OF THAT CHAOS, MOST HAD NO TIME TO EVEN GATHER THEIR BELONGINGS.
SOME, HOW-EVER, RISKED THEIR LIVES TO TAKE CARE OF CERTAIN UNFINISHED BUSINESS.
<SHE IS DEAD! THEY HAVE KILLED HER! MY GRAND-DAUGHTER, XIN RONG...STOP THEM! KILL THE MONSTERS!
<THERE! DEMONS!>

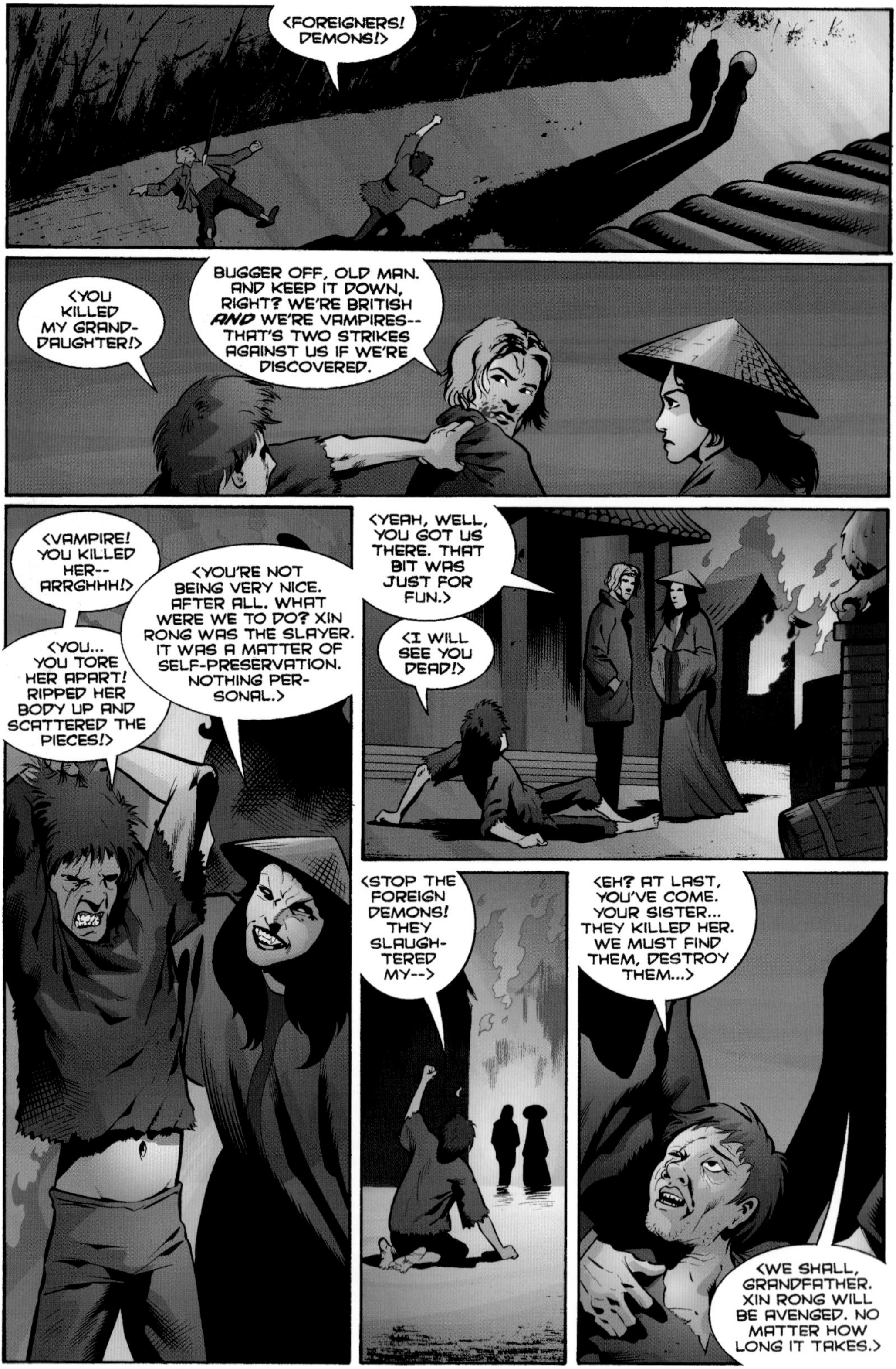

<FOREIGNERS! DEMONS!>
<YOU KILLED MY GRAND-DAUGHTER!>
BUGGER OFF, OLD MAN. AND KEEP IT DOWN, RIGHT? WE'RE BRITISH *AND* WE'RE VAMPIRES-- THAT'S TWO STRIKES AGAINST US IF WE'RE DISCOVERED.
<VAMPIRE! YOU KILLED HER-- ARRGHHH!>
<YOU... YOU TORE HER APART! RIPPED HER BODY UP AND SCATTERED THE PIECES!>
<YOU'RE NOT BEING VERY NICE. AFTER ALL. WHAT WERE WE TO DO? XIN RONG WAS THE SLAYER. IT WAS A MATTER OF SELF-PRESERVATION. NOTHING PER-SONAL.>
<YEAH, WELL, YOU GOT US THERE. THAT BIT WAS JUST FOR FUN.>
<I WILL SEE YOU DEAD!>
<STOP THE FOREIGN DEMONS! THEY SLAUGH-TERED MY-->
<EH? AT LAST, YOU'VE COME. YOUR SISTER... THEY KILLED HER. WE MUST FIND THEM, DESTROY THEM...>
<WE SHALL, GRANDFATHER. XIN RONG WILL BE AVENGED. NO MATTER HOW LONG IT TAKES.>

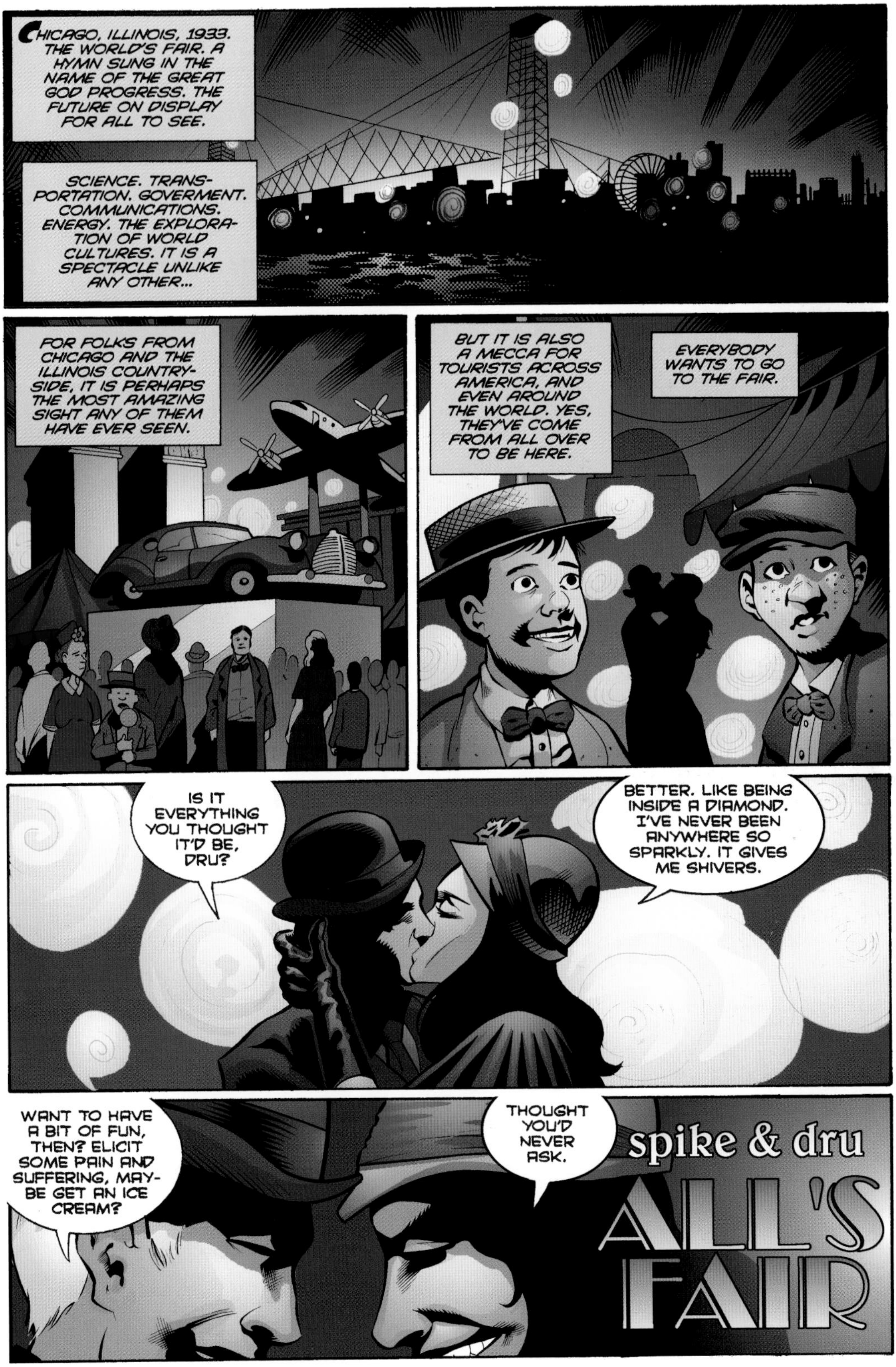
CHICAGO, ILLINOIS, 1933. THE WORLD'S FAIR. A HYMN SUNG IN THE NAME OF THE GREAT GOD PROGRESS. THE FUTURE ON DISPLAY FOR ALL TO SEE.
SCIENCE. TRANSPORTATION. GOVERMENT. COMMUNICATIONS. ENERGY. THE EXPLORATION OF WORLD CULTURES. IT IS A SPECTACLE UNLIKE ANY OTHER...
FOR FOLKS FROM CHICAGO AND THE ILLINOIS COUNTRYSIDE, IT IS PERHAPS THE MOST AMAZING SIGHT ANY OF THEM HAVE EVER SEEN.
BUT IT IS ALSO A MECCA FOR TOURISTS ACROSS AMERICA, AND EVEN AROUND THE WORLD. YES, THEY'VE COME FROM ALL OVER TO BE HERE.
EVERYBODY WANTS TO GO TO THE FAIR.
IS IT EVERYTHING YOU THOUGHT IT'D BE, DRU?
BETTER. LIKE BEING INSIDE A DIAMOND. I'VE NEVER BEEN ANYWHERE SO SPARKLY. IT GIVES ME SHIVERS.
WANT TO HAVE A BIT OF FUN, THEN? ELICIT SOME PAIN AND SUFFERING, MAYBE GET AN ICE CREAM?
THOUGHT YOU'D NEVER ASK.
spike & dru
ALL'S FAIR

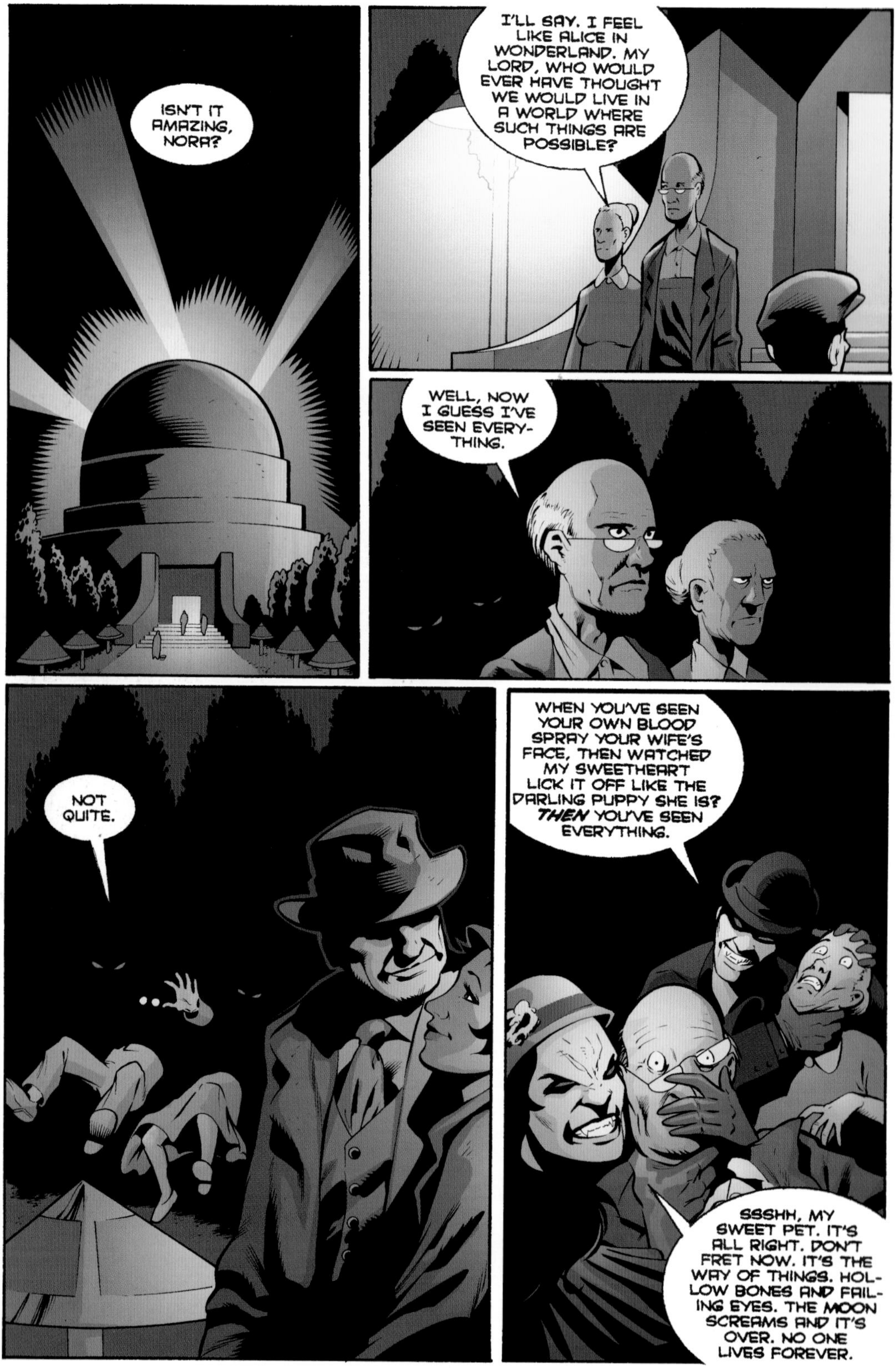
ISN'T IT AMAZING, NORA?
I'LL SAY. I FEEL LIKE ALICE IN WONDERLAND. MY LORD, WHO WOULD EVER HAVE THOUGHT WE WOULD LIVE IN A WORLD WHERE SUCH THINGS ARE POSSIBLE?
WELL, NOW I GUESS I'VE SEEN EVERY-THING.
NOT QUITE.
WHEN YOU'VE SEEN YOUR OWN BLOOD SPRAY YOUR WIFE'S FACE, THEN WATCHED MY SWEETHEART LICK IT OFF LIKE THE DARLING PUPPY SHE IS? *THEN* YOU'VE SEEN EVERYTHING.
SSSHH, MY SWEET PET. IT'S ALL RIGHT. DON'T FRET NOW. IT'S THE WAY OF THINGS. HOL-LOW BONES AND FAIL-ING EYES. THE MOON SCREAMS AND IT'S OVER. NO ONE LIVES FOREVER.

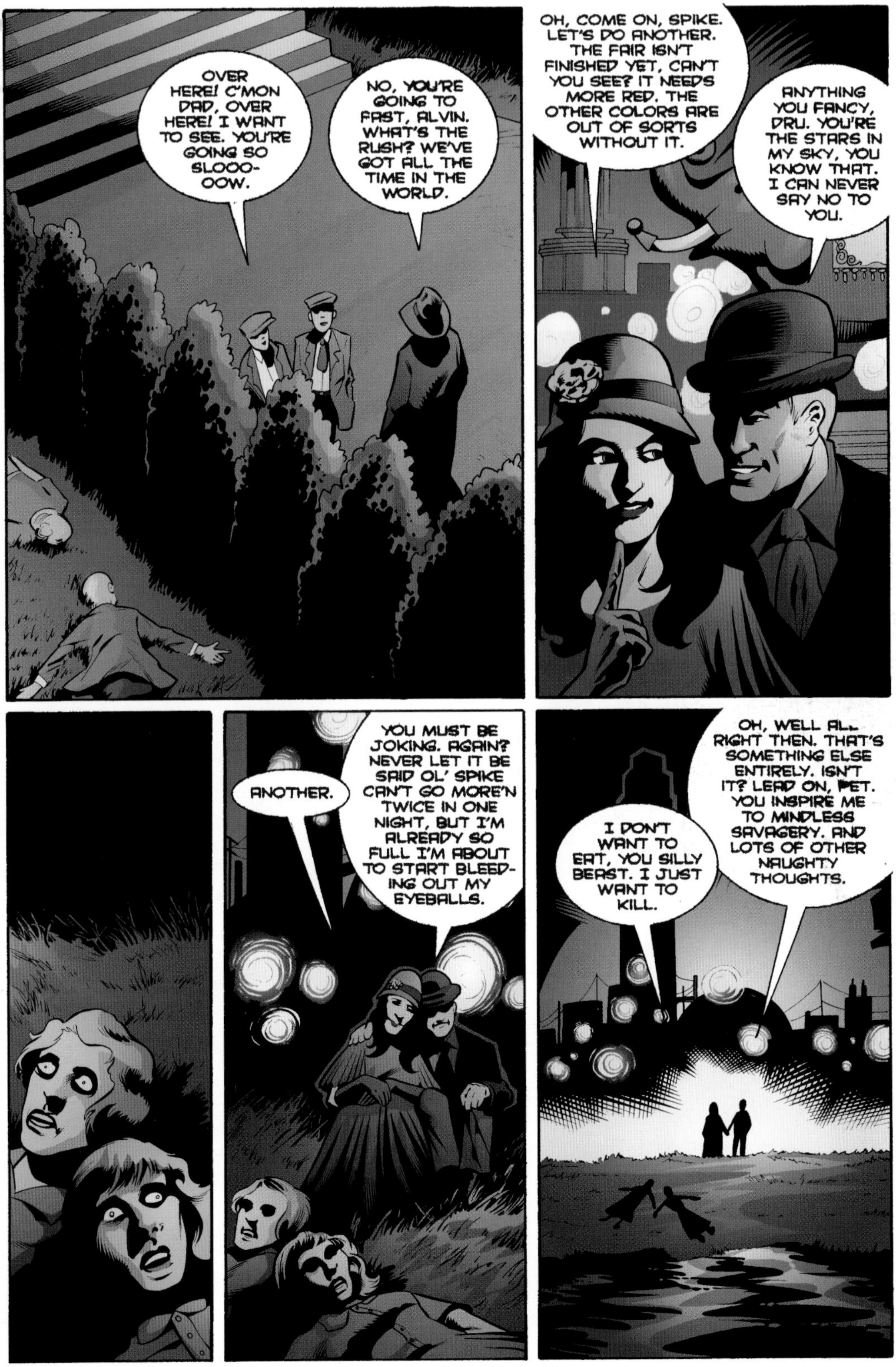
OVER HERE! C'MON DAD, OVER HERE! I WANT TO SEE. YOU'RE GOING SO SLOOO-OOW.
NO, YOU'RE GOING TO FAST, ALVIN. WHAT'S THE RUSH? WE'VE GOT ALL THE TIME IN THE WORLD.
OH, COME ON, SPIKE. LET'S DO ANOTHER. THE FAIR ISN'T FINISHED YET, CAN'T YOU SEE? IT NEEDS MORE RED. THE OTHER COLORS ARE OUT OF SORTS WITHOUT IT.
ANYTHING YOU FANCY, DRU. YOU'RE THE STARS IN MY SKY, YOU KNOW THAT. I CAN NEVER SAY NO TO YOU.
ANOTHER.
YOU MUST BE JOKING. AGAIN? NEVER LET IT BE SAID OL' SPIKE CAN'T GO MORE'N TWICE IN ONE NIGHT, BUT I'M ALREADY SO FULL I'M ABOUT TO START BLEED-ING OUT MY EYEBALLS.
I DON'T WANT TO EAT, YOU SILLY BEAST. I JUST WANT TO KILL.
OH, WELL ALL RIGHT THEN. THAT'S SOMETHING ELSE ENTIRELY. ISN'T IT? LEAD ON, PET. YOU INSPIRE ME TO MINDLESS SAVAGERY. AND LOTS OF OTHER NAUGHTY THOUGHTS.

THIS **IS** RIDICULOUS, SAM. WE CAN'T JUST PRETEND IT DIDN'T HAPPEN. PEOPLE HAVE A RIGHT TO KNOW.

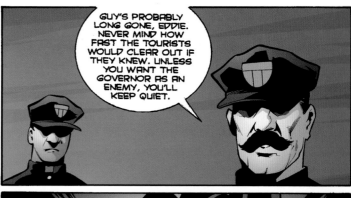

GUY'S PROBABLY LONG GONE, EDDIE. NEVER MIND HOW FAST THE TOURISTS WOULD CLEAR OUT IF THEY KNEW. UNLESS YOU WANT THE GOVERNOR AS AN ENEMY, YOU'LL KEEP QUIET.

LADIES AND GENTLEMEN, I PRESENT TO YOU AN INVENTION THAT WILL CHANGE THE WORLD.

IMAGINE AN ENDLESS POWER SOURCE. ODORLESS, SMOKE- LESS, SIMPLE TO USE, AND BEST OF ALL, FREE!

USING THE MACHINE YOU SEE BEFORE YOU, I HAVE MANAGED TO TAP INTO AN ALTERNATE DIMEN- SION, A PARALLEL WORLD BEYOND OUR UNIVERSE WHOSE VERY SUBSTANCE IS RAW ENERGY.

USING THIS MACHINE, I CAN CONVERT THAT ENERGY TO POWER. IMAGINE, IF YOU WILL, LIGHT BULBS THAT NEVER BURN OUT, AN AUTO- MOBILE THAT NEVER NEEDS GASOLINE.

IMAGINE THE WORLD'S INDUSTRIES RUN ON SAFE, CLEAN FUEL THAT COSTS NOTHING! IMAGINE HOW QUICKLY TECH- NOLOGY WILL PROGRESS THEN!

14

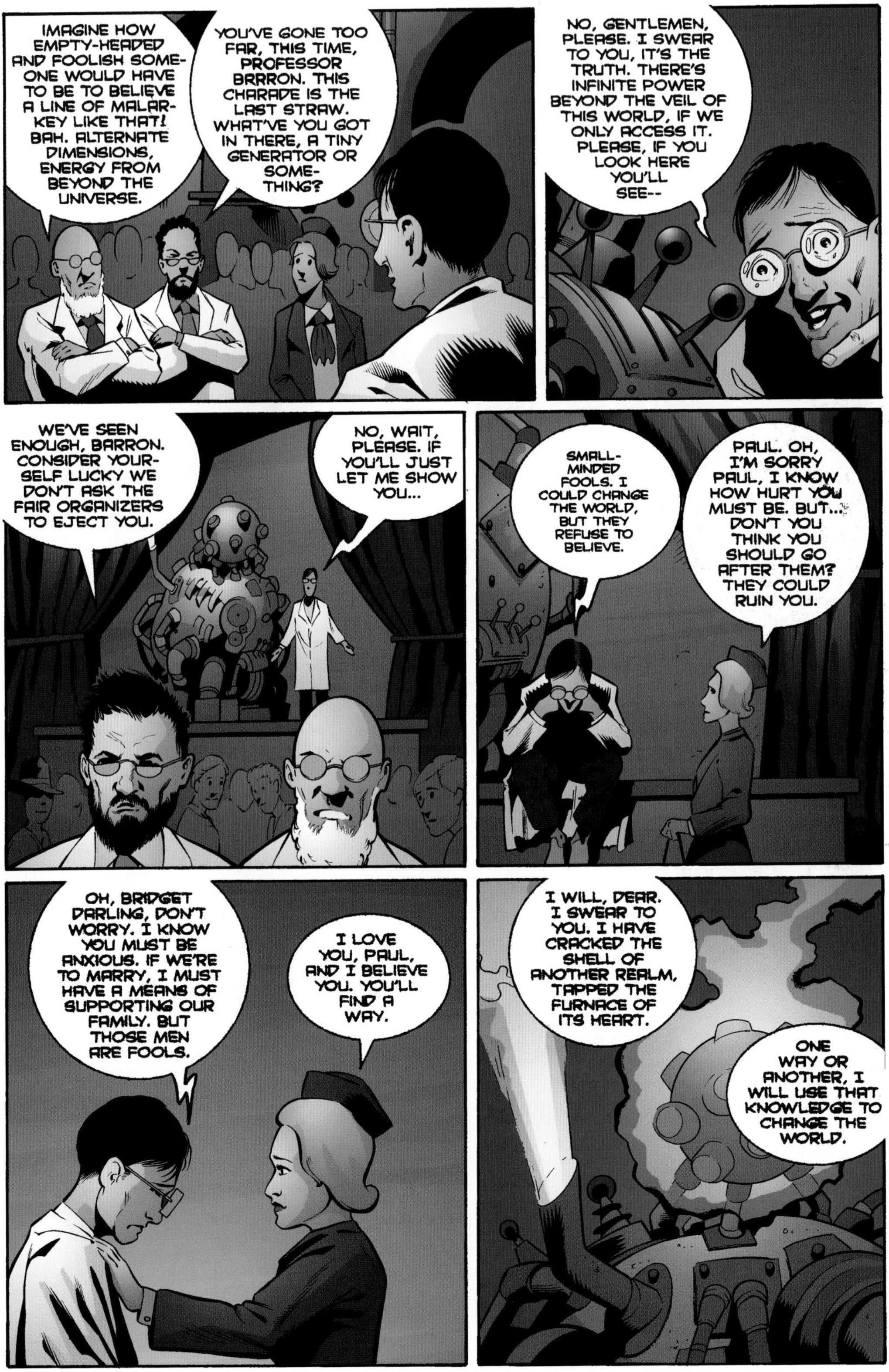
IMAGINE HOW EMPTY-HEADED AND FOOLISH SOME-ONE WOULD HAVE TO BE TO BELIEVE A LINE OF MALAR-KEY LIKE THAT! BAH. ALTERNATE DIMENSIONS, ENERGY FROM BEYOND THE UNIVERSE.
YOU'VE GONE TOO FAR, THIS TIME, PROFESSOR BARRON. THIS CHARADE IS THE LAST STRAW. WHAT'VE YOU GOT IN THERE, A TINY GENERATOR OR SOME-THING?
NO, GENTLEMEN, PLEASE. I SWEAR TO YOU, IT'S THE TRUTH. THERE'S INFINITE POWER BEYOND THE VEIL OF THIS WORLD, IF WE ONLY ACCESS IT. PLEASE, IF YOU LOOK HERE YOU'LL SEE--
WE'VE SEEN ENOUGH, BARRON. CONSIDER YOUR-SELF LUCKY WE DON'T ASK THE FAIR ORGANIZERS TO EJECT YOU.
NO, WAIT, PLEASE. IF YOU'LL JUST LET ME SHOW YOU...
SMALL-MINDED FOOLS. I COULD CHANGE THE WORLD, BUT THEY REFUSE TO BELIEVE.
PAUL. OH, I'M SORRY PAUL, I KNOW HOW HURT YOU MUST BE. BUT... DON'T YOU THINK YOU SHOULD GO AFTER THEM? THEY COULD RUIN YOU.
OH, BRIDGET DARLING, DON'T WORRY. I KNOW YOU MUST BE ANXIOUS. IF WE'RE TO MARRY, I MUST HAVE A MEANS OF SUPPORTING OUR FAMILY. BUT THOSE MEN ARE FOOLS.
I LOVE YOU, PAUL, AND I BELIEVE YOU. YOU'LL FIND A WAY.
I WILL, DEAR. I SWEAR TO YOU. I HAVE CRACKED THE SHELL OF ANOTHER REALM, TAPPED THE FURNACE OF ITS HEART.
ONE WAY OR ANOTHER, I WILL USE THAT KNOWLEDGE TO CHANGE THE WORLD.

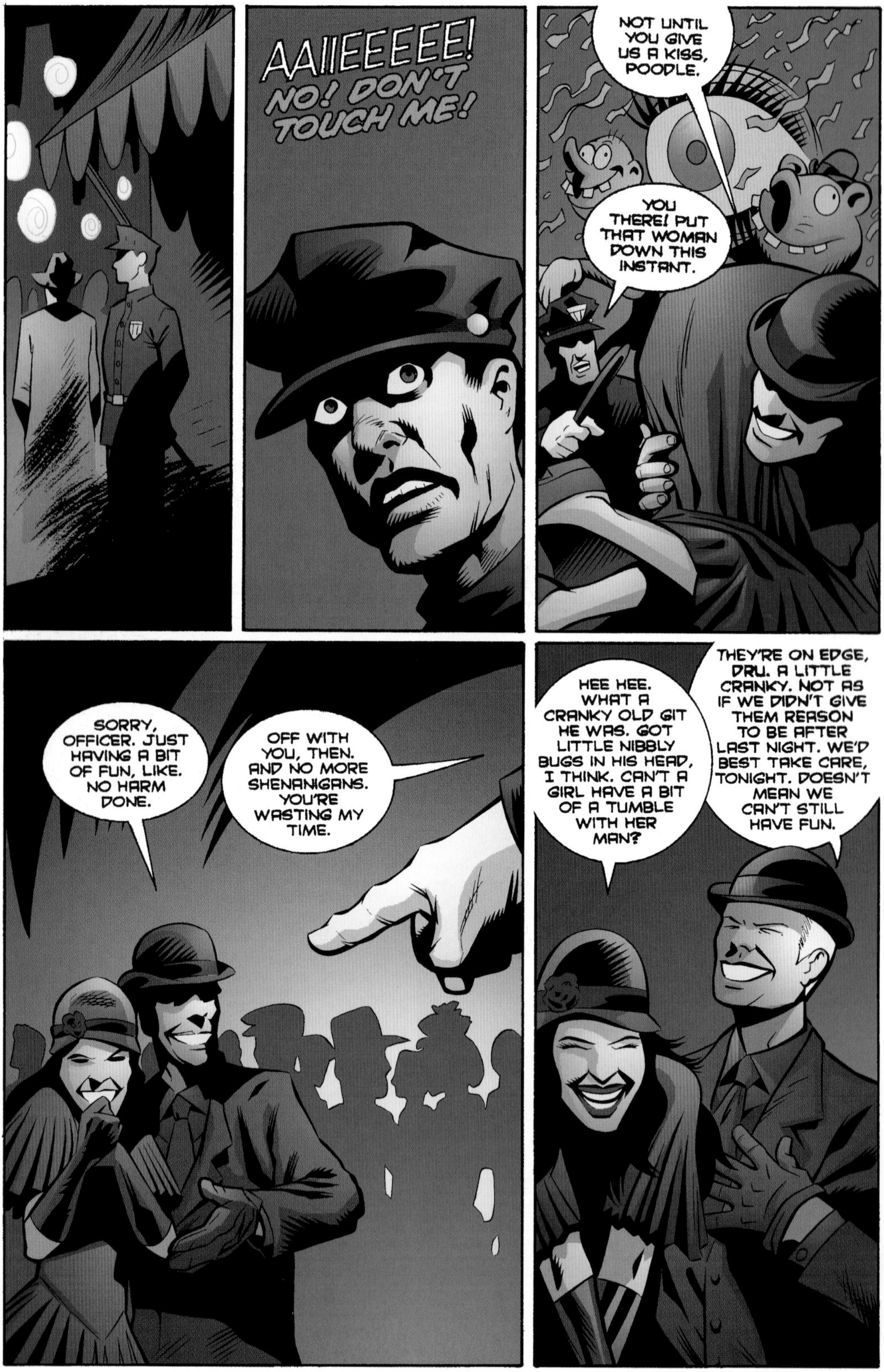
AAIIEEEEEE!
NO! DON'T TOUCH ME!
NOT UNTIL YOU GIVE US A KISS, POODLE.
YOU THERE! PUT THAT WOMAN DOWN THIS INSTANT.
SORRY, OFFICER. JUST HAVING A BIT OF FUN, LIKE. NO HARM DONE.
OFF WITH YOU, THEN. AND NO MORE SHENANIGANS. YOU'RE WASTING MY TIME.
HEE HEE. WHAT A CRANKY OLD GIT HE WAS. GOT LITTLE NIBBLY BUGS IN HIS HEAD, I THINK. CAN'T A GIRL HAVE A BIT OF A TUMBLE WITH HER MAN?
THEY'RE ON EDGE, DRU. A LITTLE CRANKY. NOT AS IF WE DIDN'T GIVE THEM REASON TO BE AFTER LAST NIGHT. WE'D BEST TAKE CARE, TONIGHT. DOESN'T MEAN WE CAN'T STILL HAVE FUN.

HERE WE ARE, THEN. ALL THESE EXHIBITS AROUND, WE MIGHT AS WELL DO A BIT OF EXPLORIN', MAYBE LEARN SOMETHING, EH? THE FAIR AIN'T ALL BLOOD AND POPCORN, Y'KNOW.

OOH, I LIKE IT HERE. WE FINALLY FOUND SOMETHING OLDER THAN WE ARE.

Exact Dinosaur Replica

MMMMMM.

DRU, WHAT IS IT? YOU ALL RIGHT, PET?

OH, NO NOT AT ALL. I CAN FEEL THEM ALL 'ROUND US, WATCHING. HATE SO UGLY AND DARK. TAKE ME AWAY.

ALL RIGHT, DRU. BUT WHERE? YOU HAD A LITTLE VISION, OR JUST SENSED SOMETHING?

I CAN FEEL THEM, SPIKE. I'M ALL SHUDDERY, DIRTY WITH THEIR EYES. TAKE ME OUT.

WE'RE GOING, POODLE. I DON'T SEE A DAMN THING, BUT WE'RE GOING.

MARVEL, LADIES AND GENTLEMEN, AT A MIRACLE OF THE FUTURE.

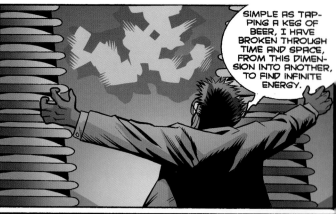

SIMPLE AS TAPPING A KEG OF BEER, I HAVE BROKEN THROUGH TIME AND SPACE, FROM THIS DIMENSION INTO ANOTHER, TO FIND INFINITE ENERGY.

EVEN A CASUAL VIEWER, ONE UNSCHOOLED IN THE SCIENCES, CAN WITNESS UP CLOSE THE ENERGY PRODUCED BY MY GENERATOR.

WITNESS LADIES AND GENTLEMEN, AS THE POWER SURGES, A CHARGE PRODUCED NOT BY ANY MECHANICAL MEANS...

...NOR ELECTRICITY-- QUITE SIMPLY, RAW POWER COLLECTED IN A BATTERY WITHIN THE GENERATOR, A CONSTANT FLOW PROVIDING CONSTANT POWER.

YEAH? IF THIS THING'S FOR REAL, THEN WHAT THE HELL ARE YOU DOING HERE WHEN YA OUGTTA BE A MILLIONAIRE?

WHAT I AM DOING HERE, AS ANY IDIOT CAN SEE, IS TRYING TO GIVE THE WORLD THE GREATEST SCIENTIFIC REVELATION IN HISTORY. BUT NARROW-MINDED FOOLS ARE ALL I SEE.

RATHER THAN BEING REVERED FOR MY ACHIEVEMENT, I AM FORCED TO DEAL WITH NEANDERTHALS SUCH AS YOURSELF WHO DON'T DESERVE TO REAP THE BENEFITS OF MY INVENTION!

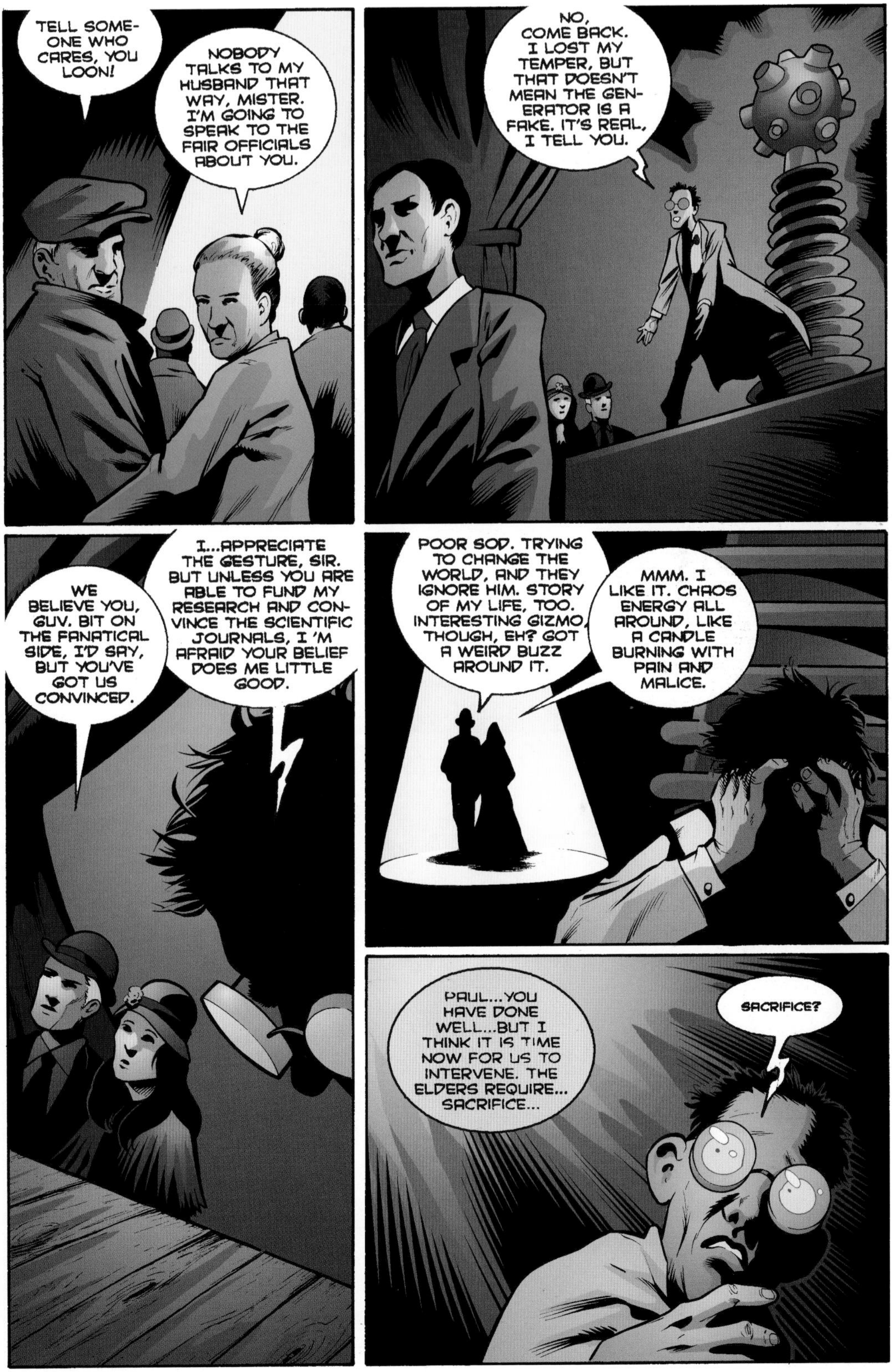
TELL SOME-ONE WHO CARES, YOU LOON!
NOBODY TALKS TO MY HUSBAND THAT WAY, MISTER. I'M GOING TO SPEAK TO THE FAIR OFFICIALS ABOUT YOU.
NO, COME BACK. I LOST MY TEMPER, BUT THAT DOESN'T MEAN THE GEN-ERATOR IS A FAKE. IT'S REAL, I TELL YOU.
WE BELIEVE YOU, GUV. BIT ON THE FANATICAL SIDE, I'D SAY, BUT YOU'VE GOT US CONVINCED.
I...APPRECIATE THE GESTURE, SIR. BUT UNLESS YOU ARE ABLE TO FUND MY RESEARCH AND CON-VINCE THE SCIENTIFIC JOURNALS, I'M AFRAID YOUR BELIEF DOES ME LITTLE GOOD.
POOR SOD. TRYING TO CHANGE THE WORLD, AND THEY IGNORE HIM. STORY OF MY LIFE, TOO. INTERESTING GIZMO, THOUGH, EH? GOT A WEIRD BUZZ AROUND IT.
MMM. I LIKE IT. CHAOS ENERGY ALL AROUND, LIKE A CANDLE BURNING WITH PAIN AND MALICE.
PAUL...YOU HAVE DONE WELL...BUT I THINK IT IS TIME NOW FOR US TO INTERVENE. THE ELDERS REQUIRE... SACRIFICE...
SACRIFICE?

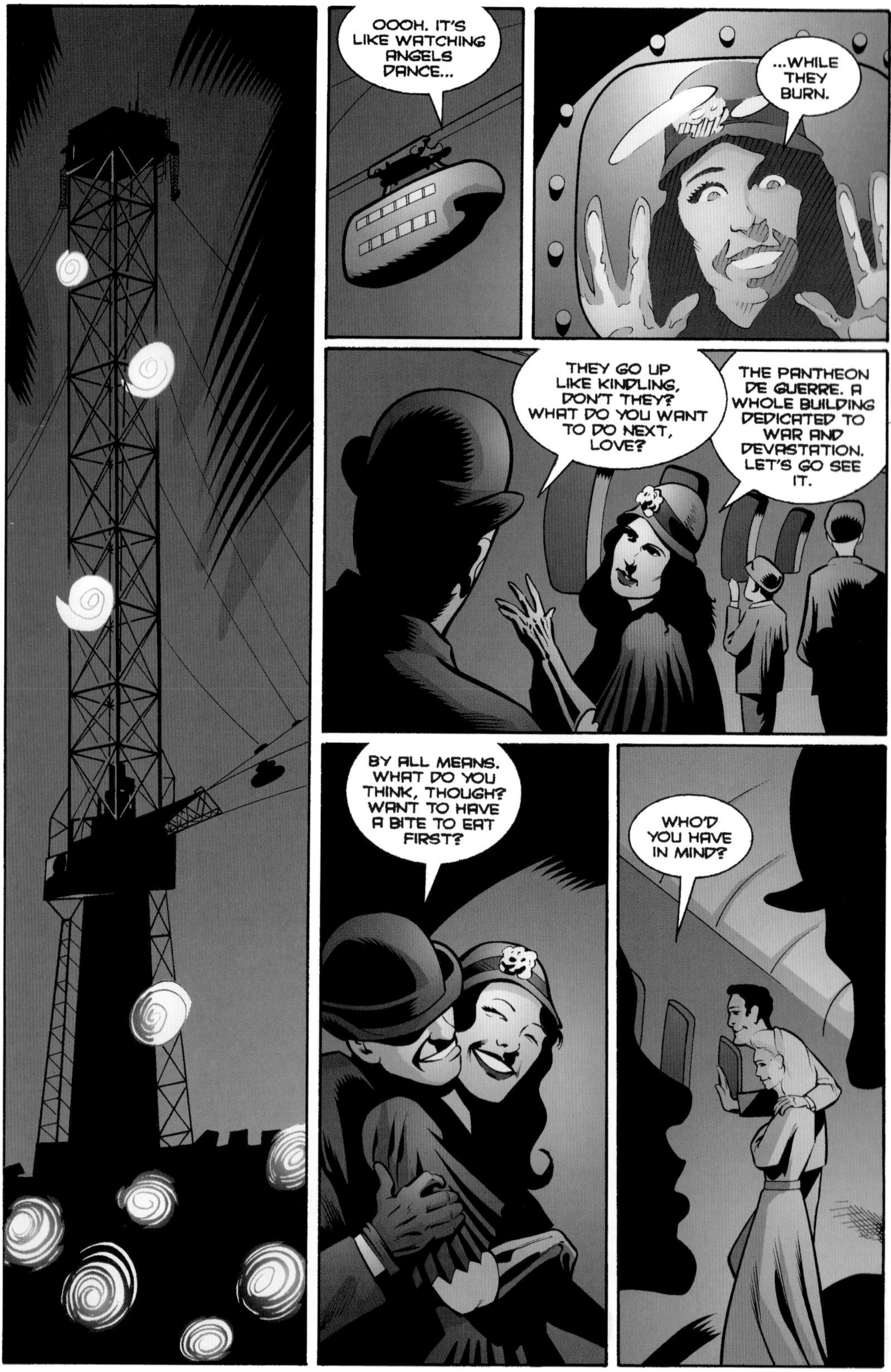
OOOH. IT'S LIKE WATCHING ANGELS DANCE...
...WHILE THEY BURN.
THEY GO UP LIKE KINDLING, DON'T THEY? WHAT DO YOU WANT TO DO NEXT, LOVE?
THE PANTHEON DE GUERRE. A WHOLE BUILDING DEDICATED TO WAR AND DEVASTATION. LET'S GO SEE IT.
BY ALL MEANS. WHAT DO YOU THINK, THOUGH? WANT TO HAVE A BITE TO EAT FIRST?
WHO'D YOU HAVE IN MIND?

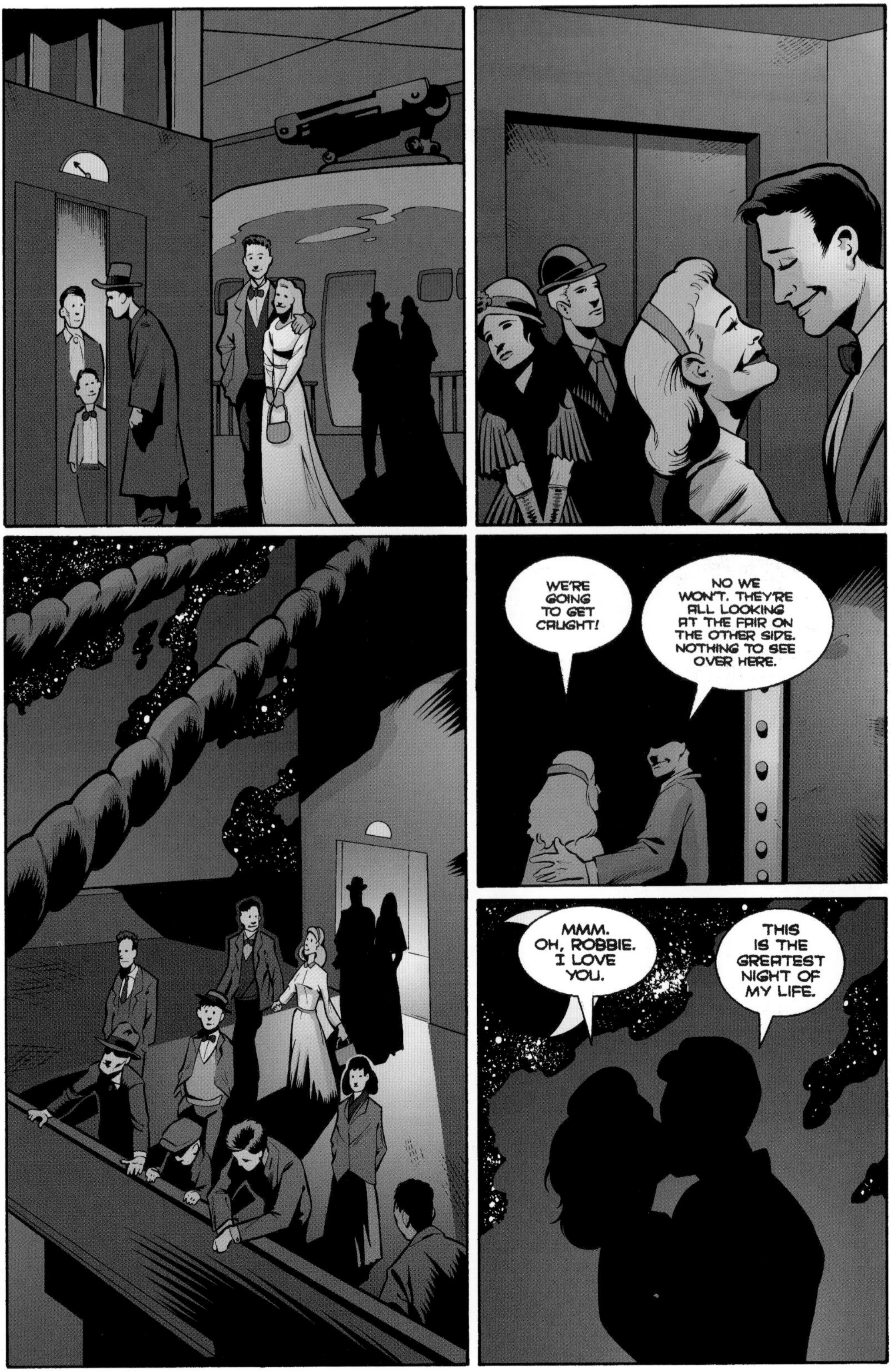
WE'RE GOING TO GET CAUGHT!
NO WE WON'T. THEY'RE ALL LOOKING AT THE FAIR ON THE OTHER SIDE. NOTHING TO SEE OVER HERE.
MMM. OH, ROBBIE. I LOVE YOU.
THIS IS THE GREATEST NIGHT OF MY LIFE.

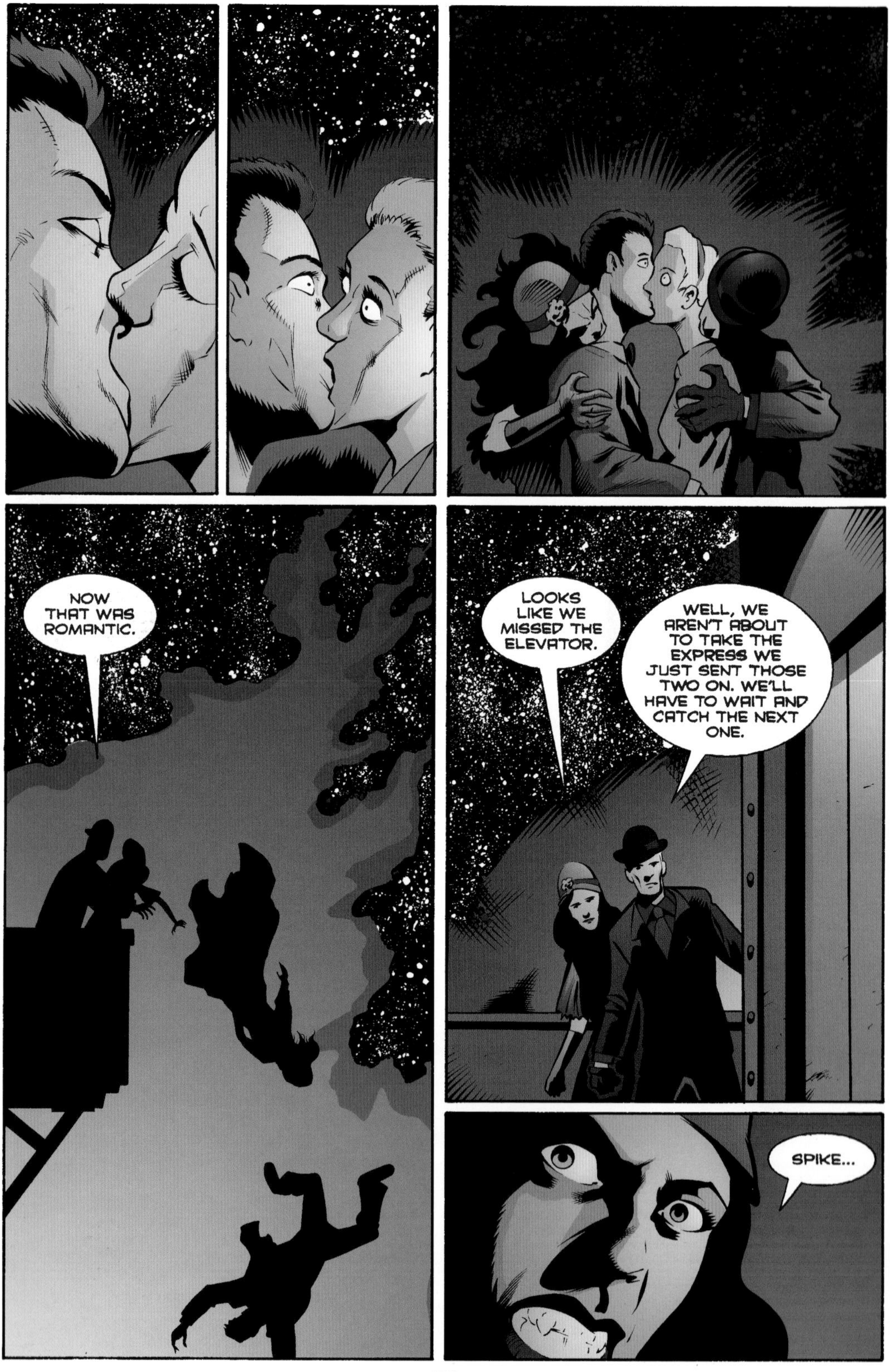
NOW THAT WAS ROMANTIC.
LOOKS LIKE WE MISSED THE ELEVATOR.
WELL, WE AREN'T ABOUT TO TAKE THE EXPRESS WE JUST SENT THOSE TWO ON. WE'LL HAVE TO WAIT AND CATCH THE NEXT ONE.
SPIKE...

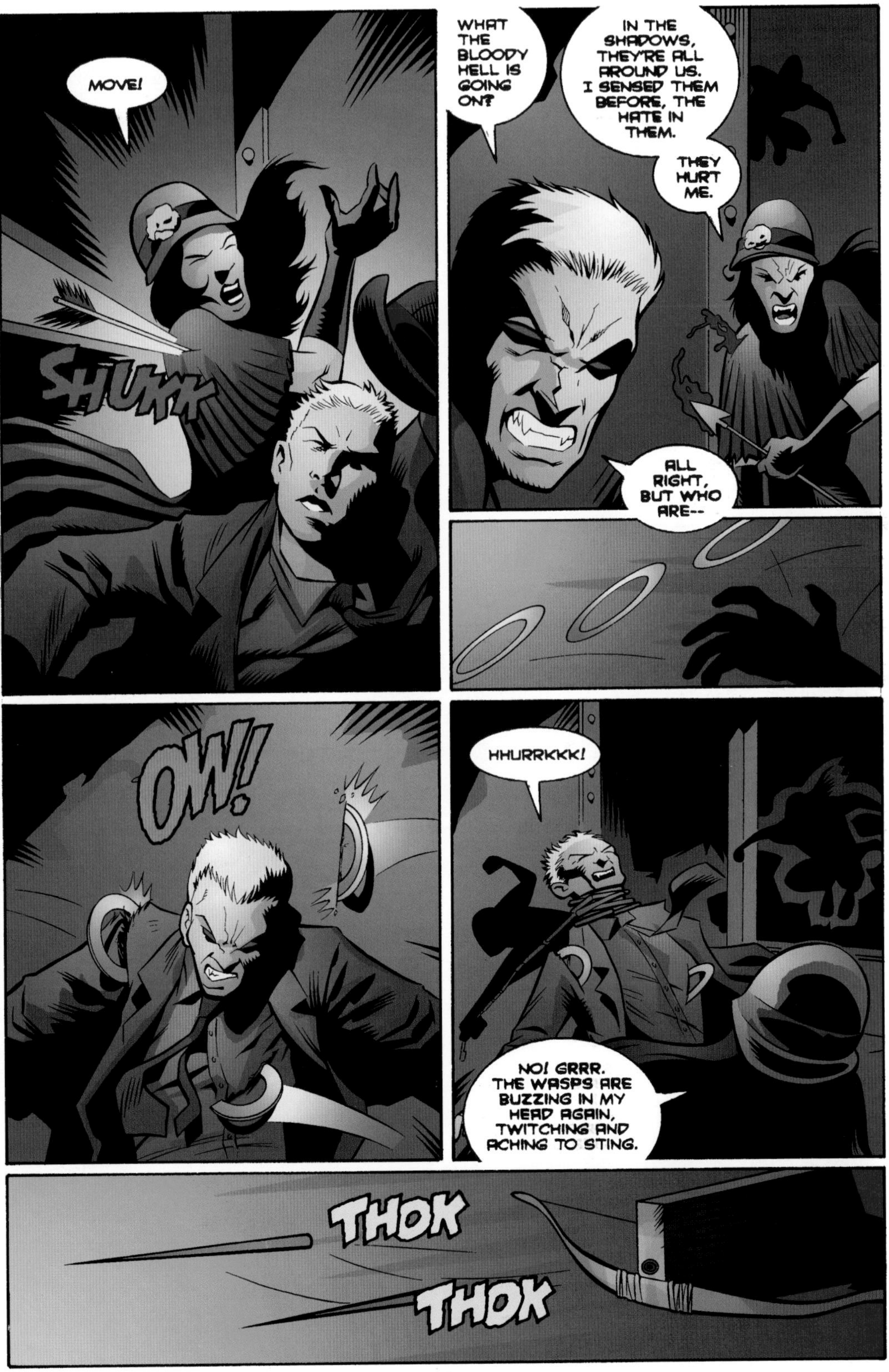
MOVE!
SHUKK
WHAT THE BLOODY HELL IS GOING ON?
IN THE SHADOWS, THEY'RE ALL AROUND US. I SENSED THEM BEFORE, THE HATE IN THEM.
THEY HURT ME.
ALL RIGHT, BUT WHO ARE--
OW!
HHURRKKK!
NO! GRRR. THE WASPS ARE BUZZING IN MY HEAD AGAIN, TWITCHING AND ACHING TO STING.
THOK
THOK

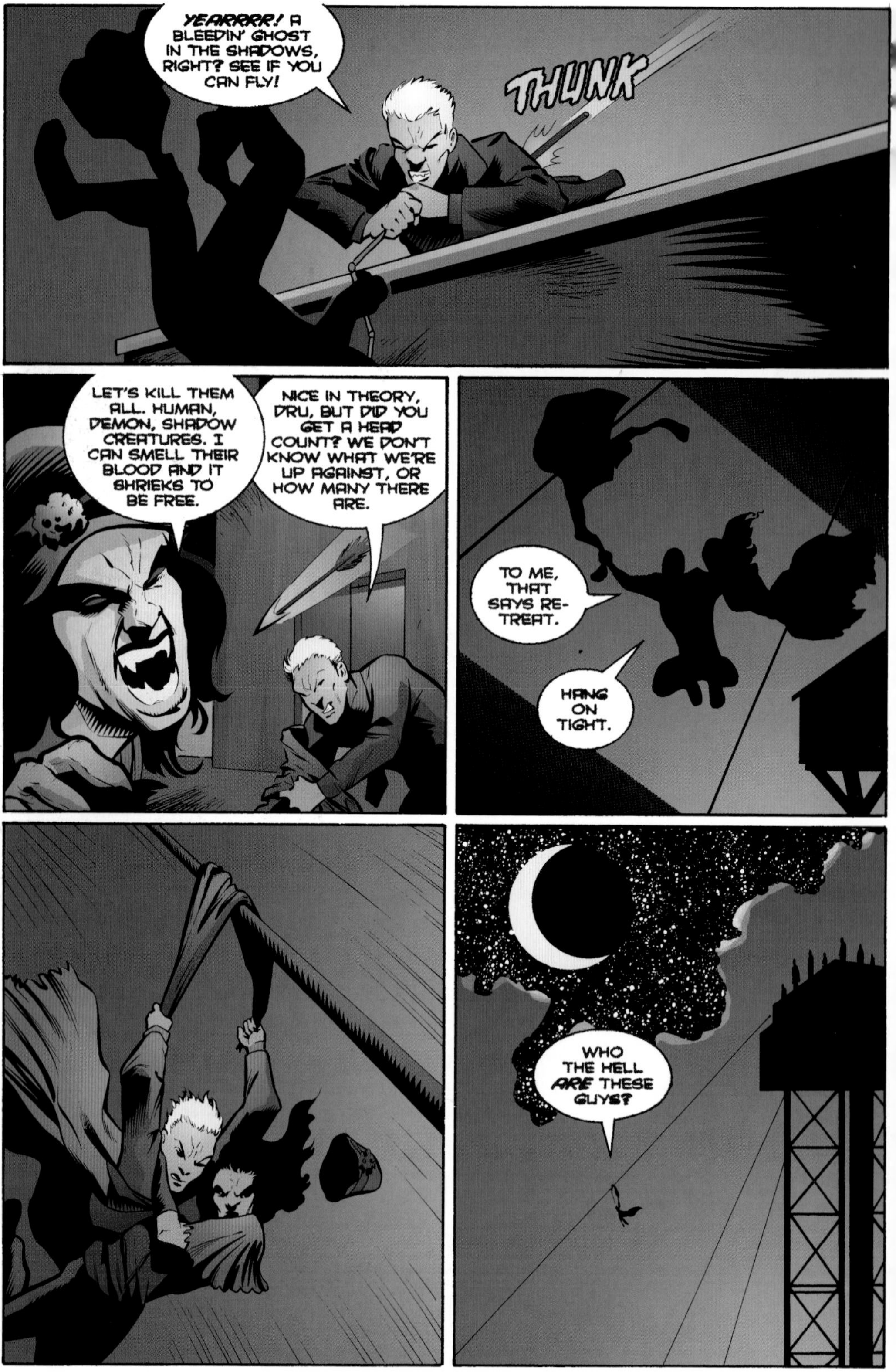
YEARRRR! A BLEEDIN' GHOST IN THE SHADOWS, RIGHT? SEE IF YOU CAN FLY!
THUNK
LET'S KILL THEM ALL. HUMAN, DEMON, SHADOW CREATURES. I CAN SMELL THEIR BLOOD AND IT SHRIEKS TO BE FREE.
NICE IN THEORY, DRU, BUT DID YOU GET A HEAD COUNT? WE DON'T KNOW WHAT WE'RE UP AGAINST, OR HOW MANY THERE ARE.
TO ME, THAT SAYS RE-TREAT.
HANG ON TIGHT.
WHO THE HELL ARE THESE GUYS?

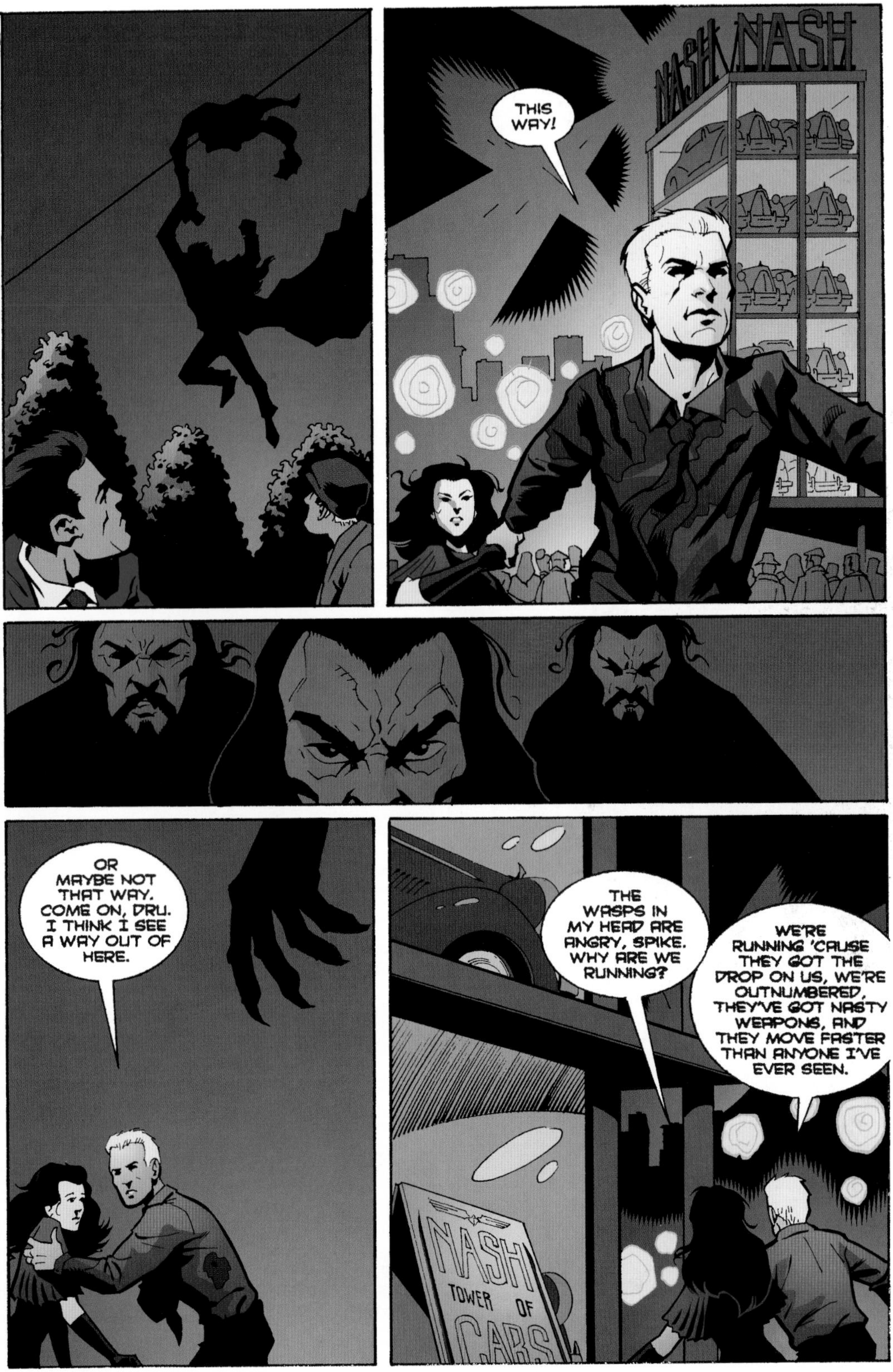
THIS WAY!
NASH
NASH
OR MAYBE NOT THAT WAY. COME ON, DRU. I THINK I SEE A WAY OUT OF HERE.
THE WASPS IN MY HEAD ARE ANGRY, SPIKE. WHY ARE WE RUNNING?
WE'RE RUNNING 'CAUSE THEY GOT THE DROP ON US, WE'RE OUTNUMBERED, THEY'VE GOT NASTY WEAPONS, AND THEY MOVE FASTER THAN ANYONE I'VE EVER SEEN.
NASH TOWER OF CARS

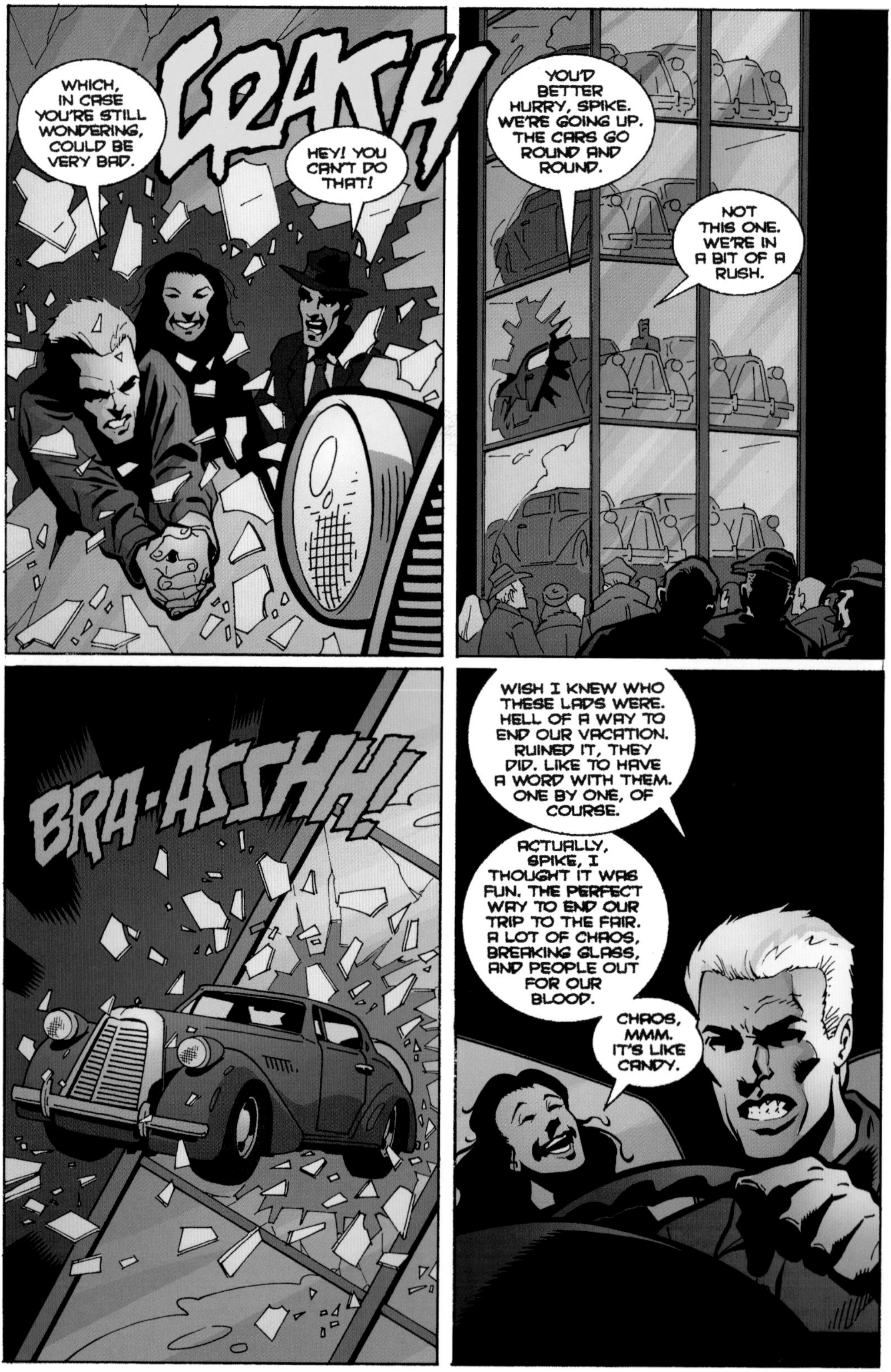
CRASH
WHICH, IN CASE YOU'RE STILL WONDERING, COULD BE VERY BAD.
HEY! YOU CAN'T DO THAT!
YOU'D BETTER HURRY, SPIKE. WE'RE GOING UP. THE CARS GO ROUND AND ROUND.
NOT THIS ONE. WE'RE IN A BIT OF A RUSH.
BRA-ASSH!
WISH I KNEW WHO THESE LADS WERE. HELL OF A WAY TO END OUR VACATION. RUINED IT, THEY DID. LIKE TO HAVE A WORD WITH THEM. ONE BY ONE, OF COURSE.
ACTUALLY, SPIKE, I THOUGHT IT WAS FUN. THE PERFECT WAY TO END OUR TRIP TO THE FAIR. A LOT OF CHAOS, BREAKING GLASS, AND PEOPLE OUT FOR OUR BLOOD.
CHAOS, MMM. IT'S LIKE CANDY.

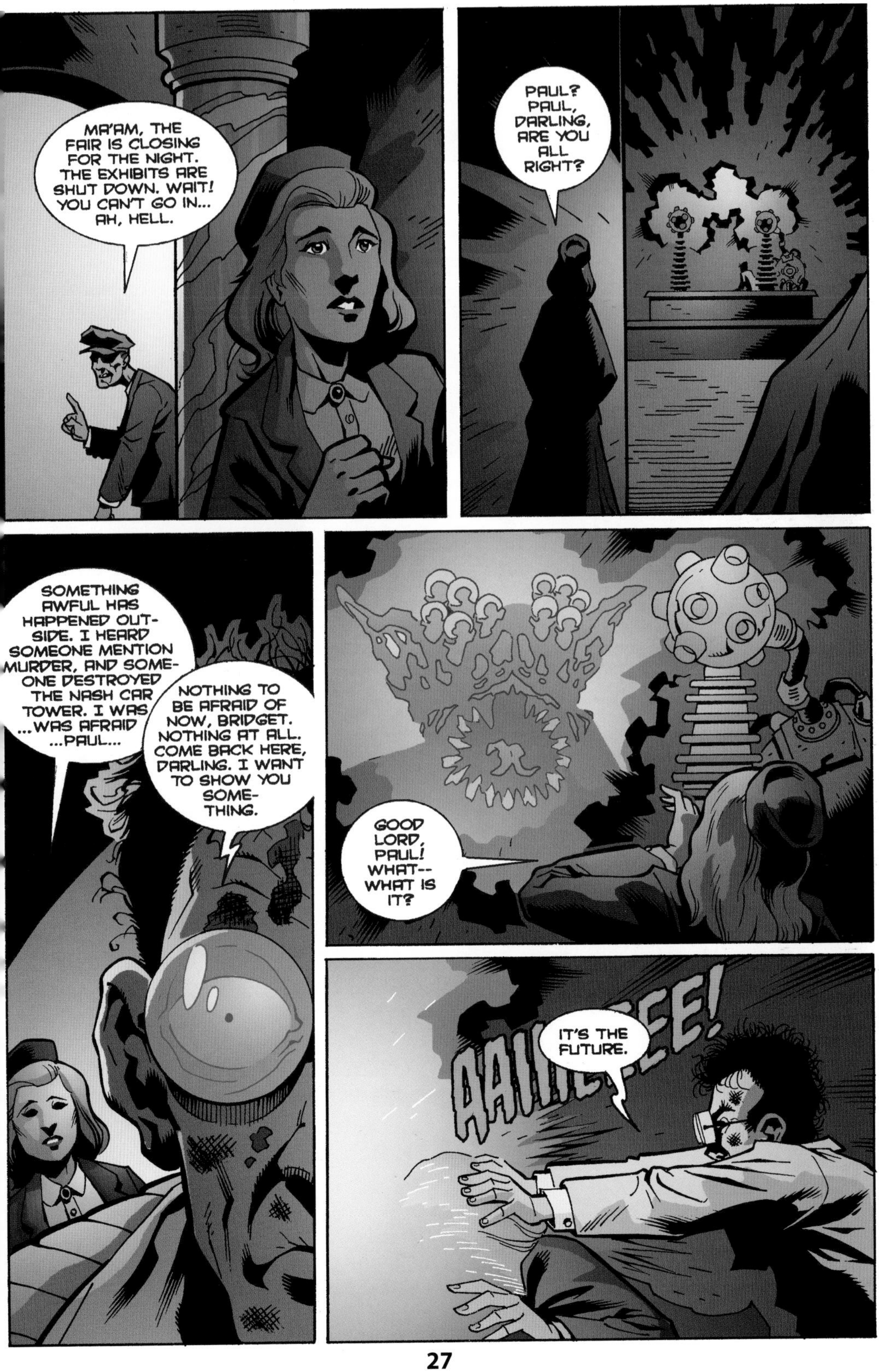
MA'AM, THE FAIR IS CLOSING FOR THE NIGHT. THE EXHIBITS ARE SHUT DOWN. WAIT! YOU CAN'T GO IN... AH, HELL.
PAUL? PAUL, DARLING, ARE YOU ALL RIGHT?
SOMETHING AWFUL HAS HAPPENED OUT-SIDE. I HEARD SOMEONE MENTION MURDER, AND SOME-ONE DESTROYED THE NASH CAR TOWER. I WAS ...WAS AFRAID ...PAUL...
NOTHING TO BE AFRAID OF NOW, BRIDGET. NOTHING AT ALL. COME BACK HERE, DARLING. I WANT TO SHOW YOU SOME-THING.
GOOD LORD, PAUL! WHAT-- WHAT IS IT?
IT'S THE FUTURE.

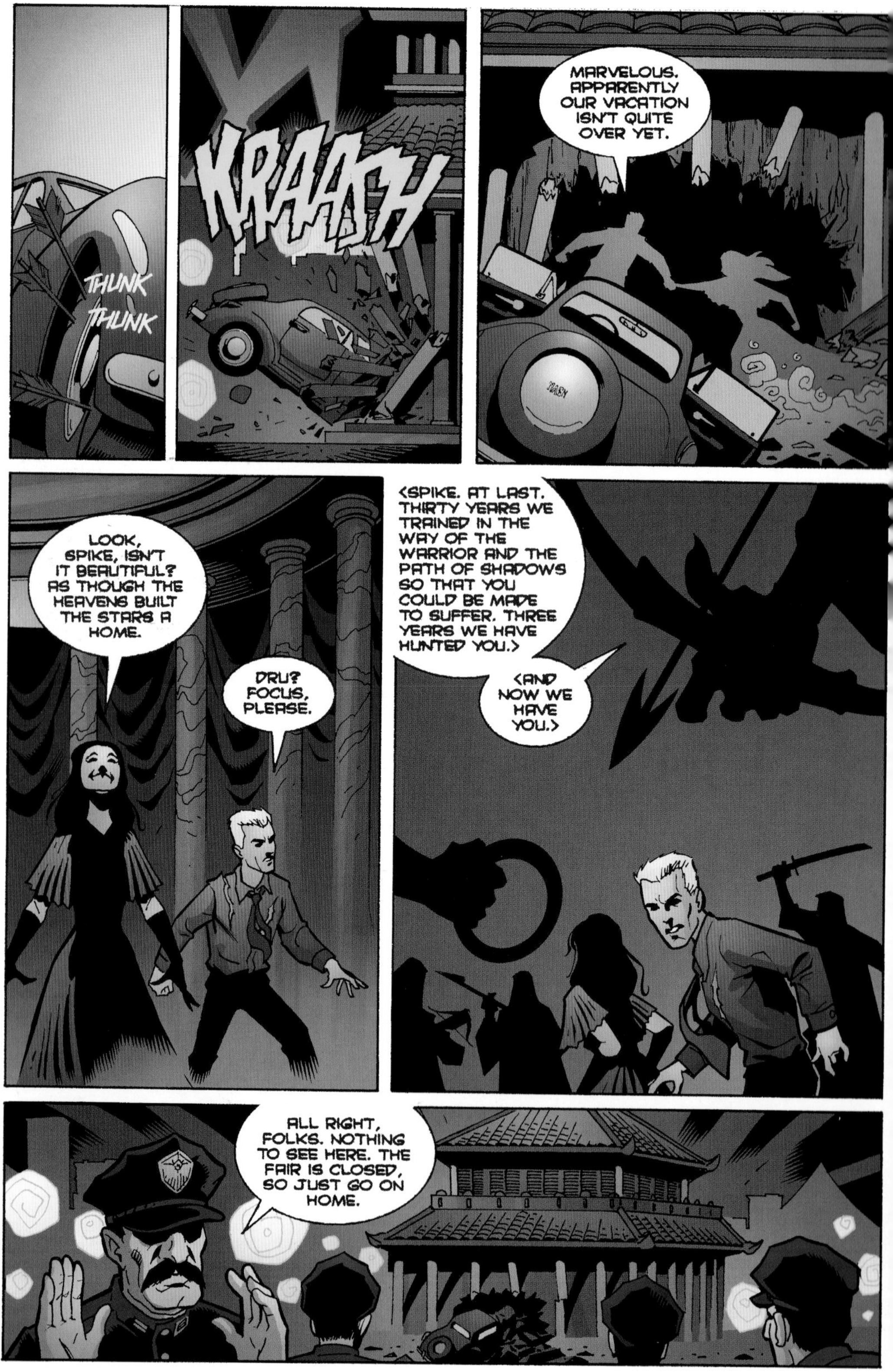
THUNK
THUNK
KRAAASH
MARVELOUS. APPARENTLY OUR VACATION ISN'T QUITE OVER YET.
LOOK, SPIKE, ISN'T IT BEAUTIFUL? AS THOUGH THE HEAVENS BUILT THE STARS A HOME.
DRU? FOCUS, PLEASE.
<SPIKE. AT LAST. THIRTY YEARS WE TRAINED IN THE WAY OF THE WARRIOR AND THE PATH OF SHADOWS SO THAT YOU COULD BE MADE TO SUFFER. THREE YEARS WE HAVE HUNTED YOU.>
<AND NOW WE HAVE YOU.>
ALL RIGHT, FOLKS. NOTHING TO SEE HERE. THE FAIR IS CLOSED, SO JUST GO ON HOME.

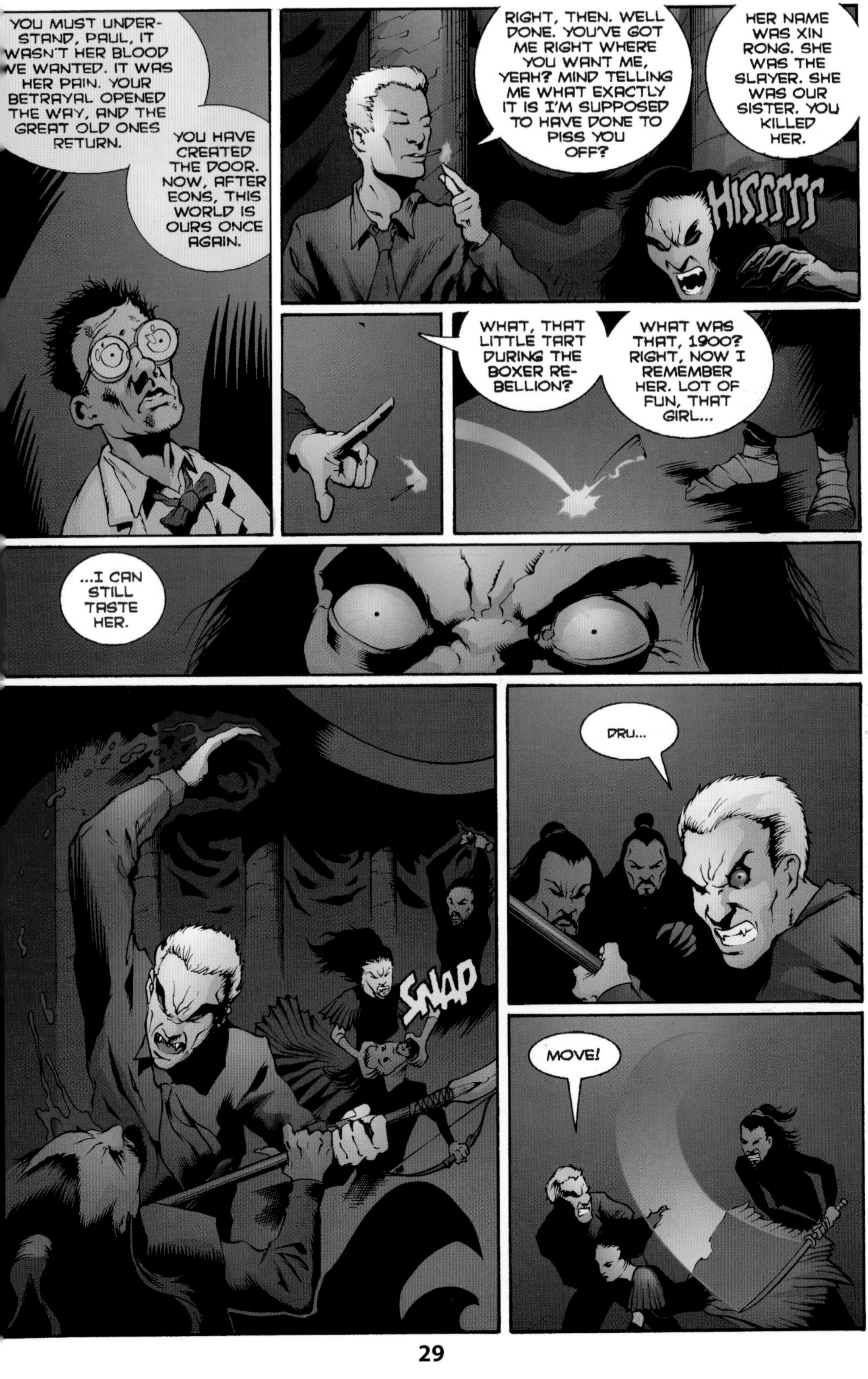
YOU MUST UNDERSTAND, PAUL, IT WASN'T HER BLOOD WE WANTED. IT WAS HER PAIN. YOUR BETRAYAL OPENED THE WAY, AND THE GREAT OLD ONES RETURN.
YOU HAVE CREATED THE DOOR. NOW, AFTER EONS, THIS WORLD IS OURS ONCE AGAIN.
RIGHT, THEN. WELL DONE. YOU'VE GOT ME RIGHT WHERE YOU WANT ME, YEAH? MIND TELLING ME WHAT EXACTLY IT IS I'M SUPPOSED TO HAVE DONE TO PISS YOU OFF?
HER NAME WAS XIN RONG. SHE WAS THE SLAYER. SHE WAS OUR SISTER. YOU KILLED HER.
HISSSSS
WHAT, THAT LITTLE TART DURING THE BOXER REBELLION?
WHAT WAS THAT, 1900? RIGHT, NOW I REMEMBER HER. LOT OF FUN, THAT GIRL...
...I CAN STILL TASTE HER.
SNAP
DRU...
MOVE!

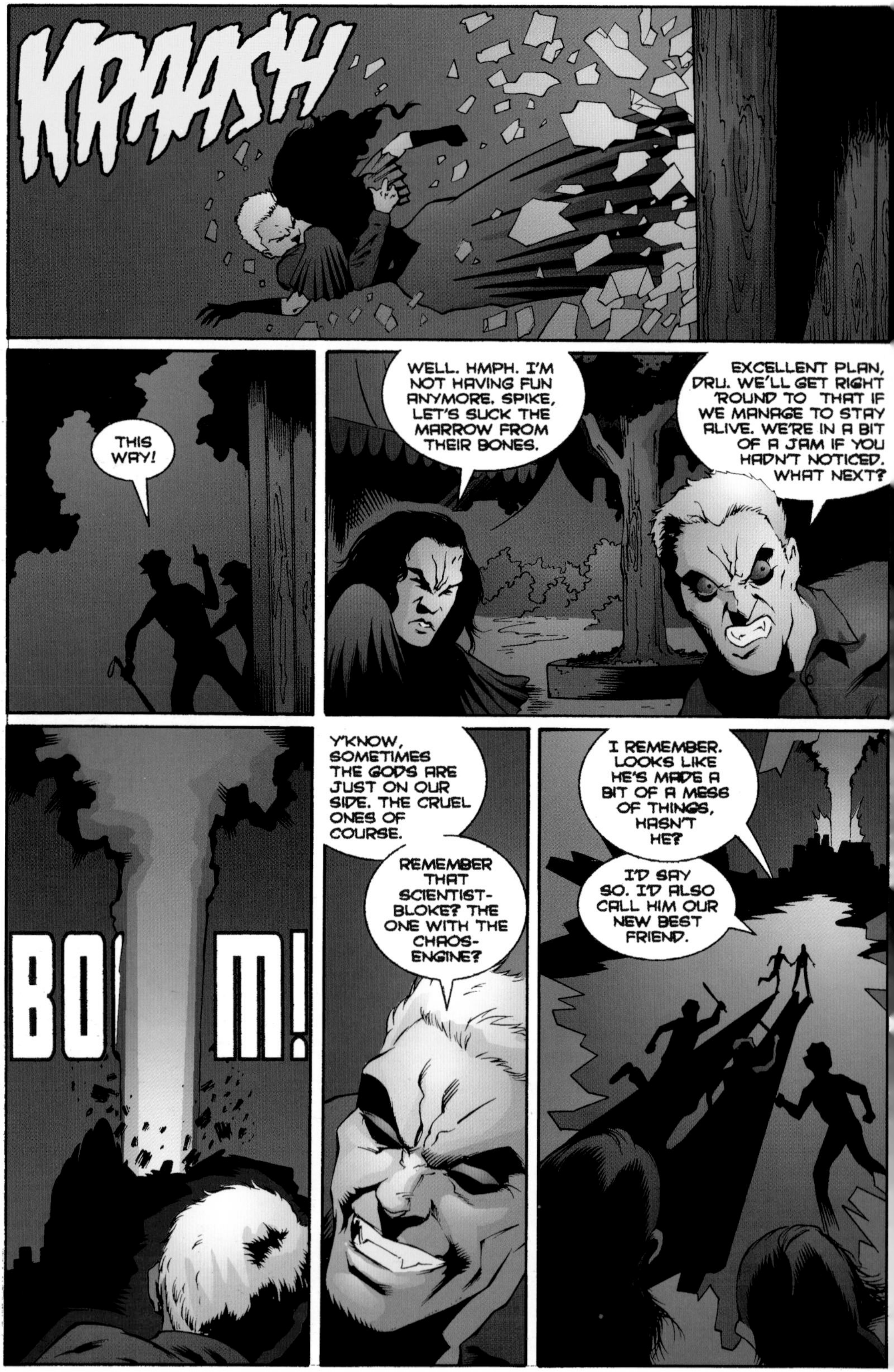
KRAASH
THIS WAY!
WELL. HMPH. I'M NOT HAVING FUN ANYMORE. SPIKE, LET'S SUCK THE MARROW FROM THEIR BONES.
EXCELLENT PLAN, DRU. WE'LL GET RIGHT 'ROUND TO THAT IF WE MANAGE TO STAY ALIVE. WE'RE IN A BIT OF A JAM IF YOU HADN'T NOTICED. WHAT NEXT?
BO M!
Y'KNOW, SOMETIMES THE GODS ARE JUST ON OUR SIDE. THE CRUEL ONES OF COURSE.
REMEMBER THAT SCIENTIST-BLOKE? THE ONE WITH THE CHAOS-ENGINE?
I REMEMBER. LOOKS LIKE HE'S MADE A BIT OF A MESS OF THINGS, HASN'T HE?
I'D SAY SO. I'D ALSO CALL HIM OUR NEW BEST FRIEND.

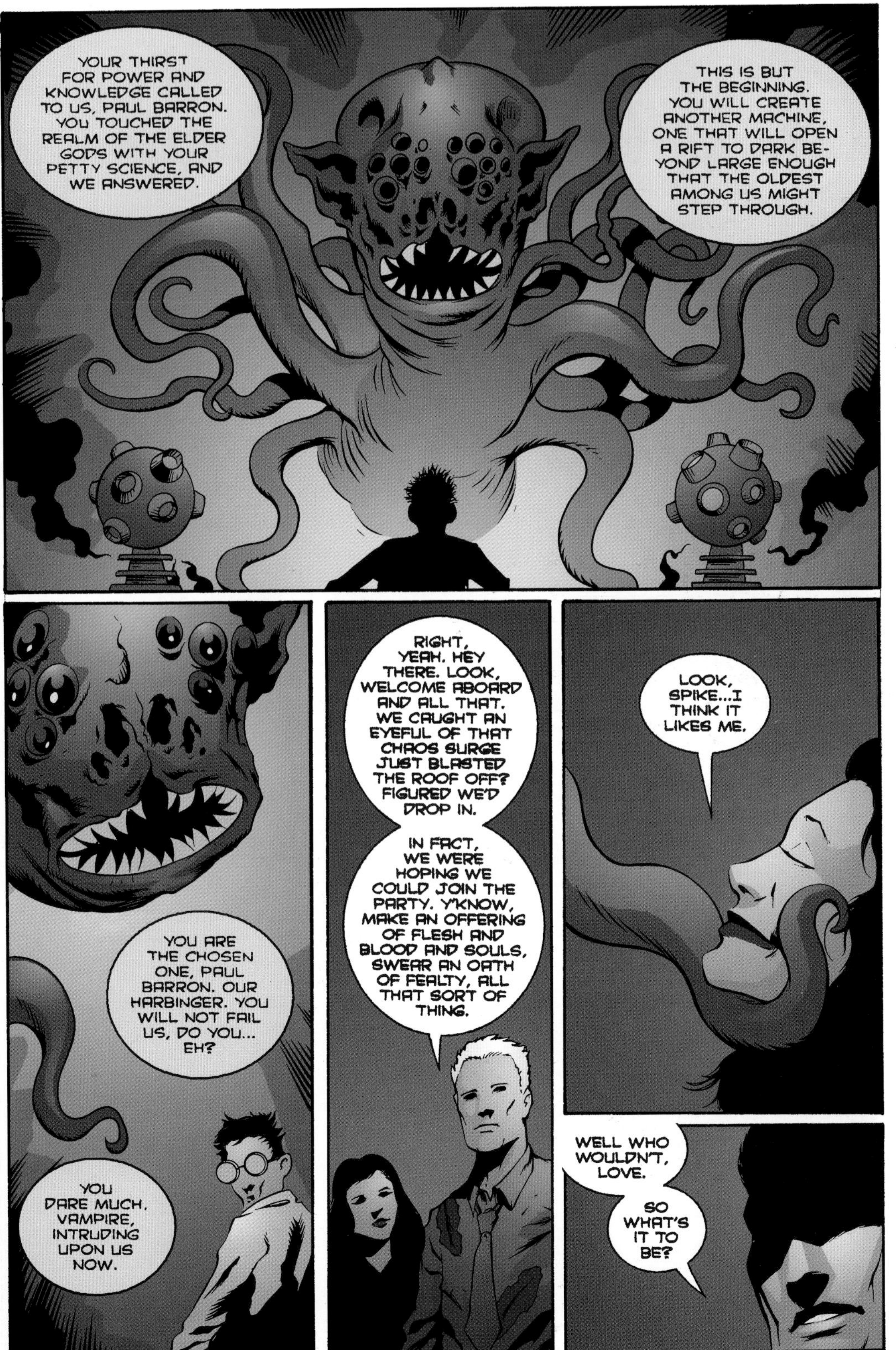
YOUR THIRST FOR POWER AND KNOWLEDGE CALLED TO US, PAUL BARRON. YOU TOUCHED THE REALM OF THE ELDER GODS WITH YOUR PETTY SCIENCE, AND WE ANSWERED.
THIS IS BUT THE BEGINNING. YOU WILL CREATE ANOTHER MACHINE, ONE THAT WILL OPEN A RIFT TO DARK BE-YOND LARGE ENOUGH THAT THE OLDEST AMONG US MIGHT STEP THROUGH.
YOU ARE THE CHOSEN ONE, PAUL BARRON. OUR HARBINGER. YOU WILL NOT FAIL US, DO YOU... EH?
YOU DARE MUCH, VAMPIRE, INTRUDING UPON US NOW.
RIGHT, YEAH. HEY THERE. LOOK, WELCOME ABOARD AND ALL THAT. WE CAUGHT AN EYEFUL OF THAT CHAOS SURGE JUST BLASTED THE ROOF OFF? FIGURED WE'D DROP IN.
IN FACT, WE WERE HOPING WE COULD JOIN THE PARTY. Y'KNOW, MAKE AN OFFERING OF FLESH AND BLOOD AND SOULS, SWEAR AN OATH OF FEALTY, ALL THAT SORT OF THING.
LOOK, SPIKE...I THINK IT LIKES ME.
WELL WHO WOULDN'T, LOVE.
SO WHAT'S IT TO BE?

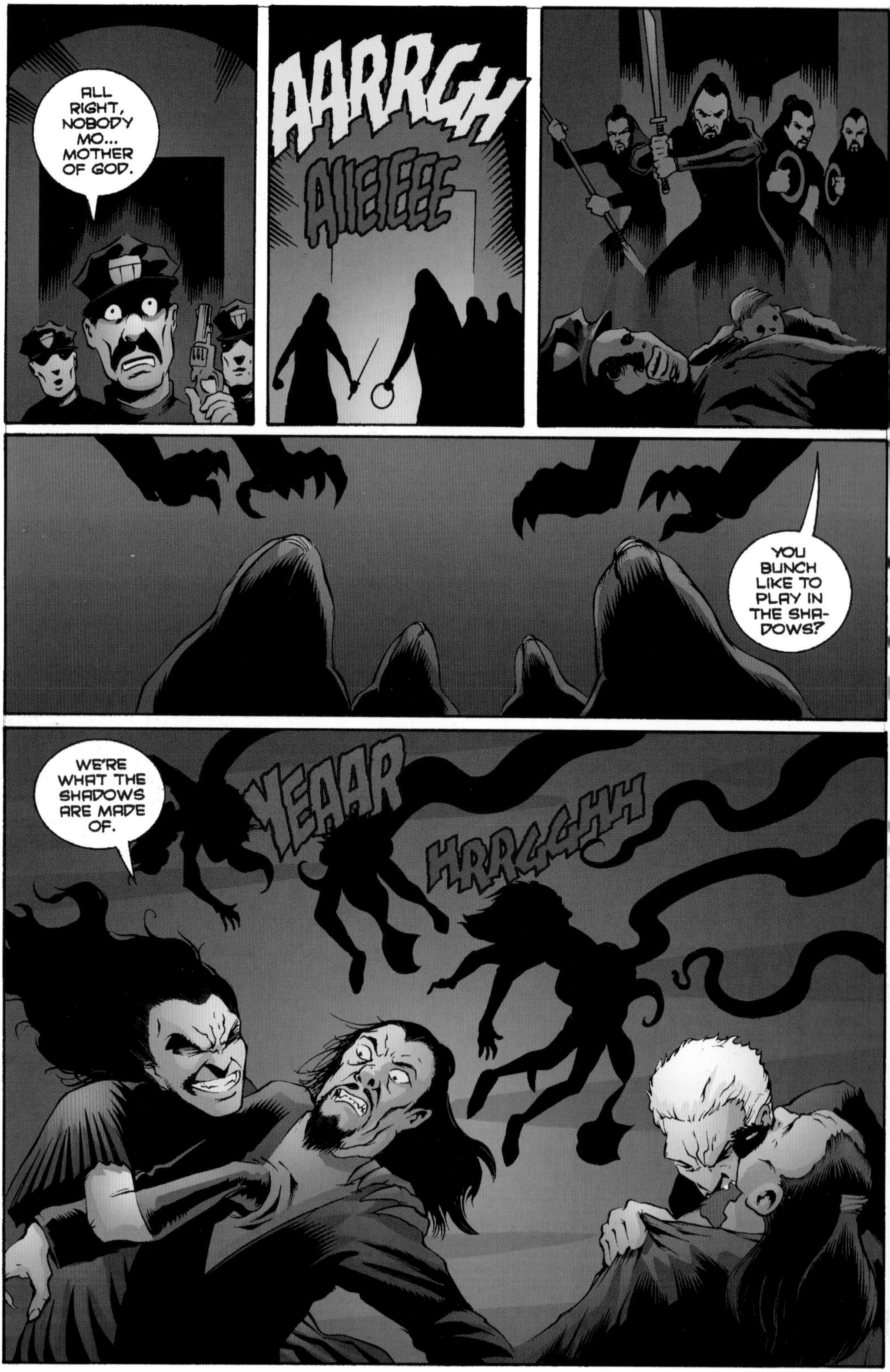
ALL RIGHT, NOBODY MO... MOTHER OF GOD.
AARRGH
AIIEIEEE
YOU BUNCH LIKE TO PLAY IN THE SHA-DOWS?
WE'RE WHAT THE SHADOWS ARE MADE OF.
YEAAR
HRRGHH

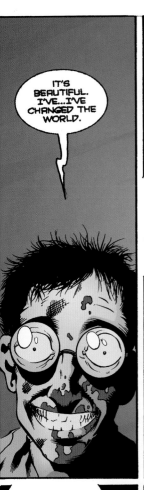

IT'S BEAUTIFUL. I'VE...I'VE CHANGED THE WORLD.

THAT WAS GLORIOUS. SCREAMS PAINT THE WALLS. IT WAS ALMOST AS THOUGH WE TORE NOT ONLY THEIR FLESH, BUT THE FLESH OF THEIR ANCESTORS GOING BACK A THOUSAND YEARS. MMM, ALL THAT SUFFERING.

YOUR HUNGER IS ADMIRABLE. YOU WILL MAKE USEFUL SER-VANTS.

YEAH, LISTEN, ABOUT THAT WHOLE OATH OF FEALTY BUSINESS?

WE LIED.

NOOOOO! YOU CAN'T!! YOU'LL DESTROY THE FUTURE! MY DESTINY!

FUTURE'S WHAT YOU MAKE IT.

33

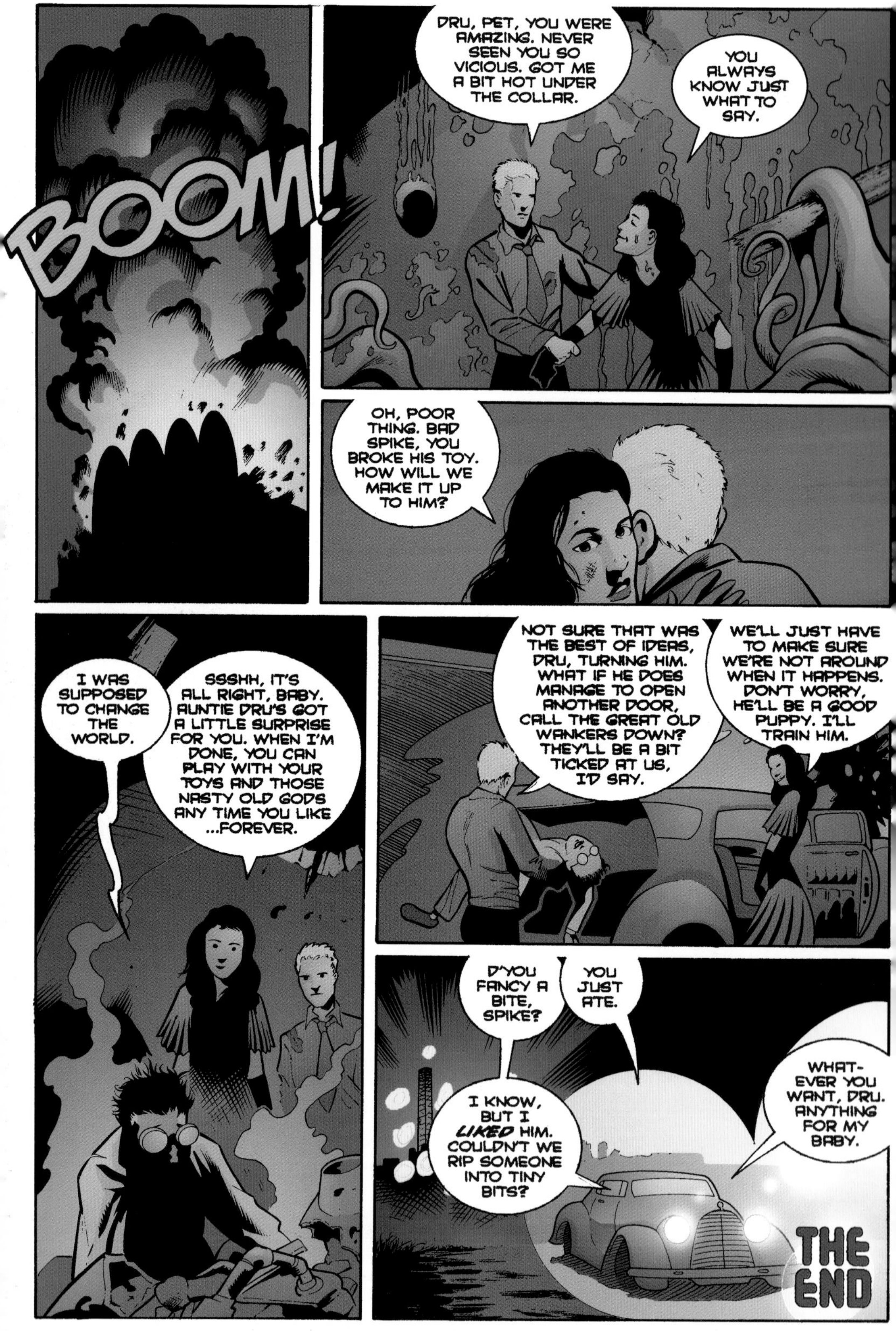
BOOM!
DRU, PET, YOU WERE AMAZING. NEVER SEEN YOU SO VICIOUS. GOT ME A BIT HOT UNDER THE COLLAR.
YOU ALWAYS KNOW JUST WHAT TO SAY.
OH, POOR THING. BAD SPIKE, YOU BROKE HIS TOY. HOW WILL WE MAKE IT UP TO HIM?
I WAS SUPPOSED TO CHANGE THE WORLD.
SSSHH, IT'S ALL RIGHT, BABY. AUNTIE DRU'S GOT A LITTLE SURPRISE FOR YOU. WHEN I'M DONE, YOU CAN PLAY WITH YOUR TOYS AND THOSE NASTY OLD GODS ANY TIME YOU LIKE ...FOREVER.
NOT SURE THAT WAS THE BEST OF IDEAS, DRU, TURNING HIM. WHAT IF HE DOES MANAGE TO OPEN ANOTHER DOOR, CALL THE GREAT OLD WANKERS DOWN? THEY'LL BE A BIT TICKED AT US, I'D SAY.
WE'LL JUST HAVE TO MAKE SURE WE'RE NOT AROUND WHEN IT HAPPENS. DON'T WORRY, HE'LL BE A GOOD PUPPY. I'LL TRAIN HIM.
D'YOU FANCY A BITE, SPIKE?
YOU JUST ATE.
I KNOW, BUT I *LIKED* HIM. COULDN'T WE RIP SOMEONE INTO TINY BITS?
WHAT-EVER YOU WANT, DRU. ANYTHING FOR MY BABY.
THE END

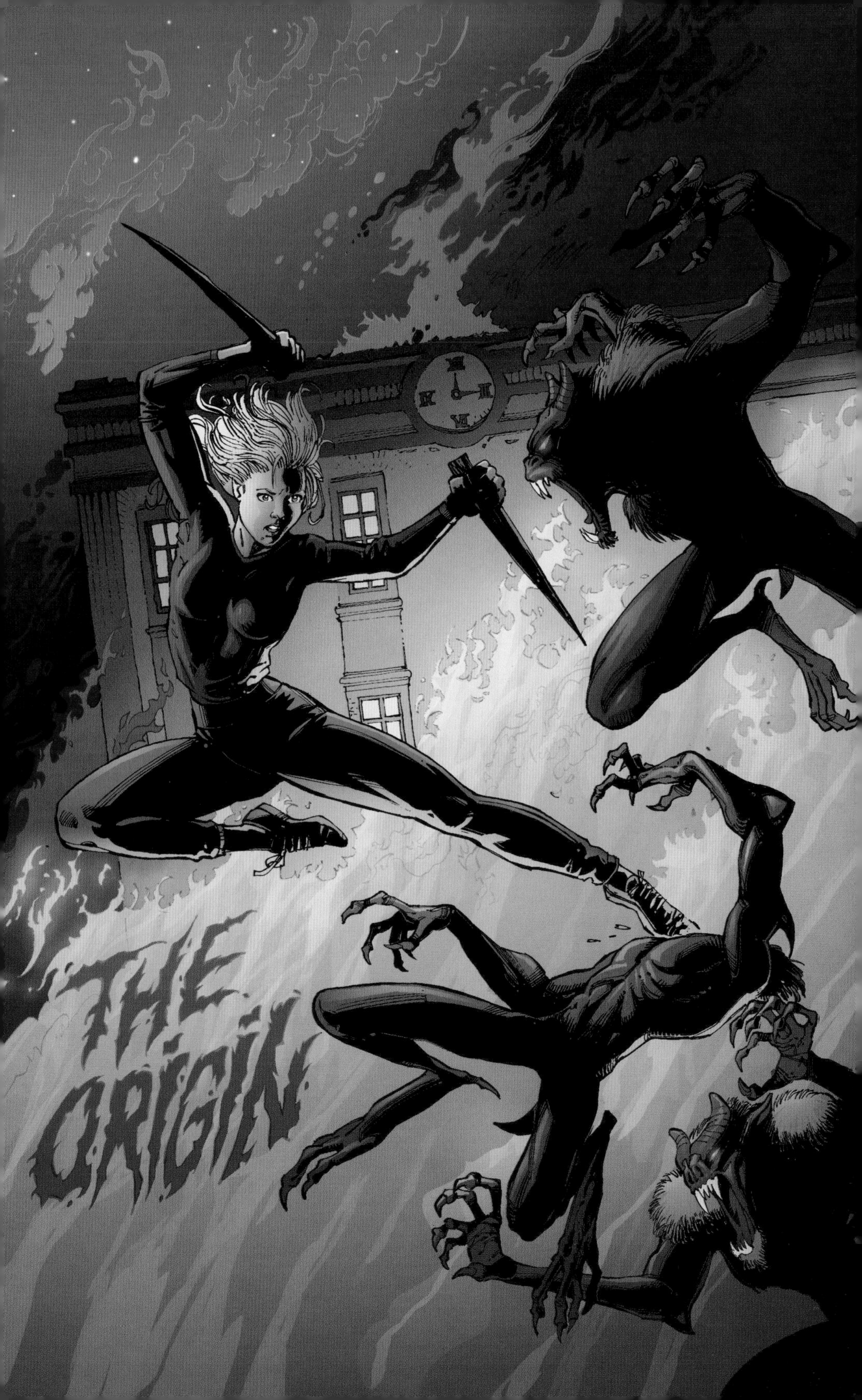
THE ORIGIN

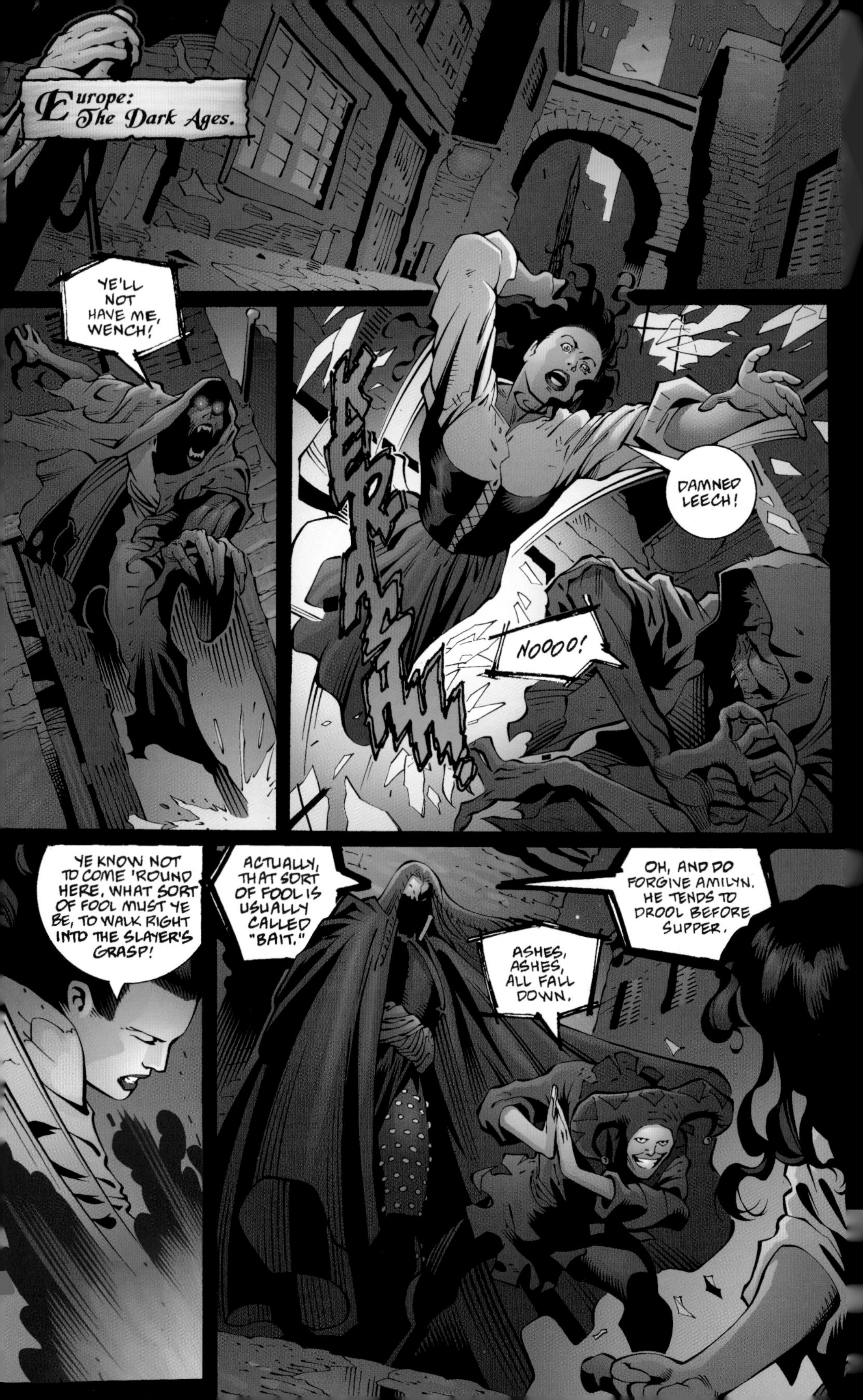
Europe: The Dark Ages.
YE'LL NOT HAVE ME, WENCH!
DAMNED LEECH!
NOOOO!
YE KNOW NOT TO COME 'ROUND HERE. WHAT SORT OF FOOL MUST YE BE, TO WALK RIGHT INTO THE SLAYER'S GRASP!
ACTUALLY, THAT SORT OF FOOL IS USUALLY CALLED "BAIT."
OH, AND DO FORGIVE AMILYN. HE TENDS TO DROOL BEFORE SUPPER.
ASHES, ASHES, ALL FALL DOWN.

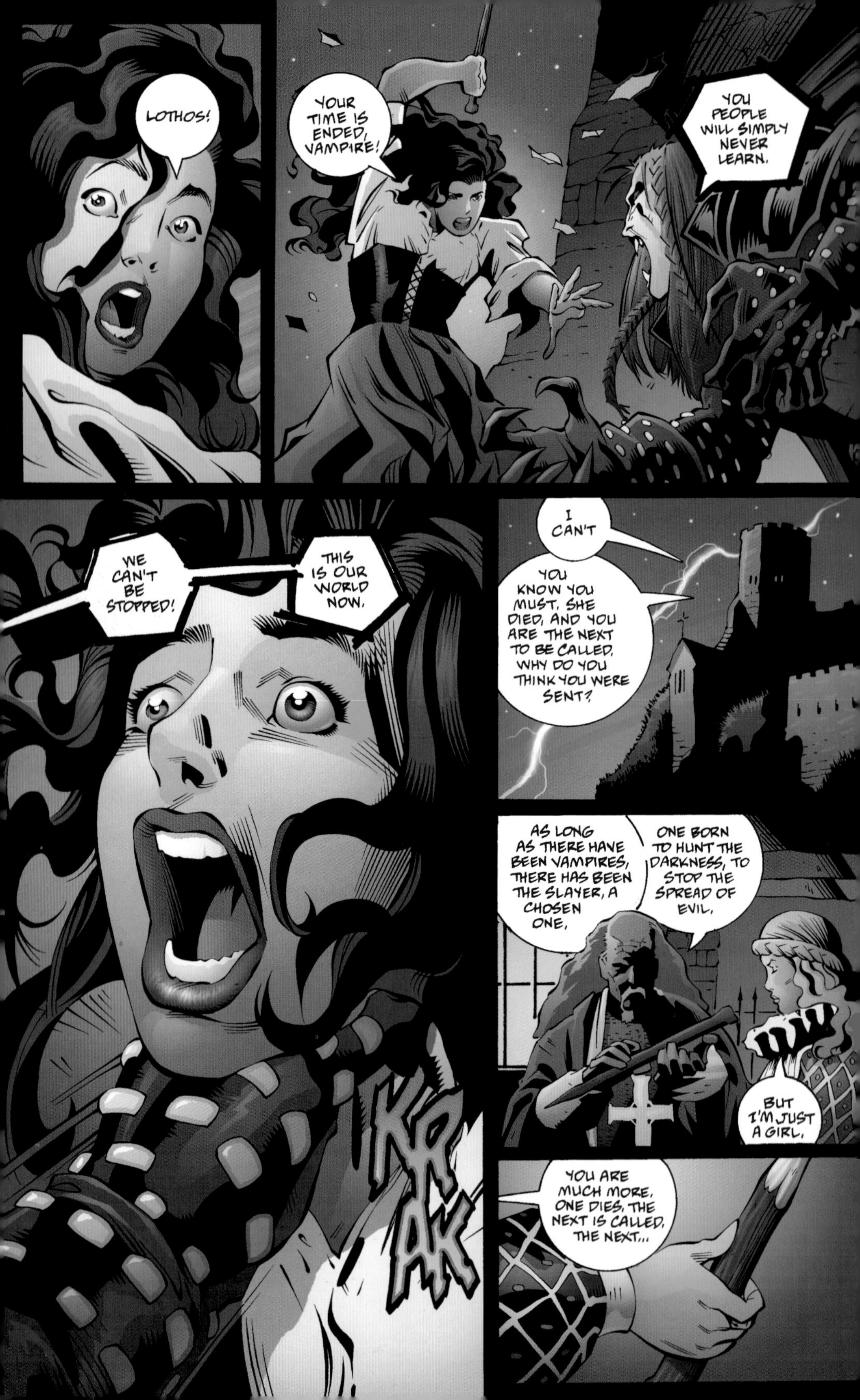
LOTHOS!
YOUR TIME IS ENDED, VAMPIRE!
YOU PEOPLE WILL SIMPLY NEVER LEARN.
WE CAN'T BE STOPPED!
THIS IS OUR WORLD NOW.
KRAK
I CAN'T
YOU KNOW YOU MUST. SHE DIED, AND YOU ARE THE NEXT TO BE CALLED. WHY DO YOU THINK YOU WERE SENT?
AS LONG AS THERE HAVE BEEN VAMPIRES, THERE HAS BEEN THE SLAYER, A CHOSEN ONE.
ONE BORN TO HUNT THE DARKNESS, TO STOP THE SPREAD OF EVIL.
BUT I'M JUST A GIRL.
YOU ARE MUCH MORE. ONE DIES, THE NEXT IS CALLED. THE NEXT...

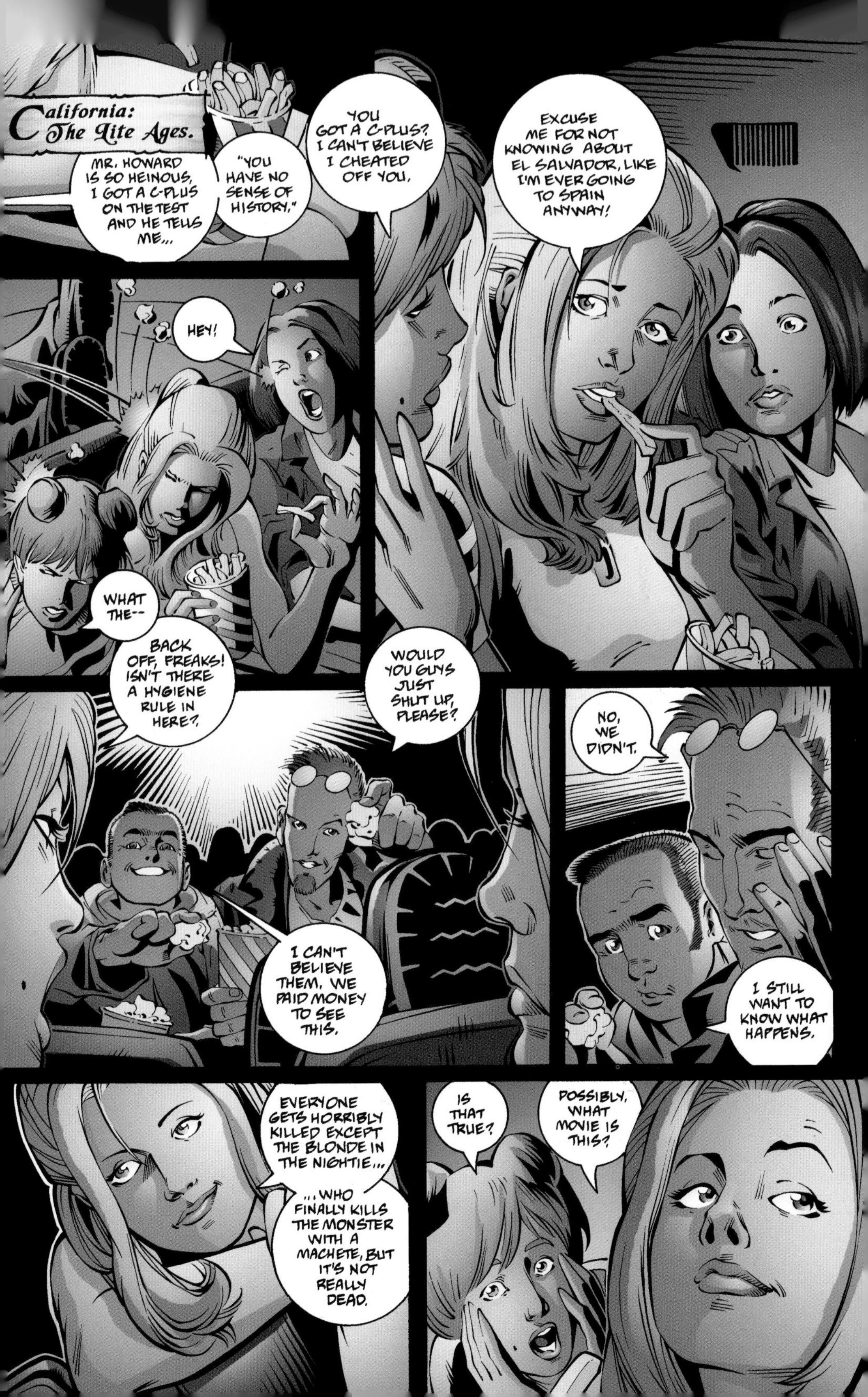
California: The Lite Ages.
MR. HOWARD IS SO HEINOUS, I GOT A C-PLUS ON THE TEST AND HE TELLS ME...
"YOU HAVE NO SENSE OF HISTORY."
YOU GOT A C-PLUS? I CAN'T BELIEVE I CHEATED OFF YOU.
EXCUSE ME FOR NOT KNOWING ABOUT EL SALVADOR, LIKE I'M EVER GOING TO SPAIN ANYWAY!
HEY!
WHAT THE--
BACK OFF, FREAKS! ISN'T THERE A HYGIENE RULE IN HERE?
WOULD YOU GUYS JUST SHUT UP, PLEASE?
I CAN'T BELIEVE THEM. WE PAID MONEY TO SEE THIS.
NO, WE DIDN'T.
I STILL WANT TO KNOW WHAT HAPPENS.
EVERYONE GETS HORRIBLY KILLED EXCEPT THE BLONDE IN THE NIGHTIE...
...WHO FINALLY KILLS THE MONSTER WITH A MACHETE, BUT IT'S NOT REALLY DEAD.
IS THAT TRUE?
POSSIBLY. WHAT MOVIE IS THIS?

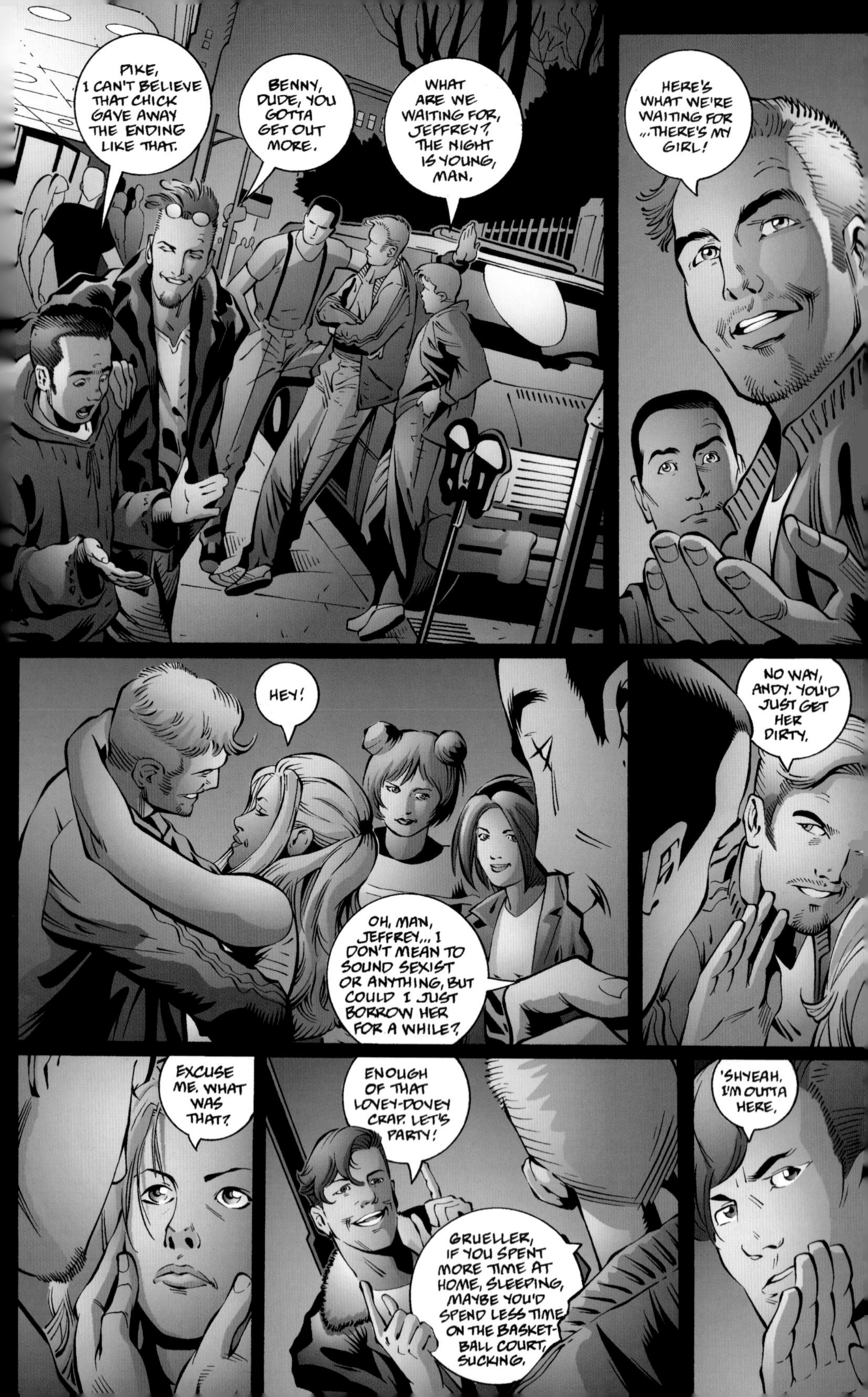
PIKE, I CAN'T BELIEVE THAT CHICK GAVE AWAY THE ENDING LIKE THAT.
BENNY, DUDE, YOU GOTTA GET OUT MORE.
WHAT ARE WE WAITING FOR, JEFFREY? THE NIGHT IS YOUNG, MAN.
HERE'S WHAT WE'RE WAITING FOR ...THERE'S MY GIRL!
HEY!
OH, MAN, JEFFREY... I DON'T MEAN TO SOUND SEXIST OR ANYTHING, BUT COULD I JUST BORROW HER FOR A WHILE?
NO WAY, ANDY. YOU'D JUST GET HER DIRTY.
EXCUSE ME. WHAT WAS THAT?
ENOUGH OF THAT LOVEY-DOVEY CRAP. LET'S PARTY!
GRUELLER, IF YOU SPENT MORE TIME AT HOME, SLEEPING, MAYBE YOU'D SPEND LESS TIME ON THE BASKET-BALL COURT, SUCKING.
'SHYEAH, I'M OUTTA HERE.

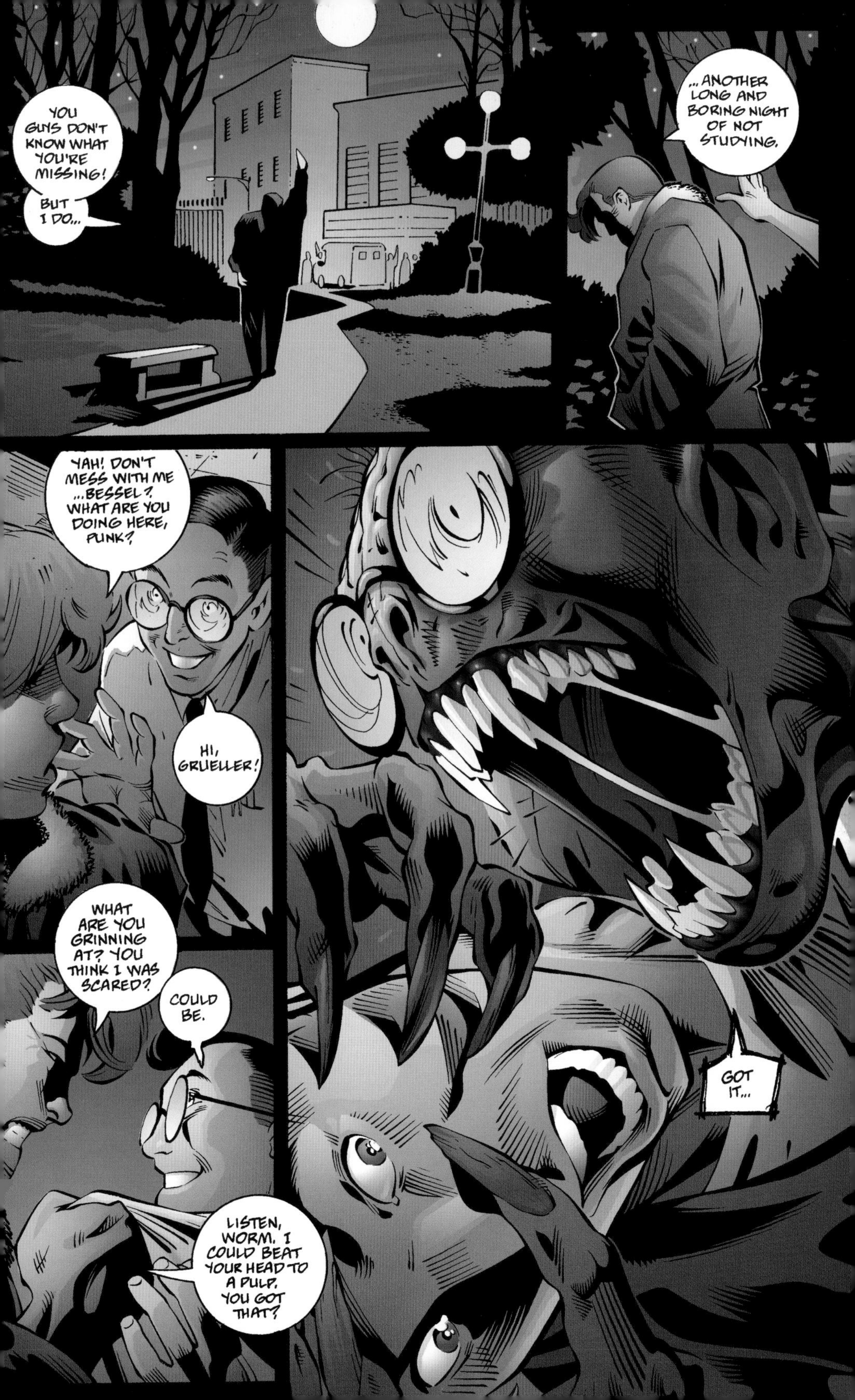
YOU GUYS DON'T KNOW WHAT YOU'RE MISSING!
BUT I DO...
...ANOTHER LONG AND BORING NIGHT OF NOT STUDYING.
YAH! DON'T MESS WITH ME ...BESSEL? WHAT ARE YOU DOING HERE, PUNK?
HI, GRUELLER!
WHAT ARE YOU GRINNING AT? YOU THINK I WAS SCARED?
COULD BE.
LISTEN, WORM. I COULD BEAT YOUR HEAD TO A PULP. YOU GOT THAT?
GOT IT...

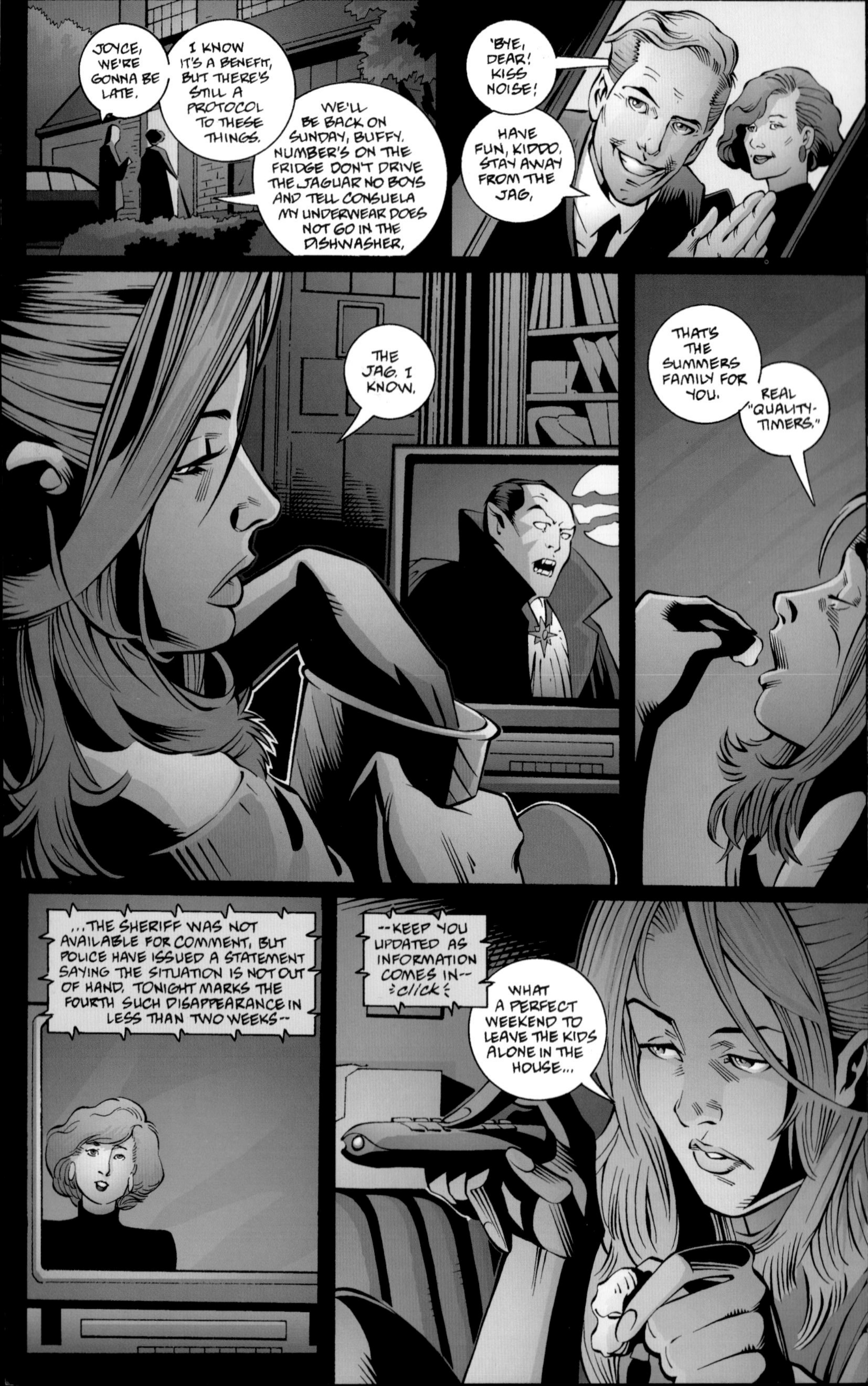
JOYCE, WE'RE GONNA BE LATE.
I KNOW IT'S A BENEFIT, BUT THERE'S STILL A PROTOCOL TO THESE THINGS.
WE'LL BE BACK ON SUNDAY, BUFFY. NUMBER'S ON THE FRIDGE DON'T DRIVE THE JAGUAR NO BOYS AND TELL CONSUELA MY UNDERWEAR DOES NOT GO IN THE DISHWASHER.
'BYE, DEAR! KISS NOISE!
HAVE FUN, KIDDO. STAY AWAY FROM THE JAG.
THE JAG. I KNOW.
THAT'S THE SUMMERS FAMILY FOR YOU.
REAL "QUALITY-TIMERS."
...THE SHERIFF WAS NOT AVAILABLE FOR COMMENT, BUT POLICE HAVE ISSUED A STATEMENT SAYING THE SITUATION IS NOT OUT OF HAND. TONIGHT MARKS THE FOURTH SUCH DISAPPEARANCE IN LESS THAN TWO WEEKS--
--KEEP YOU UPDATED AS INFORMATION COMES IN--
click
WHAT A PERFECT WEEKEND TO LEAVE THE KIDS ALONE IN THE HOUSE...

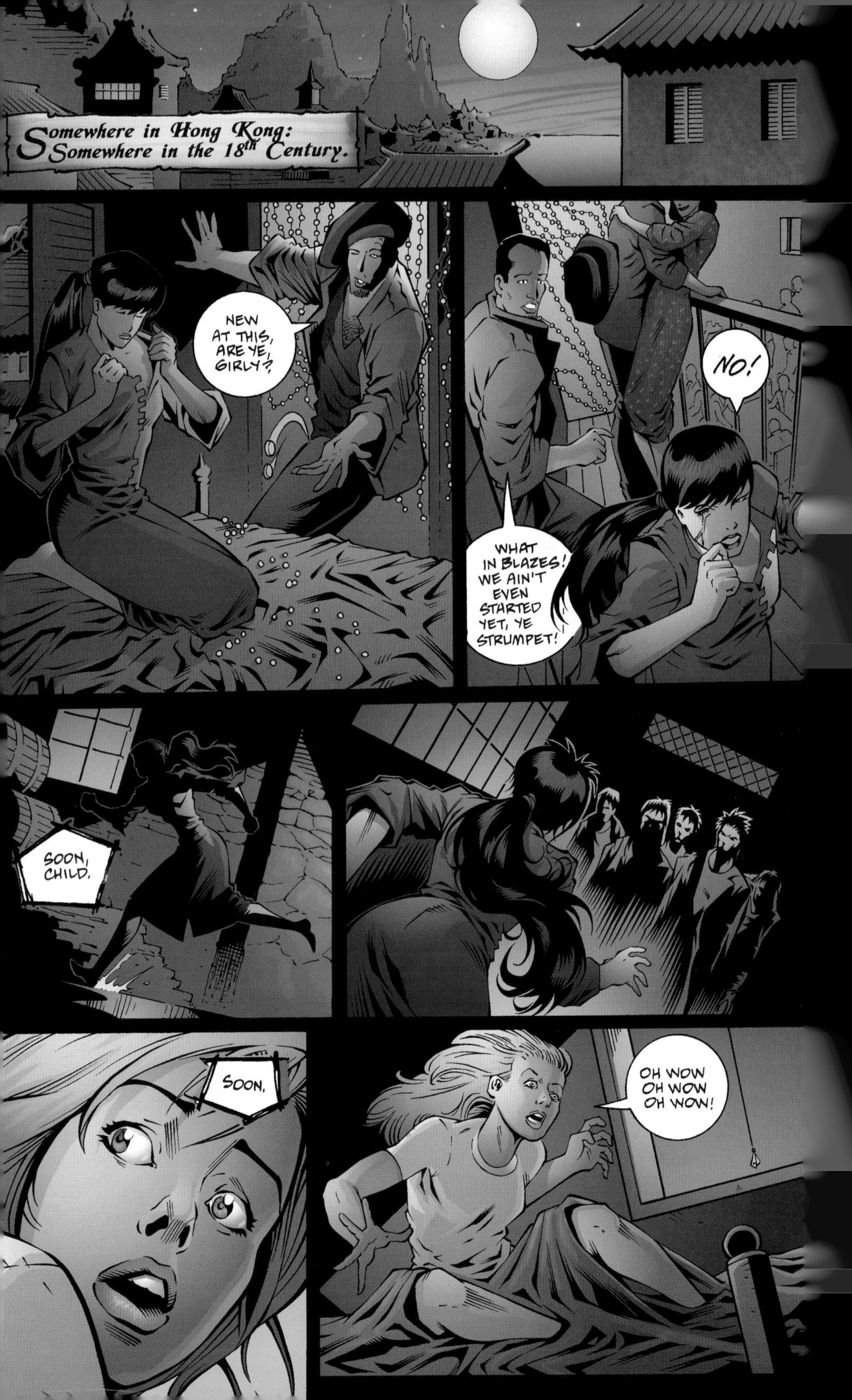
Somewhere in Hong Kong:
Somewhere in the 18th Century.
NEW AT THIS, ARE YE, GIRLY?
NO!
WHAT IN BLAZES! WE AIN'T EVEN STARTED YET, YE STRUMPET!
SOON, CHILD.
SOON.
OH WOW OH WOW OH WOW!

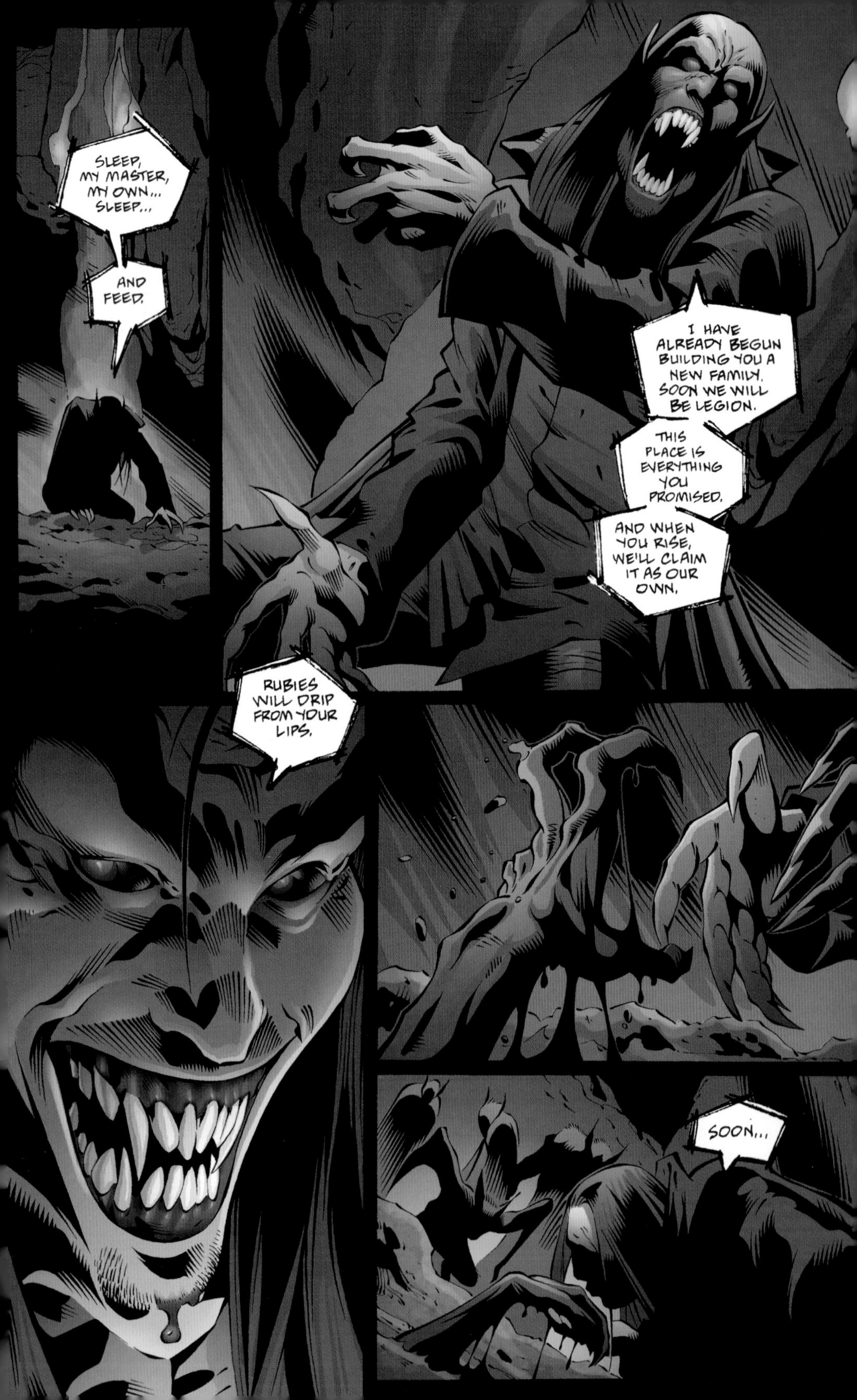
SLEEP, MY MASTER, MY OWN... SLEEP...
AND FEED.
I HAVE ALREADY BEGUN BUILDING YOU A NEW FAMILY. SOON WE WILL BE LEGION.
THIS PLACE IS EVERYTHING YOU PROMISED.
AND WHEN YOU RISE, WE'LL CLAIM IT AS OUR OWN.
RUBIES WILL DRIP FROM YOUR LIPS.
SOON...

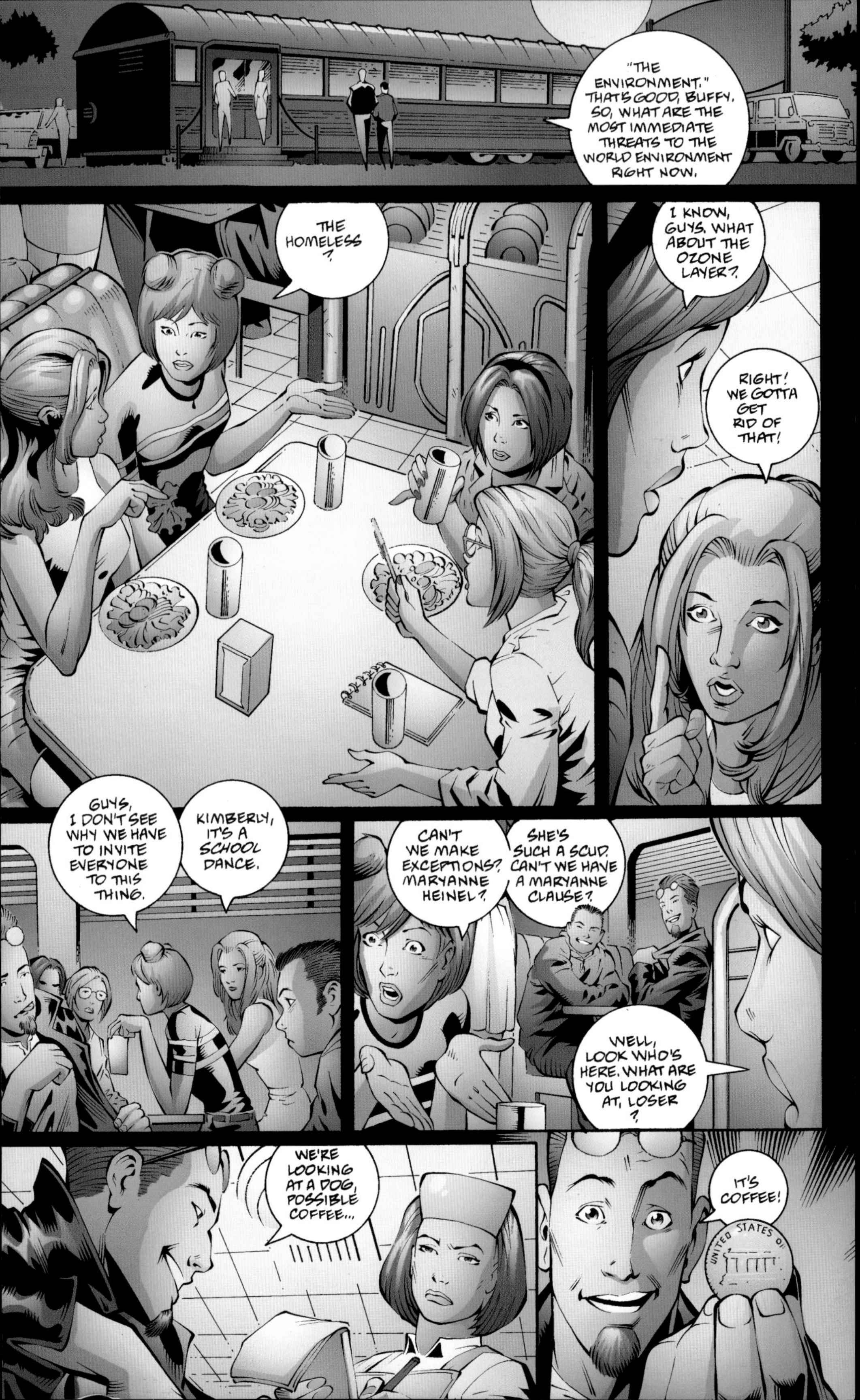
"THE ENVIRONMENT." THAT'S GOOD, BUFFY. SO, WHAT ARE THE MOST IMMEDIATE THREATS TO THE WORLD ENVIRONMENT RIGHT NOW.
THE HOMELESS?
I KNOW, GUYS. WHAT ABOUT THE OZONE LAYER?
RIGHT! WE GOTTA GET RID OF THAT!
GUYS, I DON'T SEE WHY WE HAVE TO INVITE EVERYONE TO THIS THING.
KIMBERLY, IT'S A SCHOOL DANCE.
CAN'T WE MAKE EXCEPTIONS? MARYANNE HEINEL?
SHE'S SUCH A SCUD. CAN'T WE HAVE A MARYANNE CLAUSE?
WELL, LOOK WHO'S HERE. WHAT ARE YOU LOOKING AT, LOSER?
WE'RE LOOKING AT A DOG, POSSIBLE COFFEE...
IT'S COFFEE!
UNITED STATES OF

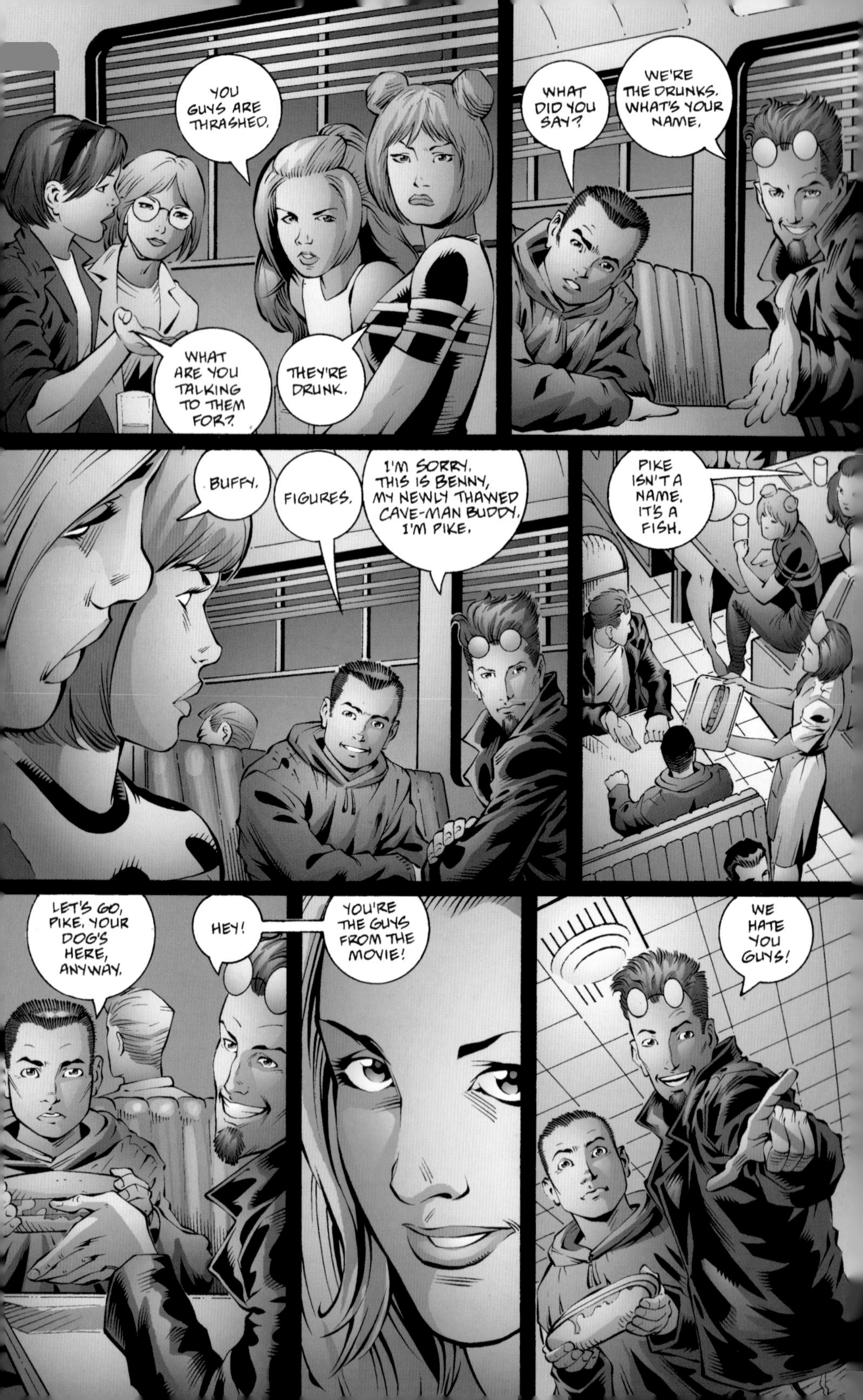

YOU GUYS ARE THRASHED.
WHAT ARE YOU TALKING TO THEM FOR?
THEY'RE DRUNK.
WHAT DID YOU SAY?
WE'RE THE DRUNKS. WHAT'S YOUR NAME.
BUFFY.
FIGURES.
I'M SORRY. THIS IS BENNY, MY NEWLY THAWED CAVE-MAN BUDDY. I'M PIKE.
PIKE ISN'T A NAME. IT'S A FISH.
LET'S GO, PIKE. YOUR DOG'S HERE, ANYWAY.
HEY!
YOU'RE THE GUYS FROM THE MOVIE!
WE HATE YOU GUYS!

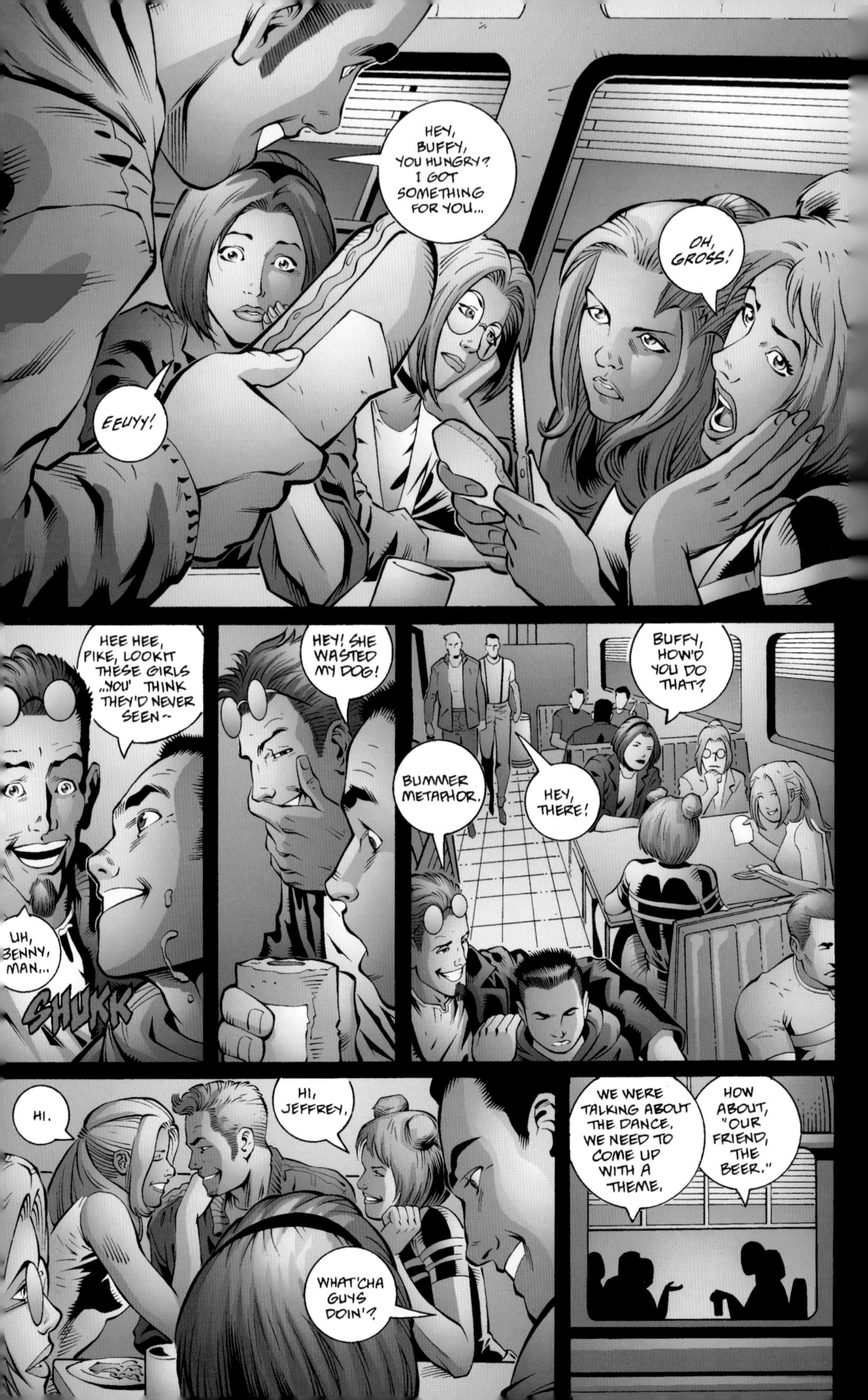
HEY, BUFFY, YOU HUNGRY? I GOT SOMETHING FOR YOU...
OH, GROSS!
EEUYY!
HEE HEE, PIKE, LOOKIT THESE GIRLS ..YOU' THINK THEY'D NEVER SEEN--
UH, BENNY, MAN...
SHUKK
HEY! SHE WASTED MY DOG!
BUFFY, HOW'D YOU DO THAT?
BUMMER METAPHOR.
HEY, THERE!
HI.
HI, JEFFREY.
WHAT'CHA GUYS DOIN'?
WE WERE TALKING ABOUT THE DANCE. WE NEED TO COME UP WITH A THEME.
HOW ABOUT, "OUR FRIEND, THE BEER."

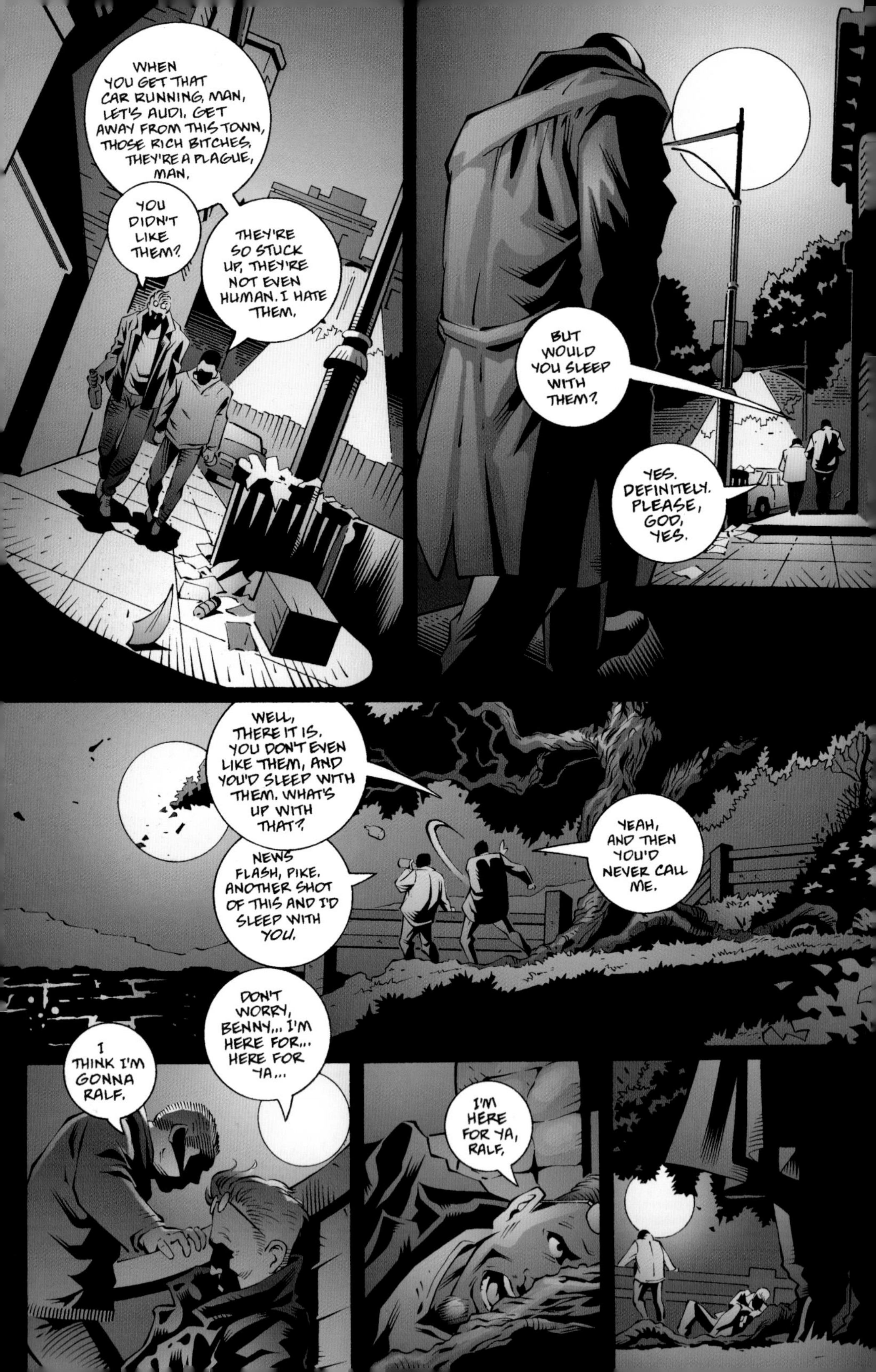
WHEN YOU GET THAT CAR RUNNING, MAN, LET'S AUDI. GET AWAY FROM THIS TOWN, THOSE RICH BITCHES. THEY'RE A PLAGUE, MAN.
YOU DIDN'T LIKE THEM?
THEY'RE SO STUCK UP, THEY'RE NOT EVEN HUMAN. I HATE THEM.
BUT WOULD YOU SLEEP WITH THEM?
YES. DEFINITELY. PLEASE, GOD, YES.
WELL, THERE IT IS. YOU DON'T EVEN LIKE THEM, AND YOU'D SLEEP WITH THEM. WHAT'S UP WITH THAT?
NEWS FLASH, PIKE. ANOTHER SHOT OF THIS AND I'D SLEEP WITH YOU.
YEAH, AND THEN YOU'D NEVER CALL ME.
I THINK I'M GONNA RALF.
DON'T WORRY, BENNY... I'M HERE FOR... HERE FOR YA...
I'M HERE FOR YA, RALF.

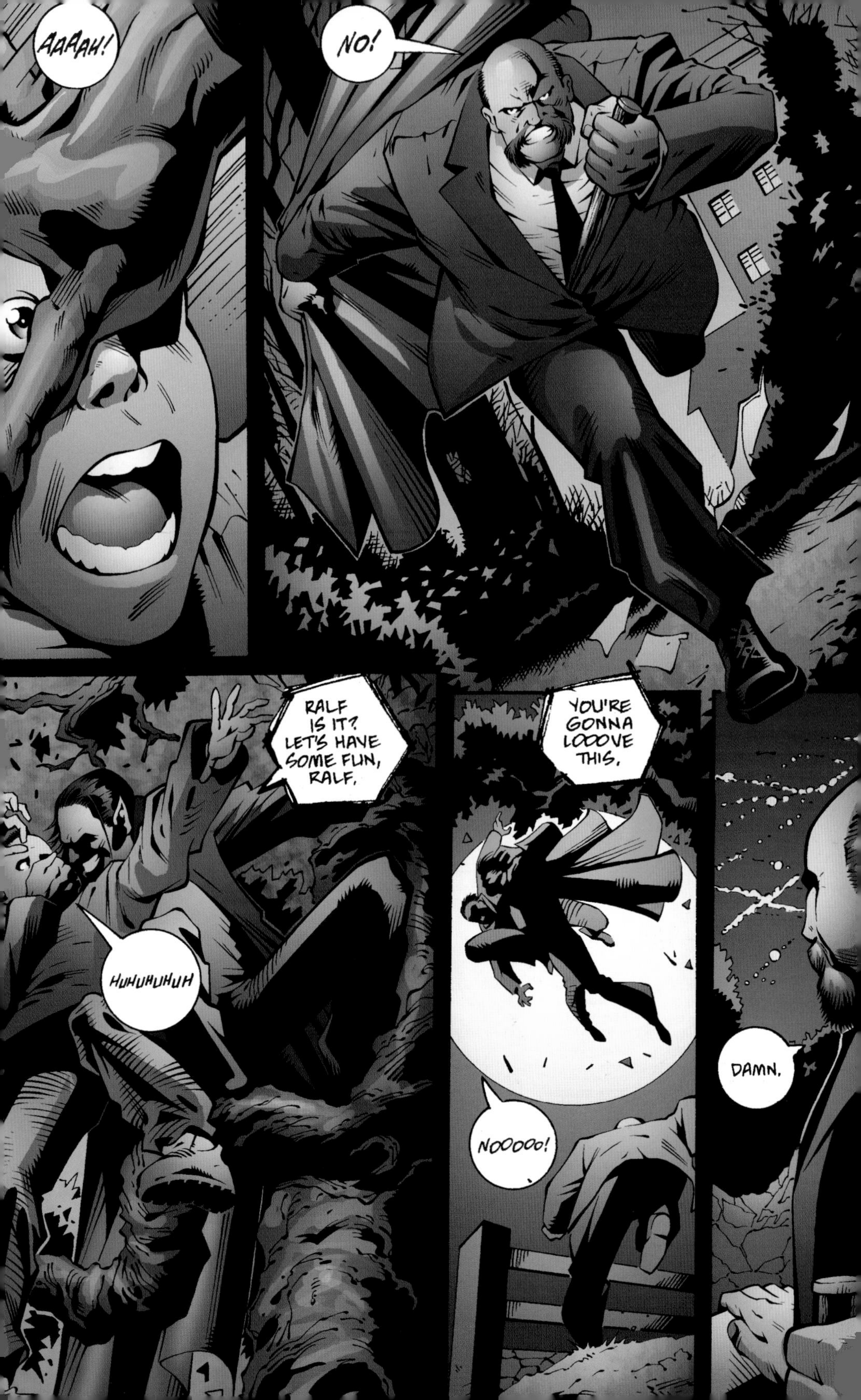
AAAAH!
NO!
RALF IS IT? LET'S HAVE SOME FUN, RALF.
HUHUHUHUH
YOU'RE GONNA LOOOVE THIS.
NOOOOO!
DAMN.

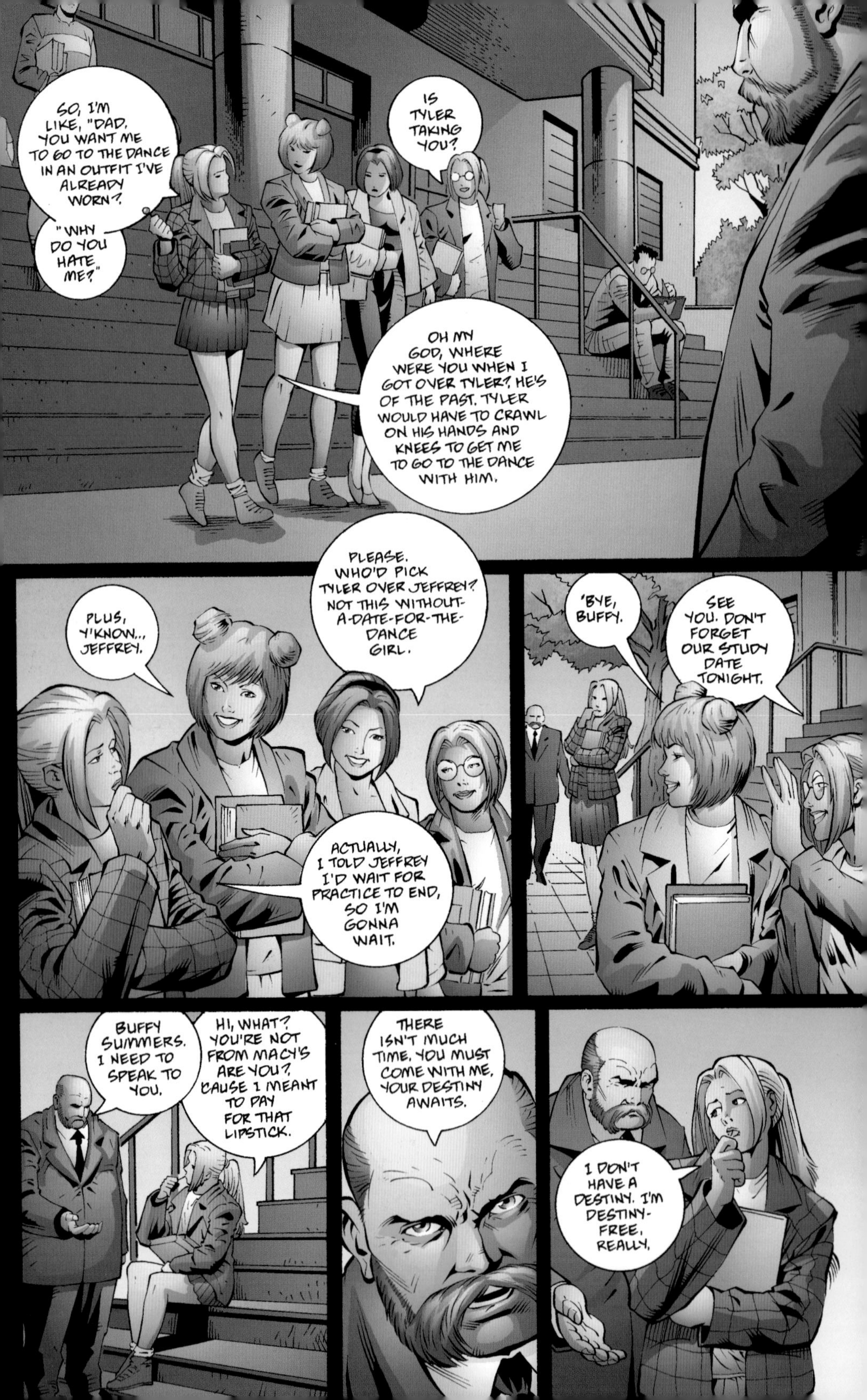
SO, I'M LIKE, "DAD, YOU WANT ME TO GO TO THE DANCE IN AN OUTFIT I'VE ALREADY WORN?
"WHY DO YOU HATE ME?"
IS TYLER TAKING YOU?
OH MY GOD, WHERE WERE YOU WHEN I GOT OVER TYLER? HE'S OF THE PAST. TYLER WOULD HAVE TO CRAWL ON HIS HANDS AND KNEES TO GET ME TO GO TO THE DANCE WITH HIM.
PLUS, Y'KNOW... JEFFREY.
PLEASE. WHO'D PICK TYLER OVER JEFFREY? NOT THIS WITHOUT-A-DATE-FOR-THE-DANCE GIRL.
ACTUALLY, I TOLD JEFFREY I'D WAIT FOR PRACTICE TO END, SO I'M GONNA WAIT.
'BYE, BUFFY.
SEE YOU. DON'T FORGET OUR STUDY DATE TONIGHT.
BUFFY SUMMERS. I NEED TO SPEAK TO YOU.
HI, WHAT? YOU'RE NOT FROM MACY'S ARE YOU? 'CAUSE I MEANT TO PAY FOR THAT LIPSTICK.
THERE ISN'T MUCH TIME. YOU MUST COME WITH ME. YOUR DESTINY AWAITS.
I DON'T HAVE A DESTINY. I'M DESTINY-FREE, REALLY.

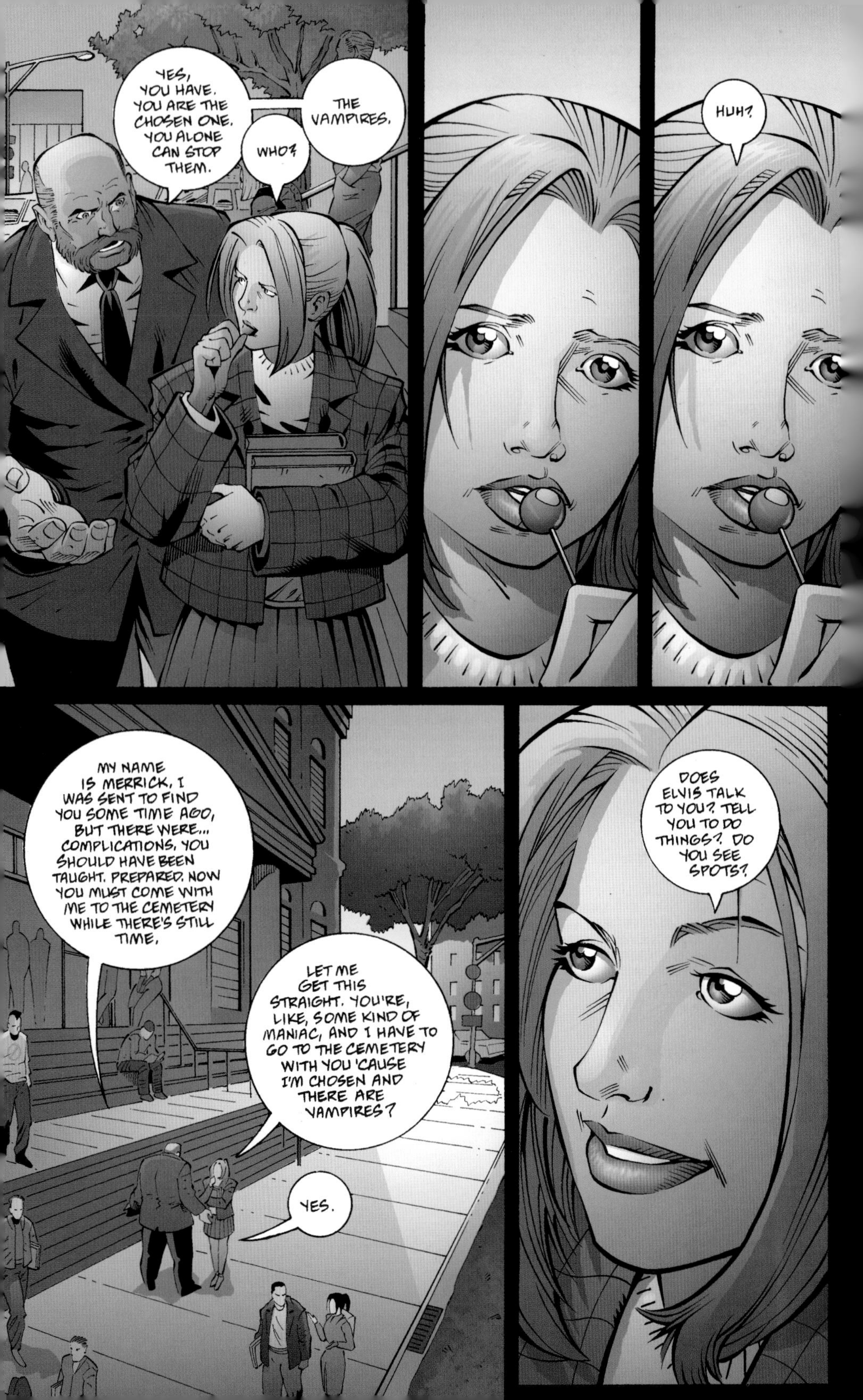
YES, YOU HAVE. YOU ARE THE CHOSEN ONE. YOU ALONE CAN STOP THEM.
WHO?
THE VAMPIRES.
HUH?
MY NAME IS MERRICK. I WAS SENT TO FIND YOU SOME TIME AGO, BUT THERE WERE... COMPLICATIONS. YOU SHOULD HAVE BEEN TAUGHT. PREPARED. NOW YOU MUST COME WITH ME TO THE CEMETERY WHILE THERE'S STILL TIME.
LET ME GET THIS STRAIGHT. YOU'RE, LIKE, SOME KIND OF MANIAC, AND I HAVE TO GO TO THE CEMETERY WITH YOU 'CAUSE I'M CHOSEN AND THERE ARE VAMPIRES?
YES.
DOES ELVIS TALK TO YOU? TELL YOU TO DO THINGS? DO YOU SEE SPOTS?

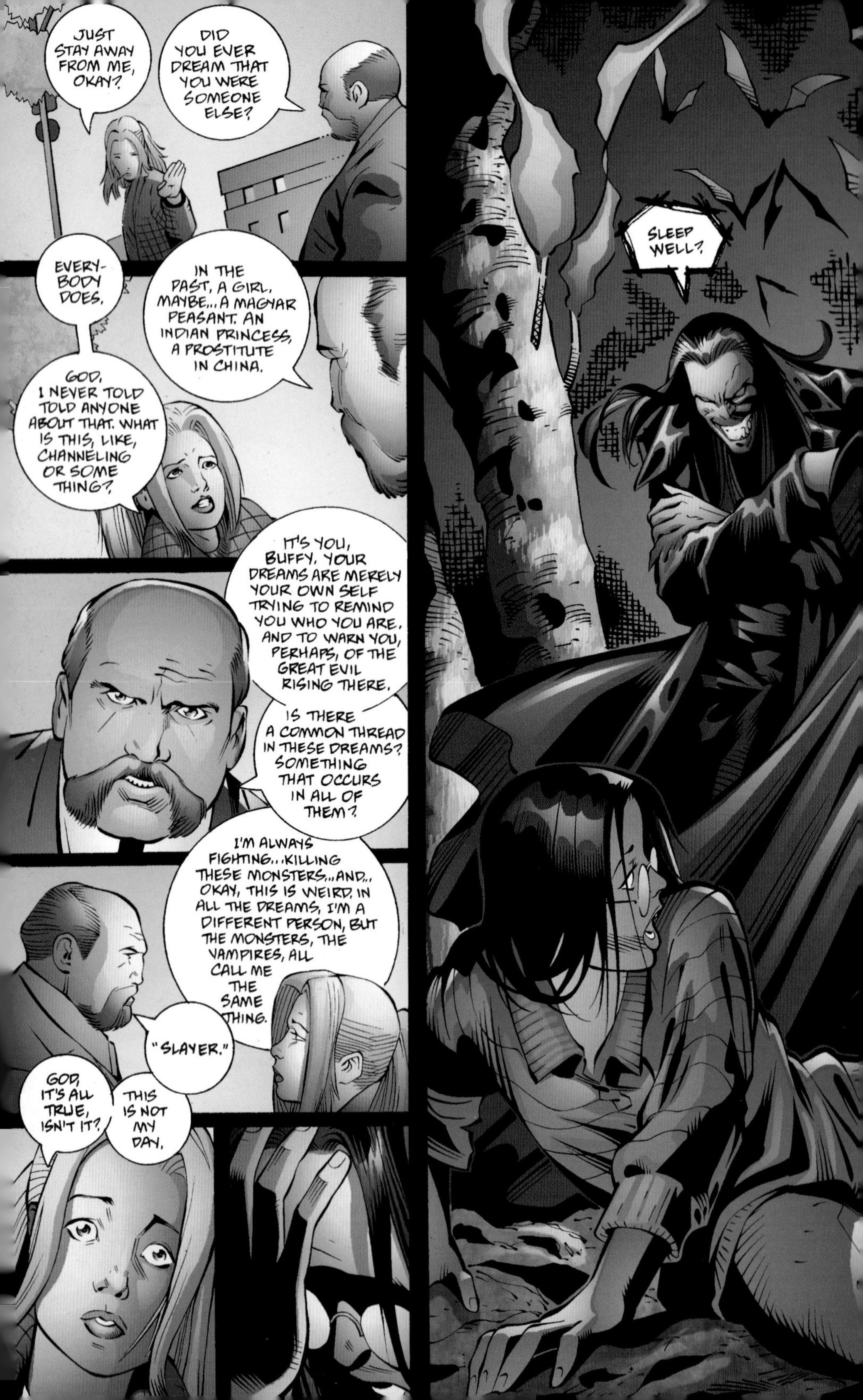
JUST STAY AWAY FROM ME, OKAY?
DID YOU EVER DREAM THAT YOU WERE SOMEONE ELSE?
EVERY-BODY DOES.
IN THE PAST, A GIRL, MAYBE... A MAGYAR PEASANT. AN INDIAN PRINCESS, A PROSTITUTE IN CHINA.
GOD, I NEVER TOLD TOLD ANYONE ABOUT THAT. WHAT IS THIS, LIKE, CHANNELING OR SOME THING?
IT'S YOU, BUFFY. YOUR DREAMS ARE MERELY YOUR OWN SELF TRYING TO REMIND YOU WHO YOU ARE, AND TO WARN YOU, PERHAPS, OF THE GREAT EVIL RISING THERE.
IS THERE A COMMON THREAD IN THESE DREAMS? SOMETHING THAT OCCURS IN ALL OF THEM?
I'M ALWAYS FIGHTING... KILLING THESE MONSTERS... AND... OKAY, THIS IS WEIRD. IN ALL THE DREAMS, I'M A DIFFERENT PERSON, BUT THE MONSTERS, THE VAMPIRES, ALL CALL ME THE SAME THING.
"SLAYER."
GOD, IT'S ALL TRUE, ISN'T IT?
THIS IS NOT MY DAY.
SLEEP WELL?

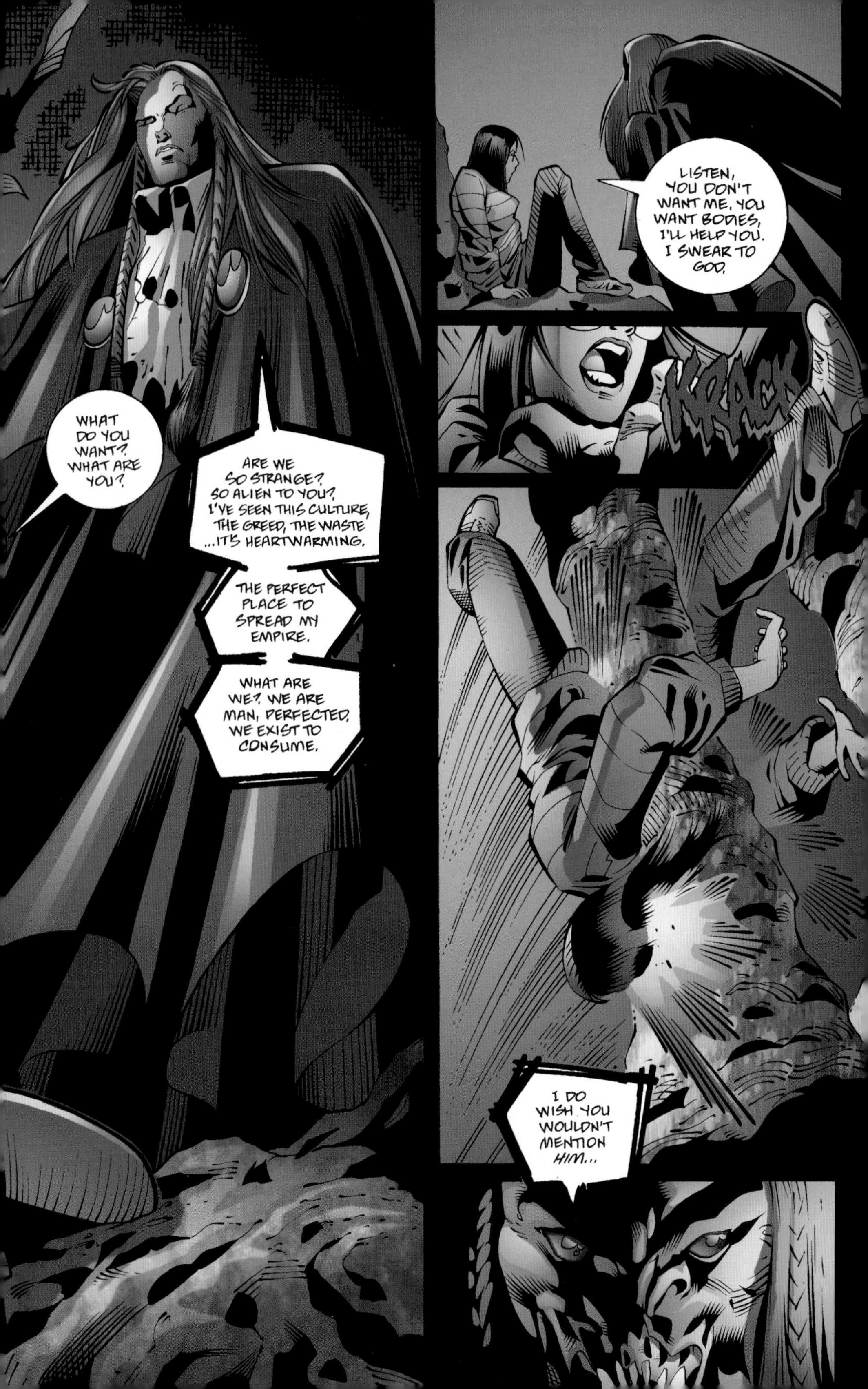

WHAT DO YOU WANT? WHAT ARE YOU?
ARE WE SO STRANGE? SO ALIEN TO YOU? I'VE SEEN THIS CULTURE, THE GREED, THE WASTE ...IT'S HEARTWARMING.
THE PERFECT PLACE TO SPREAD MY EMPIRE.
WHAT ARE WE? WE ARE MAN, PERFECTED. WE EXIST TO CONSUME.
LISTEN, YOU DON'T WANT ME, YOU WANT BODIES, I'LL HELP YOU. I SWEAR TO GOD.
KRACK
I DO WISH YOU WOULDN'T MENTION *HIM*...

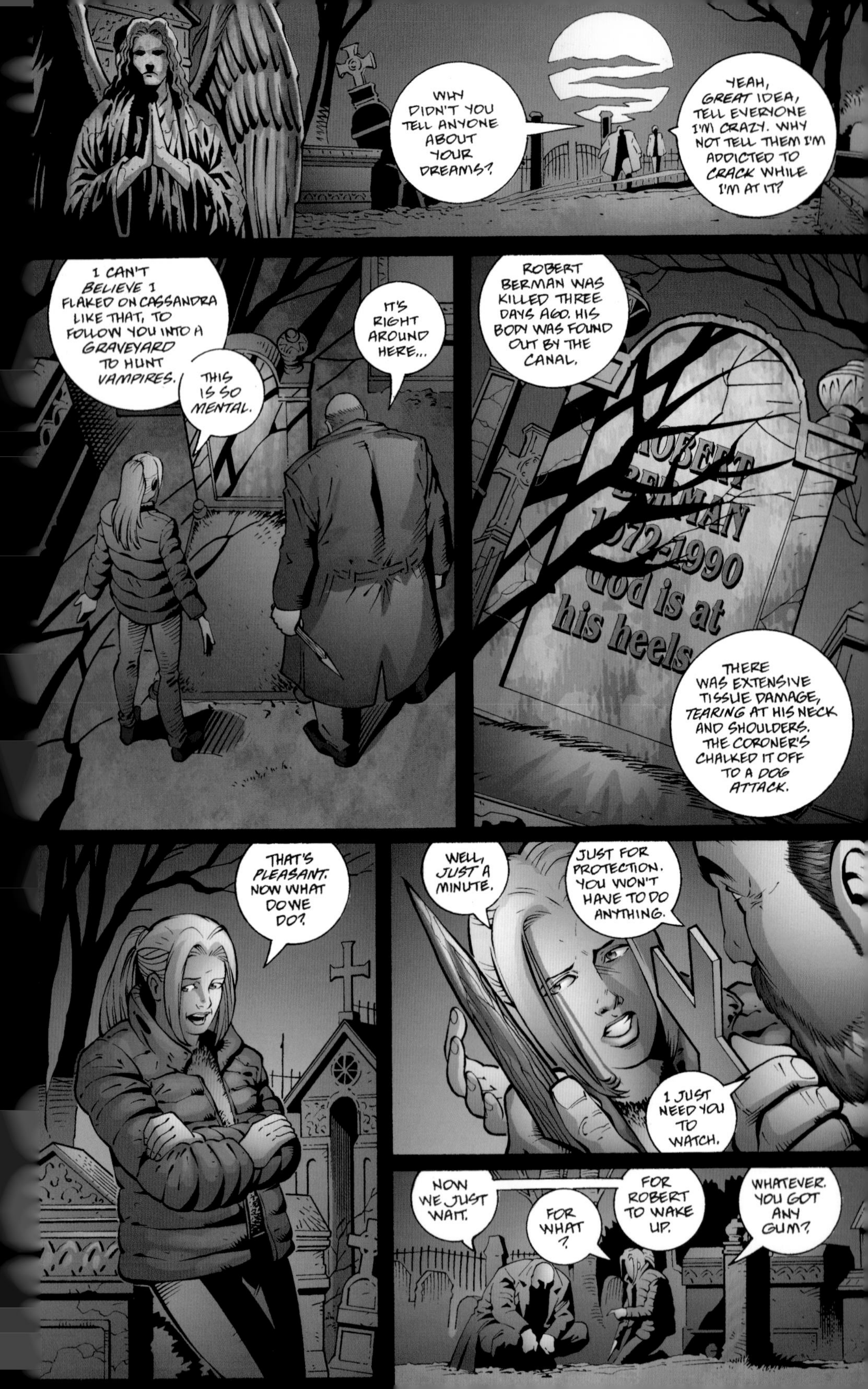
WHY DIDN'T YOU TELL ANYONE ABOUT YOUR DREAMS?
YEAH, GREAT IDEA, TELL EVERYONE I'M CRAZY. WHY NOT TELL THEM I'M ADDICTED TO CRACK WHILE I'M AT IT?
I CAN'T BELIEVE I FLAKED ON CASSANDRA LIKE THAT, TO FOLLOW YOU INTO A GRAVEYARD TO HUNT VAMPIRES.
THIS IS SO MENTAL.
IT'S RIGHT AROUND HERE...
ROBERT BERMAN WAS KILLED THREE DAYS AGO. HIS BODY WAS FOUND OUT BY THE CANAL.
ROBERT BERMAN 1972-1990 God is at his heels
THERE WAS EXTENSIVE TISSUE DAMAGE, TEARING AT HIS NECK AND SHOULDERS. THE CORONER'S CHALKED IT OFF TO A DOG ATTACK.
THAT'S PLEASANT. NOW WHAT DO WE DO?
WELL, JUST A MINUTE.
JUST FOR PROTECTION. YOU WON'T HAVE TO DO ANYTHING.
I JUST NEED YOU TO WATCH.
NOW WE JUST WAIT.
FOR WHAT?
FOR ROBERT TO WAKE UP.
WHATEVER. YOU GOT ANY GUM?

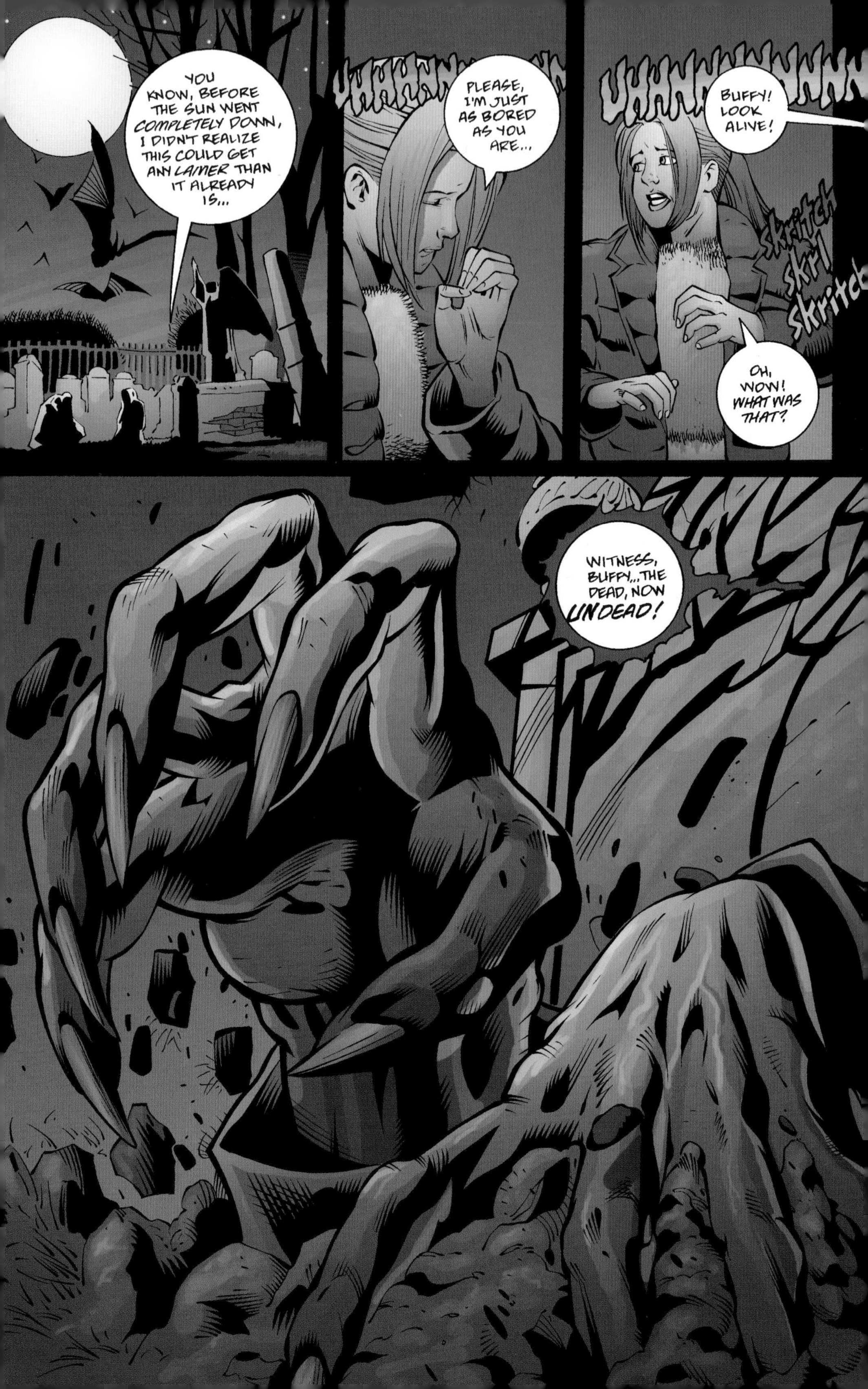
YOU KNOW, BEFORE THE SUN WENT COMPLETELY DOWN, I DIDN'T REALIZE THIS COULD GET ANY LAMER THAN IT ALREADY IS...
UHHHNNN
PLEASE, I'M JUST AS BORED AS YOU ARE...
UHHHNNNNNNNNN
BUFFY! LOOK ALIVE!
SKRITCH SKRI SKRITCH
OH, WOW! WHAT WAS THAT?
WITNESS, BUFFY... THE DEAD, NOW UNDEAD!

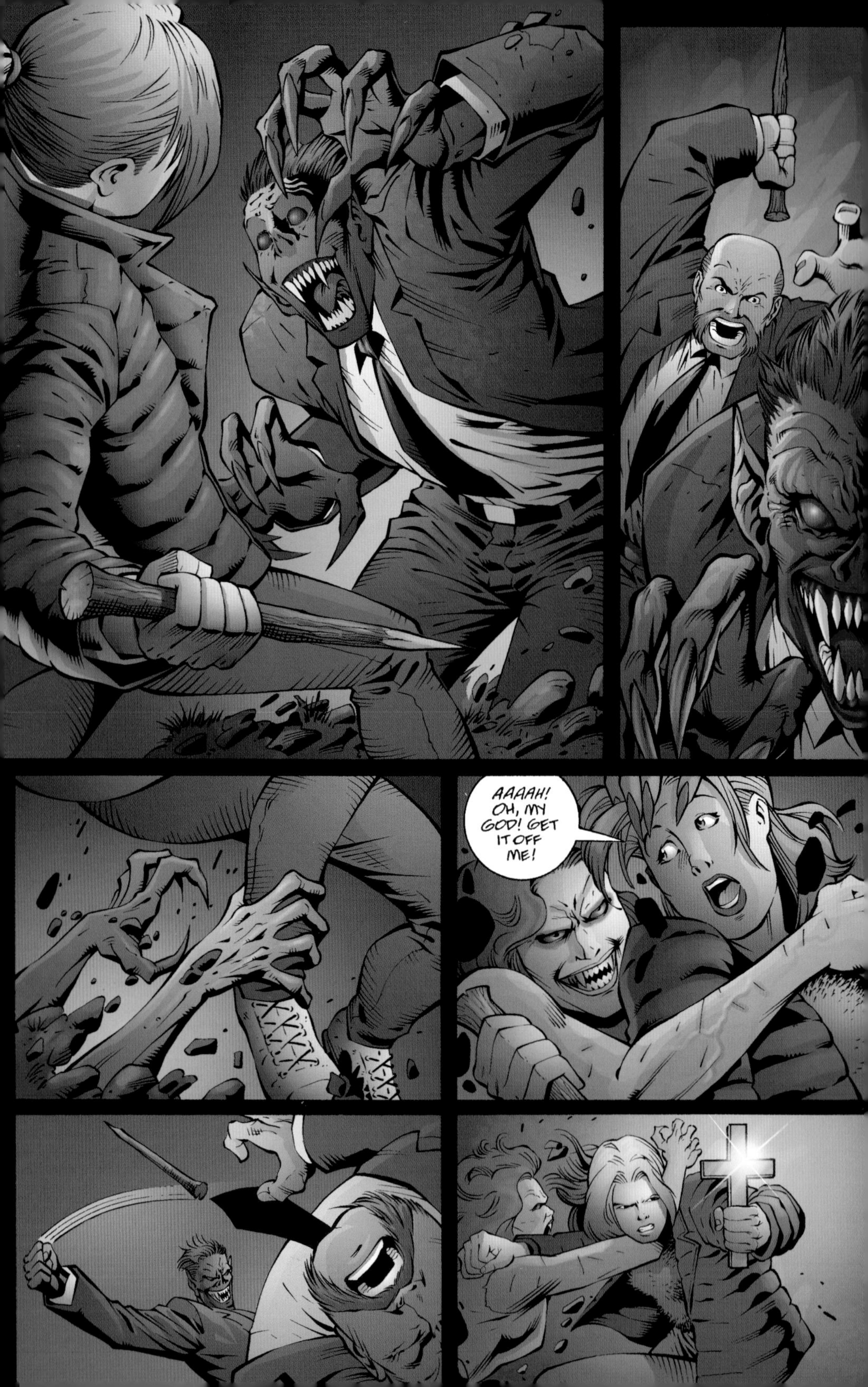
AAAAH! OH, MY GOD! GET IT OFF ME!

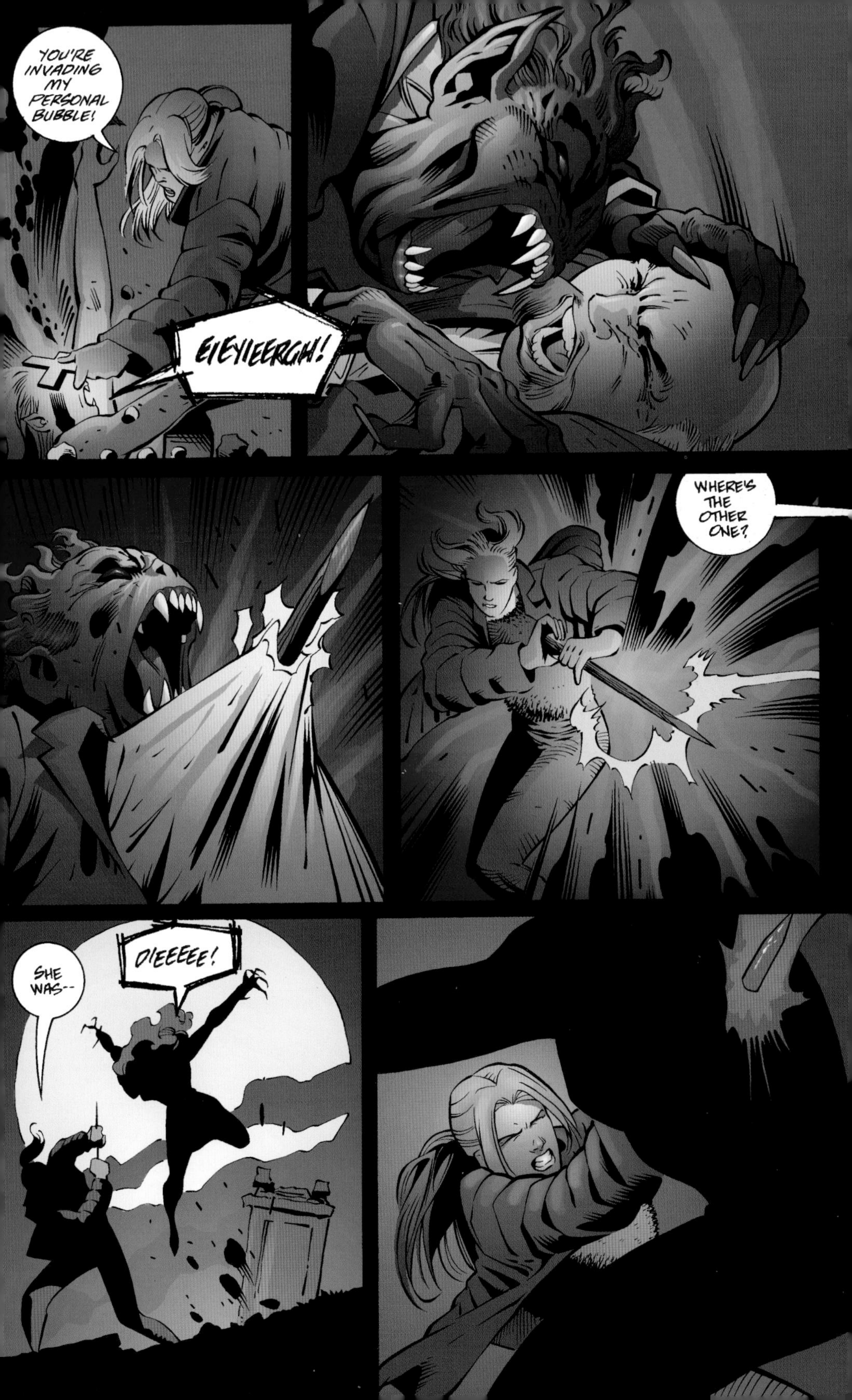
YOU'RE INVADING MY PERSONAL BUBBLE!
EIEYIEERGH!
WHERE'S THE OTHER ONE?
SHE WAS--
DIEEEEE!

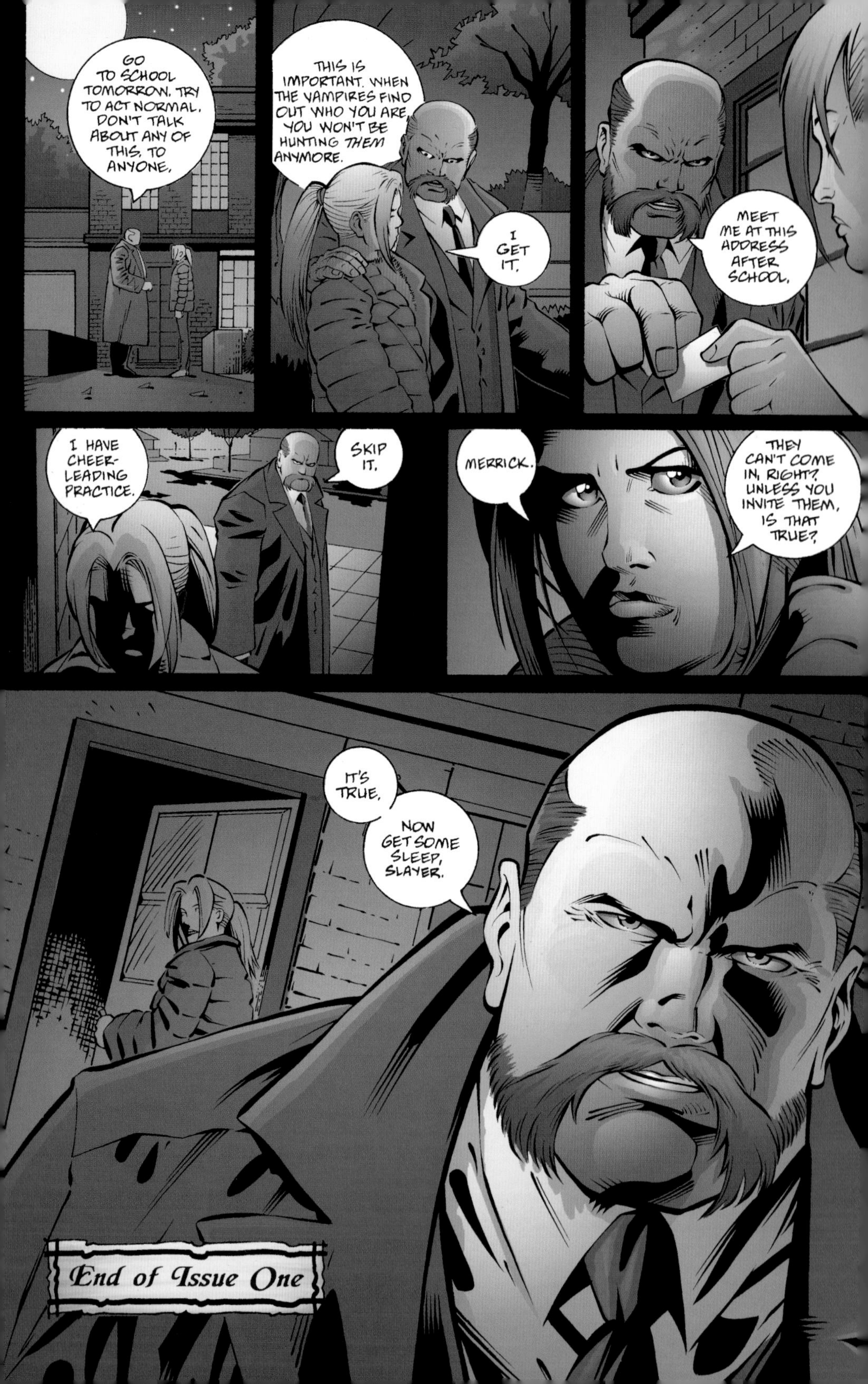
GO TO SCHOOL TOMORROW. TRY TO ACT NORMAL. DON'T TALK ABOUT ANY OF THIS. TO ANYONE.
THIS IS IMPORTANT. WHEN THE VAMPIRES FIND OUT WHO YOU ARE, YOU WON'T BE HUNTING THEM ANYMORE.
I GET IT.
MEET ME AT THIS ADDRESS AFTER SCHOOL.
I HAVE CHEER-LEADING PRACTICE.
SKIP IT.
MERRICK.
THEY CAN'T COME IN, RIGHT? UNLESS YOU INVITE THEM. IS THAT TRUE?
IT'S TRUE.
NOW GET SOME SLEEP, SLAYER.
End of Issue One

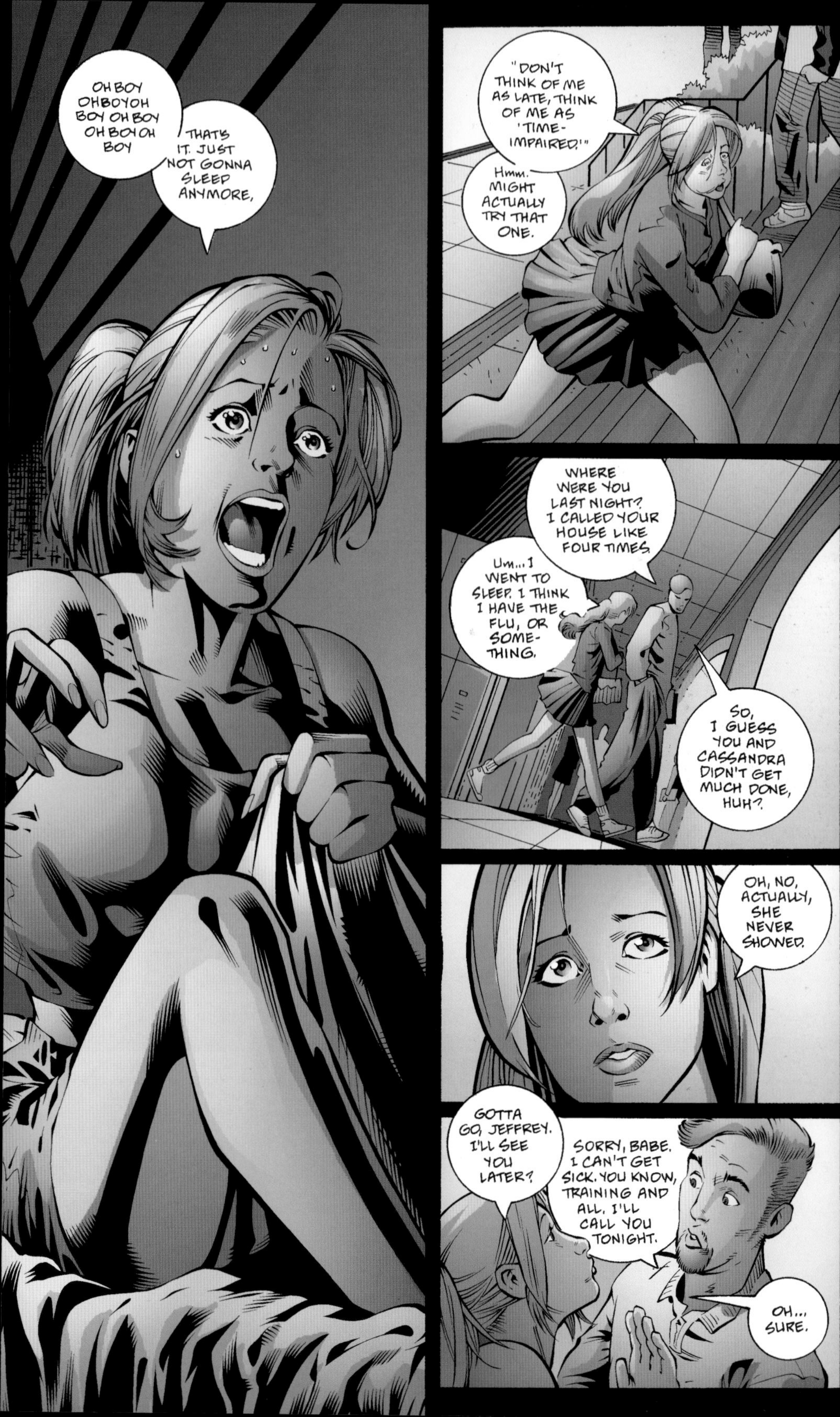
OH BOY OHBOYOH BOY OH BOY OH BOYOH BOY
THAT'S IT. JUST NOT GONNA SLEEP ANYMORE.
"DON'T THINK OF ME AS LATE, THINK OF ME AS 'TIME-IMPAIRED.'"
Hmm... MIGHT ACTUALLY TRY THAT ONE.
WHERE WERE YOU LAST NIGHT? I CALLED YOUR HOUSE LIKE FOUR TIMES.
Um... I WENT TO SLEEP. I THINK I HAVE THE FLU, OR SOME-THING.
SO, I GUESS YOU AND CASSANDRA DIDN'T GET MUCH DONE, HUH?
OH, NO, ACTUALLY, SHE NEVER SHOWED.
GOTTA GO, JEFFREY. I'LL SEE YOU LATER?
SORRY, BABE. I CAN'T GET SICK. YOU KNOW, TRAINING AND ALL. I'LL CALL YOU TONIGHT.
OH... SURE.

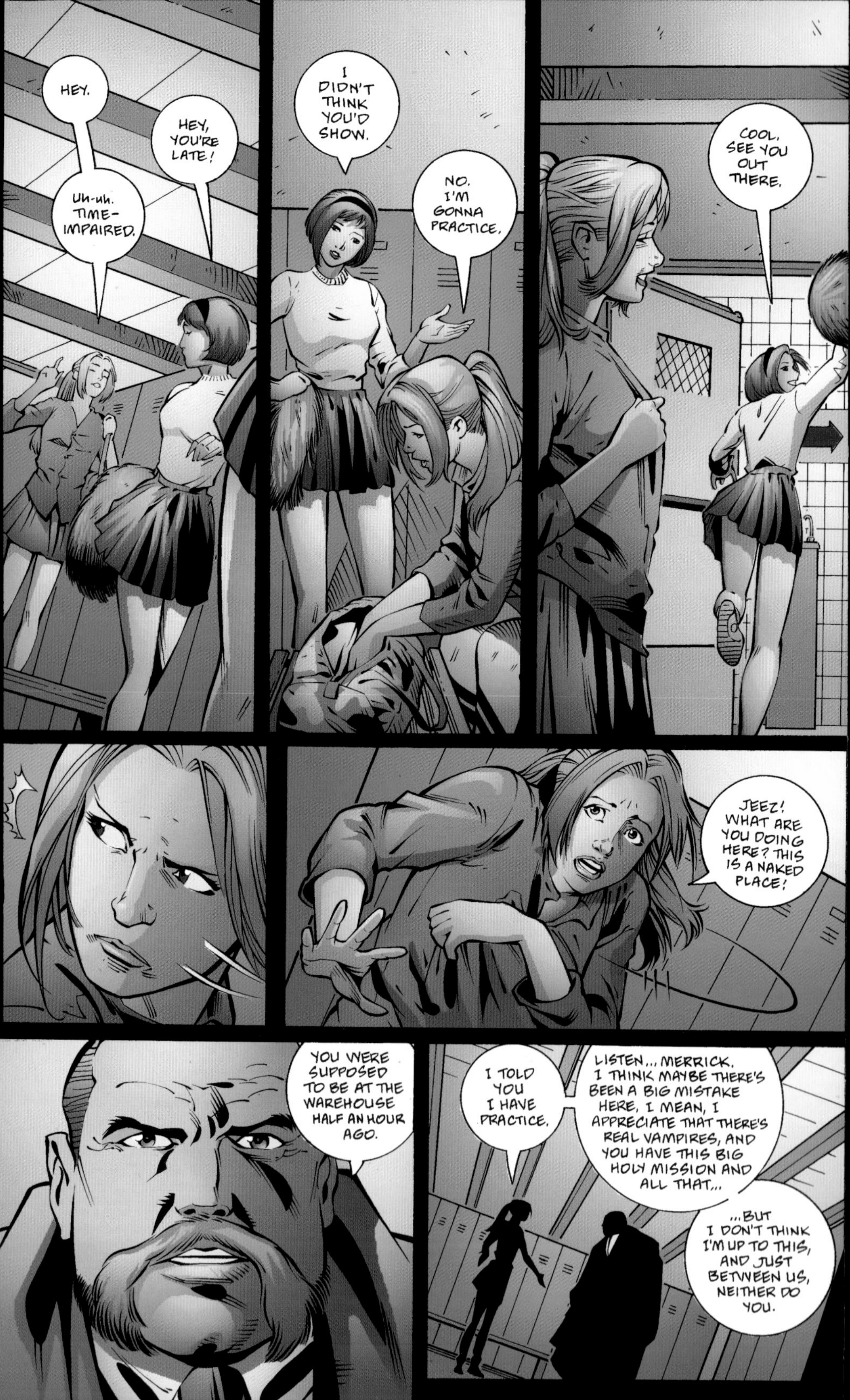
HEY.
HEY, YOU'RE LATE!
Uh-uh. TIME-IMPAIRED.
I DIDN'T THINK YOU'D SHOW.
NO. I'M GONNA PRACTICE.
COOL. SEE YOU OUT THERE.
JEEZ! WHAT ARE YOU DOING HERE? THIS IS A NAKED PLACE!
YOU WERE SUPPOSED TO BE AT THE WAREHOUSE HALF AN HOUR AGO.
I TOLD YOU I HAVE PRACTICE.
LISTEN... MERRICK. I THINK MAYBE THERE'S BEEN A BIG MISTAKE HERE. I MEAN, I APPRECIATE THAT THERE'S REAL VAMPIRES, AND YOU HAVE THIS BIG HOLY MISSION AND ALL THAT...
...BUT I DON'T THINK I'M UP TO THIS, AND JUST BETWEEN US, NEITHER DO YOU.

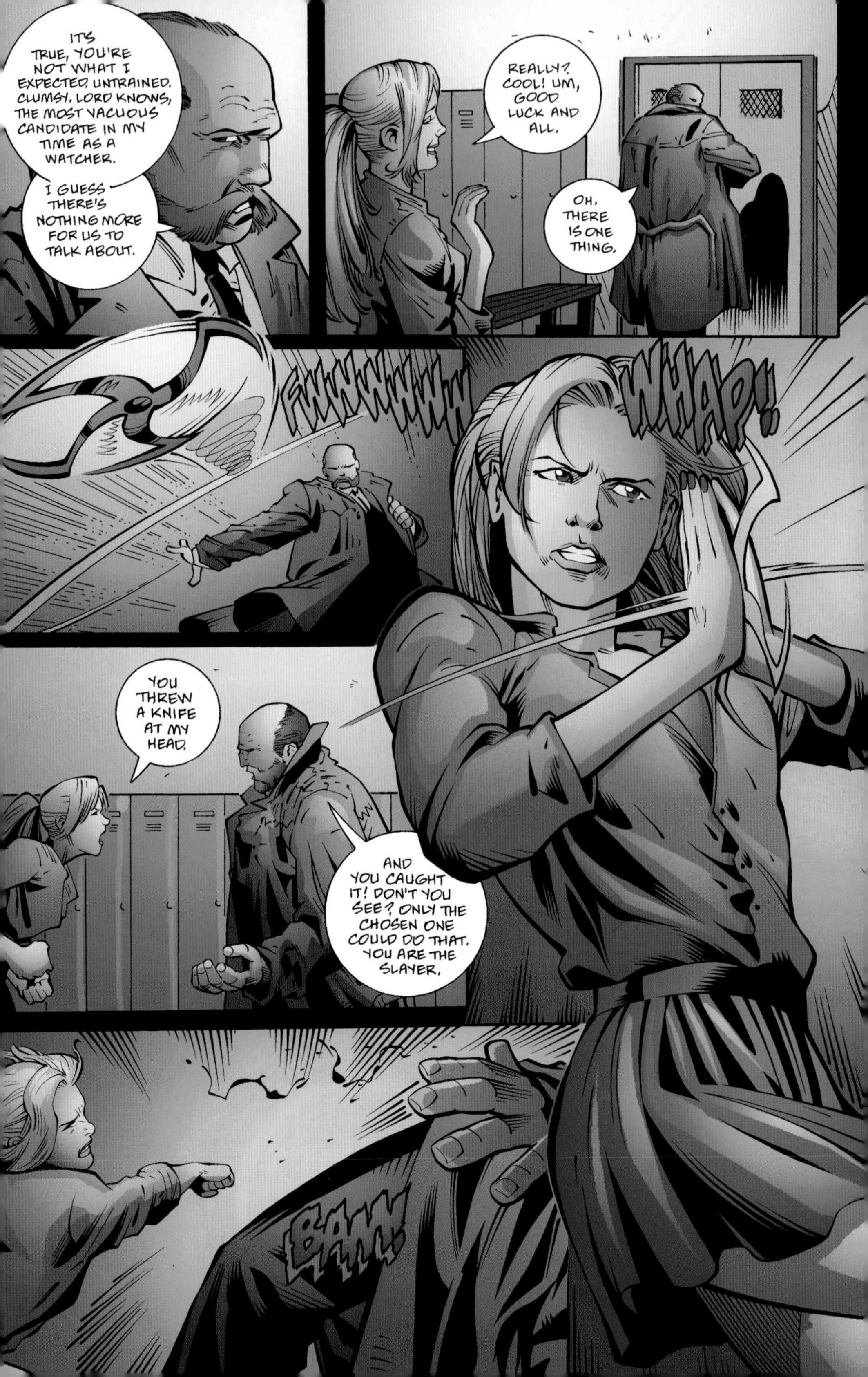
IT'S TRUE, YOU'RE NOT WHAT I EXPECTED. UNTRAINED. CLUMSY. LORD KNOWS, THE MOST VACUOUS CANDIDATE IN MY TIME AS A WATCHER.
I GUESS THERE'S NOTHING MORE FOR US TO TALK ABOUT.
REALLY? COOL! UM, GOOD LUCK AND ALL.
OH, THERE IS ONE THING.
FWWWWWWW
WHAP!
YOU THREW A KNIFE AT MY HEAD.
AND YOU CAUGHT IT! DON'T YOU SEE? ONLY THE CHOSEN ONE COULD DO THAT. YOU ARE THE SLAYER.
BAM

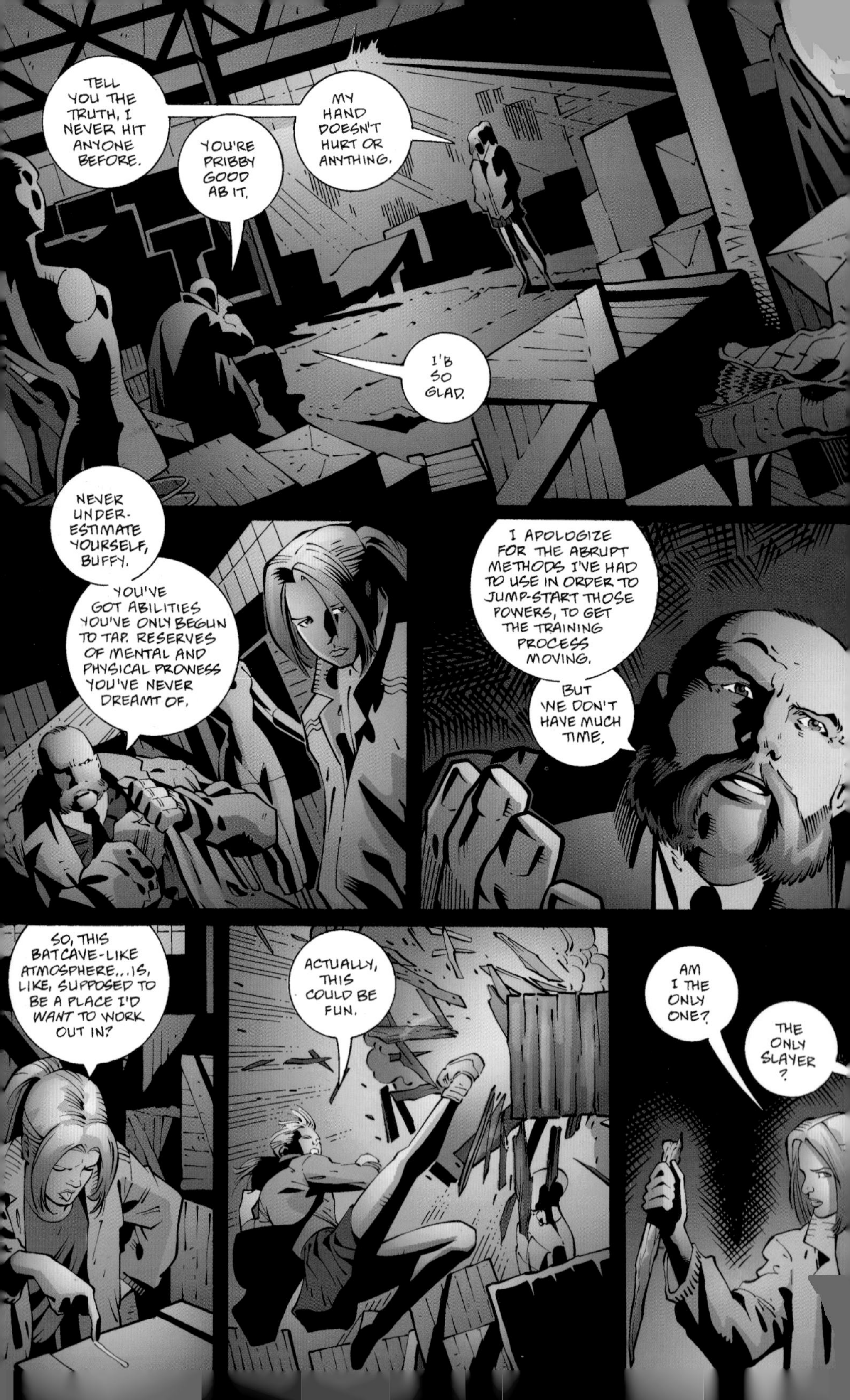
TELL YOU THE TRUTH, I NEVER HIT ANYONE BEFORE.
MY HAND DOESN'T HURT OR ANYTHING.
YOU'RE PRIBBY GOOD AB IT.
I'B SO GLAD.
NEVER UNDER-ESTIMATE YOURSELF, BUFFY.
YOU'VE GOT ABILITIES YOU'VE ONLY BEGUN TO TAP. RESERVES OF MENTAL AND PHYSICAL PROWESS YOU'VE NEVER DREAMT OF.
I APOLOGIZE FOR THE ABRUPT METHODS I'VE HAD TO USE IN ORDER TO JUMP-START THOSE POWERS, TO GET THE TRAINING PROCESS MOVING.
BUT WE DON'T HAVE MUCH TIME.
SO, THIS BATCAVE-LIKE ATMOSPHERE...IS, LIKE, SUPPOSED TO BE A PLACE I'D WANT TO WORK OUT IN?
ACTUALLY, THIS COULD BE FUN.
AM I THE ONLY ONE?
THE ONLY SLAYER?

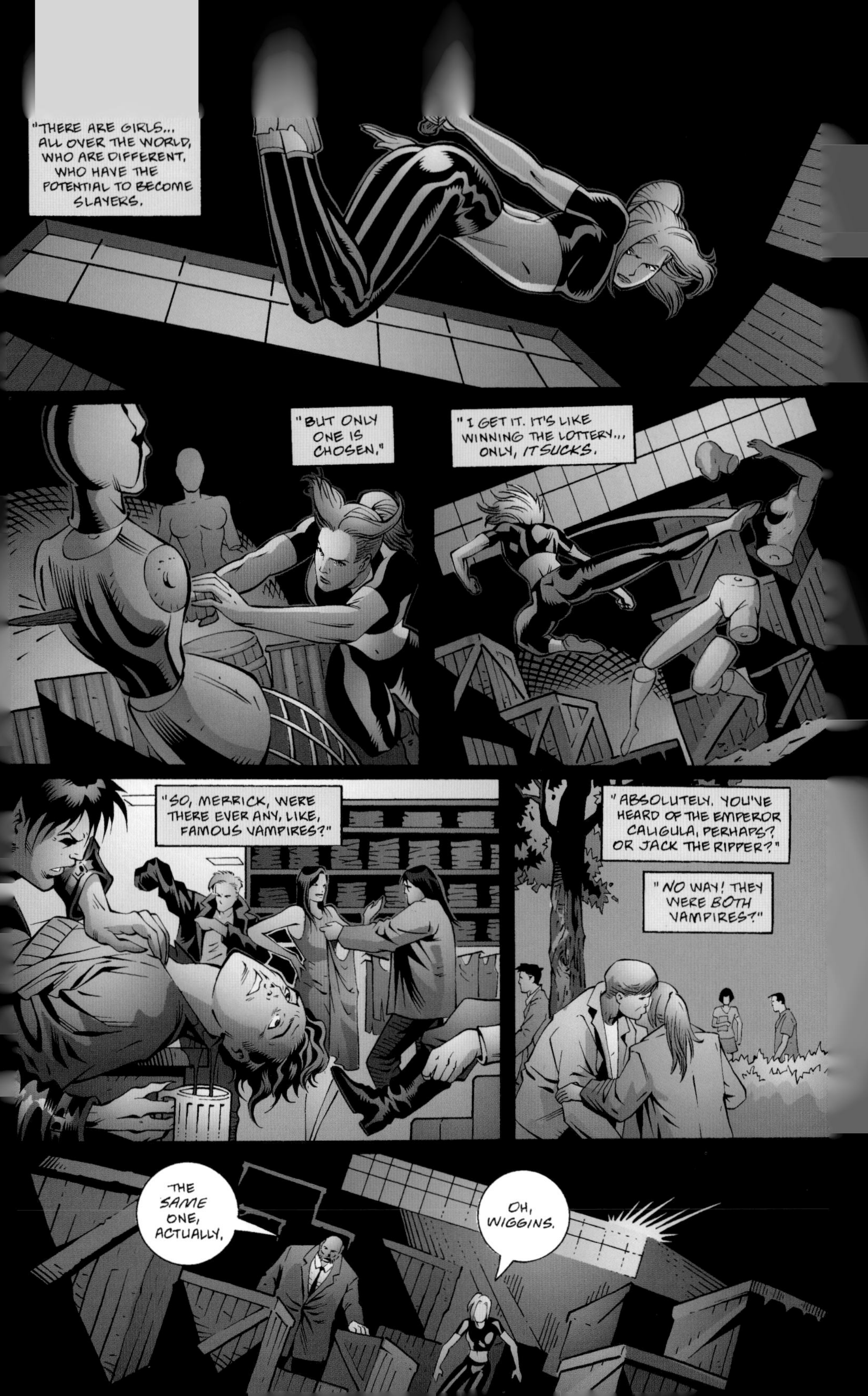
"THERE ARE GIRLS... ALL OVER THE WORLD, WHO ARE DIFFERENT, WHO HAVE THE POTENTIAL TO BECOME SLAYERS.
"BUT ONLY ONE IS CHOSEN."
"I GET IT. IT'S LIKE WINNING THE LOTTERY... ONLY, IT SUCKS.
"SO, MERRICK, WERE THERE EVER ANY, LIKE, FAMOUS VAMPIRES?"
"ABSOLUTELY. YOU'VE HEARD OF THE EMPEROR CALIGULA, PERHAPS? OR JACK THE RIPPER?"
"NO WAY! THEY WERE BOTH VAMPIRES?"
THE SAME ONE, ACTUALLY.
OH, WIGGINS.

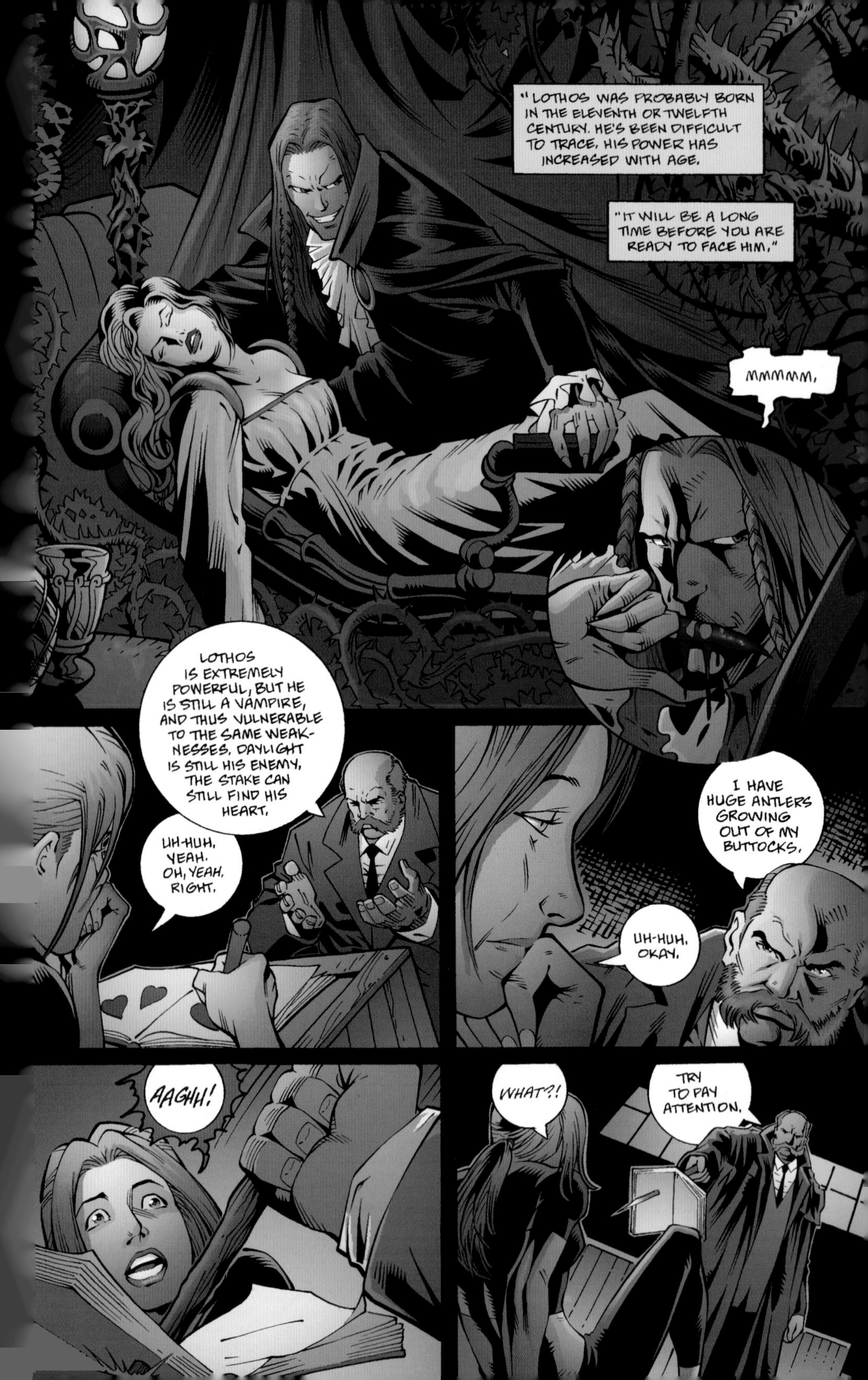
"LOTHOS WAS PROBABLY BORN IN THE ELEVENTH OR TWELFTH CENTURY. HE'S BEEN DIFFICULT TO TRACE. HIS POWER HAS INCREASED WITH AGE.
"IT WILL BE A LONG TIME BEFORE YOU ARE READY TO FACE HIM."
MMMMM.
LOTHOS IS EXTREMELY POWERFUL, BUT HE IS STILL A VAMPIRE, AND THUS VULNERABLE TO THE SAME WEAK-NESSES. DAYLIGHT IS STILL HIS ENEMY. THE STAKE CAN STILL FIND HIS HEART.
UH-HUH. YEAH. OH, YEAH. RIGHT.
I HAVE HUGE ANTLERS GROWING OUT OF MY BUTTOCKS.
UH-HUH. OKAY.
AAGHH!
WHAT?!
TRY TO PAY ATTENTION.

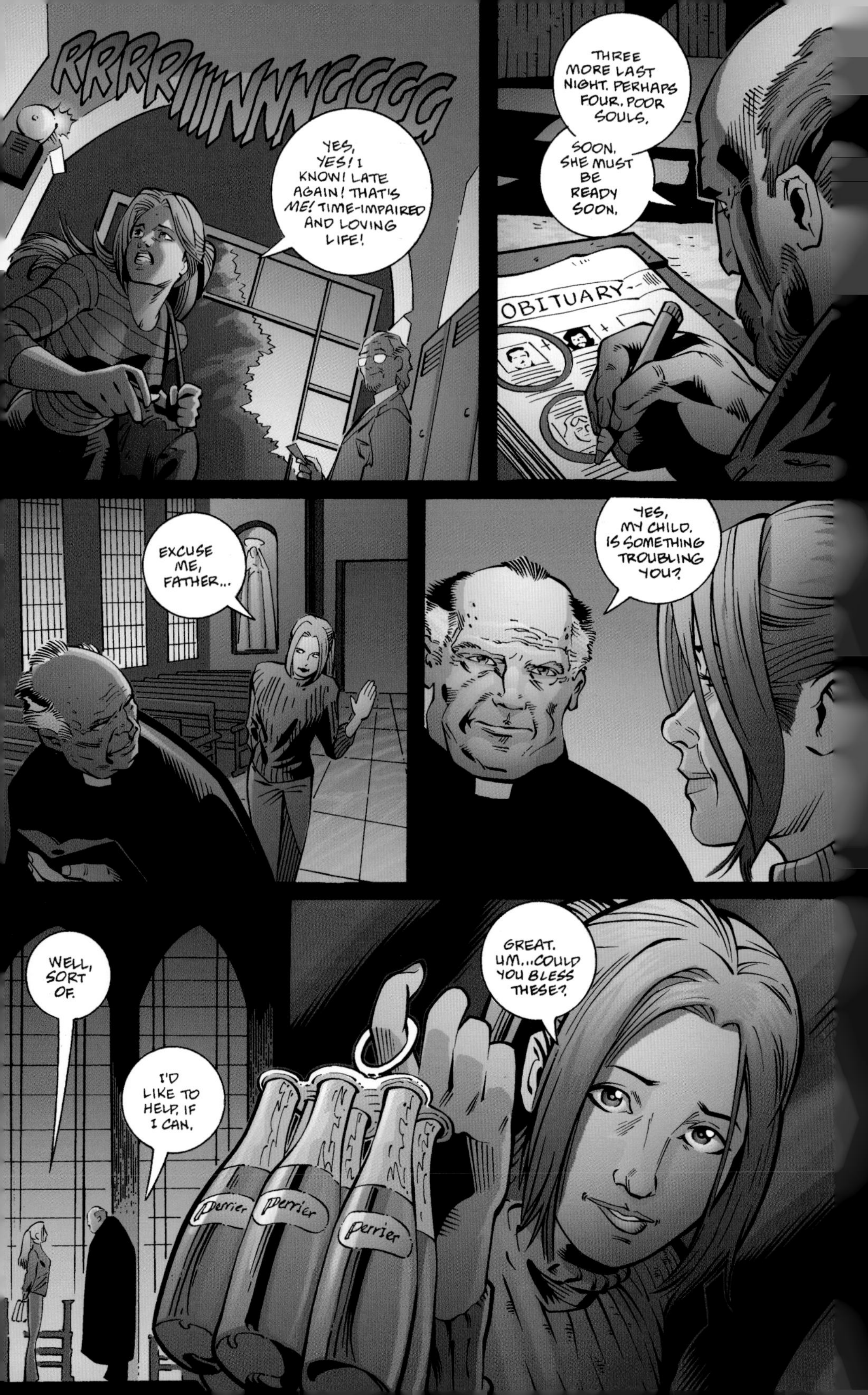
RRRRIIINNNNGGGG
YES, YES! I KNOW! LATE AGAIN! THAT'S ME! TIME-IMPAIRED AND LOVING LIFE!
THREE MORE LAST NIGHT. PERHAPS FOUR. POOR SOULS.
SOON. SHE MUST BE READY SOON.
OBITUARY
EXCUSE ME, FATHER...
YES, MY CHILD. IS SOMETHING TROUBLING YOU?
WELL, SORT OF.
I'D LIKE TO HELP, IF I CAN.
GREAT. UM...COULD YOU BLESS THESE?
Perrier
Perrier
Perrier

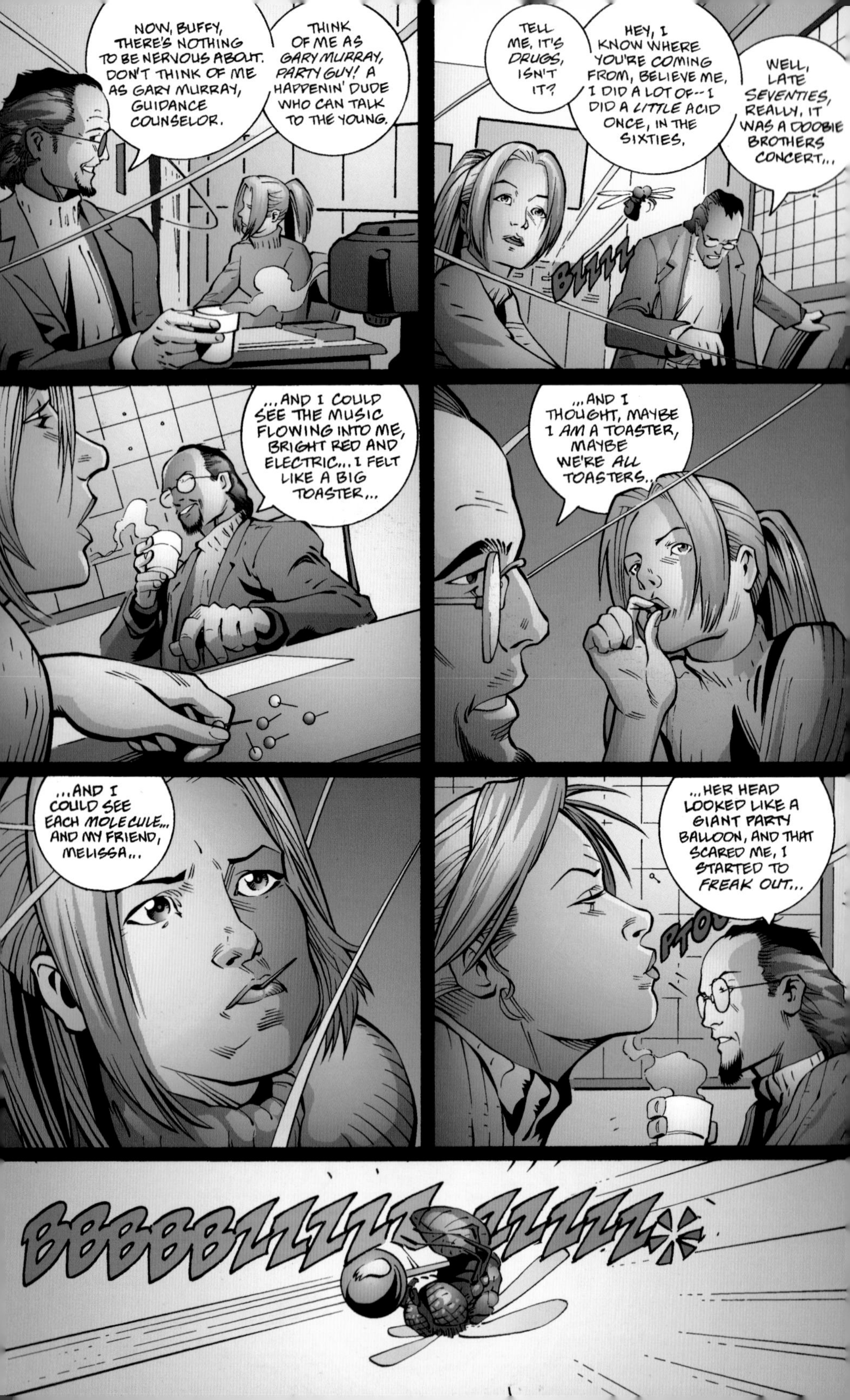
NOW, BUFFY, THERE'S NOTHING TO BE NERVOUS ABOUT. DON'T THINK OF ME AS GARY MURRAY, GUIDANCE COUNSELOR.
THINK OF ME AS GARY MURRAY, PARTY GUY! A HAPPENIN' DUDE WHO CAN TALK TO THE YOUNG.
TELL ME, IT'S DRUGS, ISN'T IT?
HEY, I KNOW WHERE YOU'RE COMING FROM, BELIEVE ME, I DID A LOT OF-- I DID A LITTLE ACID ONCE, IN THE SIXTIES.
WELL, LATE SEVENTIES, REALLY, IT WAS A DOOBIE BROTHERS CONCERT...
BZZZZ
...AND I COULD SEE THE MUSIC FLOWING INTO ME, BRIGHT RED AND ELECTRIC... I FELT LIKE A BIG TOASTER...
...AND I THOUGHT, MAYBE I AM A TOASTER, MAYBE WE'RE ALL TOASTERS...
...AND I COULD SEE EACH MOLECULE... AND MY FRIEND, MELISSA...
...HER HEAD LOOKED LIKE A GIANT PARTY BALLOON, AND THAT SCARED ME, I STARTED TO FREAK OUT...
BBBBBZZZZZ

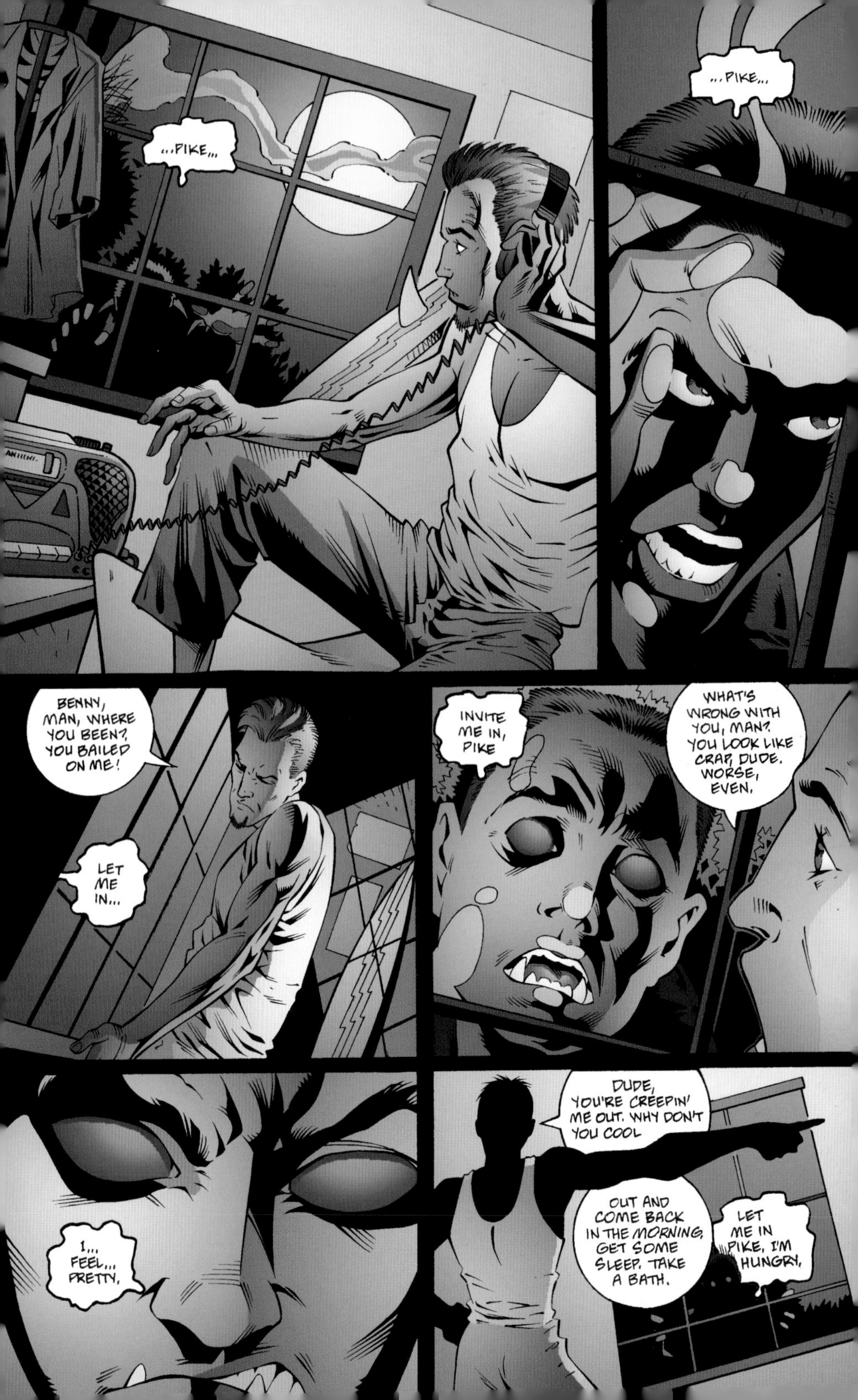
...PIKE...
...PIKE...
BENNY, MAN, WHERE YOU BEEN? YOU BAILED ON ME!
LET ME IN...
INVITE ME IN, PIKE
WHAT'S WRONG WITH YOU, MAN? YOU LOOK LIKE CRAP, DUDE. WORSE, EVEN.
I... FEEL... PRETTY.
DUDE, YOU'RE CREEPIN' ME OUT. WHY DON'T YOU COOL
OUT AND COME BACK IN THE MORNING. GET SOME SLEEP. TAKE A BATH.
LET ME IN PIKE, I'M HUNGRY.

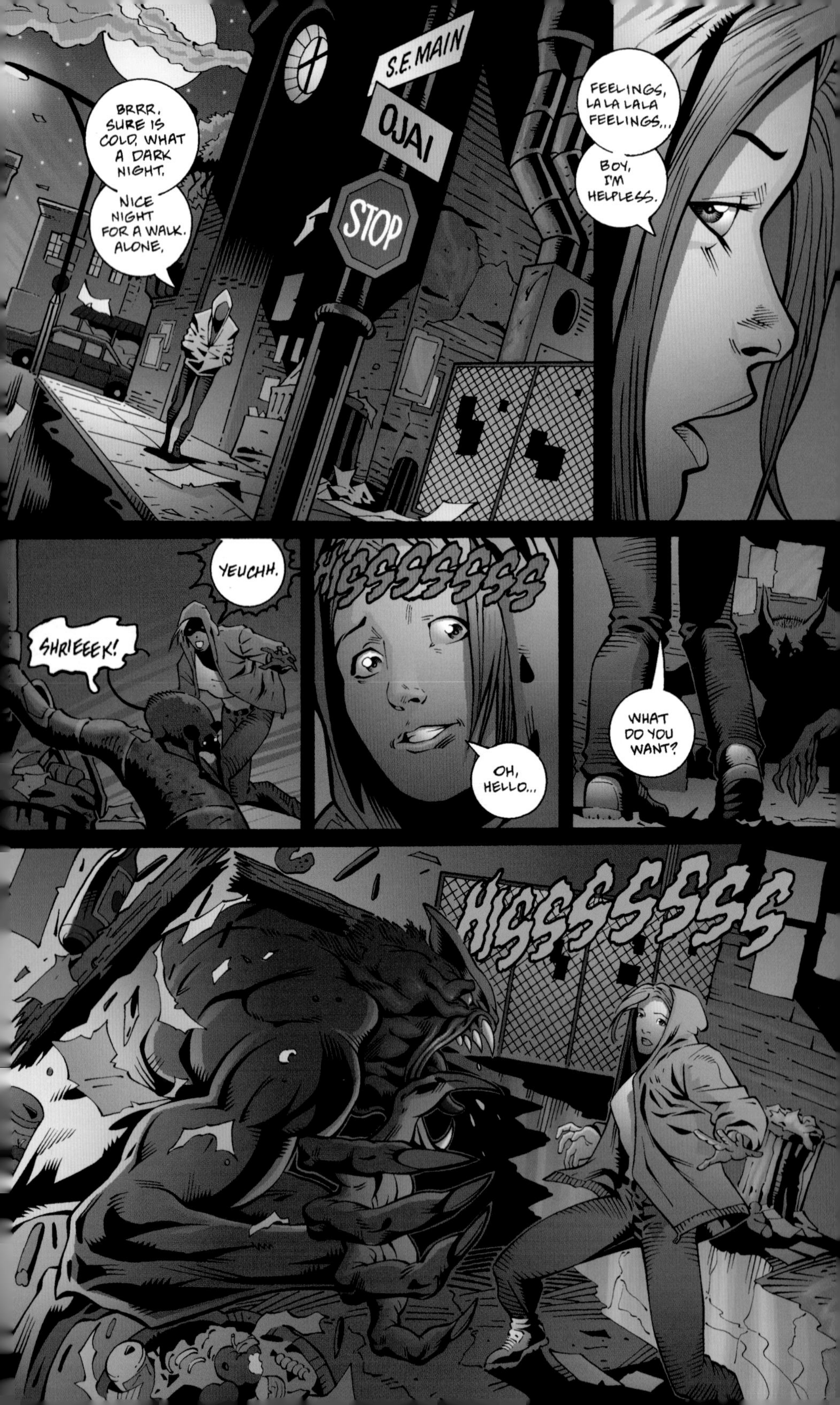

S.E. MAIN
OJAI
STOP
BRRR. SURE IS COLD. WHAT A DARK NIGHT.
NICE NIGHT FOR A WALK. ALONE.
FEELINGS, LA LA LALA FEELINGS...
BOY, I'M HELPLESS.
YEUCHH.
SHRIEEEK!
HISSSSSSS
OH, HELLO...
WHAT DO YOU WANT?
HISSSSSSSS

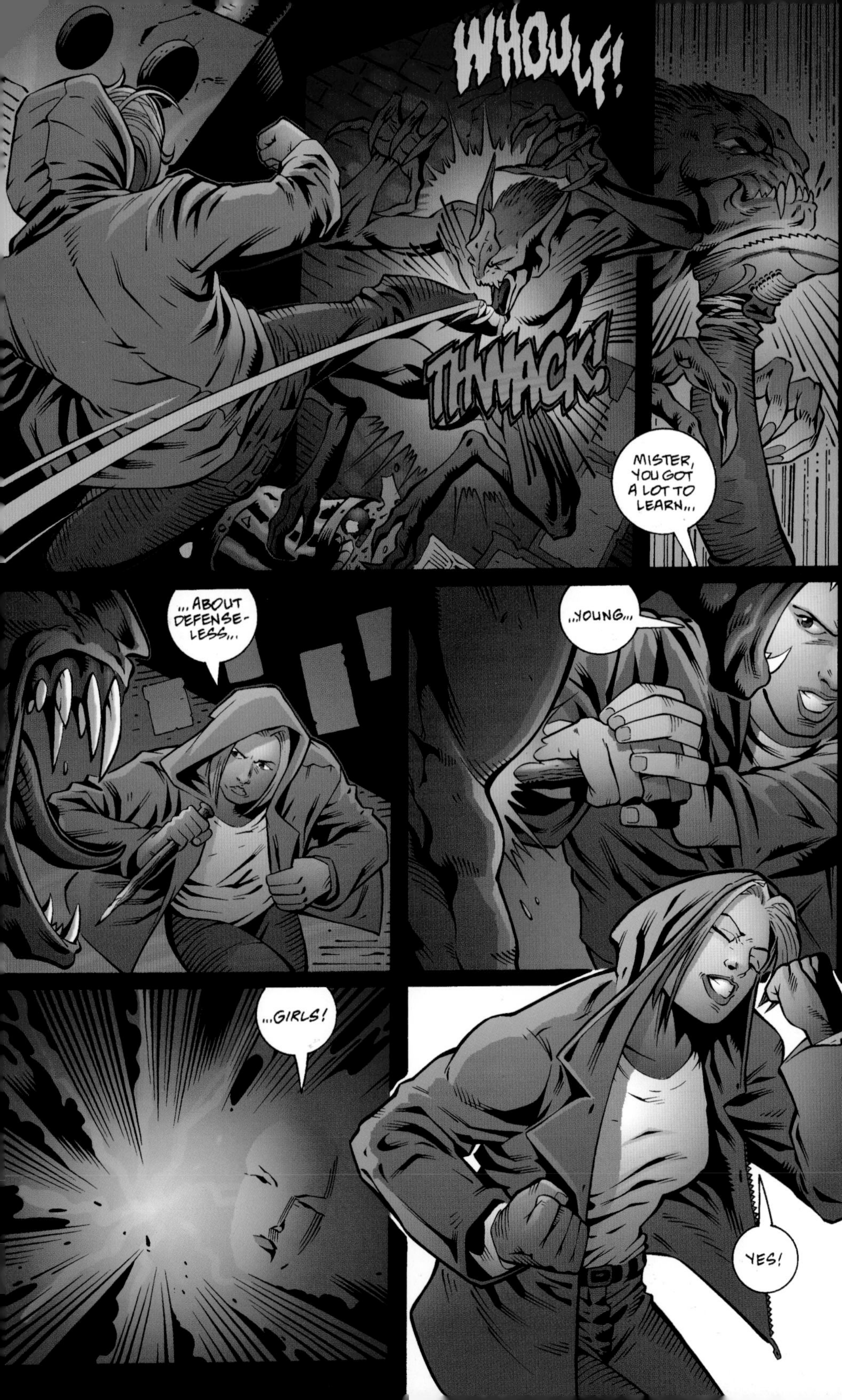
WHOULF!
THWACK!
MISTER, YOU GOT A LOT TO LEARN...
...ABOUT DEFENSE-LESS...
...YOUNG...
...GIRLS!
YES!

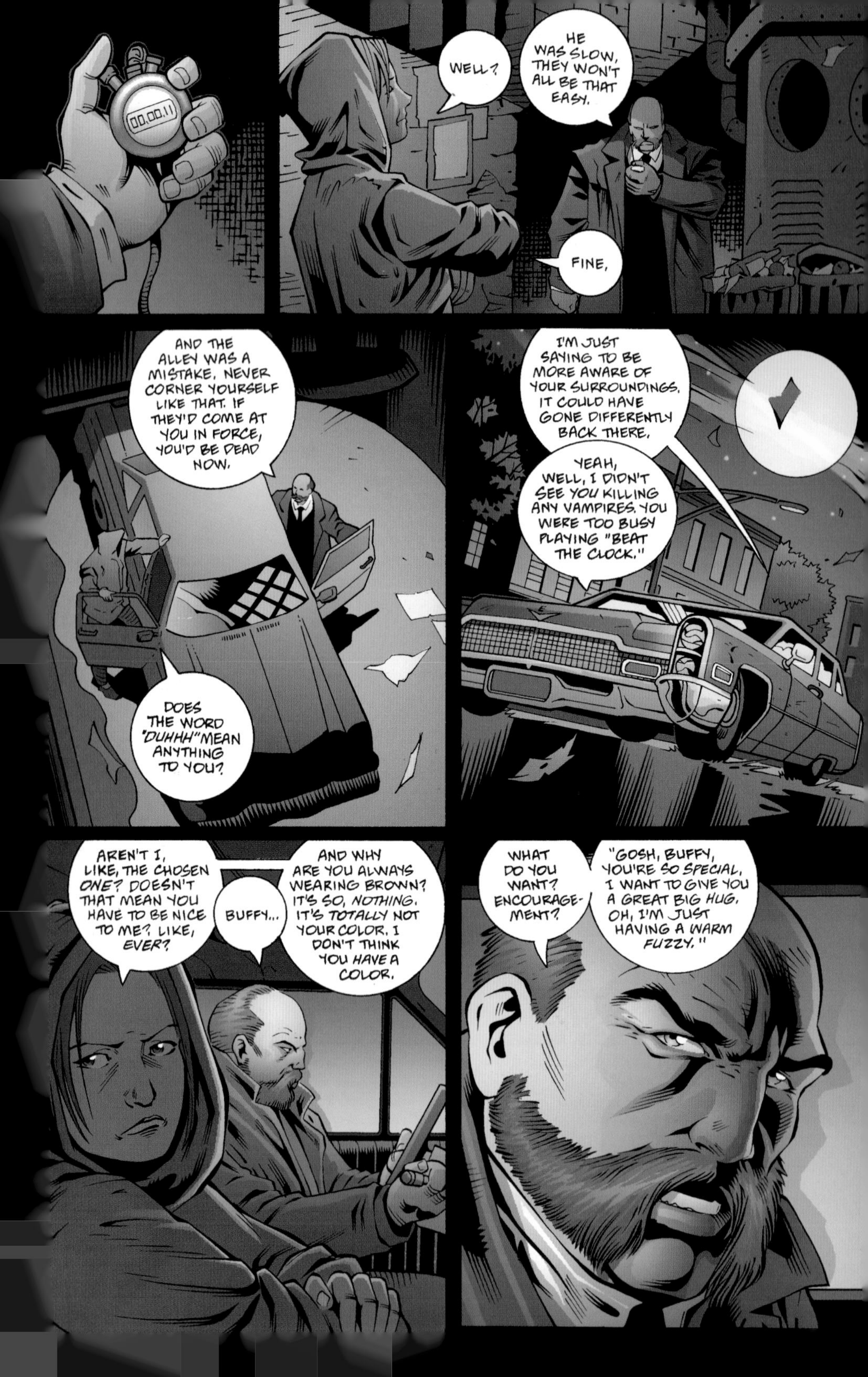
00,00,11
WELL?
HE WAS SLOW, THEY WON'T ALL BE THAT EASY.
FINE.
AND THE ALLEY WAS A MISTAKE. NEVER CORNER YOURSELF LIKE THAT. IF THEY'D COME AT YOU IN FORCE, YOU'D BE DEAD NOW.
DOES THE WORD "DUHHH" MEAN ANYTHING TO YOU?
I'M JUST SAYING TO BE MORE AWARE OF YOUR SURROUNDINGS. IT COULD HAVE GONE DIFFERENTLY BACK THERE.
YEAH, WELL, I DIDN'T SEE YOU KILLING ANY VAMPIRES. YOU WERE TOO BUSY PLAYING "BEAT THE CLOCK."
AREN'T I, LIKE, THE CHOSEN ONE? DOESN'T THAT MEAN YOU HAVE TO BE NICE TO ME? LIKE, EVER?
BUFFY...
AND WHY ARE YOU ALWAYS WEARING BROWN? IT'S SO, NOTHING. IT'S TOTALLY NOT YOUR COLOR. I DON'T THINK YOU HAVE A COLOR.
WHAT DO YOU WANT? ENCOURAGE-MENT?
"GOSH, BUFFY, YOU'RE SO SPECIAL. I WANT TO GIVE YOU A GREAT BIG HUG. OH, I'M JUST HAVING A WARM FUZZY."

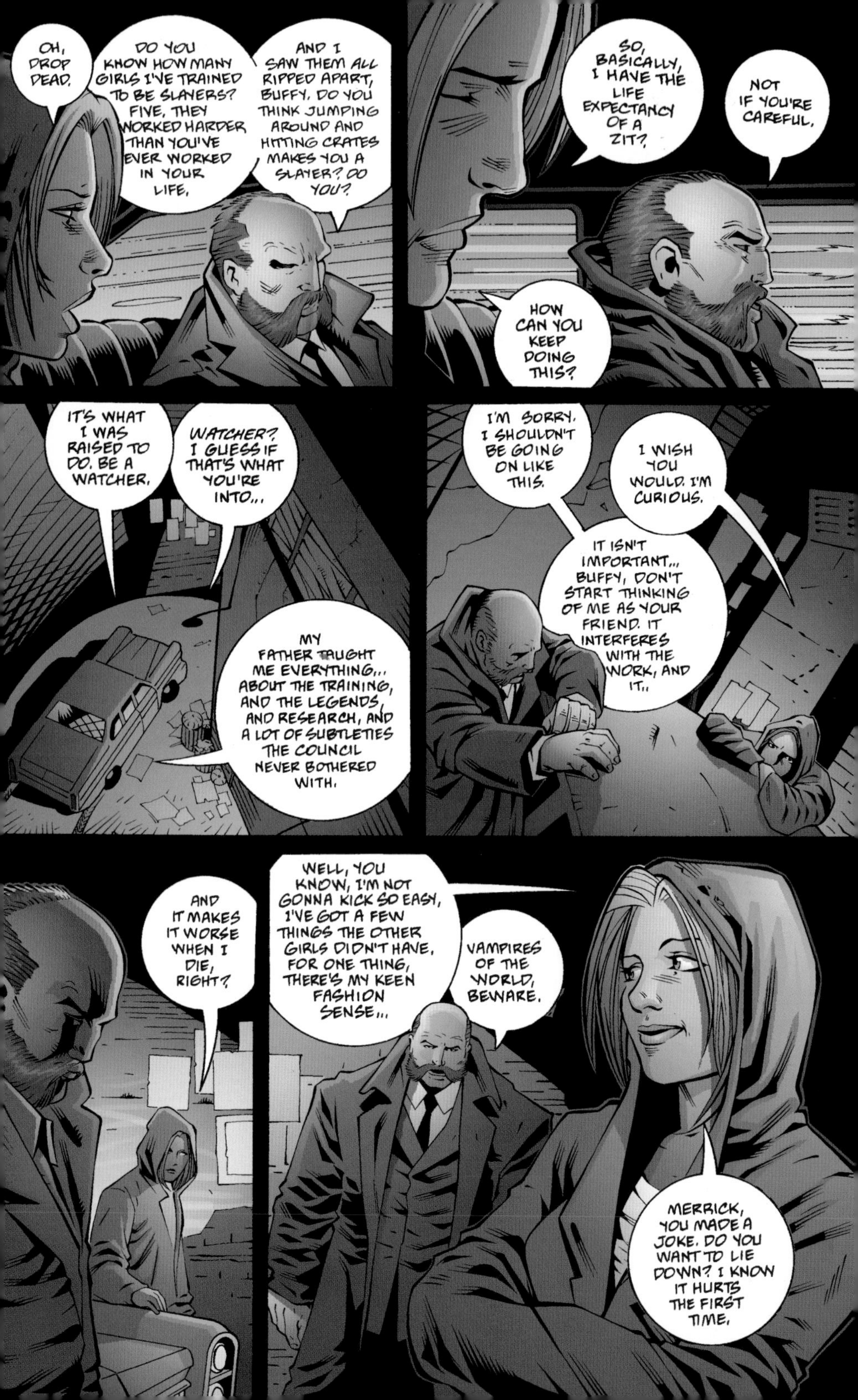
OH, DROP DEAD.
DO YOU KNOW HOW MANY GIRLS I'VE TRAINED TO BE SLAYERS? FIVE. THEY WORKED HARDER THAN YOU'VE EVER WORKED IN YOUR LIFE.
AND I SAW THEM ALL RIPPED APART, BUFFY. DO YOU THINK JUMPING AROUND AND HITTING CRATES MAKES YOU A SLAYER? DO YOU?
SO, BASICALLY, I HAVE THE LIFE EXPECTANCY OF A ZIT?
NOT IF YOU'RE CAREFUL.
HOW CAN YOU KEEP DOING THIS?
IT'S WHAT I WAS RAISED TO DO. BE A WATCHER.
WATCHER? I GUESS IF THAT'S WHAT YOU'RE INTO...
MY FATHER TAUGHT ME EVERYTHING... ABOUT THE TRAINING, AND THE LEGENDS, AND RESEARCH, AND A LOT OF SUBTLETIES THE COUNCIL NEVER BOTHERED WITH.
I'M SORRY. I SHOULDN'T BE GOING ON LIKE THIS.
I WISH YOU WOULD. I'M CURIOUS.
IT ISN'T IMPORTANT... BUFFY, DON'T START THINKING OF ME AS YOUR FRIEND. IT INTERFERES WITH THE WORK, AND IT...
AND IT MAKES IT WORSE WHEN I DIE, RIGHT?
WELL, YOU KNOW, I'M NOT GONNA KICK SO EASY. I'VE GOT A FEW THINGS THE OTHER GIRLS DIDN'T HAVE. FOR ONE THING, THERE'S MY KEEN FASHION SENSE...
VAMPIRES OF THE WORLD, BEWARE.
MERRICK, YOU MADE A JOKE. DO YOU WANT TO LIE DOWN? I KNOW IT HURTS THE FIRST TIME.

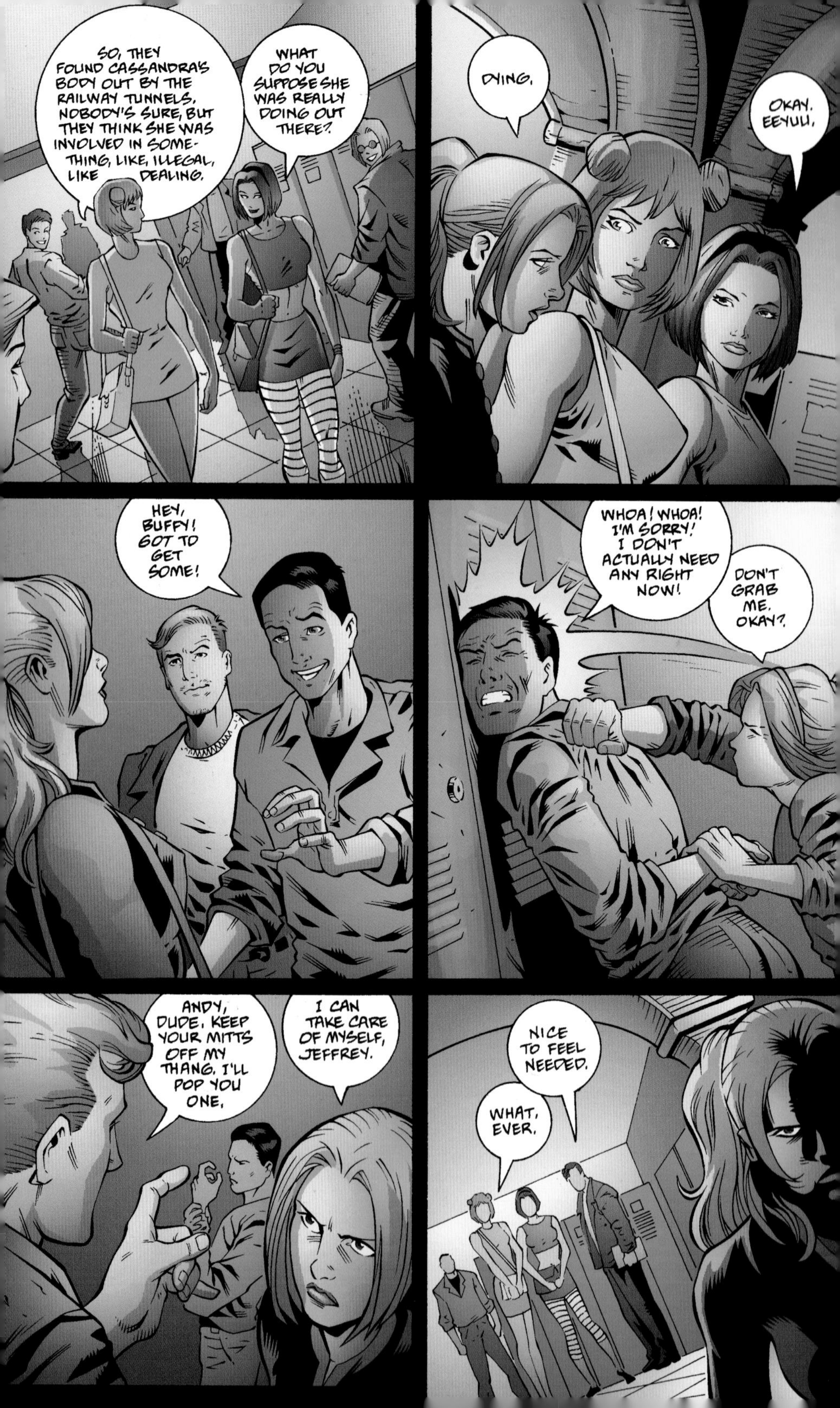
SO, THEY FOUND CASSANDRA'S BODY OUT BY THE RAILWAY TUNNELS. NOBODY'S SURE, BUT THEY THINK SHE WAS INVOLVED IN SOME-THING, LIKE, ILLEGAL, LIKE DEALING.
WHAT DO YOU SUPPOSE SHE WAS REALLY DOING OUT THERE?
DYING.
OKAY. EEYUU.
HEY, BUFFY! GOT TO GET SOME!
WHOA! WHOA! I'M SORRY! I DON'T ACTUALLY NEED ANY RIGHT NOW!
DON'T GRAB ME. OKAY?
ANDY, DUDE. KEEP YOUR MITTS OFF MY THANG. I'LL POP YOU ONE.
I CAN TAKE CARE OF MYSELF, JEFFREY.
NICE TO FEEL NEEDED.
WHAT. EVER.

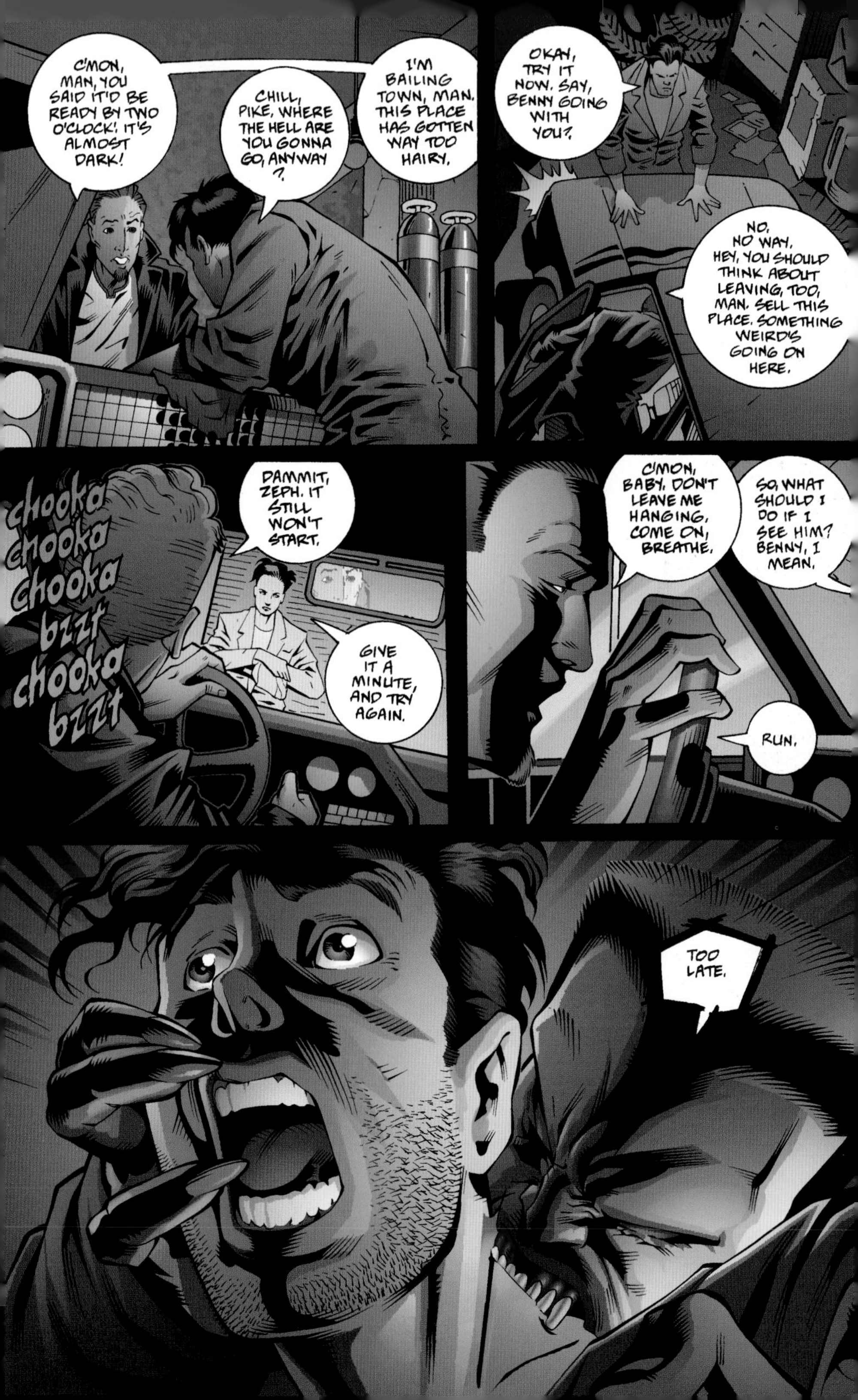
C'MON, MAN, YOU SAID IT'D BE READY BY TWO O'CLOCK! IT'S ALMOST DARK!
CHILL, PIKE, WHERE THE HELL ARE YOU GONNA GO, ANYWAY?
I'M BAILING TOWN, MAN. THIS PLACE HAS GOTTEN WAY TOO HAIRY.
OKAY, TRY IT NOW. SAY, BENNY GOING WITH YOU?
NO. NO WAY. HEY, YOU SHOULD THINK ABOUT LEAVING, TOO, MAN. SELL THIS PLACE. SOMETHING WEIRD'S GOING ON HERE.
chooka chooka chooka bzzt chooka bzzt
DAMMIT, ZEPH. IT STILL WON'T START.
GIVE IT A MINUTE, AND TRY AGAIN.
C'MON, BABY, DON'T LEAVE ME HANGING. COME ON, BREATHE.
SO, WHAT SHOULD I DO IF I SEE HIM? BENNY, I MEAN.
RUN.
TOO LATE.

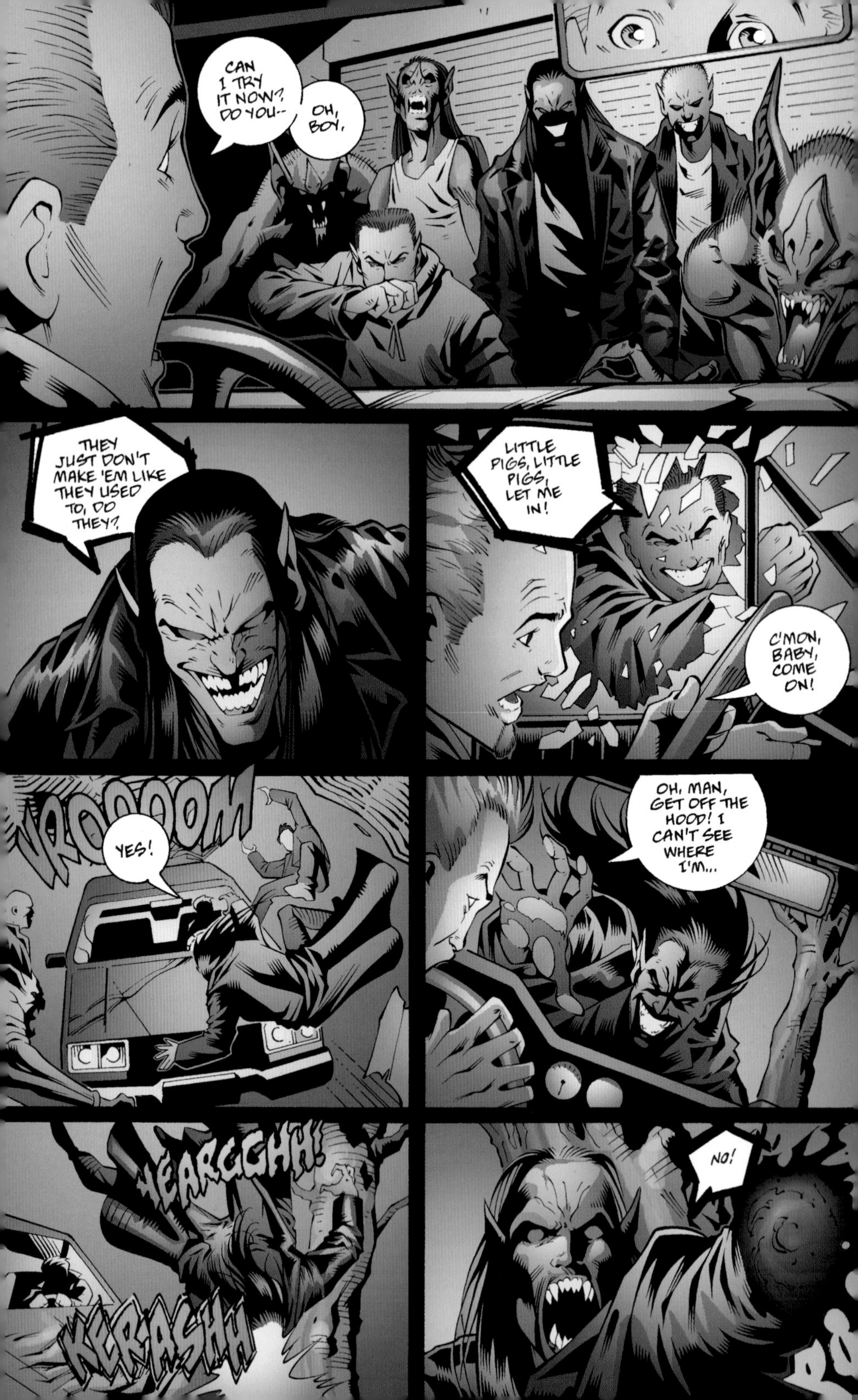
CAN I TRY IT NOW? DO YOU--
OH, BOY.
THEY JUST DON'T MAKE 'EM LIKE THEY USED TO, DO THEY?
LITTLE PIGS, LITTLE PIGS, LET ME IN!
C'MON, BABY, COME ON!
VROOOOM
YES!
OH, MAN, GET OFF THE HOOD! I CAN'T SEE WHERE I'M...
YEARGGH!
KERASHH
NO!

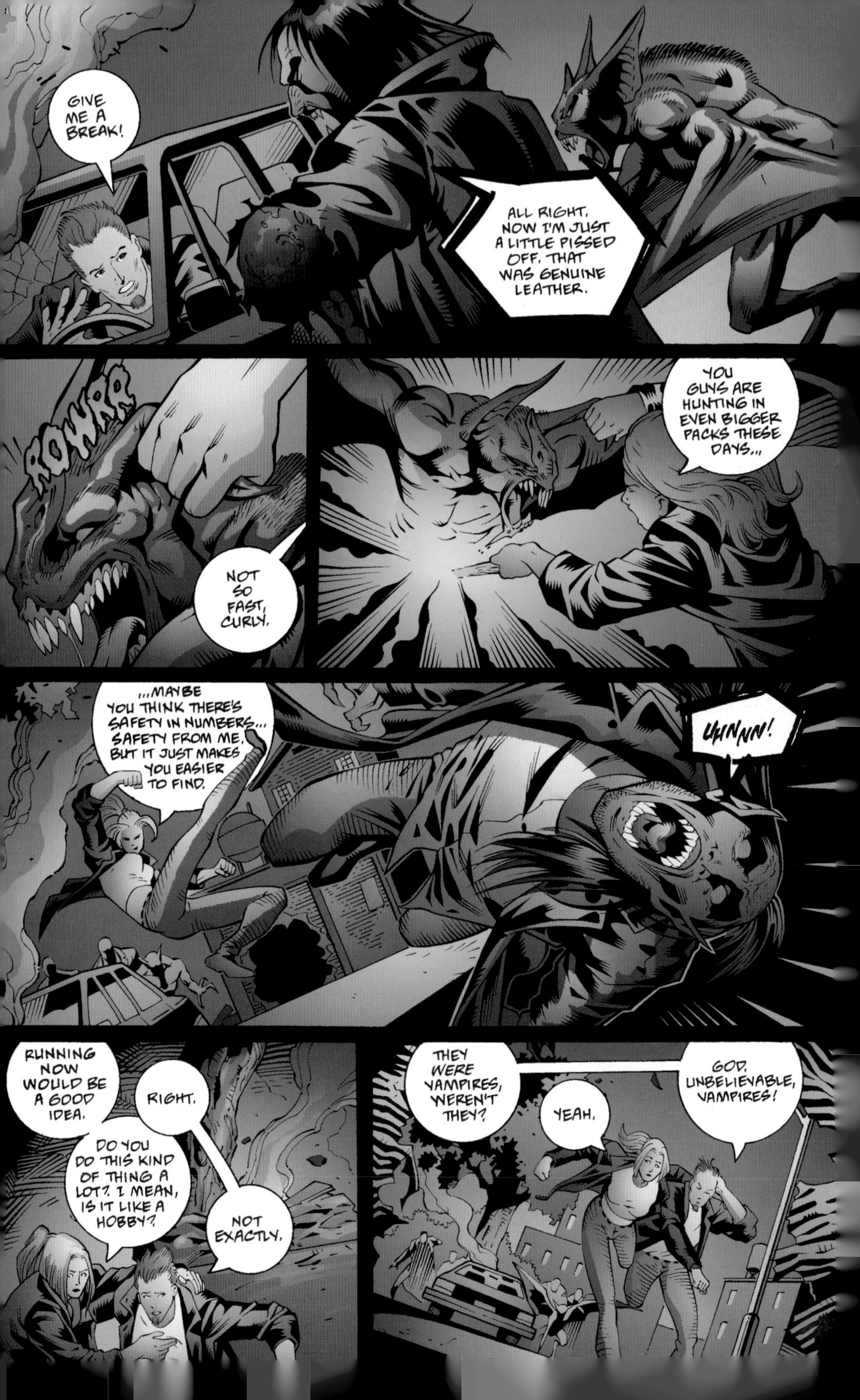
GIVE ME A BREAK!
ALL RIGHT. NOW I'M JUST A LITTLE PISSED OFF. THAT WAS GENUINE LEATHER.
ROWRR
NOT SO FAST, CURLY.
YOU GUYS ARE HUNTING IN EVEN BIGGER PACKS THESE DAYS...
...MAYBE YOU THINK THERE'S SAFETY IN NUMBERS... SAFETY FROM ME, BUT IT JUST MAKES YOU EASIER TO FIND.
UHNNN!
RUNNING NOW WOULD BE A GOOD IDEA.
RIGHT.
DO YOU DO THIS KIND OF THING A LOT? I MEAN, IS IT LIKE A HOBBY?
NOT EXACTLY.
THEY WERE VAMPIRES, WEREN'T THEY?
YEAH.
GOD. UNBELIEVABLE. VAMPIRES!

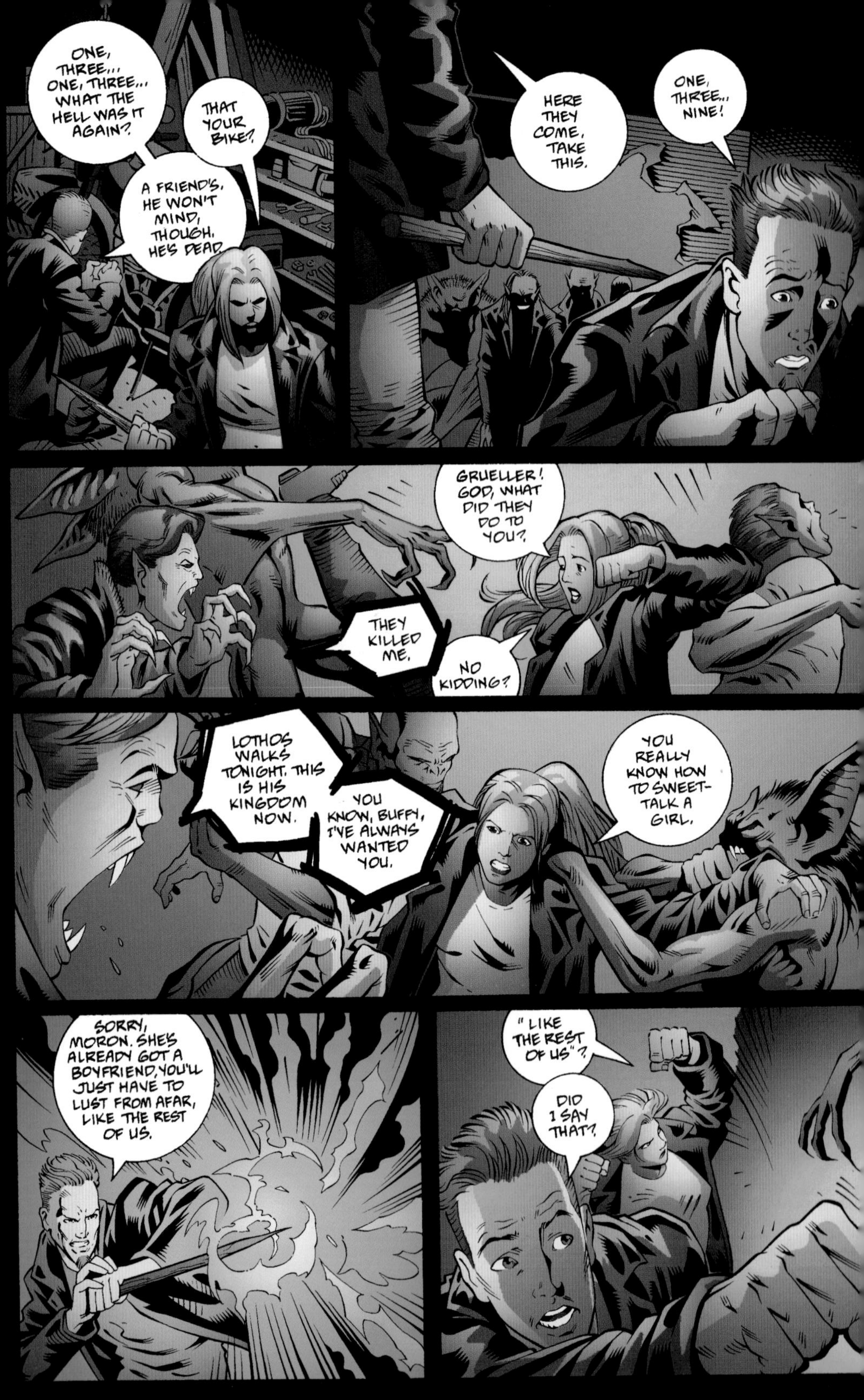
ONE, THREE... ONE, THREE... WHAT THE HELL WAS IT AGAIN?
THAT YOUR BIKE?
A FRIEND'S. HE WON'T MIND, THOUGH. HE'S DEAD.
HERE THEY COME. TAKE THIS.
ONE, THREE... NINE!
GRUELLER! GOD, WHAT DID THEY DO TO YOU?
THEY KILLED ME.
NO KIDDING?
LOTHOS WALKS TONIGHT. THIS IS HIS KINGDOM NOW.
YOU KNOW, BUFFY, I'VE ALWAYS WANTED YOU.
YOU REALLY KNOW HOW TO SWEET-TALK A GIRL.
SORRY, MORON. SHE'S ALREADY GOT A BOYFRIEND. YOU'LL JUST HAVE TO LUST FROM AFAR, LIKE THE REST OF US.
"LIKE THE REST OF US"?
DID I SAY THAT?

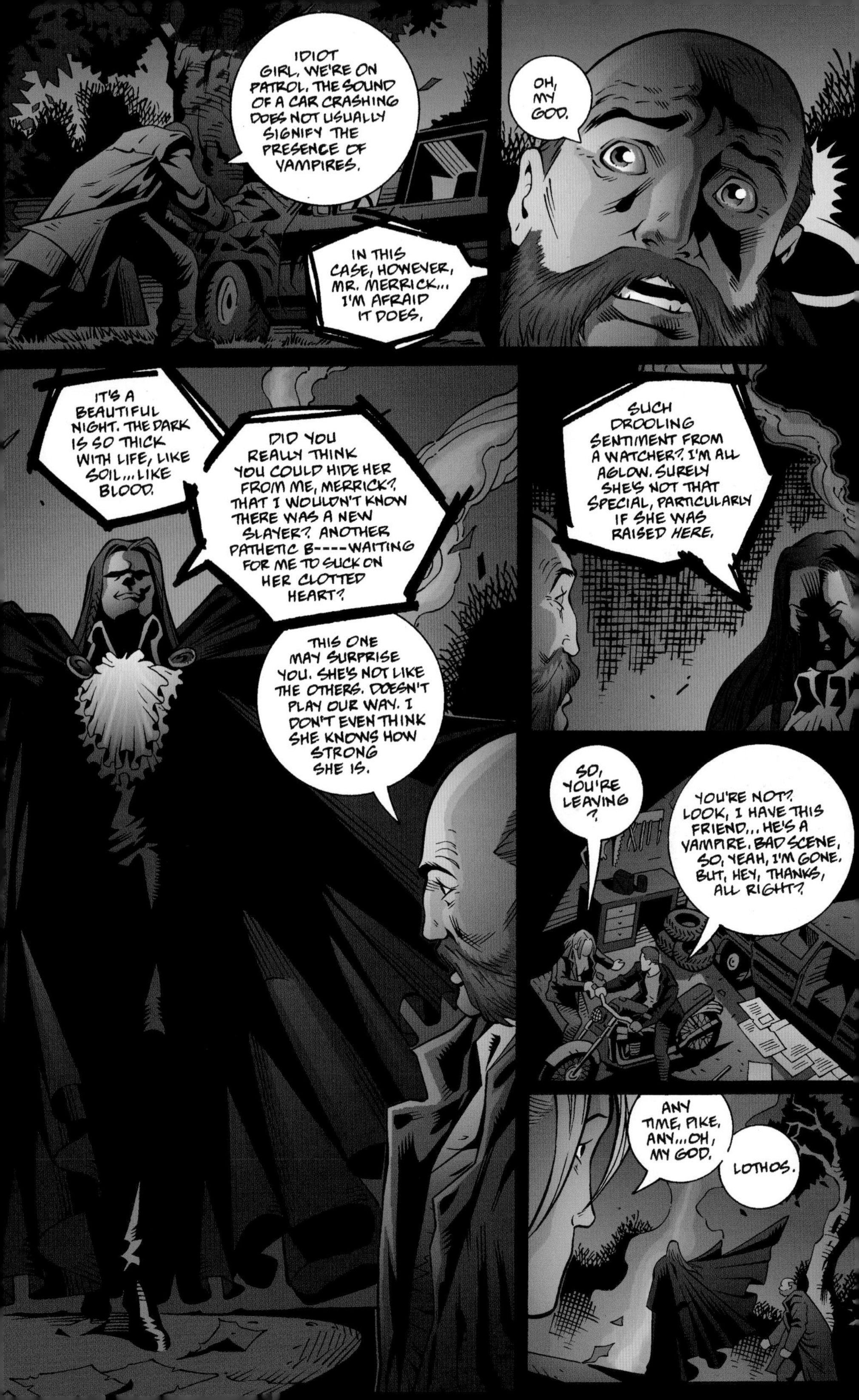
IDIOT GIRL, WE'RE ON PATROL. THE SOUND OF A CAR CRASHING DOES NOT USUALLY SIGNIFY THE PRESENCE OF VAMPIRES.
IN THIS CASE, HOWEVER, MR. MERRICK... I'M AFRAID IT DOES.
OH, MY GOD.
IT'S A BEAUTIFUL NIGHT. THE DARK IS SO THICK WITH LIFE, LIKE SOIL... LIKE BLOOD.
DID YOU REALLY THINK YOU COULD HIDE HER FROM ME, MERRICK? THAT I WOULDN'T KNOW THERE WAS A NEW SLAYER? ANOTHER PATHETIC B----WAITING FOR ME TO SUCK ON HER CLOTTED HEART?
THIS ONE MAY SURPRISE YOU. SHE'S NOT LIKE THE OTHERS. DOESN'T PLAY OUR WAY. I DON'T EVEN THINK SHE KNOWS HOW STRONG SHE IS.
SUCH DROOLING SENTIMENT FROM A WATCHER? I'M ALL AGLOW. SURELY SHE'S NOT THAT SPECIAL, PARTICULARLY IF SHE WAS RAISED *HERE*.
SO, YOU'RE LEAVING?
YOU'RE NOT? LOOK, I HAVE THIS FRIEND... HE'S A VAMPIRE. BAD SCENE. SO, YEAH, I'M GONE. BUT, HEY, THANKS, ALL RIGHT?
ANY TIME, PIKE, ANY... OH, MY GOD.
LOTHOS.

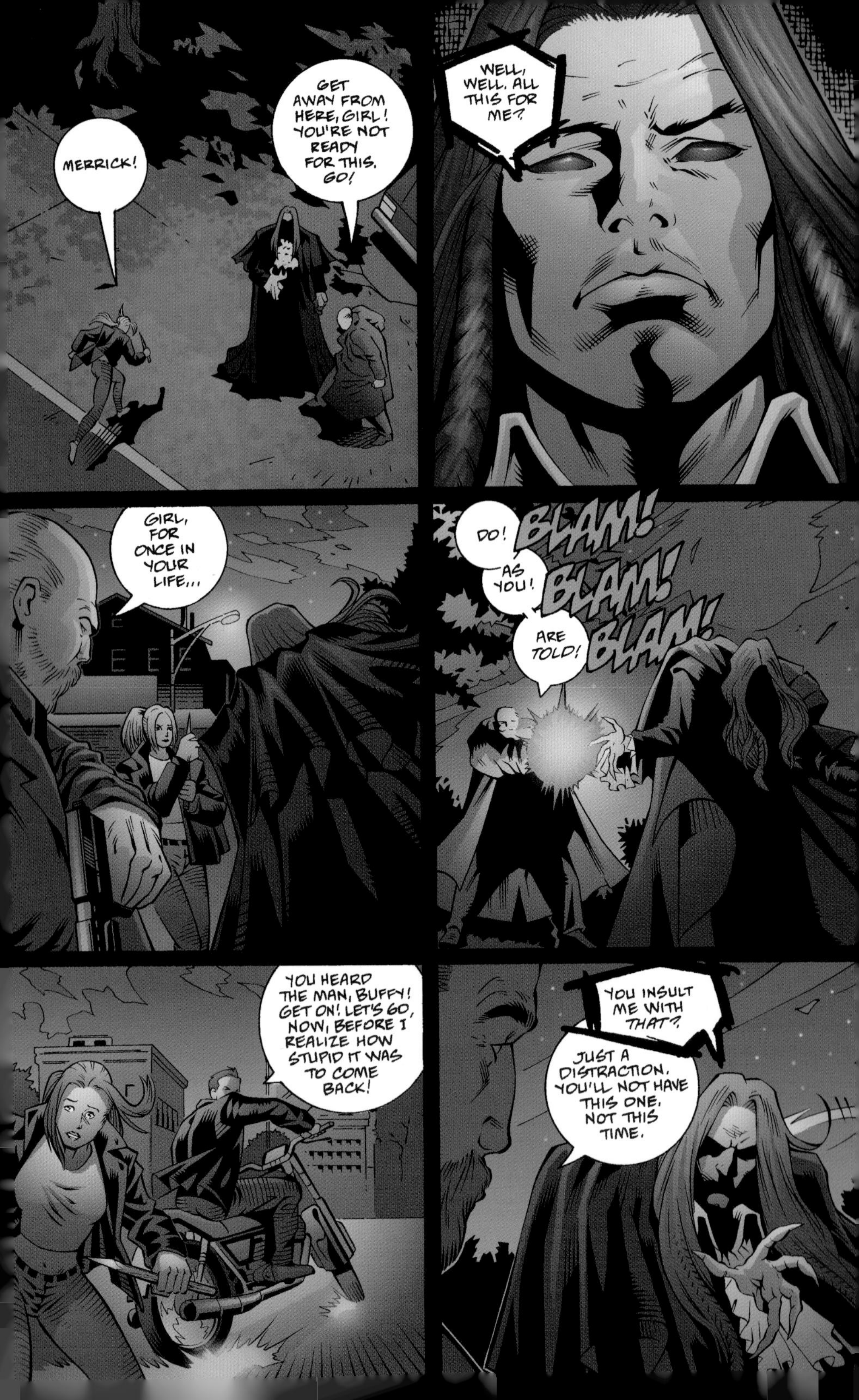
MERRICK!
GET AWAY FROM HERE, GIRL! YOU'RE NOT READY FOR THIS. GO!
WELL, WELL. ALL THIS FOR ME?
GIRL, FOR ONCE IN YOUR LIFE...
DO!
BLAM!
AS YOU!
BLAM!
ARE TOLD!
BLAM!
YOU HEARD THE MAN, BUFFY! GET ON! LET'S GO, NOW, BEFORE I REALIZE HOW STUPID IT WAS TO COME BACK!
YOU INSULT ME WITH *THAT*?
JUST A DISTRACTION. YOU'LL NOT HAVE THIS ONE, NOT THIS TIME.

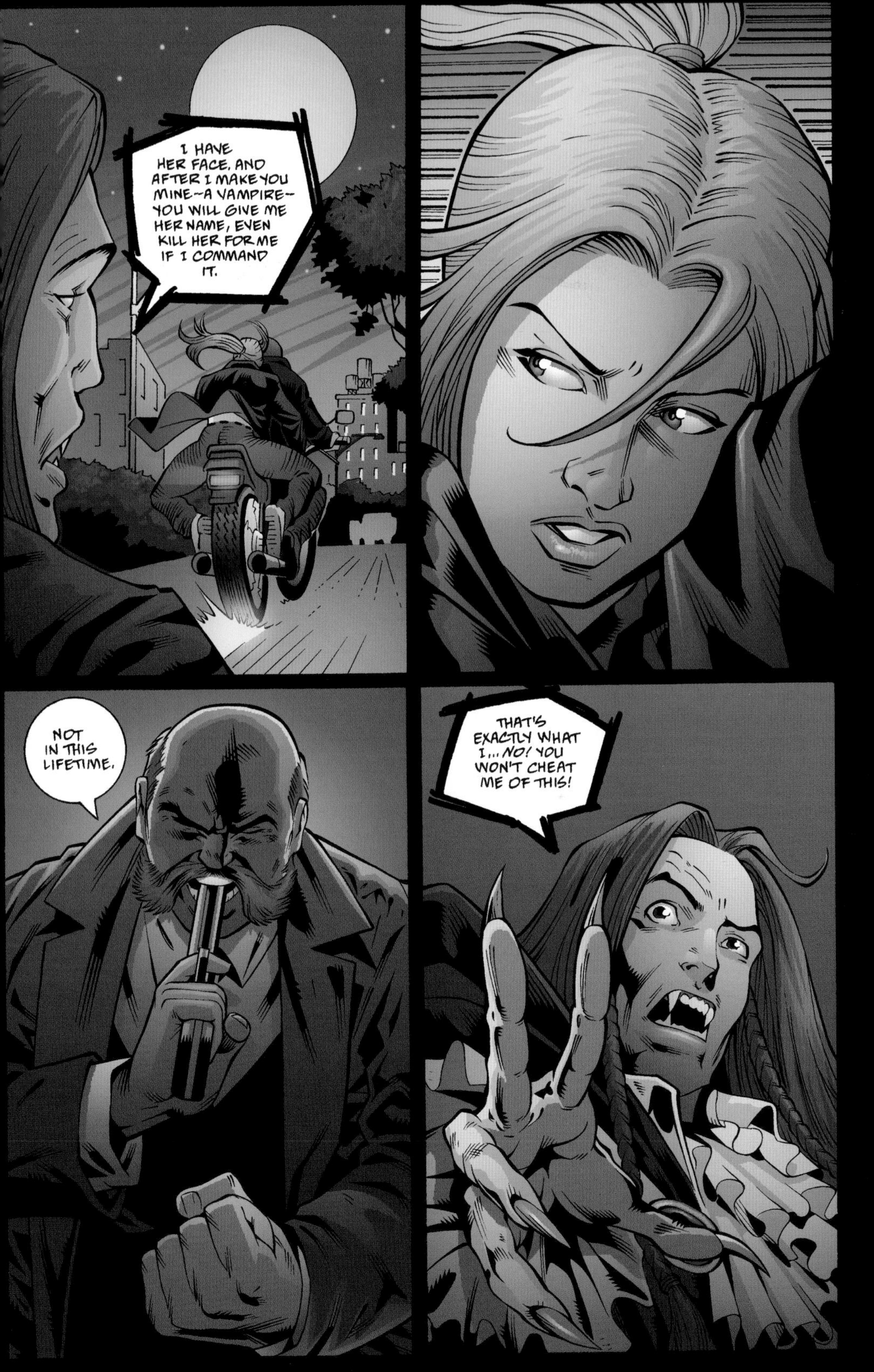
I HAVE HER FACE, AND AFTER I MAKE YOU MINE--A VAMPIRE--YOU WILL GIVE ME HER NAME, EVEN KILL HER FOR ME IF I COMMAND IT.
NOT IN THIS LIFETIME.
THAT'S EXACTLY WHAT I... NO! YOU WON'T CHEAT ME OF THIS!

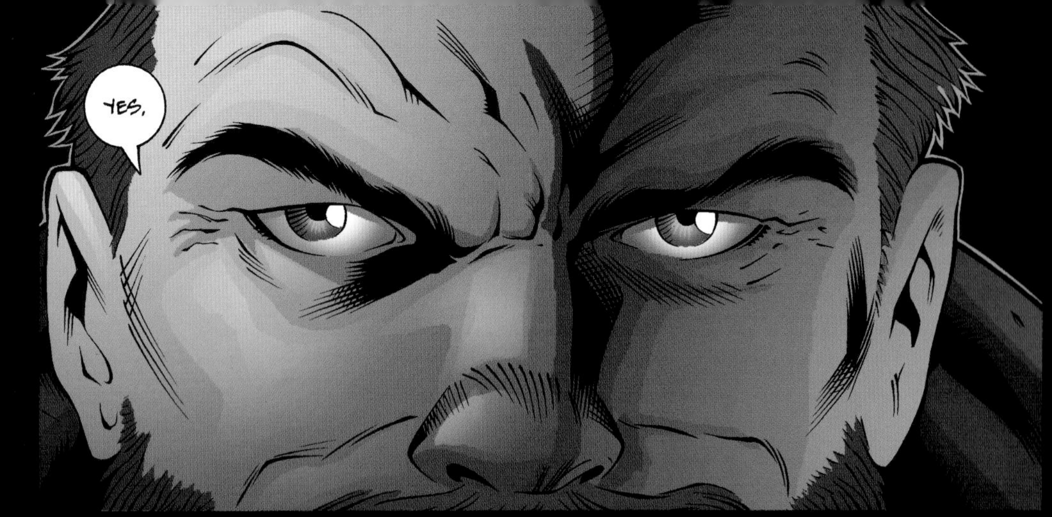
YES,

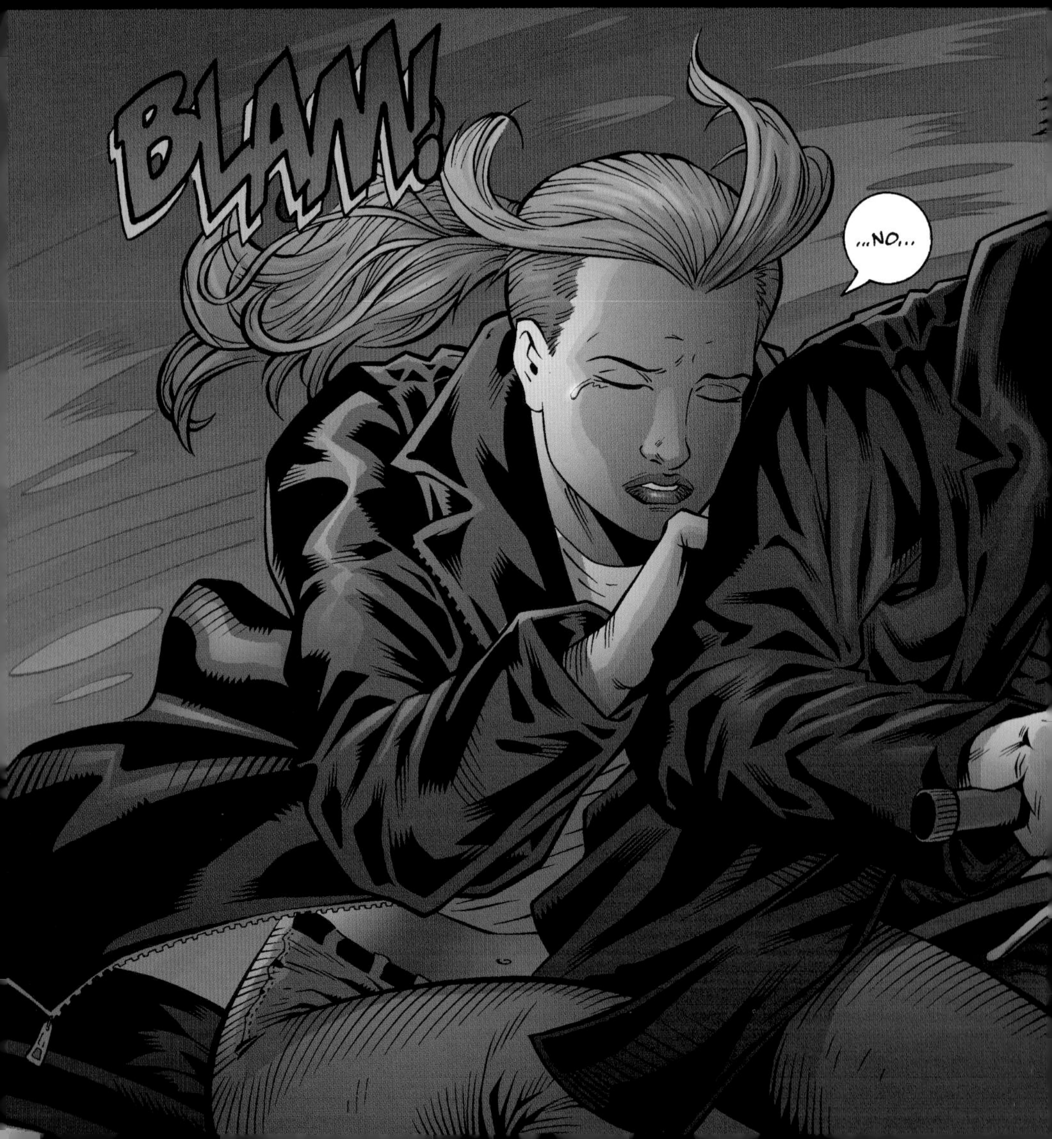
BLAM!
...NO...

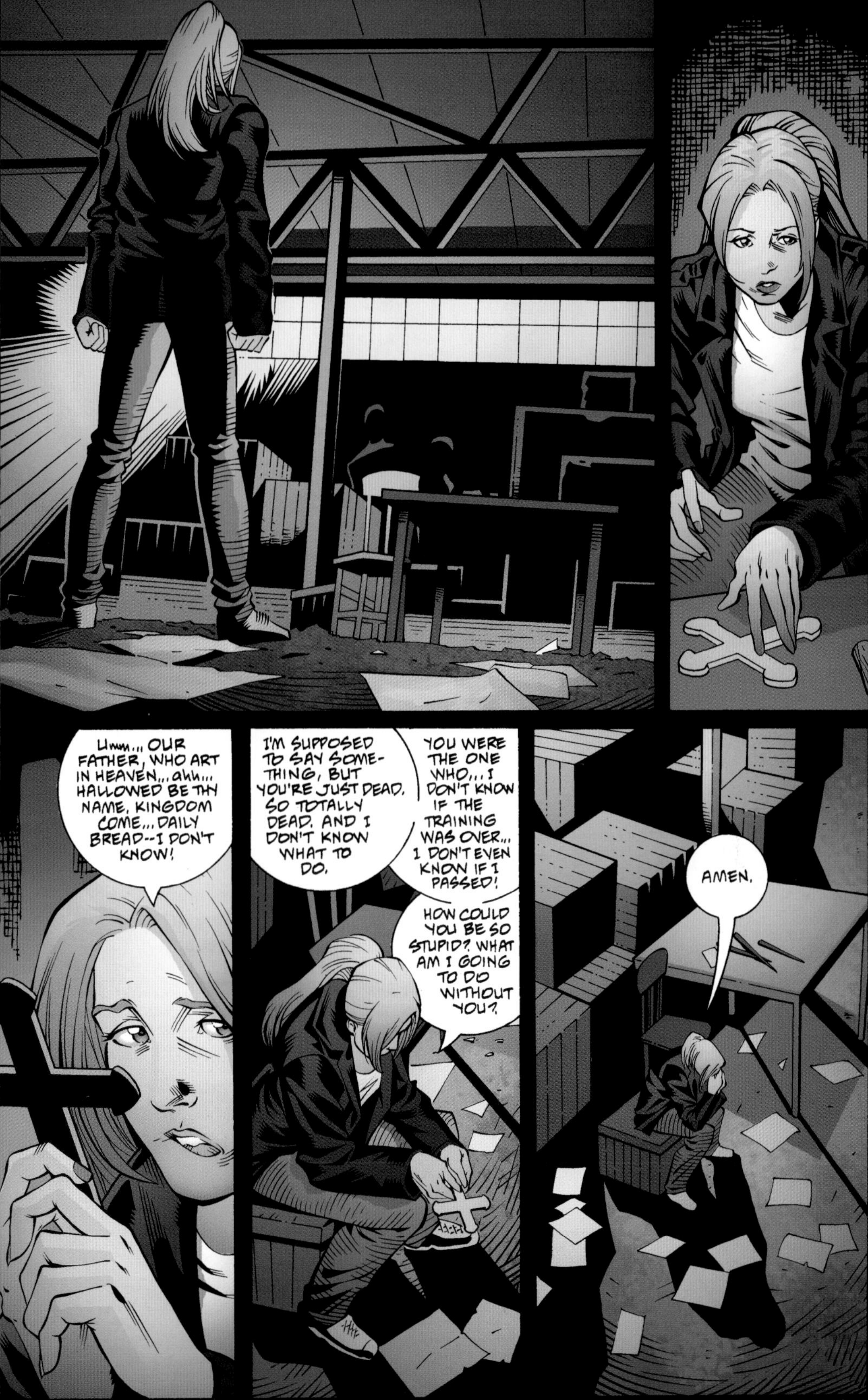
UMM... OUR FATHER, WHO ART IN HEAVEN... AHH... HALLOWED BE THY NAME, KINGDOM COME... DAILY BREAD--I DON'T KNOW!
I'M SUPPOSED TO SAY SOME-THING, BUT YOU'RE JUST DEAD. SO TOTALLY DEAD. AND I DON'T KNOW WHAT TO DO.
YOU WERE THE ONE WHO... I DON'T KNOW IF THE TRAINING WAS OVER... I DON'T EVEN KNOW IF I PASSED!
HOW COULD YOU BE SO STUPID? WHAT AM I GOING TO DO WITHOUT YOU?
AMEN.

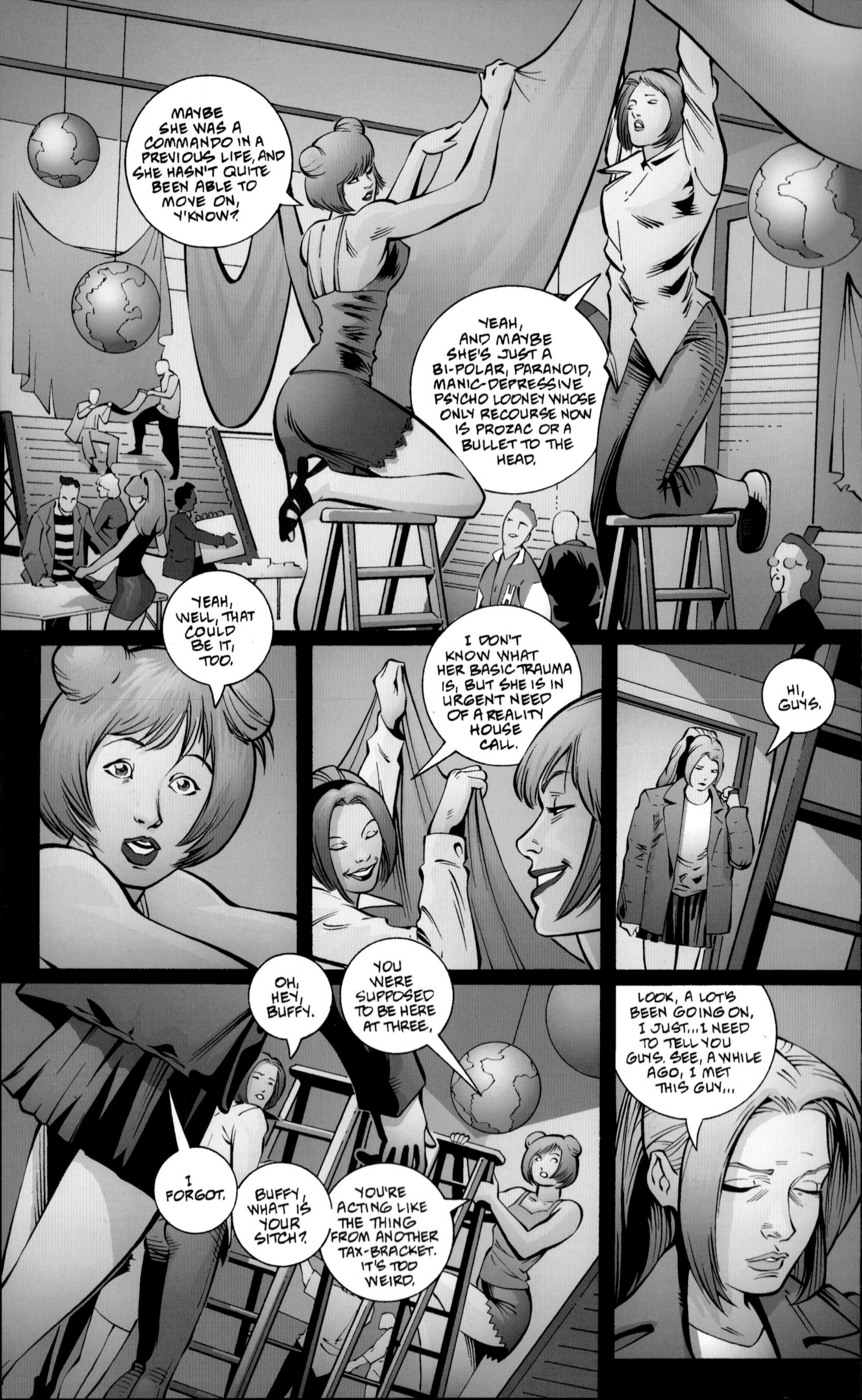
MAYBE SHE WAS A COMMANDO IN A PREVIOUS LIFE, AND SHE HASN'T QUITE BEEN ABLE TO MOVE ON, Y'KNOW?
YEAH, AND MAYBE SHE'S JUST A BI-POLAR, PARANOID, MANIC-DEPRESSIVE PSYCHO LOONEY WHOSE ONLY RECOURSE NOW IS PROZAC OR A BULLET TO THE HEAD.
YEAH, WELL, THAT COULD BE IT, TOO.
I DON'T KNOW WHAT HER BASIC TRAUMA IS, BUT SHE IS IN URGENT NEED OF A REALITY HOUSE CALL.
HI, GUYS.
OH, HEY, BUFFY.
YOU WERE SUPPOSED TO BE HERE AT THREE.
I FORGOT.
BUFFY, WHAT IS YOUR SITCH?
YOU'RE ACTING LIKE THE THING FROM ANOTHER TAX-BRACKET. IT'S TOO WEIRD.
LOOK, A LOT'S BEEN GOING ON. I JUST... I NEED TO TELL YOU GUYS. SEE, A WHILE AGO, I MET THIS GUY...

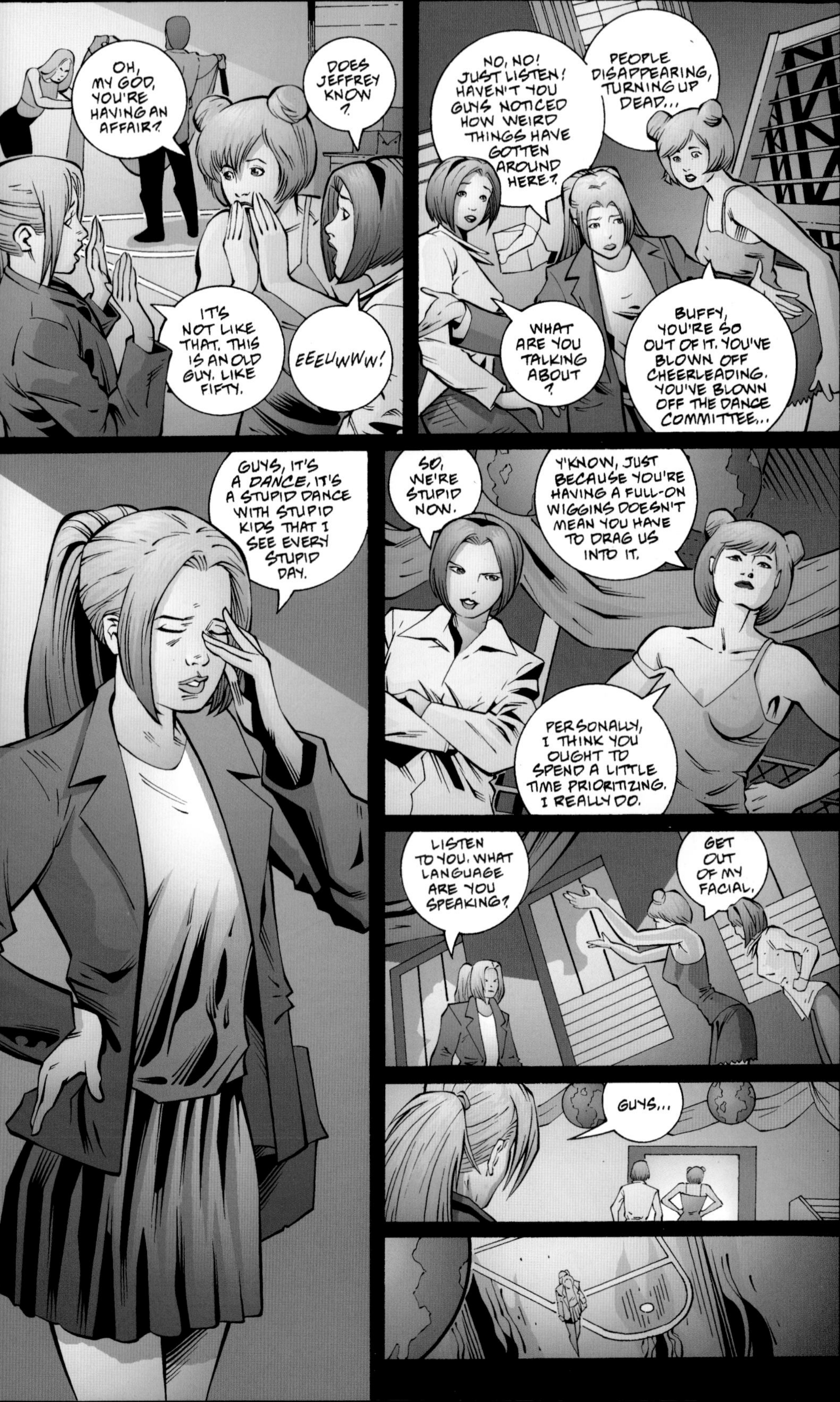
OH, MY GOD, YOU'RE HAVING AN AFFAIR?
DOES JEFFREY KNOW?
IT'S NOT LIKE THAT. THIS IS AN OLD GUY. LIKE FIFTY.
EEEUWWW!
NO, NO! JUST LISTEN! HAVEN'T YOU GUYS NOTICED HOW WEIRD THINGS HAVE GOTTEN AROUND HERE?
PEOPLE DISAPPEARING, TURNING UP DEAD...
WHAT ARE YOU TALKING ABOUT?
BUFFY, YOU'RE SO OUT OF IT. YOU'VE BLOWN OFF CHEERLEADING. YOU'VE BLOWN OFF THE DANCE COMMITTEE...
GUYS, IT'S A DANCE, IT'S A STUPID DANCE WITH STUPID KIDS THAT I SEE EVERY STUPID DAY.
SO, WE'RE STUPID NOW.
Y'KNOW, JUST BECAUSE YOU'RE HAVING A FULL-ON WIGGINS DOESN'T MEAN YOU HAVE TO DRAG US INTO IT.
PERSONALLY, I THINK YOU OUGHT TO SPEND A LITTLE TIME PRIORITIZING. I REALLY DO.
LISTEN TO YOU. WHAT LANGUAGE ARE YOU SPEAKING?
GET OUT OF MY FACIAL.
GUYS...

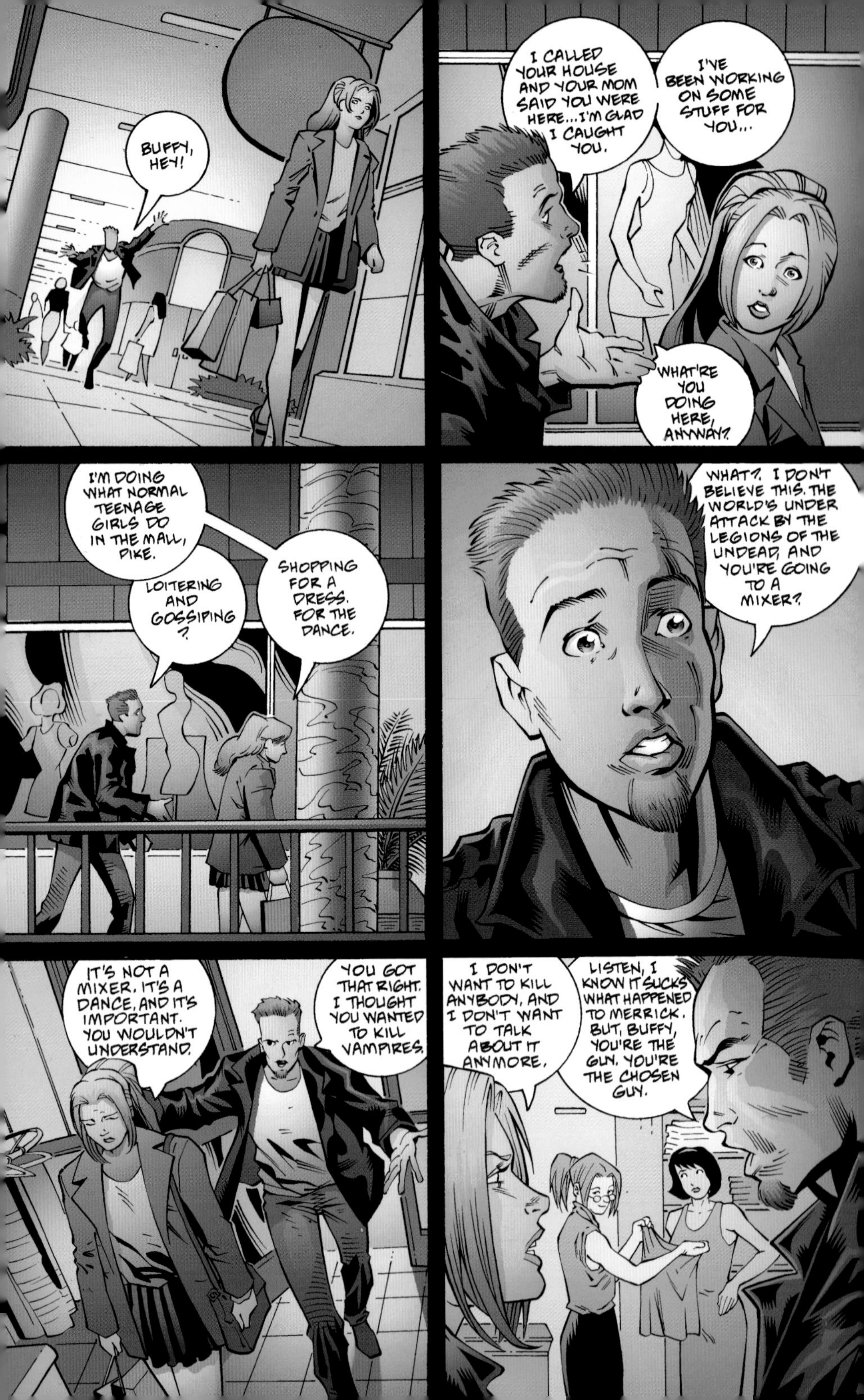
BUFFY, HEY!
I CALLED YOUR HOUSE AND YOUR MOM SAID YOU WERE HERE... I'M GLAD I CAUGHT YOU.
I'VE BEEN WORKING ON SOME STUFF FOR YOU...
WHAT'RE YOU DOING HERE, ANYWAY?
I'M DOING WHAT NORMAL TEENAGE GIRLS DO IN THE MALL, PIKE.
LOITERING AND GOSSIPING?
SHOPPING FOR A DRESS. FOR THE DANCE.
WHAT? I DON'T BELIEVE THIS. THE WORLD'S UNDER ATTACK BY THE LEGIONS OF THE UNDEAD, AND YOU'RE GOING TO A MIXER?
IT'S NOT A MIXER. IT'S A DANCE, AND IT'S IMPORTANT. YOU WOULDN'T UNDERSTAND.
YOU GOT THAT RIGHT. I THOUGHT YOU WANTED TO KILL VAMPIRES.
I DON'T WANT TO KILL ANYBODY, AND I DON'T WANT TO TALK ABOUT IT ANYMORE.
LISTEN, I KNOW IT SUCKS WHAT HAPPENED TO MERRICK. BUT, BUFFY, YOU'RE THE GUY. YOU'RE THE CHOSEN GUY.

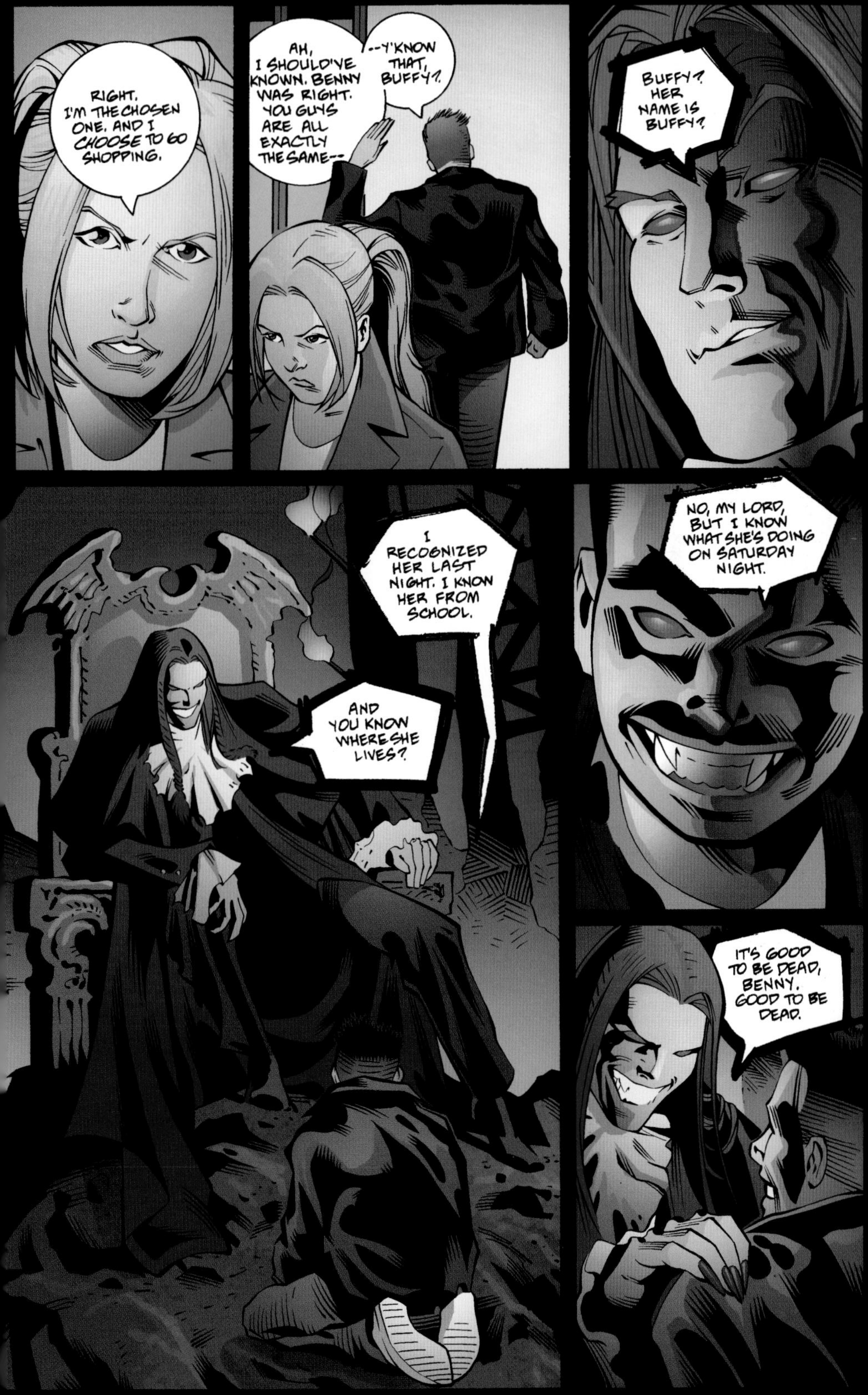
RIGHT. I'M THE CHOSEN ONE. AND I CHOOSE TO GO SHOPPING.
AH, I SHOULD'VE KNOWN. BENNY WAS RIGHT. YOU GUYS ARE ALL EXACTLY THE SAME--
--Y'KNOW THAT, BUFFY?
BUFFY? HER NAME IS BUFFY?
I RECOGNIZED HER LAST NIGHT. I KNOW HER FROM SCHOOL.
AND YOU KNOW WHERE SHE LIVES?
NO, MY LORD, BUT I KNOW WHAT SHE'S DOING ON SATURDAY NIGHT.
IT'S GOOD TO BE DEAD, BENNY. GOOD TO BE DEAD.

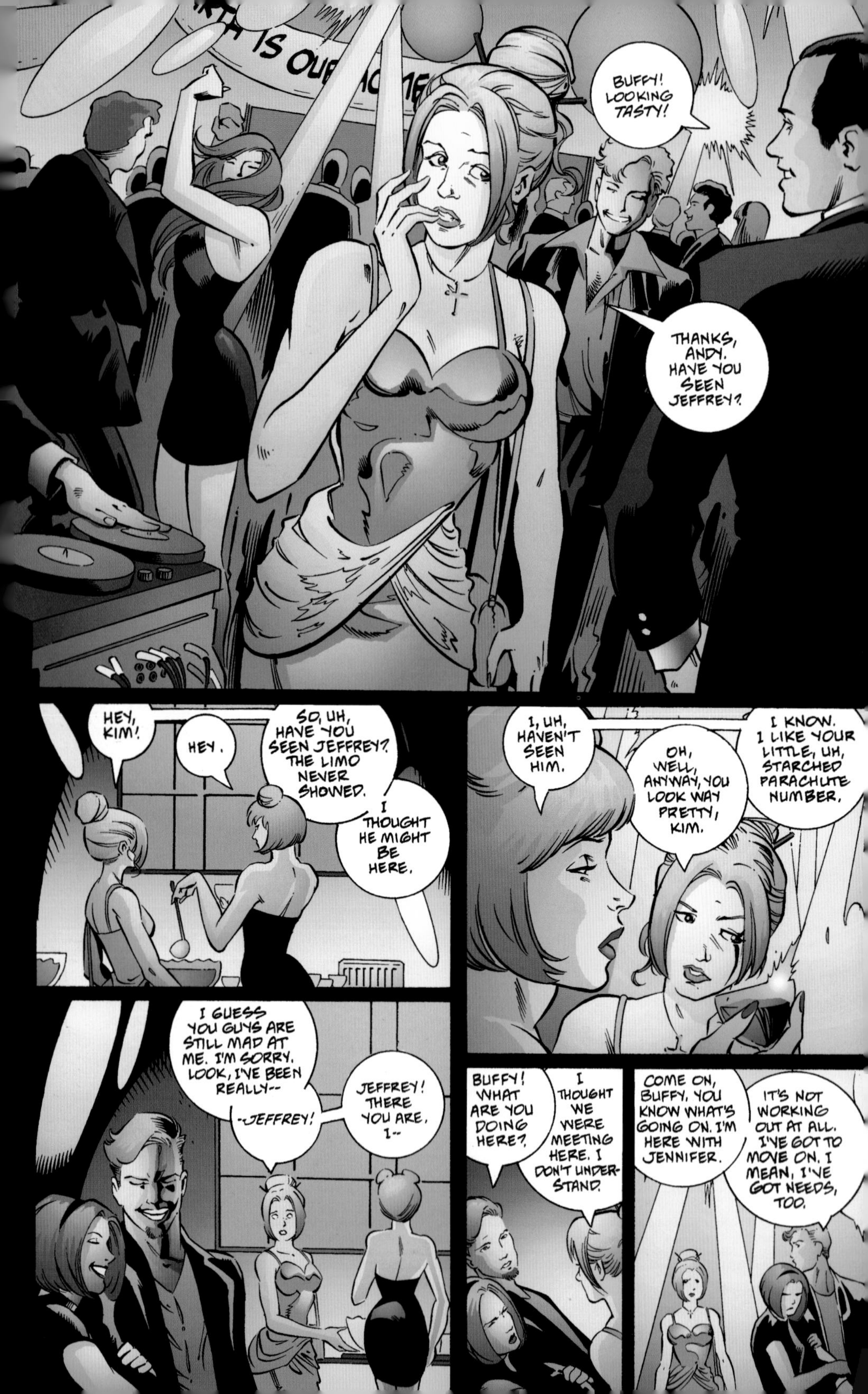

...RTH IS OUR HOME
BUFFY! LOOKING TASTY!
THANKS, ANDY. HAVE YOU SEEN JEFFREY?
HEY, KIM!
HEY.
SO, UH, HAVE YOU SEEN JEFFREY? THE LIMO NEVER SHOWED.
I THOUGHT HE MIGHT BE HERE.
I, UH, HAVEN'T SEEN HIM.
OH, WELL, ANYWAY, YOU LOOK WAY PRETTY, KIM.
I KNOW. I LIKE YOUR LITTLE, UH, STARCHED PARACHUTE NUMBER.
I GUESS YOU GUYS ARE STILL MAD AT ME. I'M SORRY. LOOK, I'VE BEEN REALLY--
--JEFFREY!
JEFFREY! THERE YOU ARE. I--
BUFFY! WHAT ARE YOU DOING HERE?
I THOUGHT WE WERE MEETING HERE. I DON'T UNDERSTAND.
COME ON, BUFFY. YOU KNOW WHAT'S GOING ON. I'M HERE WITH JENNIFER.
IT'S NOT WORKING OUT AT ALL. I'VE GOT TO MOVE ON. I MEAN, I'VE GOT NEEDS, TOO.

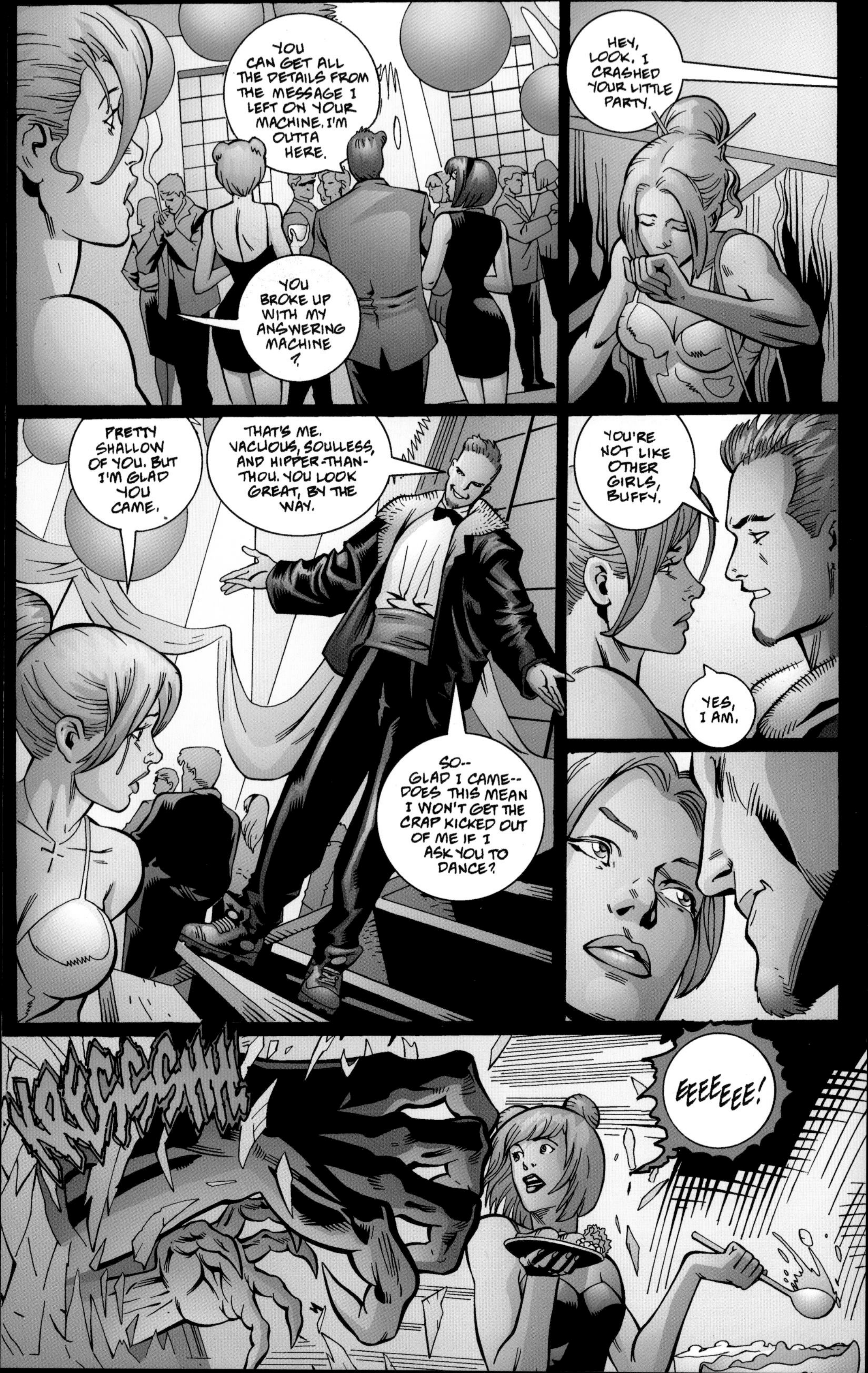
YOU CAN GET ALL THE DETAILS FROM THE MESSAGE I LEFT ON YOUR MACHINE. I'M OUTTA HERE.
YOU BROKE UP WITH MY ANSWERING MACHINE?
HEY, LOOK. I CRASHED YOUR LITTLE PARTY.
PRETTY SHALLOW OF YOU. BUT I'M GLAD YOU CAME.
THAT'S ME. VACUOUS, SOULLESS, AND HIPPER-THAN-THOU. YOU LOOK GREAT, BY THE WAY.
SO-- GLAD I CAME-- DOES THIS MEAN I WON'T GET THE CRAP KICKED OUT OF ME IF I ASK YOU TO DANCE?
YOU'RE NOT LIKE OTHER GIRLS, BUFFY.
YES, I AM.
EEEEEEE!

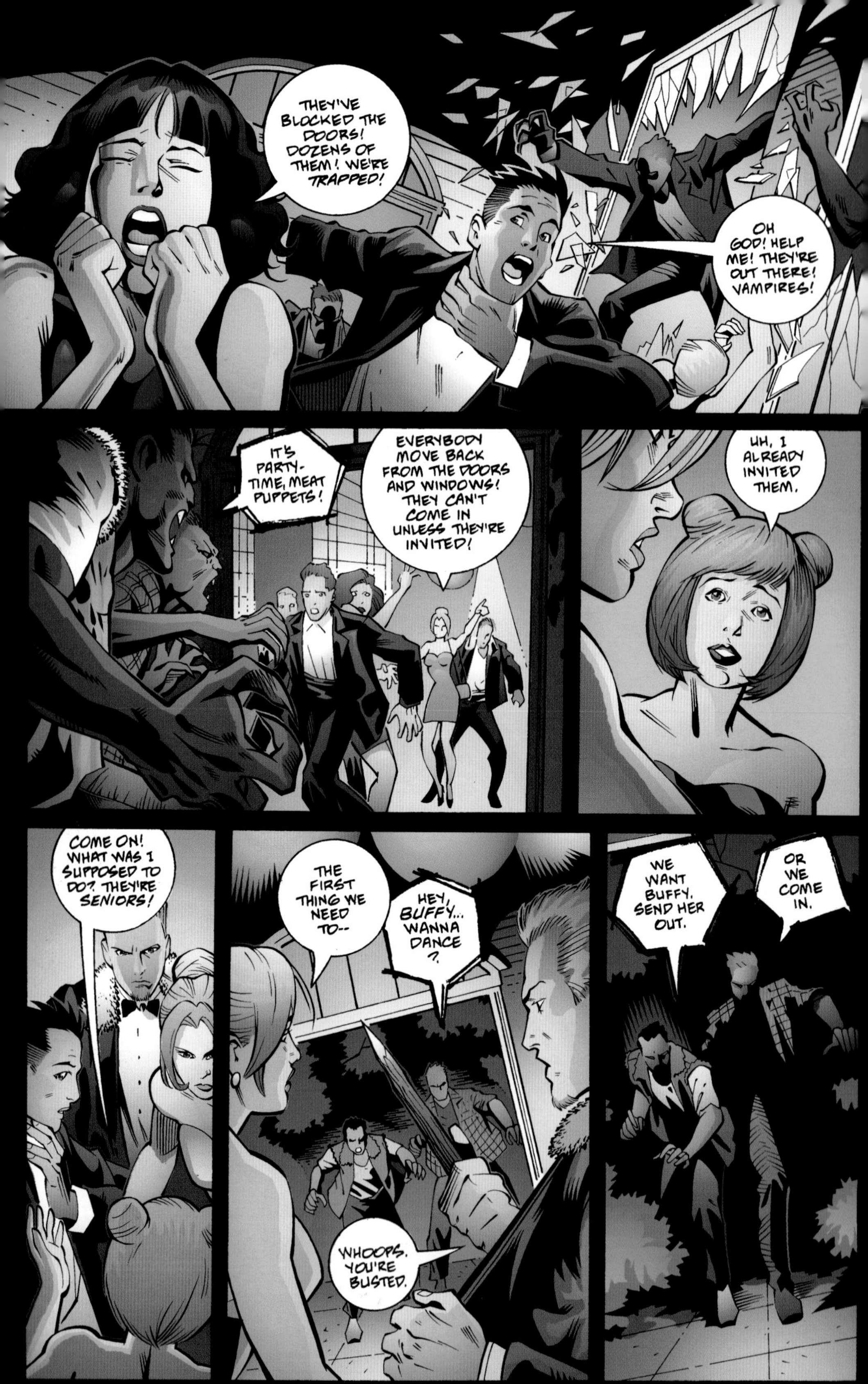
THEY'VE BLOCKED THE DOORS! DOZENS OF THEM! WE'RE TRAPPED!
OH GOD! HELP ME! THEY'RE OUT THERE! VAMPIRES!
IT'S PARTY-TIME, MEAT PUPPETS!
EVERYBODY MOVE BACK FROM THE DOORS AND WINDOWS! THEY CAN'T COME IN UNLESS THEY'RE INVITED!
UH, I ALREADY INVITED THEM.
COME ON! WHAT WAS I SUPPOSED TO DO? THEY'RE SENIORS!
THE FIRST THING WE NEED TO--
HEY, BUFFY... WANNA DANCE?
WHOOPS. YOU'RE BUSTED.
WE WANT BUFFY. SEND HER OUT.
OR WE COME IN.

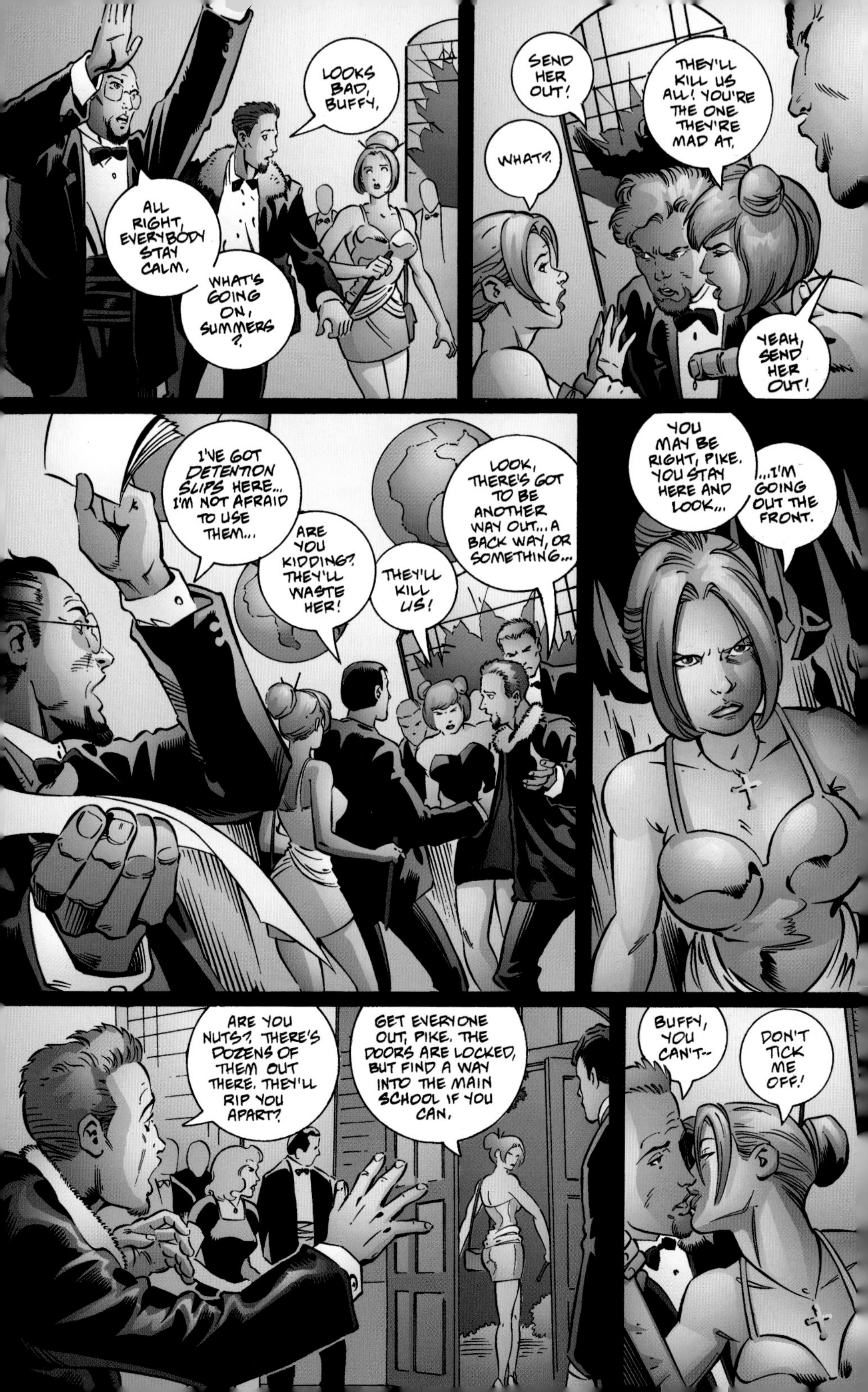
LOOKS BAD, BUFFY.
ALL RIGHT, EVERYBODY STAY CALM.
WHAT'S GOING ON, SUMMERS?
SEND HER OUT!
WHAT?
THEY'LL KILL US ALL! YOU'RE THE ONE THEY'RE MAD AT.
YEAH, SEND HER OUT!
I'VE GOT DETENTION SLIPS HERE... I'M NOT AFRAID TO USE THEM...
ARE YOU KIDDING? THEY'LL WASTE HER!
THEY'LL KILL US!
LOOK, THERE'S GOT TO BE ANOTHER WAY OUT... A BACK WAY, OR SOMETHING...
YOU MAY BE RIGHT, PIKE. YOU STAY HERE AND LOOK...
...I'M GOING OUT THE FRONT.
ARE YOU NUTS? THERE'S DOZENS OF THEM OUT THERE. THEY'LL RIP YOU APART?
GET EVERYONE OUT, PIKE. THE DOORS ARE LOCKED, BUT FIND A WAY INTO THE MAIN SCHOOL IF YOU CAN.
BUFFY, YOU CAN'T--
DON'T TICK ME OFF!

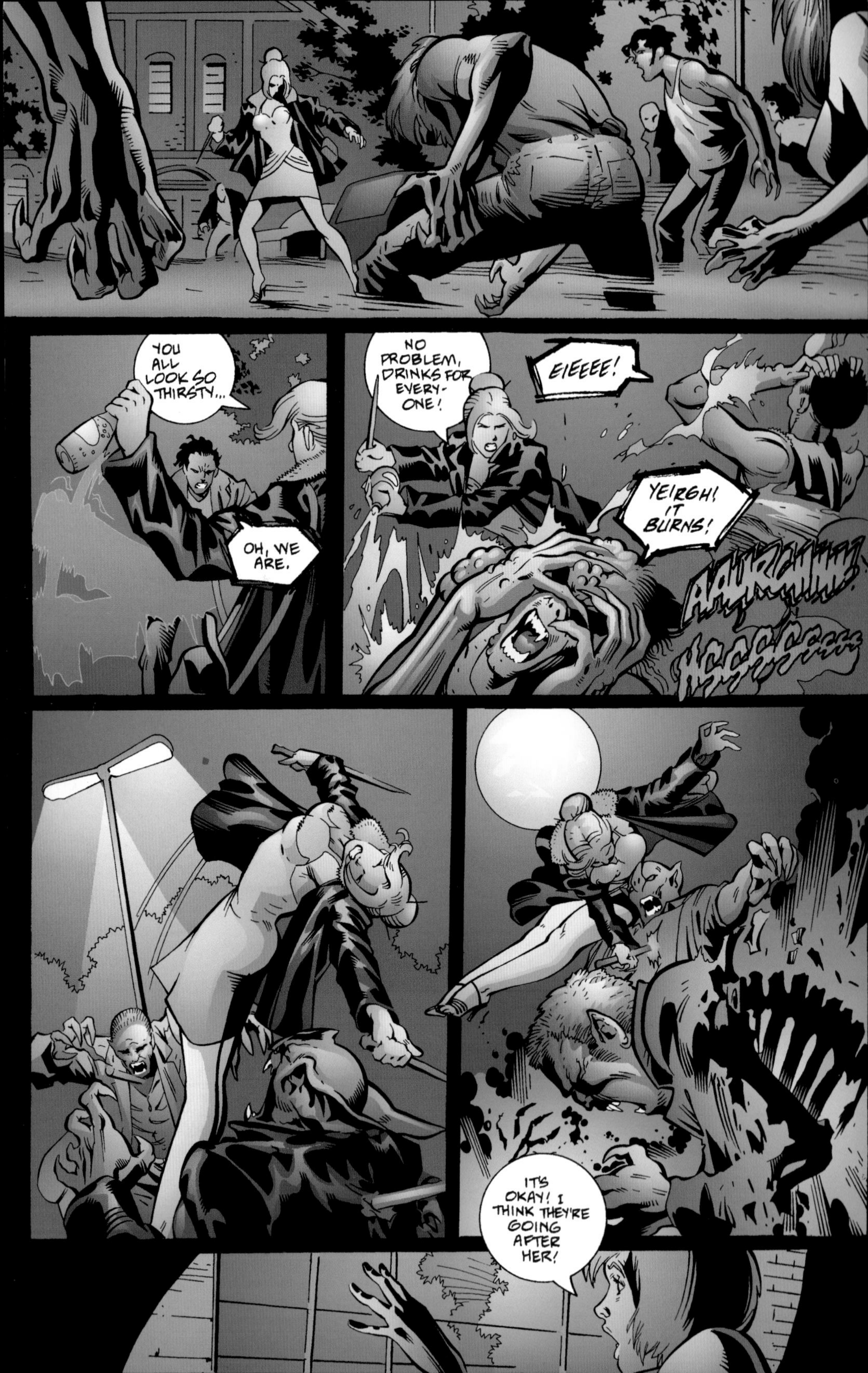
YOU ALL LOOK SO THIRSTY...
OH, WE ARE.
NO PROBLEM, DRINKS FOR EVERY-ONE!
EIEEEE!
YEIRGH! IT BURNS!
IT'S OKAY! I THINK THEY'RE GOING AFTER HER!

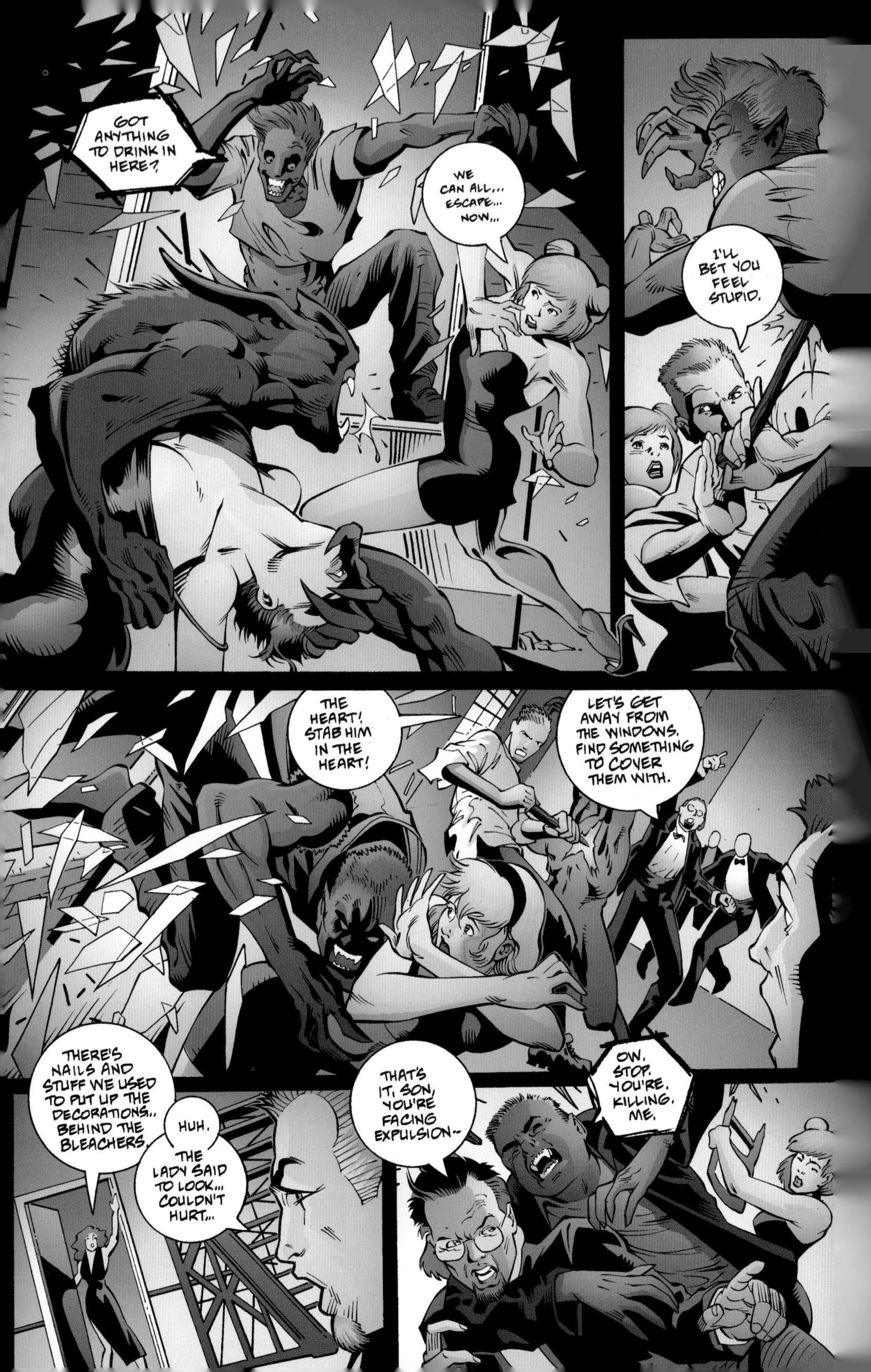
GOT ANYTHING TO DRINK IN HERE?
WE CAN ALL... ESCAPE... NOW...
I'LL BET YOU FEEL STUPID.
THE HEART! STAB HIM IN THE HEART!
LET'S GET AWAY FROM THE WINDOWS. FIND SOMETHING TO COVER THEM WITH.
THERE'S NAILS AND STUFF WE USED TO PUT UP THE DECORATIONS.. BEHIND THE BLEACHERS.
HUH.
THE LADY SAID TO LOOK... COULDN'T HURT...
THAT'S IT, SON, YOU'RE FACING EXPULSION--
OW. STOP. YOU'RE. KILLING. ME.

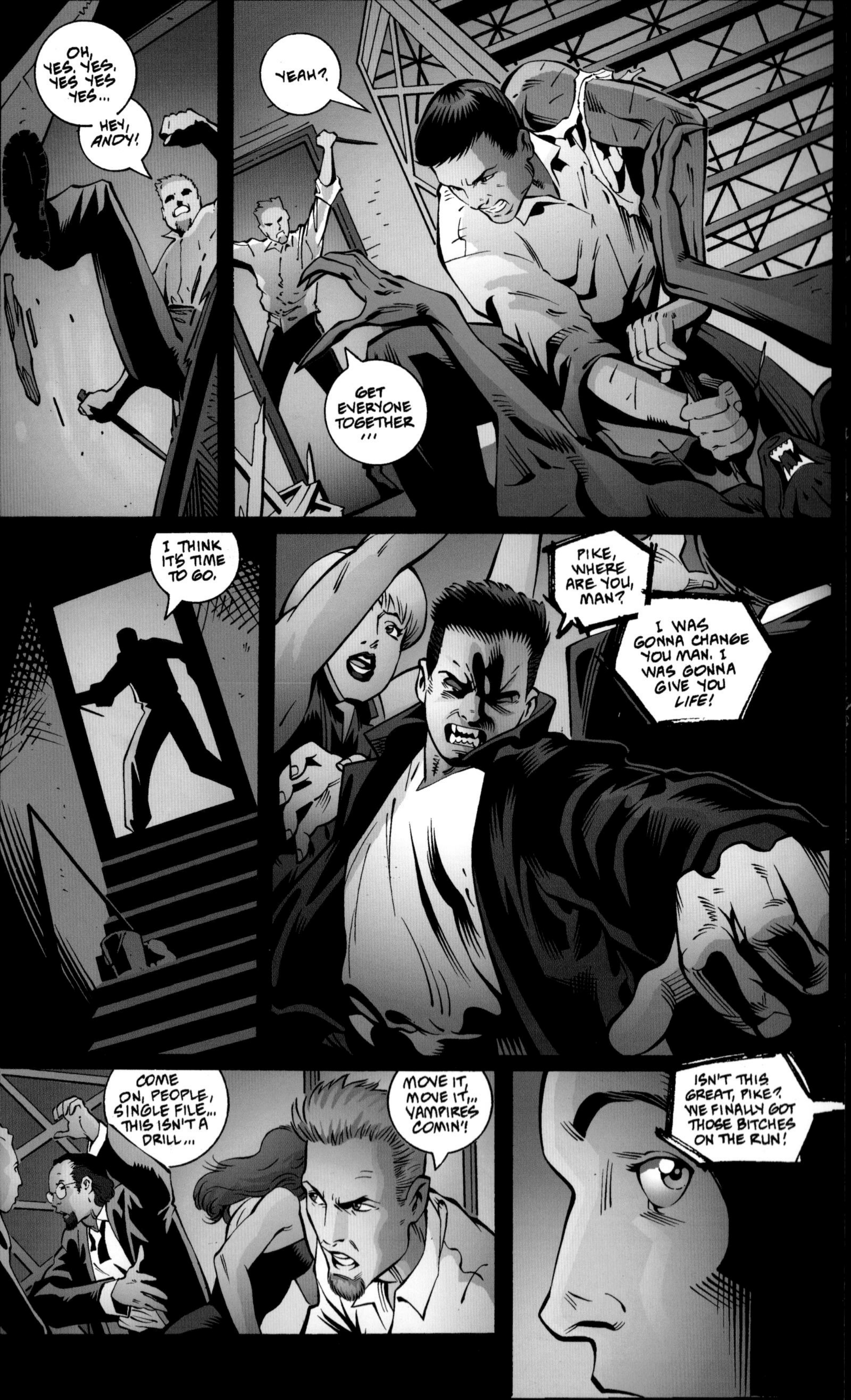
OH, YES. YES. YES YES YES...
HEY, ANDY!
YEAH?
GET EVERYONE TOGETHER ...
I THINK IT'S TIME TO GO.
PIKE, WHERE ARE YOU, MAN?
I WAS GONNA CHANGE YOU MAN. I WAS GONNA GIVE YOU LIFE!
COME ON, PEOPLE, SINGLE FILE... THIS ISN'T A DRILL...
MOVE IT, MOVE IT... VAMPIRES COMIN'!
ISN'T THIS GREAT, PIKE? WE FINALLY GOT THOSE BITCHES ON THE RUN!

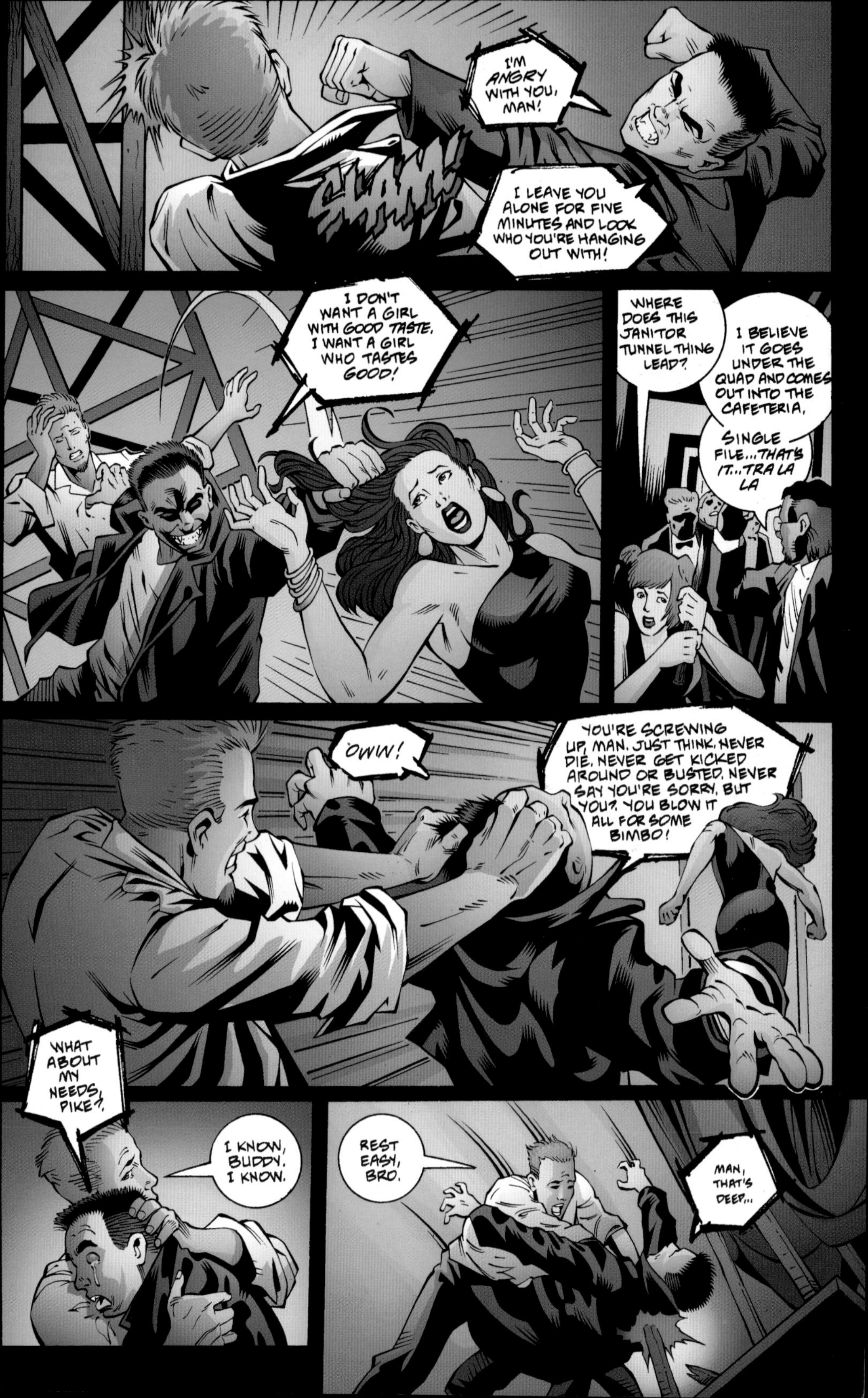
I'M ANGRY WITH YOU, MAN!
SLAM!
I LEAVE YOU ALONE FOR FIVE MINUTES AND LOOK WHO YOU'RE HANGING OUT WITH!
I DON'T WANT A GIRL WITH GOOD TASTE. I WANT A GIRL WHO TASTES GOOD!
WHERE DOES THIS JANITOR TUNNEL THING LEAD?
I BELIEVE IT GOES UNDER THE QUAD AND COMES OUT INTO THE CAFETERIA.
SINGLE FILE... THAT'S IT... TRA LA LA
OWW!
YOU'RE SCREWING UP, MAN. JUST THINK. NEVER DIE. NEVER GET KICKED AROUND OR BUSTED. NEVER SAY YOU'RE SORRY. BUT YOU? YOU BLOW IT ALL FOR SOME BIMBO!
WHAT ABOUT MY NEEDS, PIKE?
I KNOW, BUDDY. I KNOW.
REST EASY, BRO.
MAN, THAT'S DEEP...

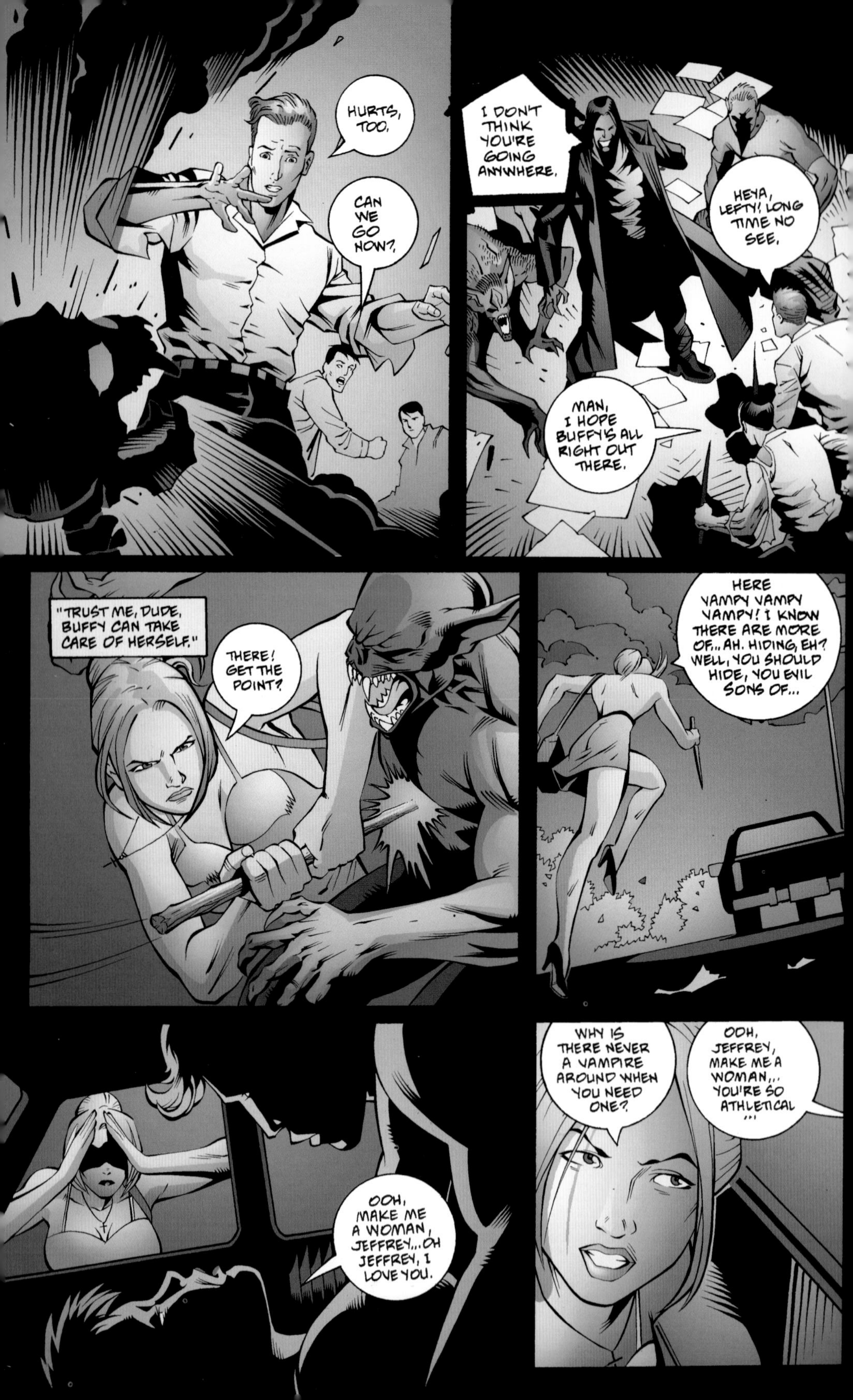
HURTS, TOO.
CAN WE GO NOW?
I DON'T THINK YOU'RE GOING ANYWHERE.
HEYA, LEFTY! LONG TIME NO SEE.
MAN, I HOPE BUFFY'S ALL RIGHT OUT THERE.
"TRUST ME, DUDE, BUFFY CAN TAKE CARE OF HERSELF."
THERE! GET THE POINT?
HERE VAMPY VAMPY VAMPY! I KNOW THERE ARE MORE OF... AH. HIDING, EH? WELL, YOU SHOULD HIDE, YOU EVIL SONS OF...
OOH, MAKE ME A WOMAN, JEFFREY... OH JEFFREY, I LOVE YOU.
WHY IS THERE NEVER A VAMPIRE AROUND WHEN YOU NEED ONE?
OOH, JEFFREY, MAKE ME A WOMAN... YOU'RE SO ATHLETICAL...

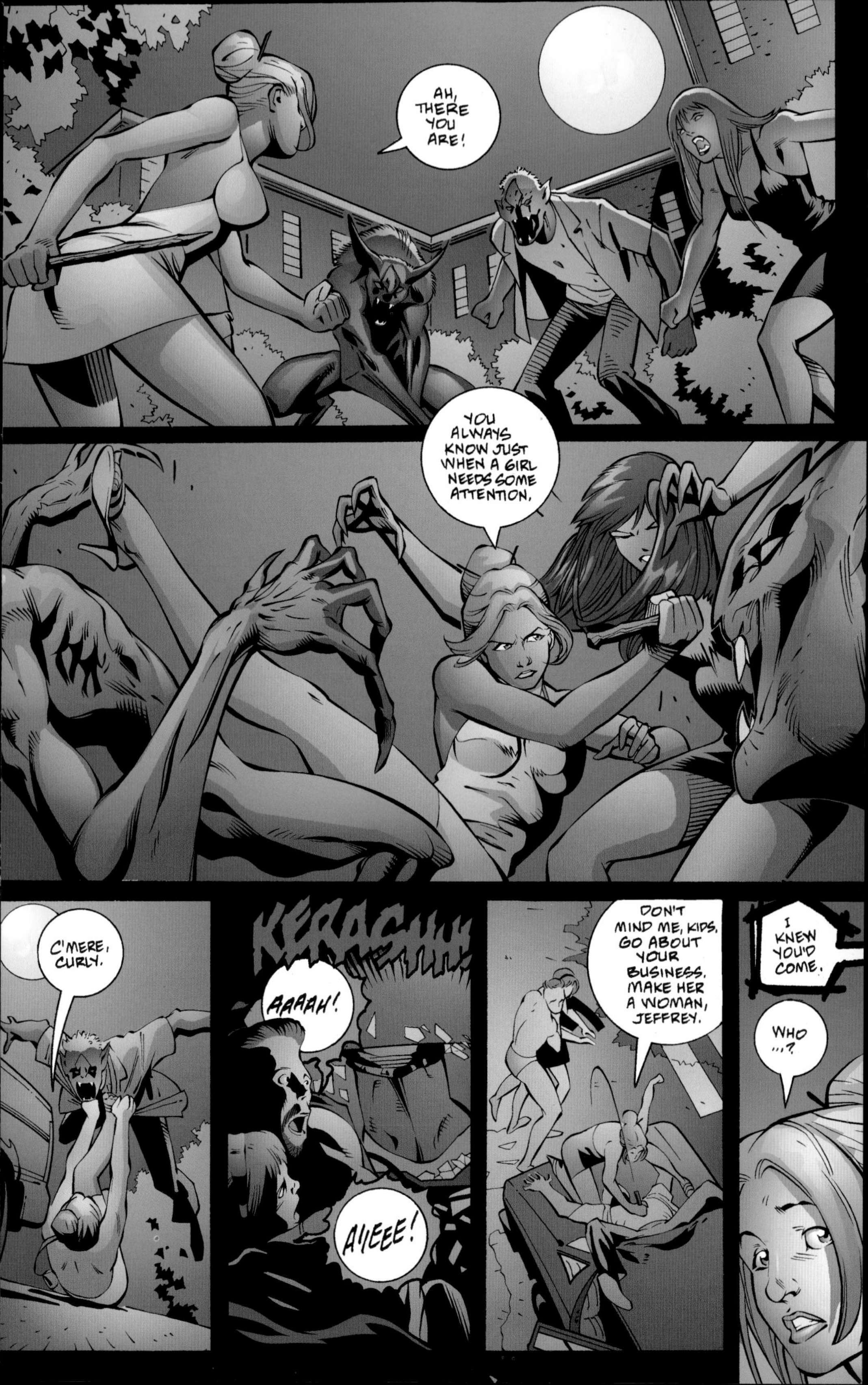
AH, THERE YOU ARE!
YOU ALWAYS KNOW JUST WHEN A GIRL NEEDS SOME ATTENTION.
C'MERE, CURLY.
AAAAH!
AIIEEE!
DON'T MIND ME, KIDS, GO ABOUT YOUR BUSINESS. MAKE HER A WOMAN, JEFFREY.
I KNEW YOU'D COME.
WHO ...?

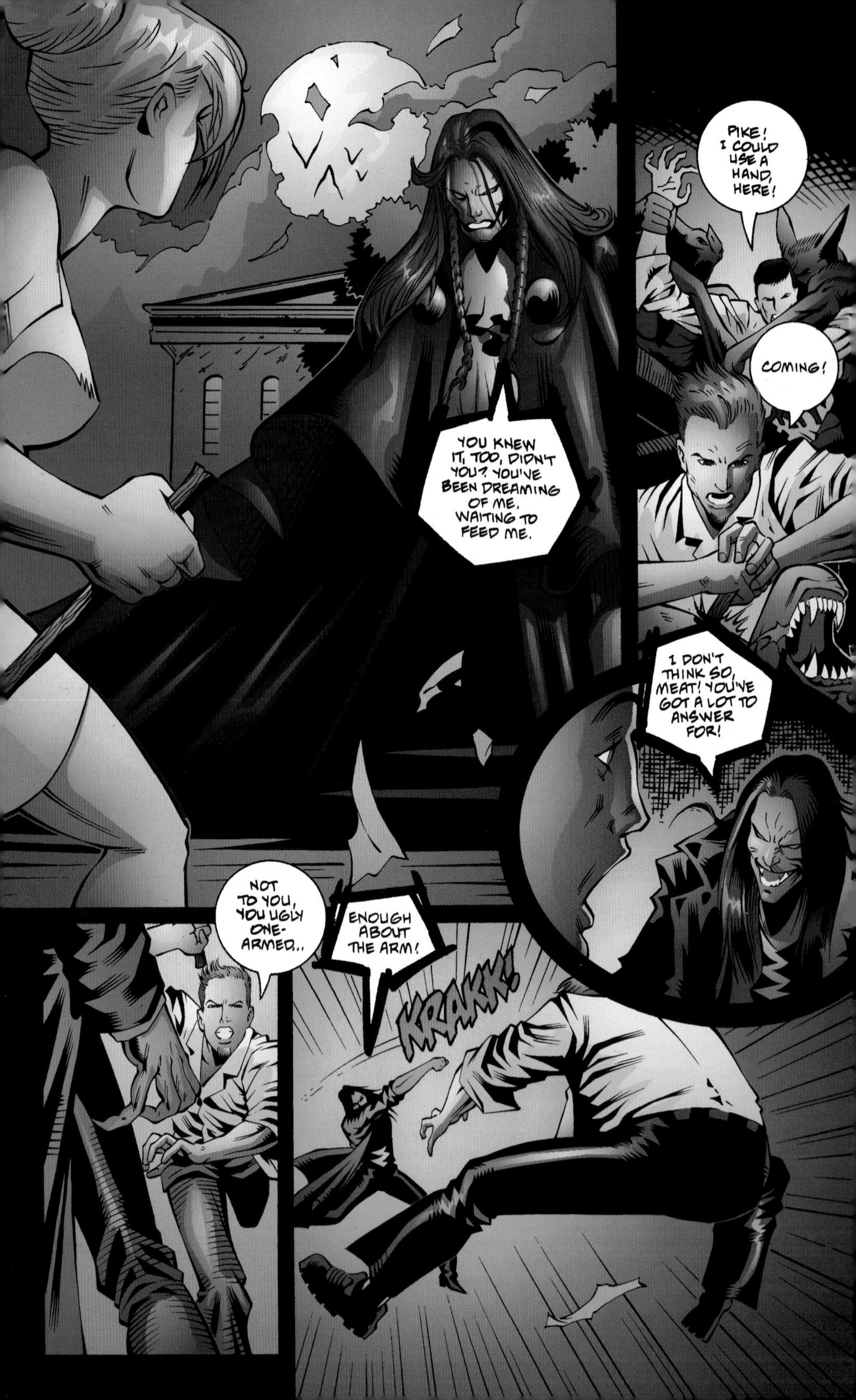
YOU KNEW IT, TOO, DIDN'T YOU? YOU'VE BEEN DREAMING OF ME, WAITING TO FEED ME.
PIKE! I COULD USE A HAND, HERE!
COMING!
I DON'T THINK SO, MEAT! YOU'VE GOT A LOT TO ANSWER FOR!
NOT TO YOU, YOU UGLY ONE-ARMED...
ENOUGH ABOUT THE ARM!
KRAKK!

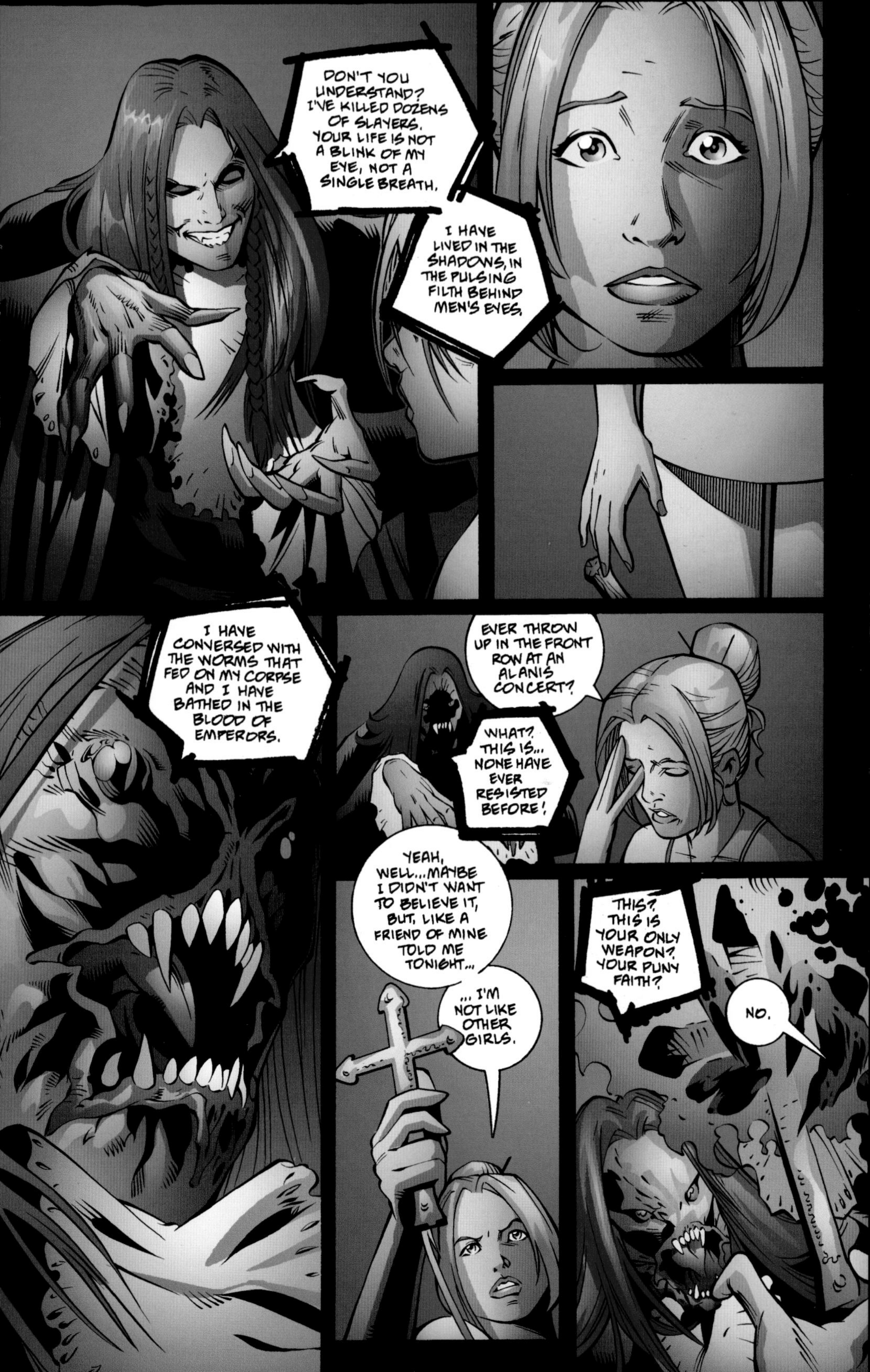
DON'T YOU UNDERSTAND? I'VE KILLED DOZENS OF SLAYERS. YOUR LIFE IS NOT A BLINK OF MY EYE, NOT A SINGLE BREATH.
I HAVE LIVED IN THE SHADOWS, IN THE PULSING FILTH BEHIND MEN'S EYES.
I HAVE CONVERSED WITH THE WORMS THAT FED ON MY CORPSE AND I HAVE BATHED IN THE BLOOD OF EMPERORS.
EVER THROW UP IN THE FRONT ROW AT AN ALANIS CONCERT?
WHAT? THIS IS... NONE HAVE EVER RESISTED BEFORE!
YEAH, WELL... MAYBE I DIDN'T WANT TO BELIEVE IT, BUT, LIKE A FRIEND OF MINE TOLD ME TONIGHT...
... I'M NOT LIKE OTHER GIRLS.
THIS? THIS IS YOUR ONLY WEAPON? YOUR PUNY FAITH?
NO.

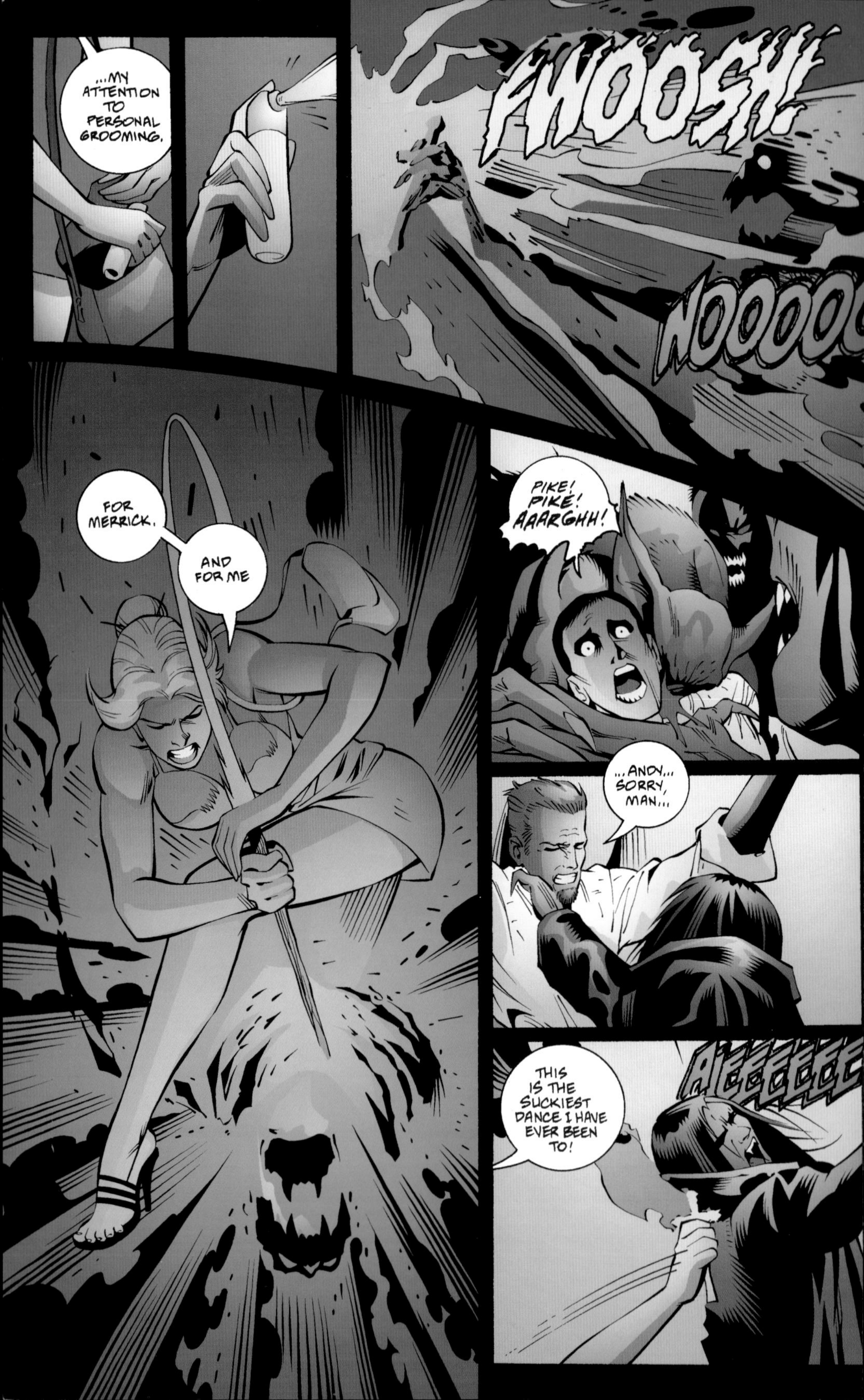
...MY ATTENTION TO PERSONAL GROOMING.
FWOOSH!
NOOOOO
FOR MERRICK.
AND FOR ME
PIKE! PIKE! AAARGHH!
...ANDY... SORRY, MAN...
AEEEEE
THIS IS THE SUCKIEST DANCE I HAVE EVER BEEN TO!

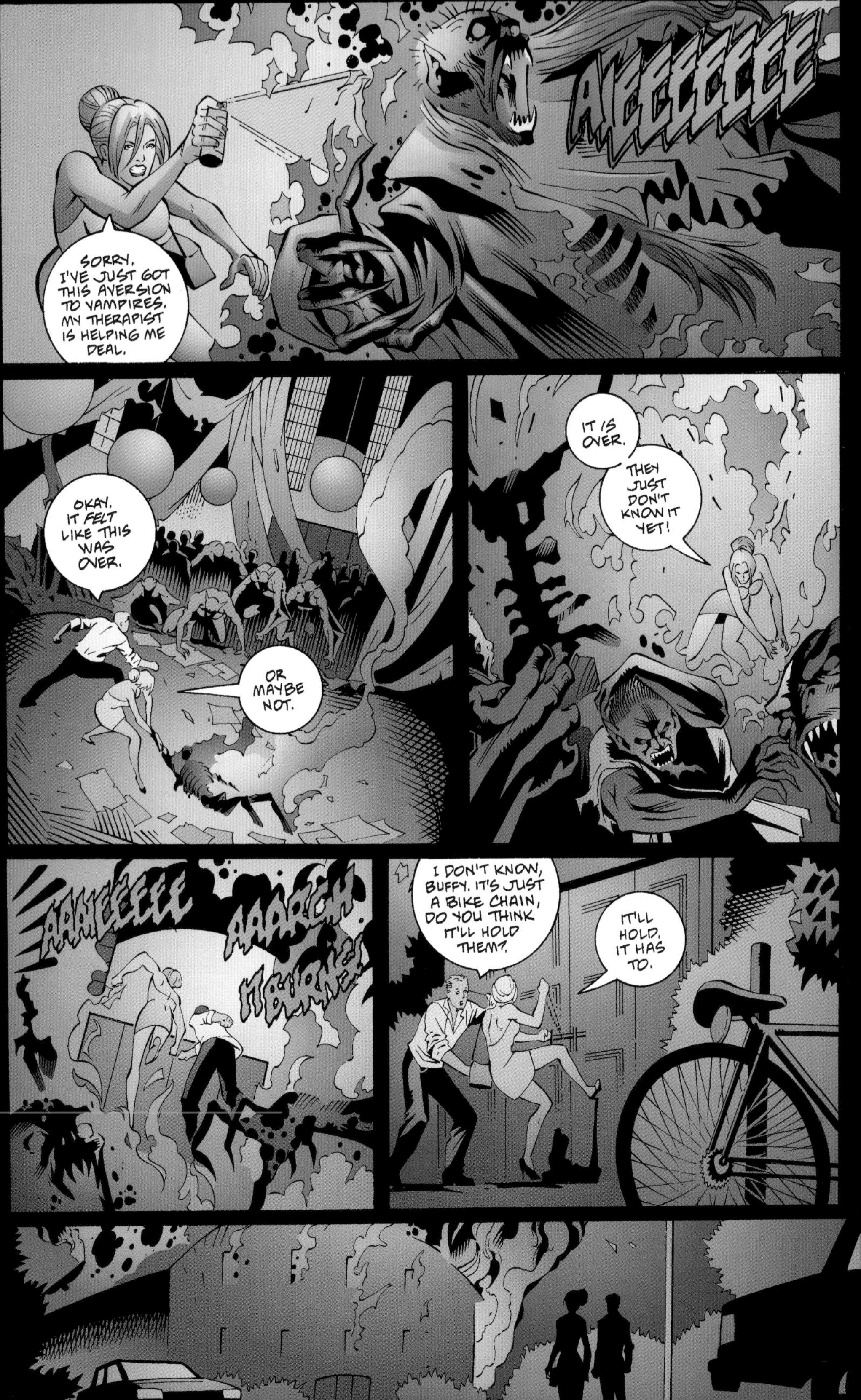
AIEEEEEEE
SORRY. I'VE JUST GOT THIS AVERSION TO VAMPIRES. MY THERAPIST IS HELPING ME DEAL.
OKAY. IT FELT LIKE THIS WAS OVER.
OR MAYBE NOT.
IT IS OVER.
THEY JUST DON'T KNOW IT YET!
AAAIEEEE
AAARGH
IT BURNS!
I DON'T KNOW, BUFFY. IT'S JUST A BIKE CHAIN, DO YOU THINK IT'LL HOLD THEM?
IT'LL HOLD. IT HAS TO.

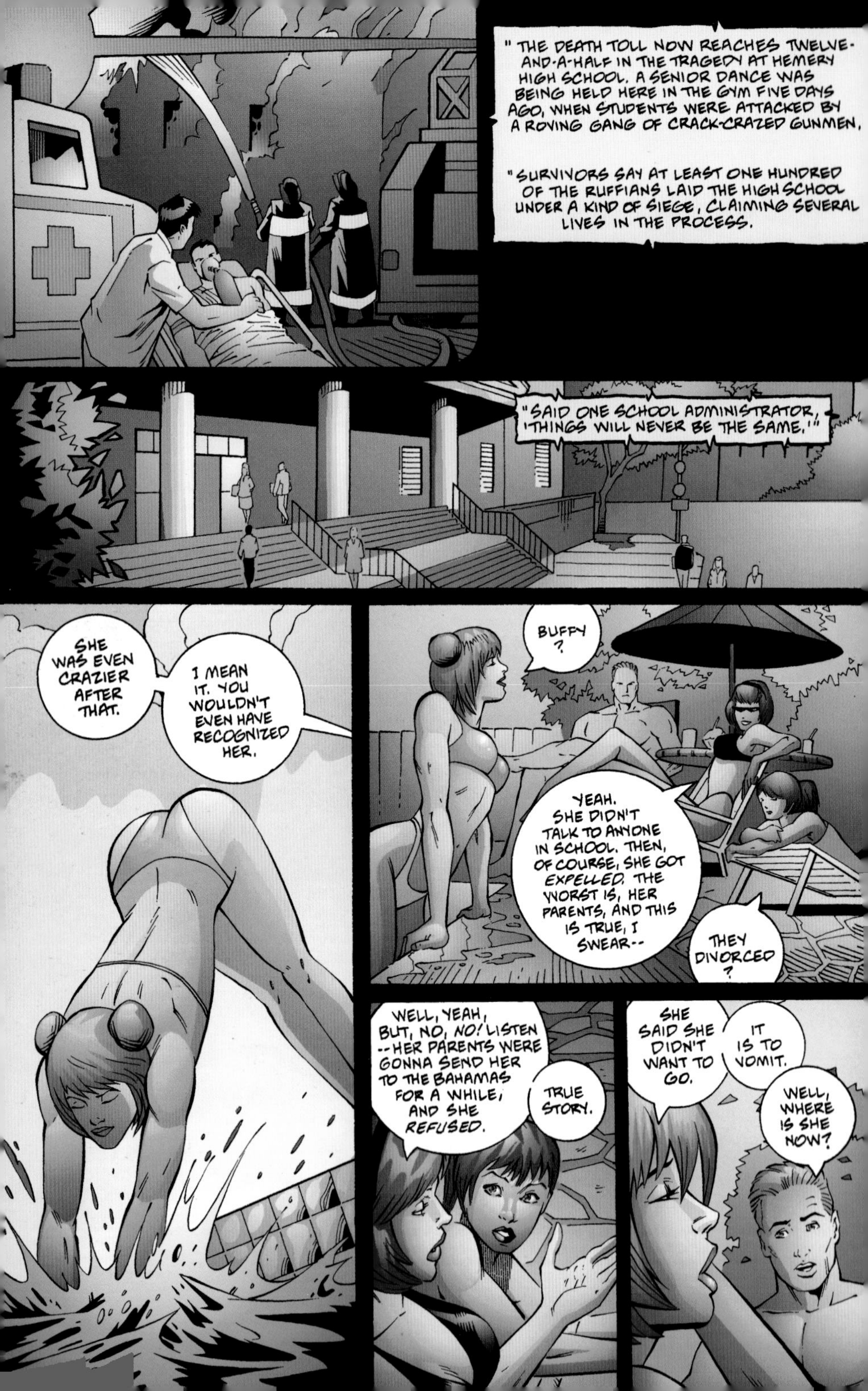
"THE DEATH TOLL NOW REACHES TWELVE-AND-A-HALF IN THE TRAGEDY AT HEMERY HIGH SCHOOL. A SENIOR DANCE WAS BEING HELD HERE IN THE GYM FIVE DAYS AGO, WHEN STUDENTS WERE ATTACKED BY A ROVING GANG OF CRACK-CRAZED GUNMEN.
"SURVIVORS SAY AT LEAST ONE HUNDRED OF THE RUFFIANS LAID THE HIGH SCHOOL UNDER A KIND OF SIEGE, CLAIMING SEVERAL LIVES IN THE PROCESS.
"SAID ONE SCHOOL ADMINISTRATOR, 'THINGS WILL NEVER BE THE SAME.'"
SHE WAS EVEN CRAZIER AFTER THAT.
I MEAN IT. YOU WOULDN'T EVEN HAVE RECOGNIZED HER.
BUFFY?
YEAH. SHE DIDN'T TALK TO ANYONE IN SCHOOL. THEN, OF COURSE, SHE GOT EXPELLED. THE WORST IS, HER PARENTS, AND THIS IS TRUE, I SWEAR--
THEY DIVORCED?
WELL, YEAH, BUT, NO, NO! LISTEN --HER PARENTS WERE GONNA SEND HER TO THE BAHAMAS FOR A WHILE, AND SHE REFUSED.
TRUE STORY.
SHE SAID SHE DIDN'T WANT TO GO.
IT IS TO VOMIT.
WELL, WHERE IS SHE NOW?

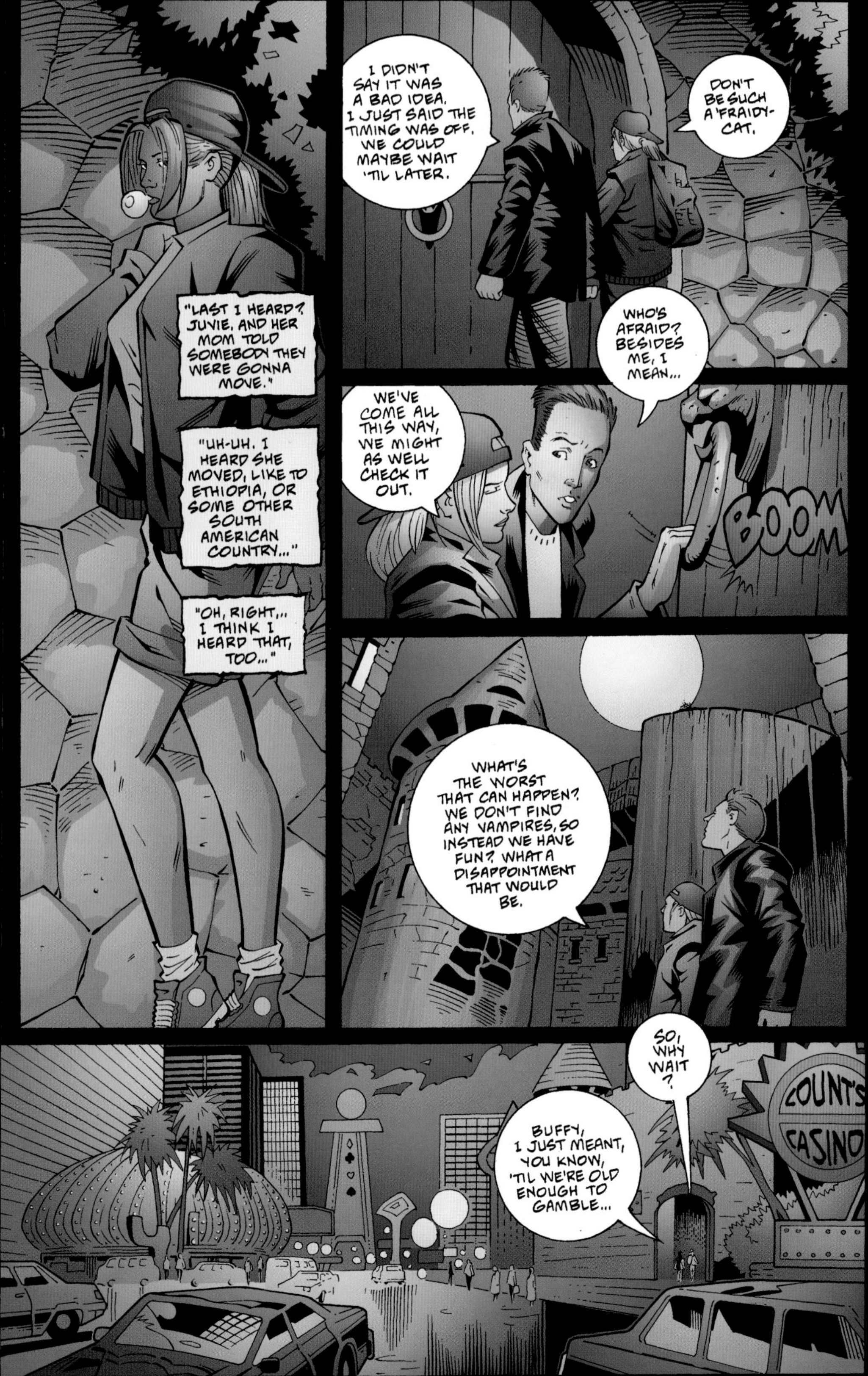
"LAST I HEARD? JUVIE. AND HER MOM TOLD SOMEBODY THEY WERE GONNA MOVE."
"UH-UH. I HEARD SHE MOVED, LIKE TO ETHIOPIA, OR SOME OTHER SOUTH AMERICAN COUNTRY..."
"OH, RIGHT... I THINK I HEARD THAT, TOO..."
I DIDN'T SAY IT WAS A BAD IDEA. I JUST SAID THE TIMING WAS OFF. WE COULD MAYBE WAIT 'TIL LATER.
DON'T BE SUCH A 'FRAIDY-CAT.
WHO'S AFRAID? BESIDES ME, I MEAN...
WE'VE COME ALL THIS WAY, WE MIGHT AS WELL CHECK IT OUT.
BOOM
WHAT'S THE WORST THAT CAN HAPPEN? WE DON'T FIND ANY VAMPIRES, SO INSTEAD WE HAVE FUN? WHAT A DISAPPOINTMENT THAT WOULD BE.
SO, WHY WAIT?
BUFFY, I JUST MEANT, YOU KNOW, 'TIL WE'RE OLD ENOUGH TO GAMBLE...
COUNT'S CASINO

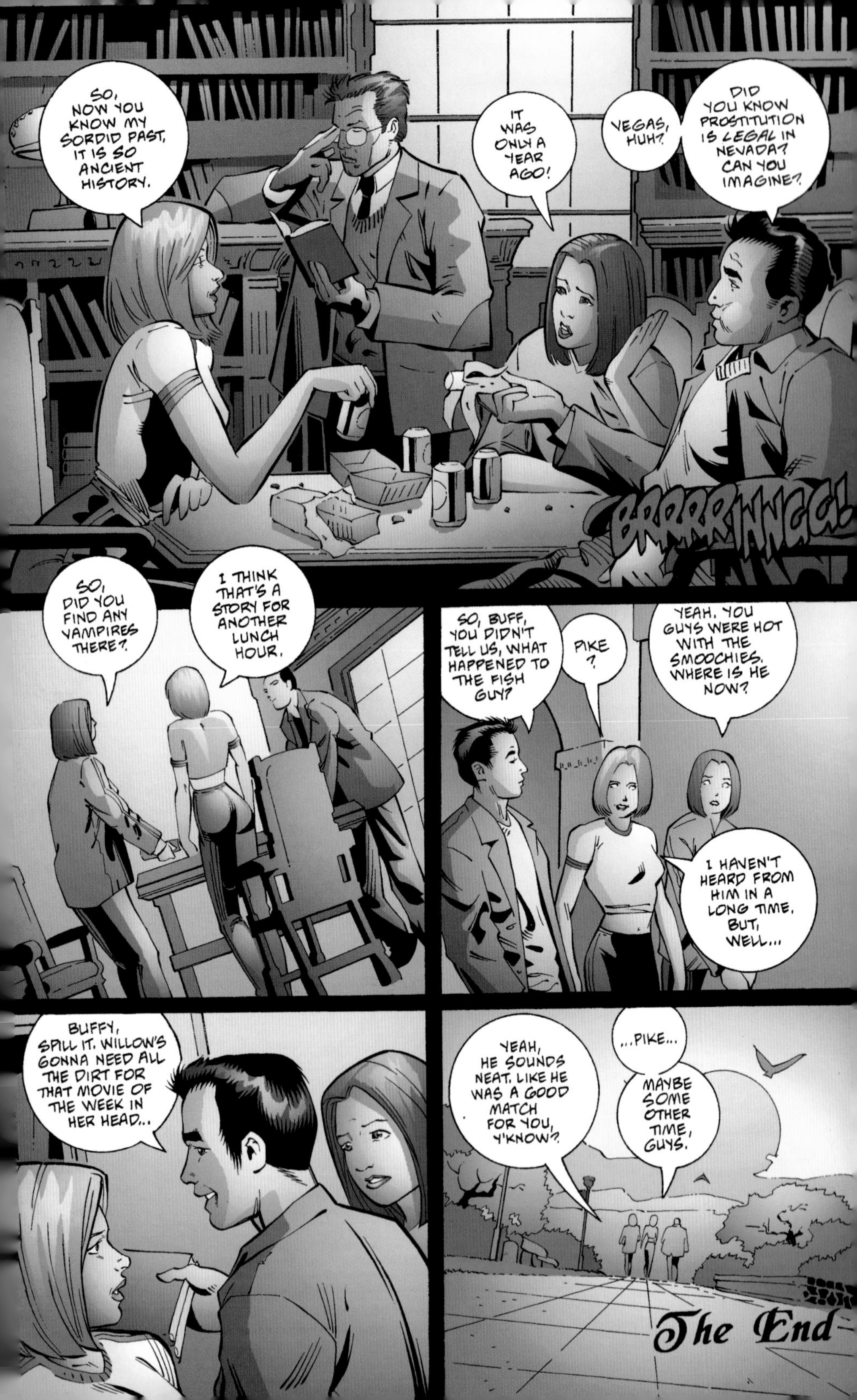
SO, NOW YOU KNOW MY SORDID PAST, IT IS SO ANCIENT HISTORY.
IT WAS ONLY A YEAR AGO!
VEGAS, HUH?
DID YOU KNOW PROSTITUTION IS LEGAL IN NEVADA? CAN YOU IMAGINE?
BRRRRINNGG!
SO, DID YOU FIND ANY VAMPIRES THERE?
I THINK THAT'S A STORY FOR ANOTHER LUNCH HOUR.
SO, BUFF, YOU DIDN'T TELL US, WHAT HAPPENED TO THE FISH GUY?
PIKE?
YEAH. YOU GUYS WERE HOT WITH THE SMOOCHIES. WHERE IS HE NOW?
I HAVEN'T HEARD FROM HIM IN A LONG TIME. BUT, WELL...
BUFFY, SPILL IT. WILLOW'S GONNA NEED ALL THE DIRT FOR THAT MOVIE OF THE WEEK IN HER HEAD...
YEAH, HE SOUNDS NEAT. LIKE HE WAS A GOOD MATCH FOR YOU, Y'KNOW?
...PIKE...
MAYBE SOME OTHER TIME, GUYS.
The End

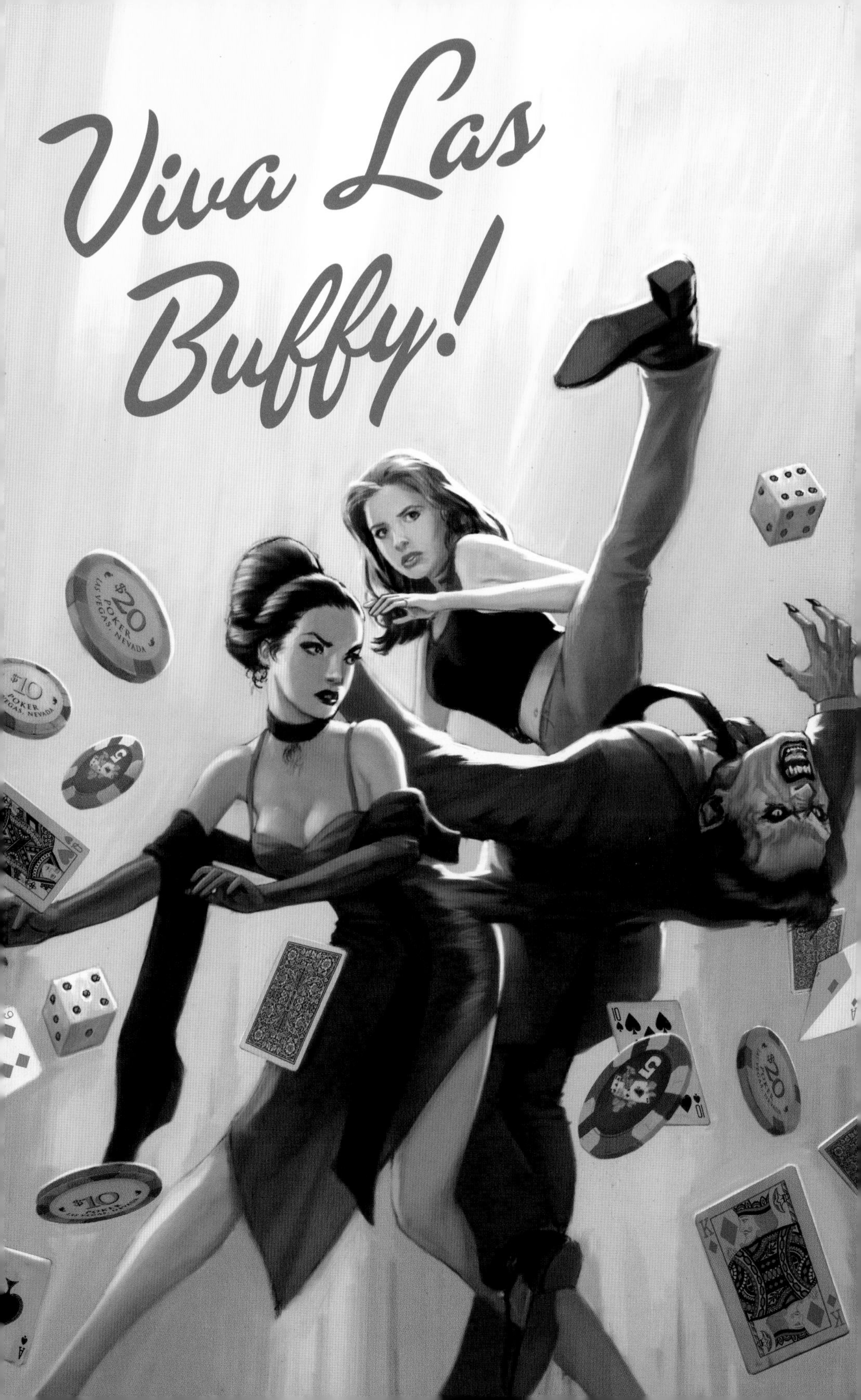

Viva Las Buffy!
$20 POKER LAS VEGAS, NEVADA

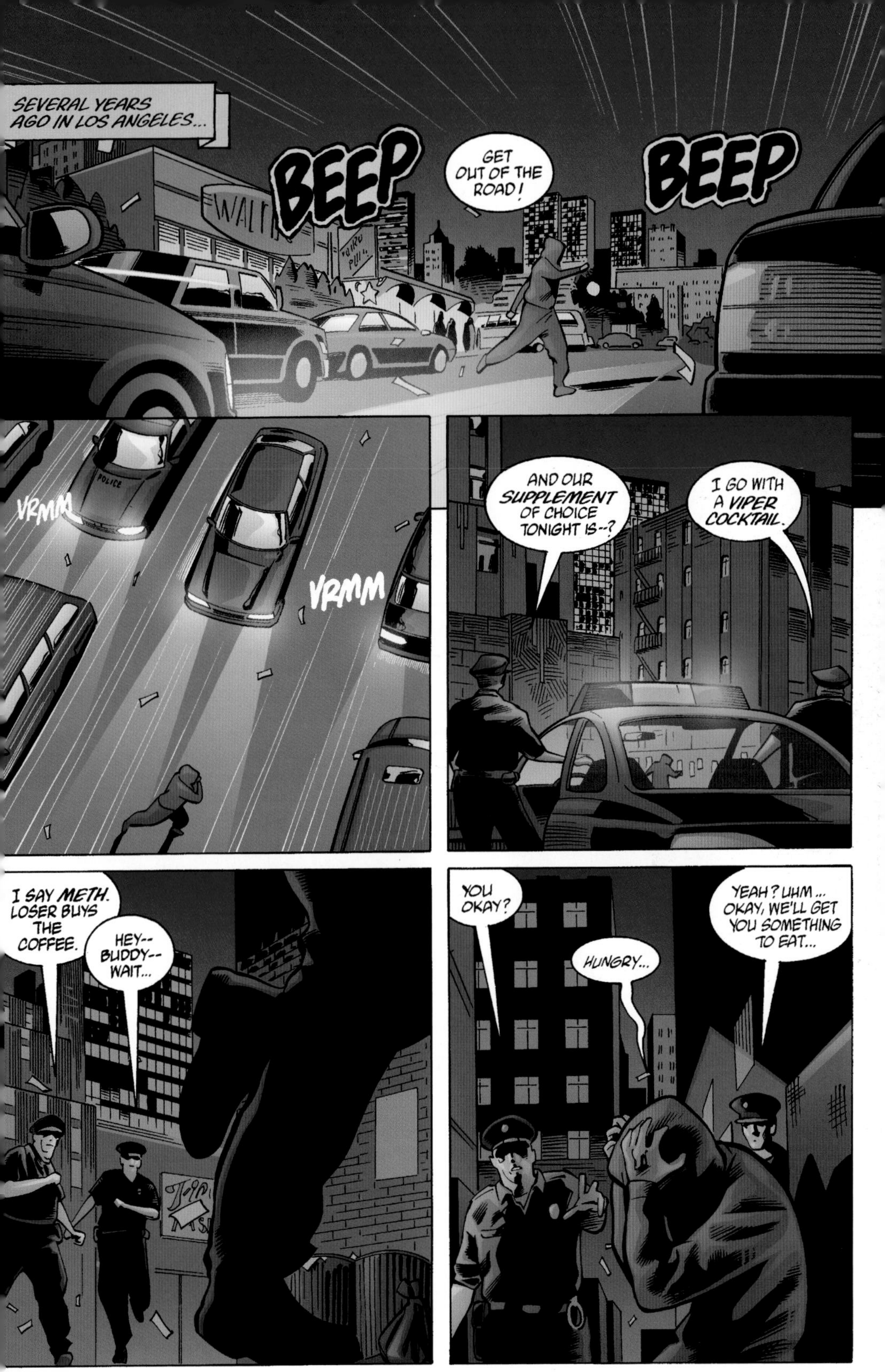
SEVERAL YEARS AGO IN LOS ANGELES...
BEEP
GET OUT OF THE ROAD!
BEEP
VRMM
VRMM
AND OUR SUPPLEMENT OF CHOICE TONIGHT IS--?
I GO WITH A VIPER COCKTAIL.
I SAY METH. LOSER BUYS THE COFFEE.
HEY-- BUDDY-- WAIT...
YOU OKAY?
HUNGRY...
YEAH? UHM... OKAY, WE'LL GET YOU SOMETHING TO EAT...

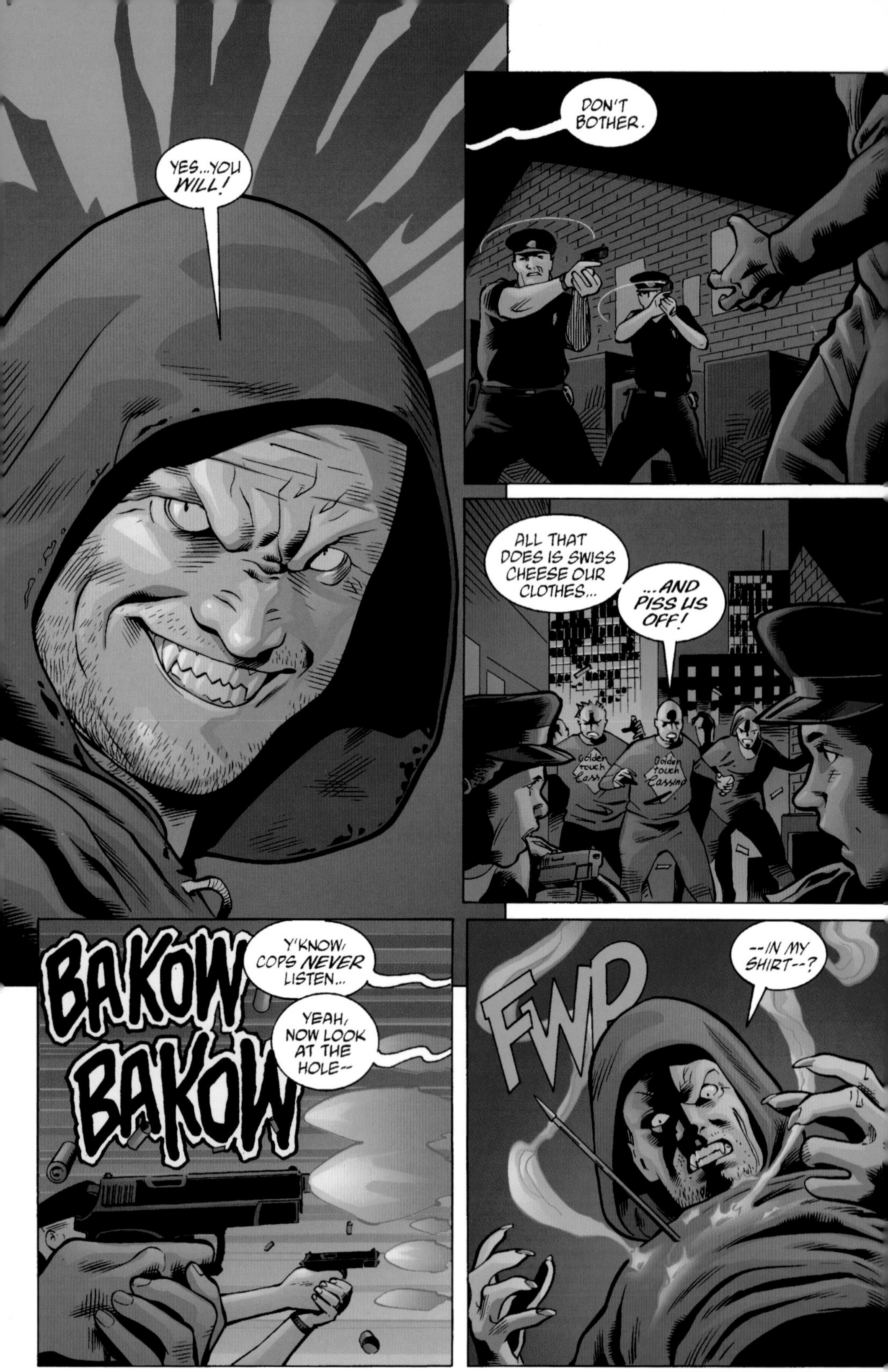
YES...YOU WILL!
DON'T BOTHER.
ALL THAT DOES IS SWISS CHEESE OUR CLOTHES...
...AND PISS US OFF!
Golden touch Casino
Golden touch Cassino
BAKOW
BAKOW
Y'KNOW, COPS NEVER LISTEN...
YEAH, NOW LOOK AT THE HOLE--
FWP
--IN MY SHIRT--?

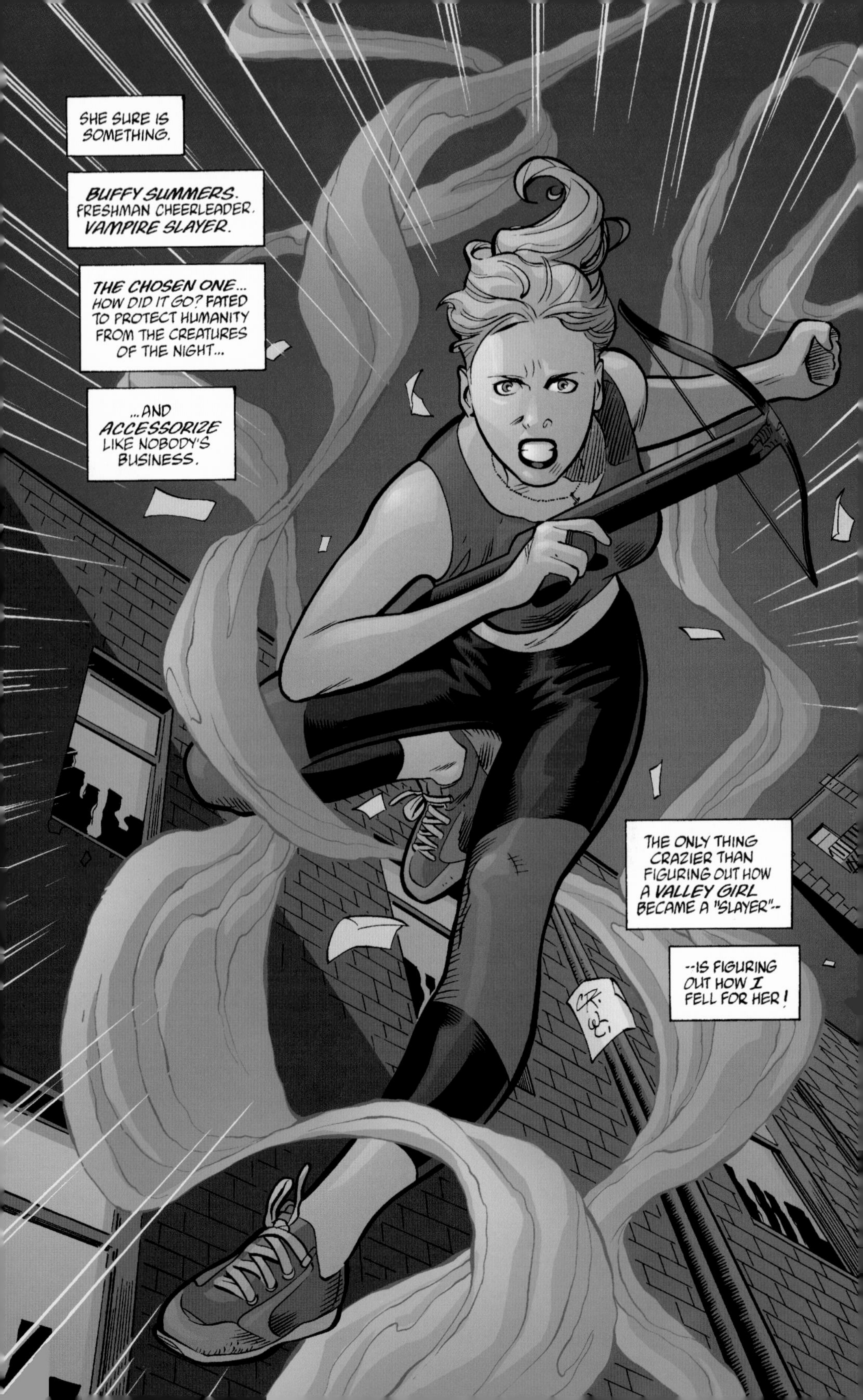
SHE SURE IS SOMETHING.
BUFFY SUMMERS. FRESHMAN CHEERLEADER. VAMPIRE SLAYER.
THE CHOSEN ONE... HOW DID IT GO? FATED TO PROTECT HUMANITY FROM THE CREATURES OF THE NIGHT...
...AND ACCESSORIZE LIKE NOBODY'S BUSINESS.
THE ONLY THING CRAZIER THAN FIGURING OUT HOW A VALLEY GIRL BECAME A "SLAYER"--
--IS FIGURING OUT HOW I FELL FOR HER!

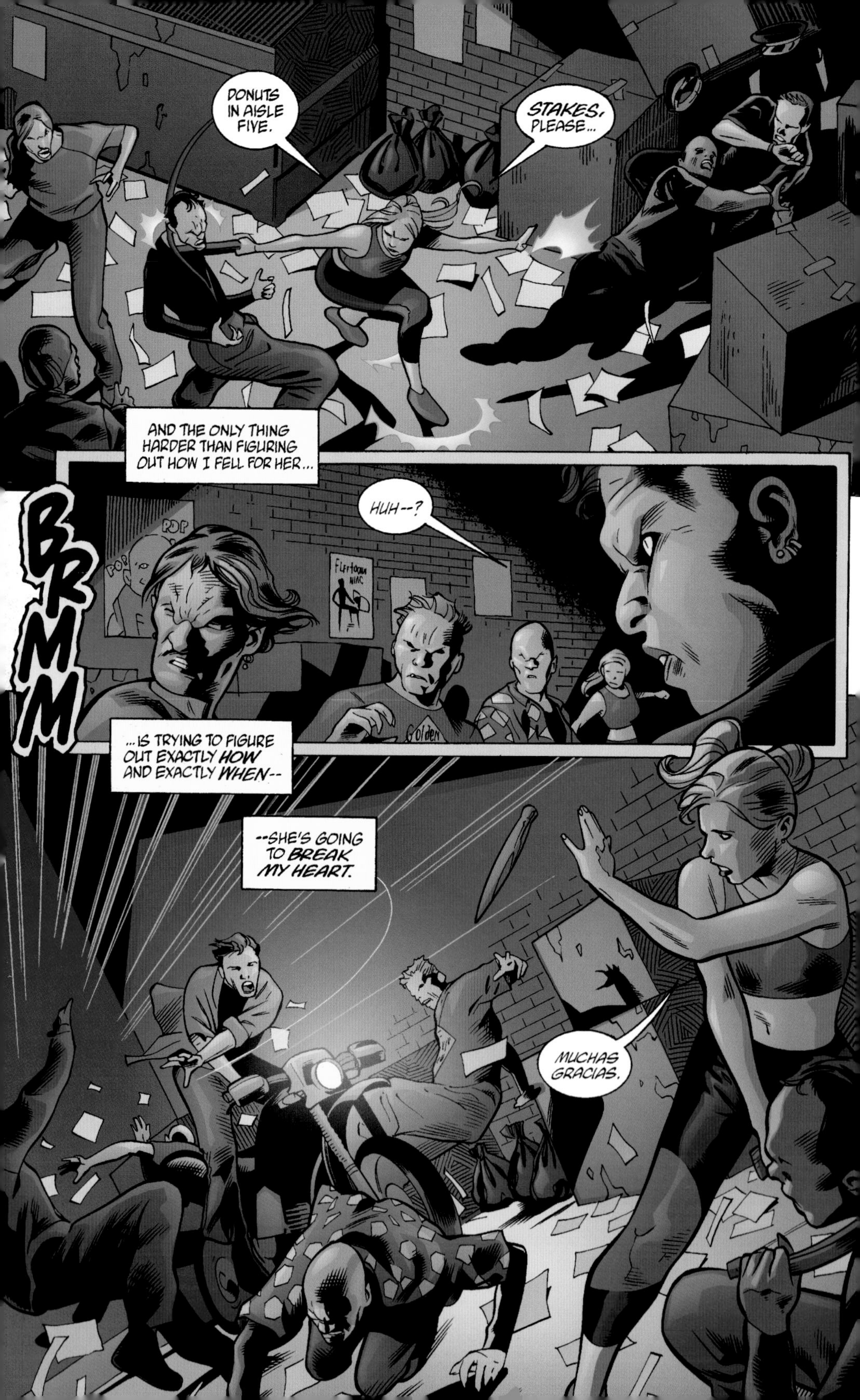
DONUTS IN AISLE FIVE.
STAKES, PLEASE...
AND THE ONLY THING HARDER THAN FIGURING OUT HOW I FELL FOR HER...
BRMMM
HUH--?
...IS TRYING TO FIGURE OUT EXACTLY HOW AND EXACTLY WHEN--
--SHE'S GOING TO BREAK MY HEART.
MUCHAS GRACIAS.

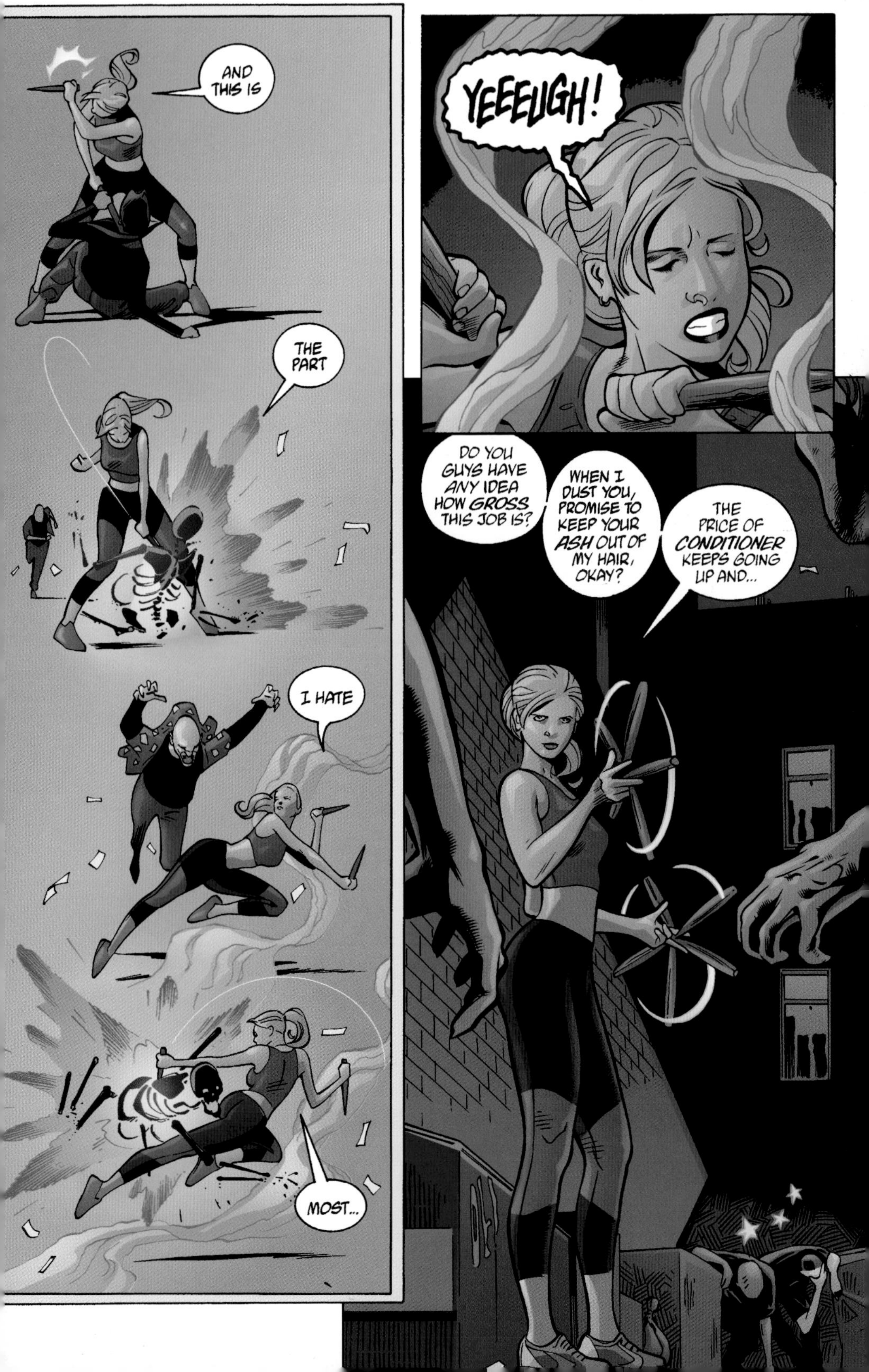
AND THIS IS
THE PART
I HATE
MOST...
YEEEUGH!
DO YOU GUYS HAVE ANY IDEA HOW GROSS THIS JOB IS?
WHEN I DUST YOU, PROMISE TO KEEP YOUR ASH OUT OF MY HAIR, OKAY?
THE PRICE OF CONDITIONER KEEPS GOING UP AND...

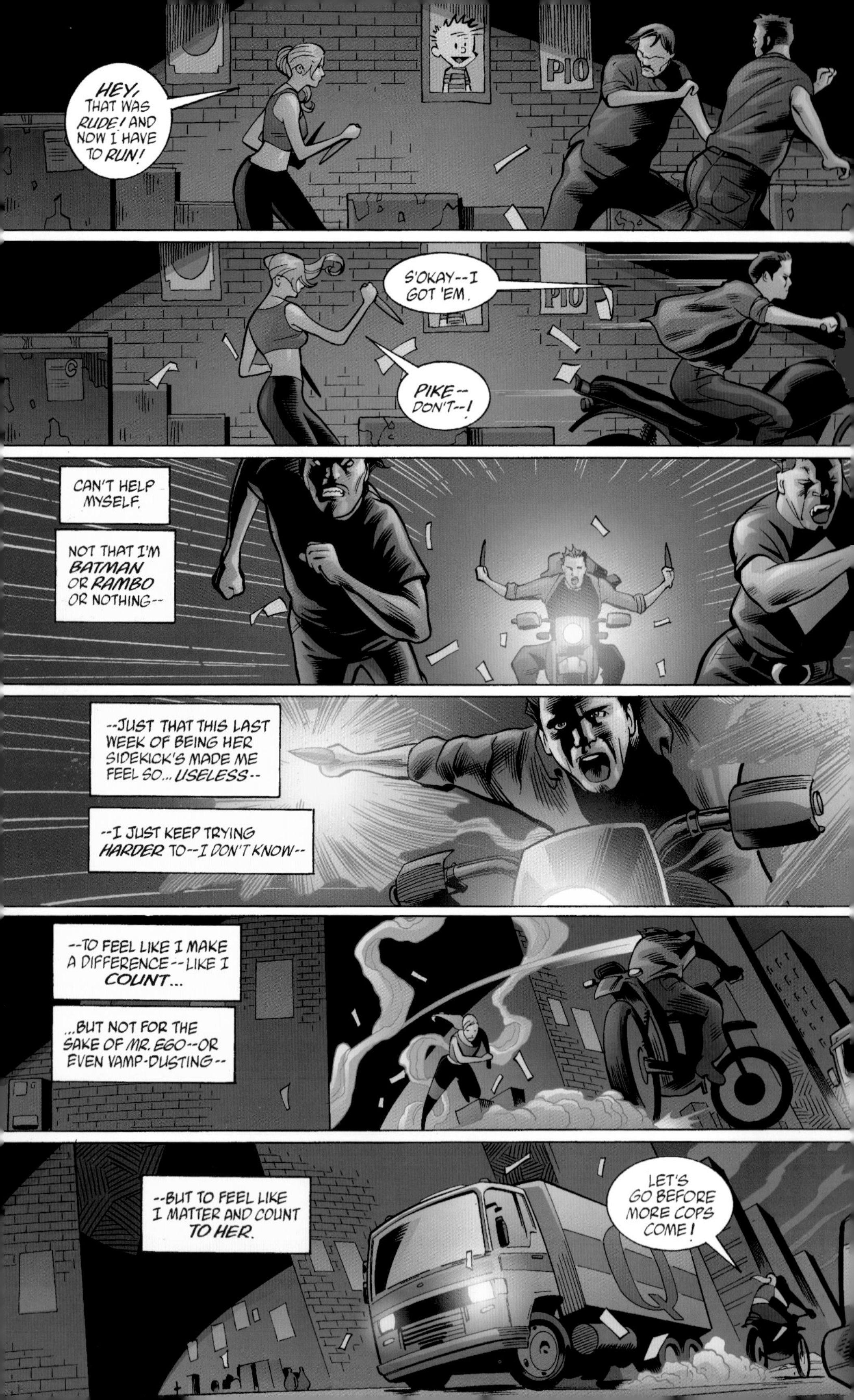
HEY, THAT WAS RUDE! AND NOW I HAVE TO RUN!
S'OKAY--I GOT 'EM.
PIKE-- DON'T--!
CAN'T HELP MYSELF.
NOT THAT I'M BATMAN OR RAMBO OR NOTHING--
--JUST THAT THIS LAST WEEK OF BEING HER SIDEKICK'S MADE ME FEEL SO... USELESS--
--I JUST KEEP TRYING HARDER TO--I DON'T KNOW--
--TO FEEL LIKE I MAKE A DIFFERENCE--LIKE I COUNT...
...BUT NOT FOR THE SAKE OF MR. EGO--OR EVEN VAMP-DUSTING--
--BUT TO FEEL LIKE I MATTER AND COUNT TO HER.
LET'S GO BEFORE MORE COPS COME!

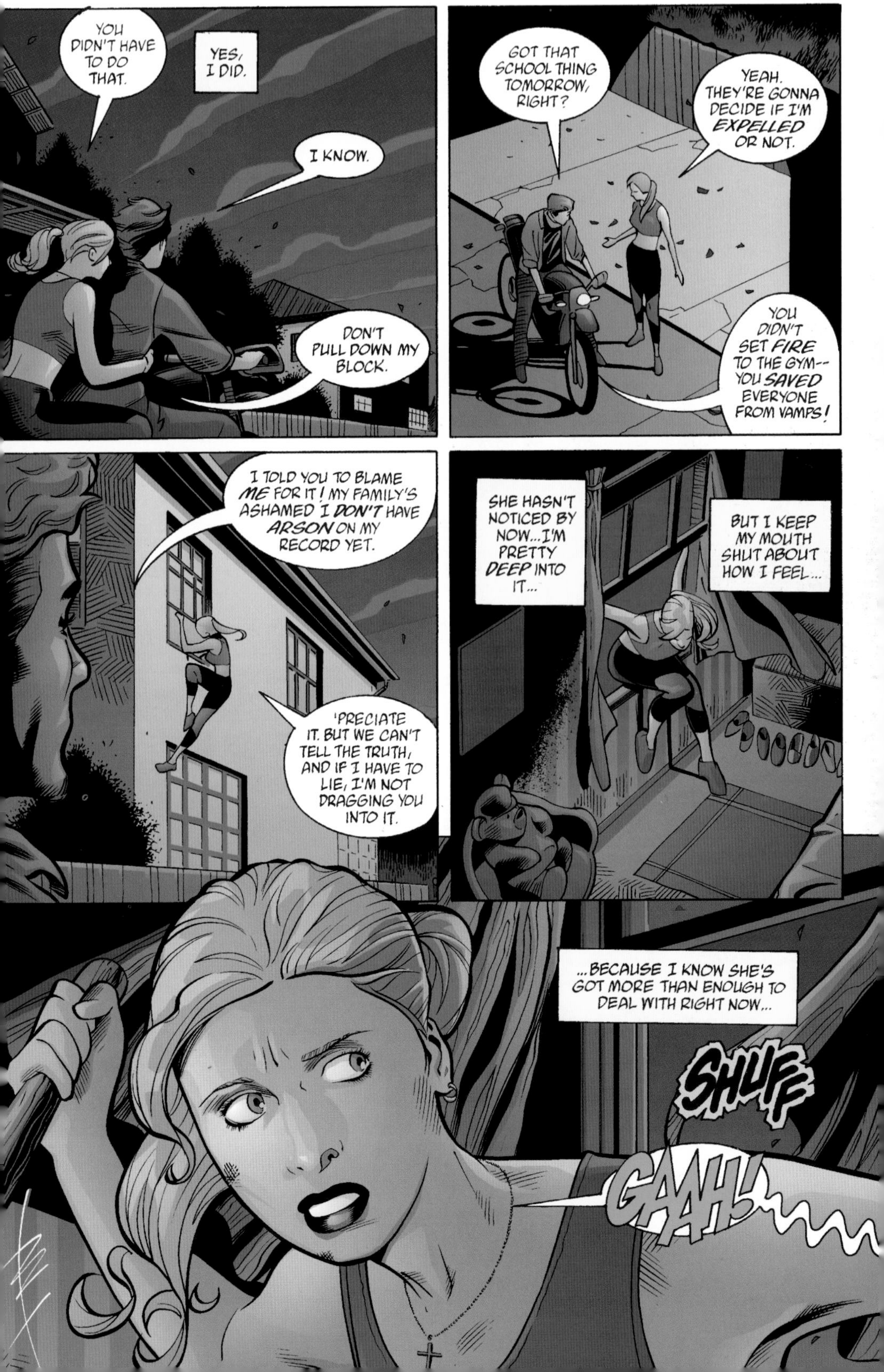
YOU DIDN'T HAVE TO DO THAT.
YES, I DID.
I KNOW.
DON'T PULL DOWN MY BLOCK.
GOT THAT SCHOOL THING TOMORROW, RIGHT?
YEAH. THEY'RE GONNA DECIDE IF I'M EXPELLED OR NOT.
YOU DIDN'T SET FIRE TO THE GYM-- YOU SAVED EVERYONE FROM VAMPS!
I TOLD YOU TO BLAME ME FOR IT! MY FAMILY'S ASHAMED I DON'T HAVE ARSON ON MY RECORD YET.
'PRECIATE IT. BUT WE CAN'T TELL THE TRUTH, AND IF I HAVE TO LIE, I'M NOT DRAGGING YOU INTO IT.
SHE HASN'T NOTICED BY NOW...I'M PRETTY DEEP INTO IT...
BUT I KEEP MY MOUTH SHUT ABOUT HOW I FEEL...
...BECAUSE I KNOW SHE'S GOT MORE THAN ENOUGH TO DEAL WITH RIGHT NOW...
SHUFF
GAAH!

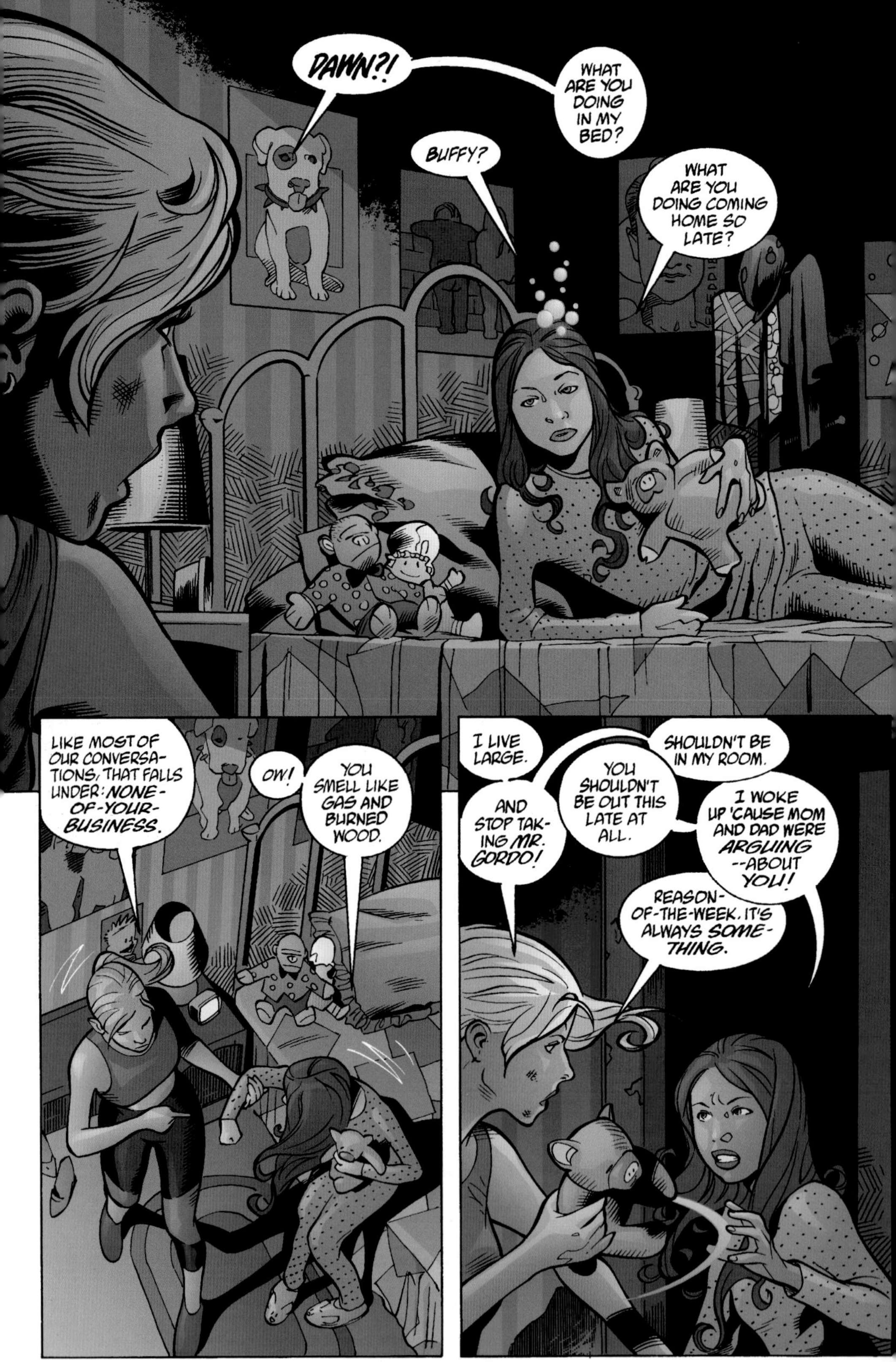
DAWN?!
WHAT ARE YOU DOING IN MY BED?
BUFFY?
WHAT ARE YOU DOING COMING HOME SO LATE?
LIKE MOST OF OUR CONVERSATIONS, THAT FALLS UNDER: NONE-OF-YOUR-BUSINESS.
OW!
YOU SMELL LIKE GAS AND BURNED WOOD.
I LIVE LARGE.
SHOULDN'T BE IN MY ROOM.
AND STOP TAKING MR. GORDO!
YOU SHOULDN'T BE OUT THIS LATE AT ALL.
I WOKE UP 'CAUSE MOM AND DAD WERE ARGUING --ABOUT YOU!
REASON-OF-THE-WEEK. IT'S ALWAYS SOMETHING.

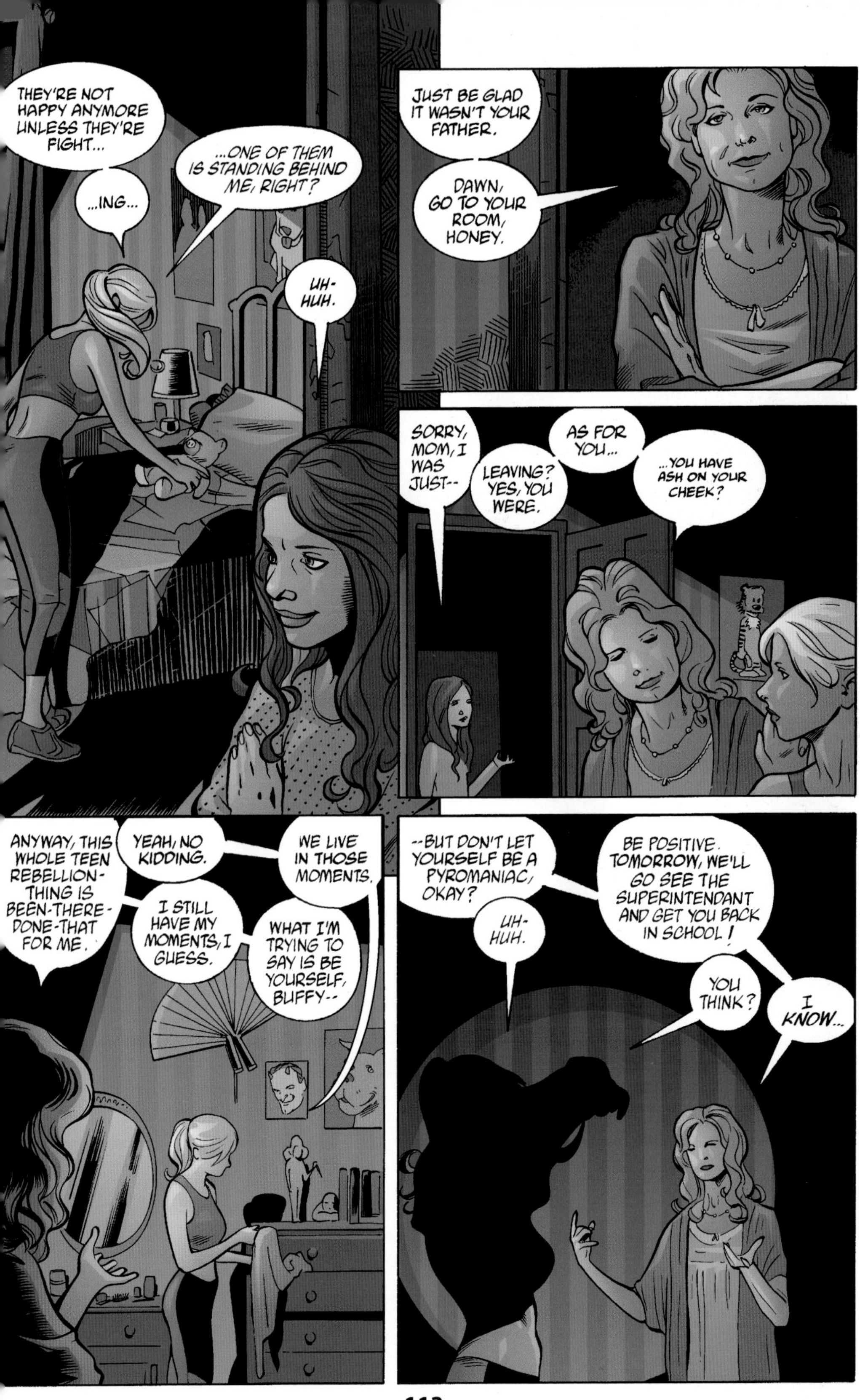
THEY'RE NOT HAPPY ANYMORE UNLESS THEY'RE FIGHT...
...ING...
...ONE OF THEM IS STANDING BEHIND ME, RIGHT?
UH-HUH.
JUST BE GLAD IT WASN'T YOUR FATHER.
DAWN, GO TO YOUR ROOM, HONEY.
SORRY, MOM, I WAS JUST--
LEAVING? YES, YOU WERE.
AS FOR YOU...
...YOU HAVE ASH ON YOUR CHEEK?
ANYWAY, THIS WHOLE TEEN REBELLION-THING IS BEEN-THERE-DONE-THAT FOR ME.
YEAH, NO KIDDING.
I STILL HAVE MY MOMENTS, I GUESS.
WE LIVE IN THOSE MOMENTS.
WHAT I'M TRYING TO SAY IS BE YOURSELF, BUFFY--
--BUT DON'T LET YOURSELF BE A PYROMANIAC, OKAY?
UH-HUH.
BE POSITIVE. TOMORROW, WE'LL GO SEE THE SUPERINTENDANT AND GET YOU BACK IN SCHOOL!
YOU THINK?
I KNOW...

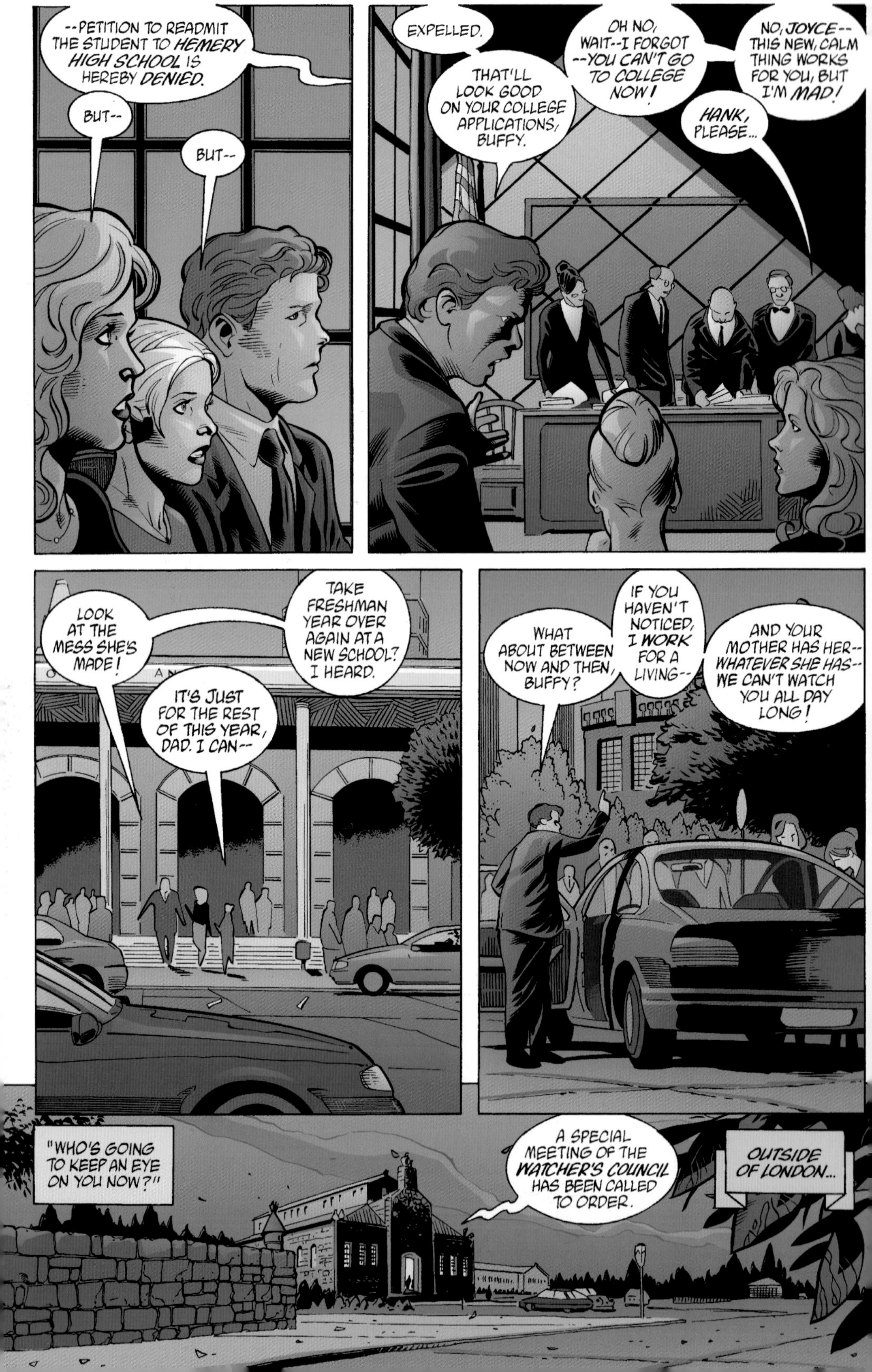
--PETITION TO READMIT THE STUDENT TO HEMERY HIGH SCHOOL IS HEREBY DENIED.
BUT--
BUT--
EXPELLED.
THAT'LL LOOK GOOD ON YOUR COLLEGE APPLICATIONS, BUFFY.
OH NO, WAIT--I FORGOT --YOU CAN'T GO TO COLLEGE NOW!
NO, JOYCE-- THIS NEW, CALM THING WORKS FOR YOU, BUT I'M MAD!
HANK, PLEASE...
LOOK AT THE MESS SHE'S MADE!
TAKE FRESHMAN YEAR OVER AGAIN AT A NEW SCHOOL? I HEARD.
IT'S JUST FOR THE REST OF THIS YEAR, DAD. I CAN--
WHAT ABOUT BETWEEN NOW AND THEN, BUFFY?
IF YOU HAVEN'T NOTICED, I WORK FOR A LIVING--
AND YOUR MOTHER HAS HER-- WHATEVER SHE HAS-- WE CAN'T WATCH YOU ALL DAY LONG!
"WHO'S GOING TO KEEP AN EYE ON YOU NOW?"
A SPECIAL MEETING OF THE WATCHER'S COUNCIL HAS BEEN CALLED TO ORDER.
OUTSIDE OF LONDON...

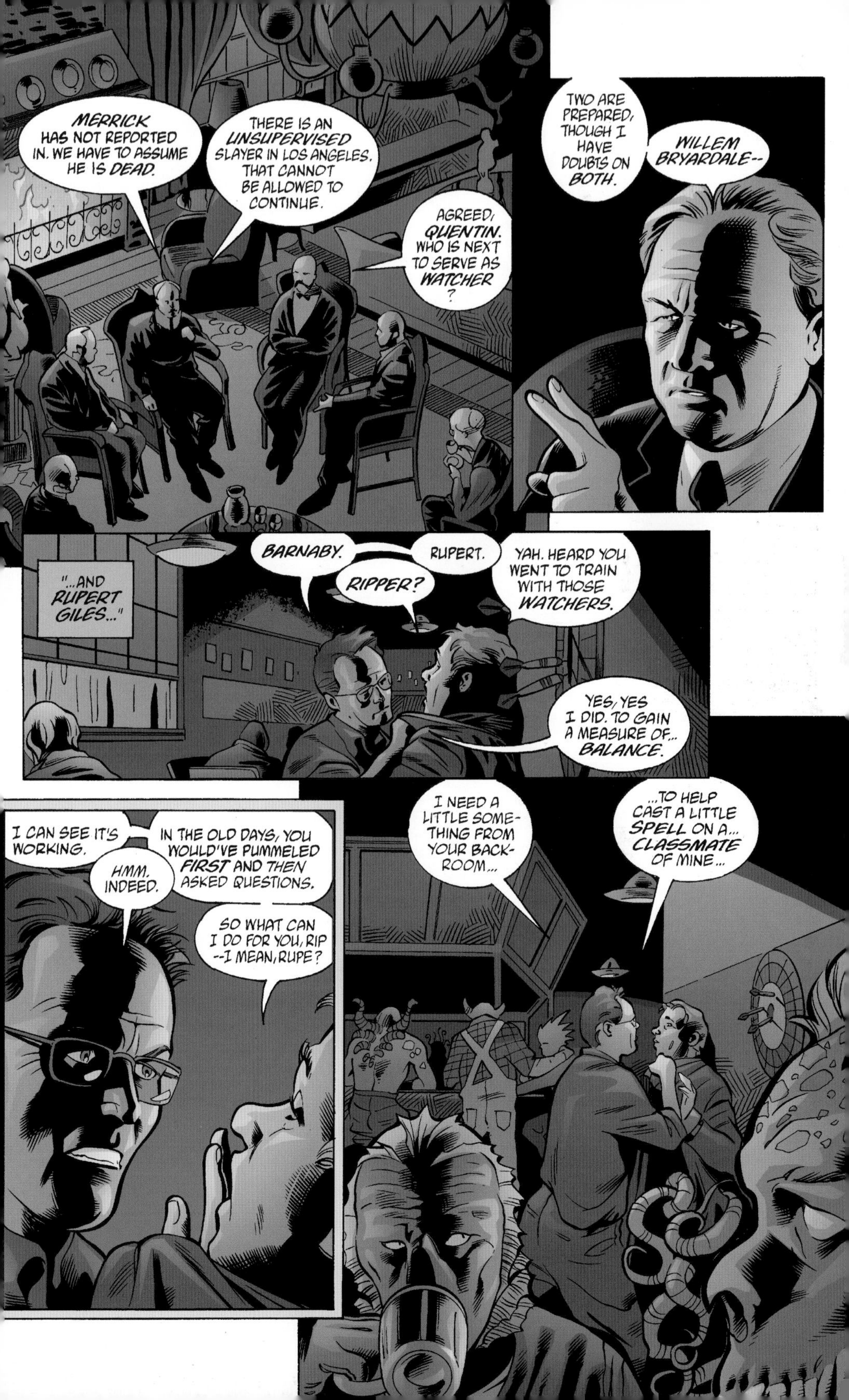
MERRICK HAS NOT REPORTED IN. WE HAVE TO ASSUME HE IS DEAD.
THERE IS AN UNSUPERVISED SLAYER IN LOS ANGELES. THAT CANNOT BE ALLOWED TO CONTINUE.
AGREED, QUENTIN. WHO IS NEXT TO SERVE AS WATCHER?
TWO ARE PREPARED, THOUGH I HAVE DOUBTS ON BOTH.
WILLEM BRYARDALE--
"...AND RUPERT GILES..."
BARNABY.
RUPERT.
RIPPER?
YAH. HEARD YOU WENT TO TRAIN WITH THOSE WATCHERS.
YES, YES I DID. TO GAIN A MEASURE OF... BALANCE.
I CAN SEE IT'S WORKING.
IN THE OLD DAYS, YOU WOULD'VE PUMMELED FIRST AND THEN ASKED QUESTIONS.
HMM. INDEED.
SO WHAT CAN I DO FOR YOU, RIP --I MEAN, RUPE?
I NEED A LITTLE SOME-THING FROM YOUR BACK-ROOM...
...TO HELP CAST A LITTLE SPELL ON A... CLASSMATE OF MINE...

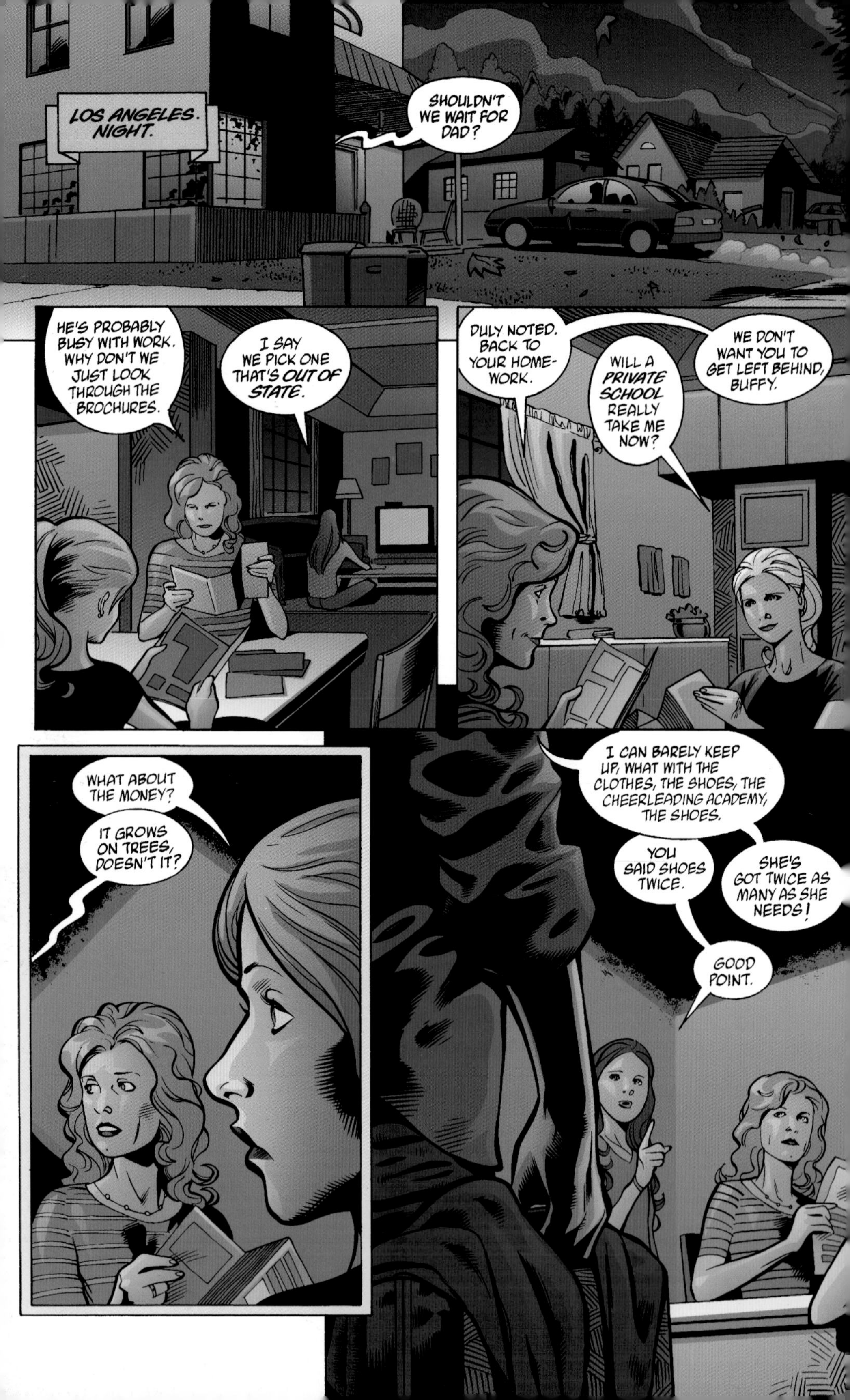
LOS ANGELES. NIGHT.
SHOULDN'T WE WAIT FOR DAD?
HE'S PROBABLY BUSY WITH WORK. WHY DON'T WE JUST LOOK THROUGH THE BROCHURES.
I SAY WE PICK ONE THAT'S OUT OF STATE.
DULY NOTED. BACK TO YOUR HOME-WORK.
WE DON'T WANT YOU TO GET LEFT BEHIND, BUFFY.
WILL A PRIVATE SCHOOL REALLY TAKE ME NOW?
WHAT ABOUT THE MONEY?
IT GROWS ON TREES, DOESN'T IT?
I CAN BARELY KEEP UP, WHAT WITH THE CLOTHES, THE SHOES, THE CHEERLEADING ACADEMY, THE SHOES.
YOU SAID SHOES TWICE.
SHE'S GOT TWICE AS MANY AS SHE NEEDS!
GOOD POINT.

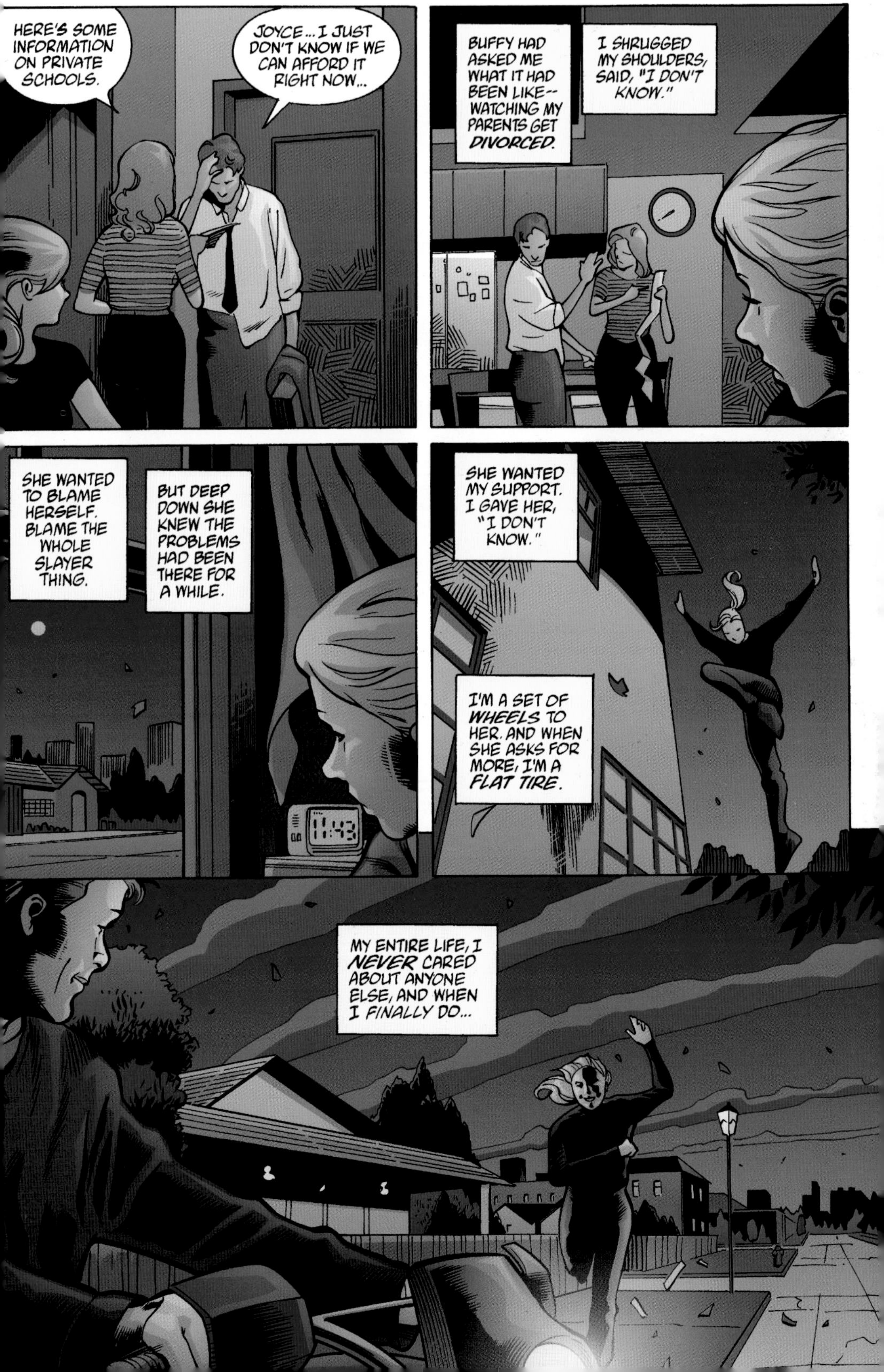
HERE'S SOME INFORMATION ON PRIVATE SCHOOLS.
JOYCE... I JUST DON'T KNOW IF WE CAN AFFORD IT RIGHT NOW...
BUFFY HAD ASKED ME WHAT IT HAD BEEN LIKE-- WATCHING MY PARENTS GET DIVORCED.
I SHRUGGED MY SHOULDERS, SAID, "I DON'T KNOW."
SHE WANTED TO BLAME HERSELF. BLAME THE WHOLE SLAYER THING.
BUT DEEP DOWN SHE KNEW THE PROBLEMS HAD BEEN THERE FOR A WHILE.
SHE WANTED MY SUPPORT. I GAVE HER, "I DON'T KNOW."
I'M A SET OF WHEELS TO HER. AND WHEN SHE ASKS FOR MORE, I'M A FLAT TIRE.
MY ENTIRE LIFE, I NEVER CARED ABOUT ANYONE ELSE, AND WHEN I FINALLY DO...

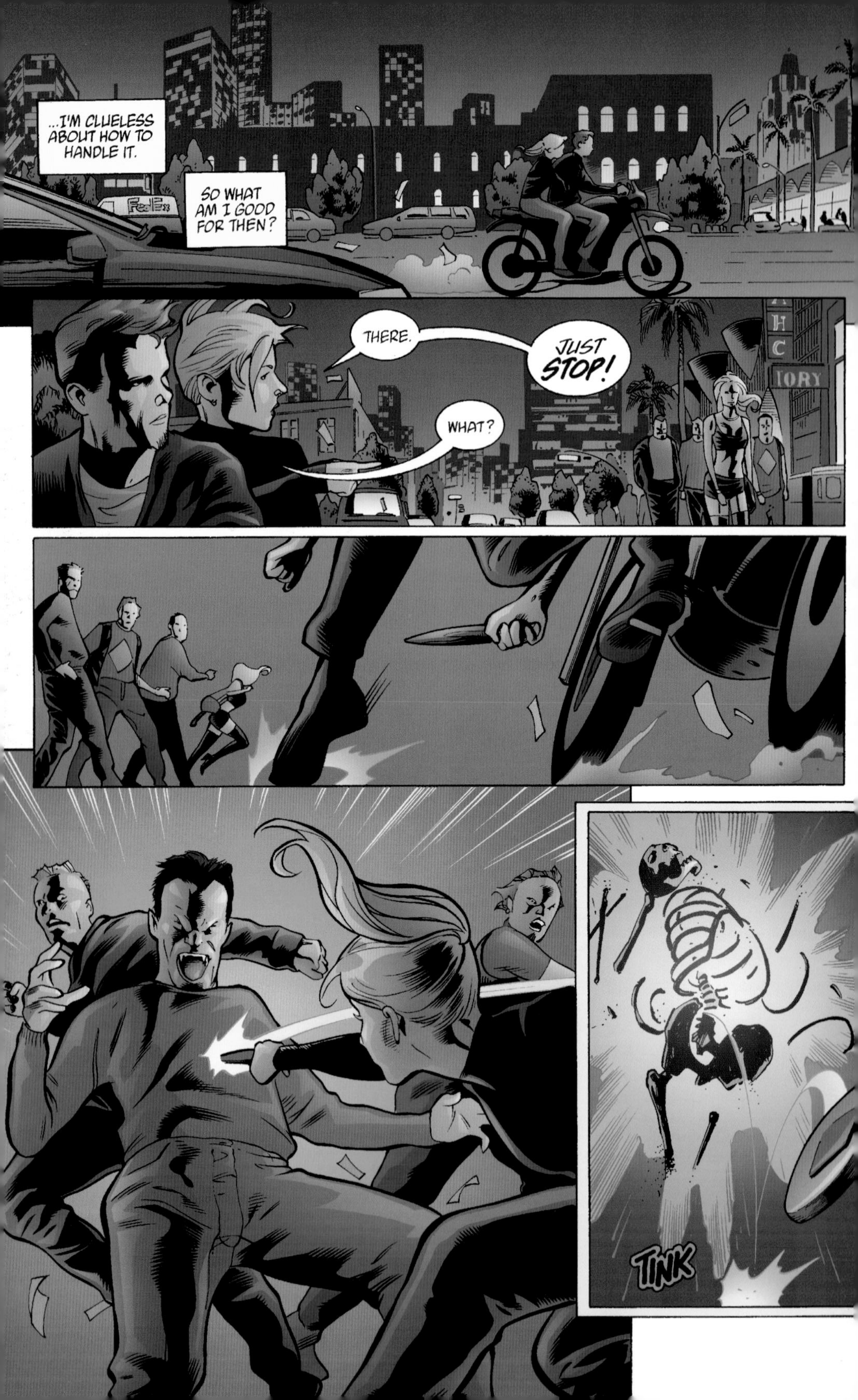

...I'M CLUELESS ABOUT HOW TO HANDLE IT.
SO WHAT AM I GOOD FOR THEN?
FedEx
THERE.
JUST STOP!
WHAT?
TINK

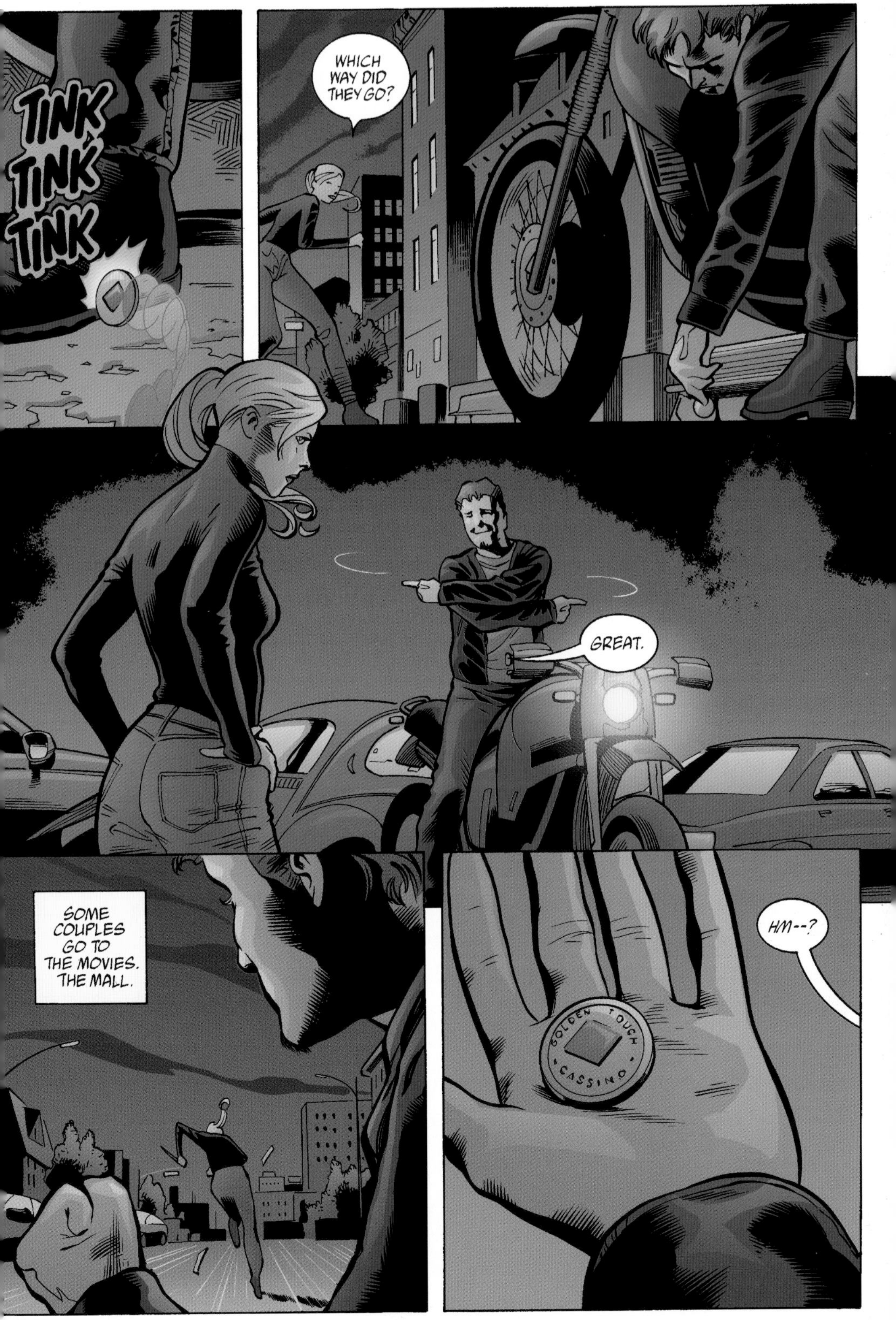
TINK TINK TINK
WHICH WAY DID THEY GO?
GREAT.
SOME COUPLES GO TO THE MOVIES. THE MALL.
HM--?
GOLDEN TOUCH CASSINO

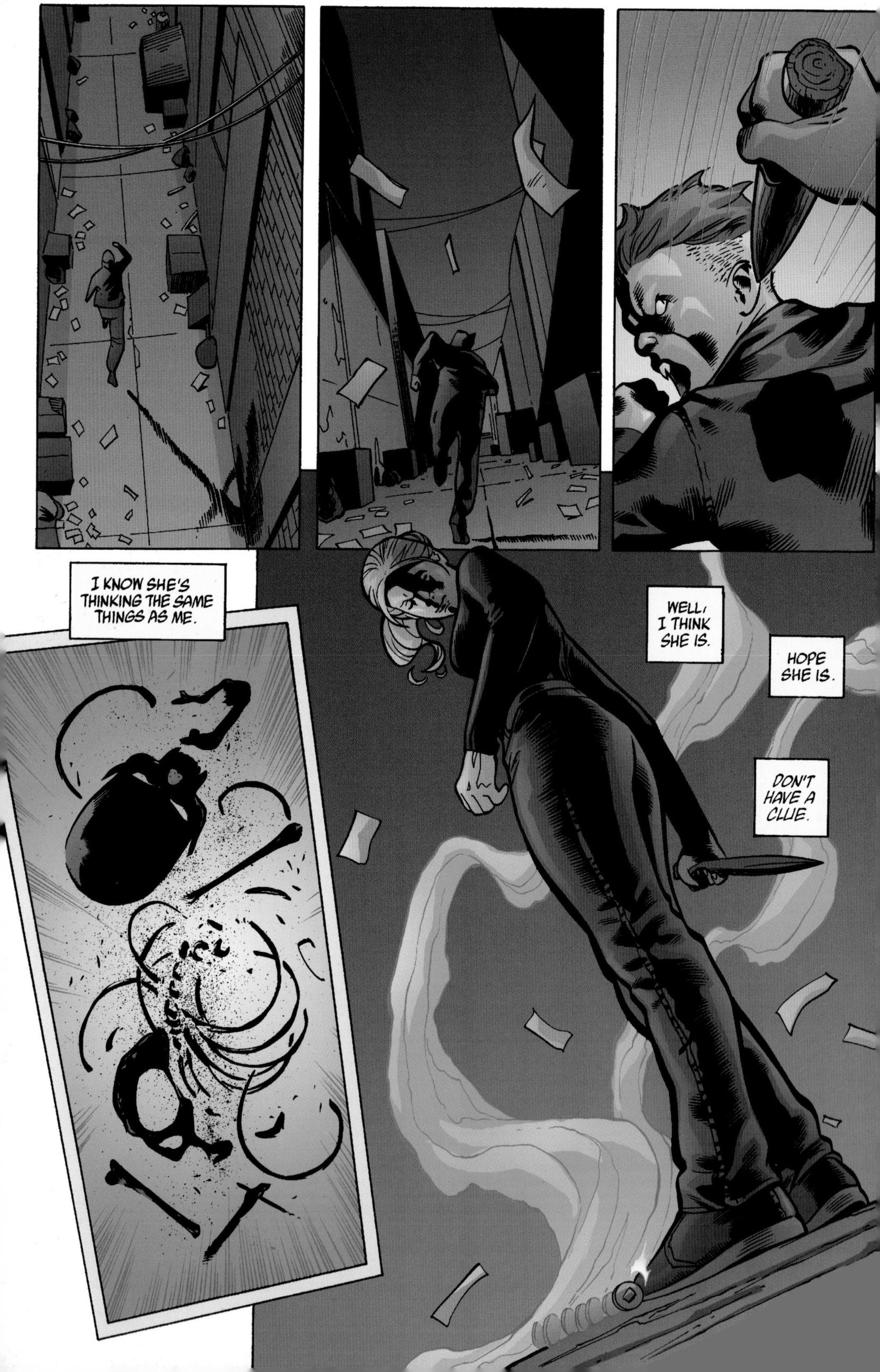

I KNOW SHE'S THINKING THE SAME THINGS AS ME.
WELL, I THINK SHE IS.
HOPE SHE IS.
DON'T HAVE A CLUE.

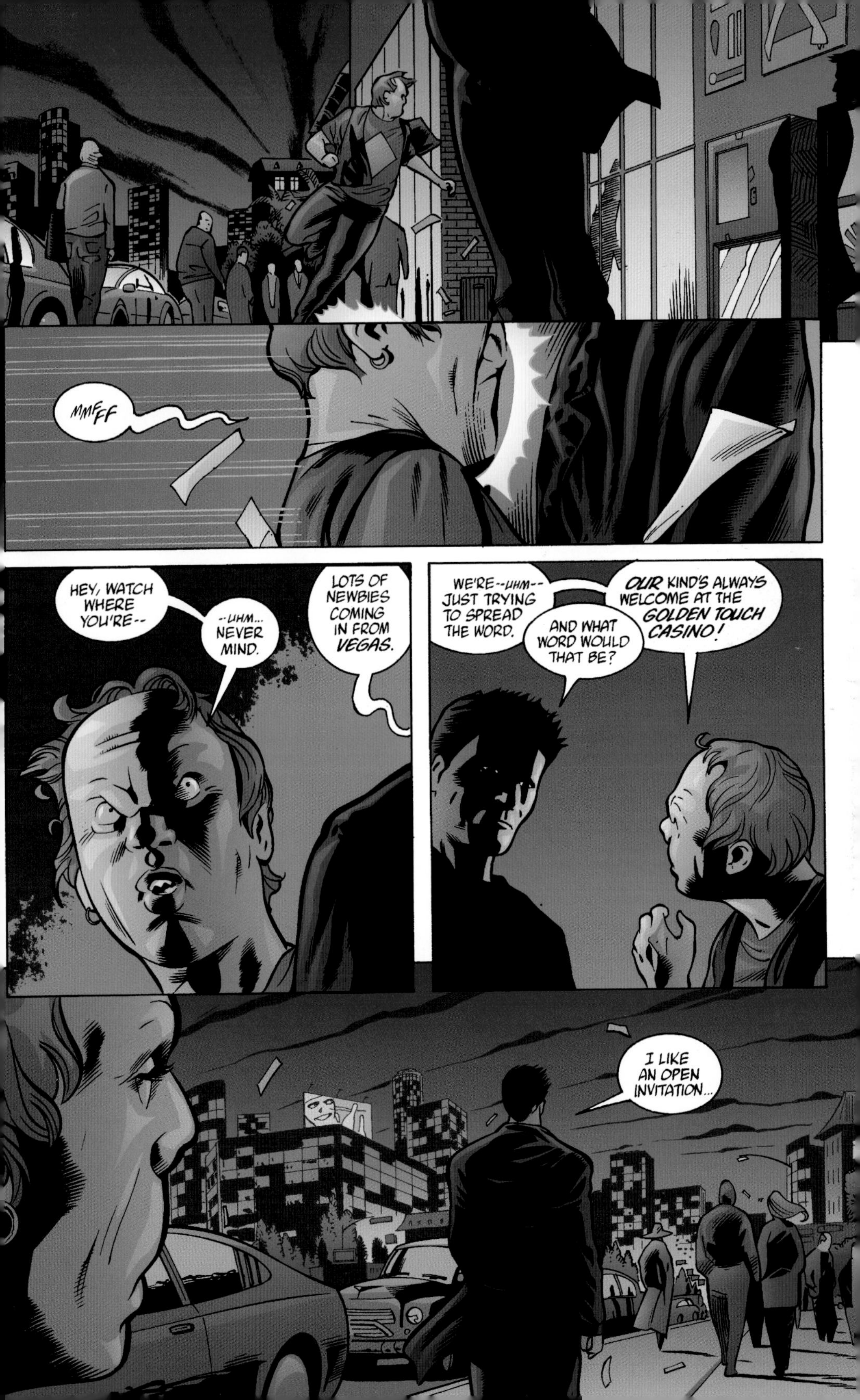
MMFFF
HEY, WATCH WHERE YOU'RE--
--UHM... NEVER MIND.
LOTS OF NEWBIES COMING IN FROM VEGAS.
WE'RE--UHM--JUST TRYING TO SPREAD THE WORD.
OUR KIND'S ALWAYS WELCOME AT THE GOLDEN TOUCH CASINO!
AND WHAT WORD WOULD THAT BE?
I LIKE AN OPEN INVITATION...

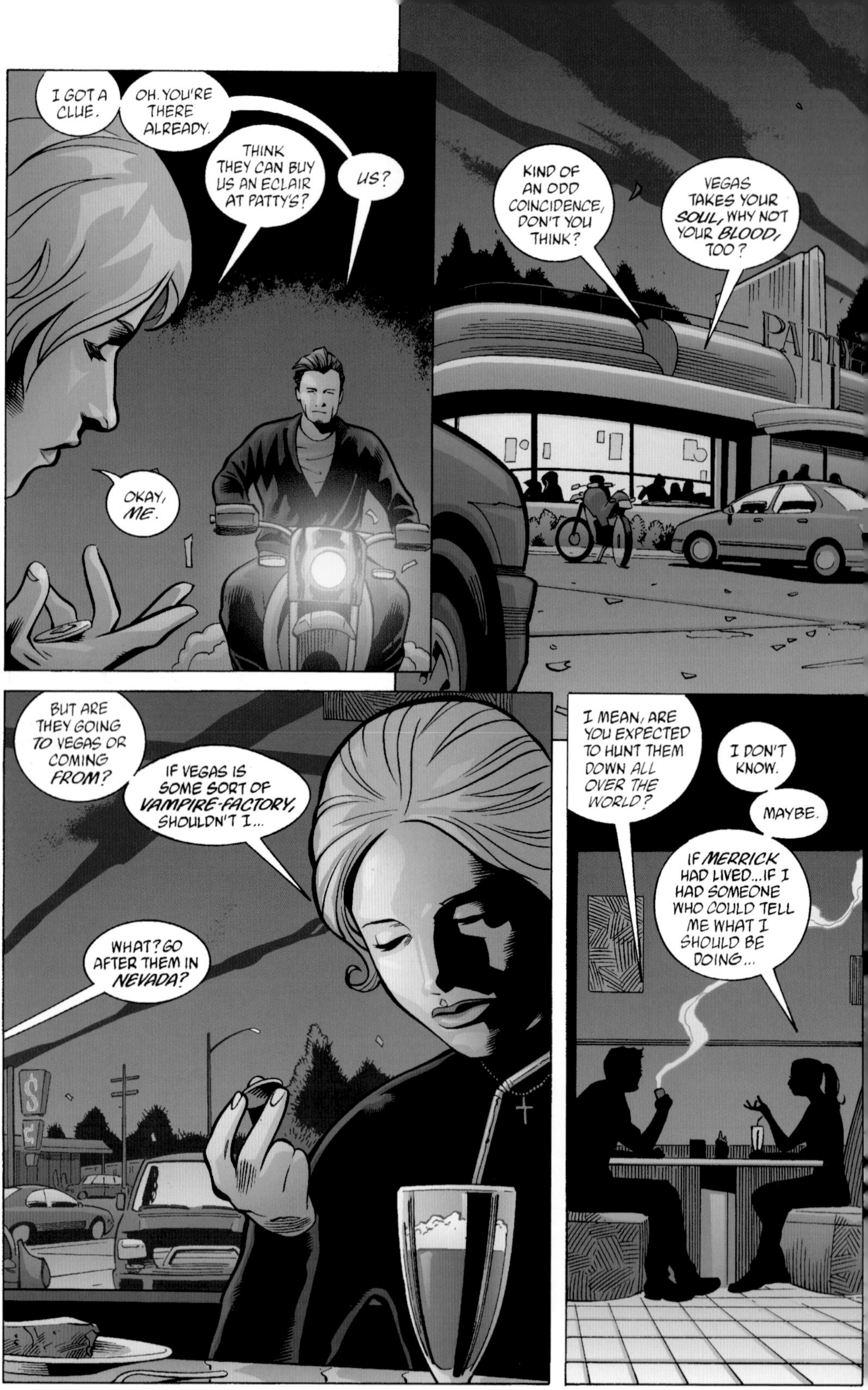
I GOT A CLUE.
OH. YOU'RE THERE ALREADY.
THINK THEY CAN BUY US AN ECLAIR AT PATTY'S?
US?
OKAY, ME.
KIND OF AN ODD COINCIDENCE, DON'T YOU THINK?
VEGAS TAKES YOUR SOUL, WHY NOT YOUR BLOOD, TOO?
PATTY
BUT ARE THEY GOING TO VEGAS OR COMING FROM?
IF VEGAS IS SOME SORT OF VAMPIRE-FACTORY, SHOULDN'T I...
WHAT? GO AFTER THEM IN NEVADA?
I MEAN, ARE YOU EXPECTED TO HUNT THEM DOWN ALL OVER THE WORLD?
I DON'T KNOW.
MAYBE.
IF MERRICK HAD LIVED...IF I HAD SOMEONE WHO COULD TELL ME WHAT I SHOULD BE DOING...

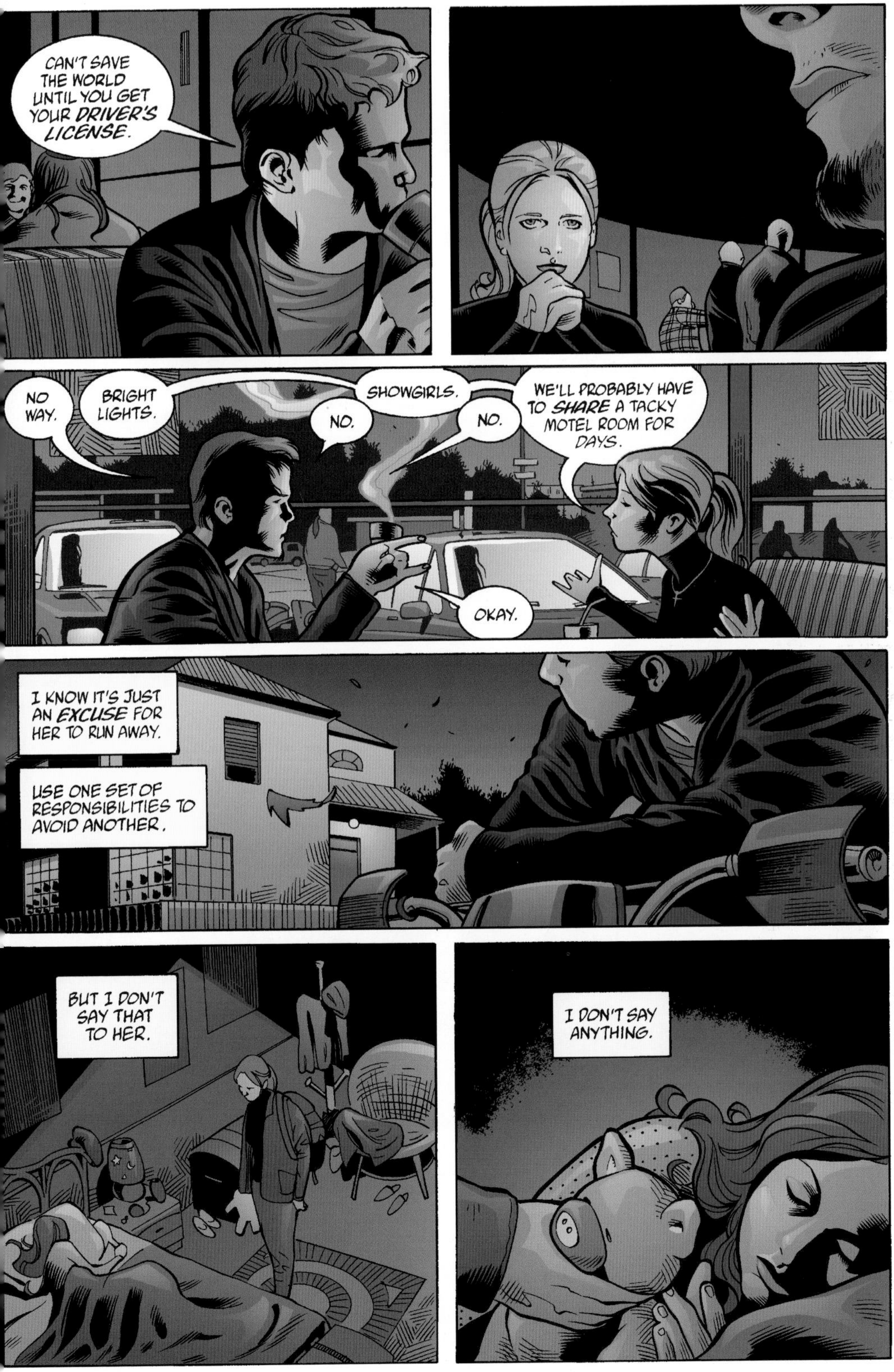
CAN'T SAVE THE WORLD UNTIL YOU GET YOUR DRIVER'S LICENSE.
NO WAY.
BRIGHT LIGHTS.
NO.
SHOWGIRLS.
NO.
WE'LL PROBABLY HAVE TO SHARE A TACKY MOTEL ROOM FOR DAYS.
OKAY.
I KNOW IT'S JUST AN EXCUSE FOR HER TO RUN AWAY.
USE ONE SET OF RESPONSIBILITIES TO AVOID ANOTHER.
BUT I DON'T SAY THAT TO HER.
I DON'T SAY ANYTHING.

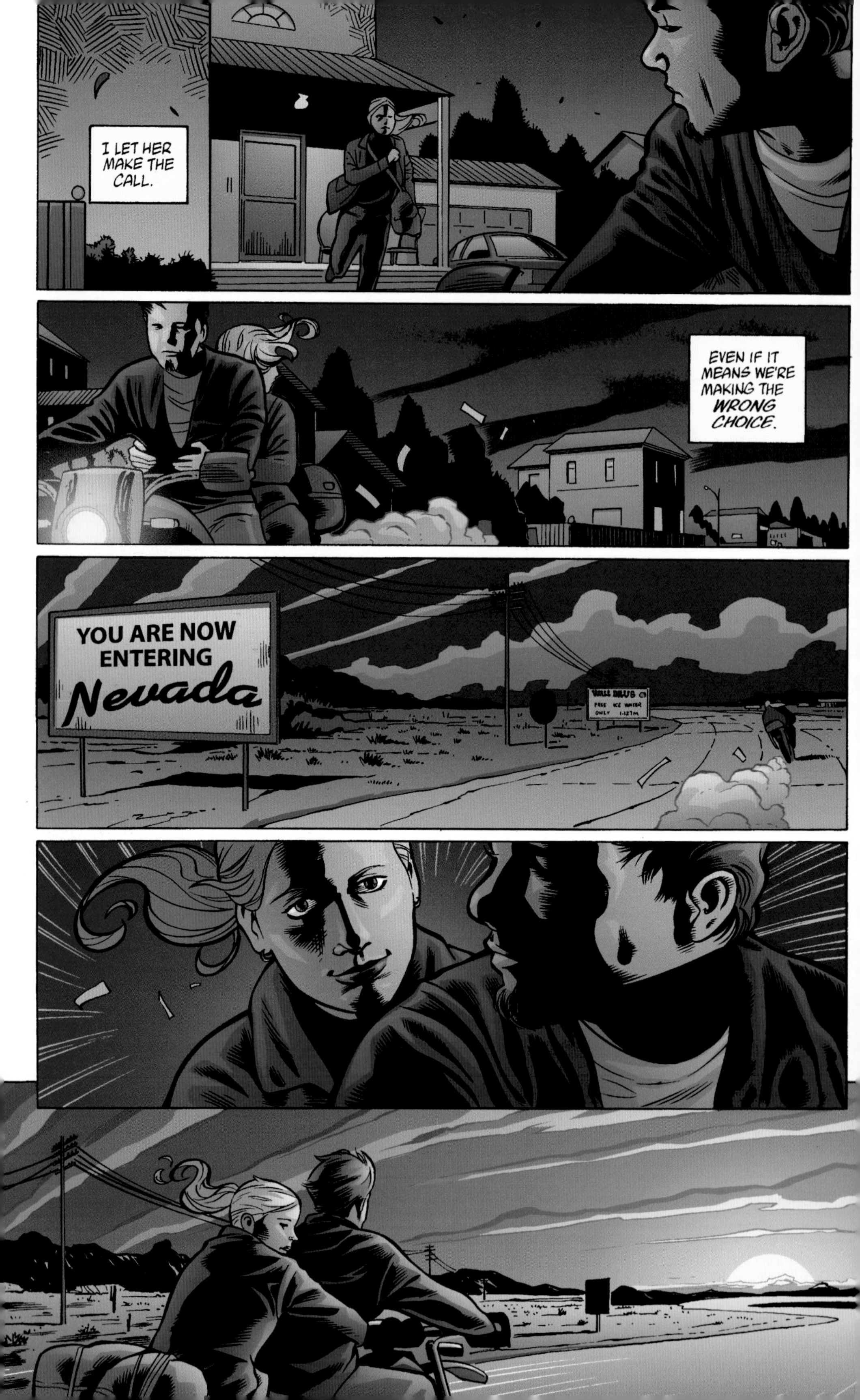
I LET HER MAKE THE CALL.
EVEN IF IT MEANS WE'RE MAKING THE *WRONG CHOICE*.
YOU ARE NOW ENTERING Nevada

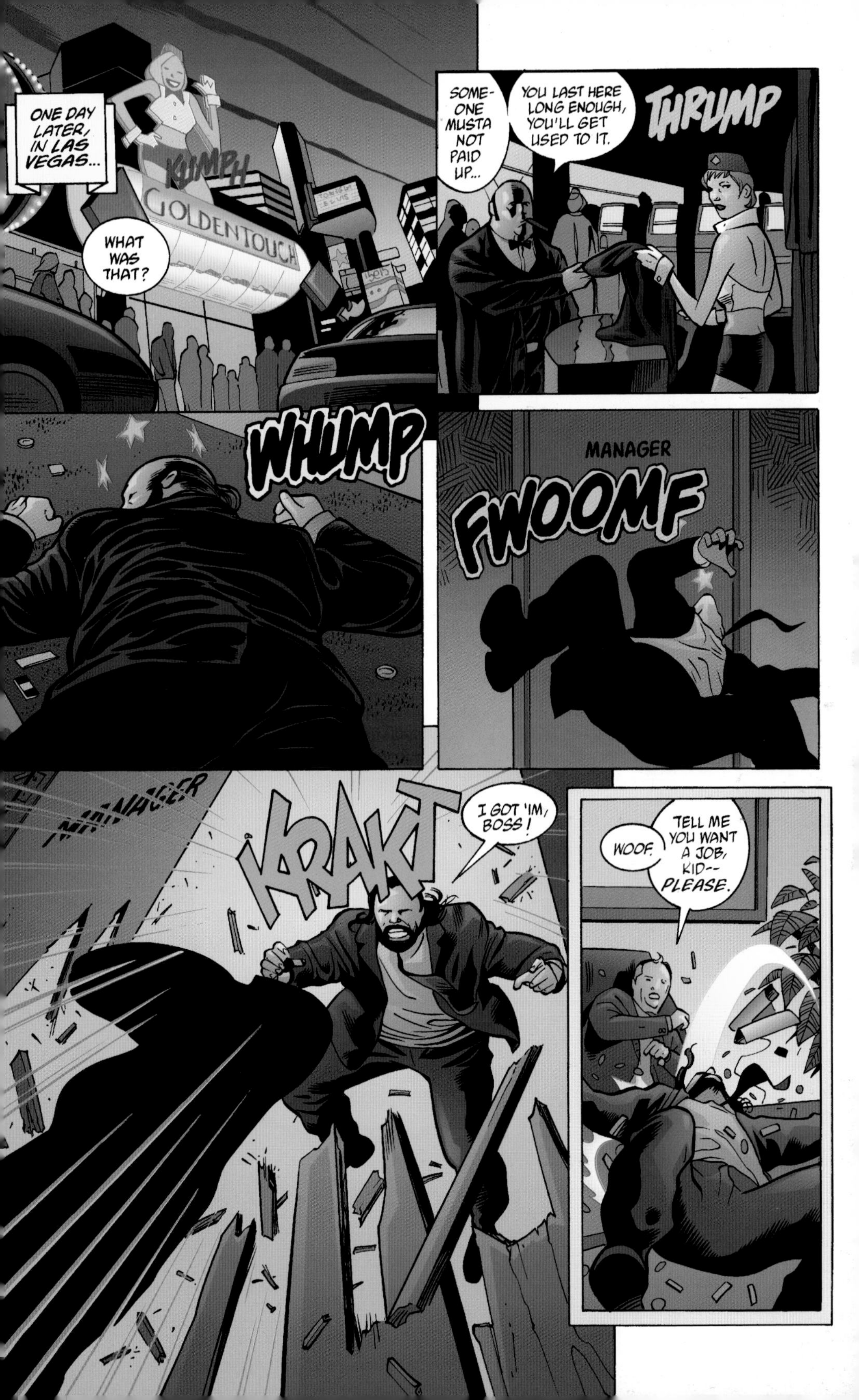
ONE DAY LATER, IN LAS VEGAS...
KLUMPH
GOLDENTOUCH
WHAT WAS THAT?
SOME-ONE MUSTA NOT PAID UP...
YOU LAST HERE LONG ENOUGH, YOU'LL GET USED TO IT.
THRUMP
WHUMP
MANAGER
FWOOMF
KRAKT
I GOT 'IM, BOSS!
WOOF.
TELL ME YOU WANT A JOB, KID-- PLEASE.

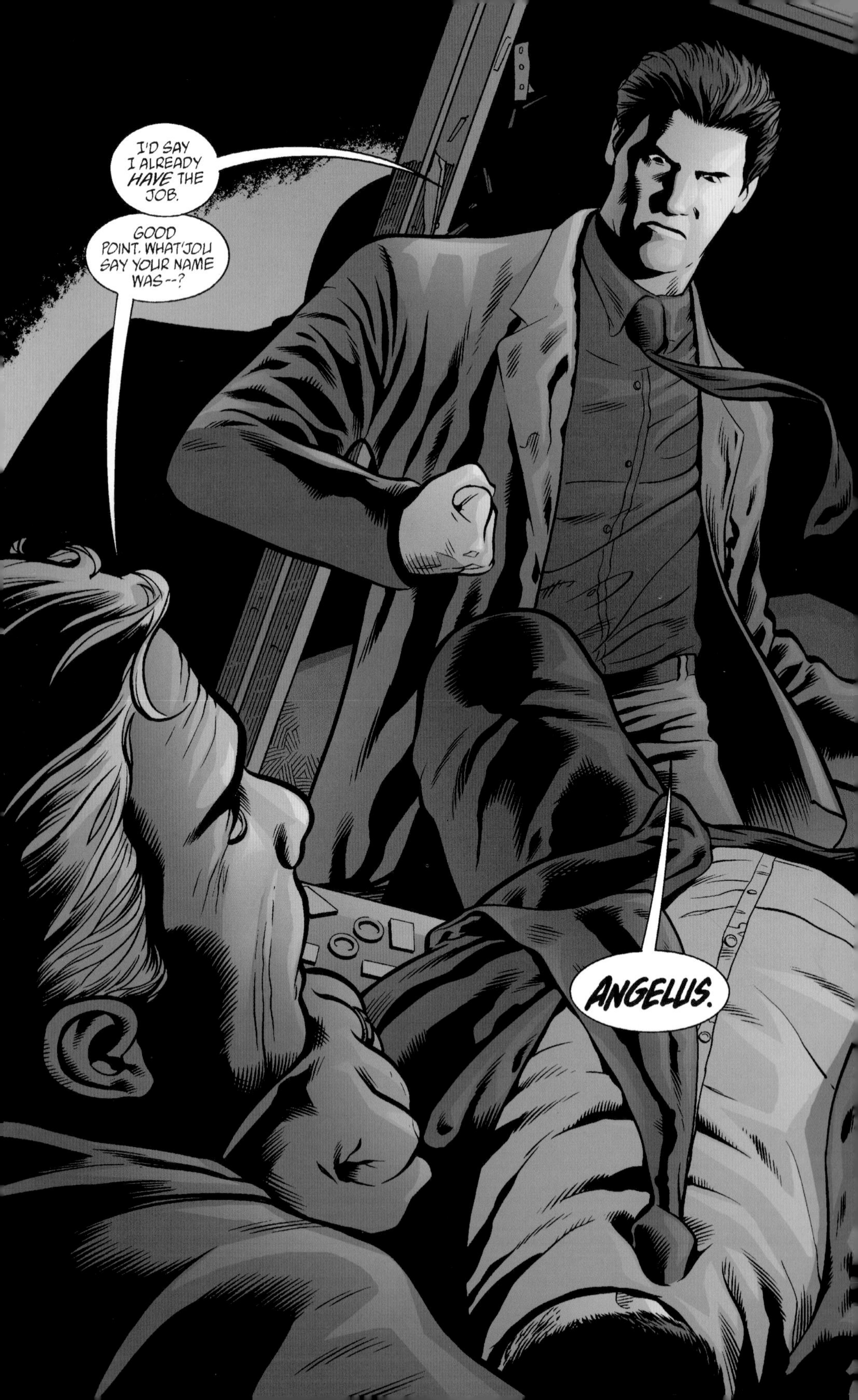
I'D SAY I ALREADY *HAVE* THE JOB.
GOOD POINT. WHAT'JOU SAY YOUR NAME WAS--?
ANGELUS.

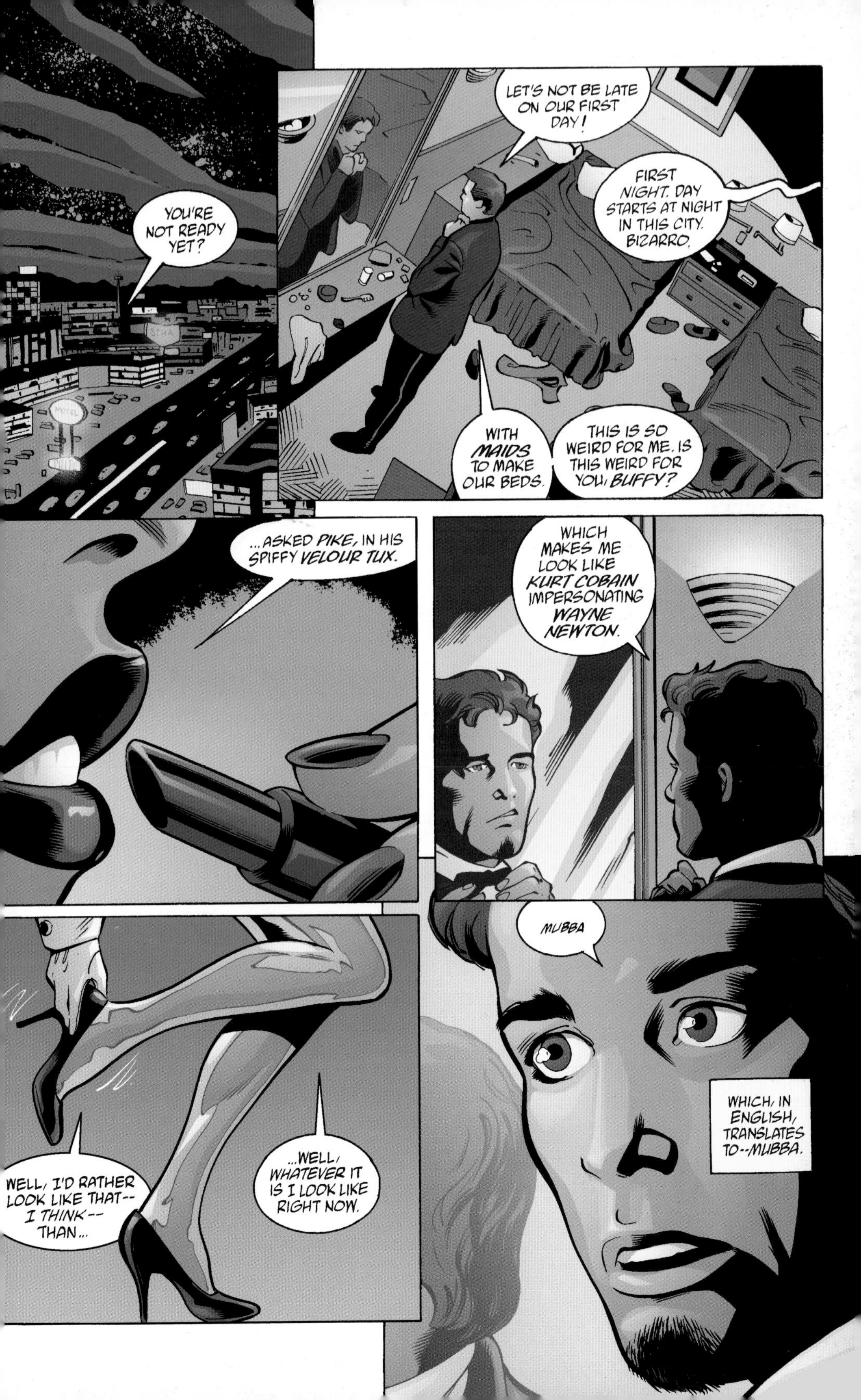
YOU'RE NOT READY YET?
LET'S NOT BE LATE ON OUR FIRST DAY!
FIRST NIGHT. DAY STARTS AT NIGHT IN THIS CITY. BIZARRO.
WITH MAIDS TO MAKE OUR BEDS.
THIS IS SO WEIRD FOR ME. IS THIS WEIRD FOR YOU, BUFFY?
...ASKED PIKE, IN HIS SPIFFY VELOUR TUX.
WHICH MAKES ME LOOK LIKE KURT COBAIN IMPERSONATING WAYNE NEWTON.
WELL, I'D RATHER LOOK LIKE THAT-- I THINK-- THAN...
...WELL, WHATEVER IT IS I LOOK LIKE RIGHT NOW.
MUBBA
WHICH, IN ENGLISH, TRANSLATES TO--MUBBA.

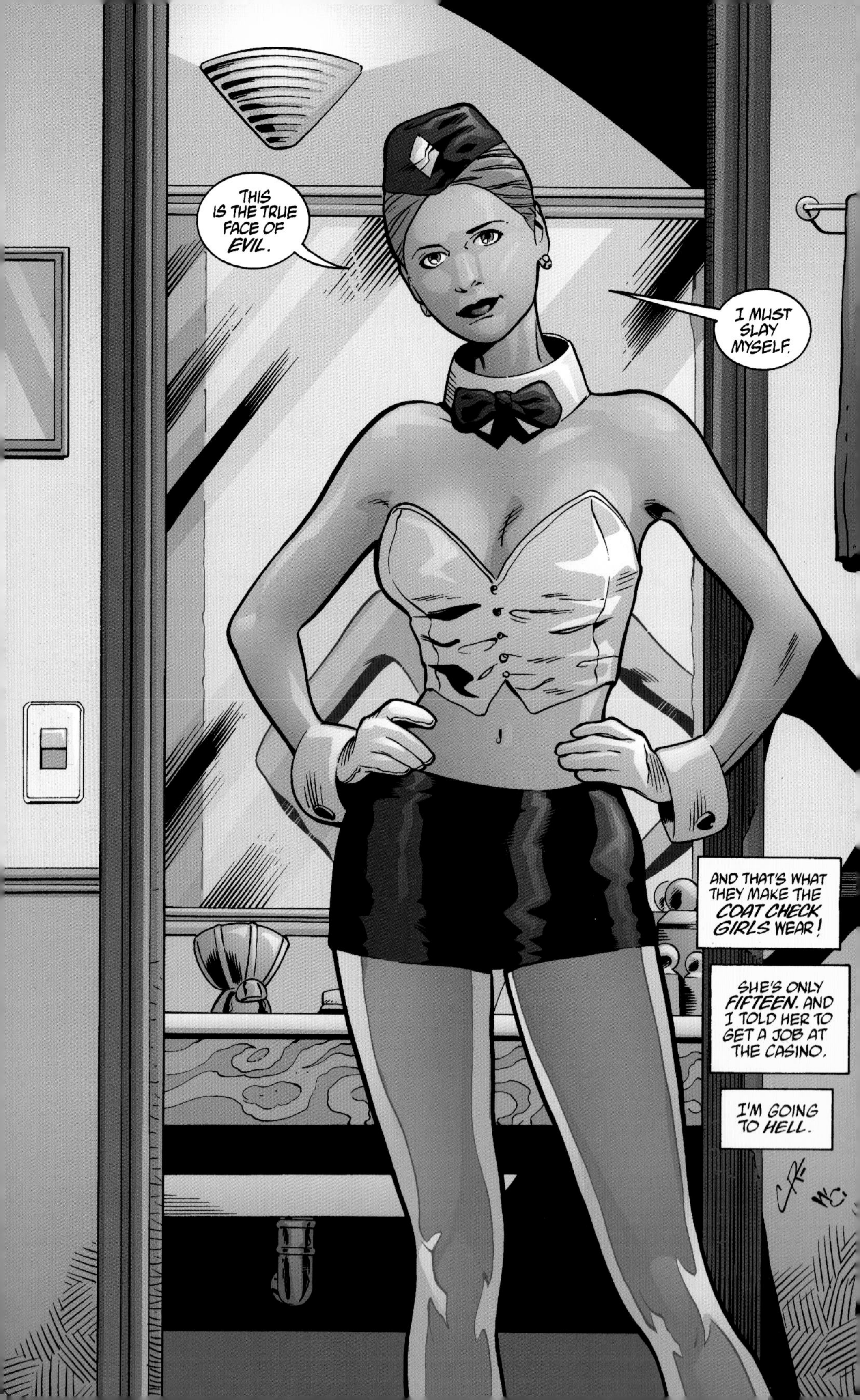
THIS IS THE TRUE FACE OF EVIL.
I MUST SLAY MYSELF.
AND THAT'S WHAT THEY MAKE THE COAT CHECK GIRLS WEAR!
SHE'S ONLY FIFTEEN. AND I TOLD HER TO GET A JOB AT THE CASINO.
I'M GOING TO HELL.

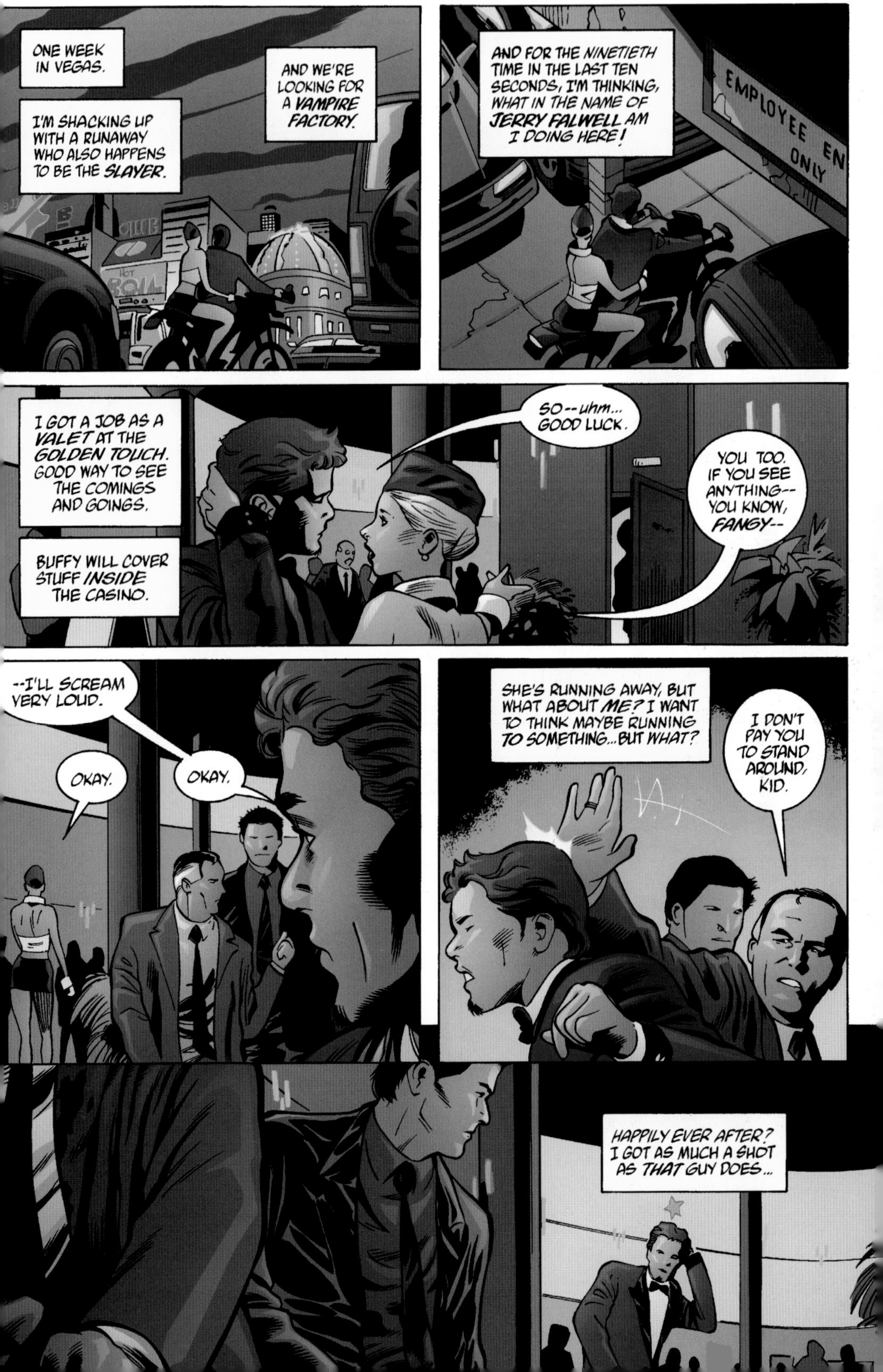
ONE WEEK IN VEGAS.
I'M SHACKING UP WITH A RUNAWAY WHO ALSO HAPPENS TO BE THE SLAYER.
AND WE'RE LOOKING FOR A VAMPIRE FACTORY.
AND FOR THE NINETIETH TIME IN THE LAST TEN SECONDS, I'M THINKING, WHAT IN THE NAME OF JERRY FALWELL AM I DOING HERE!
EMPLOYEE EN ONLY
I GOT A JOB AS A VALET AT THE GOLDEN TOUCH. GOOD WAY TO SEE THE COMINGS AND GOINGS.
BUFFY WILL COVER STUFF INSIDE THE CASINO.
SO--uhm... GOOD LUCK.
YOU TOO. IF YOU SEE ANYTHING--YOU KNOW, FANGY--
--I'LL SCREAM VERY LOUD.
OKAY.
OKAY.
SHE'S RUNNING AWAY, BUT WHAT ABOUT ME? I WANT TO THINK MAYBE RUNNING TO SOMETHING... BUT WHAT?
I DON'T PAY YOU TO STAND AROUND, KID.
HAPPILY EVER AFTER? I GOT AS MUCH A SHOT AS THAT GUY DOES...

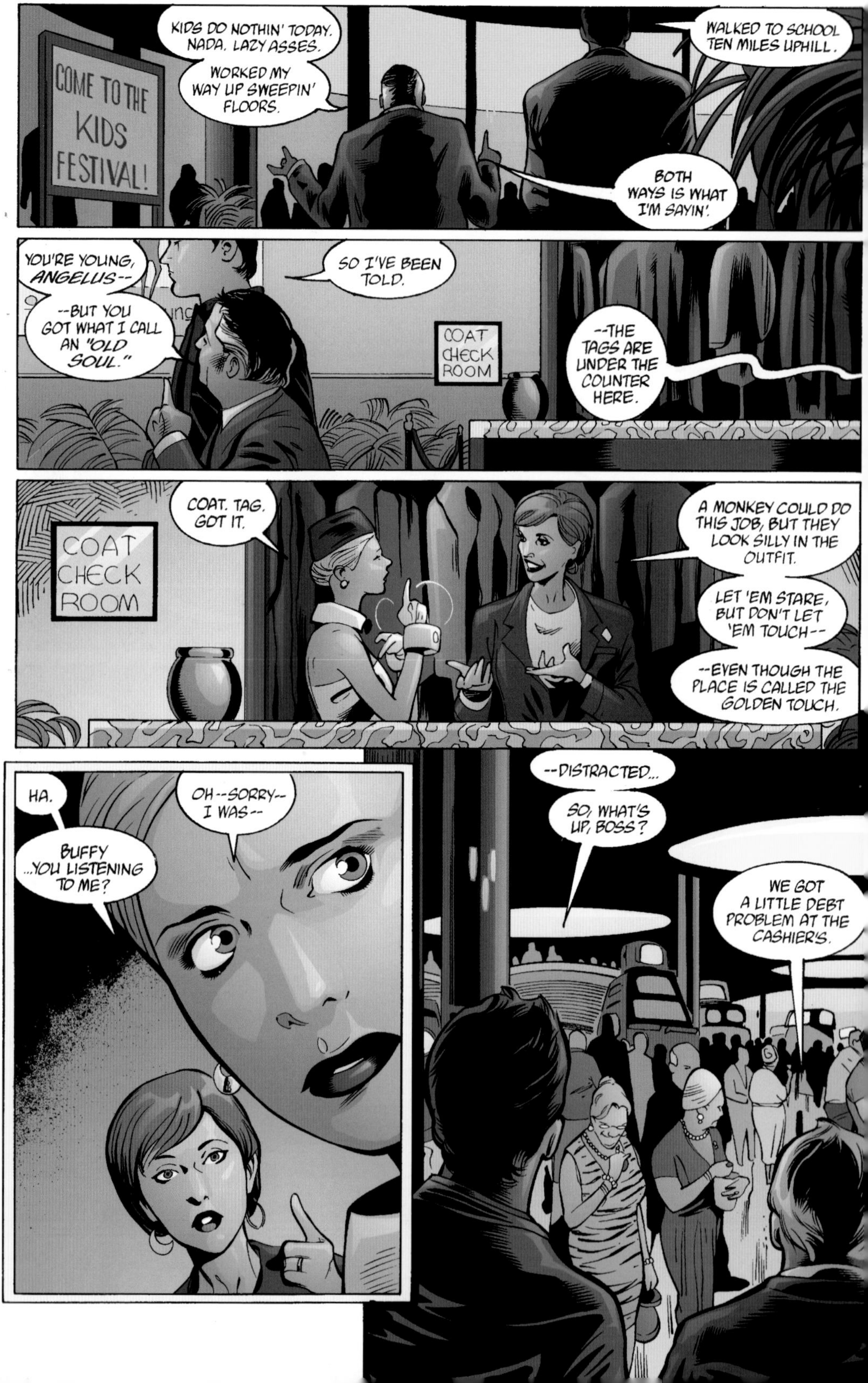
COME TO THE KIDS FESTIVAL!
KIDS DO NOTHIN' TODAY. NADA. LAZY ASSES.
WORKED MY WAY UP SWEEPIN' FLOORS.
WALKED TO SCHOOL TEN MILES UPHILL.
BOTH WAYS IS WHAT I'M SAYIN'.
YOU'RE YOUNG, ANGELUS--
--BUT YOU GOT WHAT I CALL AN "OLD SOUL."
SO I'VE BEEN TOLD.
COAT CHECK ROOM
--THE TAGS ARE UNDER THE COUNTER HERE.
COAT CHECK ROOM
COAT. TAG. GOT IT.
A MONKEY COULD DO THIS JOB, BUT THEY LOOK SILLY IN THE OUTFIT.
LET 'EM STARE, BUT DON'T LET 'EM TOUCH--
--EVEN THOUGH THE PLACE IS CALLED THE GOLDEN TOUCH.
HA.
BUFFY ...YOU LISTENING TO ME?
OH--SORRY-- I WAS--
--DISTRACTED...
SO, WHAT'S UP, BOSS?
WE GOT A LITTLE DEBT PROBLEM AT THE CASHIER'S.

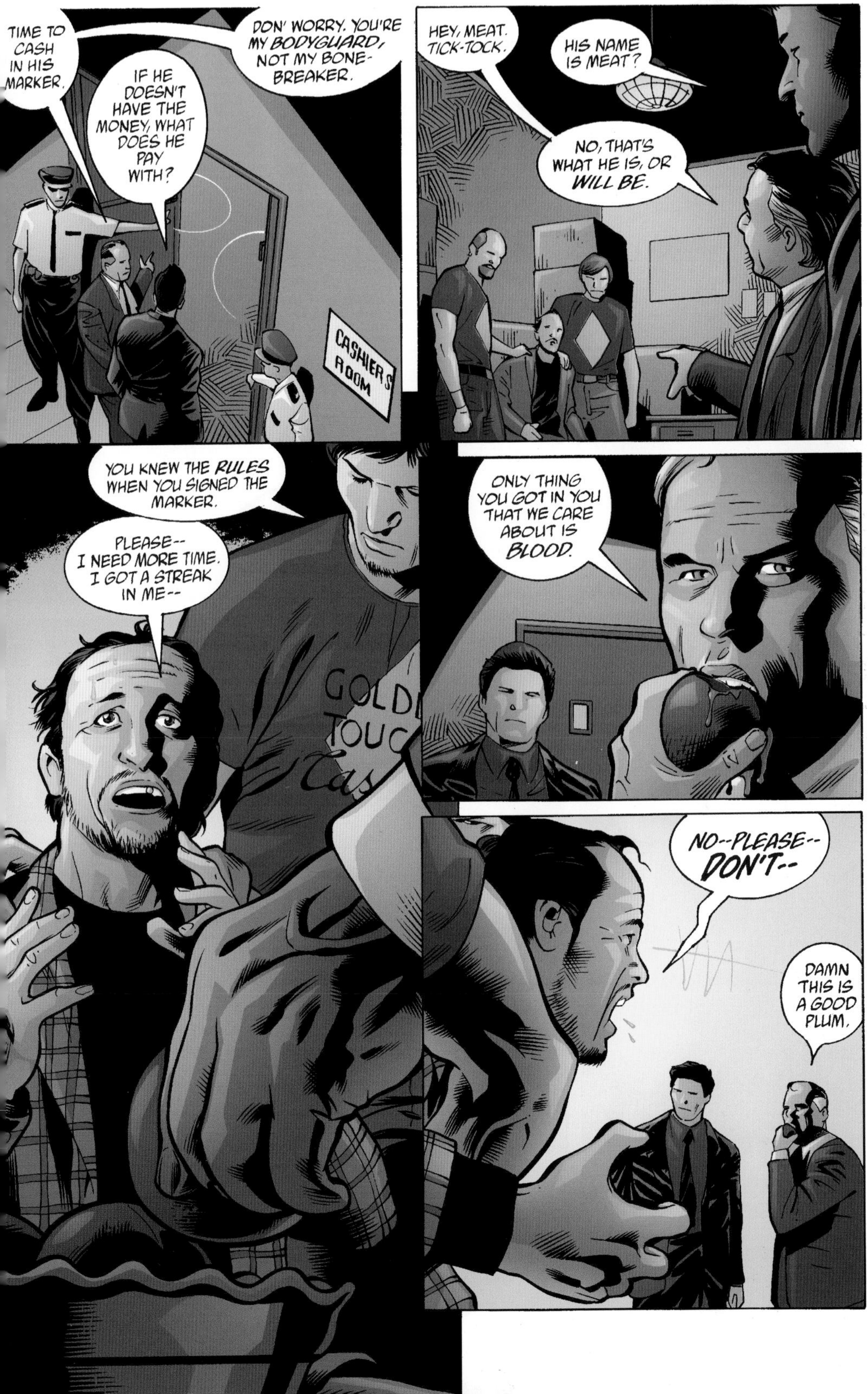
TIME TO CASH IN HIS MARKER.
IF HE DOESN'T HAVE THE MONEY, WHAT DOES HE PAY WITH?
DON' WORRY. YOU'RE MY BODYGUARD, NOT MY BONE-BREAKER.
CASHIER'S ROOM
HEY, MEAT. TICK-TOCK.
HIS NAME IS MEAT?
NO, THAT'S WHAT HE IS, OR WILL BE.
YOU KNEW THE RULES WHEN YOU SIGNED THE MARKER.
PLEASE-- I NEED MORE TIME. I GOT A STREAK IN ME--
ONLY THING YOU GOT IN YOU THAT WE CARE ABOUT IS BLOOD.
NO--PLEASE--DON'T--
DAMN THIS IS A GOOD PLUM.

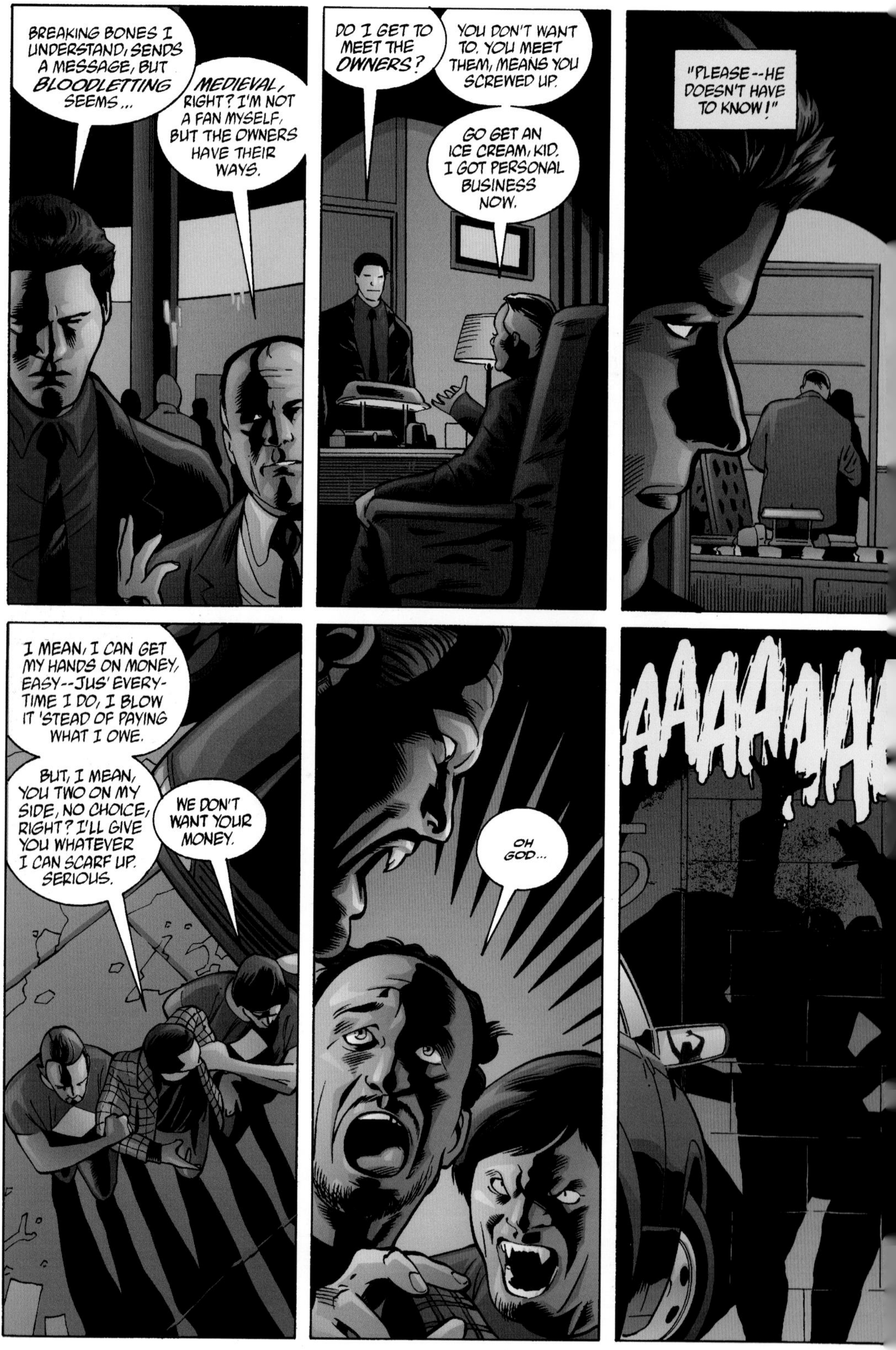
BREAKING BONES I UNDERSTAND, SENDS A MESSAGE, BUT BLOODLETTING SEEMS...
MEDIEVAL, RIGHT? I'M NOT A FAN MYSELF, BUT THE OWNERS HAVE THEIR WAYS.
DO I GET TO MEET THE OWNERS?
YOU DON'T WANT TO. YOU MEET THEM, MEANS YOU SCREWED UP.
GO GET AN ICE CREAM, KID. I GOT PERSONAL BUSINESS NOW.
"PLEASE--HE DOESN'T HAVE TO KNOW!"
I MEAN, I CAN GET MY HANDS ON MONEY, EASY--JUS' EVERY-TIME I DO, I BLOW IT 'STEAD OF PAYING WHAT I OWE.
BUT, I MEAN, YOU TWO ON MY SIDE, NO CHOICE, RIGHT? I'LL GIVE YOU WHATEVER I CAN SCARF UP. SERIOUS.
WE DON'T WANT YOUR MONEY.
OH GOD...
AAAAAA

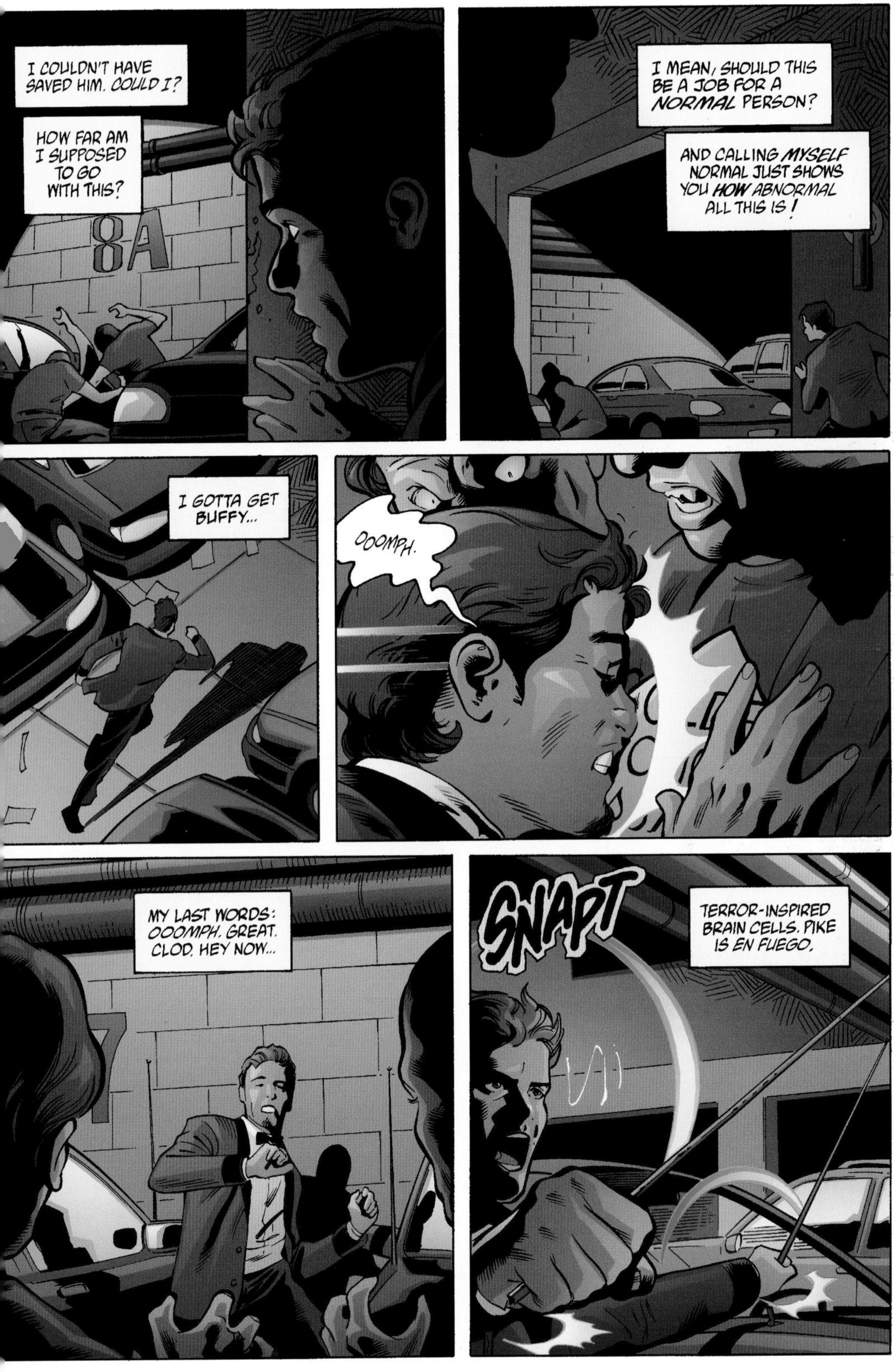
I COULDN'T HAVE SAVED HIM. COULD I?
HOW FAR AM I SUPPOSED TO GO WITH THIS?
8A
I MEAN, SHOULD THIS BE A JOB FOR A NORMAL PERSON?
AND CALLING MYSELF NORMAL JUST SHOWS YOU HOW ABNORMAL ALL THIS IS!
I GOTTA GET BUFFY...
OOOMPH.
MY LAST WORDS: OOOMPH. GREAT. CLOD. HEY NOW...
SNAPT
TERROR-INSPIRED BRAIN CELLS. PIKE IS EN FUEGO.

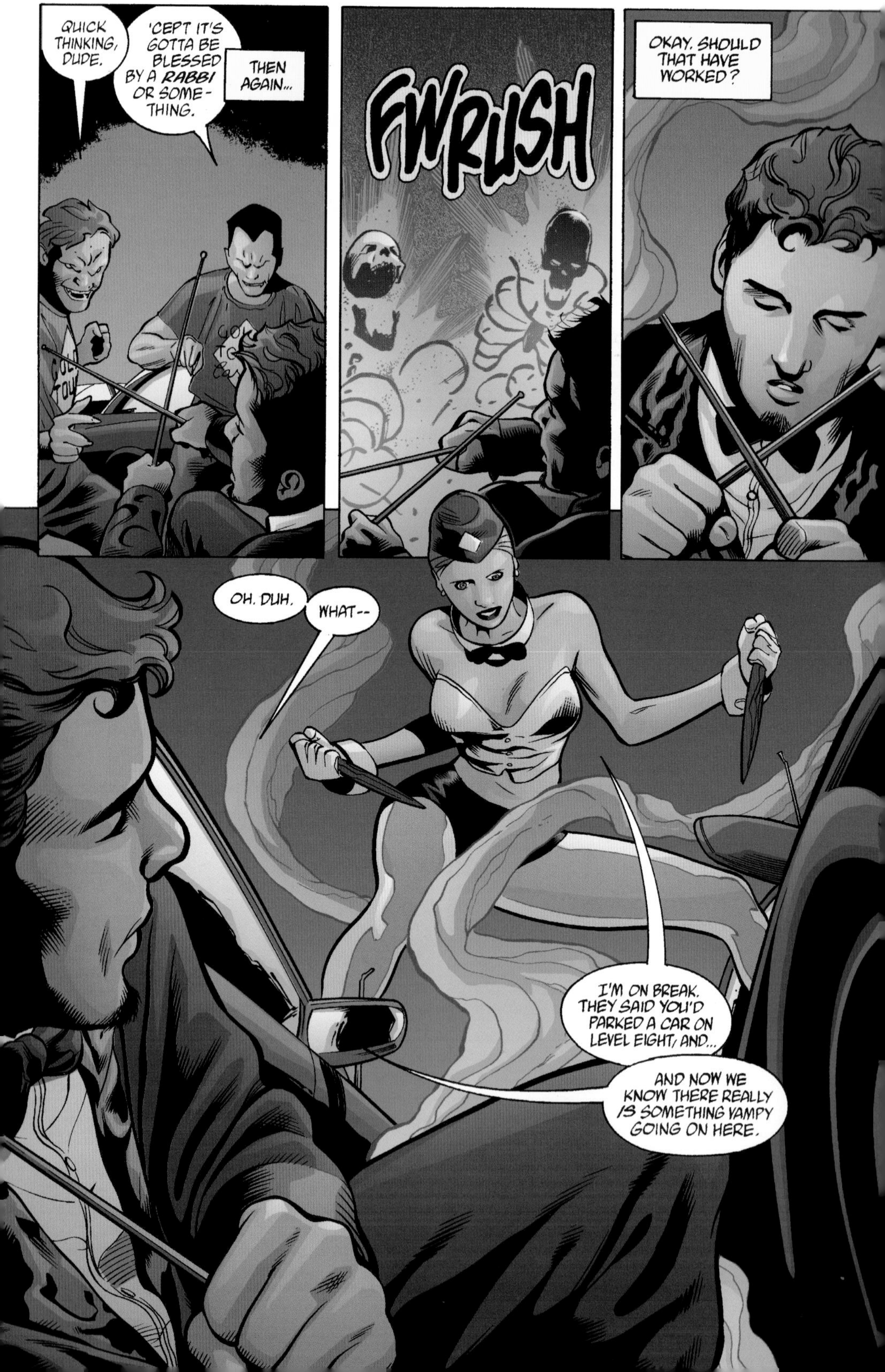
QUICK THINKING, DUDE.
'CEPT IT'S GOTTA BE BLESSED BY A RABBI OR SOMETHING.
THEN AGAIN...
FWRUSH
OKAY. SHOULD THAT HAVE WORKED?
OH. DUH.
WHAT--
I'M ON BREAK. THEY SAID YOU'D PARKED A CAR ON LEVEL EIGHT, AND...
AND NOW WE KNOW THERE REALLY IS SOMETHING VAMPY GOING ON HERE.

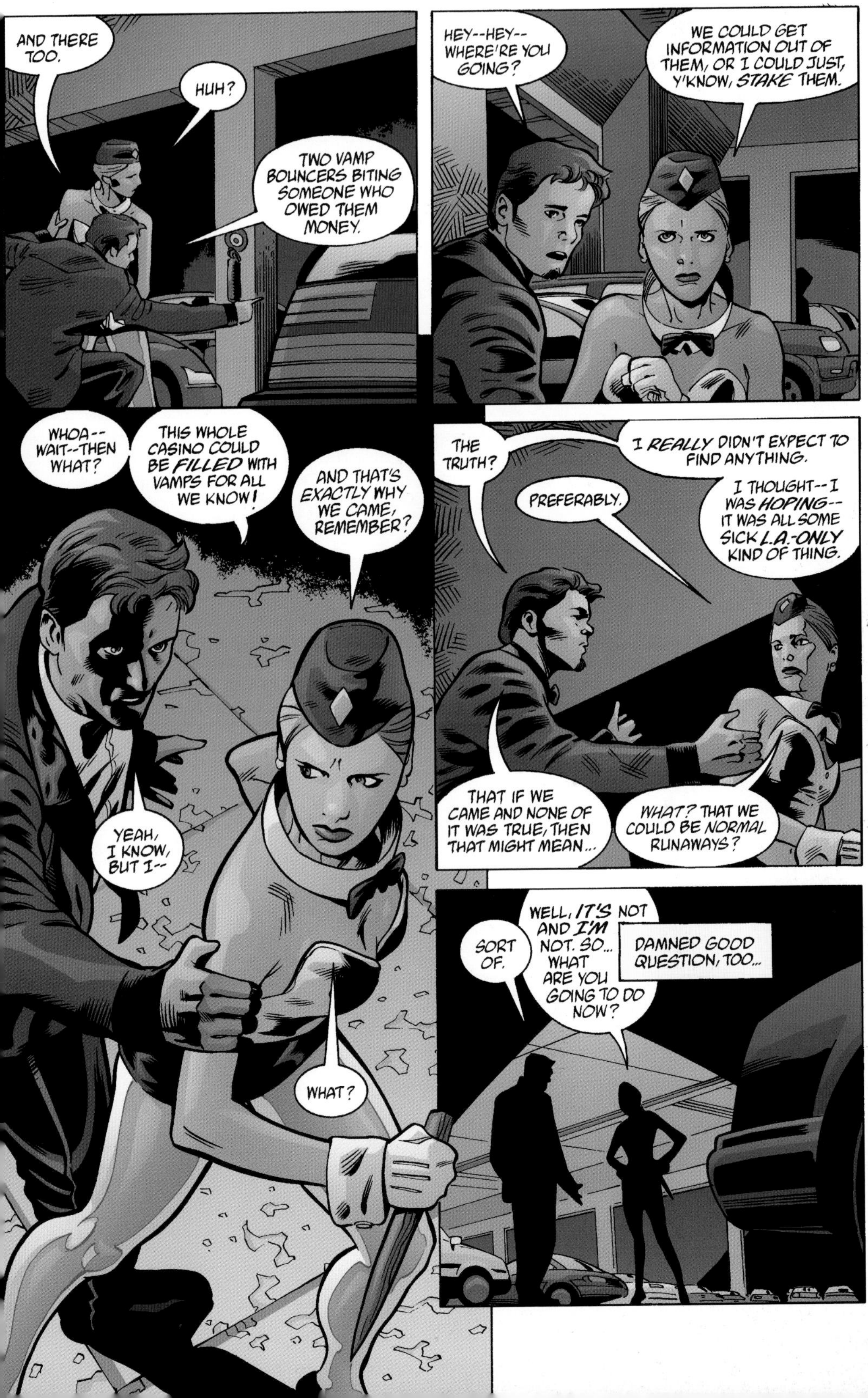

AND THERE TOO.
HUH?
TWO VAMP BOUNCERS BITING SOMEONE WHO OWED THEM MONEY.
HEY--HEY--WHERE'RE YOU GOING?
WE COULD GET INFORMATION OUT OF THEM, OR I COULD JUST, Y'KNOW, *STAKE* THEM.
WHOA--WAIT--THEN WHAT?
THIS WHOLE CASINO COULD BE *FILLED* WITH VAMPS FOR ALL WE KNOW!
AND THAT'S EXACTLY WHY WE CAME, REMEMBER?
YEAH, I KNOW, BUT I--
WHAT?
THE TRUTH?
I *REALLY* DIDN'T EXPECT TO FIND ANYTHING.
PREFERABLY.
I THOUGHT--I WAS *HOPING*--IT WAS ALL SOME SICK *L.A.-ONLY* KIND OF THING.
THAT IF WE CAME AND NONE OF IT WAS TRUE, THEN THAT MIGHT MEAN...
WHAT? THAT WE COULD BE *NORMAL* RUNAWAYS?
SORT OF.
WELL, *IT'S* NOT AND *I'M* NOT. SO... WHAT ARE YOU GOING TO DO NOW?
DAMNED GOOD QUESTION, TOO...

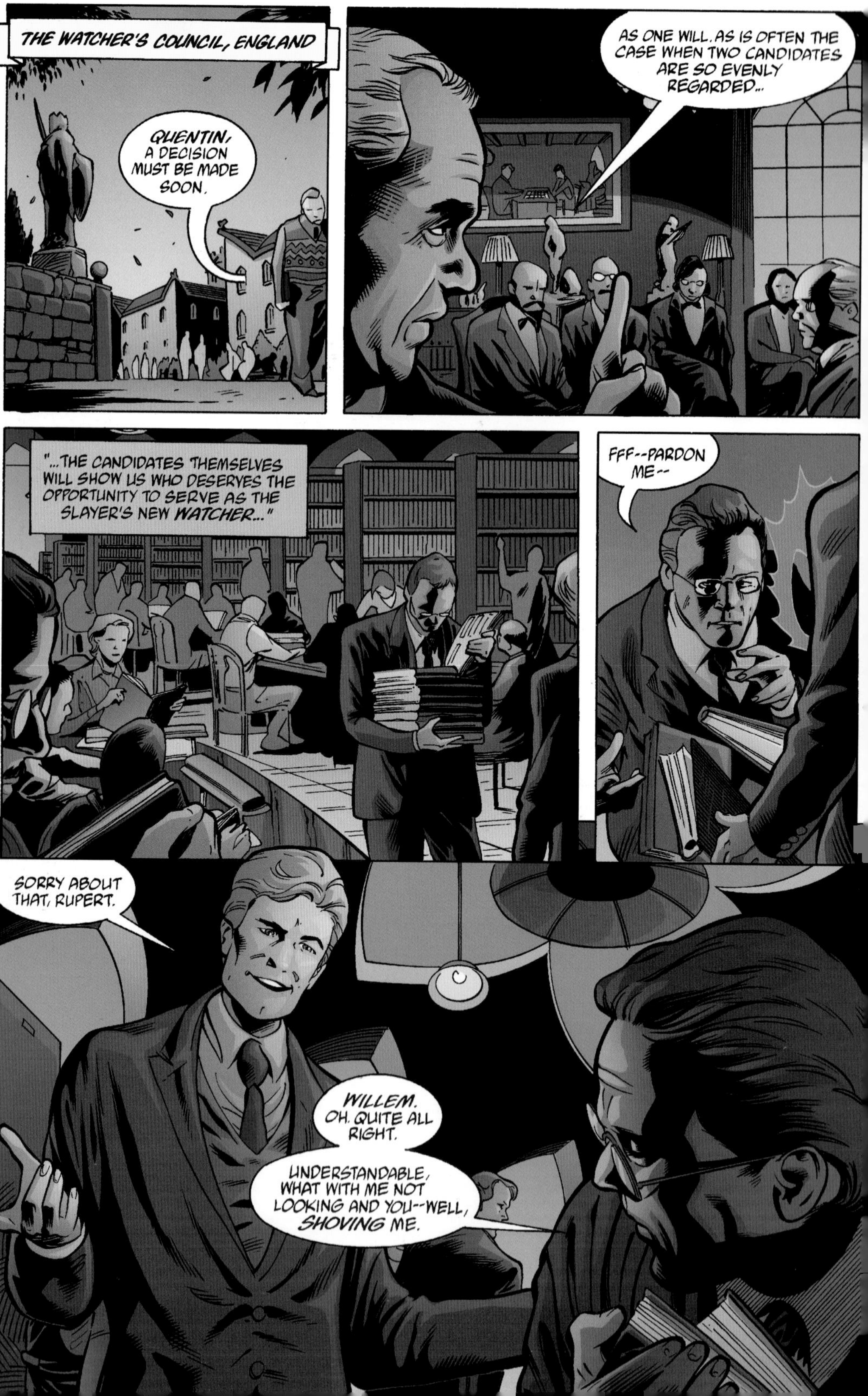
THE WATCHER'S COUNCIL, ENGLAND
QUENTIN, A DECISION MUST BE MADE SOON.
AS ONE WILL. AS IS OFTEN THE CASE WHEN TWO CANDIDATES ARE SO EVENLY REGARDED...
"...THE CANDIDATES THEMSELVES WILL SHOW US WHO DESERVES THE OPPORTUNITY TO SERVE AS THE SLAYER'S NEW WATCHER..."
FFF--PARDON ME--
SORRY ABOUT THAT, RUPERT.
WILLEM. OH. QUITE ALL RIGHT.
UNDERSTANDABLE, WHAT WITH ME NOT LOOKING AND YOU--WELL, SHOVING ME.

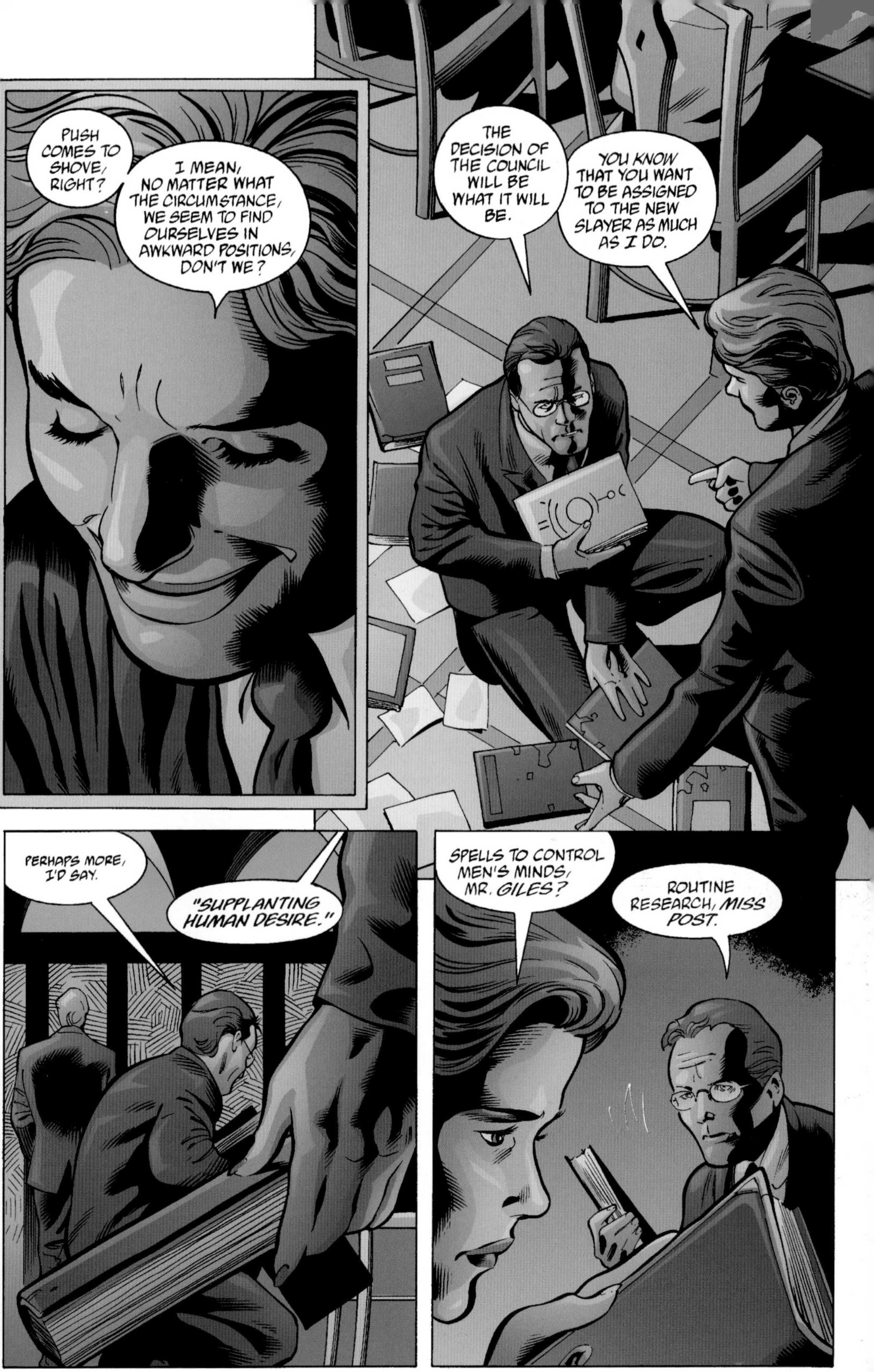

PUSH COMES TO SHOVE, RIGHT?
I MEAN, NO MATTER WHAT THE CIRCUMSTANCE, WE SEEM TO FIND OURSELVES IN AWKWARD POSITIONS, DON'T WE?
THE DECISION OF THE COUNCIL WILL BE WHAT IT WILL BE.
YOU KNOW THAT YOU WANT TO BE ASSIGNED TO THE NEW SLAYER AS MUCH AS I DO.
PERHAPS MORE, I'D SAY.
"SUPPLANTING HUMAN DESIRE."
SPELLS TO CONTROL MEN'S MINDS, MR. GILES?
ROUTINE RESEARCH, MISS POST.

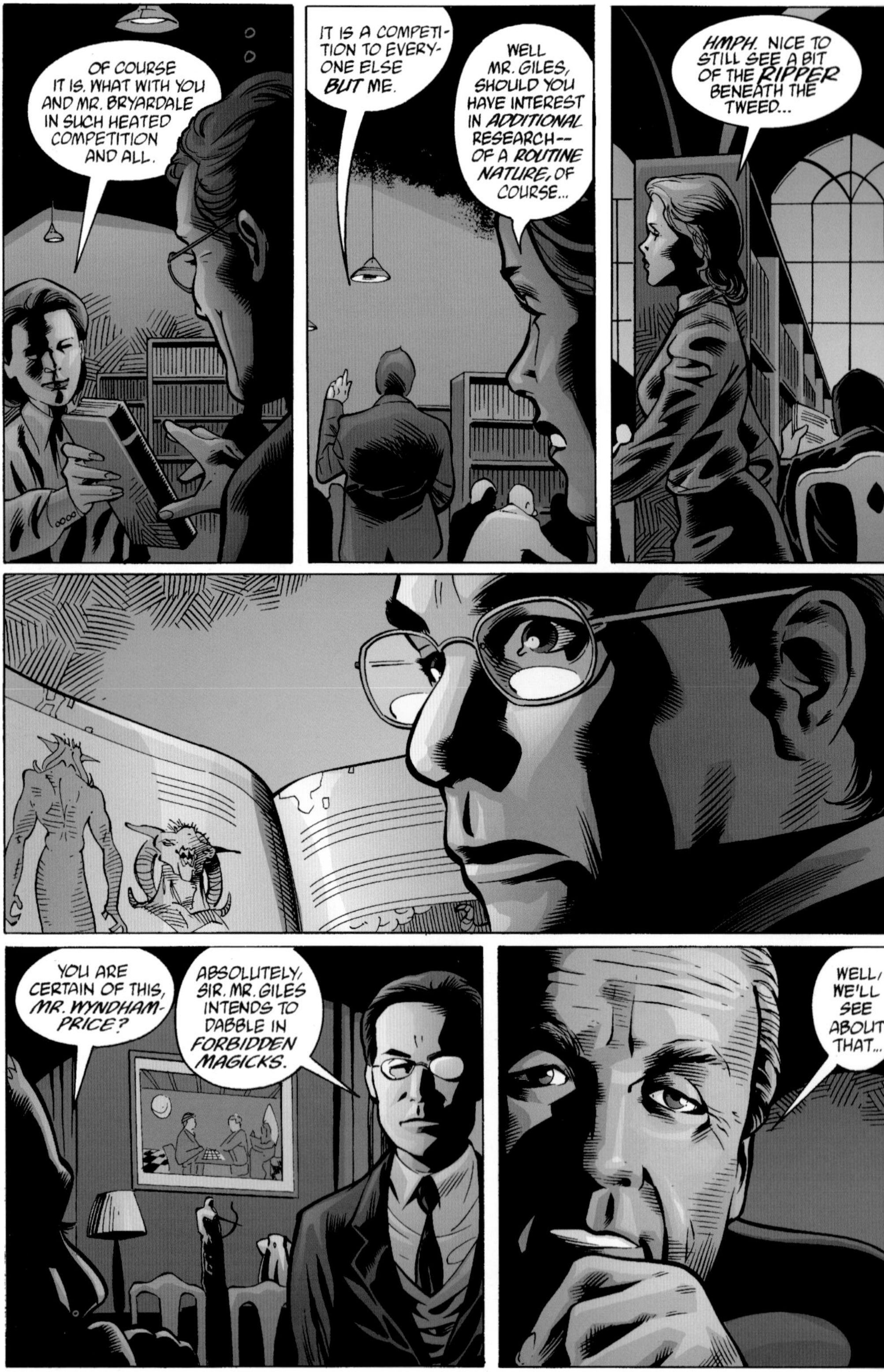
OF COURSE IT IS. WHAT WITH YOU AND MR. BRYARDALE IN SUCH HEATED COMPETITION AND ALL.
IT IS A COMPETITION TO EVERYONE ELSE BUT ME.
WELL MR. GILES, SHOULD YOU HAVE INTEREST IN ADDITIONAL RESEARCH-- OF A ROUTINE NATURE, OF COURSE...
HMPH. NICE TO STILL SEE A BIT OF THE RIPPER BENEATH THE TWEED...
YOU ARE CERTAIN OF THIS, MR. WYNDHAM-PRICE?
ABSOLUTELY, SIR. MR. GILES INTENDS TO DABBLE IN FORBIDDEN MAGICKS.
WELL, WE'LL SEE ABOUT THAT...

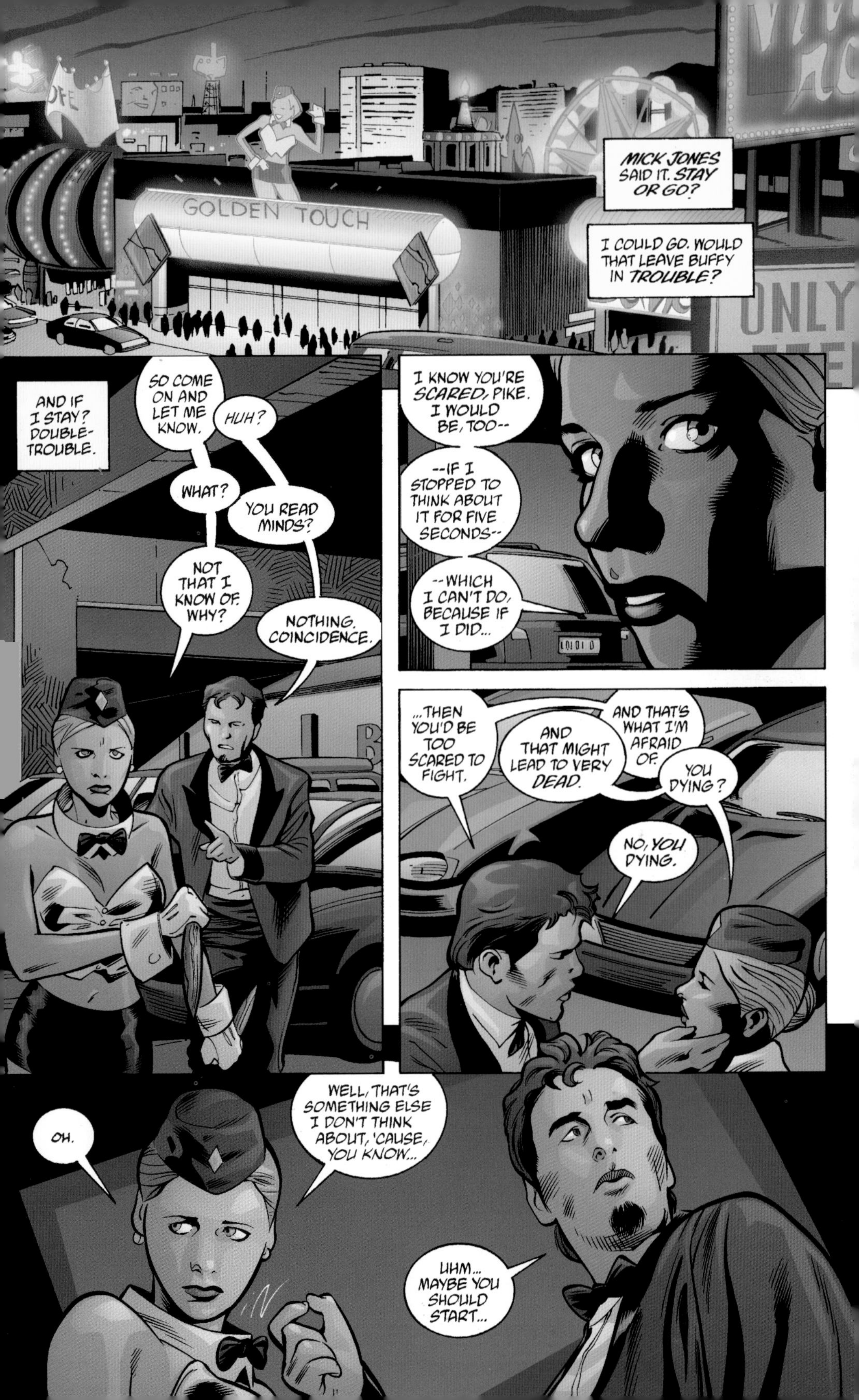
GOLDEN TOUCH
MICK JONES SAID IT. STAY OR GO?
I COULD GO. WOULD THAT LEAVE BUFFY IN TROUBLE?
ONLY
AND IF I STAY? DOUBLE-TROUBLE.
SO COME ON AND LET ME KNOW.
HUH?
WHAT?
YOU READ MINDS?
NOT THAT I KNOW OF. WHY?
NOTHING. COINCIDENCE.
I KNOW YOU'RE SCARED, PIKE. I WOULD BE, TOO--
--IF I STOPPED TO THINK ABOUT IT FOR FIVE SECONDS--
--WHICH I CAN'T DO, BECAUSE IF I DID...
...THEN YOU'D BE TOO SCARED TO FIGHT.
AND THAT MIGHT LEAD TO VERY DEAD.
AND THAT'S WHAT I'M AFRAID OF.
YOU DYING?
NO, YOU DYING.
OH.
WELL, THAT'S SOMETHING ELSE I DON'T THINK ABOUT, 'CAUSE, YOU KNOW...
UHM... MAYBE YOU SHOULD START...

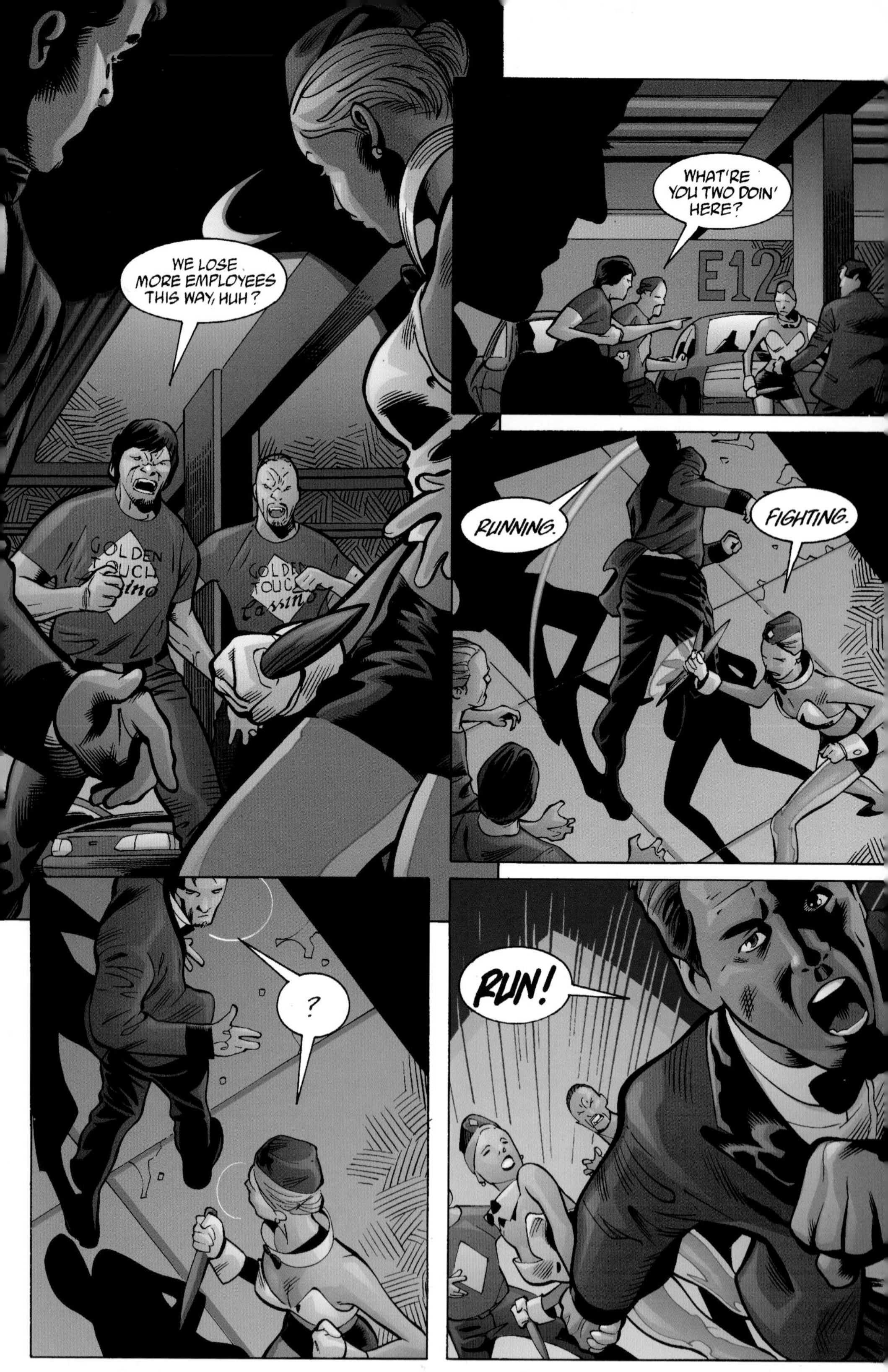
WE LOSE MORE EMPLOYEES THIS WAY, HUH?
GOLDEN TOUCH Casino
WHAT'RE YOU TWO DOIN' HERE?
E12
RUNNING.
FIGHTING.
?
RUN!

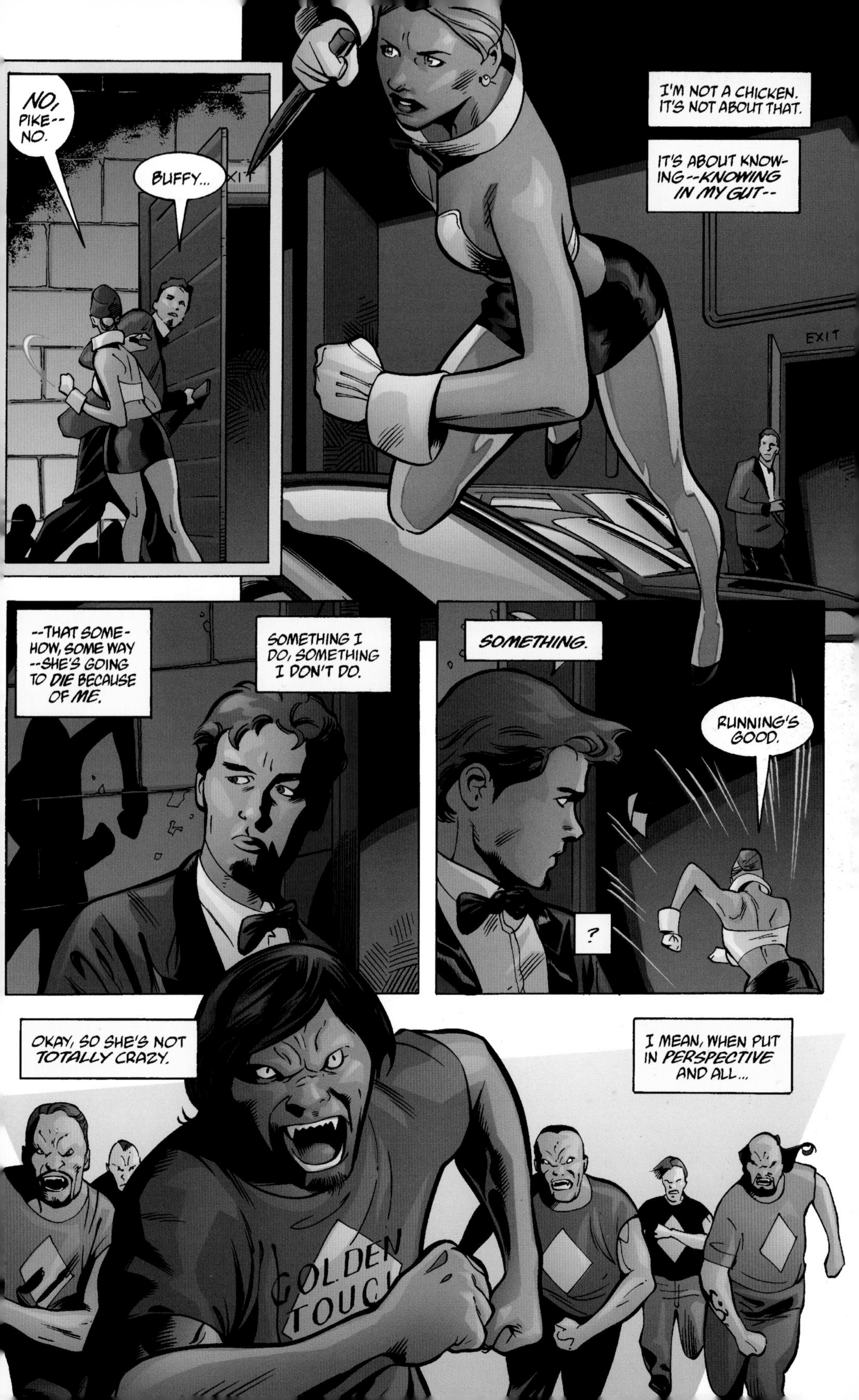
NO, PIKE-- NO.
BUFFY...
EXIT
I'M NOT A CHICKEN. IT'S NOT ABOUT THAT.
IT'S ABOUT KNOWING--KNOWING IN MY GUT--
EXIT
--THAT SOMEHOW, SOME WAY --SHE'S GOING TO DIE BECAUSE OF ME.
SOMETHING I DO, SOMETHING I DON'T DO.
SOMETHING.
RUNNING'S GOOD.
?
OKAY, SO SHE'S NOT TOTALLY CRAZY.
I MEAN, WHEN PUT IN PERSPECTIVE AND ALL...
GOLDEN TOUC

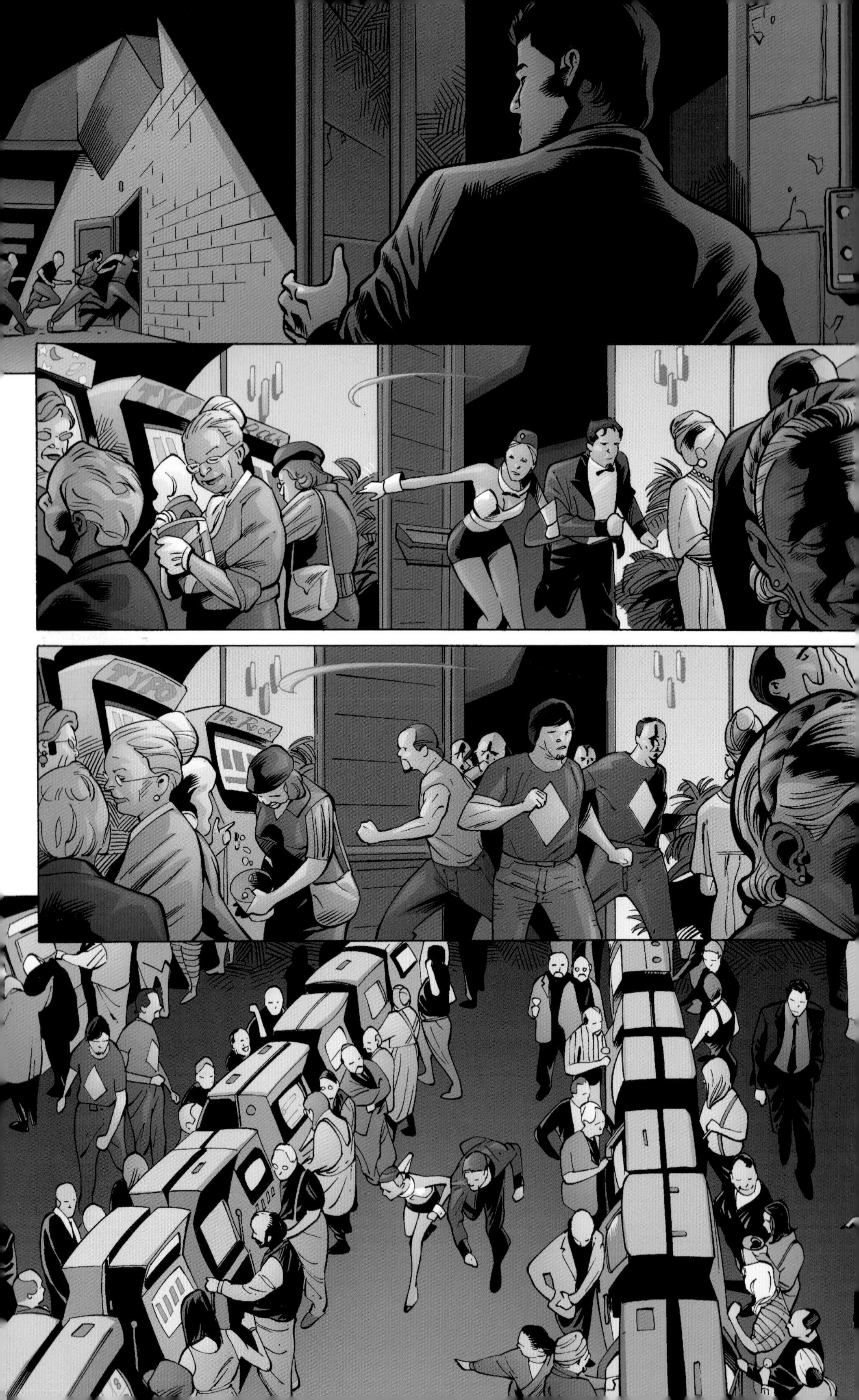
TYPO
The Rock

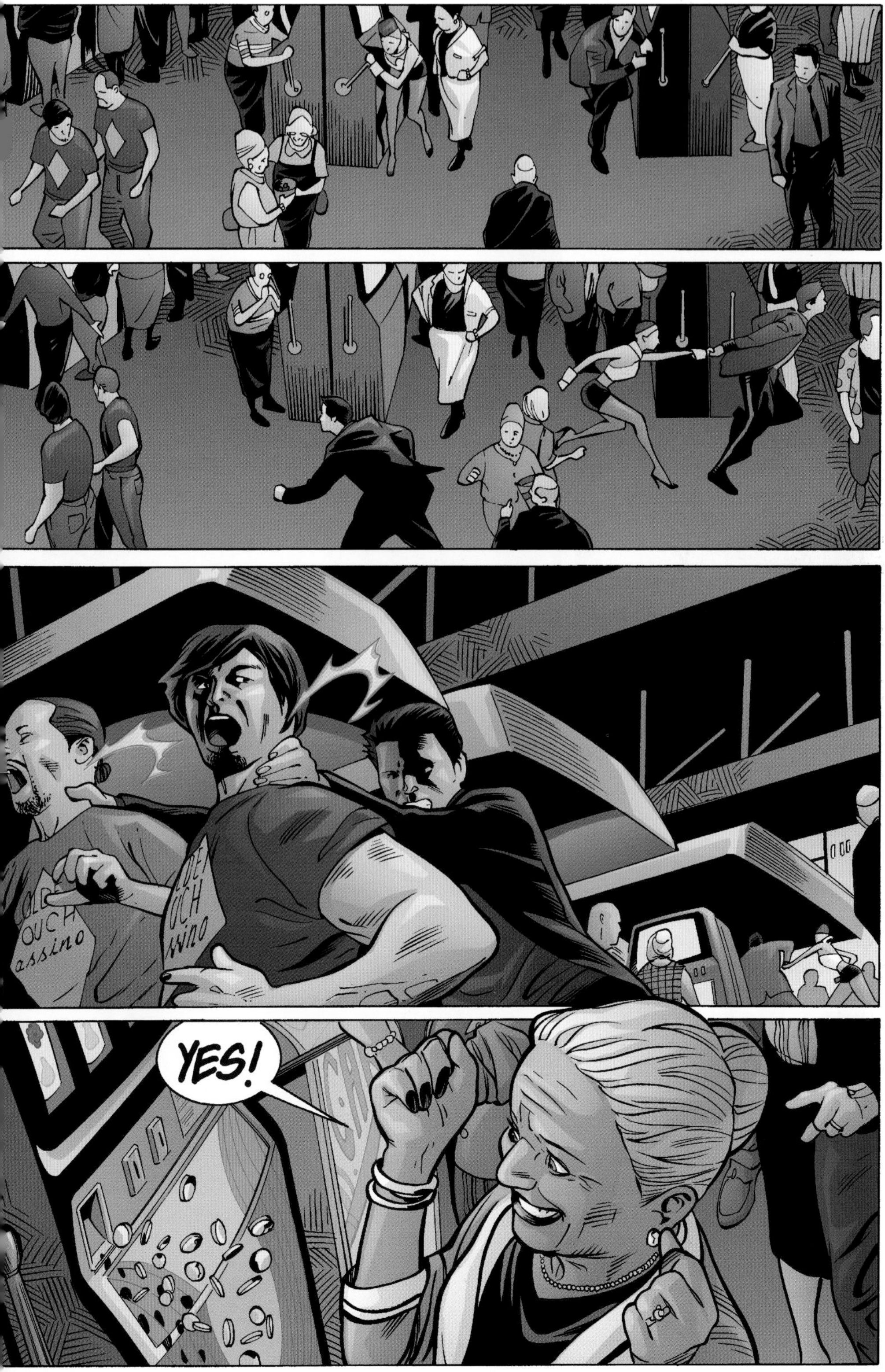
YES!

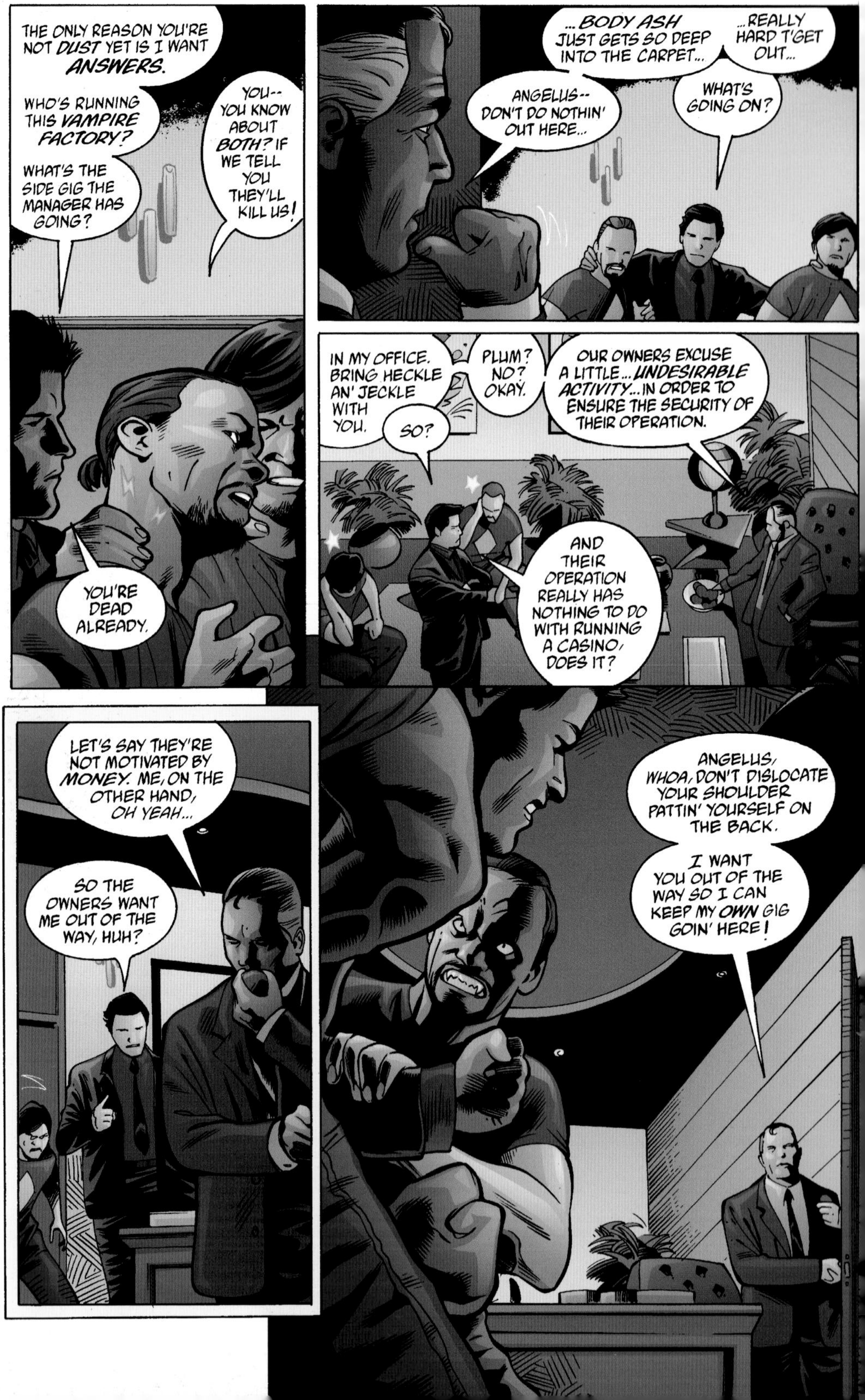
THE ONLY REASON YOU'RE NOT DUST YET IS I WANT ANSWERS.
WHO'S RUNNING THIS VAMPIRE FACTORY?
WHAT'S THE SIDE GIG THE MANAGER HAS GOING?
YOU-- YOU KNOW ABOUT BOTH? IF WE TELL YOU THEY'LL KILL US!
...BODY ASH JUST GETS SO DEEP INTO THE CARPET...
...REALLY HARD T'GET OUT...
ANGELUS-- DON'T DO NOTHIN' OUT HERE...
WHAT'S GOING ON?
YOU'RE DEAD ALREADY.
IN MY OFFICE. BRING HECKLE AN' JECKLE WITH YOU.
PLUM? NO? OKAY.
OUR OWNERS EXCUSE A LITTLE... UNDESIRABLE ACTIVITY... IN ORDER TO ENSURE THE SECURITY OF THEIR OPERATION.
SO?
AND THEIR OPERATION REALLY HAS NOTHING TO DO WITH RUNNING A CASINO, DOES IT?
LET'S SAY THEY'RE NOT MOTIVATED BY MONEY. ME, ON THE OTHER HAND, OH YEAH...
SO THE OWNERS WANT ME OUT OF THE WAY, HUH?
ANGELUS, WHOA, DON'T DISLOCATE YOUR SHOULDER PATTIN' YOURSELF ON THE BACK.
I WANT YOU OUT OF THE WAY SO I CAN KEEP MY OWN GIG GOIN' HERE!

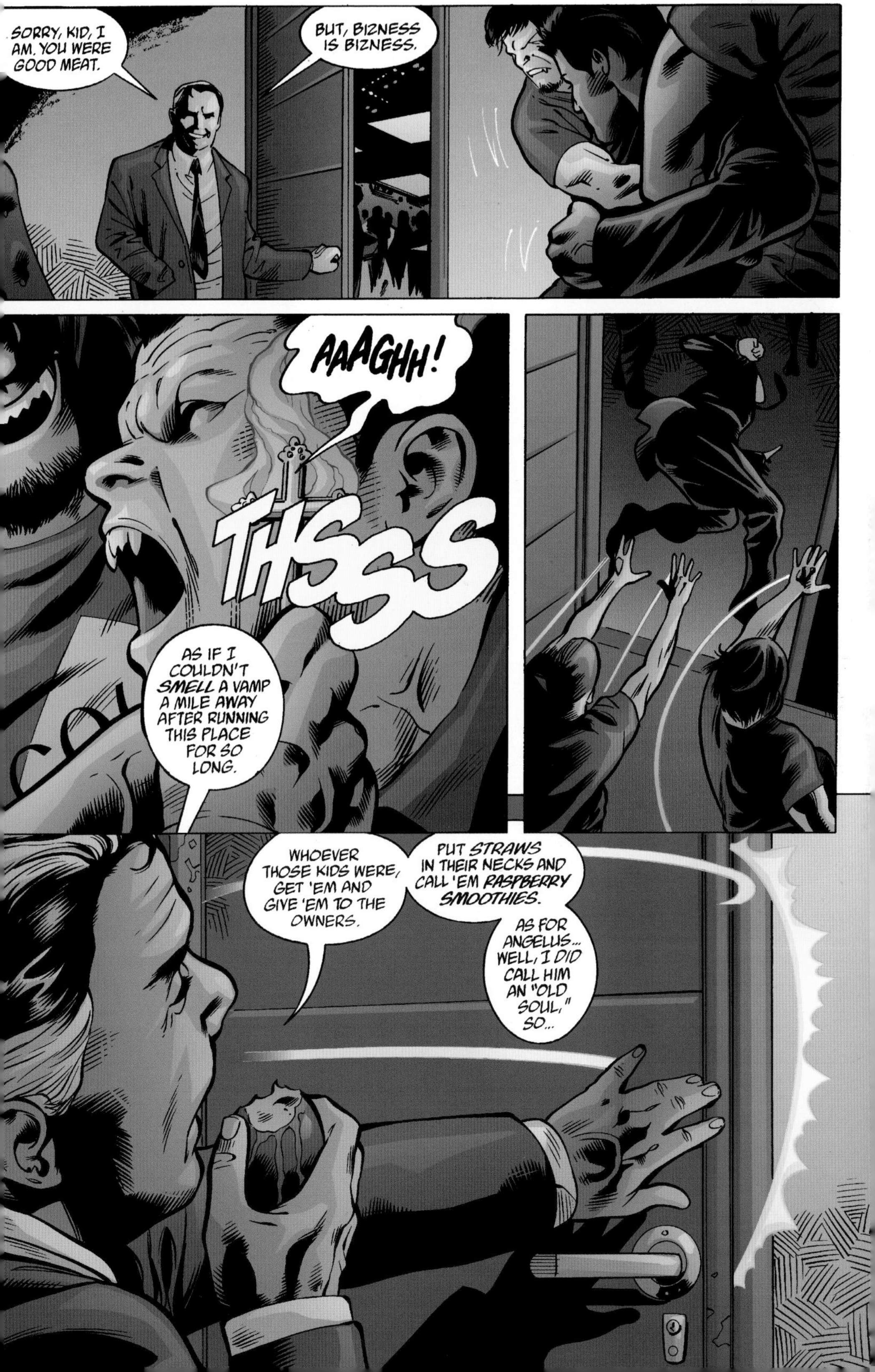
SORRY, KID, I AM. YOU WERE GOOD MEAT.
BUT, BIZNESS IS BIZNESS.
AAAGHH!
THSSS
AS IF I COULDN'T SMELL A VAMP A MILE AWAY AFTER RUNNING THIS PLACE FOR SO LONG.
WHOEVER THOSE KIDS WERE, GET 'EM AND GIVE 'EM TO THE OWNERS.
PUT STRAWS IN THEIR NECKS AND CALL 'EM RASPBERRY SMOOTHIES.
AS FOR ANGELUS... WELL, I DID CALL HIM AN "OLD SOUL," SO...

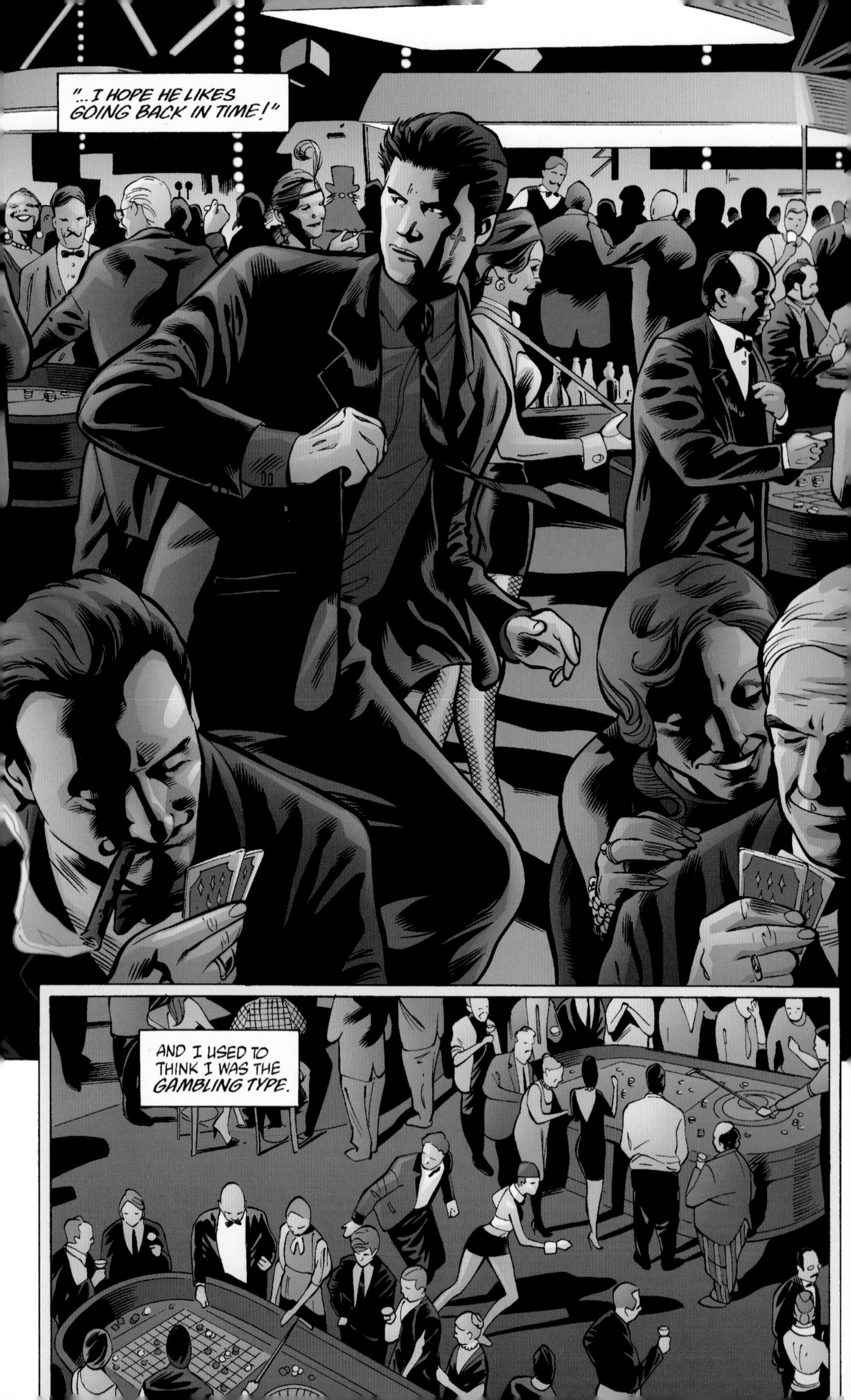
"...I HOPE HE LIKES GOING BACK IN TIME!"
AND I USED TO THINK I WAS THE *GAMBLING TYPE*.

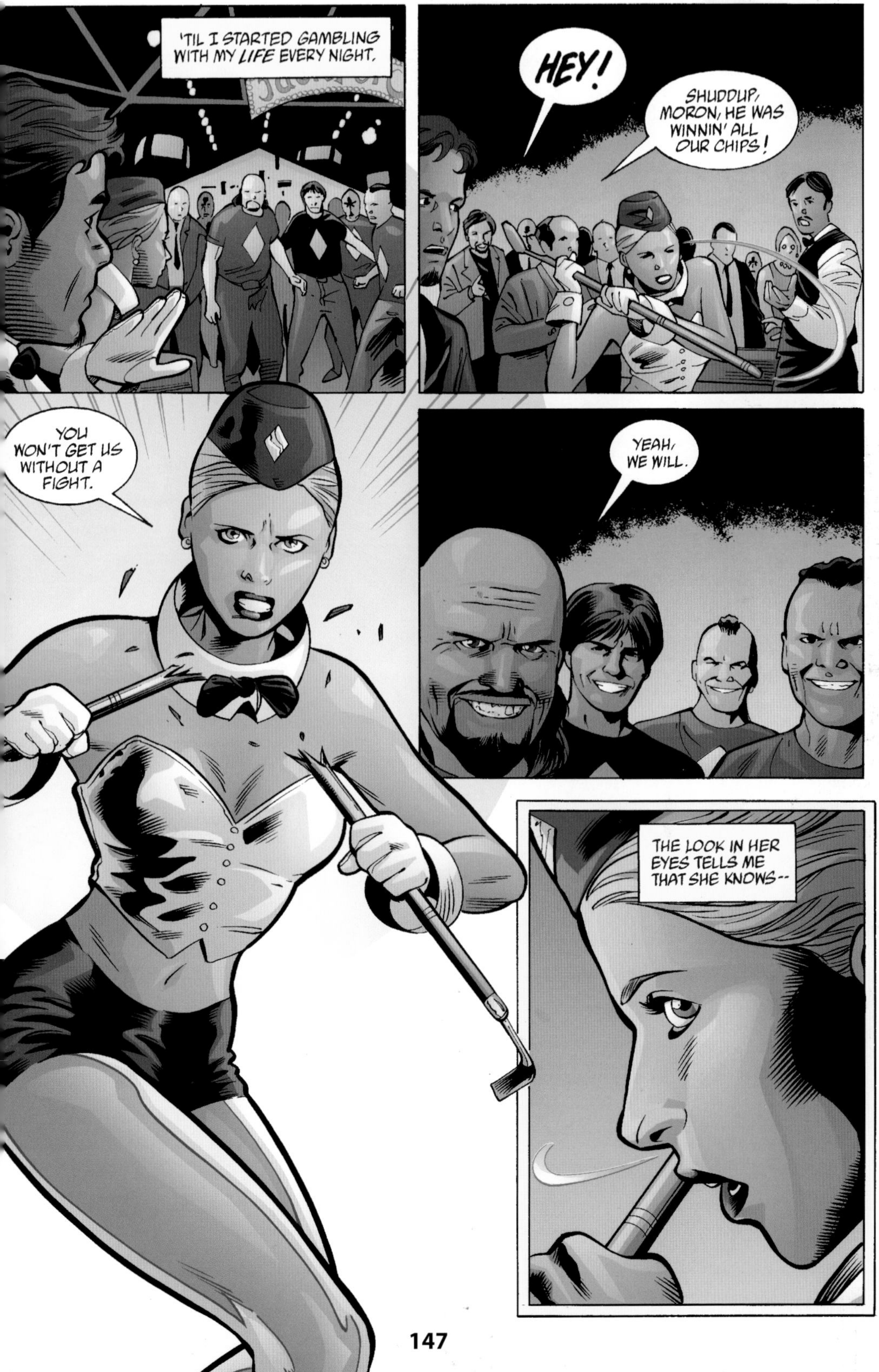
'TIL I STARTED GAMBLING WITH MY *LIFE* EVERY NIGHT.
HEY!
SHUDDUP, MORON, HE WAS WINNIN' ALL OUR CHIPS!
YOU WON'T GET US WITHOUT A FIGHT.
YEAH, WE WILL.
THE LOOK IN HER EYES TELLS ME THAT SHE KNOWS--

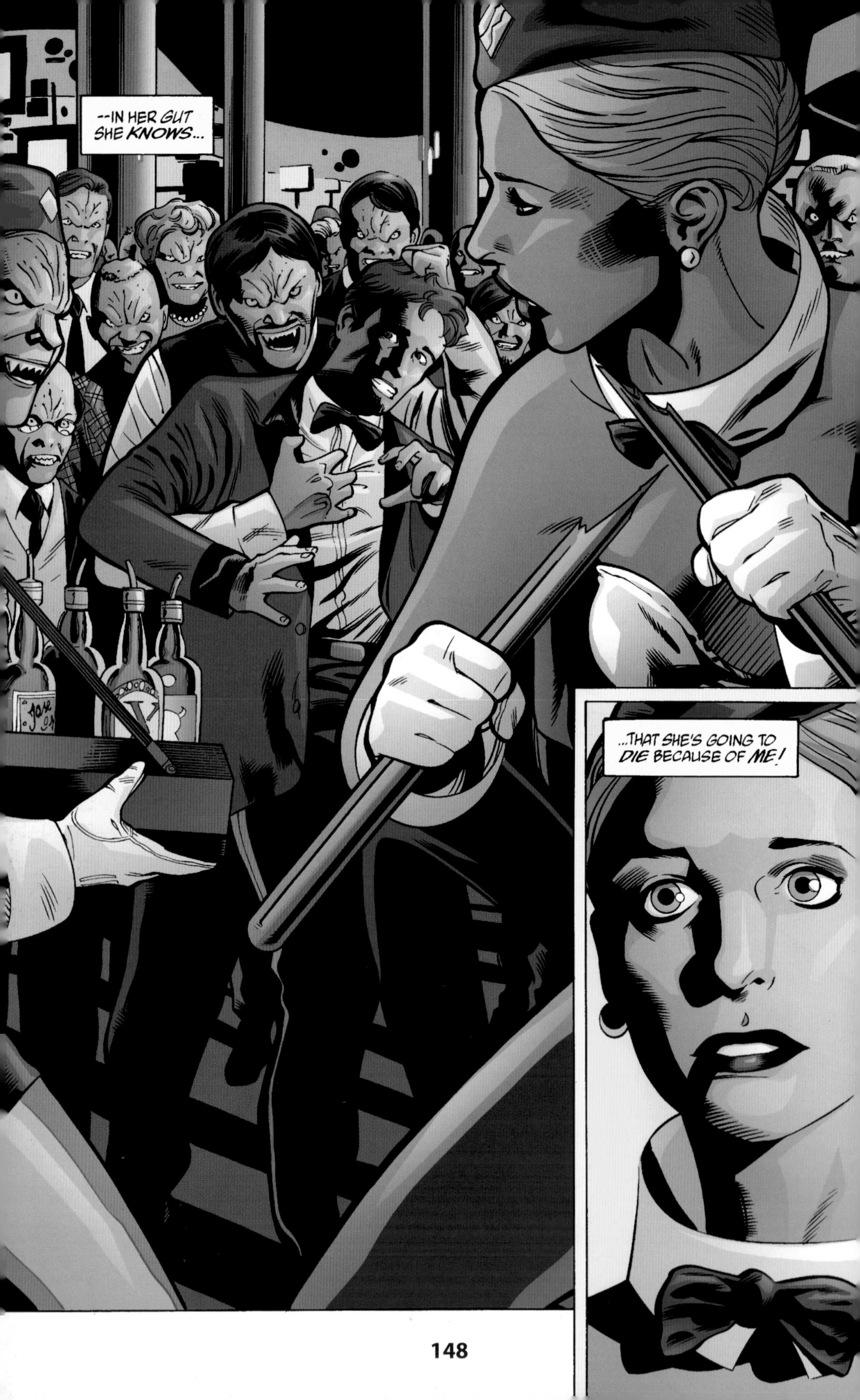
--IN HER GUT SHE KNOWS...
...THAT SHE'S GOING TO DIE BECAUSE OF ME!

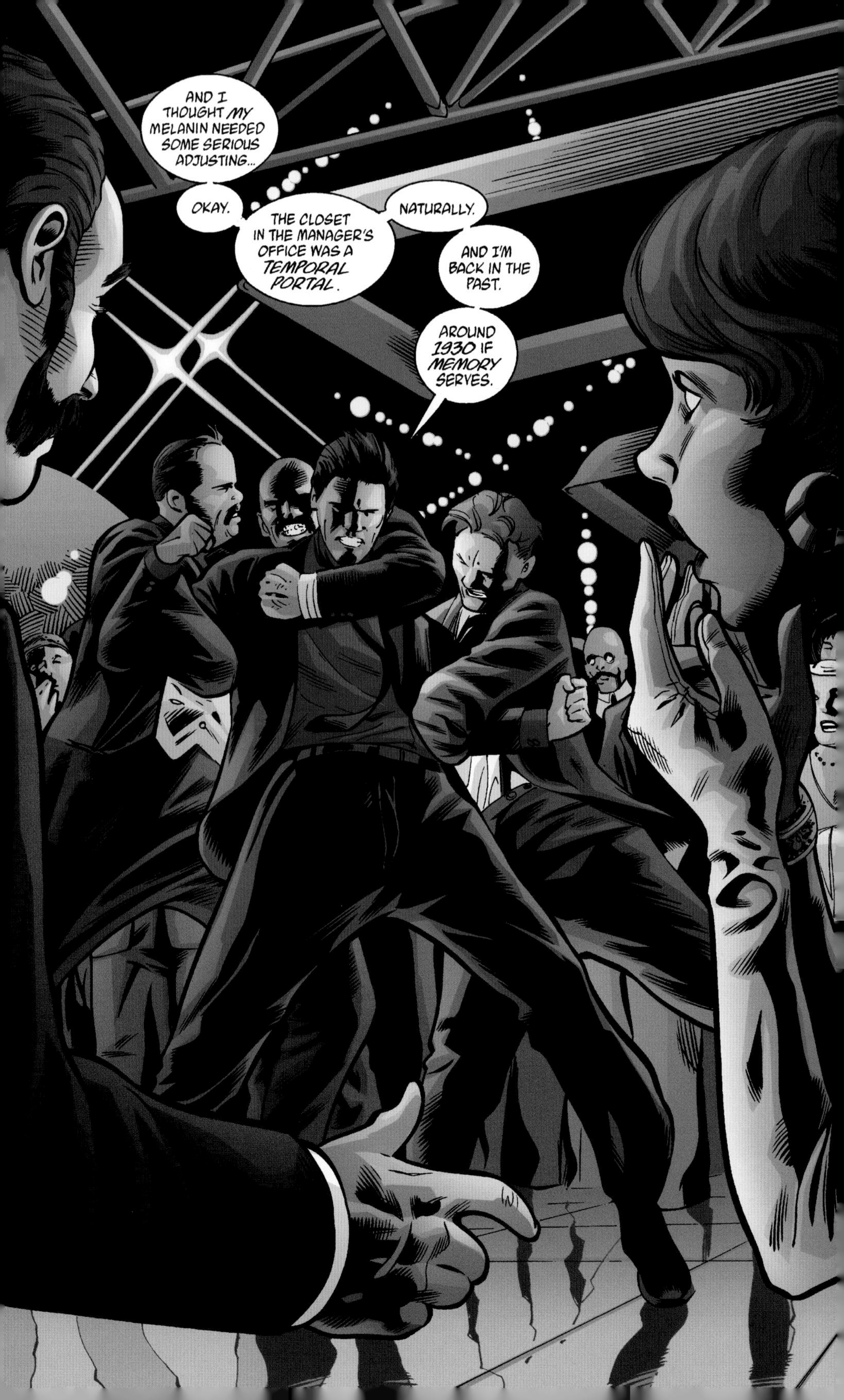
AND I THOUGHT *MY* MELANIN NEEDED SOME SERIOUS ADJUSTING...
OKAY.
THE CLOSET IN THE MANAGER'S OFFICE WAS A *TEMPORAL PORTAL*.
NATURALLY.
AND I'M BACK IN THE PAST.
AROUND *1930* IF *MEMORY* SERVES.

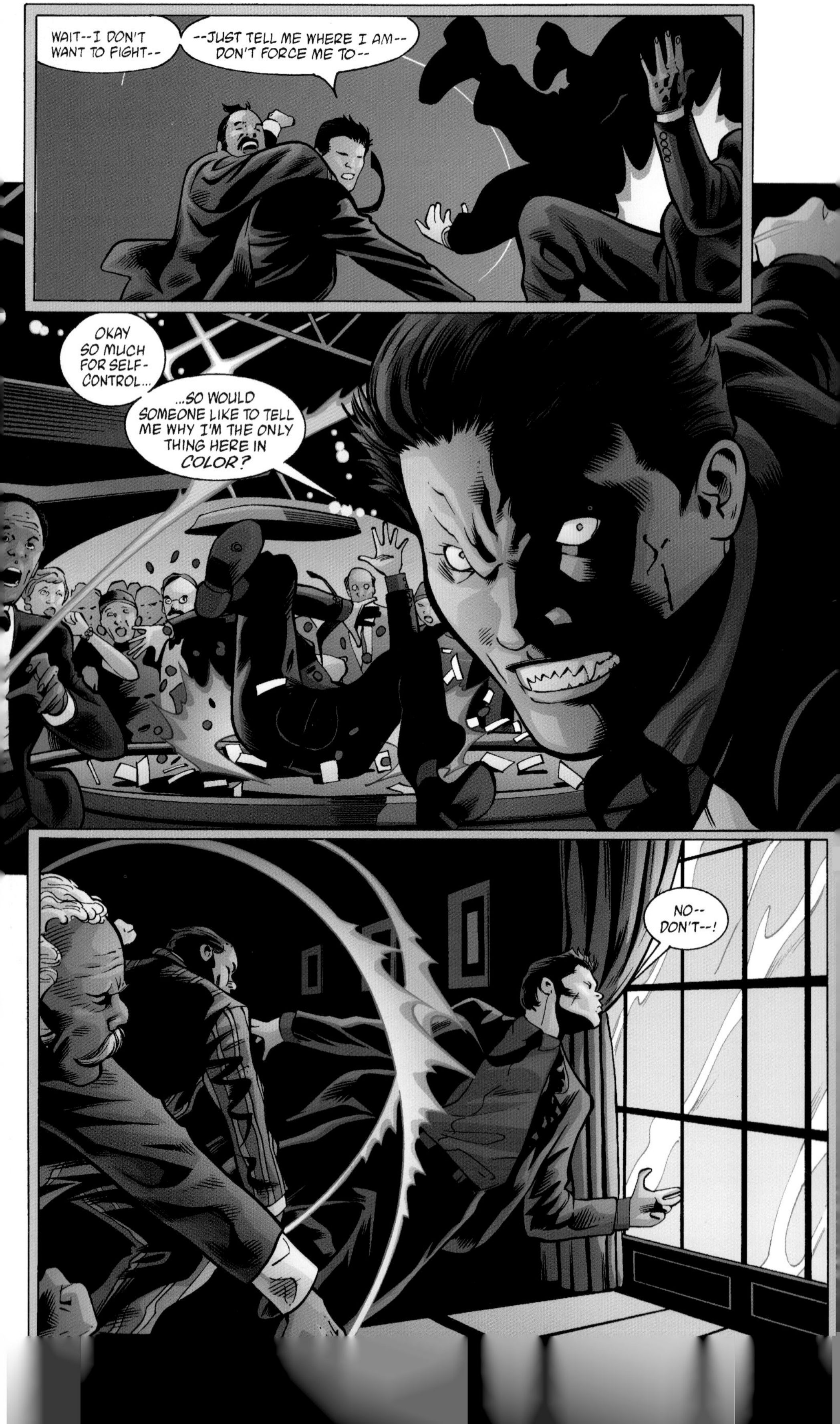
WAIT--I DON'T WANT TO FIGHT--
--JUST TELL ME WHERE I AM-- DON'T FORCE ME TO--
OKAY SO MUCH FOR SELF-CONTROL...
...SO WOULD SOMEONE LIKE TO TELL ME WHY I'M THE ONLY THING HERE IN COLOR?
NO-- DON'T--!

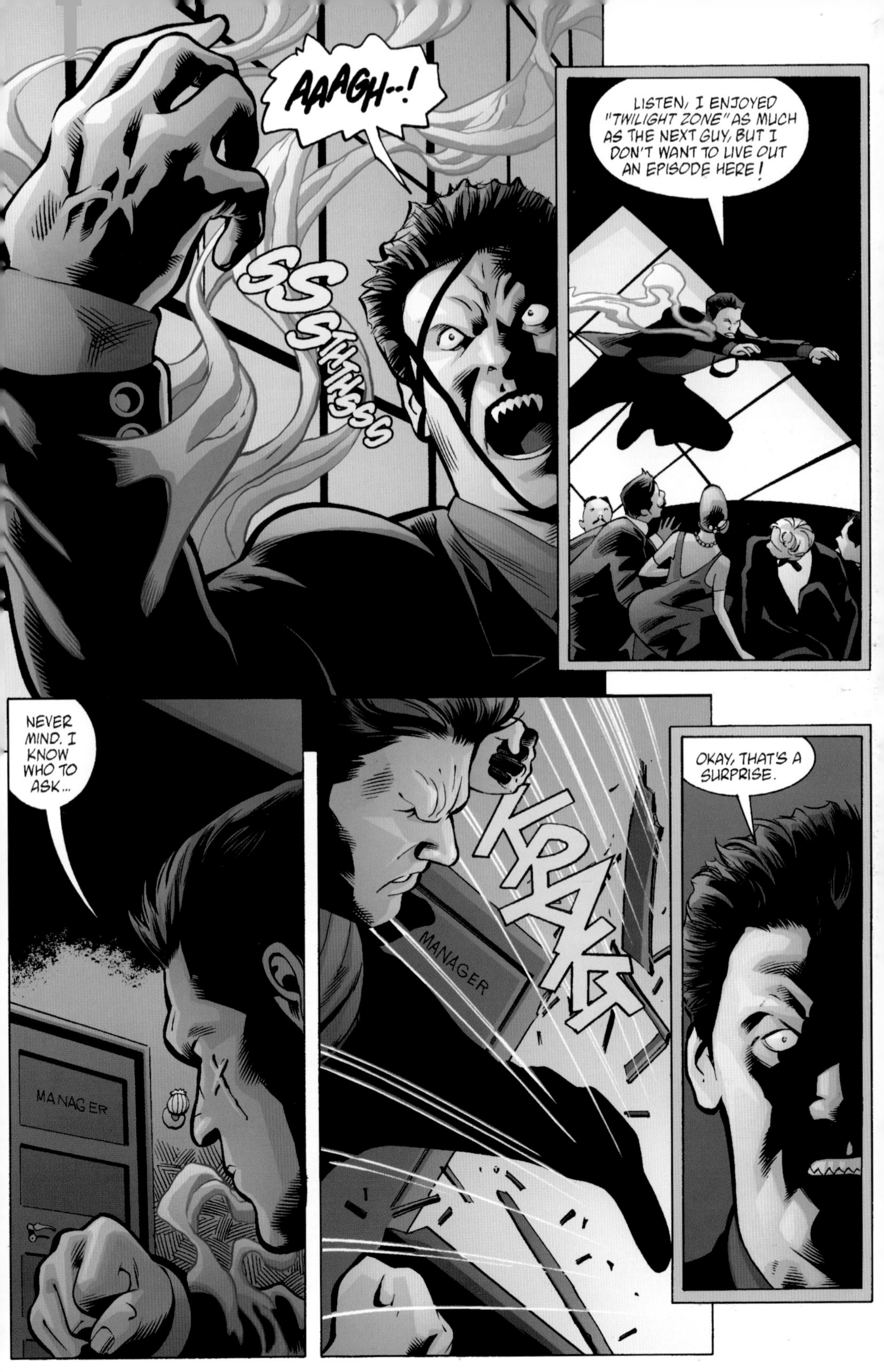

AAAGH--!
SSSTHHSSS
LISTEN, I ENJOYED "TWILIGHT ZONE" AS MUCH AS THE NEXT GUY, BUT I DON'T WANT TO LIVE OUT AN EPISODE HERE!
NEVER MIND. I KNOW WHO TO ASK...
MANAGER
MANAGER
KRAK
OKAY, THAT'S A SURPRISE.

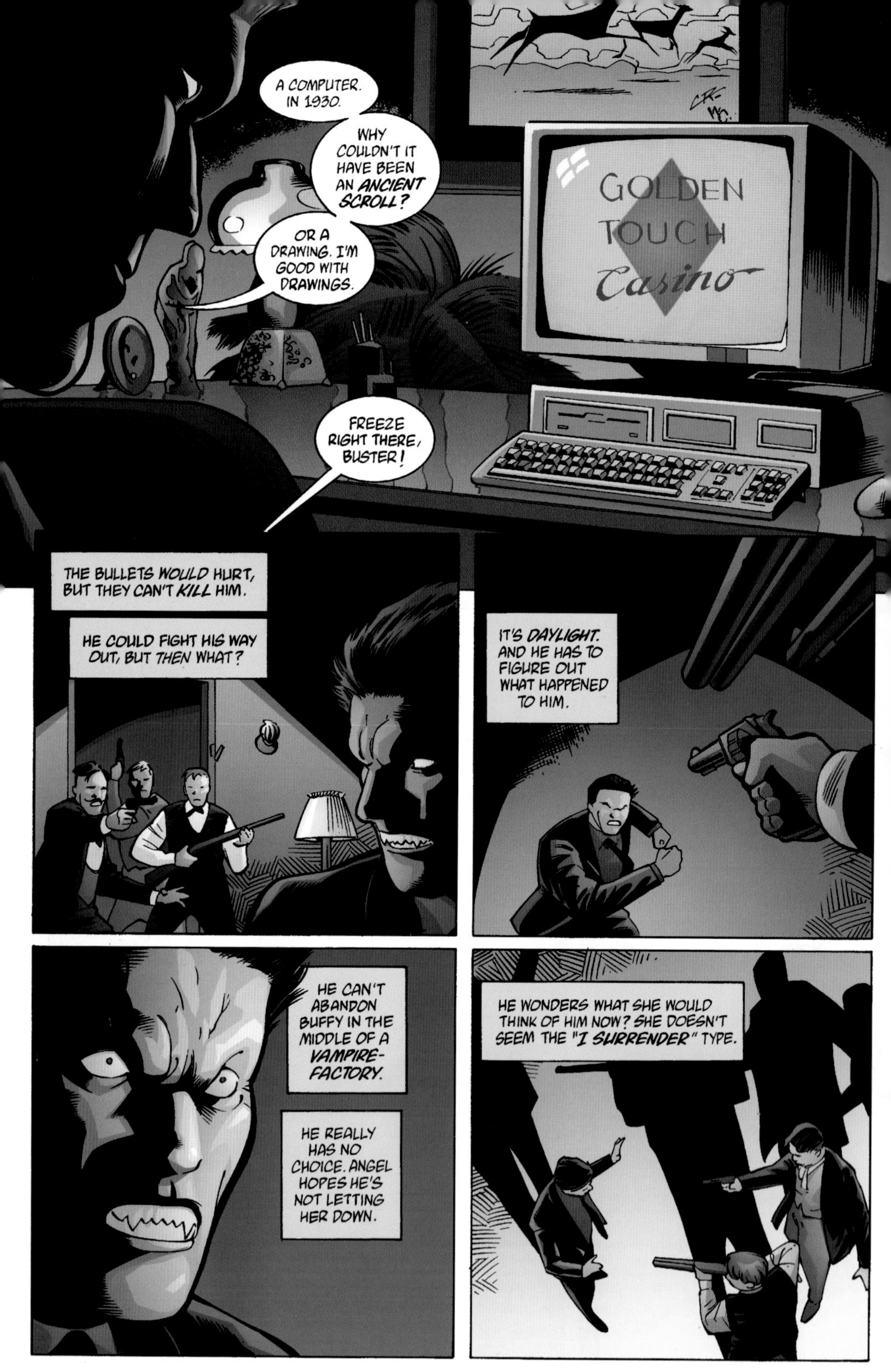
A COMPUTER. IN 1930.
WHY COULDN'T IT HAVE BEEN AN ANCIENT SCROLL?
OR A DRAWING. I'M GOOD WITH DRAWINGS.
GOLDEN TOUCH Casino
FREEZE RIGHT THERE, BUSTER!
THE BULLETS WOULD HURT, BUT THEY CAN'T KILL HIM.
HE COULD FIGHT HIS WAY OUT, BUT THEN WHAT?
IT'S DAYLIGHT. AND HE HAS TO FIGURE OUT WHAT HAPPENED TO HIM.
HE CAN'T ABANDON BUFFY IN THE MIDDLE OF A VAMPIRE-FACTORY.
HE REALLY HAS NO CHOICE. ANGEL HOPES HE'S NOT LETTING HER DOWN.
HE WONDERS WHAT SHE WOULD THINK OF HIM NOW? SHE DOESN'T SEEM THE "I SURRENDER" TYPE.

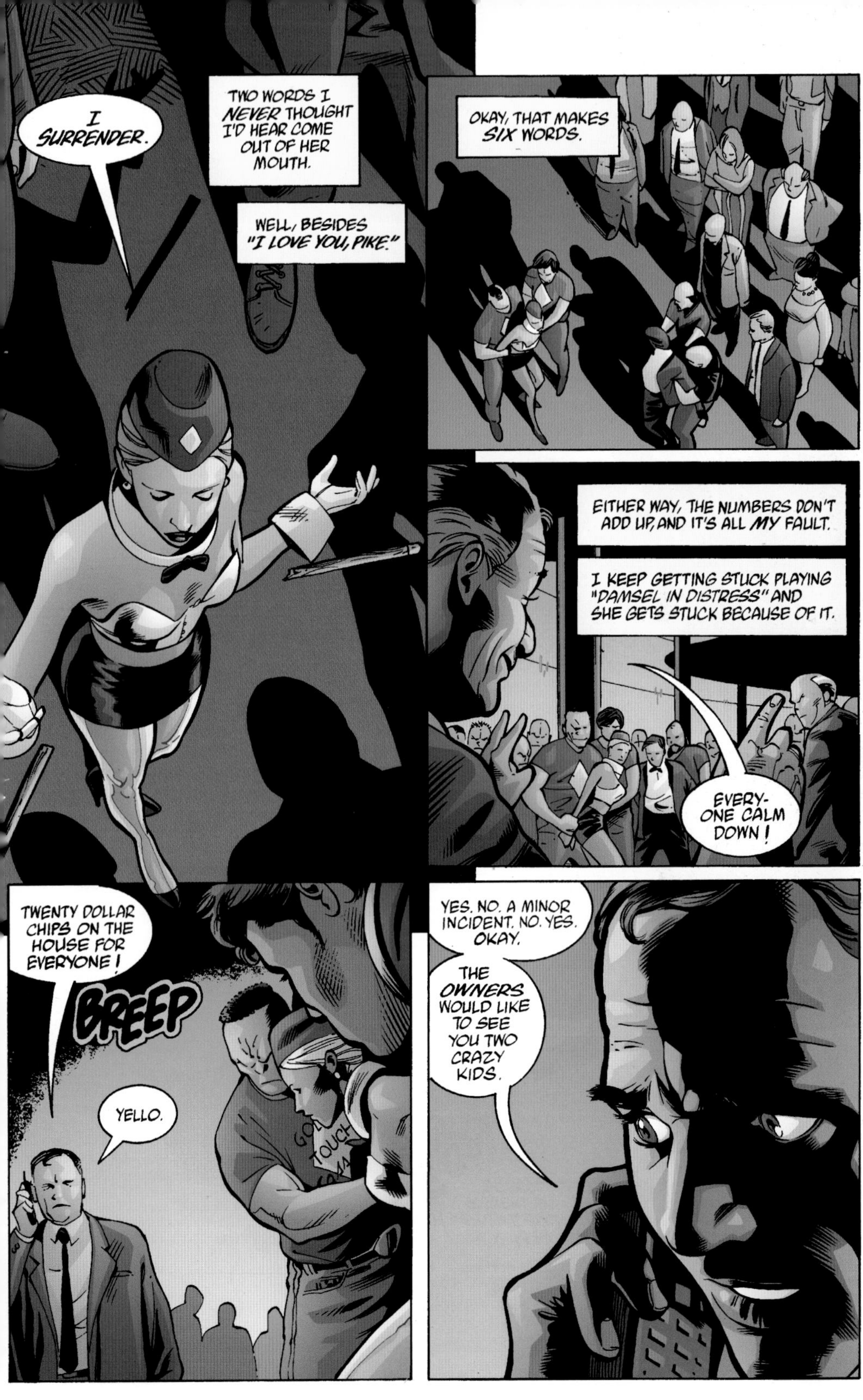
I SURRENDER.
TWO WORDS I NEVER THOUGHT I'D HEAR COME OUT OF HER MOUTH.
WELL, BESIDES "I LOVE YOU, PIKE."
OKAY, THAT MAKES SIX WORDS.
EITHER WAY, THE NUMBERS DON'T ADD UP, AND IT'S ALL MY FAULT.
I KEEP GETTING STUCK PLAYING "DAMSEL IN DISTRESS" AND SHE GETS STUCK BECAUSE OF IT.
EVERY-ONE CALM DOWN!
TWENTY DOLLAR CHIPS ON THE HOUSE FOR EVERYONE!
BREEP
YELLO.
YES. NO. A MINOR INCIDENT. NO. YES. OKAY.
THE OWNERS WOULD LIKE TO SEE YOU TWO CRAZY KIDS.

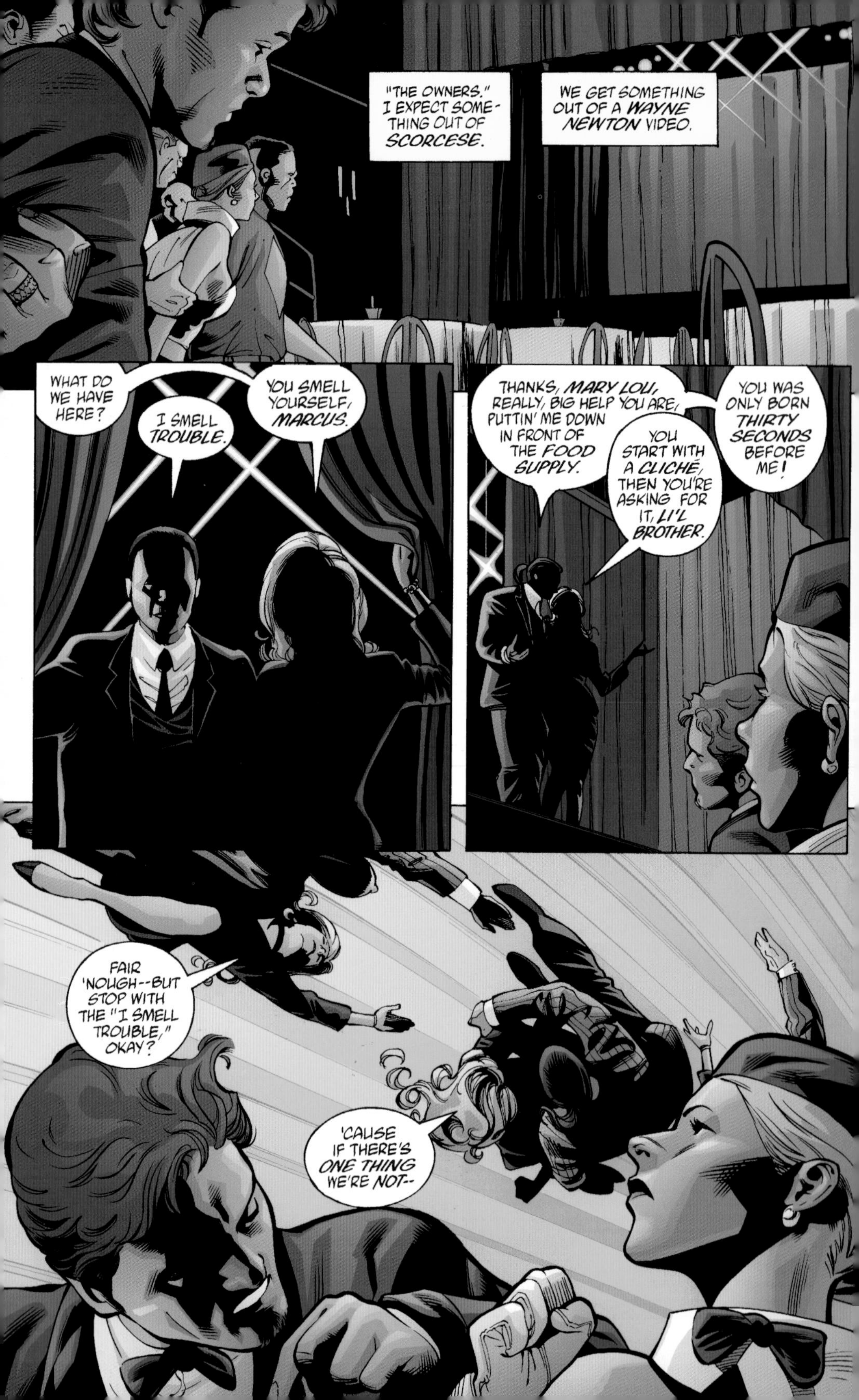
"THE OWNERS." I EXPECT SOMETHING OUT OF SCORCESE.
WE GET SOMETHING OUT OF A WAYNE NEWTON VIDEO.
WHAT DO WE HAVE HERE?
I SMELL TROUBLE.
YOU SMELL YOURSELF, MARCUS.
THANKS, MARY LOU, REALLY, BIG HELP YOU ARE, PUTTIN' ME DOWN IN FRONT OF THE FOOD SUPPLY.
YOU WAS ONLY BORN THIRTY SECONDS BEFORE ME!
YOU START WITH A CLICHÉ, THEN YOU'RE ASKING FOR IT, LI'L BROTHER.
FAIR 'NOUGH--BUT STOP WITH THE "I SMELL TROUBLE," OKAY?
'CAUSE IF THERE'S ONE THING WE'RE NOT--

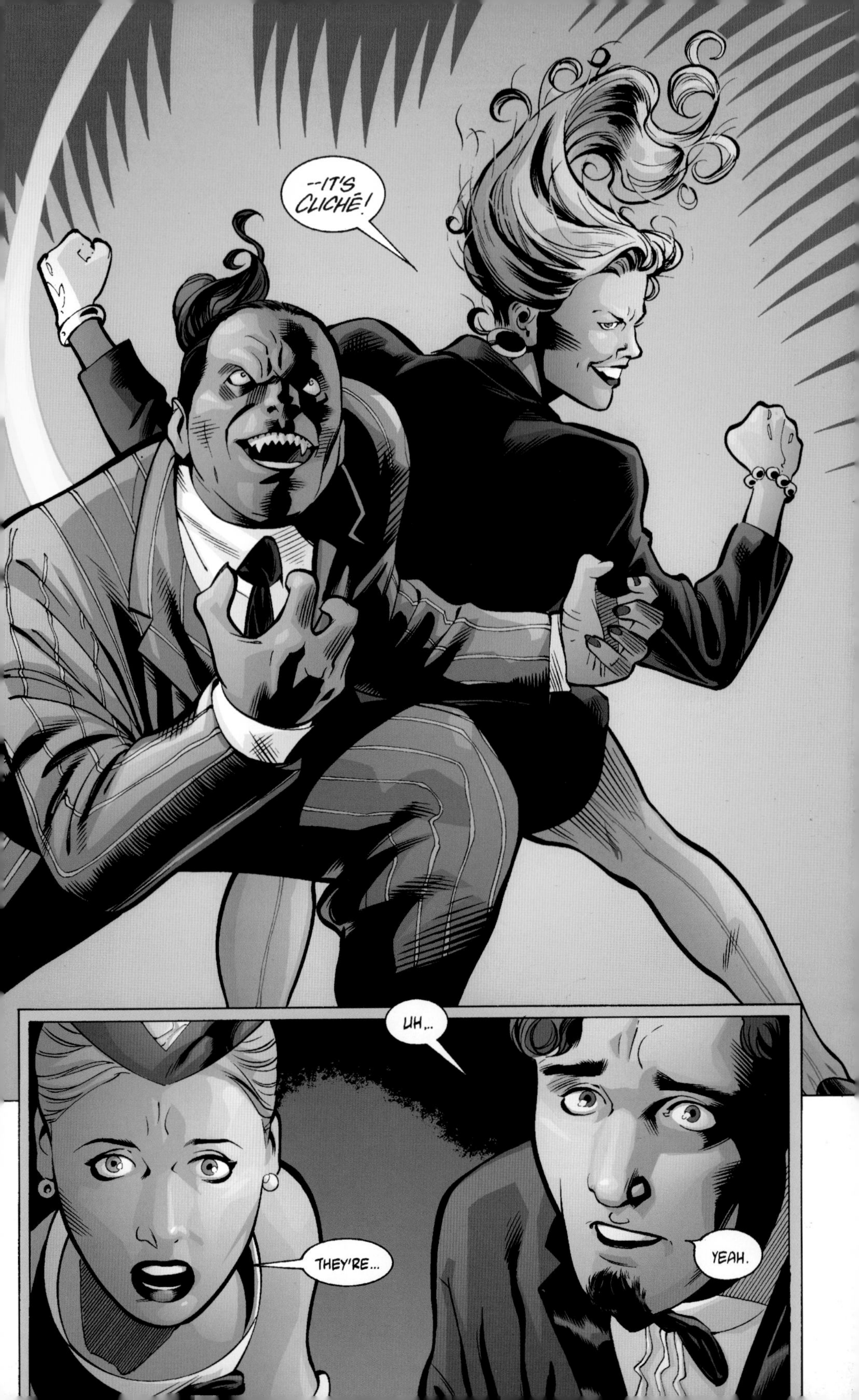
--IT'S CLICHÉ!
UH...
THEY'RE...
YEAH.

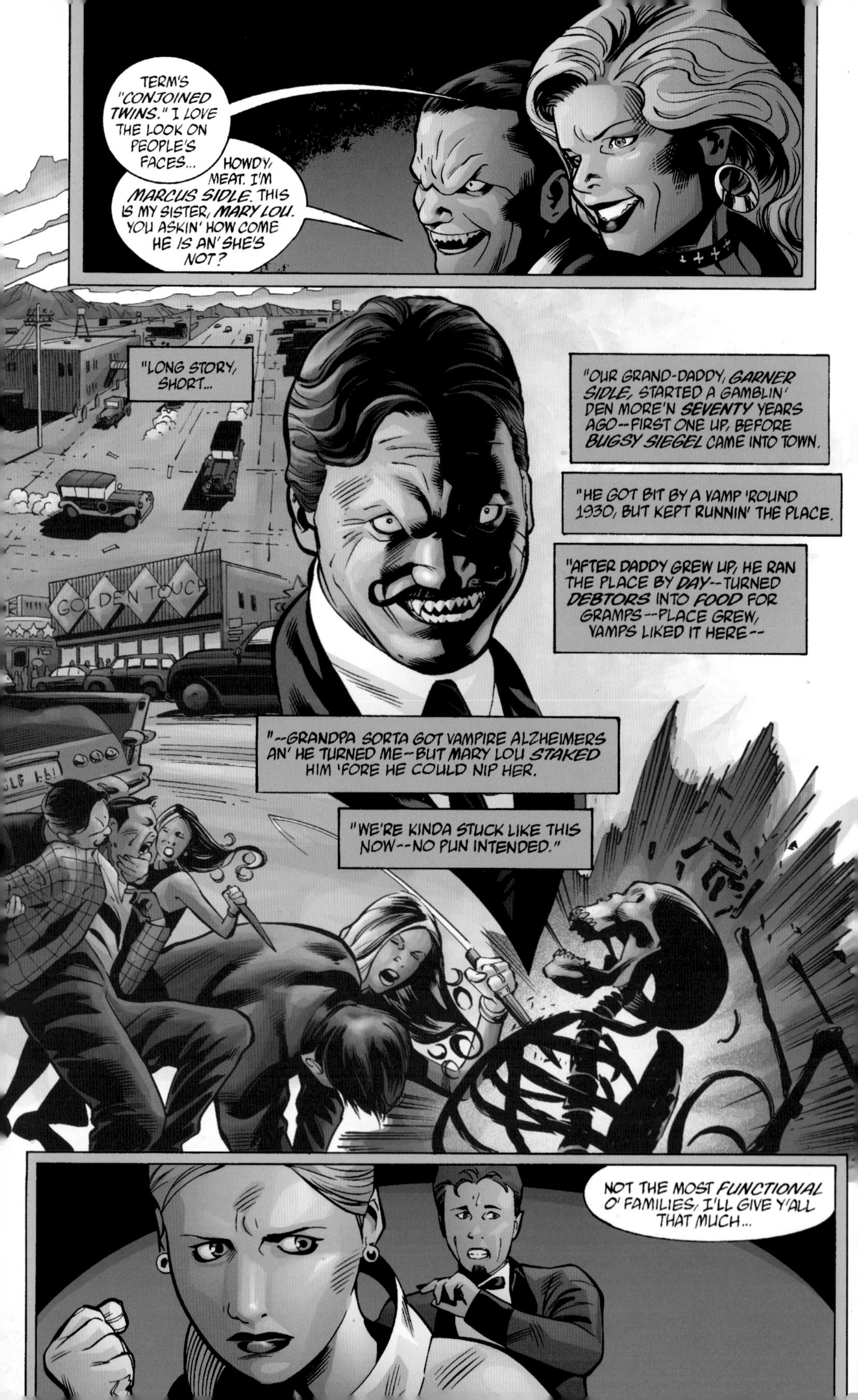
TERM'S "CONJOINED TWINS." I LOVE THE LOOK ON PEOPLE'S FACES...
HOWDY, MEAT. I'M MARCUS SIDLE. THIS IS MY SISTER, MARY LOU. YOU ASKIN' HOW COME HE IS AN' SHE'S NOT?
"LONG STORY, SHORT...
"OUR GRAND-DADDY, GARNER SIDLE, STARTED A GAMBLIN' DEN MORE'N SEVENTY YEARS AGO--FIRST ONE UP, BEFORE BUGSY SIEGEL CAME INTO TOWN.
"HE GOT BIT BY A VAMP 'ROUND 1930, BUT KEPT RUNNIN' THE PLACE.
"AFTER DADDY GREW UP, HE RAN THE PLACE BY DAY--TURNED DEBTORS INTO FOOD FOR GRAMPS--PLACE GREW, VAMPS LIKED IT HERE--
GOLDEN TOUCH
"--GRANDPA SORTA GOT VAMPIRE ALZHEIMERS AN' HE TURNED ME--BUT MARY LOU STAKED HIM 'FORE HE COULD NIP HER.
"WE'RE KINDA STUCK LIKE THIS NOW--NO PUN INTENDED."
NOT THE MOST FUNCTIONAL O' FAMILIES, I'LL GIVE Y'ALL THAT MUCH...

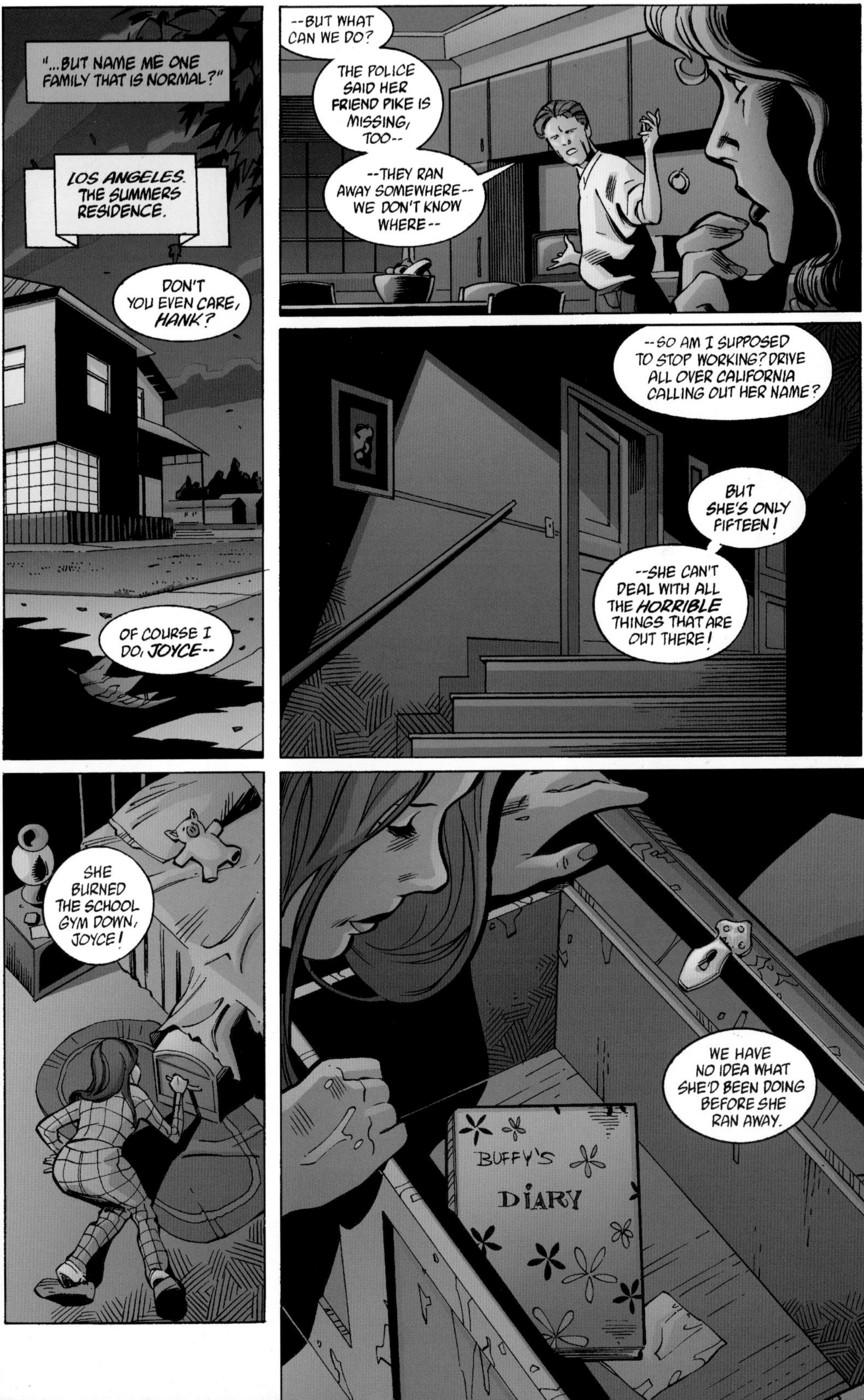

"...BUT NAME ME ONE FAMILY THAT IS NORMAL?"
LOS ANGELES. THE SUMMERS RESIDENCE.
DON'T YOU EVEN CARE, HANK?
OF COURSE I DO, JOYCE--
--BUT WHAT CAN WE DO?
THE POLICE SAID HER FRIEND PIKE IS MISSING, TOO--
--THEY RAN AWAY SOMEWHERE-- WE DON'T KNOW WHERE--
--SO AM I SUPPOSED TO STOP WORKING? DRIVE ALL OVER CALIFORNIA CALLING OUT HER NAME?
BUT SHE'S ONLY FIFTEEN!
--SHE CAN'T DEAL WITH ALL THE HORRIBLE THINGS THAT ARE OUT THERE!
SHE BURNED THE SCHOOL GYM DOWN, JOYCE!
WE HAVE NO IDEA WHAT SHE'D BEEN DOING BEFORE SHE RAN AWAY.
BUFFY'S DIARY

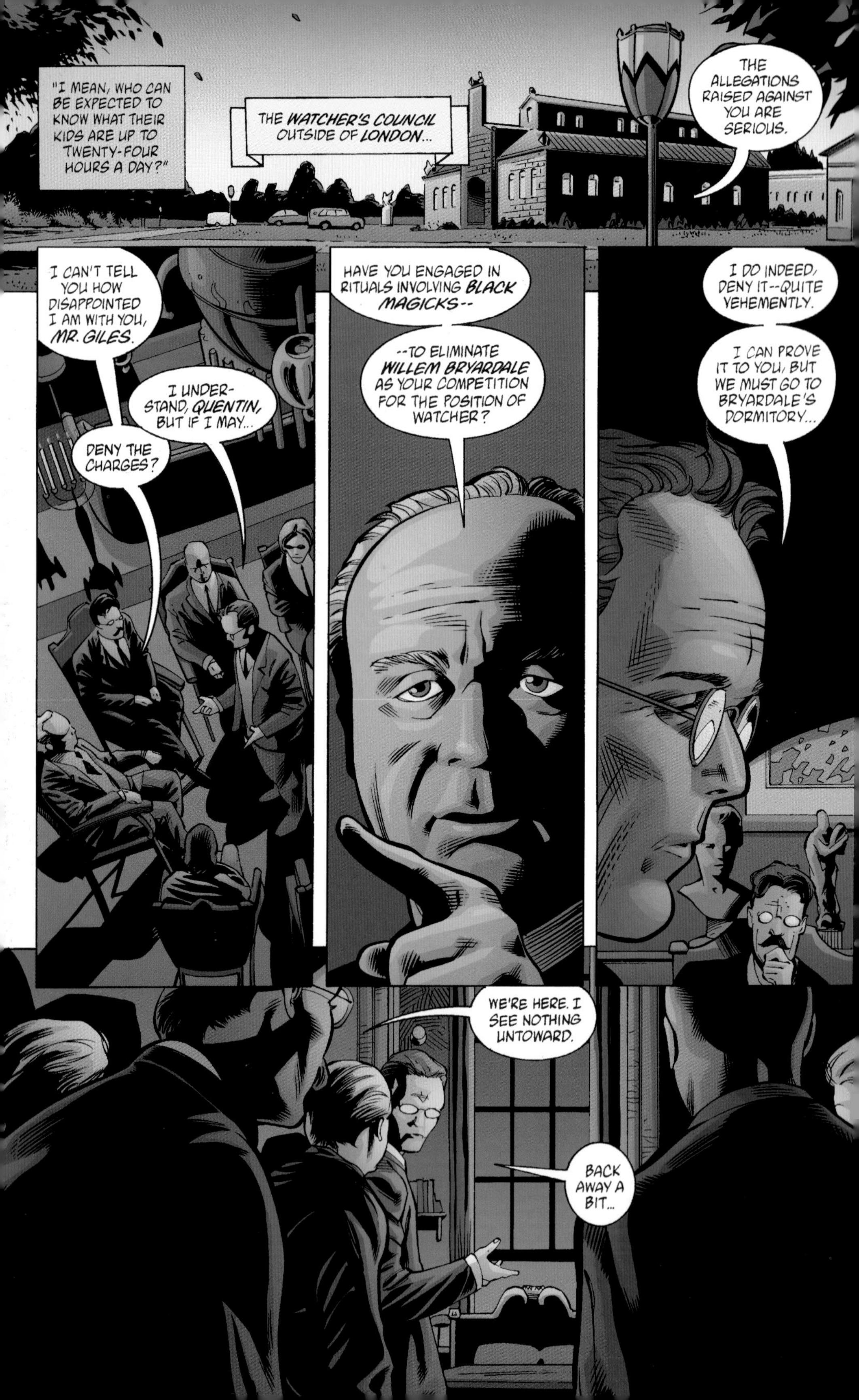
"I MEAN, WHO CAN BE EXPECTED TO KNOW WHAT THEIR KIDS ARE UP TO TWENTY-FOUR HOURS A DAY?"
THE WATCHER'S COUNCIL OUTSIDE OF LONDON...
THE ALLEGATIONS RAISED AGAINST YOU ARE SERIOUS.
I CAN'T TELL YOU HOW DISAPPOINTED I AM WITH YOU, MR. GILES.
I UNDERSTAND, QUENTIN, BUT IF I MAY...
DENY THE CHARGES?
HAVE YOU ENGAGED IN RITUALS INVOLVING BLACK MAGICKS--
--TO ELIMINATE WILLEM BRYARDALE AS YOUR COMPETITION FOR THE POSITION OF WATCHER?
I DO INDEED, DENY IT--QUITE YEHEMENTLY.
I CAN PROVE IT TO YOU, BUT WE MUST GO TO BRYARDALE'S DORMITORY...
WE'RE HERE. I SEE NOTHING UNTOWARD.
BACK AWAY A BIT...

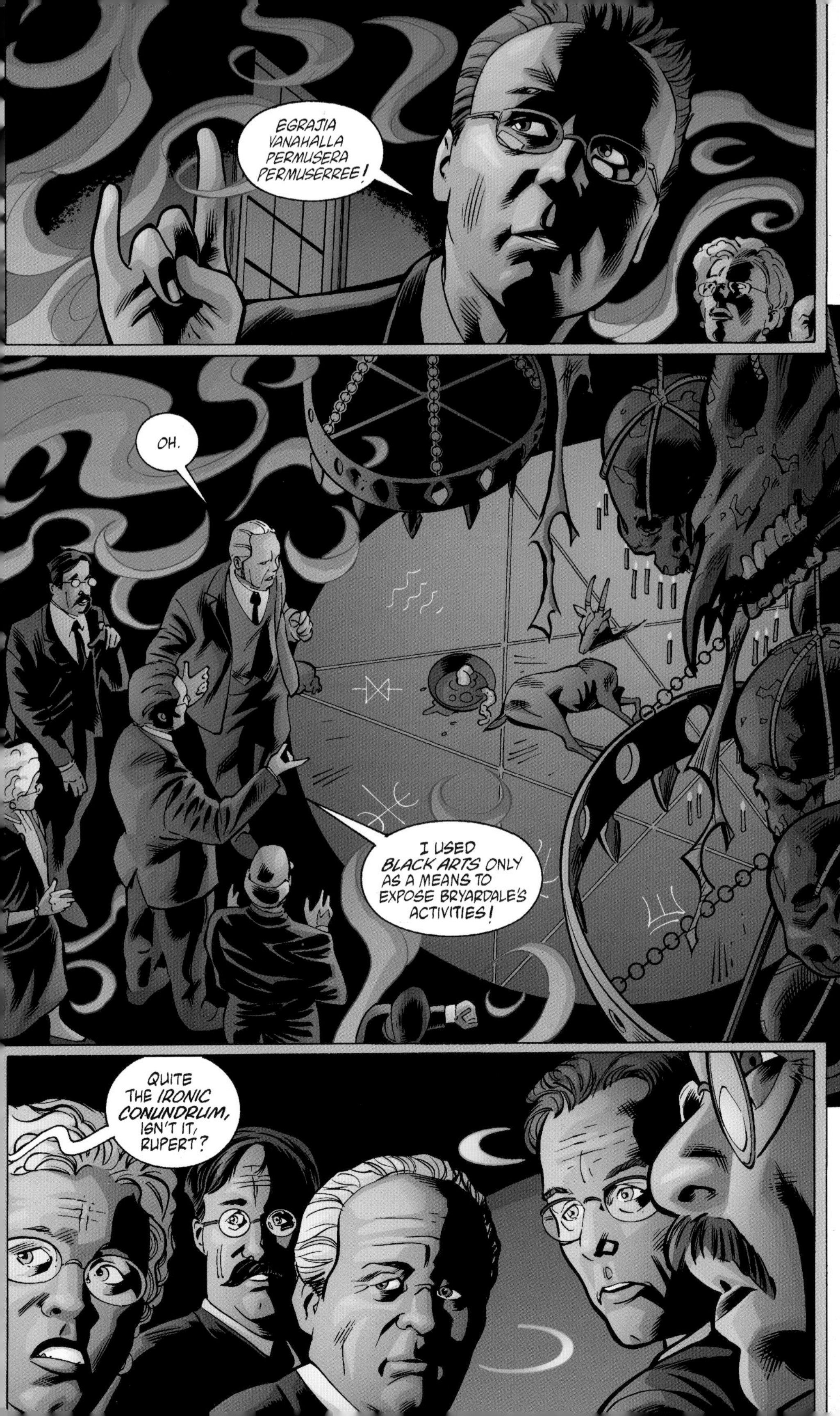
EGRAJIA VANAHALLA PERMUSERA PERMUSERREE!
OH.
I USED BLACK ARTS ONLY AS A MEANS TO EXPOSE BRYARDALE'S ACTIVITIES!
QUITE THE IRONIC CONUNDRUM, ISN'T IT, RUPERT?

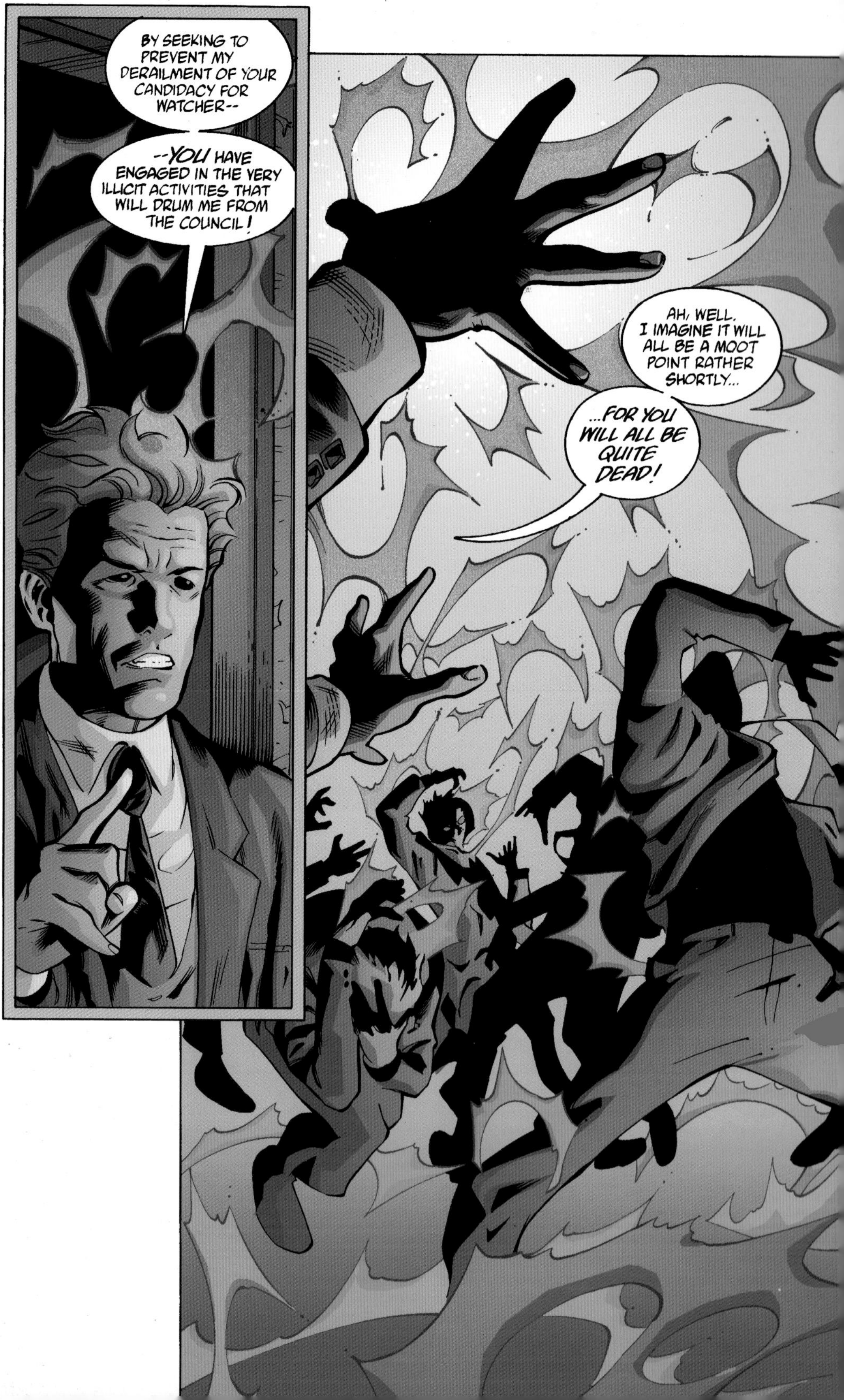
BY SEEKING TO PREVENT MY DERAILMENT OF YOUR CANDIDACY FOR WATCHER--
--YOU HAVE ENGAGED IN THE VERY ILLICIT ACTIVITIES THAT WILL DRUM ME FROM THE COUNCIL!
AH, WELL. I IMAGINE IT WILL ALL BE A MOOT POINT RATHER SHORTLY...
...FOR YOU WILL ALL BE QUITE DEAD!

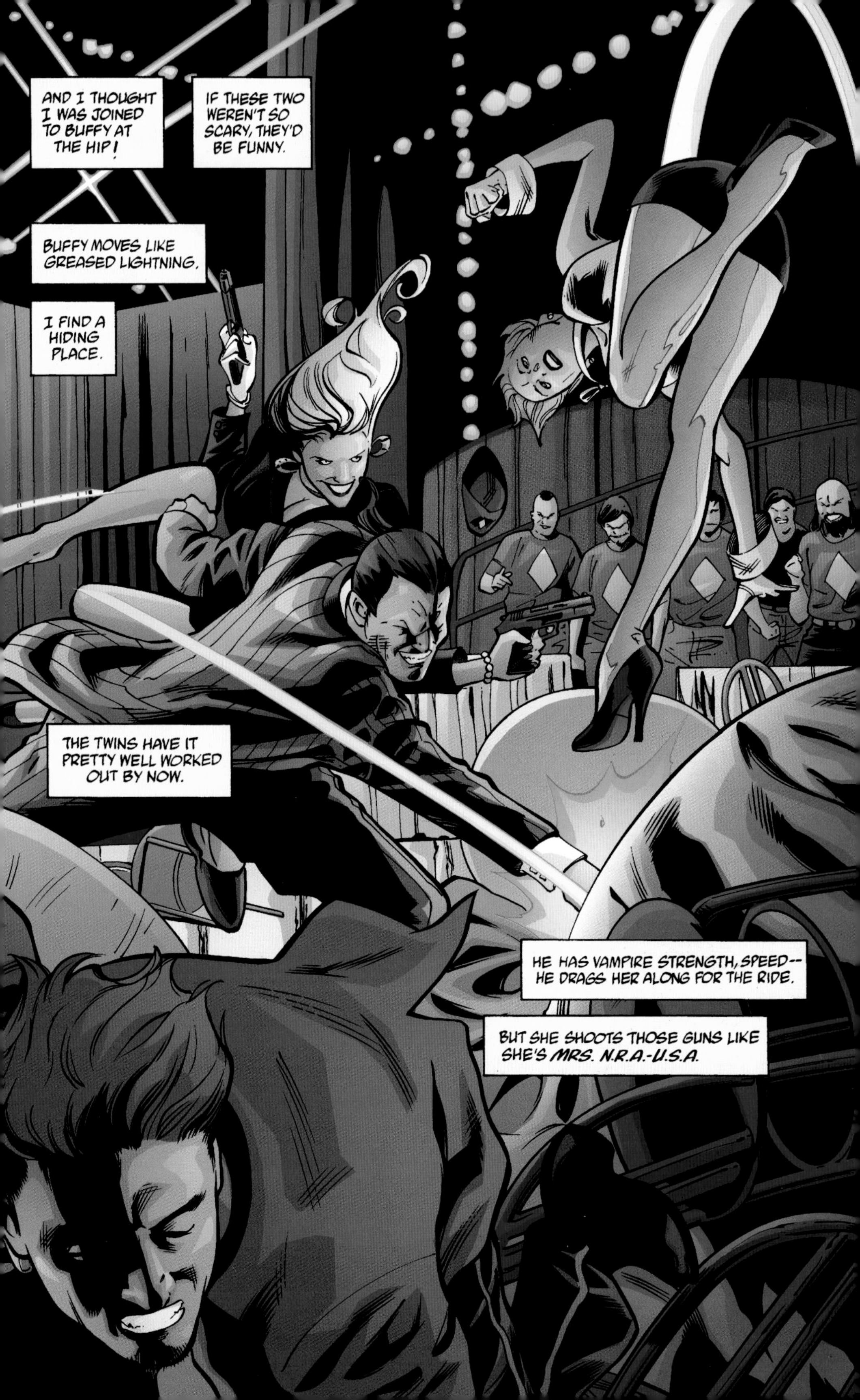
AND I THOUGHT I WAS JOINED TO BUFFY AT THE HIP!
IF THESE TWO WEREN'T SO SCARY, THEY'D BE FUNNY.
BUFFY MOVES LIKE GREASED LIGHTNING.
I FIND A HIDING PLACE.
THE TWINS HAVE IT PRETTY WELL WORKED OUT BY NOW.
HE HAS VAMPIRE STRENGTH, SPEED-- HE DRAGS HER ALONG FOR THE RIDE.
BUT SHE SHOOTS THOSE GUNS LIKE SHE'S *MRS. N.R.A.-U.S.A.*

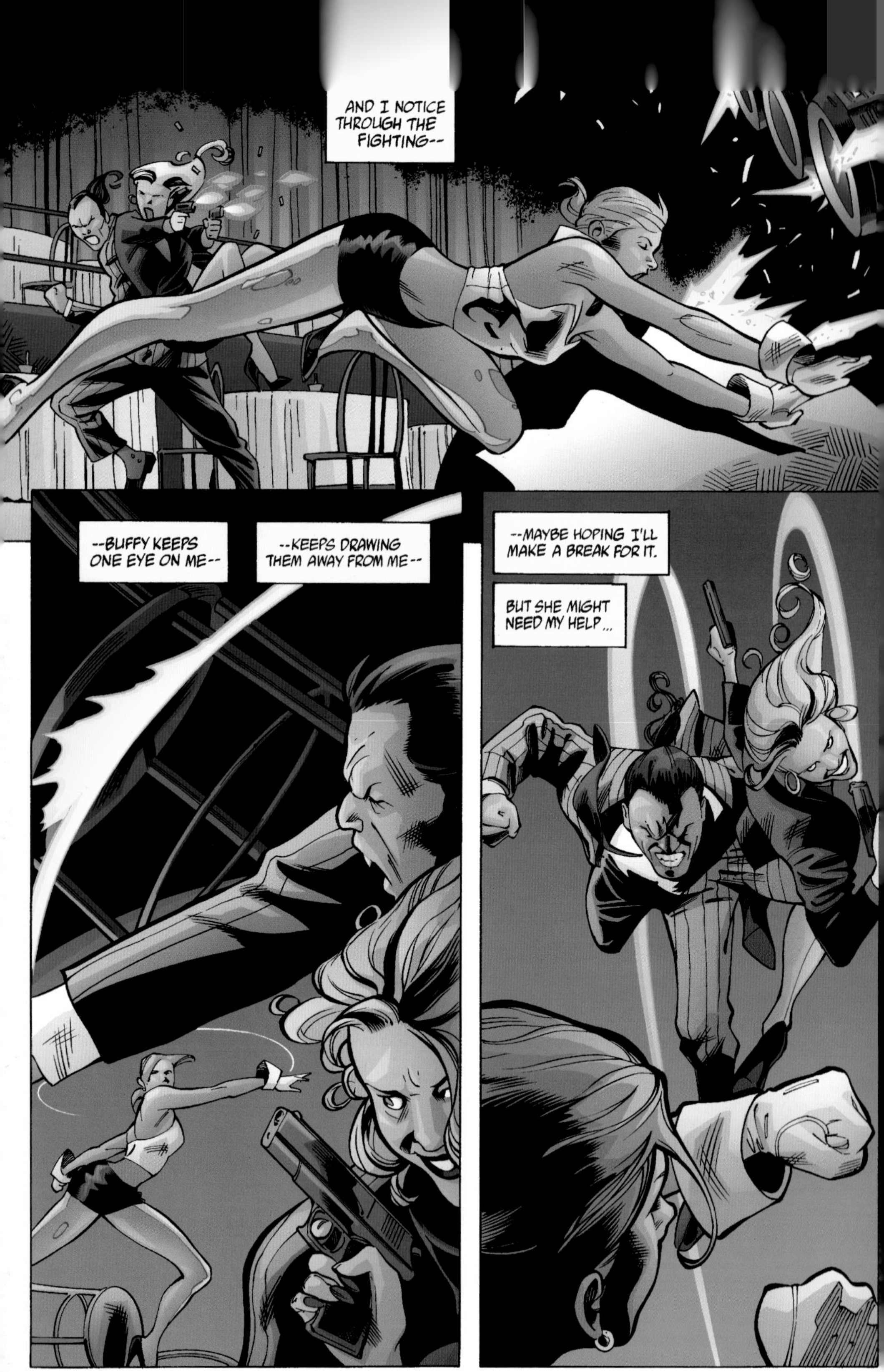
AND I NOTICE THROUGH THE FIGHTING--
--BUFFY KEEPS ONE EYE ON ME--
--KEEPS DRAWING THEM AWAY FROM ME--
--MAYBE HOPING I'LL MAKE A BREAK FOR IT.
BUT SHE MIGHT NEED MY HELP...

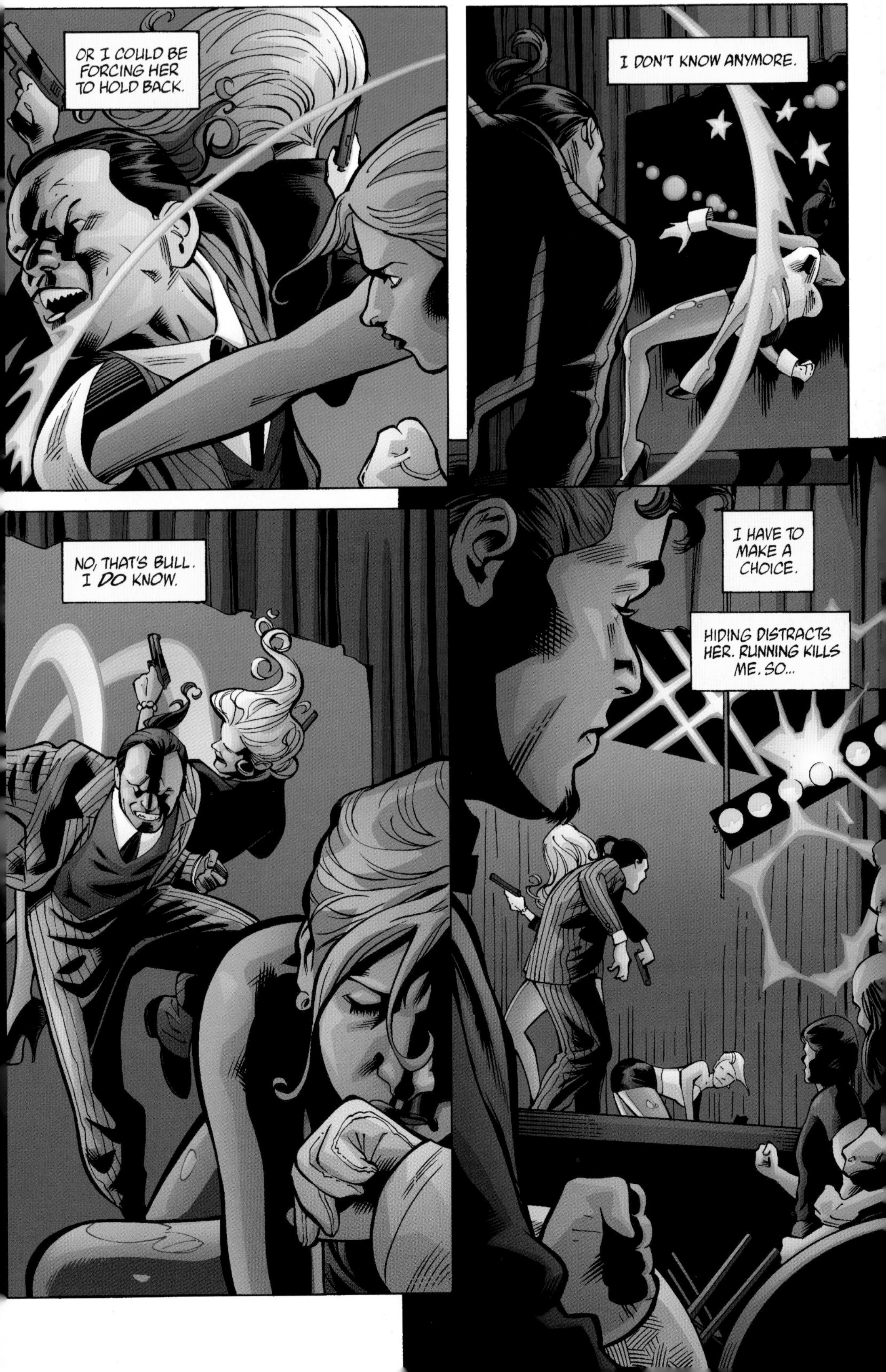
OR I COULD BE FORCING HER TO HOLD BACK.
I DON'T KNOW ANYMORE.
NO, THAT'S BULL. I DO KNOW.
I HAVE TO MAKE A CHOICE.
HIDING DISTRACTS HER. RUNNING KILLS ME. SO...

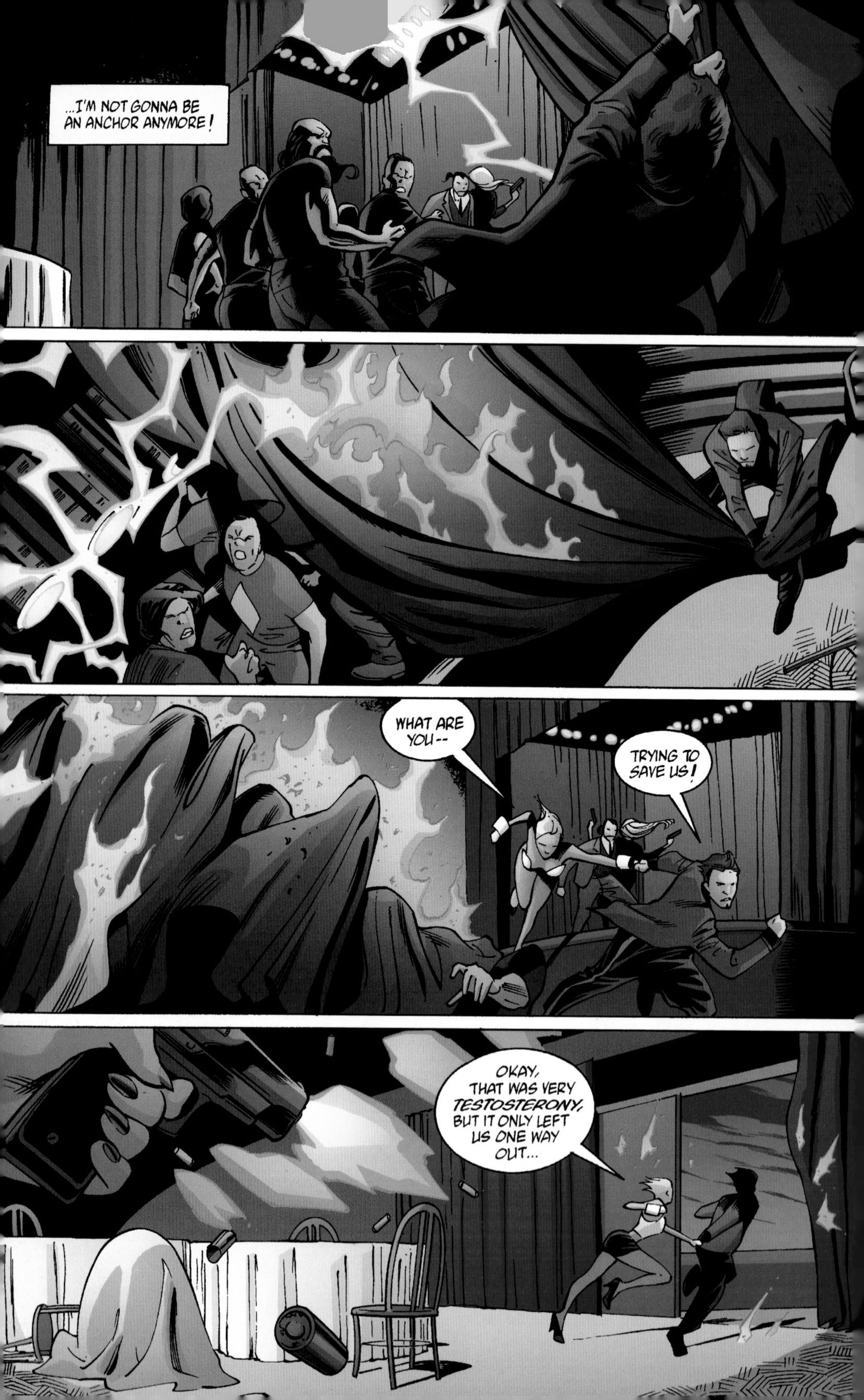
...I'M NOT GONNA BE AN ANCHOR ANYMORE!
WHAT ARE YOU--
TRYING TO SAVE US!
OKAY, THAT WAS VERY *TESTOSTERONY,* BUT IT ONLY LEFT US ONE WAY OUT...

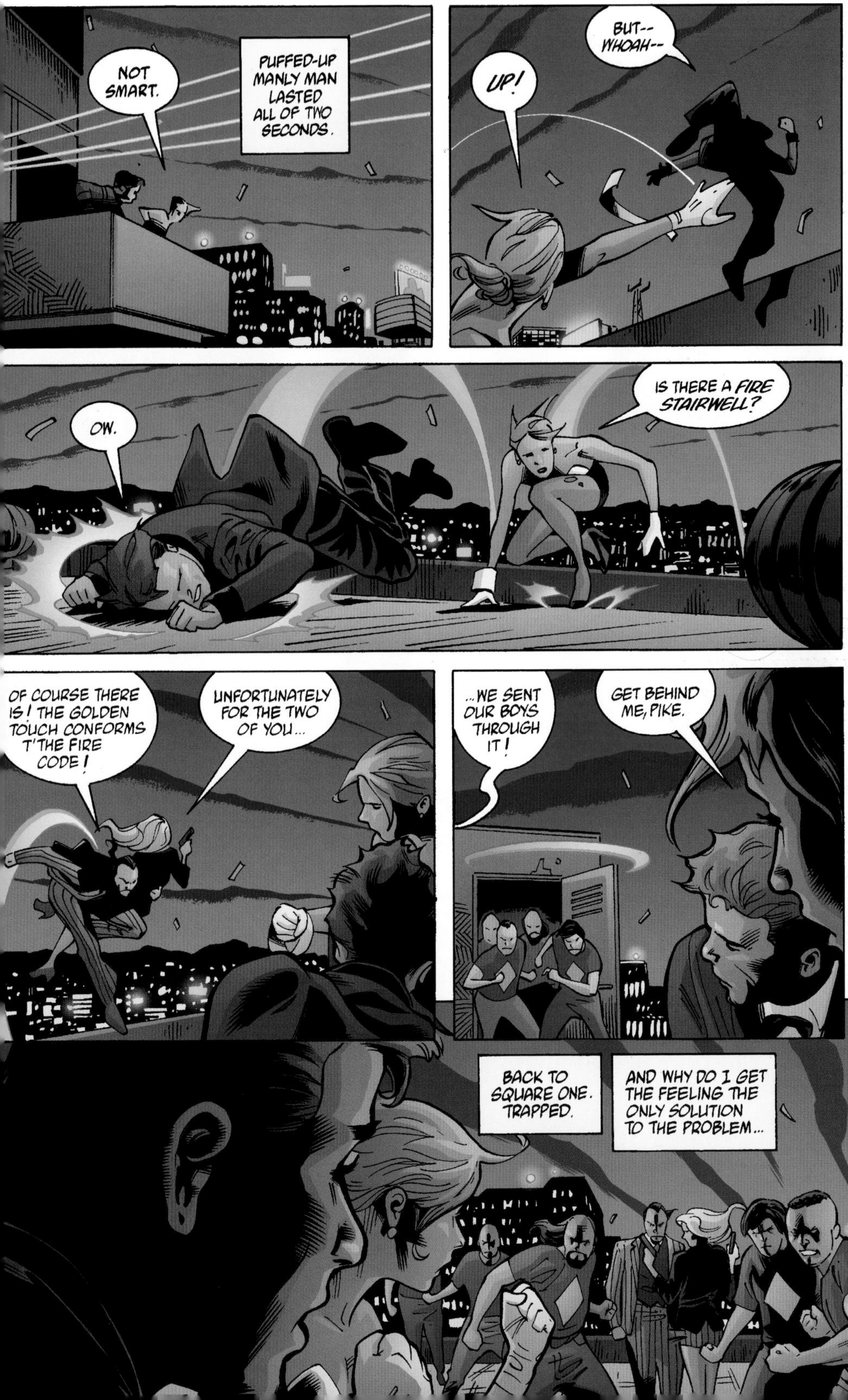
PUFFED-UP MANLY MAN LASTED ALL OF TWO SECONDS.
NOT SMART.
BUT-- WHOAH--
UP!
OW.
IS THERE A FIRE STAIRWELL?
OF COURSE THERE IS! THE GOLDEN TOUCH CONFORMS T'THE FIRE CODE!
UNFORTUNATELY FOR THE TWO OF YOU...
...WE SENT OUR BOYS THROUGH IT!
GET BEHIND ME, PIKE.
BACK TO SQUARE ONE. TRAPPED.
AND WHY DO I GET THE FEELING THE ONLY SOLUTION TO THE PROBLEM...

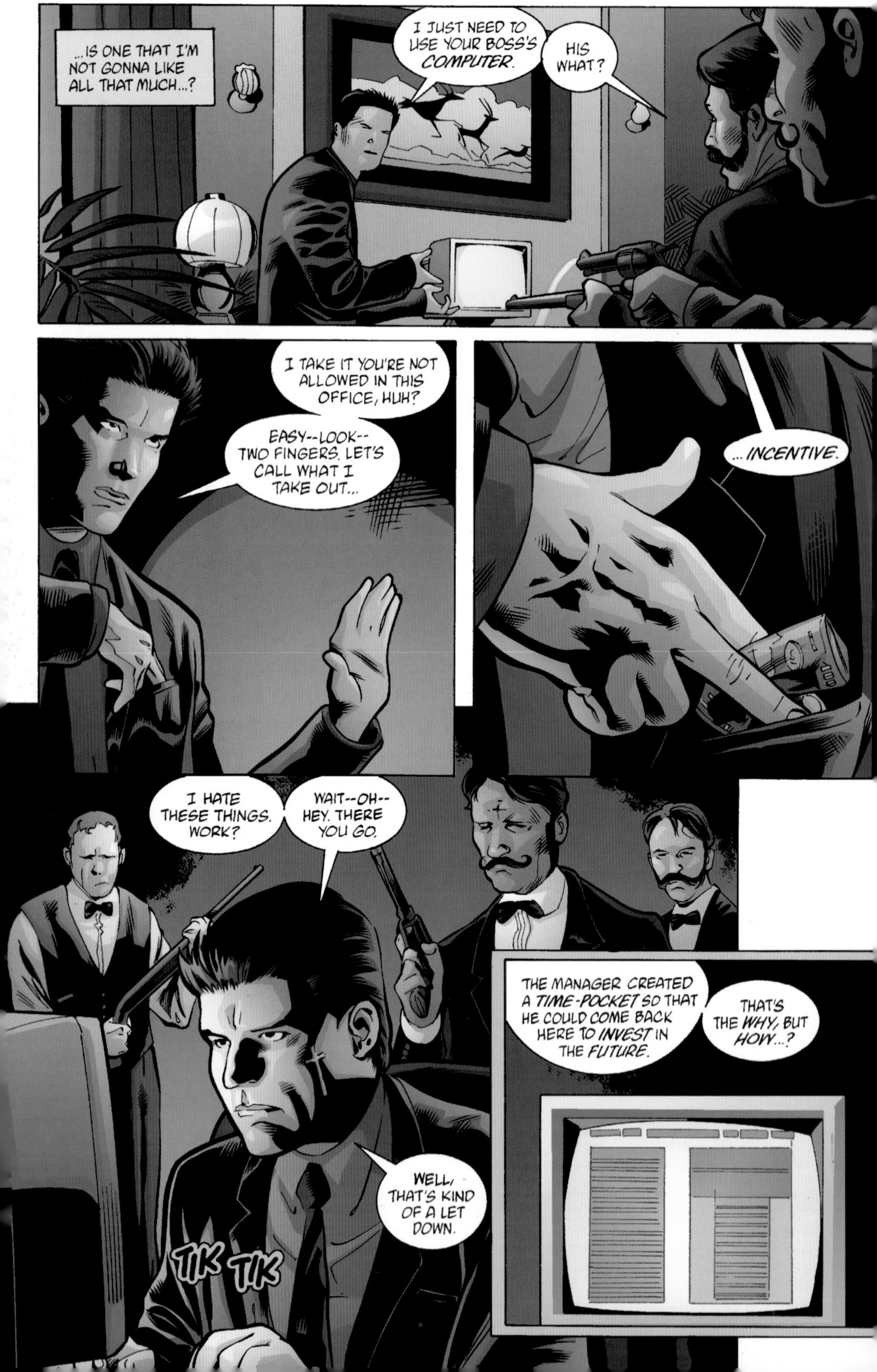
...IS ONE THAT I'M NOT GONNA LIKE ALL THAT MUCH...?
I JUST NEED TO USE YOUR BOSS'S COMPUTER.
HIS WHAT?
I TAKE IT YOU'RE NOT ALLOWED IN THIS OFFICE, HUH?
EASY--LOOK-- TWO FINGERS. LET'S CALL WHAT I TAKE OUT...
...INCENTIVE.
I HATE THESE THINGS. WORK?
WAIT--OH-- HEY. THERE YOU GO.
WELL, THAT'S KIND OF A LET DOWN.
TIK TIK
THE MANAGER CREATED A TIME-POCKET SO THAT HE COULD COME BACK HERE TO INVEST IN THE FUTURE.
THAT'S THE WHY, BUT HOW...?

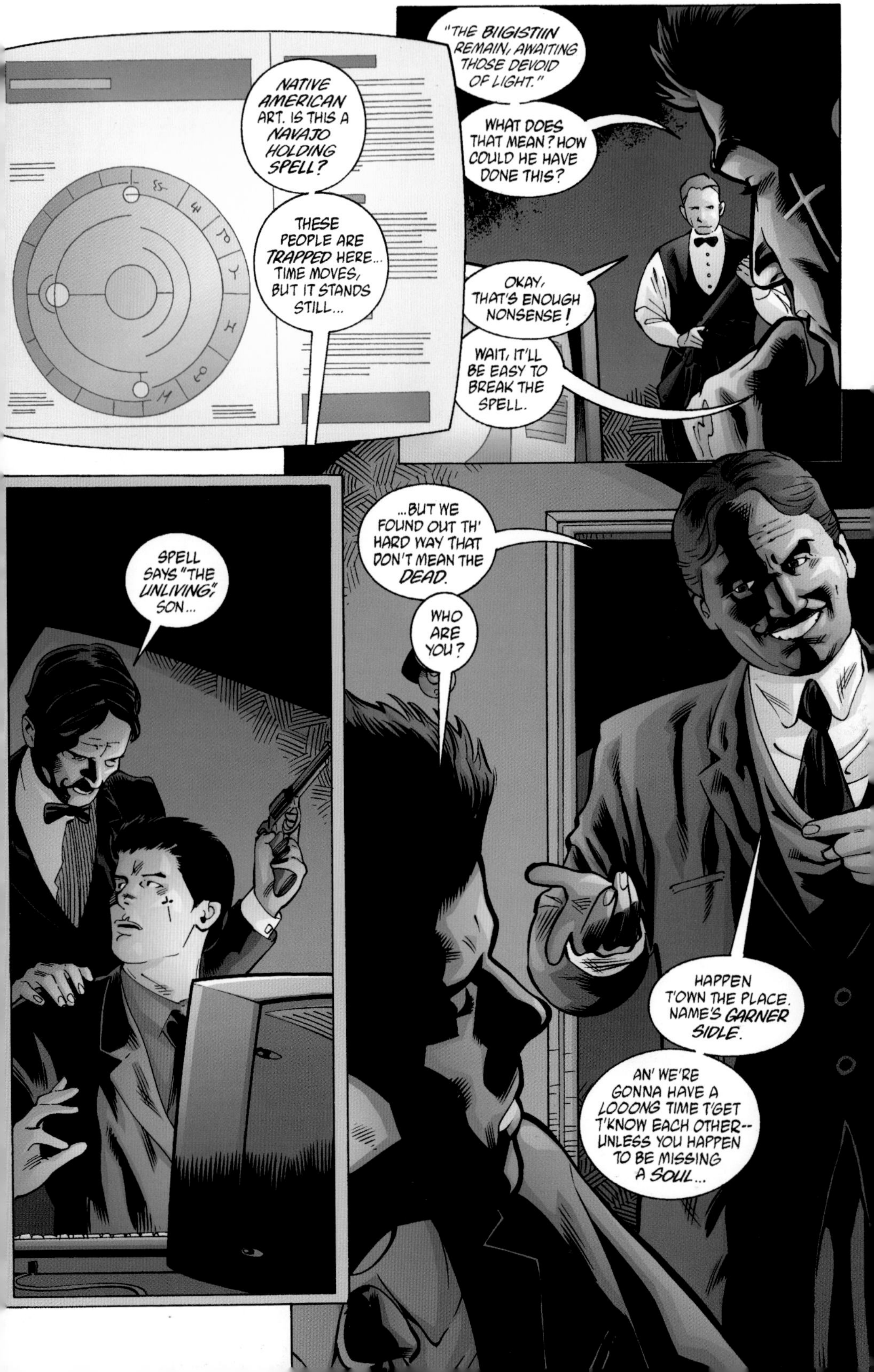
NATIVE AMERICAN ART. IS THIS A NAVAJO HOLDING SPELL?
THESE PEOPLE ARE TRAPPED HERE... TIME MOVES, BUT IT STANDS STILL...
"THE BIIGISTIIN REMAIN, AWAITING THOSE DEVOID OF LIGHT."
WHAT DOES THAT MEAN? HOW COULD HE HAVE DONE THIS?
OKAY, THAT'S ENOUGH NONSENSE!
WAIT, IT'LL BE EASY TO BREAK THE SPELL.
SPELL SAYS "THE UNLIVING," SON...
...BUT WE FOUND OUT TH' HARD WAY THAT DON'T MEAN THE DEAD.
WHO ARE YOU?
HAPPEN T'OWN THE PLACE. NAME'S GARNER SIDLE.
AN' WE'RE GONNA HAVE A LOOONG TIME T'GET T'KNOW EACH OTHER-- UNLESS YOU HAPPEN TO BE MISSING A SOUL...

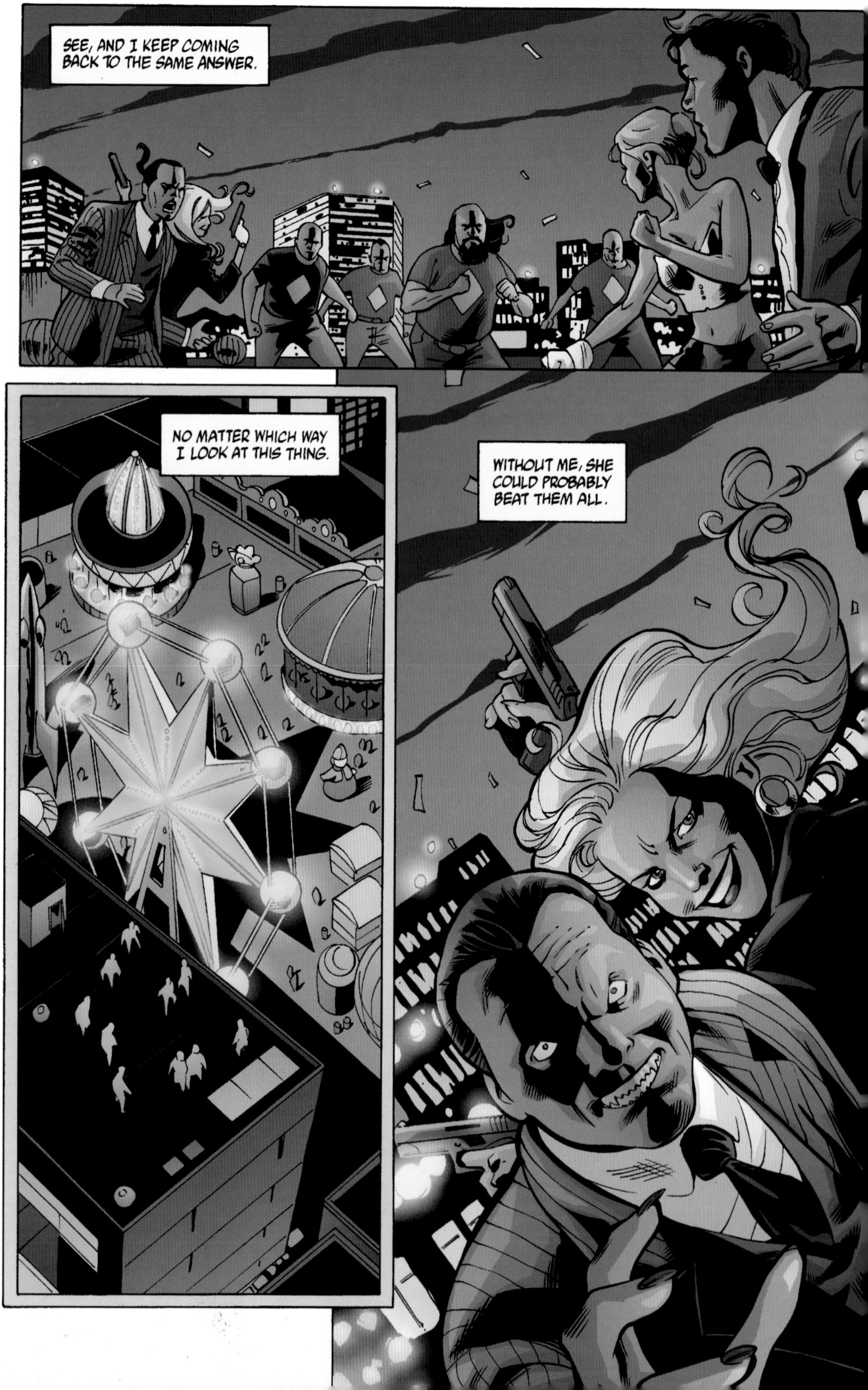
SEE, AND I KEEP COMING BACK TO THE SAME ANSWER.
NO MATTER WHICH WAY I LOOK AT THIS THING.
WITHOUT ME, SHE COULD PROBABLY BEAT THEM ALL.

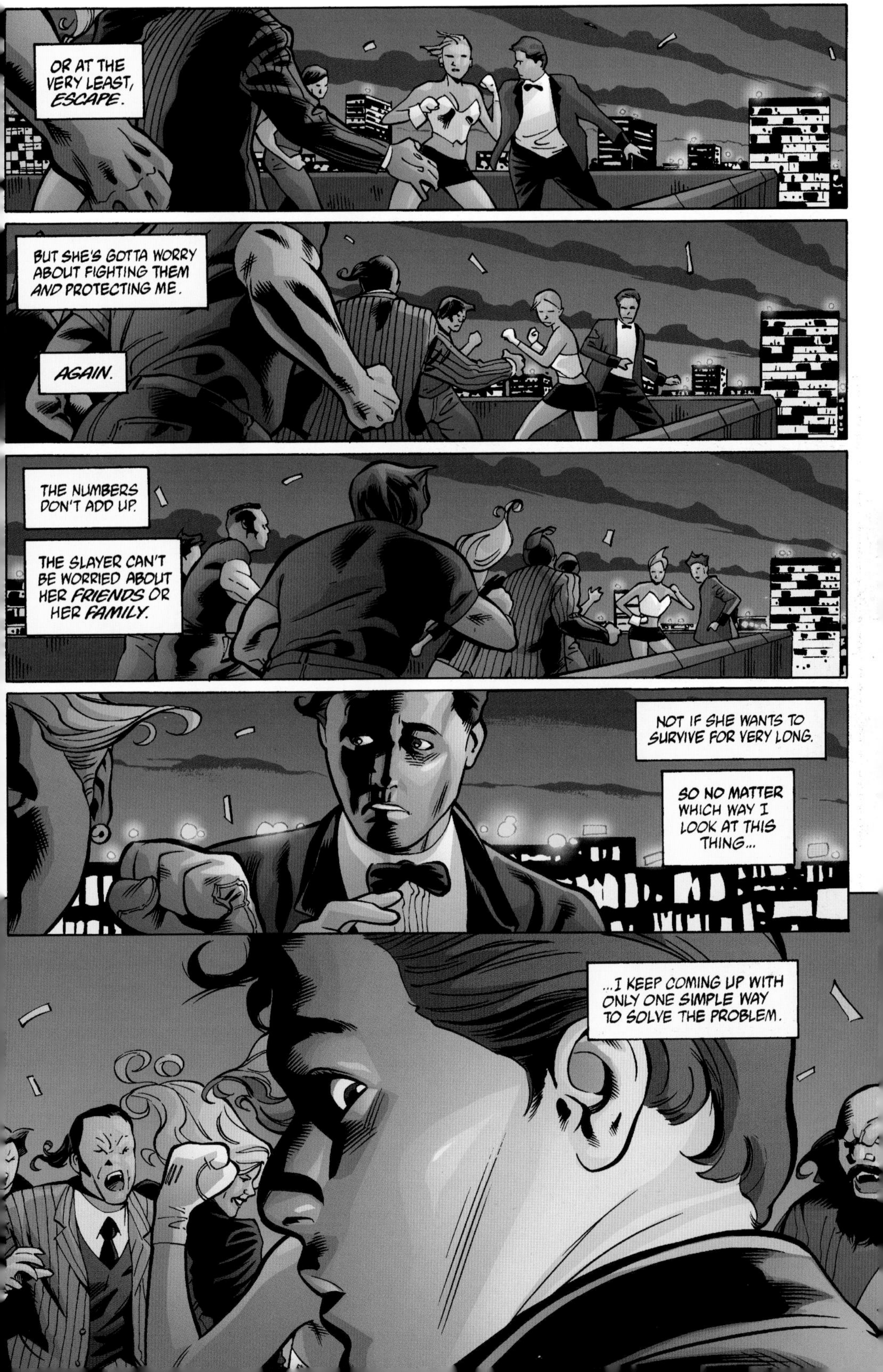
OR AT THE VERY LEAST, ESCAPE.
BUT SHE'S GOTTA WORRY ABOUT FIGHTING THEM AND PROTECTING ME.
AGAIN.
THE NUMBERS DON'T ADD UP.
THE SLAYER CAN'T BE WORRIED ABOUT HER FRIENDS OR HER FAMILY.
NOT IF SHE WANTS TO SURVIVE FOR VERY LONG.
SO NO MATTER WHICH WAY I LOOK AT THIS THING...
...I KEEP COMING UP WITH ONLY ONE SIMPLE WAY TO SOLVE THE PROBLEM.

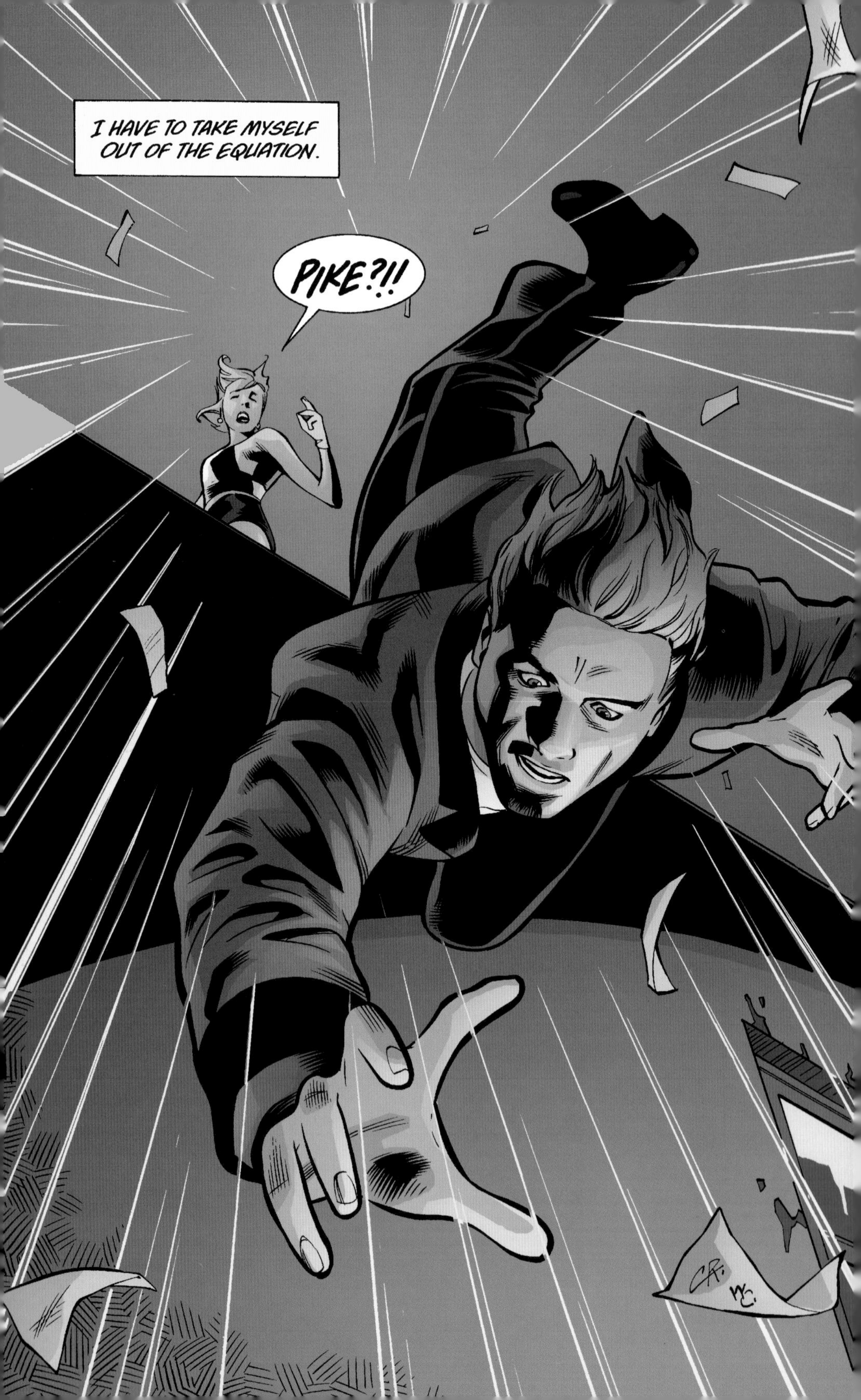
I HAVE TO TAKE MYSELF OUT OF THE EQUATION.
PIKE?!!

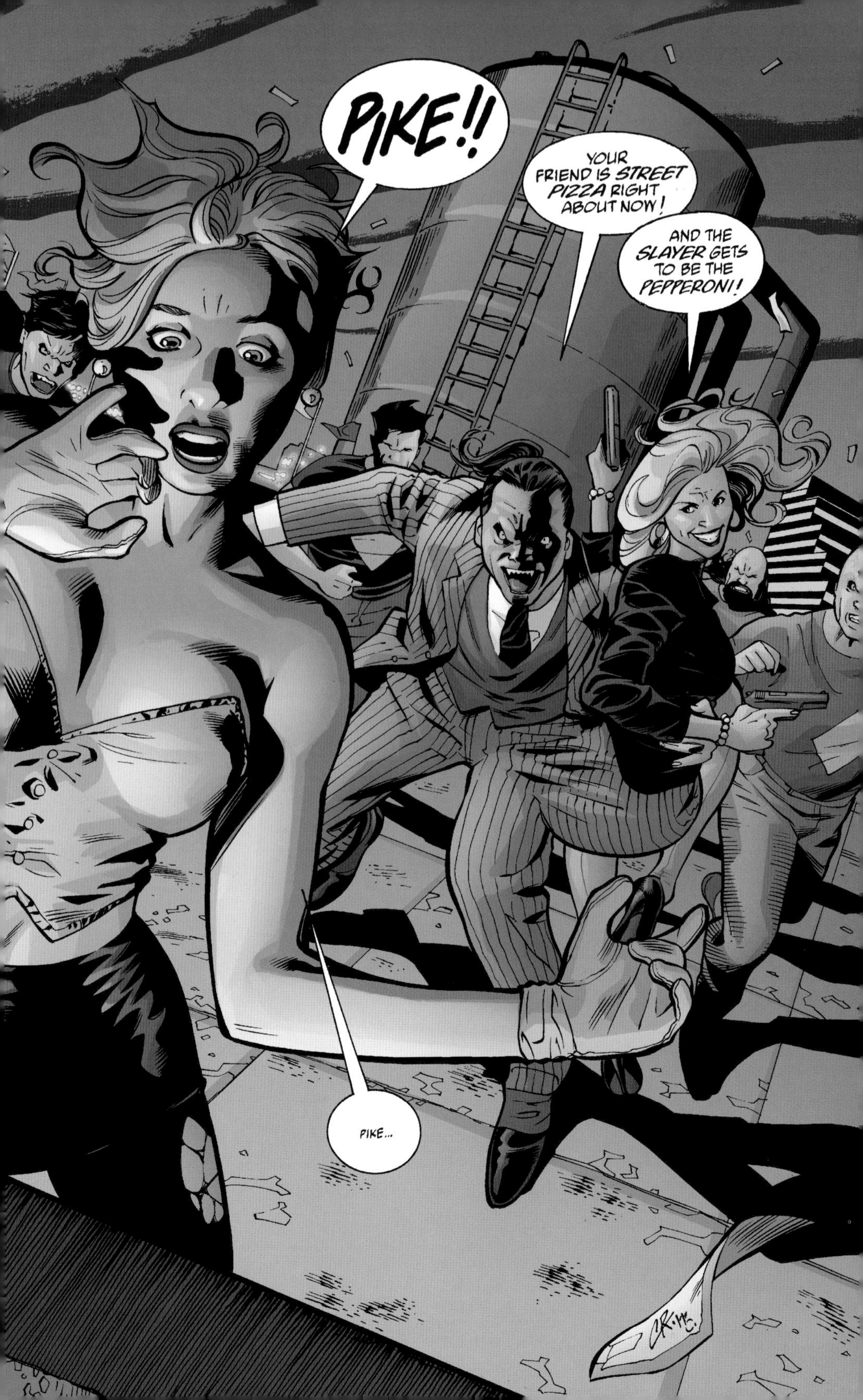
PIKE!!
YOUR FRIEND IS STREET PIZZA RIGHT ABOUT NOW!
AND THE SLAYER GETS TO BE THE PEPPERONI!
PIKE...

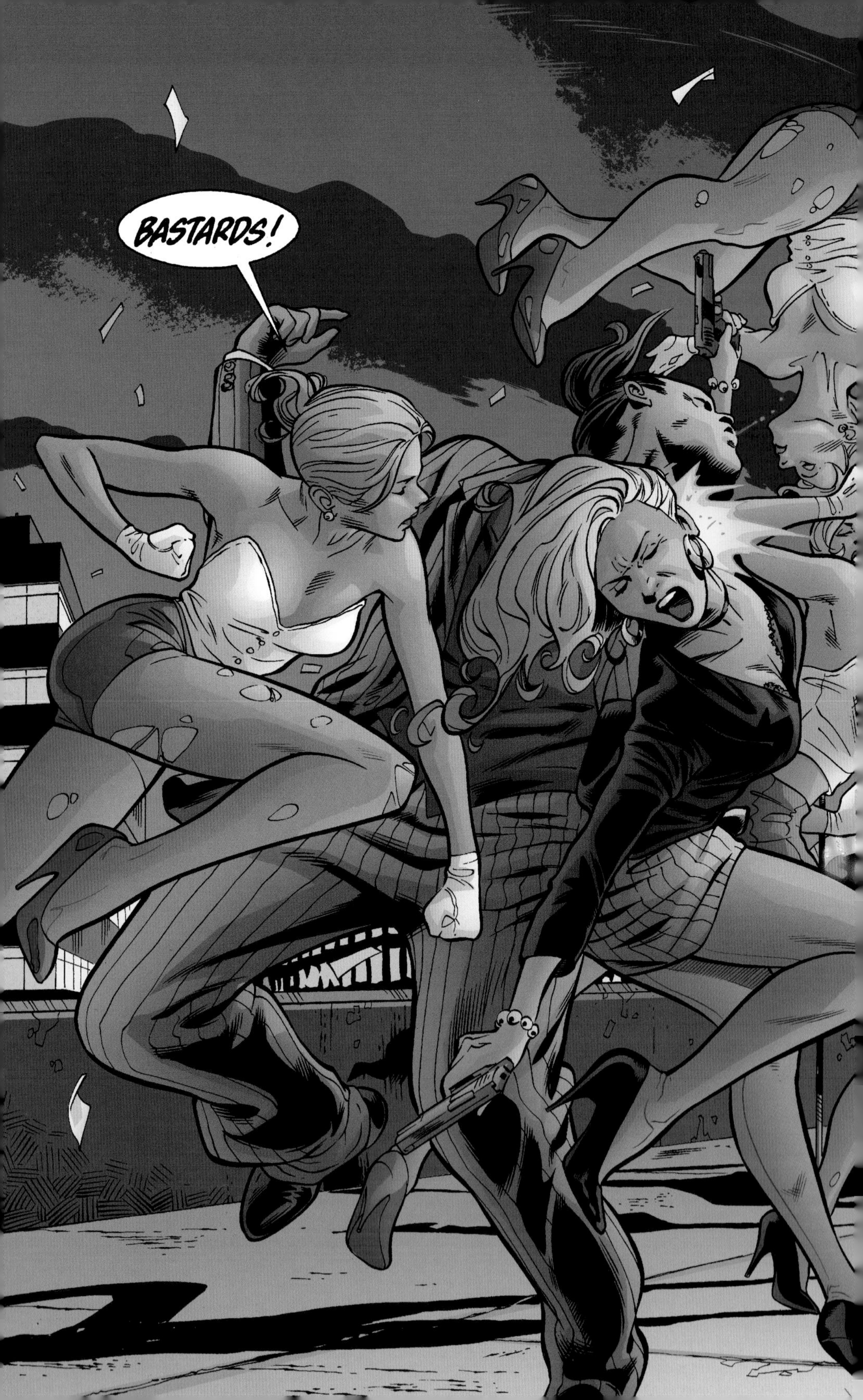
BASTARDS!

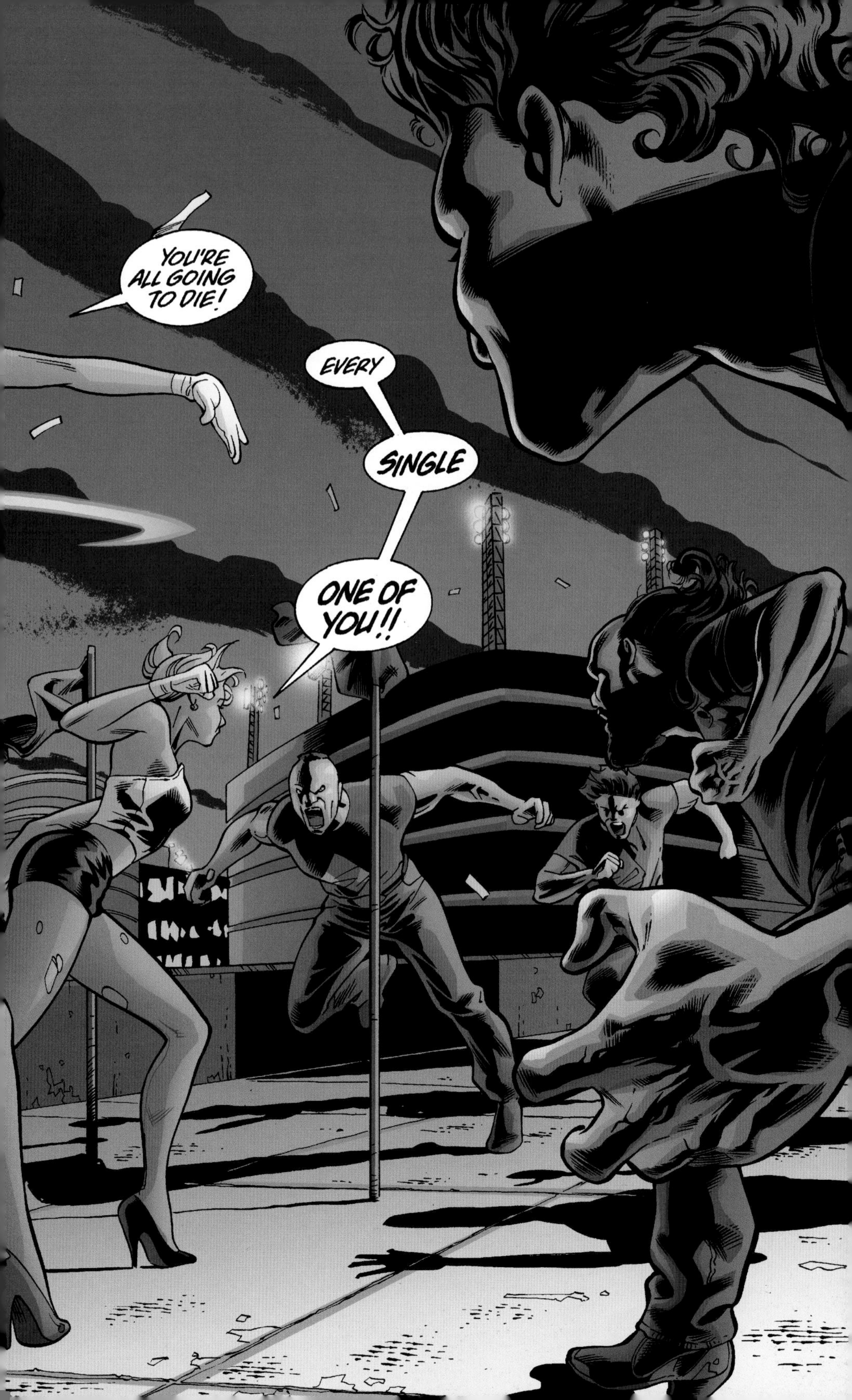
YOU'RE ALL GOING TO DIE!
EVERY
SINGLE
ONE OF YOU!!

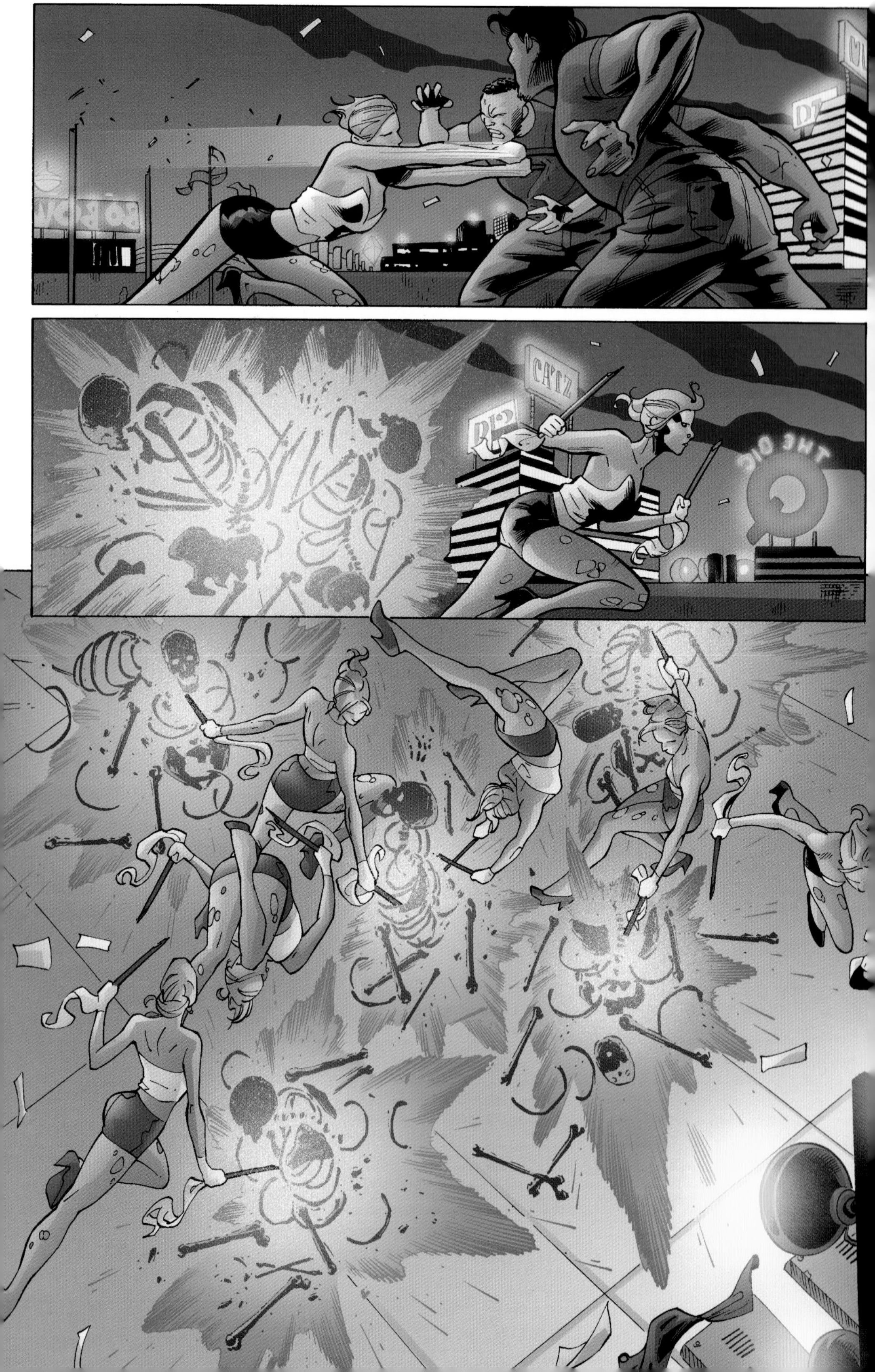
CAT'Z

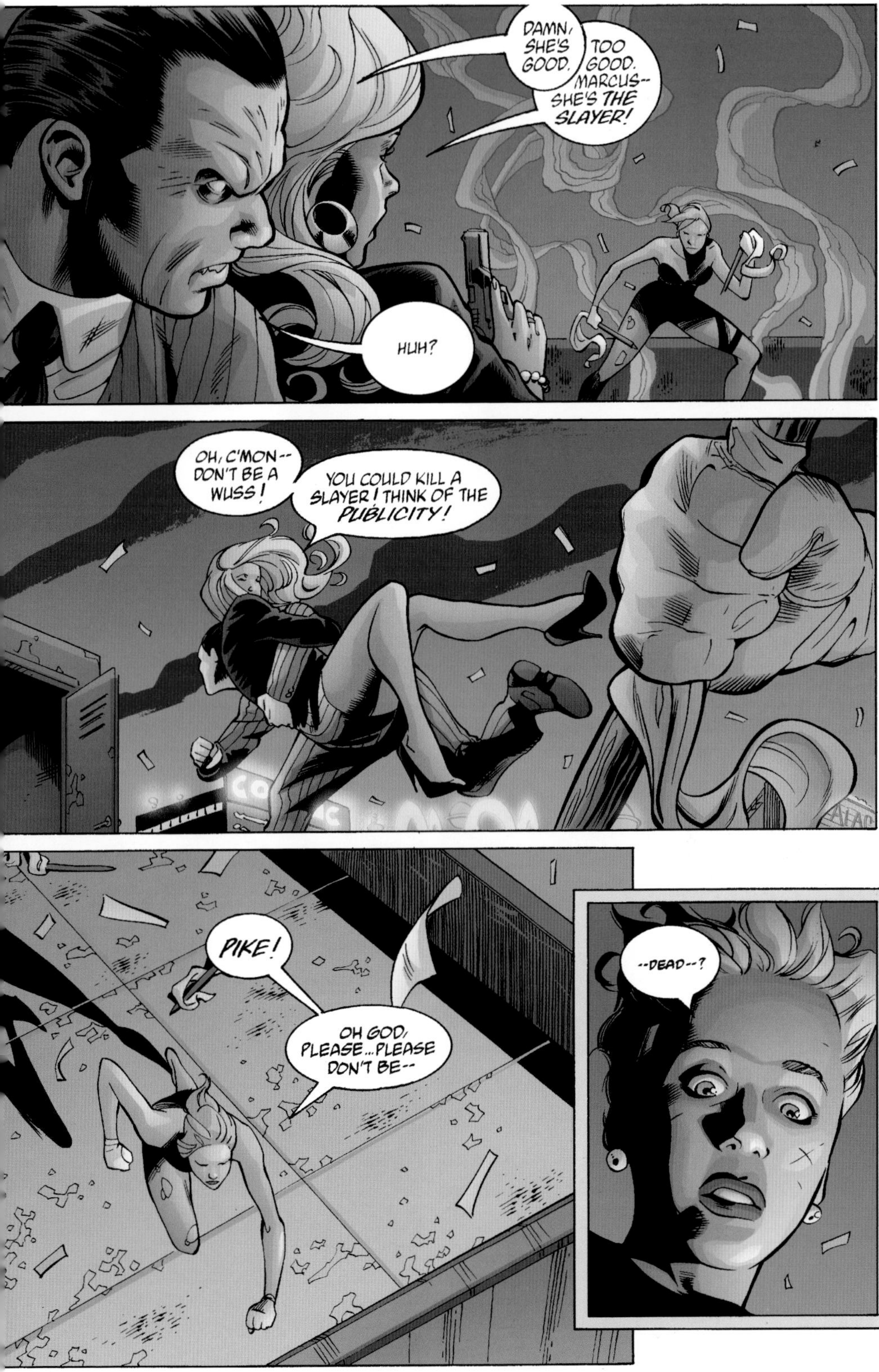
DAMN, SHE'S GOOD.
TOO GOOD. MARCUS-- SHE'S THE SLAYER!
HUH?
OH, C'MON-- DON'T BE A WUSS!
YOU COULD KILL A SLAYER! THINK OF THE PUBLICITY!
PIKE!
OH GOD, PLEASE...PLEASE DON'T BE--
--DEAD--?

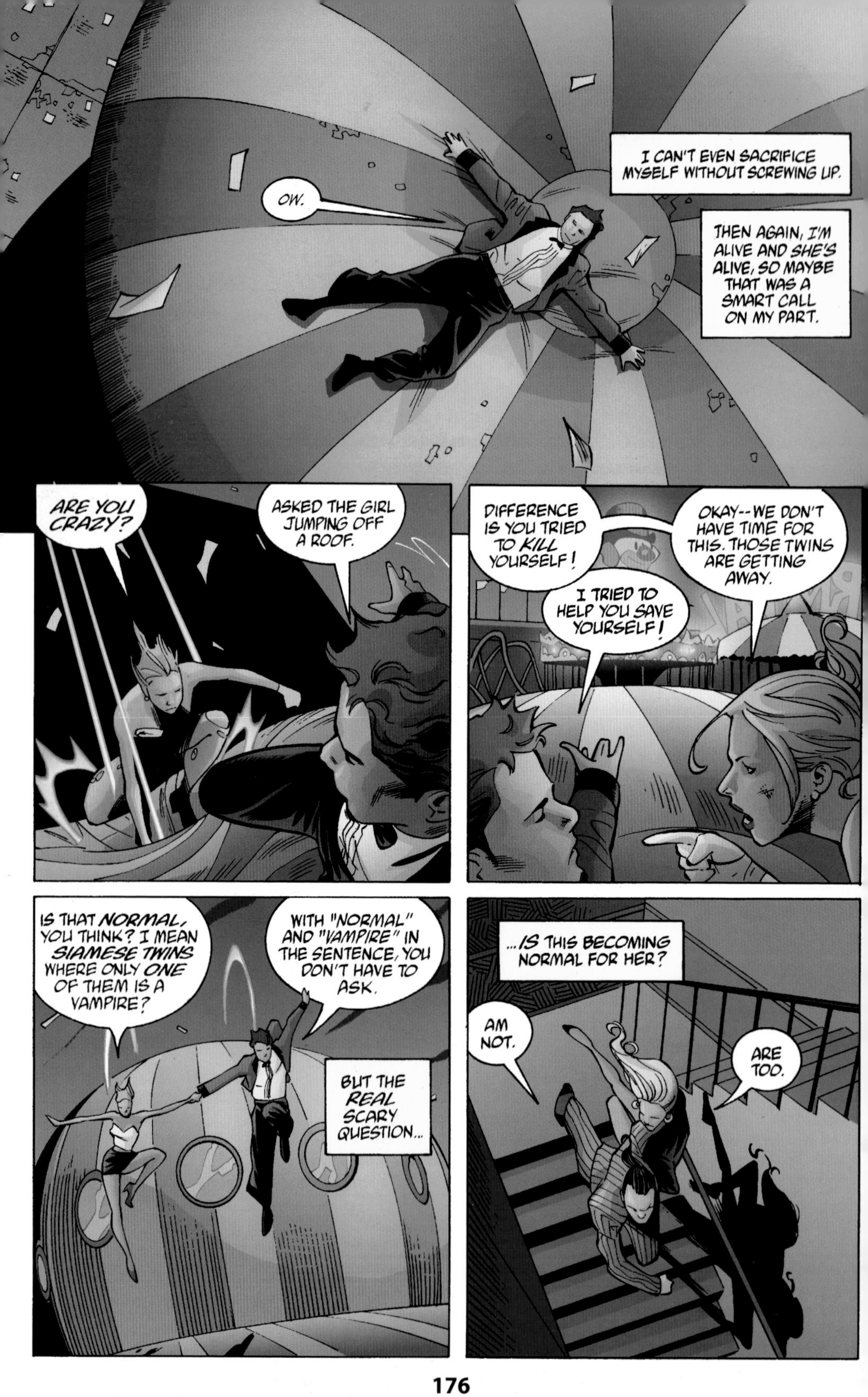
I CAN'T EVEN SACRIFICE MYSELF WITHOUT SCREWING UP.
OW.
THEN AGAIN, I'M ALIVE AND SHE'S ALIVE, SO MAYBE THAT WAS A SMART CALL ON MY PART.
ARE YOU CRAZY?
ASKED THE GIRL JUMPING OFF A ROOF.
DIFFERENCE IS YOU TRIED TO KILL YOURSELF!
I TRIED TO HELP YOU SAVE YOURSELF!
OKAY--WE DON'T HAVE TIME FOR THIS. THOSE TWINS ARE GETTING AWAY.
IS THAT NORMAL, YOU THINK? I MEAN SIAMESE TWINS WHERE ONLY ONE OF THEM IS A VAMPIRE?
WITH "NORMAL" AND "VAMPIRE" IN THE SENTENCE, YOU DON'T HAVE TO ASK.
BUT THE REAL SCARY QUESTION...
...IS THIS BECOMING NORMAL FOR HER?
AM NOT.
ARE TOO.

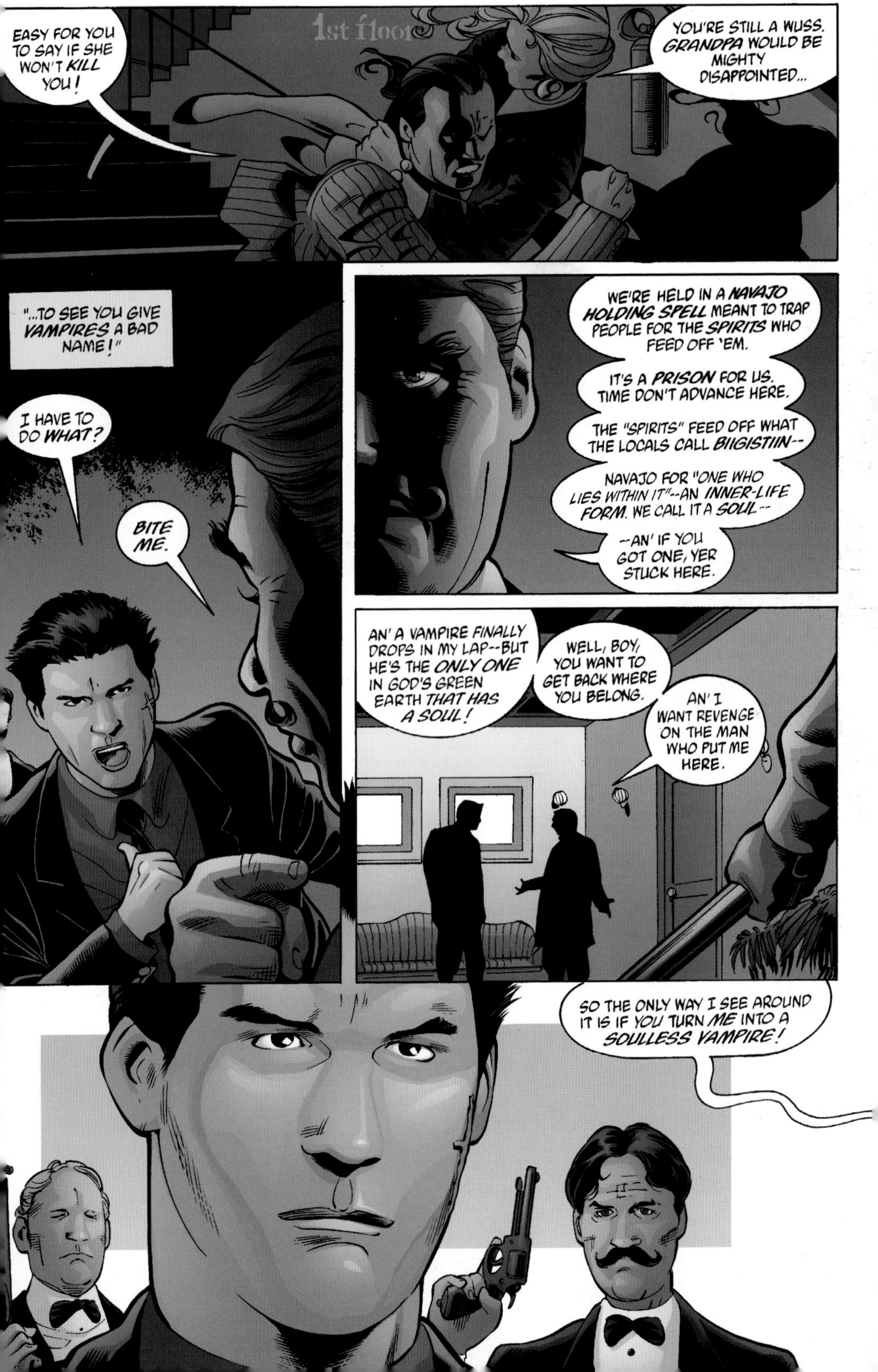

1st floor
EASY FOR YOU TO SAY IF SHE WON'T KILL YOU!
YOU'RE STILL A WUSS. GRANDPA WOULD BE MIGHTY DISAPPOINTED...
"...TO SEE YOU GIVE VAMPIRES A BAD NAME!"
I HAVE TO DO WHAT?
BITE ME.
WE'RE HELD IN A NAVAJO HOLDING SPELL MEANT TO TRAP PEOPLE FOR THE SPIRITS WHO FEED OFF 'EM.
IT'S A PRISON FOR US. TIME DON'T ADVANCE HERE.
THE "SPIRITS" FEED OFF WHAT THE LOCALS CALL BIIGISTIIN--
NAVAJO FOR "ONE WHO LIES WITHIN IT"--AN INNER-LIFE FORM. WE CALL IT A SOUL--
--AN' IF YOU GOT ONE, YER STUCK HERE.
AN' A VAMPIRE FINALLY DROPS IN MY LAP--BUT HE'S THE ONLY ONE IN GOD'S GREEN EARTH THAT HAS A SOUL!
WELL, BOY, YOU WANT TO GET BACK WHERE YOU BELONG.
AN' I WANT REVENGE ON THE MAN WHO PUT ME HERE.
SO THE ONLY WAY I SEE AROUND IT IS IF YOU TURN ME INTO A SOULLESS VAMPIRE!

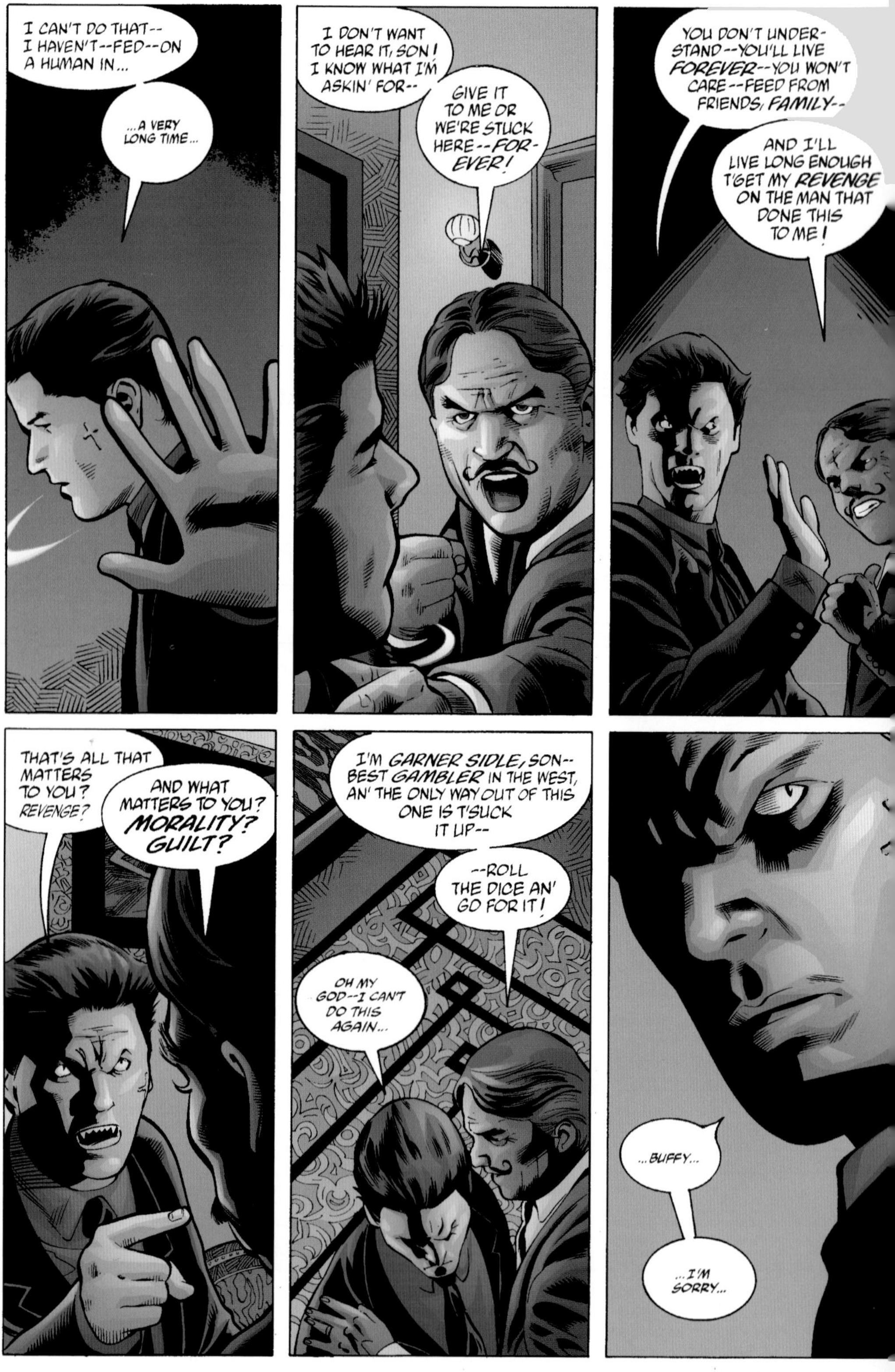
I CAN'T DO THAT--
I HAVEN'T--FED--ON
A HUMAN IN...
...A VERY LONG TIME...
I DON'T WANT TO HEAR IT, SON! I KNOW WHAT I'M ASKIN' FOR--
GIVE IT TO ME OR WE'RE STUCK HERE--FOR-EVER!
YOU DON'T UNDER-STAND--YOU'LL LIVE FOREVER--YOU WON'T CARE--FEED FROM FRIENDS, FAMILY--
AND I'LL LIVE LONG ENOUGH T'GET MY REVENGE ON THE MAN THAT DONE THIS TO ME!
THAT'S ALL THAT MATTERS TO YOU? REVENGE?
AND WHAT MATTERS TO YOU? MORALITY? GUILT?
I'M GARNER SIDLE, SON-- BEST GAMBLER IN THE WEST, AN' THE ONLY WAY OUT OF THIS ONE IS T'SUCK IT UP--
--ROLL THE DICE AN' GO FOR IT!
OH MY GOD--I CAN'T DO THIS AGAIN...
...BUFFY...
...I'M SORRY...

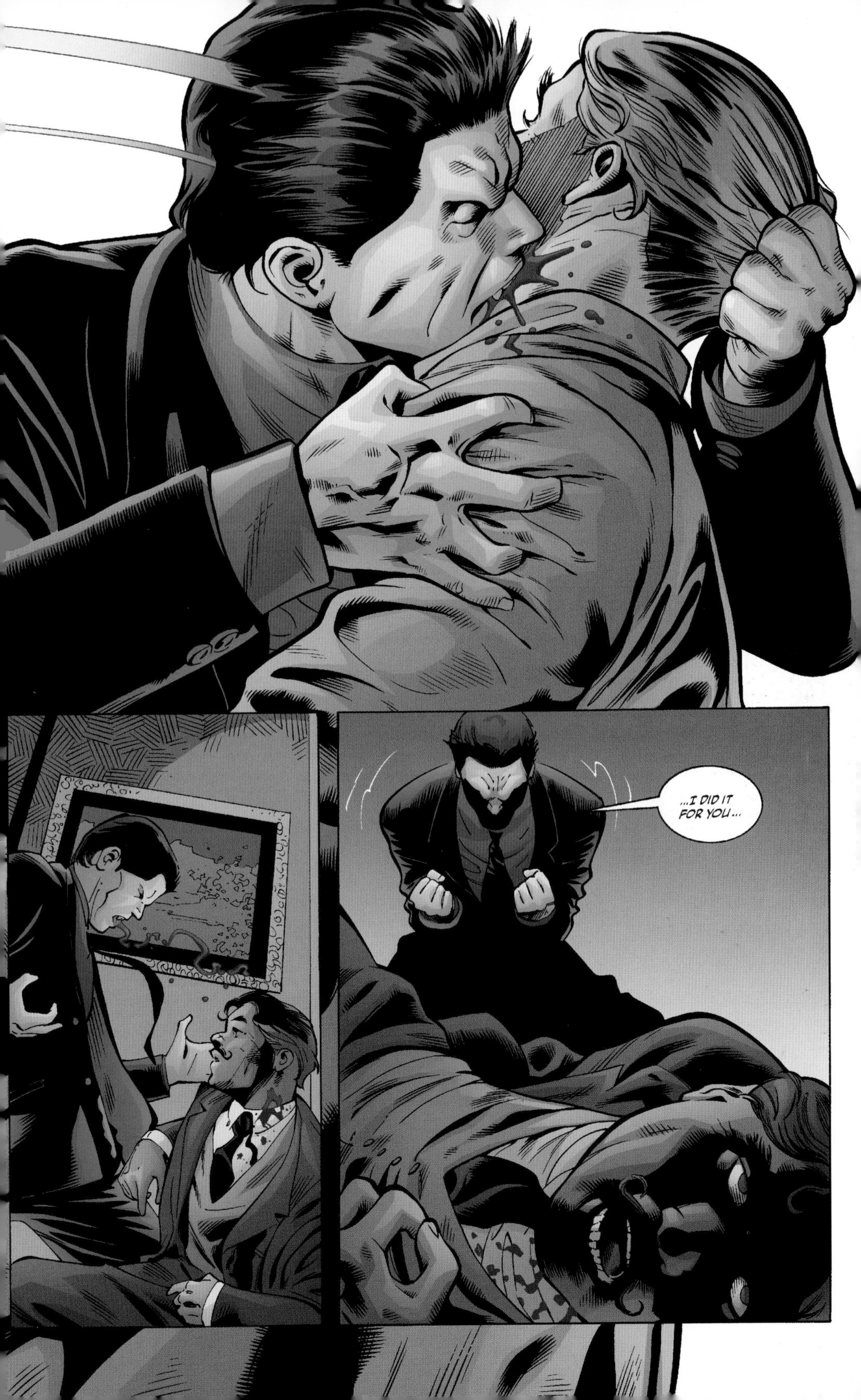
...I DID IT
FOR YOU...

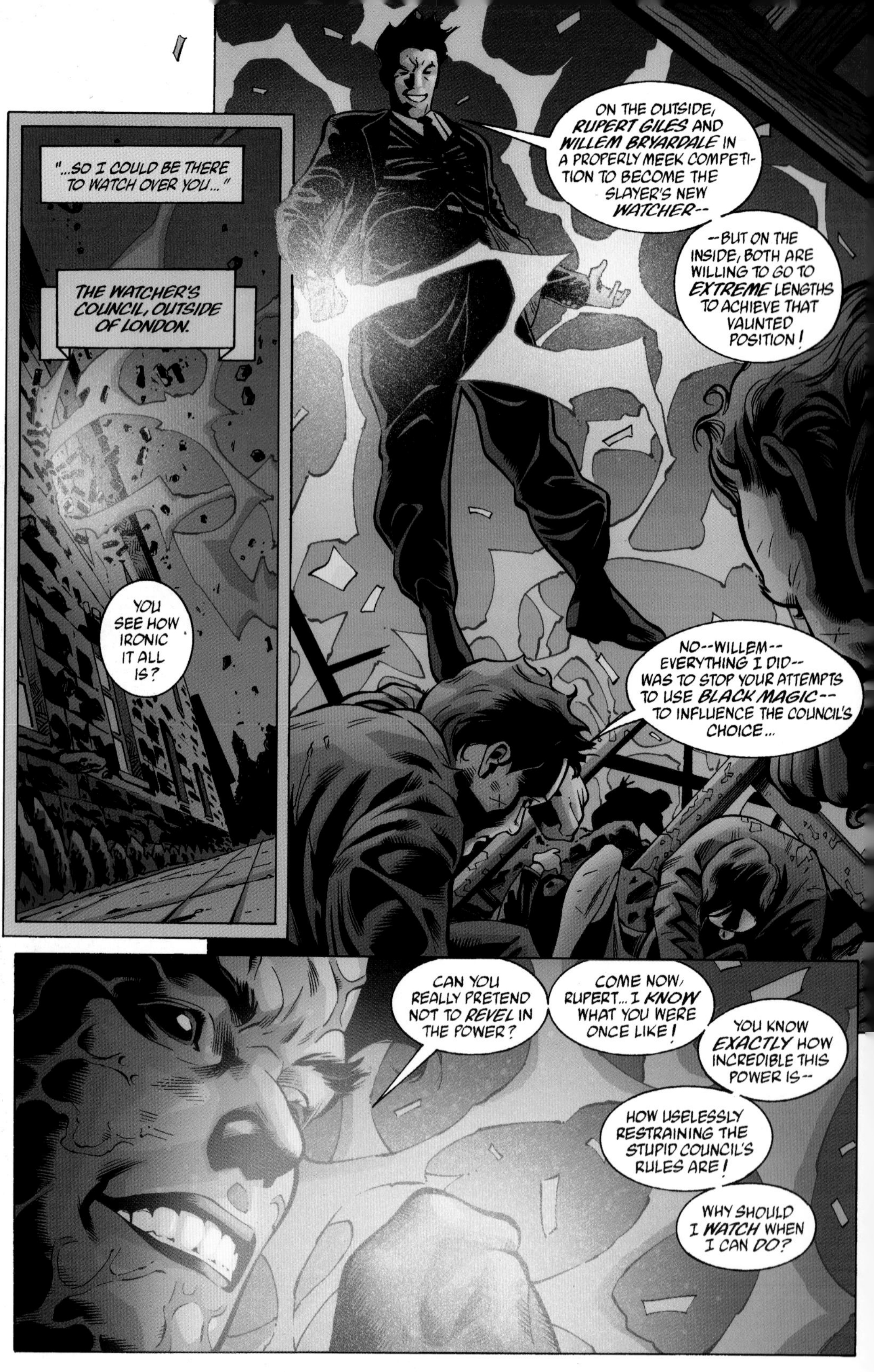
"...SO I COULD BE THERE TO WATCH OVER YOU..."
THE WATCHER'S COUNCIL, OUTSIDE OF LONDON.
ON THE OUTSIDE, RUPERT GILES AND WILLEM BRYARDALE IN A PROPERLY MEEK COMPETITION TO BECOME THE SLAYER'S NEW WATCHER--
--BUT ON THE INSIDE, BOTH ARE WILLING TO GO TO EXTREME LENGTHS TO ACHIEVE THAT VAUNTED POSITION!
YOU SEE HOW IRONIC IT ALL IS?
NO--WILLEM--EVERYTHING I DID--WAS TO STOP YOUR ATTEMPTS TO USE BLACK MAGIC--TO INFLUENCE THE COUNCIL'S CHOICE...
CAN YOU REALLY PRETEND NOT TO REVEL IN THE POWER?
COME NOW, RUPERT... I KNOW WHAT YOU WERE ONCE LIKE!
YOU KNOW EXACTLY HOW INCREDIBLE THIS POWER IS--
HOW USELESSLY RESTRAINING THE STUPID COUNCIL'S RULES ARE!
WHY SHOULD I WATCH WHEN I CAN DO?

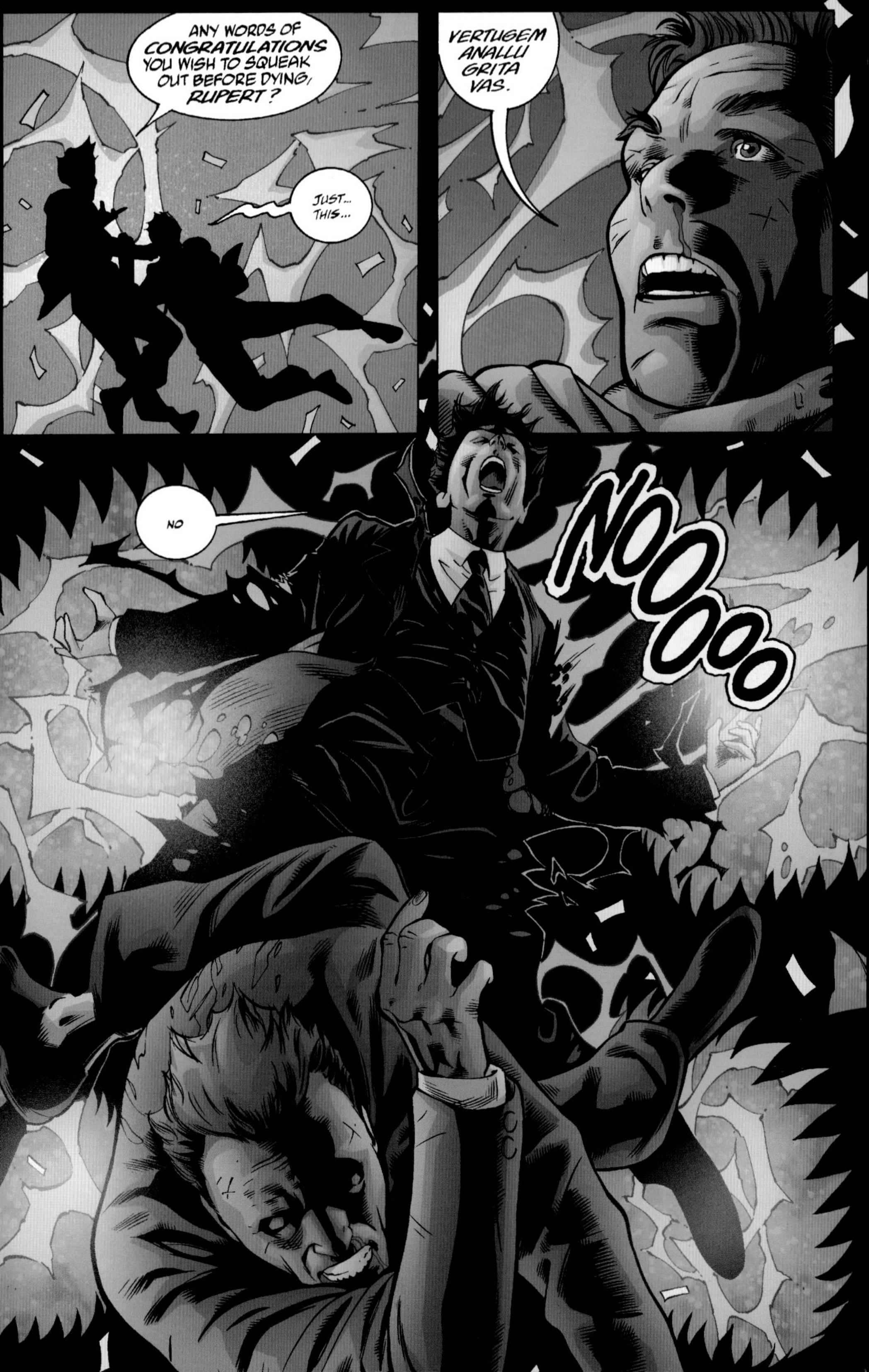
ANY WORDS OF CONGRATULATIONS YOU WISH TO SQUEAK OUT BEFORE DYING, RUPERT?
JUST... THIS...
VERTUGEM ANALLU GRITA VAS.
NO
NOOOOO

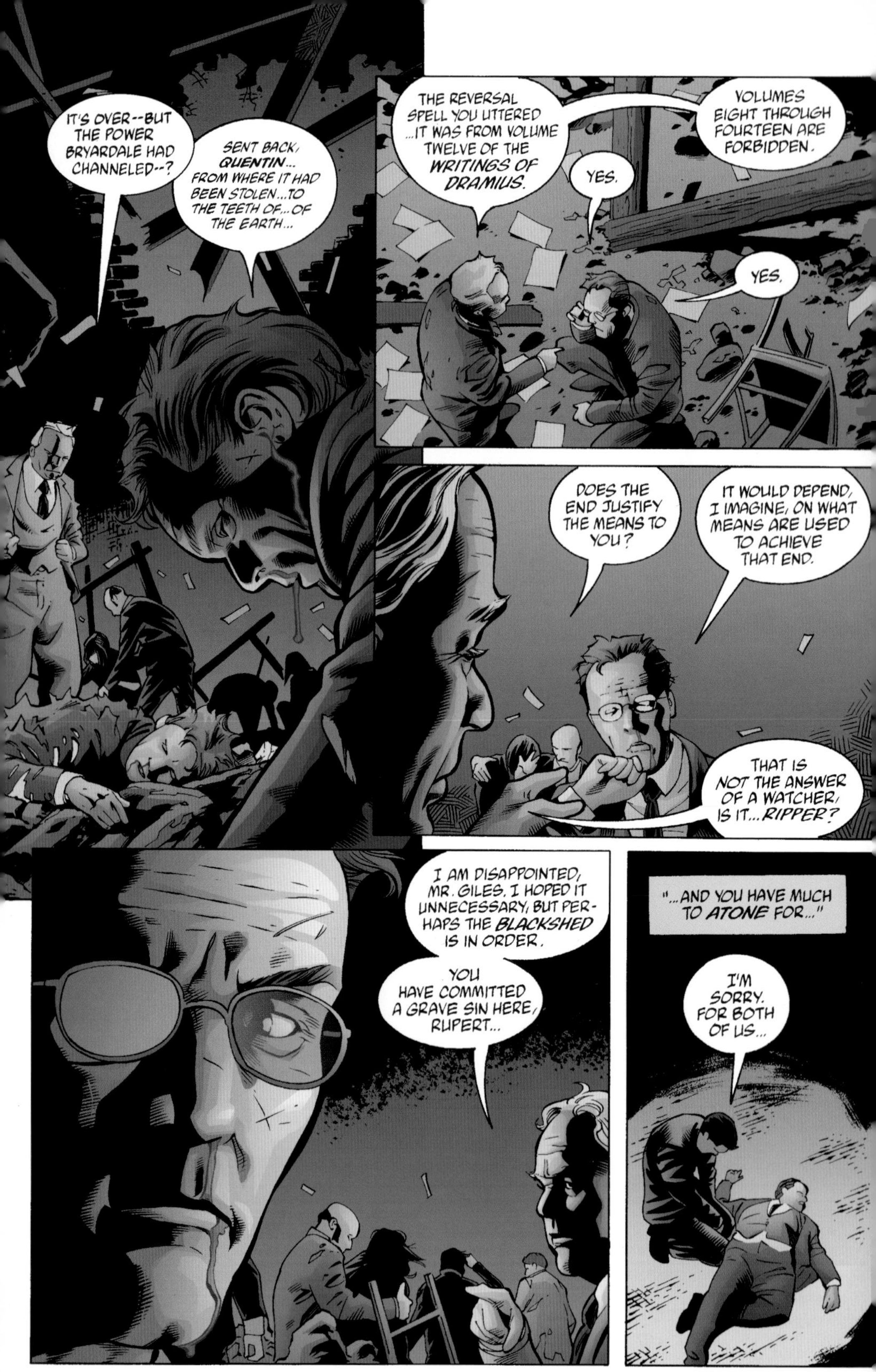
IT'S OVER--BUT THE POWER BRYARDALE HAD CHANNELED--?
SENT BACK, QUENTIN... FROM WHERE IT HAD BEEN STOLEN...TO THE TEETH OF...OF THE EARTH...
THE REVERSAL SPELL YOU UTTERED ...IT WAS FROM VOLUME TWELVE OF THE WRITINGS OF DRAMIUS.
YES.
VOLUMES EIGHT THROUGH FOURTEEN ARE FORBIDDEN.
YES.
DOES THE END JUSTIFY THE MEANS TO YOU?
IT WOULD DEPEND, I IMAGINE, ON WHAT MEANS ARE USED TO ACHIEVE THAT END.
THAT IS NOT THE ANSWER OF A WATCHER, IS IT...RIPPER?
I AM DISAPPOINTED, MR. GILES. I HOPED IT UNNECESSARY, BUT PERHAPS THE BLACKSHED IS IN ORDER.
YOU HAVE COMMITTED A GRAVE SIN HERE, RUPERT...
"...AND YOU HAVE MUCH TO ATONE FOR..."
I'M SORRY. FOR BOTH OF US...

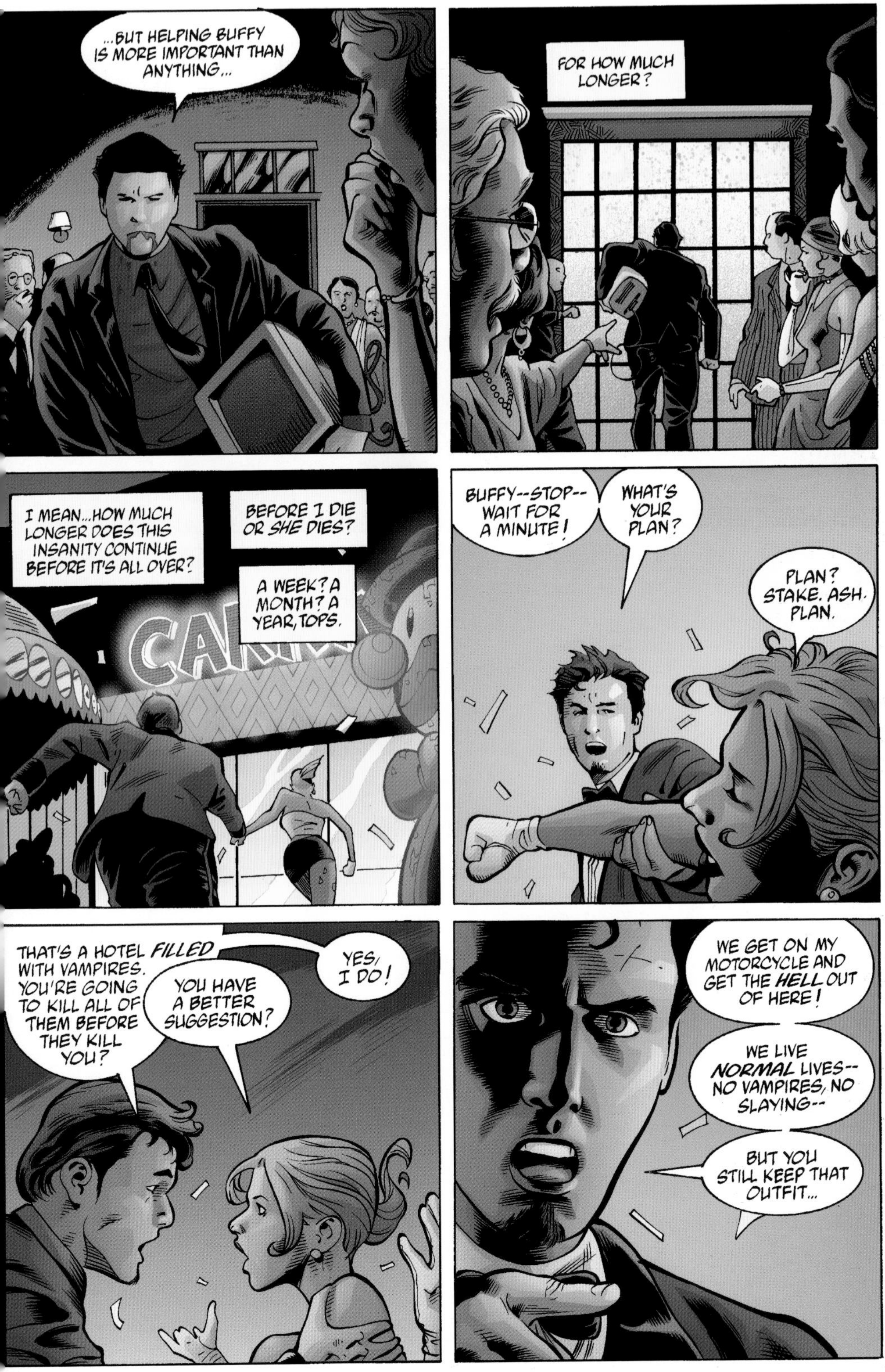
...BUT HELPING BUFFY IS MORE IMPORTANT THAN ANYTHING...
FOR HOW MUCH LONGER?
I MEAN...HOW MUCH LONGER DOES THIS INSANITY CONTINUE BEFORE IT'S ALL OVER?
BEFORE I DIE OR SHE DIES?
A WEEK? A MONTH? A YEAR, TOPS.
BUFFY--STOP-- WAIT FOR A MINUTE!
WHAT'S YOUR PLAN?
PLAN? STAKE. ASH. PLAN.
THAT'S A HOTEL FILLED WITH VAMPIRES. YOU'RE GOING TO KILL ALL OF THEM BEFORE THEY KILL YOU?
YES, I DO!
YOU HAVE A BETTER SUGGESTION?
WE GET ON MY MOTORCYCLE AND GET THE HELL OUT OF HERE!
WE LIVE NORMAL LIVES-- NO VAMPIRES, NO SLAYING--
BUT YOU STILL KEEP THAT OUTFIT...

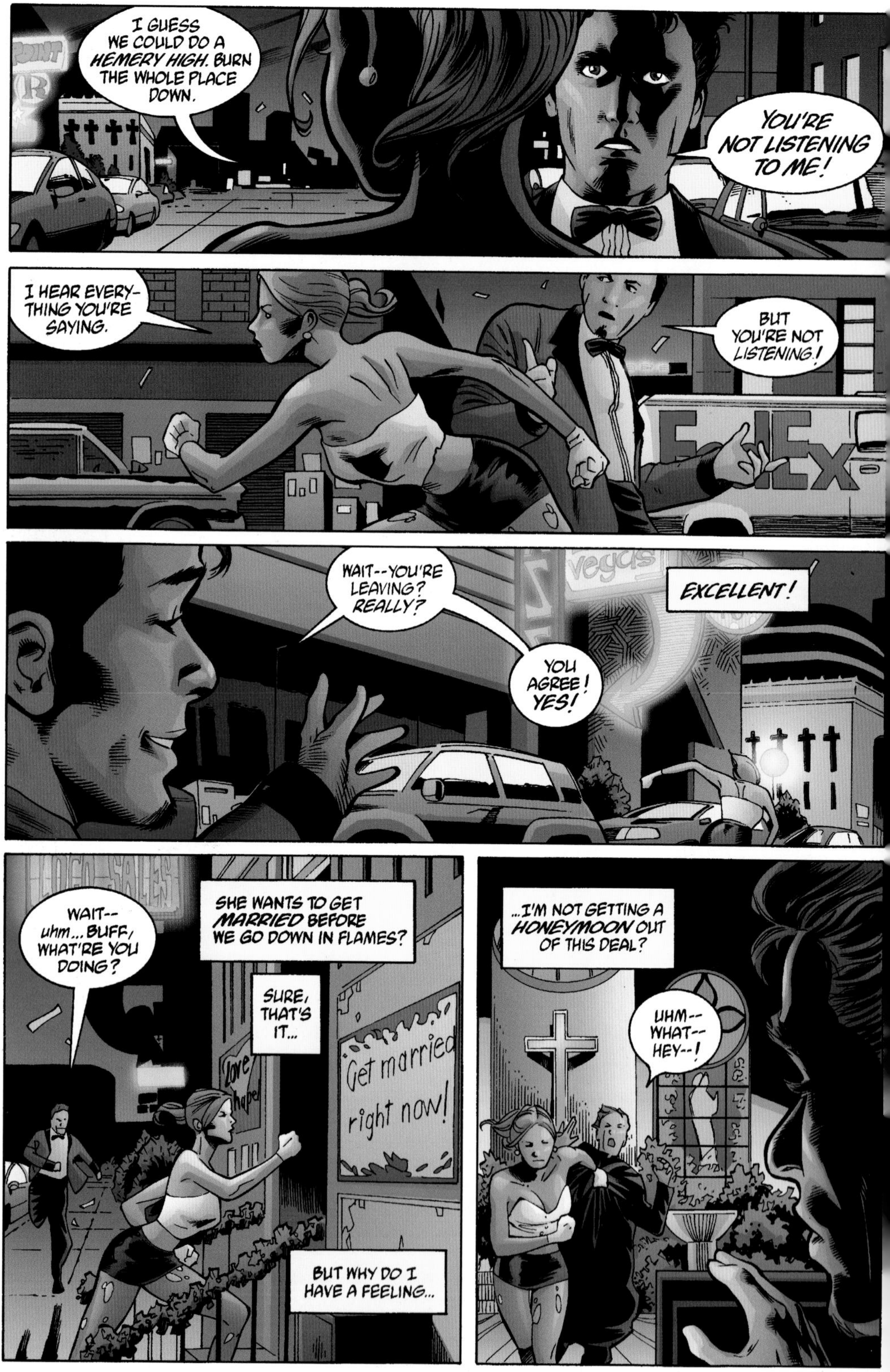

I GUESS WE COULD DO A *HEMERY HIGH*. BURN THE WHOLE PLACE DOWN.
YOU'RE NOT LISTENING TO ME!
I HEAR EVERYTHING YOU'RE SAYING.
BUT YOU'RE NOT LISTENING!
WAIT--YOU'RE LEAVING? REALLY?
YOU AGREE! YES!
EXCELLENT!
WAIT-- uhm... BUFF, WHAT'RE YOU DOING?
SHE WANTS TO GET *MARRIED* BEFORE WE GO DOWN IN FLAMES?
SURE, THAT'S IT...
Love Chapel
Get married right now!
BUT WHY DO I HAVE A FEELING...
...I'M NOT GETTING A *HONEYMOON* OUT OF THIS DEAL?
UHM-- WHAT-- HEY--!

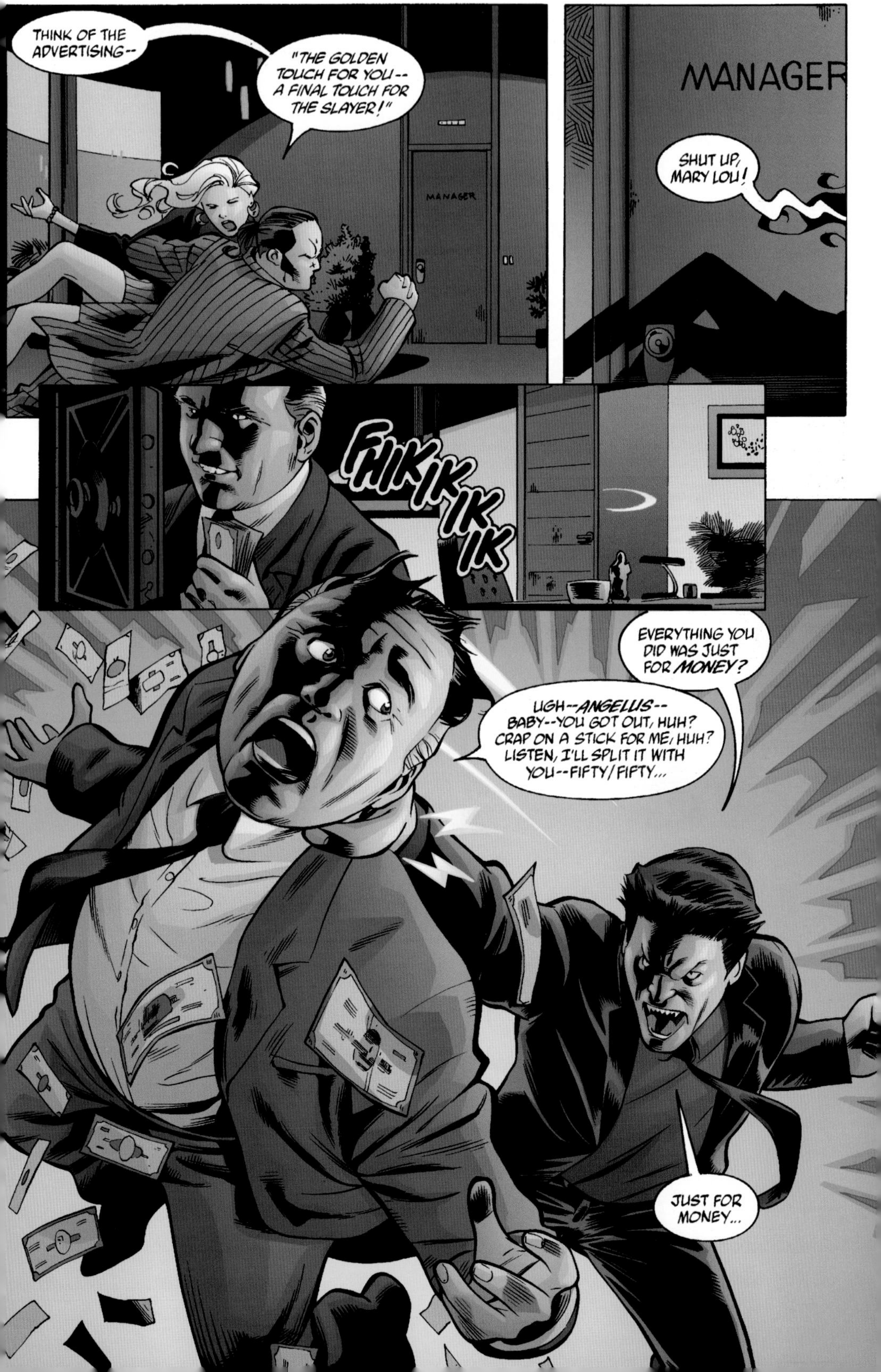
THINK OF THE ADVERTISING--
"THE GOLDEN TOUCH FOR YOU-- A FINAL TOUCH FOR THE SLAYER!"
MANAGER
MANAGER
SHUT UP, MARY LOU!
FHIKIKIKIK
EVERYTHING YOU DID WAS JUST FOR *MONEY*?
UGH--*ANGELUS*-- BABY--YOU GOT OUT, HUH? CRAP ON A STICK FOR ME, HUH? LISTEN, I'LL SPLIT IT WITH YOU--FIFTY/FIFTY...
JUST FOR MONEY...

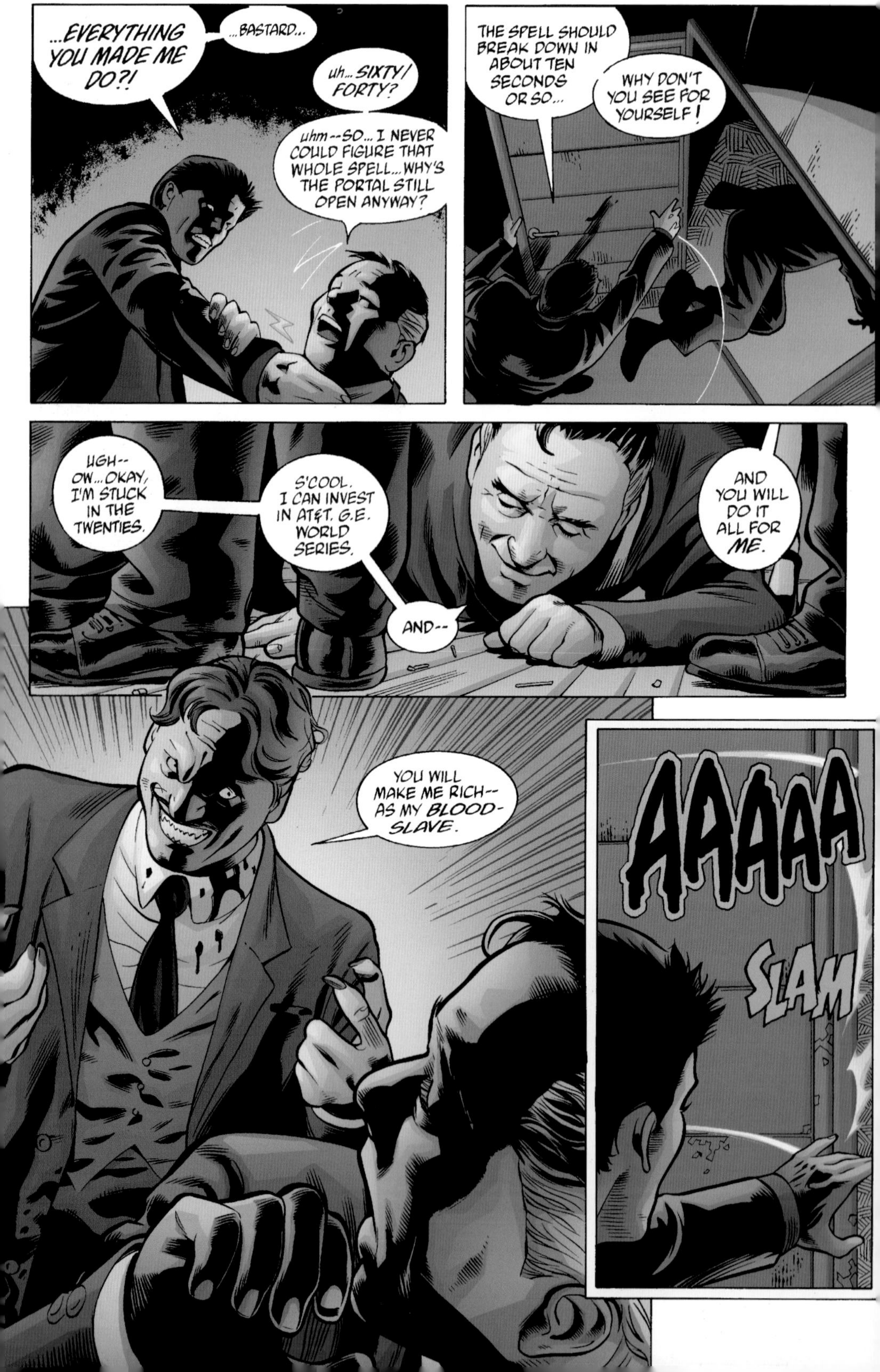
...EVERYTHING YOU MADE ME DO?!
...BASTARD...
uh... SIXTY/ FORTY?
uhm--SO... I NEVER COULD FIGURE THAT WHOLE SPELL... WHY'S THE PORTAL STILL OPEN ANYWAY?
THE SPELL SHOULD BREAK DOWN IN ABOUT TEN SECONDS OR SO...
WHY DON'T YOU SEE FOR YOURSELF!
UGH--OW... OKAY, I'M STUCK IN THE TWENTIES.
S'COOL. I CAN INVEST IN AT&T. G.E. WORLD SERIES.
AND--
AND YOU WILL DO IT ALL FOR ME.
YOU WILL MAKE ME RICH--AS MY BLOOD-SLAVE.
AAAAA
SLAM

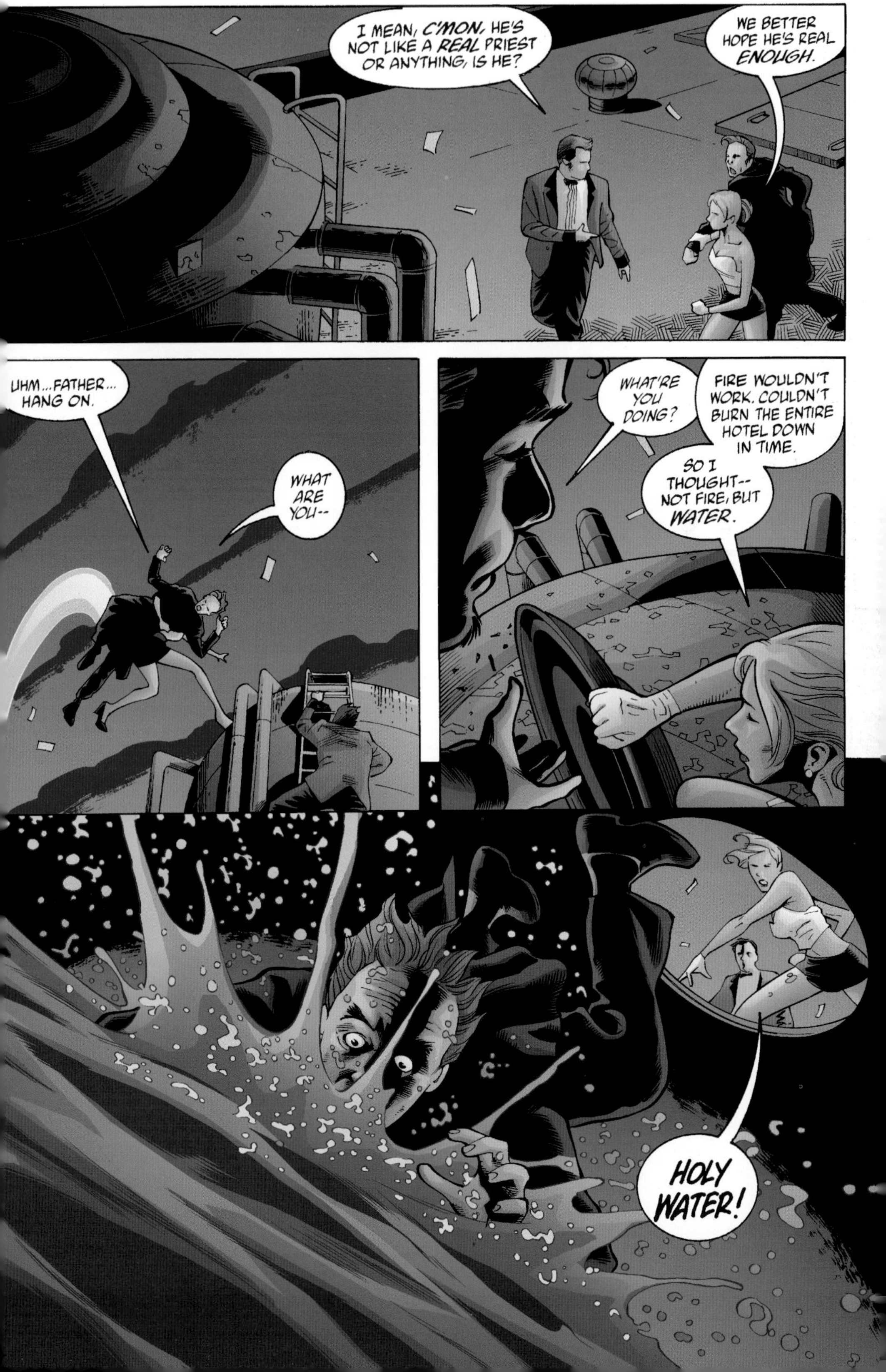
I MEAN, C'MON, HE'S NOT LIKE A REAL PRIEST OR ANYTHING, IS HE?
WE BETTER HOPE HE'S REAL ENOUGH.
UHM...FATHER... HANG ON.
WHAT ARE YOU--
WHAT'RE YOU DOING?
FIRE WOULDN'T WORK. COULDN'T BURN THE ENTIRE HOTEL DOWN IN TIME.
SO I THOUGHT--NOT FIRE, BUT WATER.
HOLY WATER!

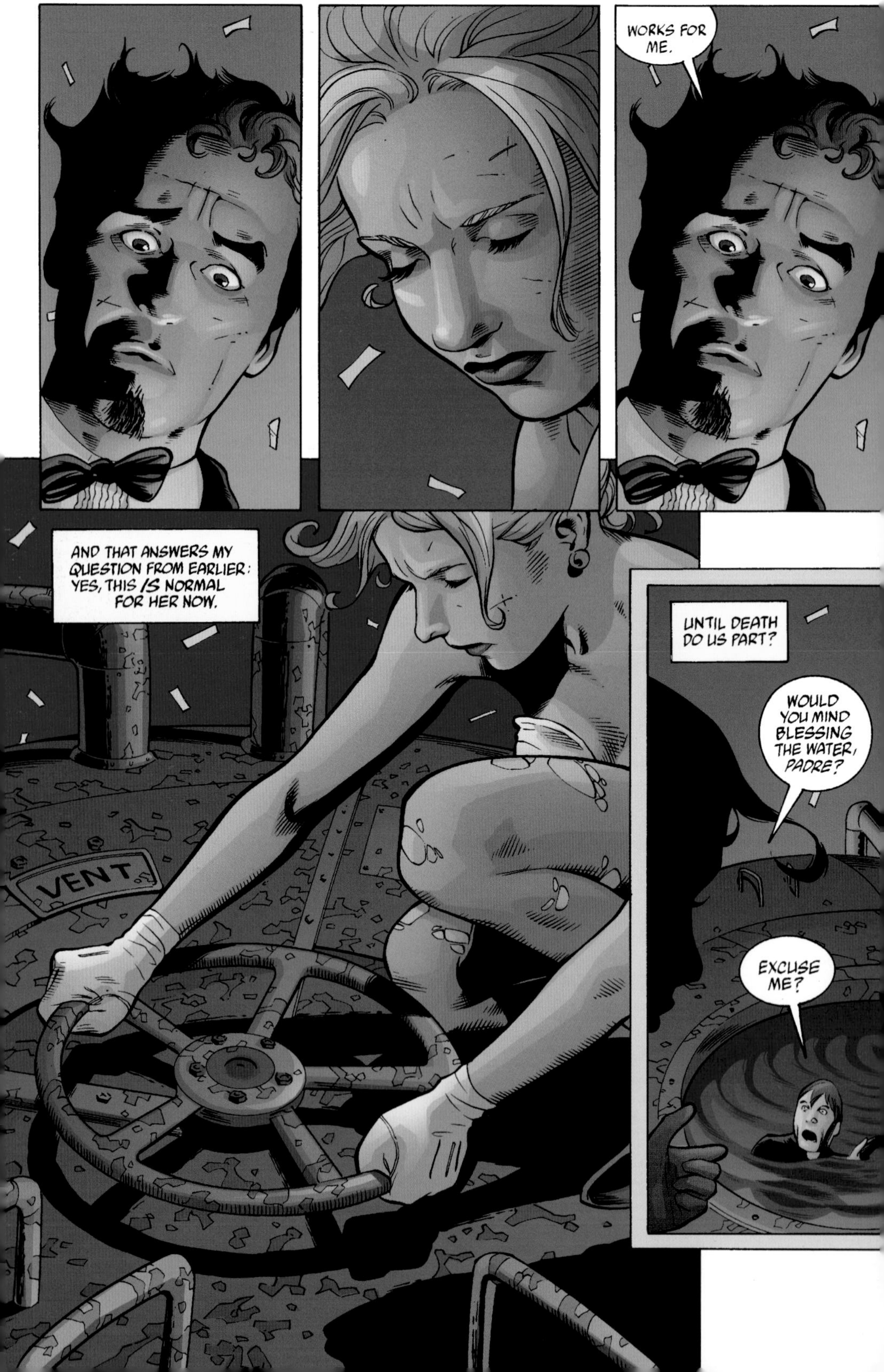
WORKS FOR ME.
AND THAT ANSWERS MY QUESTION FROM EARLIER: YES, THIS *IS* NORMAL FOR HER NOW.
VENT
UNTIL DEATH DO US PART?
WOULD YOU MIND BLESSING THE WATER, *PADRE?*
EXCUSE ME?

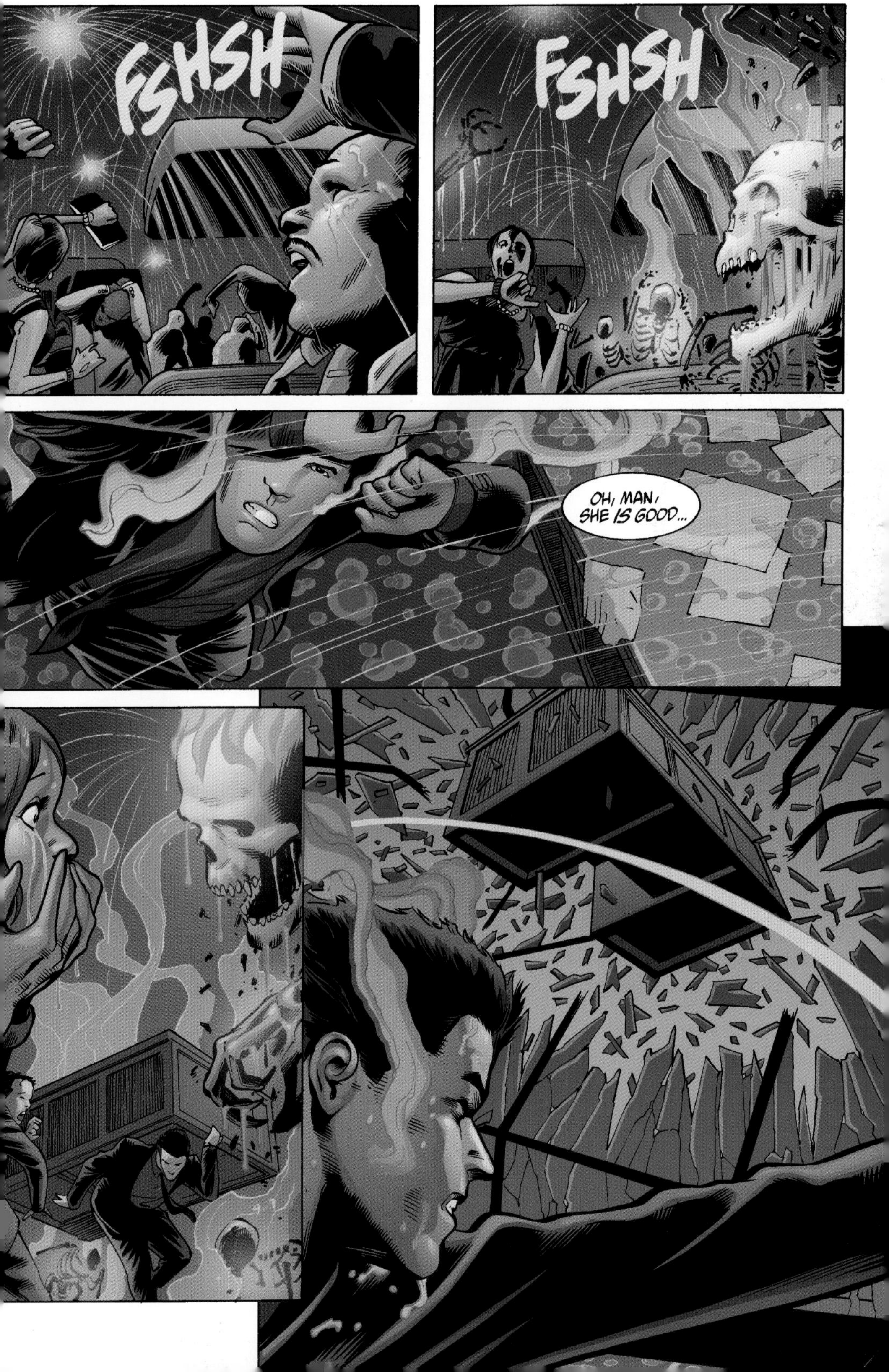
FSHSH
FSHSH
OH, MAN, SHE IS GOOD...

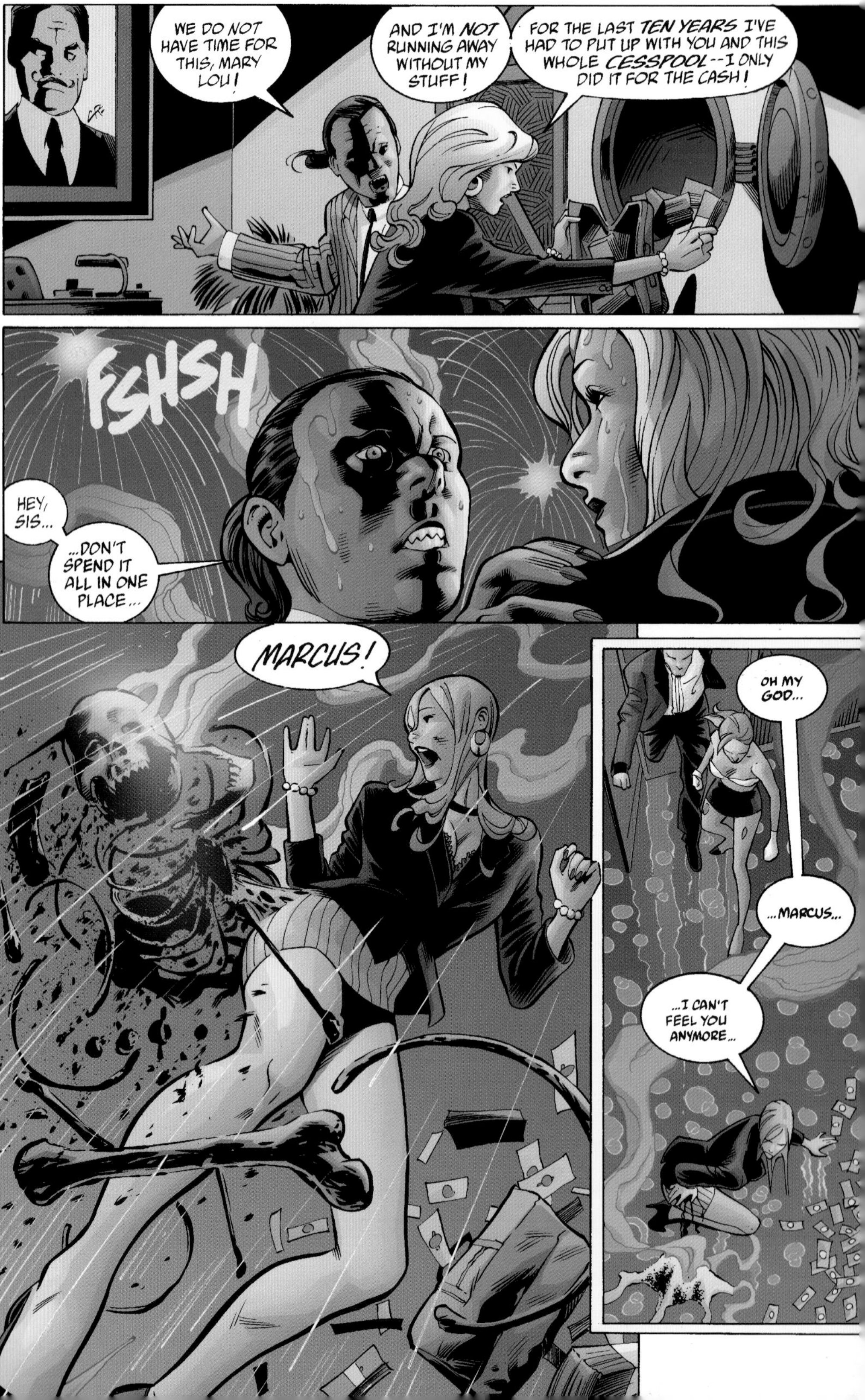
WE DO NOT HAVE TIME FOR THIS, MARY LOU!
AND I'M NOT RUNNING AWAY WITHOUT MY STUFF!
FOR THE LAST TEN YEARS I'VE HAD TO PUT UP WITH YOU AND THIS WHOLE CESSPOOL--I ONLY DID IT FOR THE CASH!
FSHSH
HEY, SIS...
...DON'T SPEND IT ALL IN ONE PLACE...
MARCUS!
OH MY GOD...
...MARCUS...
...I CAN'T FEEL YOU ANYMORE...

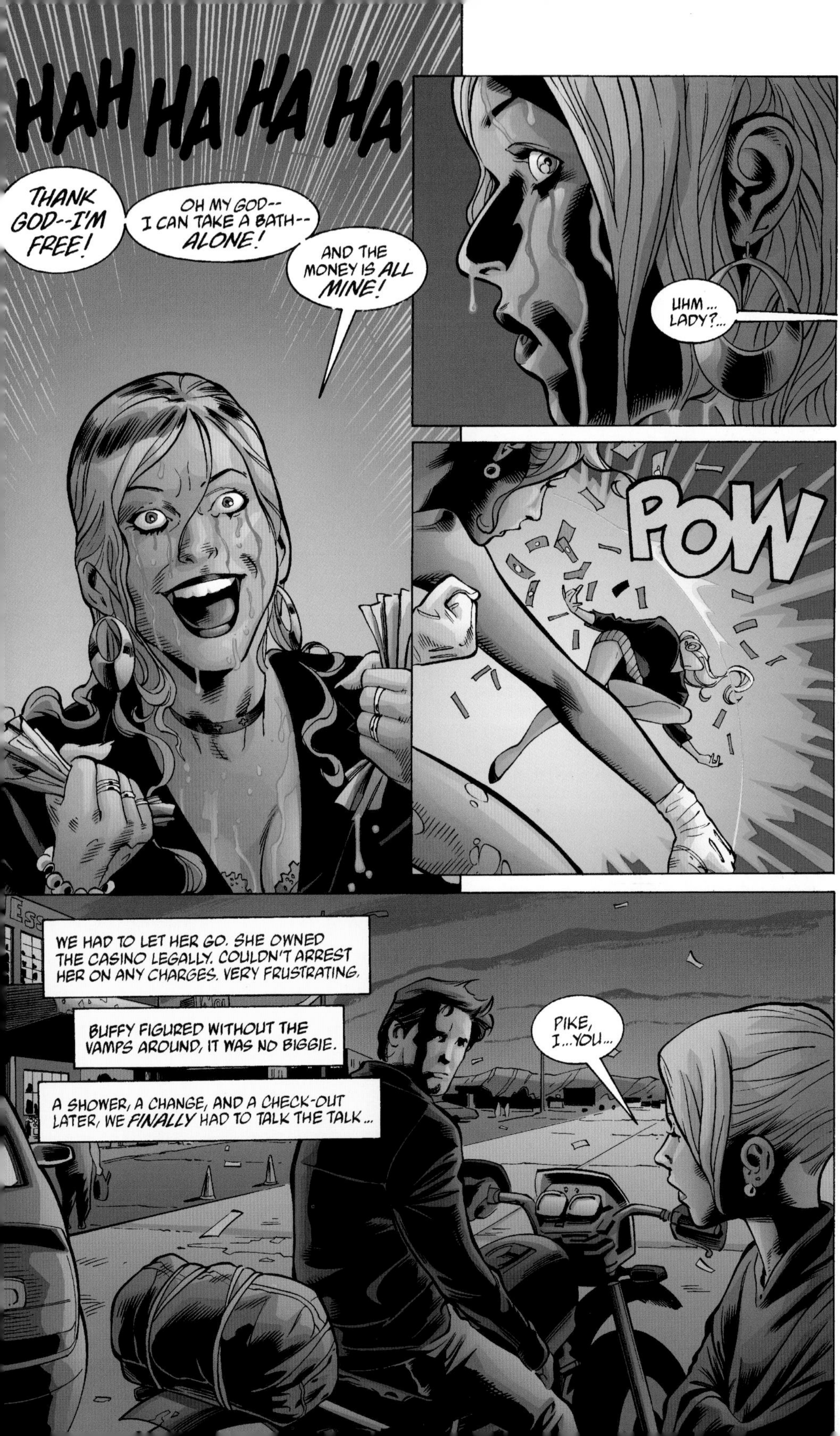
HAH HA HA HA HA
THANK GOD--I'M FREE!
OH MY GOD-- I CAN TAKE A BATH-- ALONE!
AND THE MONEY IS ALL MINE!
UHM ... LADY?...
POW
WE HAD TO LET HER GO. SHE OWNED THE CASINO LEGALLY. COULDN'T ARREST HER ON ANY CHARGES. VERY FRUSTRATING.
BUFFY FIGURED WITHOUT THE VAMPS AROUND, IT WAS NO BIGGIE.
A SHOWER, A CHANGE, AND A CHECK-OUT LATER, WE FINALLY HAD TO TALK THE TALK...
PIKE, I...YOU...

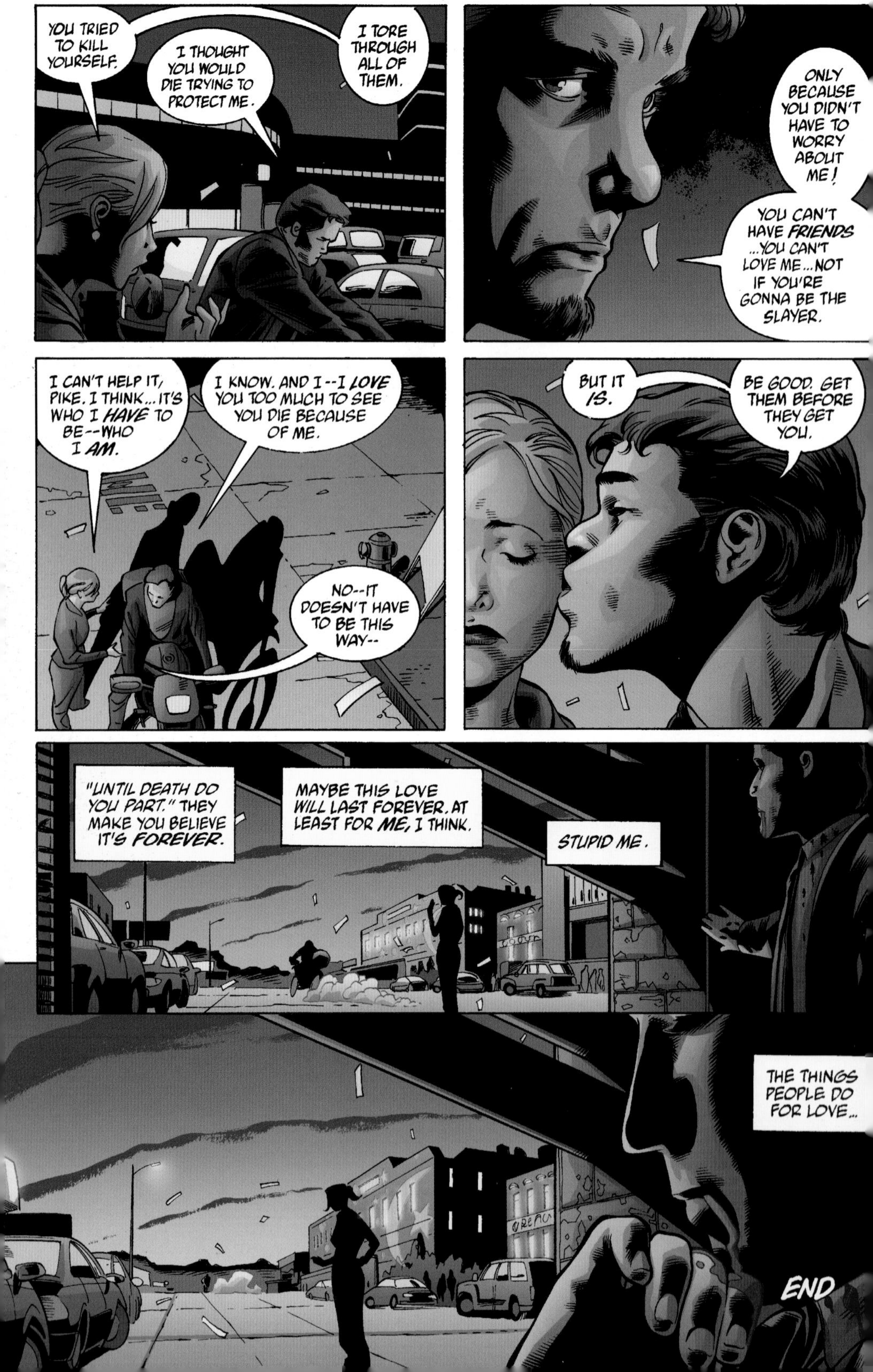
YOU TRIED TO KILL YOURSELF.
I THOUGHT YOU WOULD DIE TRYING TO PROTECT ME.
I TORE THROUGH ALL OF THEM.
ONLY BECAUSE YOU DIDN'T HAVE TO WORRY ABOUT ME!
YOU CAN'T HAVE FRIENDS ...YOU CAN'T LOVE ME... NOT IF YOU'RE GONNA BE THE SLAYER.
I CAN'T HELP IT, PIKE. I THINK... IT'S WHO I HAVE TO BE--WHO I AM.
I KNOW. AND I--I LOVE YOU TOO MUCH TO SEE YOU DIE BECAUSE OF ME.
NO--IT DOESN'T HAVE TO BE THIS WAY--
BUT IT IS.
BE GOOD. GET THEM BEFORE THEY GET YOU.
"UNTIL DEATH DO YOU PART." THEY MAKE YOU BELIEVE IT'S FOREVER.
MAYBE THIS LOVE WILL LAST FOREVER. AT LEAST FOR ME, I THINK.
STUPID ME.
THE THINGS PEOPLE DO FOR LOVE...
END

Dawn & Hoopy the Bear

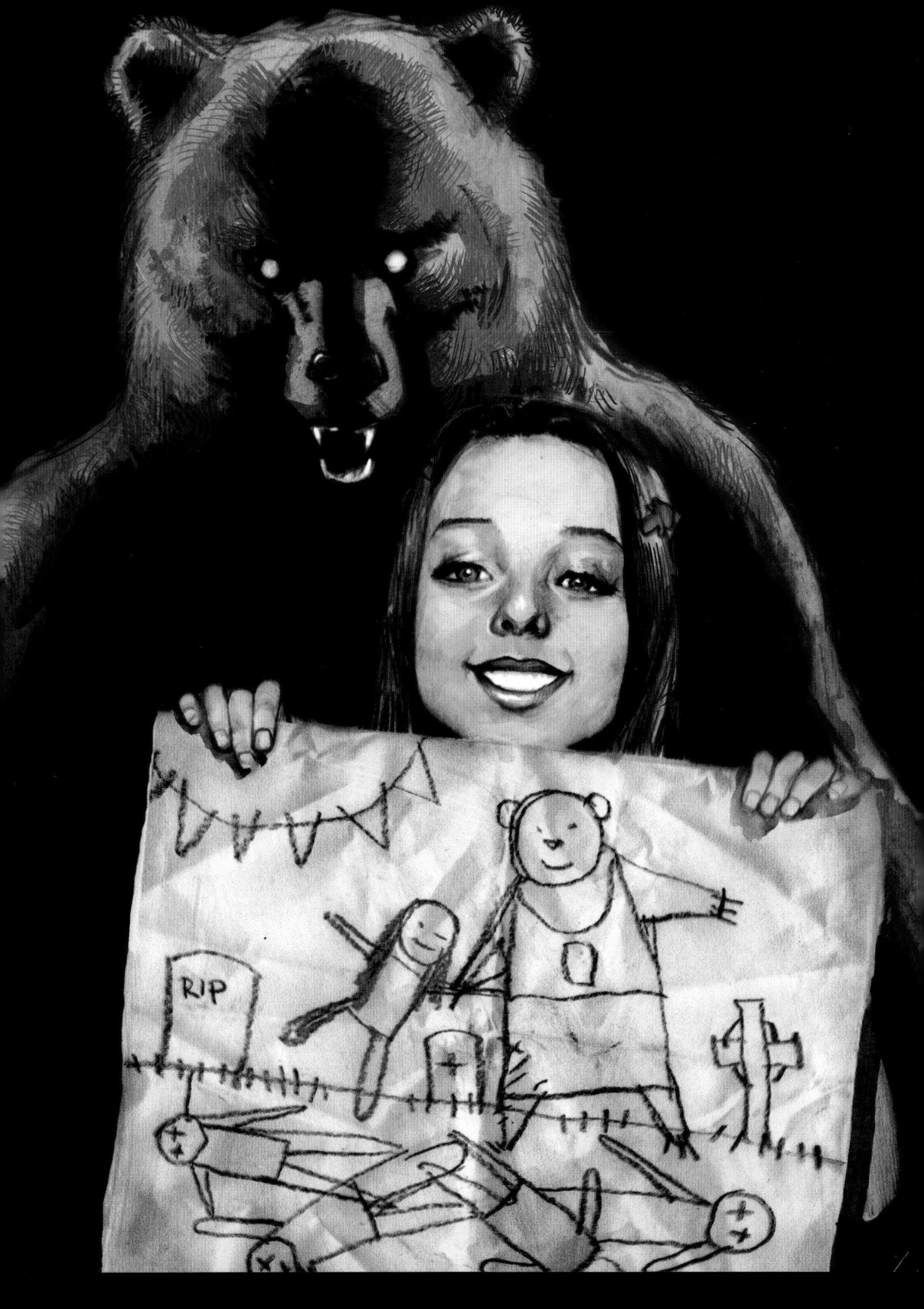
RIP

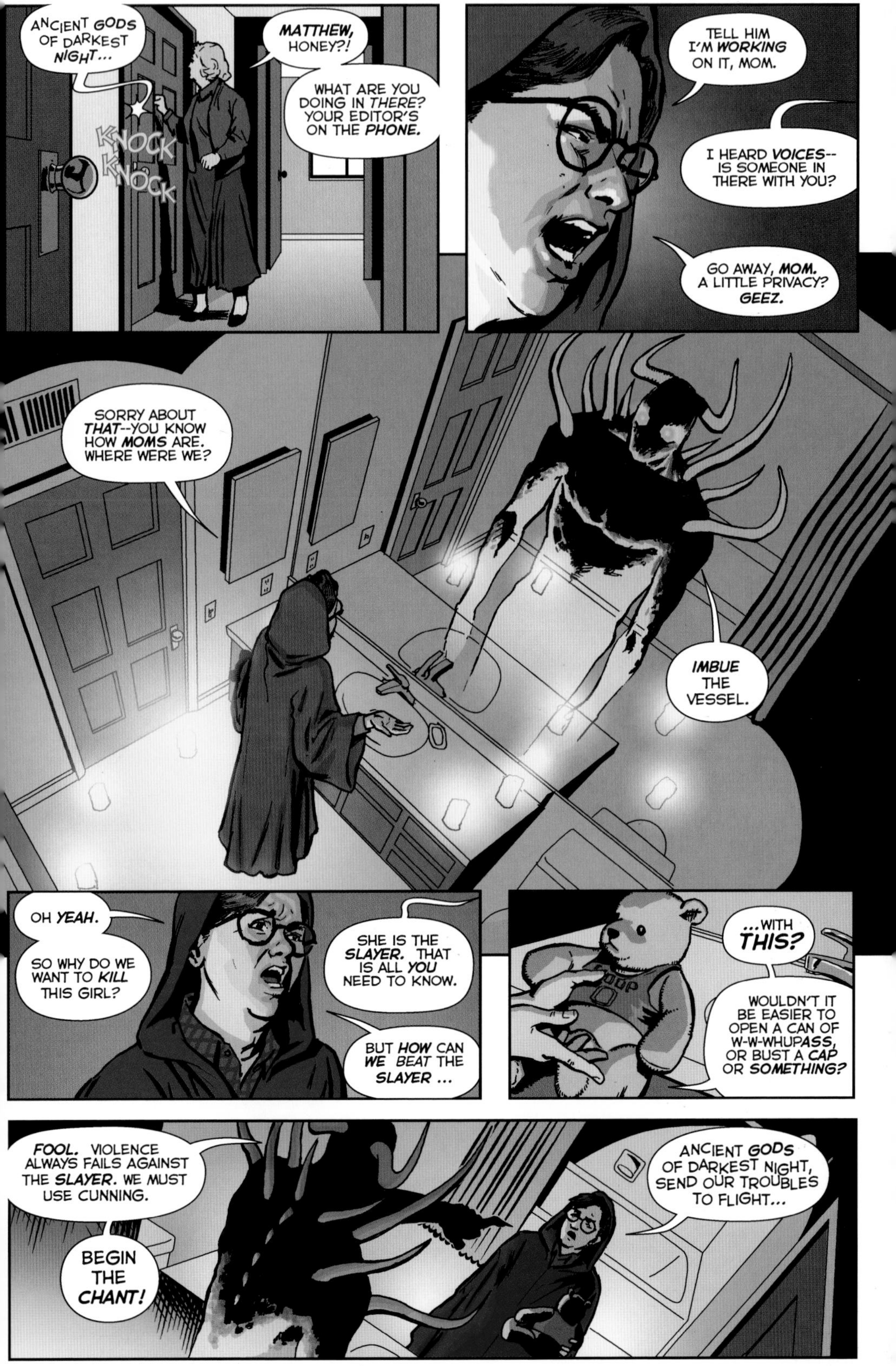
ANCIENT GODS OF DARKEST NIGHT...
KNOCK KNOCK
MATTHEW, HONEY?!
WHAT ARE YOU DOING IN THERE? YOUR EDITOR'S ON THE PHONE.
TELL HIM I'M WORKING ON IT, MOM.
I HEARD VOICES-- IS SOMEONE IN THERE WITH YOU?
GO AWAY, MOM. A LITTLE PRIVACY? GEEZ.
SORRY ABOUT THAT--YOU KNOW HOW MOMS ARE. WHERE WERE WE?
IMBUE THE VESSEL.
OH YEAH.
SO WHY DO WE WANT TO KILL THIS GIRL?
SHE IS THE SLAYER. THAT IS ALL YOU NEED TO KNOW.
BUT HOW CAN WE BEAT THE SLAYER ...
...WITH THIS?
WOULDN'T IT BE EASIER TO OPEN A CAN OF W-W-WHUPASS, OR BUST A CAP OR SOMETHING?
FOOL. VIOLENCE ALWAYS FAILS AGAINST THE SLAYER. WE MUST USE CUNNING.
BEGIN THE CHANT!
ANCIENT GODS OF DARKEST NIGHT, SEND OUR TROUBLES TO FLIGHT...

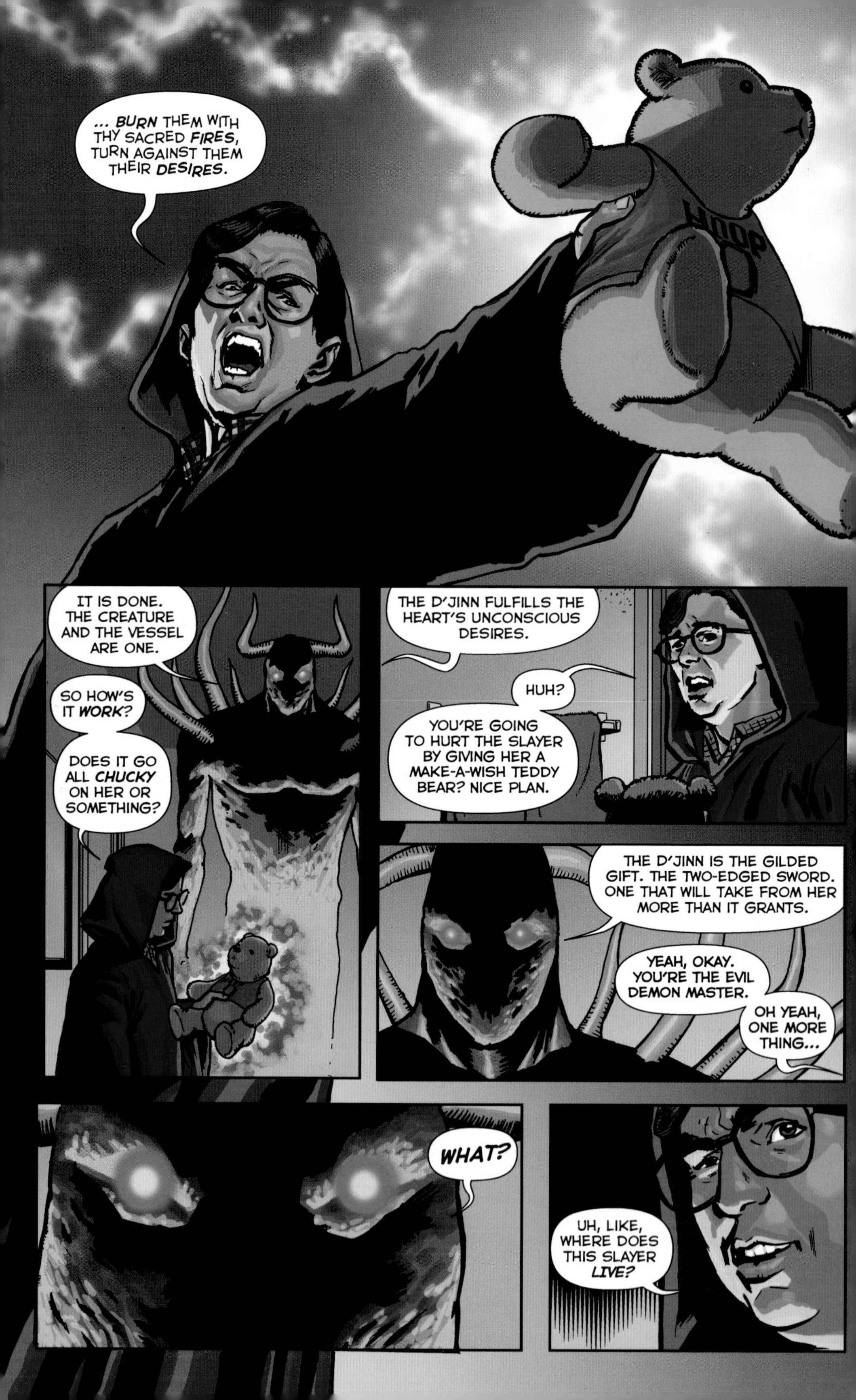
... BURN THEM WITH THY SACRED FIRES, TURN AGAINST THEM THEIR DESIRES.
HOOP
IT IS DONE. THE CREATURE AND THE VESSEL ARE ONE.
SO HOW'S IT WORK?
DOES IT GO ALL CHUCKY ON HER OR SOMETHING?
THE D'JINN FULFILLS THE HEART'S UNCONSCIOUS DESIRES.
HUH?
YOU'RE GOING TO HURT THE SLAYER BY GIVING HER A MAKE-A-WISH TEDDY BEAR? NICE PLAN.
THE D'JINN IS THE GILDED GIFT. THE TWO-EDGED SWORD. ONE THAT WILL TAKE FROM HER MORE THAN IT GRANTS.
YEAH, OKAY. YOU'RE THE EVIL DEMON MASTER.
OH YEAH, ONE MORE THING...
WHAT?
UH, LIKE, WHERE DOES THIS SLAYER LIVE?

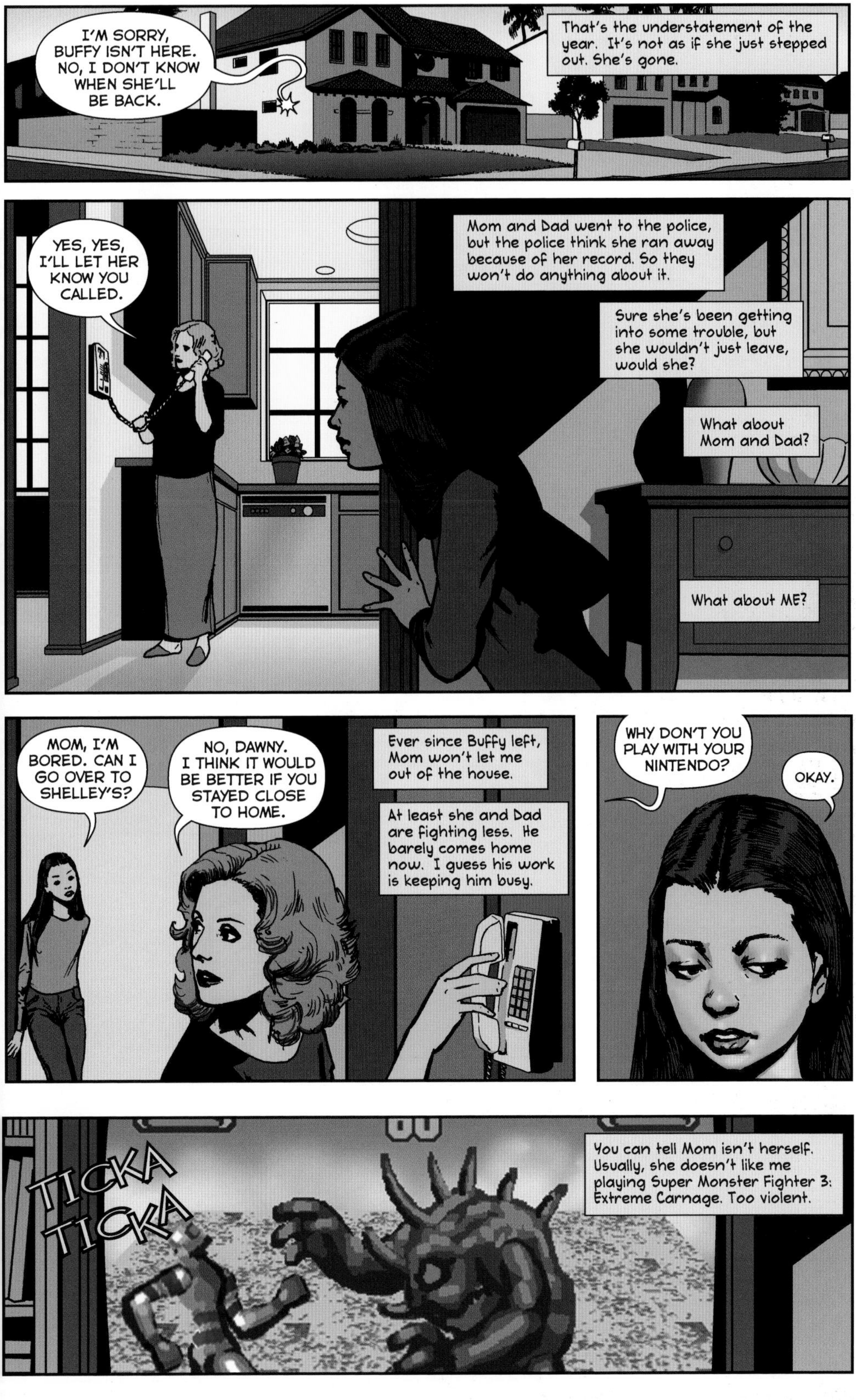

I'M SORRY, BUFFY ISN'T HERE. NO, I DON'T KNOW WHEN SHE'LL BE BACK.
That's the understatement of the year. It's not as if she just stepped out. She's gone.
YES, YES, I'LL LET HER KNOW YOU CALLED.
Mom and Dad went to the police, but the police think she ran away because of her record. So they won't do anything about it.
Sure she's been getting into some trouble, but she wouldn't just leave, would she?
What about Mom and Dad?
What about ME?
MOM, I'M BORED. CAN I GO OVER TO SHELLEY'S?
NO, DAWNY. I THINK IT WOULD BE BETTER IF YOU STAYED CLOSE TO HOME.
Ever since Buffy left, Mom won't let me out of the house.
At least she and Dad are fighting less. He barely comes home now. I guess his work is keeping him busy.
WHY DON'T YOU PLAY WITH YOUR NINTENDO?
OKAY.
TICKA TICKA
You can tell Mom isn't herself. Usually, she doesn't like me playing Super Monster Fighter 3: Extreme Carnage. Too violent.

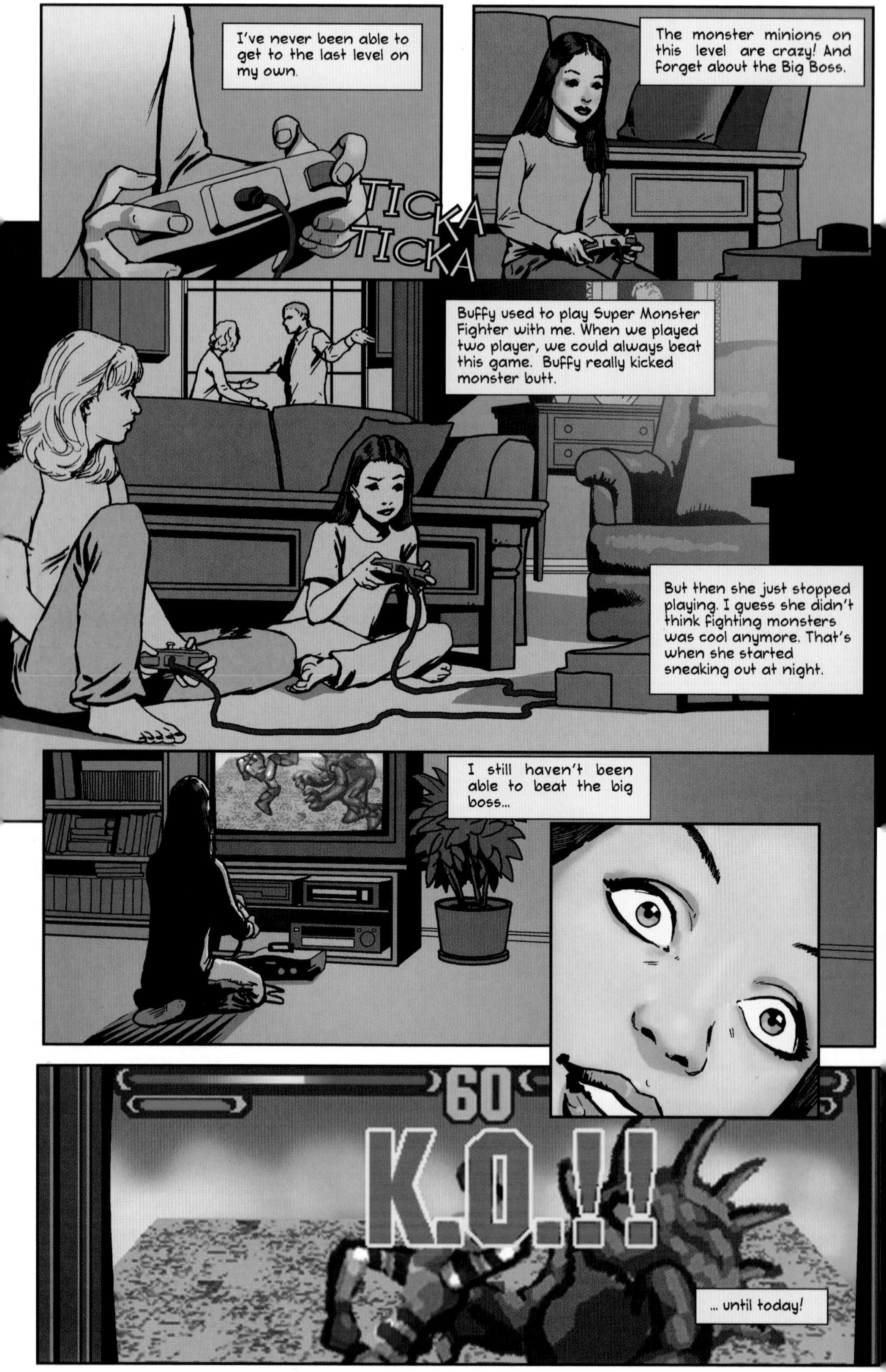
I've never been able to get to the last level on my own.
TICKA TICKA
The monster minions on this level are crazy! And forget about the Big Boss.
Buffy used to play Super Monster Fighter with me. When we played two player, we could always beat this game. Buffy really kicked monster butt.
But then she just stopped playing. I guess she didn't think fighting monsters was cool anymore. That's when she started sneaking out at night.
I still haven't been able to beat the big boss...
60
K.O.!!
... until today!

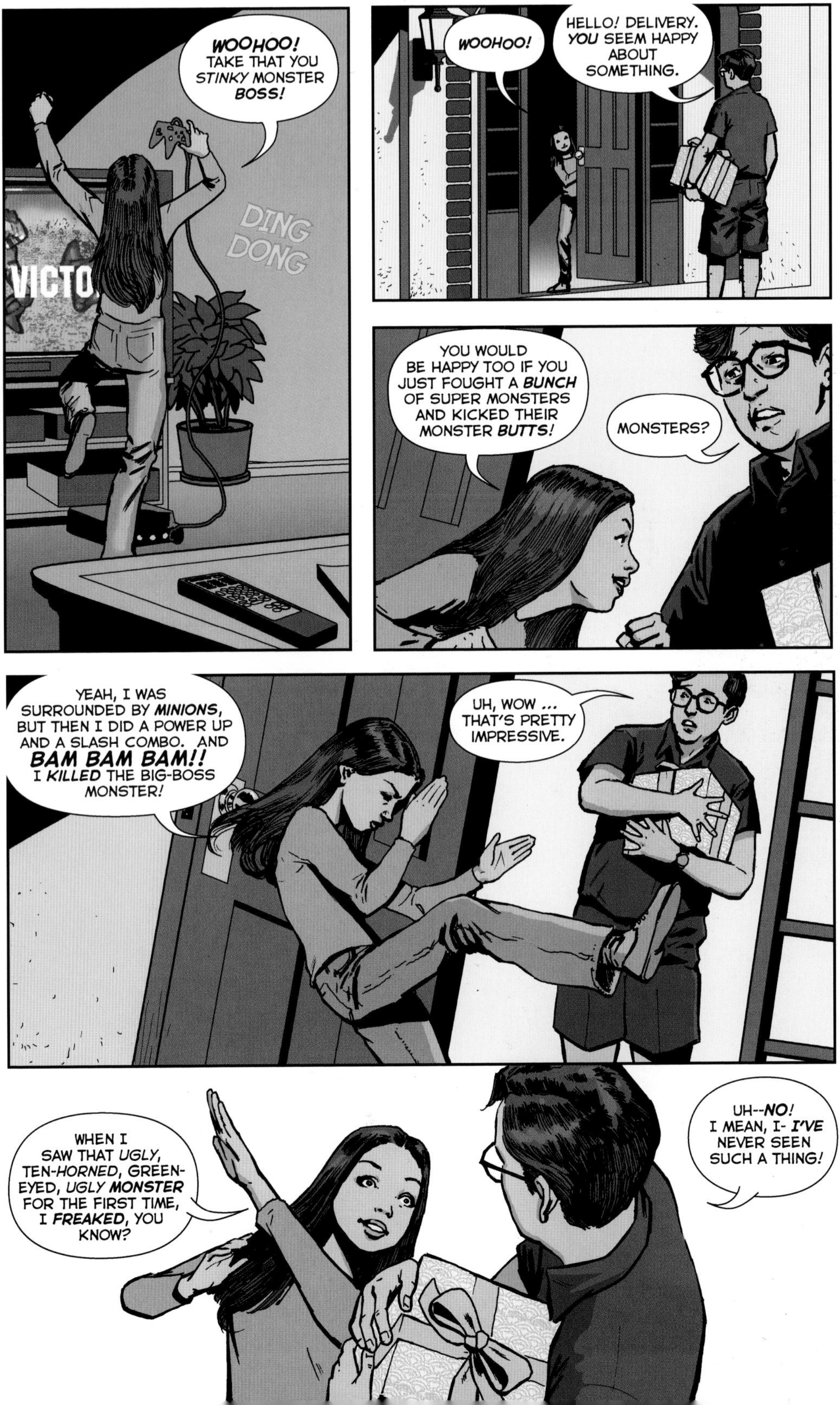
WOOHOO! TAKE THAT YOU STINKY MONSTER BOSS!
VICTO
DING DONG
WOOHOO!
HELLO! DELIVERY. YOU SEEM HAPPY ABOUT SOMETHING.
YOU WOULD BE HAPPY TOO IF YOU JUST FOUGHT A BUNCH OF SUPER MONSTERS AND KICKED THEIR MONSTER BUTTS!
MONSTERS?
YEAH, I WAS SURROUNDED BY MINIONS, BUT THEN I DID A POWER UP AND A SLASH COMBO. AND BAM BAM BAM!! I KILLED THE BIG-BOSS MONSTER!
UH, WOW ... THAT'S PRETTY IMPRESSIVE.
WHEN I SAW THAT UGLY, TEN-HORNED, GREEN-EYED, UGLY MONSTER FOR THE FIRST TIME, I FREAKED, YOU KNOW?
UH--NO! I MEAN, I- I'VE NEVER SEEN SUCH A THING!

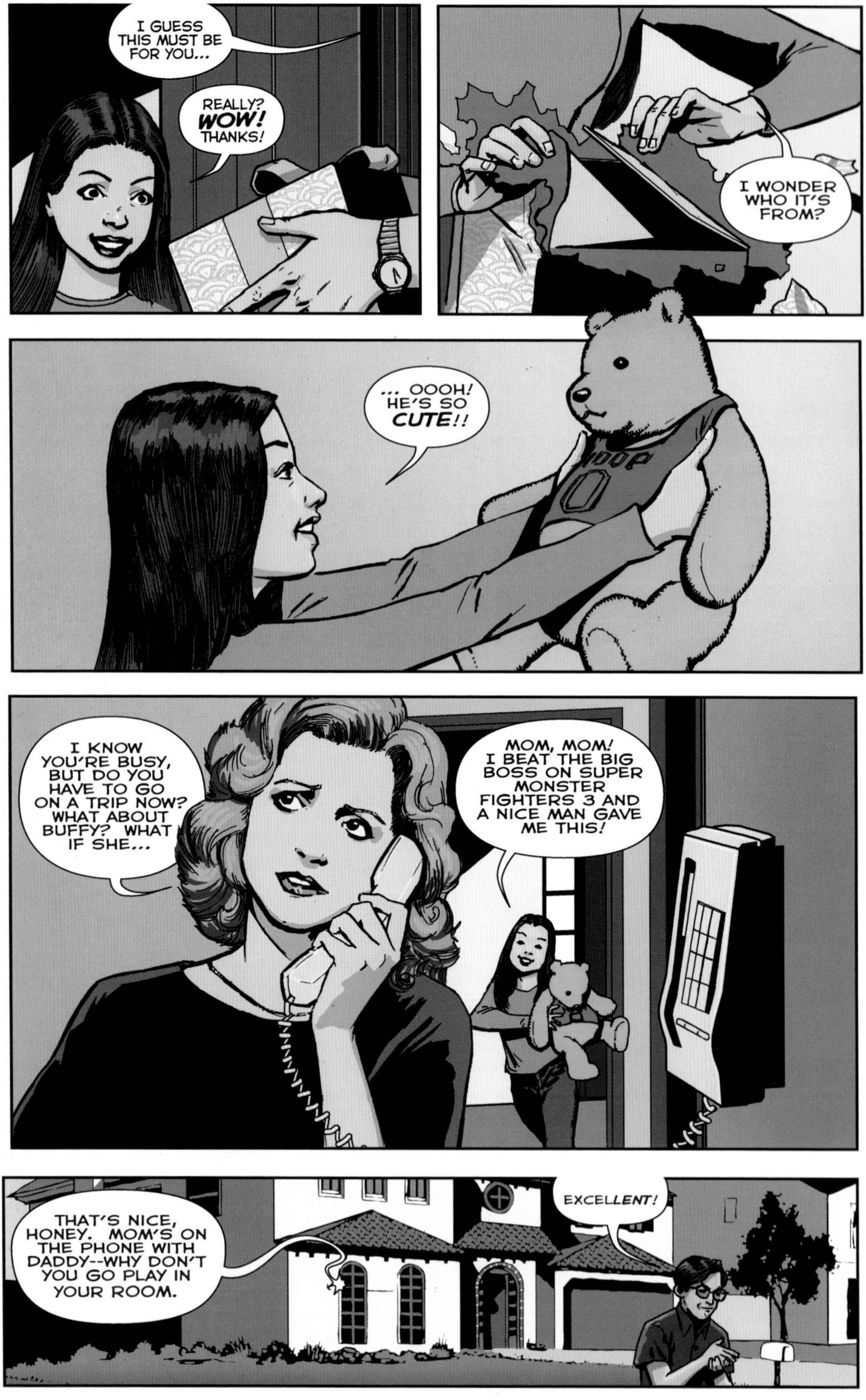

I GUESS THIS MUST BE FOR YOU...
REALLY? WOW! THANKS!
I WONDER WHO IT'S FROM?
... OOOH! HE'S SO CUTE!!
I KNOW YOU'RE BUSY, BUT DO YOU HAVE TO GO ON A TRIP NOW? WHAT ABOUT BUFFY? WHAT IF SHE...
MOM, MOM! I BEAT THE BIG BOSS ON SUPER MONSTER FIGHTERS 3 AND A NICE MAN GAVE ME THIS!
THAT'S NICE, HONEY. MOM'S ON THE PHONE WITH DADDY--WHY DON'T YOU GO PLAY IN YOUR ROOM.
EXCELLENT!

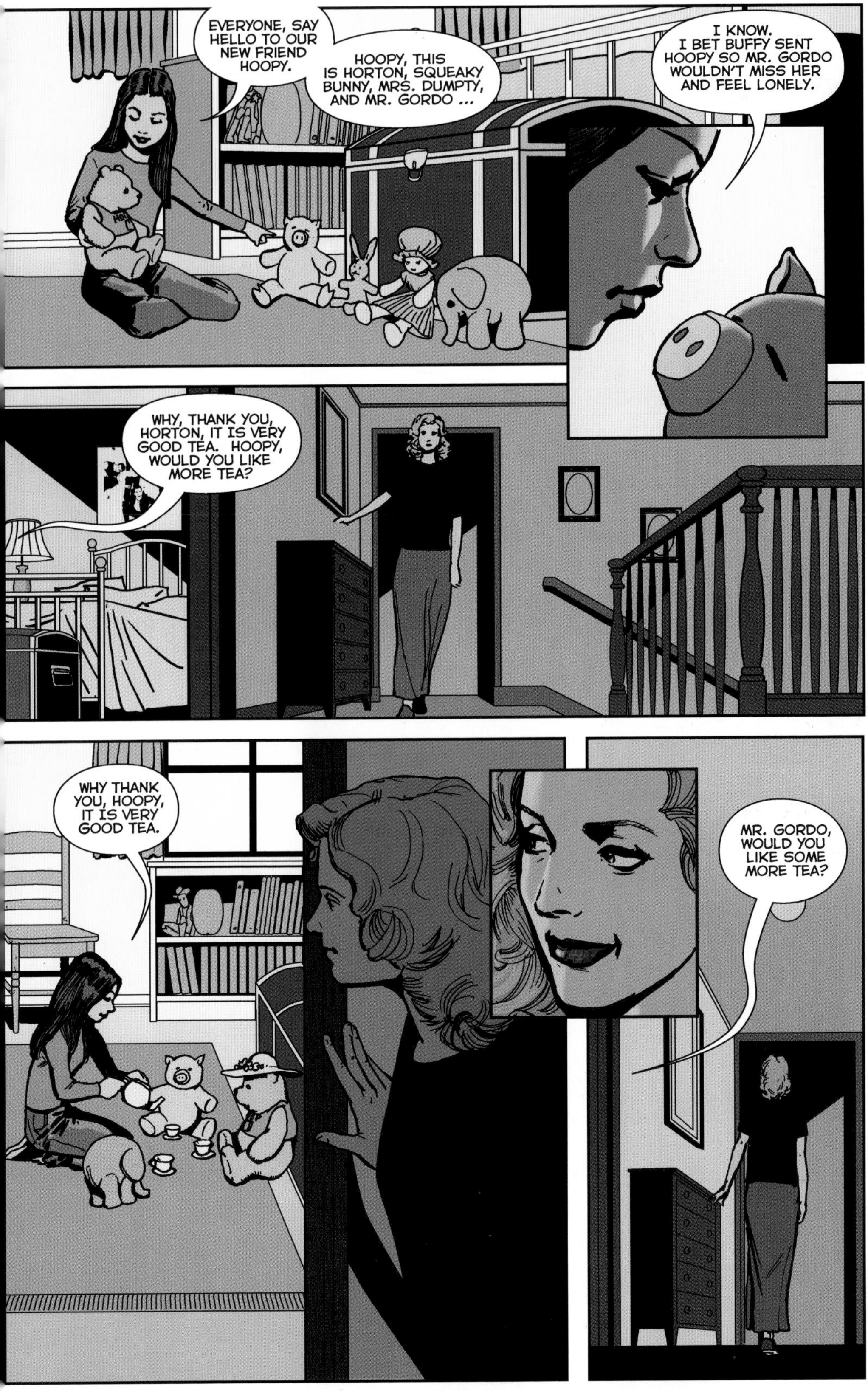
EVERYONE, SAY HELLO TO OUR NEW FRIEND HOOPY.
HOOPY, THIS IS HORTON, SQUEAKY BUNNY, MRS. DUMPTY, AND MR. GORDO ...
I KNOW. I BET BUFFY SENT HOOPY SO MR. GORDO WOULDN'T MISS HER AND FEEL LONELY.
WHY, THANK YOU, HORTON, IT IS VERY GOOD TEA. HOOPY, WOULD YOU LIKE MORE TEA?
WHY THANK YOU, HOOPY, IT IS VERY GOOD TEA.
MR. GORDO, WOULD YOU LIKE SOME MORE TEA?

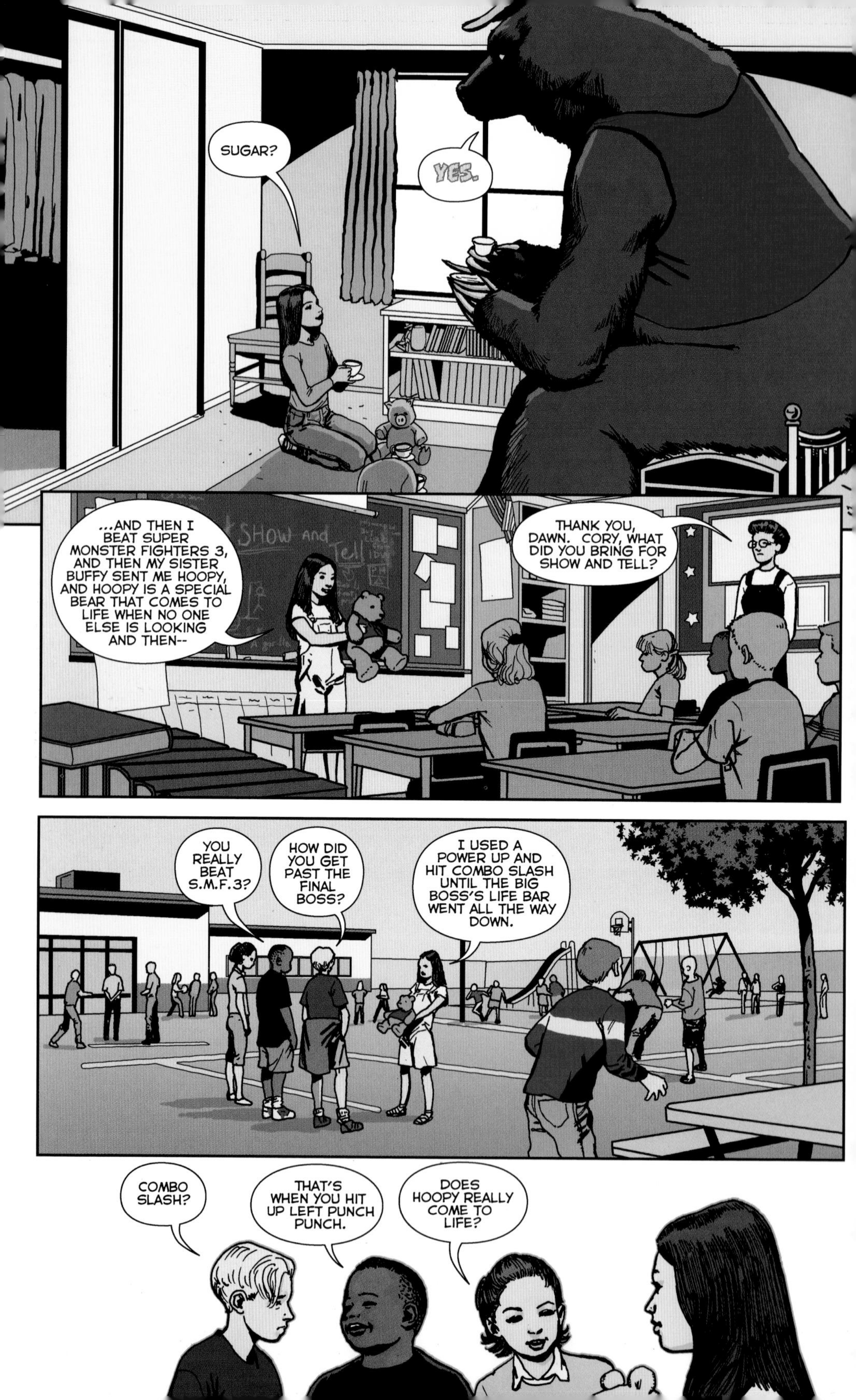
SUGAR?
YES.
...AND THEN I BEAT SUPER MONSTER FIGHTERS 3, AND THEN MY SISTER BUFFY SENT ME HOOPY, AND HOOPY IS A SPECIAL BEAR THAT COMES TO LIFE WHEN NO ONE ELSE IS LOOKING AND THEN--
THANK YOU, DAWN. CORY, WHAT DID YOU BRING FOR SHOW AND TELL?
YOU REALLY BEAT S.M.F.3?
HOW DID YOU GET PAST THE FINAL BOSS?
I USED A POWER UP AND HIT COMBO SLASH UNTIL THE BIG BOSS'S LIFE BAR WENT ALL THE WAY DOWN.
COMBO SLASH?
THAT'S WHEN YOU HIT UP LEFT PUNCH PUNCH.
DOES HOOPY REALLY COME TO LIFE?

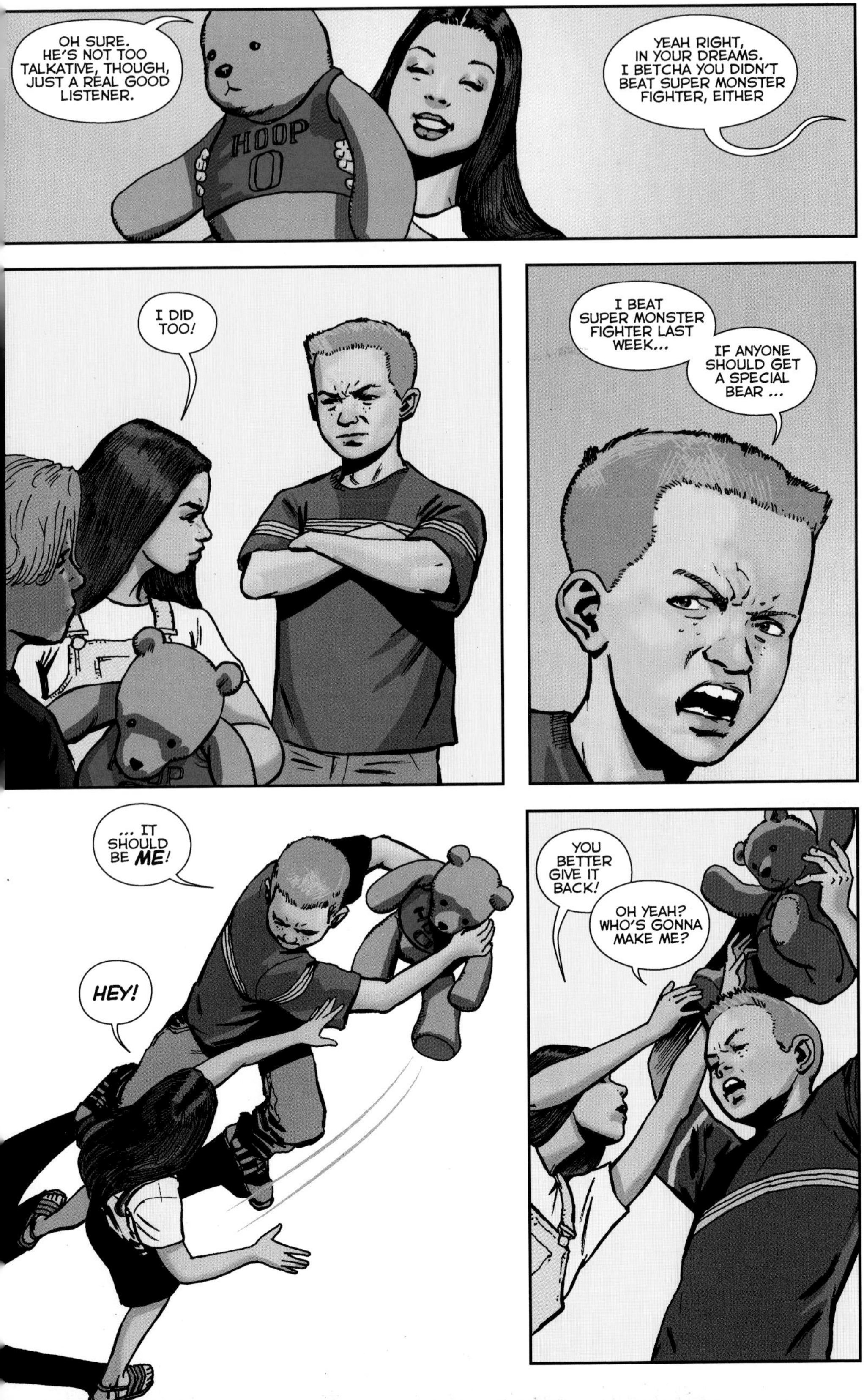
OH SURE. HE'S NOT TOO TALKATIVE, THOUGH, JUST A REAL GOOD LISTENER.
YEAH RIGHT, IN YOUR DREAMS. I BETCHA YOU DIDN'T BEAT SUPER MONSTER FIGHTER, EITHER
HOOP 0
I DID TOO!
I BEAT SUPER MONSTER FIGHTER LAST WEEK...
IF ANYONE SHOULD GET A SPECIAL BEAR ...
... IT SHOULD BE *ME*!
HEY!
YOU BETTER GIVE IT BACK!
OH YEAH? WHO'S GONNA MAKE ME?

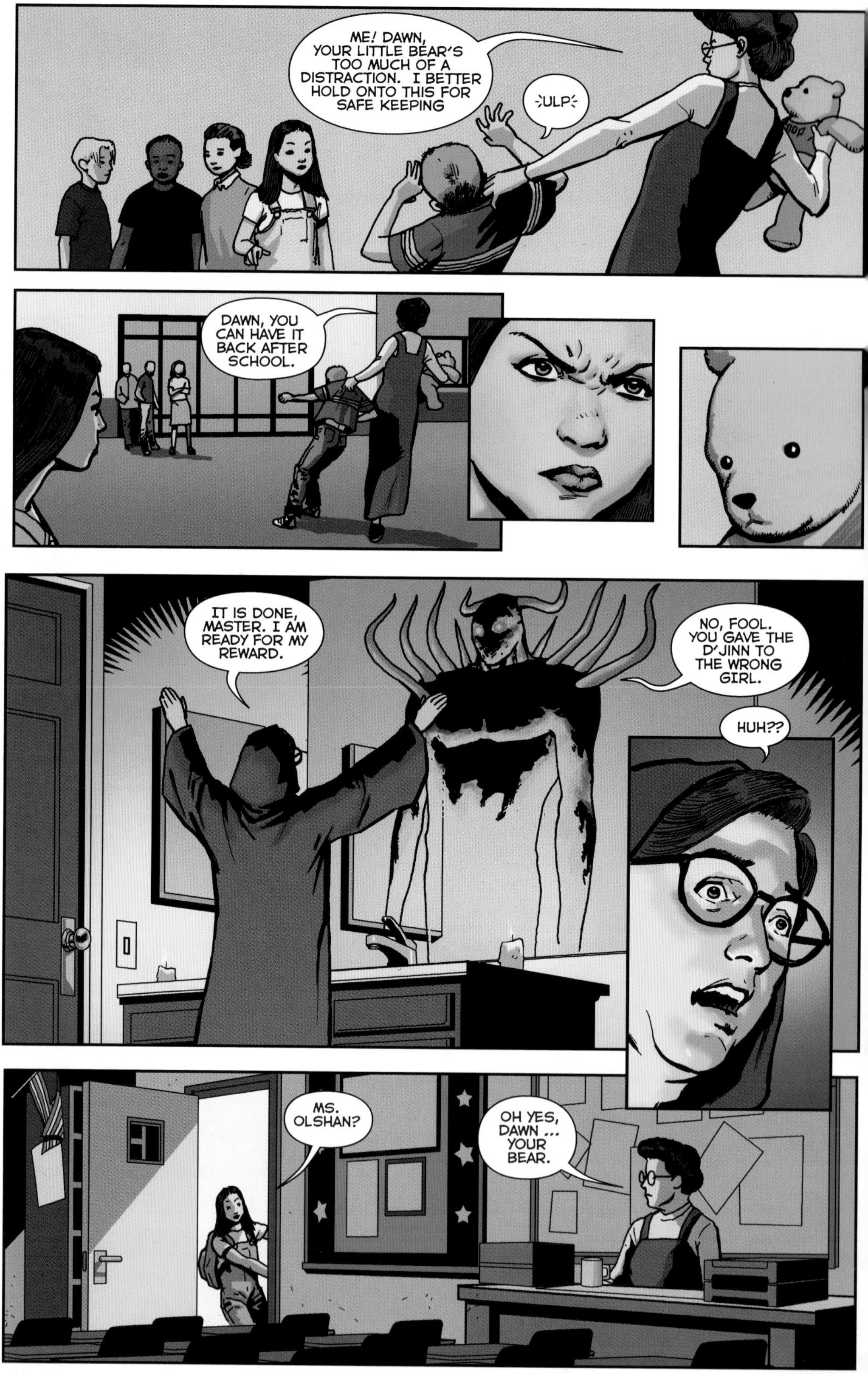
ME! DAWN, YOUR LITTLE BEAR'S TOO MUCH OF A DISTRACTION. I BETTER HOLD ONTO THIS FOR SAFE KEEPING
ULP
DAWN, YOU CAN HAVE IT BACK AFTER SCHOOL.
IT IS DONE, MASTER. I AM READY FOR MY REWARD.
NO, FOOL. YOU GAVE THE D'JINN TO THE WRONG GIRL.
HUH??
MS. OLSHAN?
OH YES, DAWN ... YOUR BEAR.

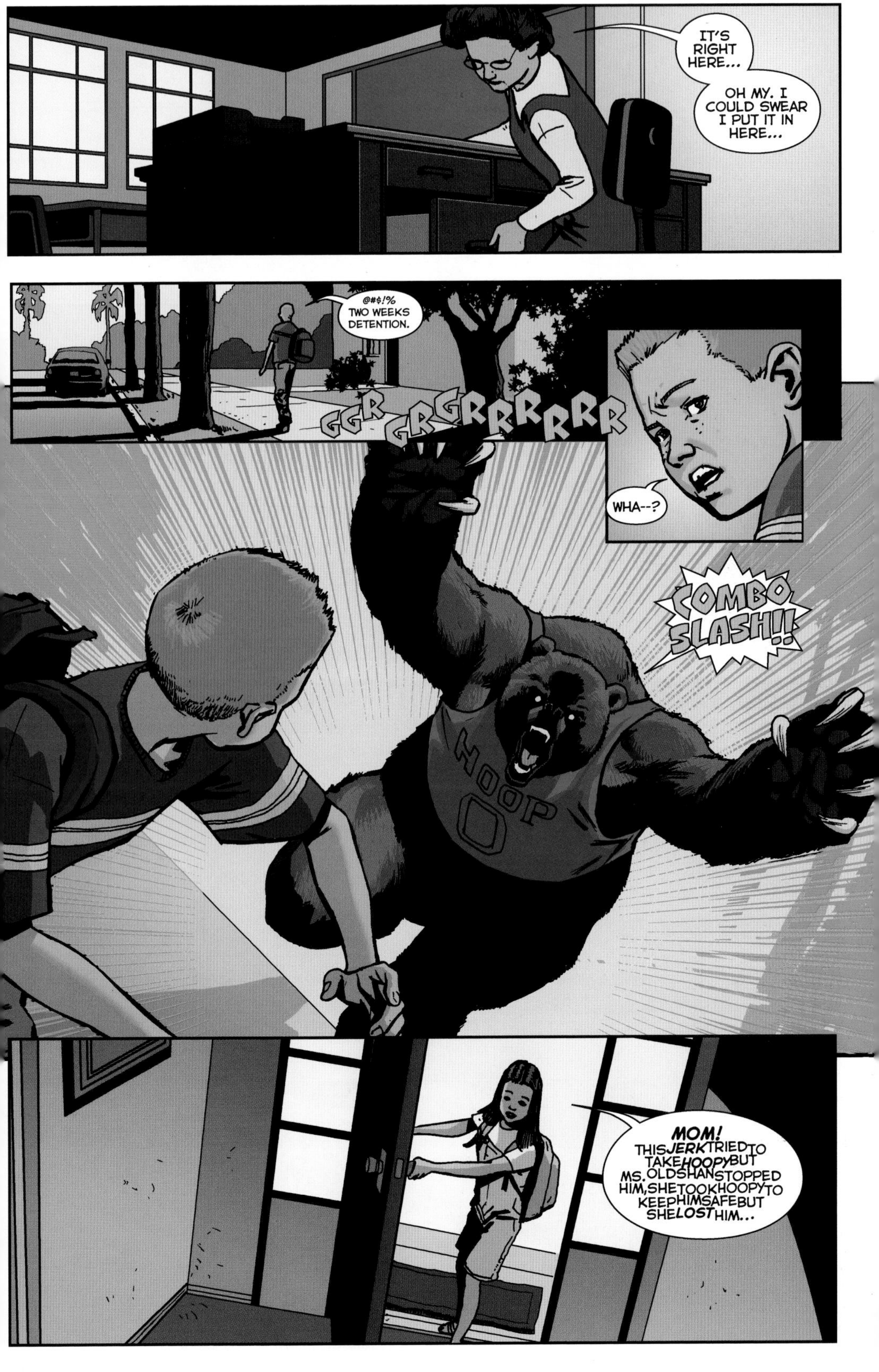

IT'S RIGHT HERE...
OH MY. I COULD SWEAR I PUT IT IN HERE...
@#$!% TWO WEEKS DETENTION.
GGR GRGRRRRRR
WHA--?
COMBO SLASH!!
HOOP 0
MOM! THIS JERK TRIED TO TAKE HOOPY BUT MS. OLDSHAN STOPPED HIM, SHE TOOK HOOPY TO KEEP HIM SAFE BUT SHE LOST HIM...

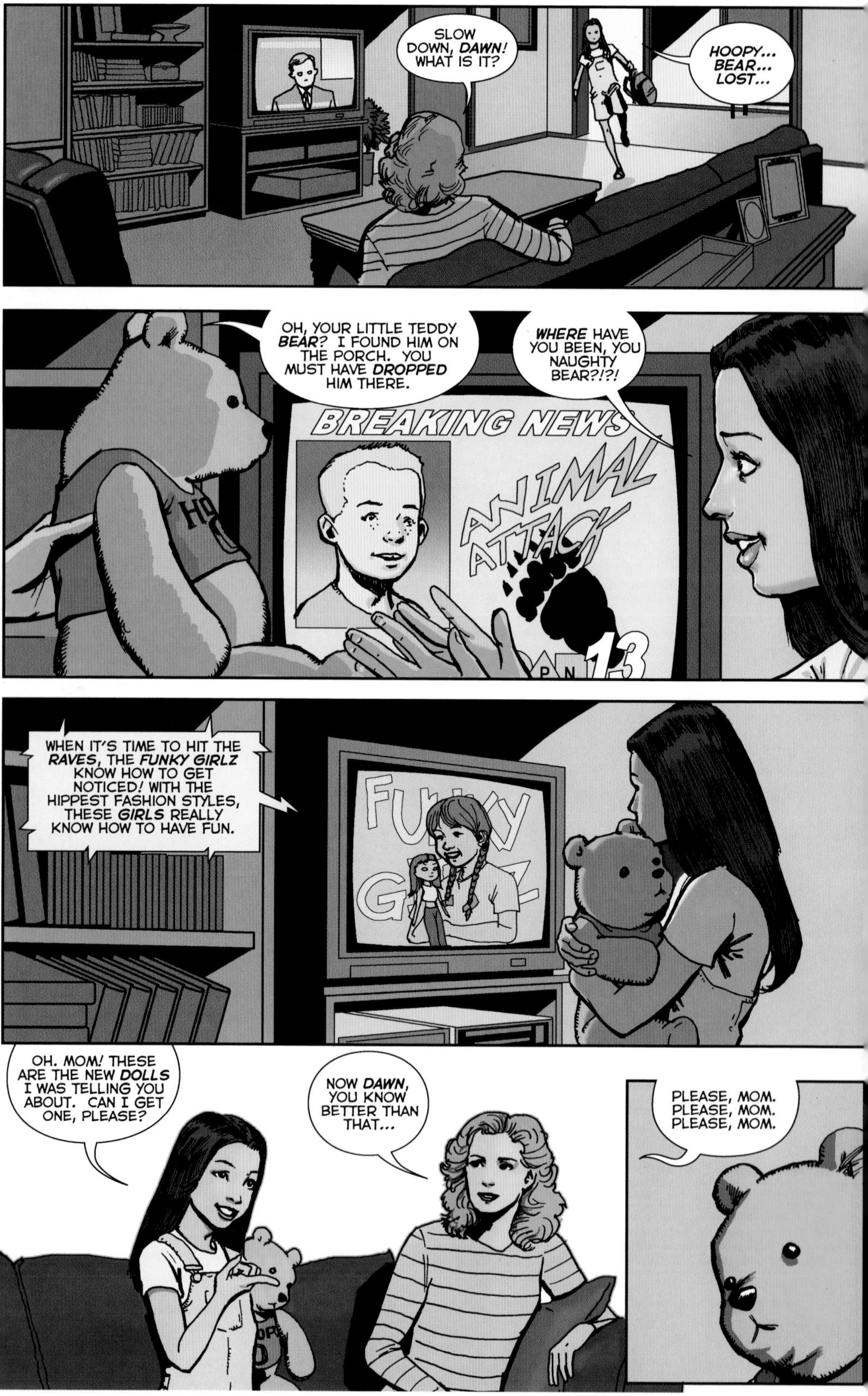
SLOW DOWN, DAWN! WHAT IS IT?
HOOPY... BEAR... LOST...
OH, YOUR LITTLE TEDDY BEAR? I FOUND HIM ON THE PORCH. YOU MUST HAVE DROPPED HIM THERE.
WHERE HAVE YOU BEEN, YOU NAUGHTY BEAR?!?!
BREAKING NEWS
ANIMAL ATTACK
WHEN IT'S TIME TO HIT THE RAVES, THE FUNKY GIRLZ KNOW HOW TO GET NOTICED! WITH THE HIPPEST FASHION STYLES, THESE GIRLS REALLY KNOW HOW TO HAVE FUN.
OH. MOM! THESE ARE THE NEW DOLLS I WAS TELLING YOU ABOUT. CAN I GET ONE, PLEASE?
NOW DAWN, YOU KNOW BETTER THAN THAT...
PLEASE, MOM. PLEASE, MOM. PLEASE, MOM.

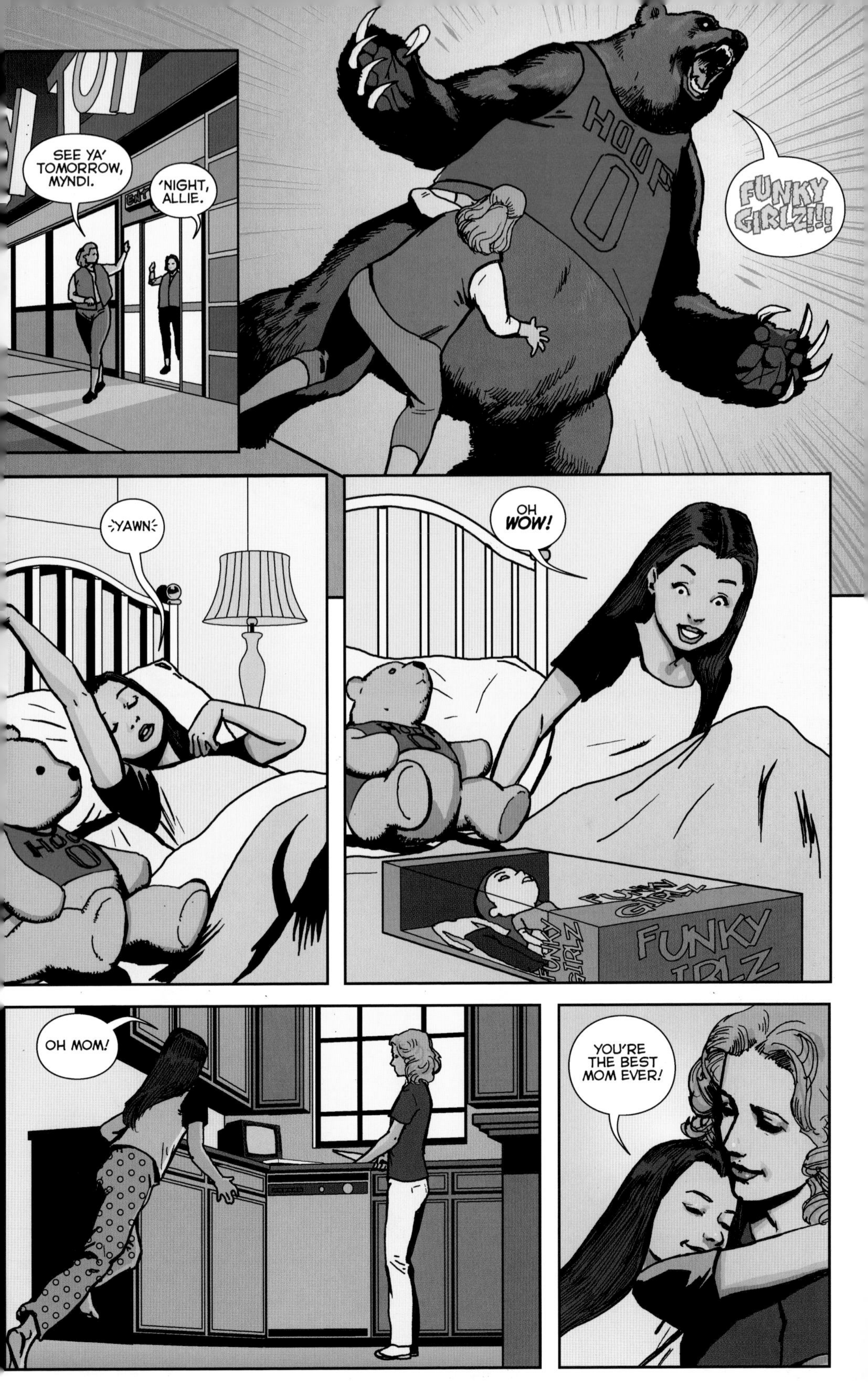
SEE YA' TOMORROW, MYNDI.
'NIGHT, ALLIE.
FUNKY GIRLZ!!!
-YAWN-
OH WOW!
FUNKY GIRLZ
OH MOM!
YOU'RE THE BEST MOM EVER!

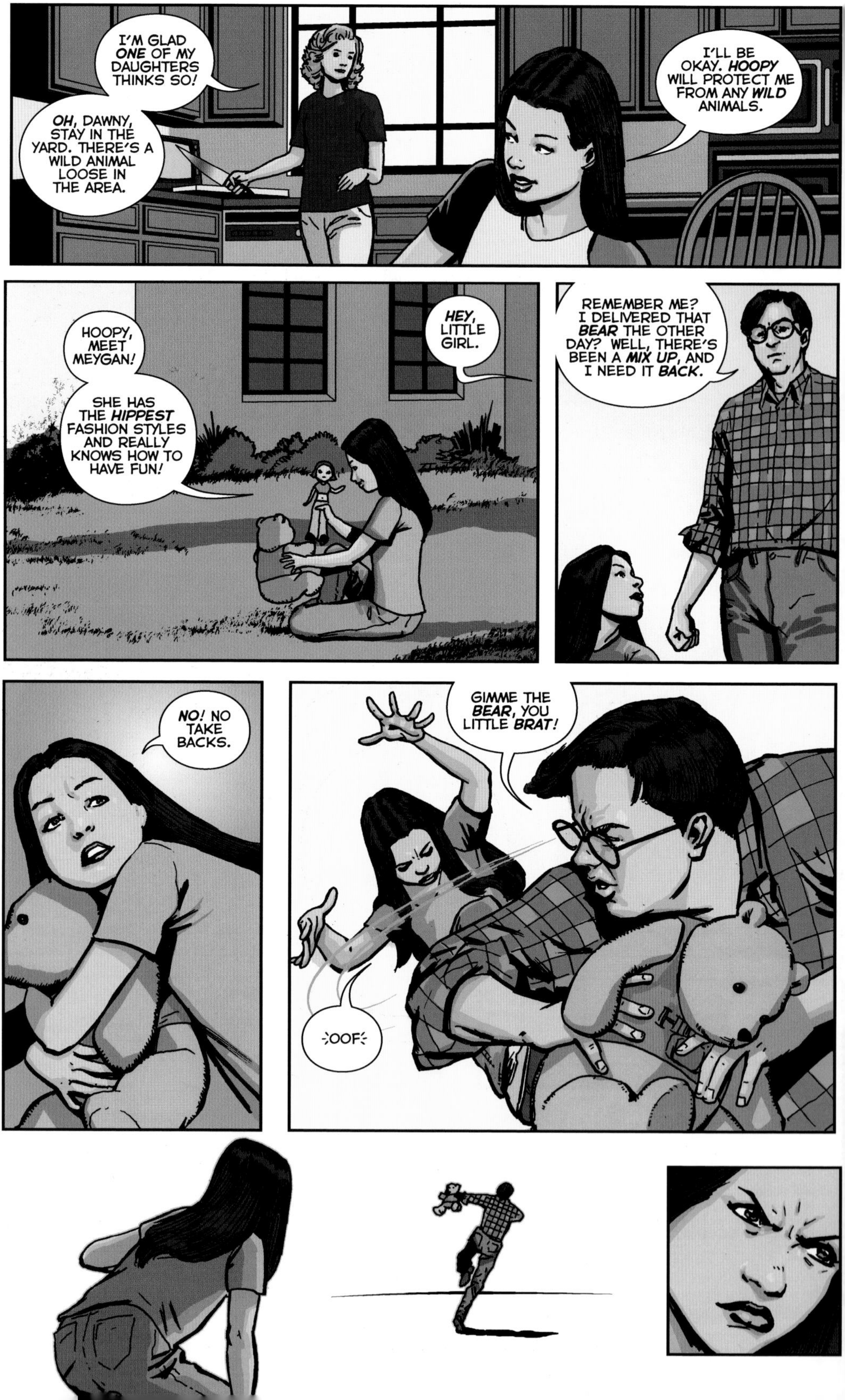
OH, DAWNY, STAY IN THE YARD. THERE'S A WILD ANIMAL LOOSE IN THE AREA.
I'LL BE OKAY. HOOPY WILL PROTECT ME FROM ANY WILD ANIMALS.
I'M GLAD ONE OF MY DAUGHTERS THINKS SO!
HOOPY, MEET MEYGAN!
SHE HAS THE HIPPEST FASHION STYLES AND REALLY KNOWS HOW TO HAVE FUN!
HEY, LITTLE GIRL.
REMEMBER ME? I DELIVERED THAT BEAR THE OTHER DAY? WELL, THERE'S BEEN A MIX UP, AND I NEED IT BACK.
NO! NO TAKE BACKS.
GIMME THE BEAR, YOU LITTLE BRAT!
OOF

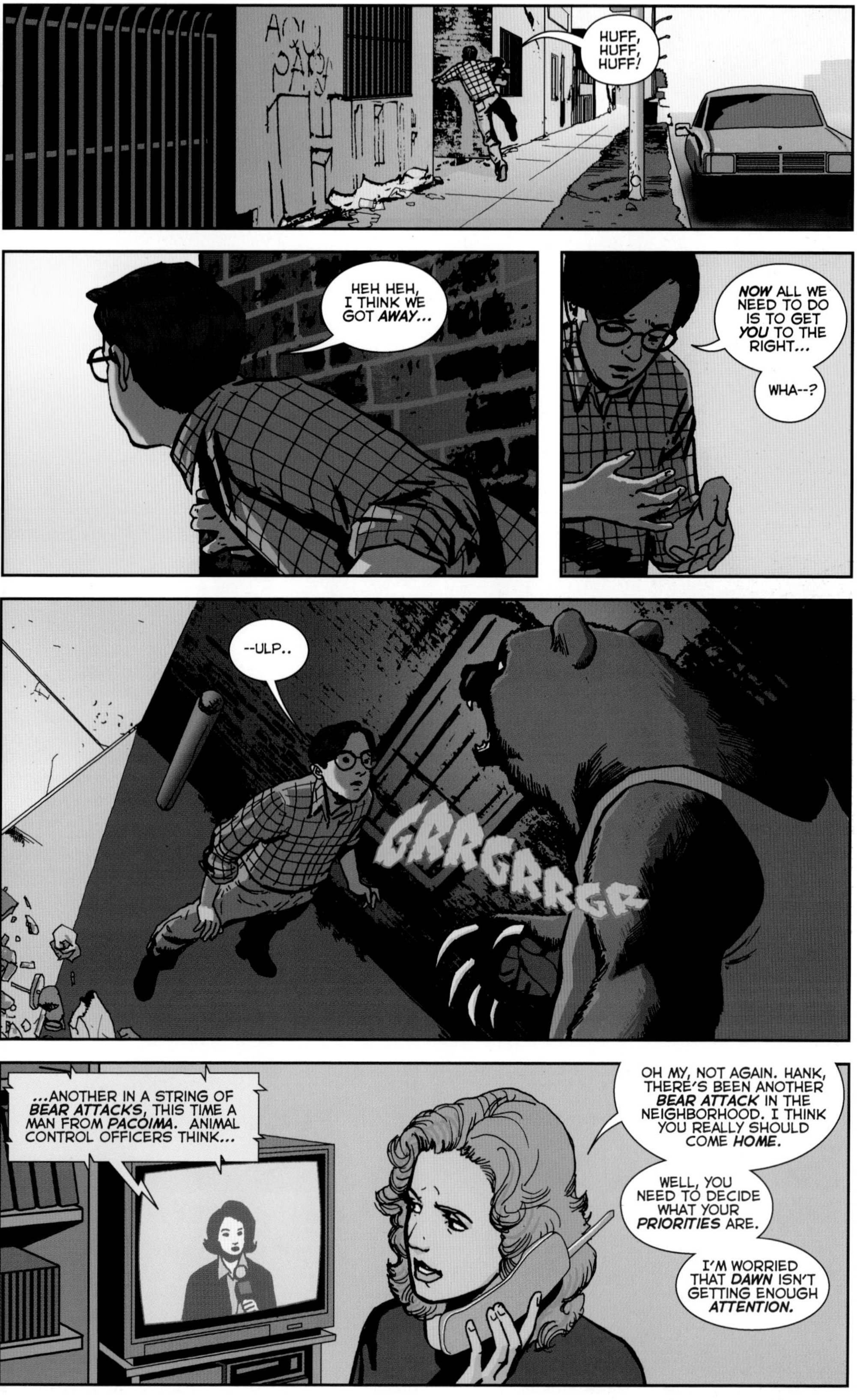

HUFF, HUFF, HUFF!
HEH HEH, I THINK WE GOT AWAY...
NOW ALL WE NEED TO DO IS TO GET YOU TO THE RIGHT...
WHA--?
--ULP..
GRRGRRRGR
...ANOTHER IN A STRING OF BEAR ATTACKS, THIS TIME A MAN FROM PACOIMA. ANIMAL CONTROL OFFICERS THINK...
OH MY, NOT AGAIN. HANK, THERE'S BEEN ANOTHER BEAR ATTACK IN THE NEIGHBORHOOD. I THINK YOU REALLY SHOULD COME HOME.
WELL, YOU NEED TO DECIDE WHAT YOUR PRIORITIES ARE.
I'M WORRIED THAT DAWN ISN'T GETTING ENOUGH ATTENTION.

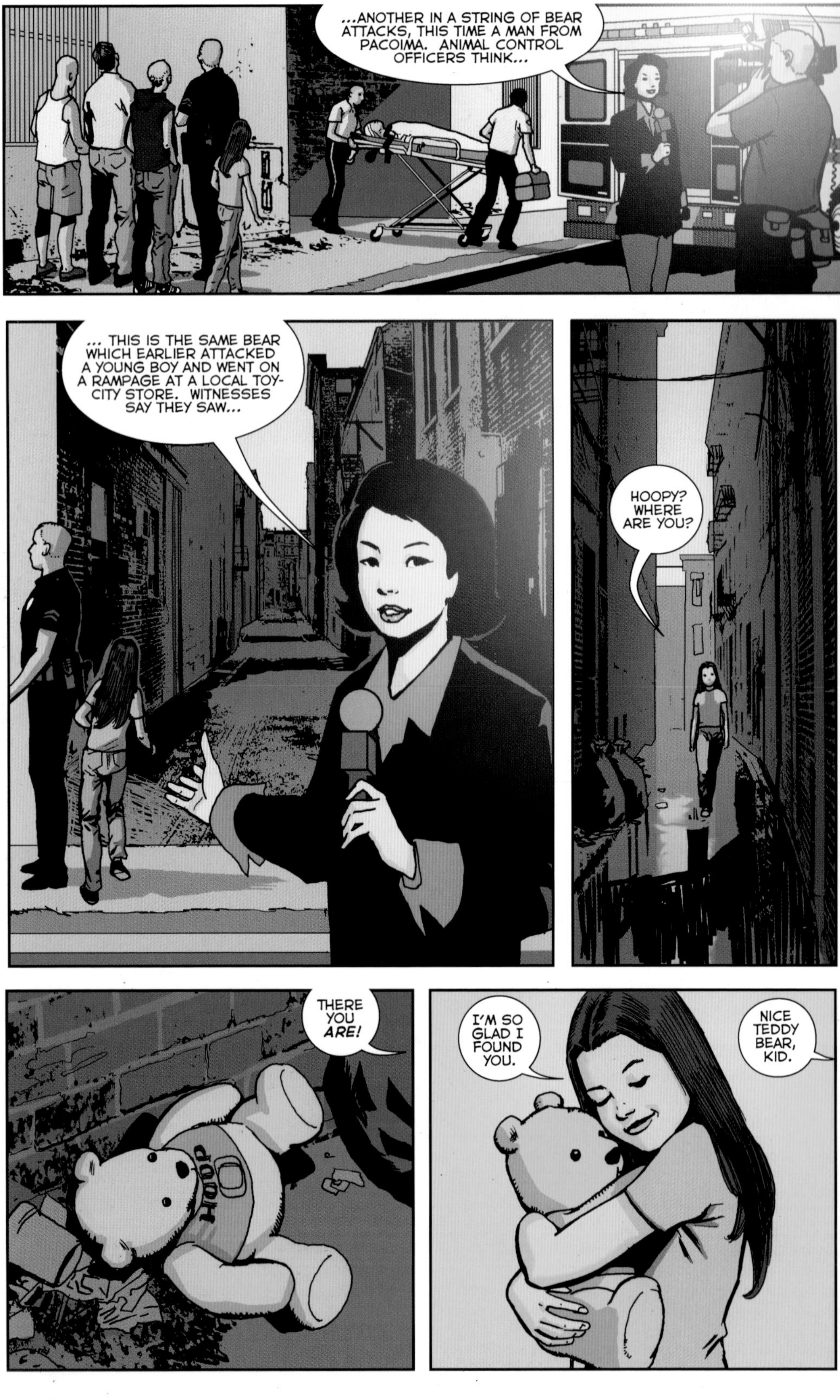
...ANOTHER IN A STRING OF BEAR ATTACKS, THIS TIME A MAN FROM PACOIMA. ANIMAL CONTROL OFFICERS THINK...
... THIS IS THE SAME BEAR WHICH EARLIER ATTACKED A YOUNG BOY AND WENT ON A RAMPAGE AT A LOCAL TOY-CITY STORE. WITNESSES SAY THEY SAW...
HOOPY? WHERE ARE YOU?
THERE YOU *ARE!*
I'M SO GLAD I FOUND YOU.
NICE TEDDY BEAR, KID.

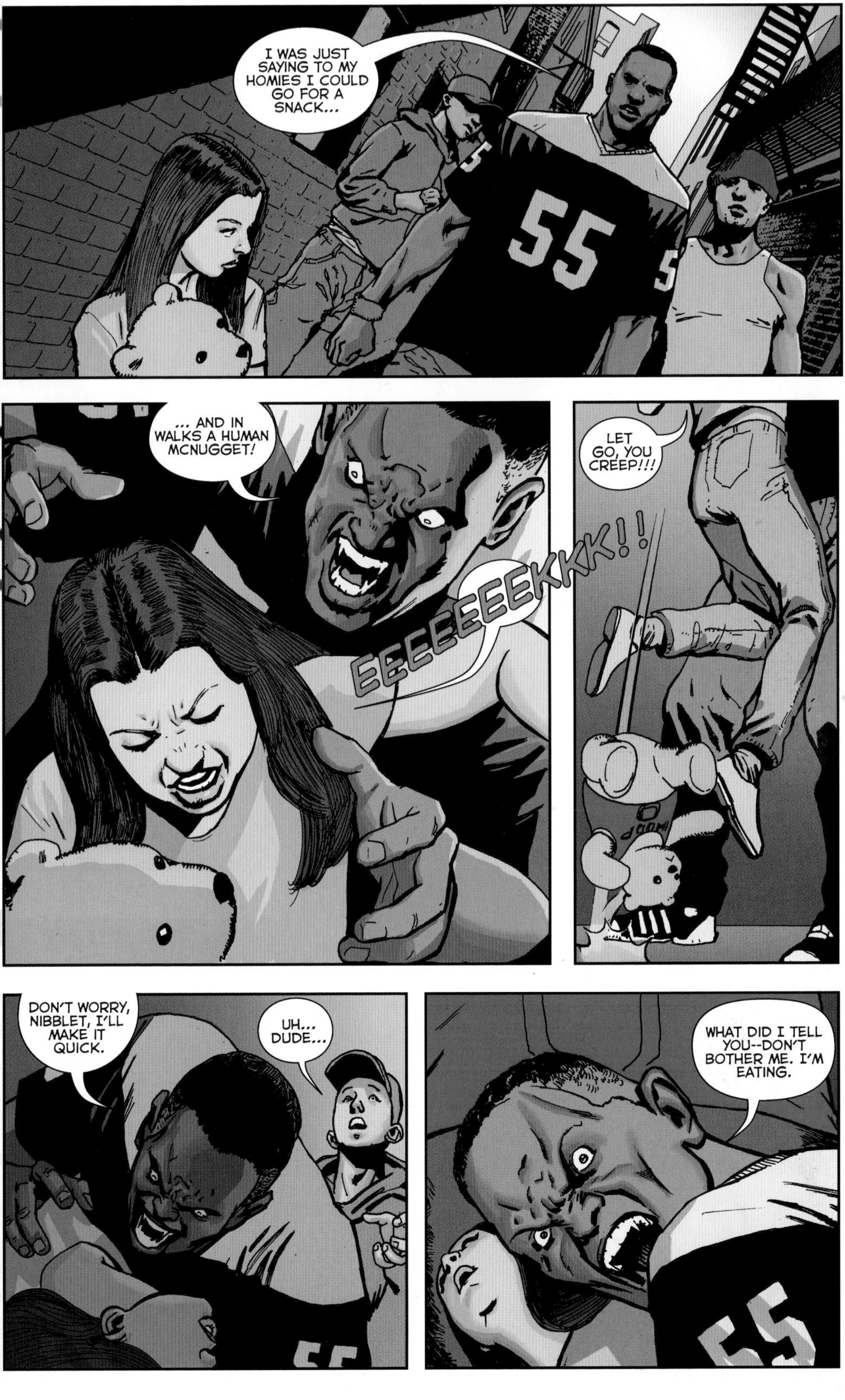

I WAS JUST SAYING TO MY HOMIES I COULD GO FOR A SNACK...
... AND IN WALKS A HUMAN MCNUGGET!
EEEEEEEEEKKK!!
LET GO, YOU CREEP!!!
DON'T WORRY, NIBBLET, I'LL MAKE IT QUICK.
UH... DUDE...
WHAT DID I TELL YOU--DON'T BOTHER ME. I'M EATING.

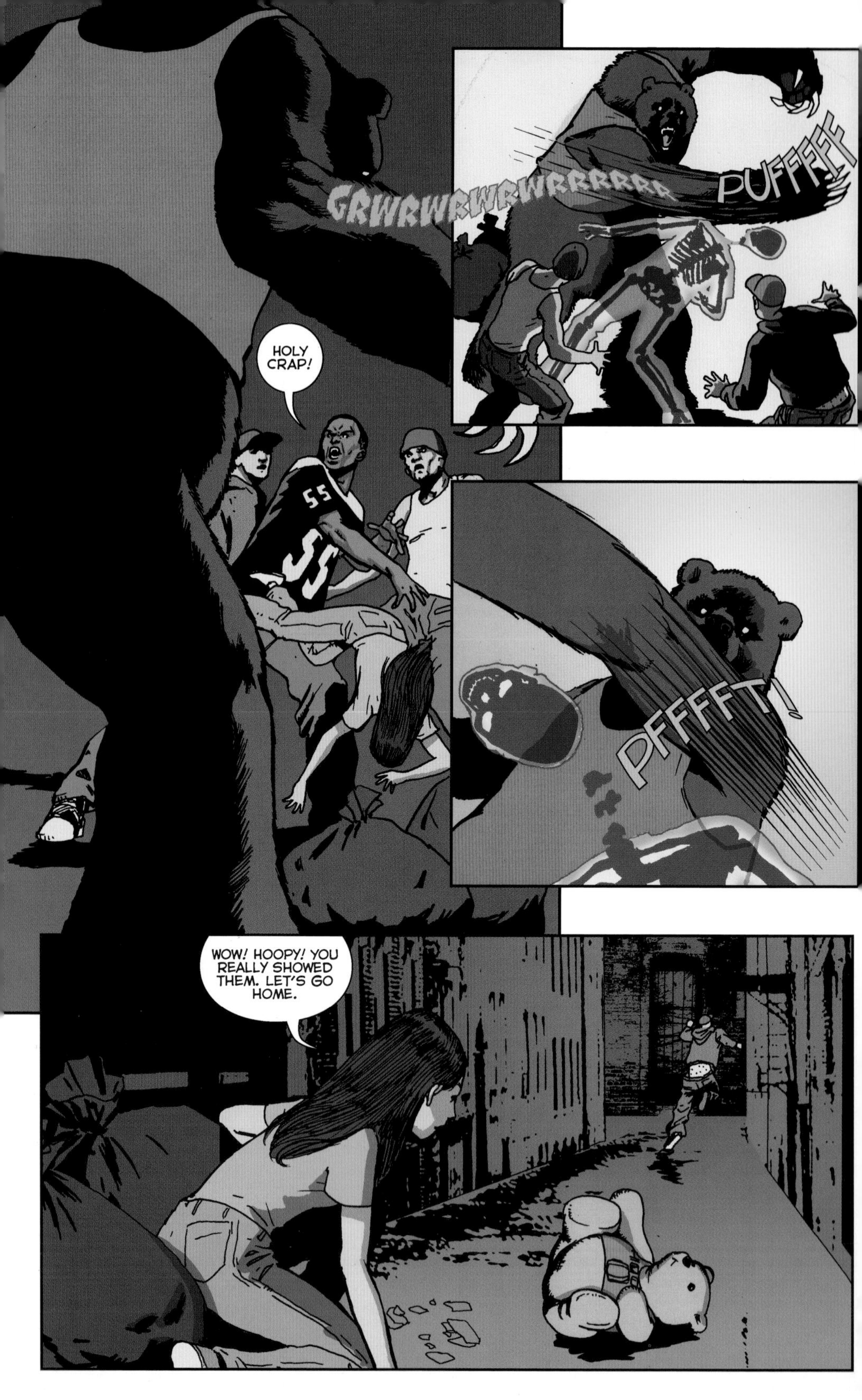
GRWRWRWRWRRRRRR
PUFFFFF
HOLY CRAP!
PFFFFT!
WOW! HOOPY! YOU REALLY SHOWED THEM. LET'S GO HOME.

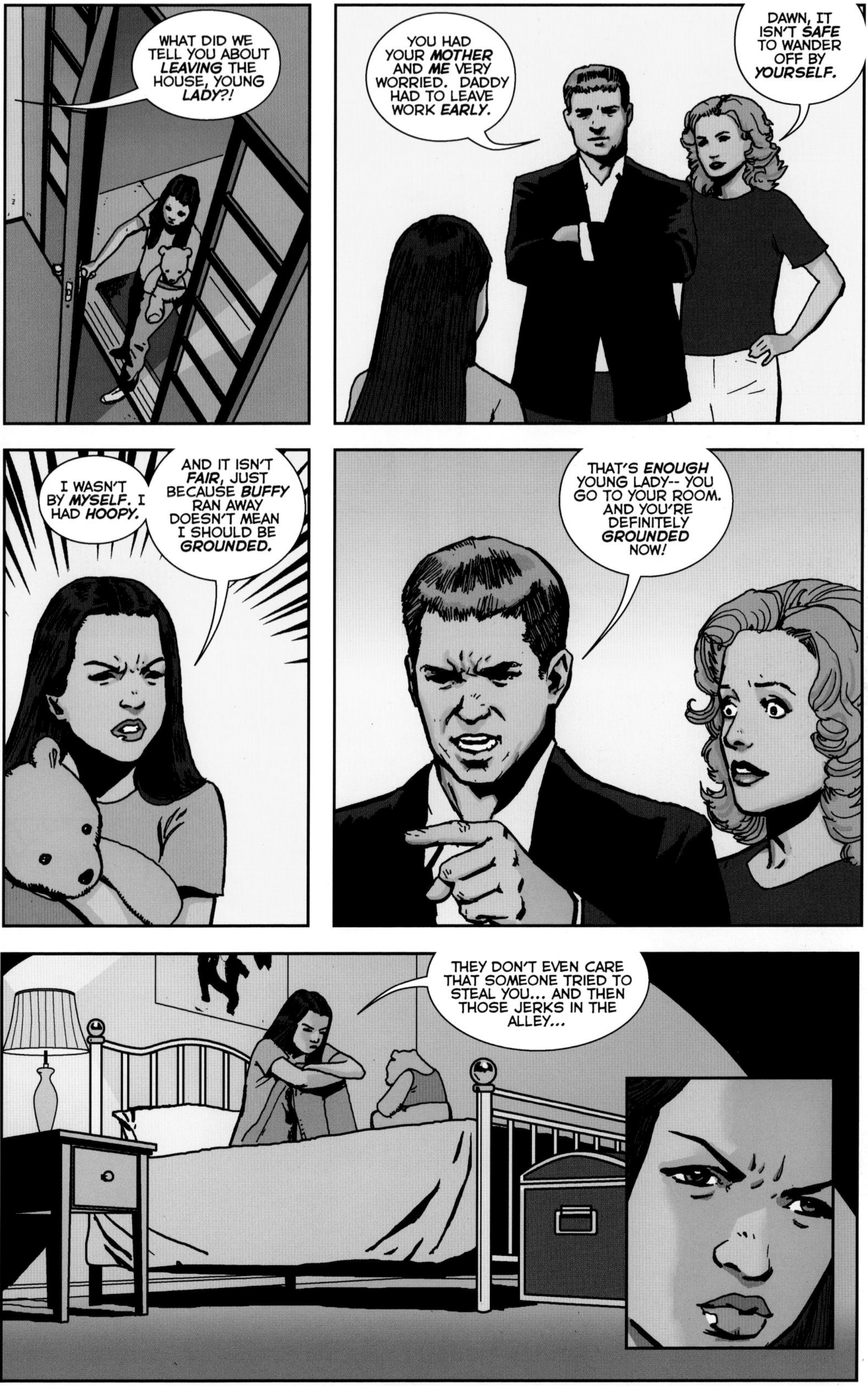
WHAT DID WE TELL YOU ABOUT LEAVING THE HOUSE, YOUNG LADY?!
YOU HAD YOUR MOTHER AND ME VERY WORRIED. DADDY HAD TO LEAVE WORK EARLY.
DAWN, IT ISN'T SAFE TO WANDER OFF BY YOURSELF.
I WASN'T BY MYSELF. I HAD HOOPY.
AND IT ISN'T FAIR, JUST BECAUSE BUFFY RAN AWAY DOESN'T MEAN I SHOULD BE GROUNDED.
THAT'S ENOUGH YOUNG LADY-- YOU GO TO YOUR ROOM. AND YOU'RE DEFINITELY GROUNDED NOW!
THEY DON'T EVEN CARE THAT SOMEONE TRIED TO STEAL YOU... AND THEN THOSE JERKS IN THE ALLEY...

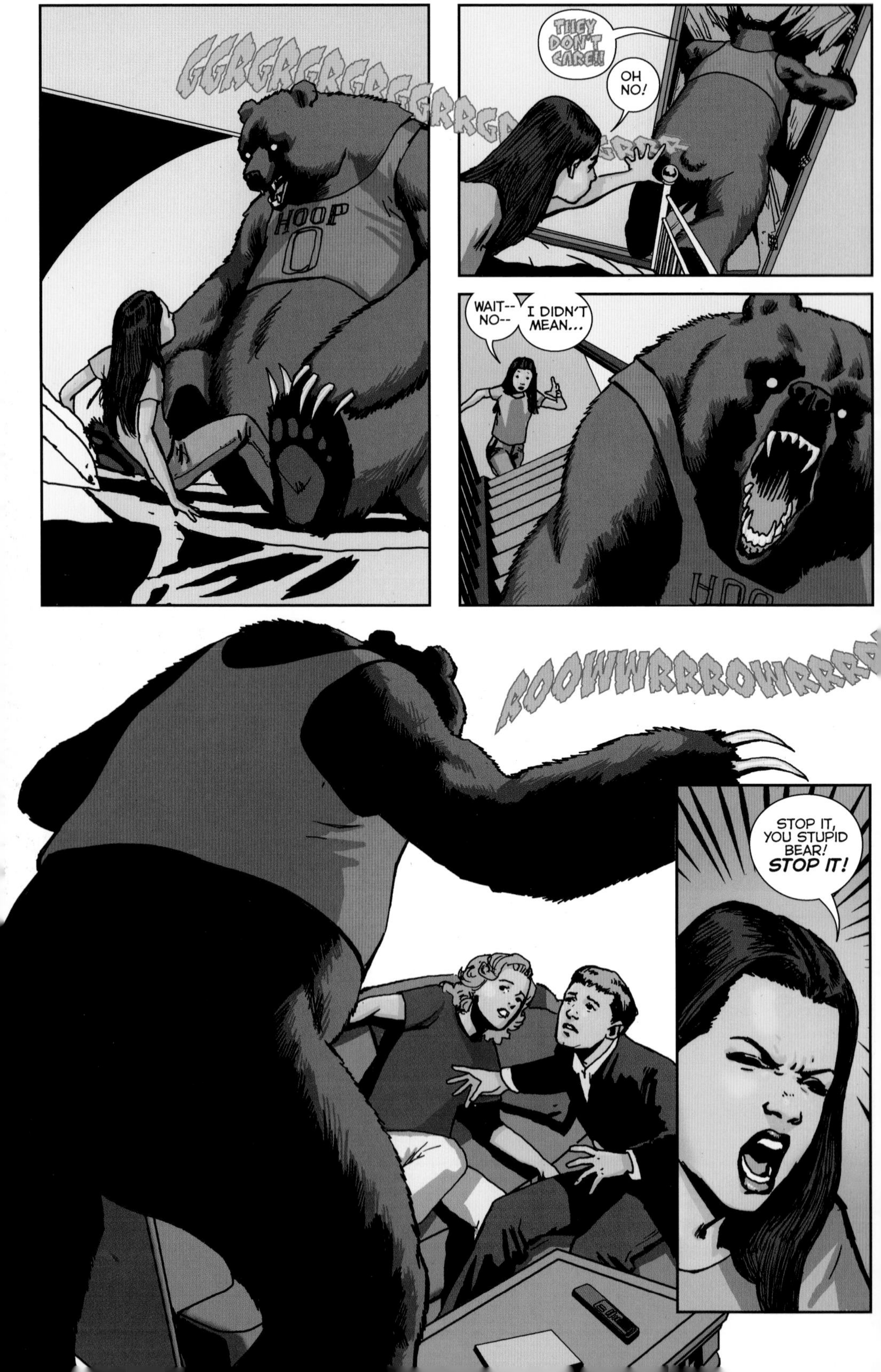
HOOP
0
THEY DON'T CARE!!
OH NO!
WAIT-- NO--
I DIDN'T MEAN...
ROOWWRRROWRRR
STOP IT, YOU STUPID BEAR! STOP IT!

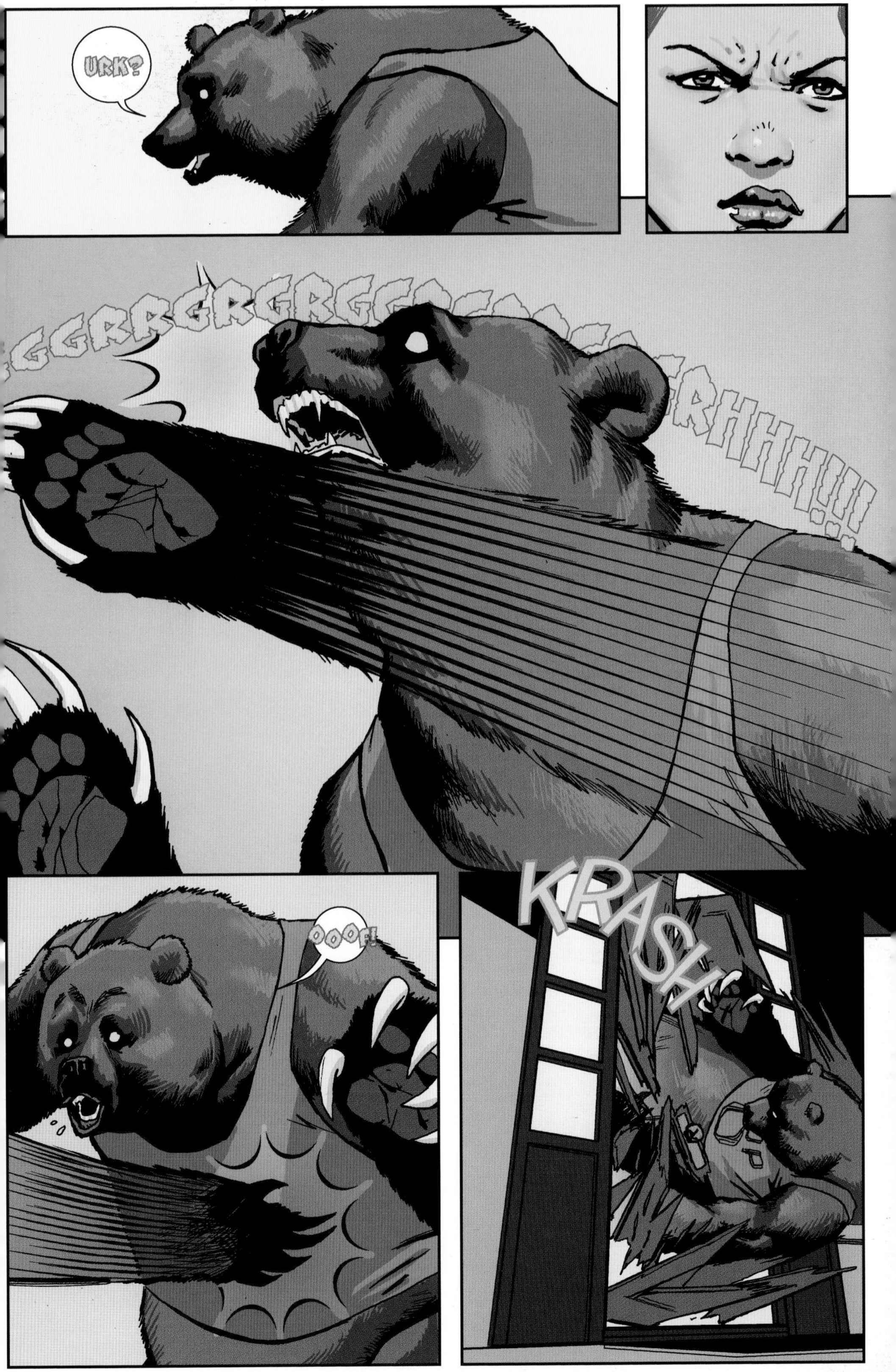
URK?
GGRRGRGRGG
RHHHH!!!
OOOF!
KRASH

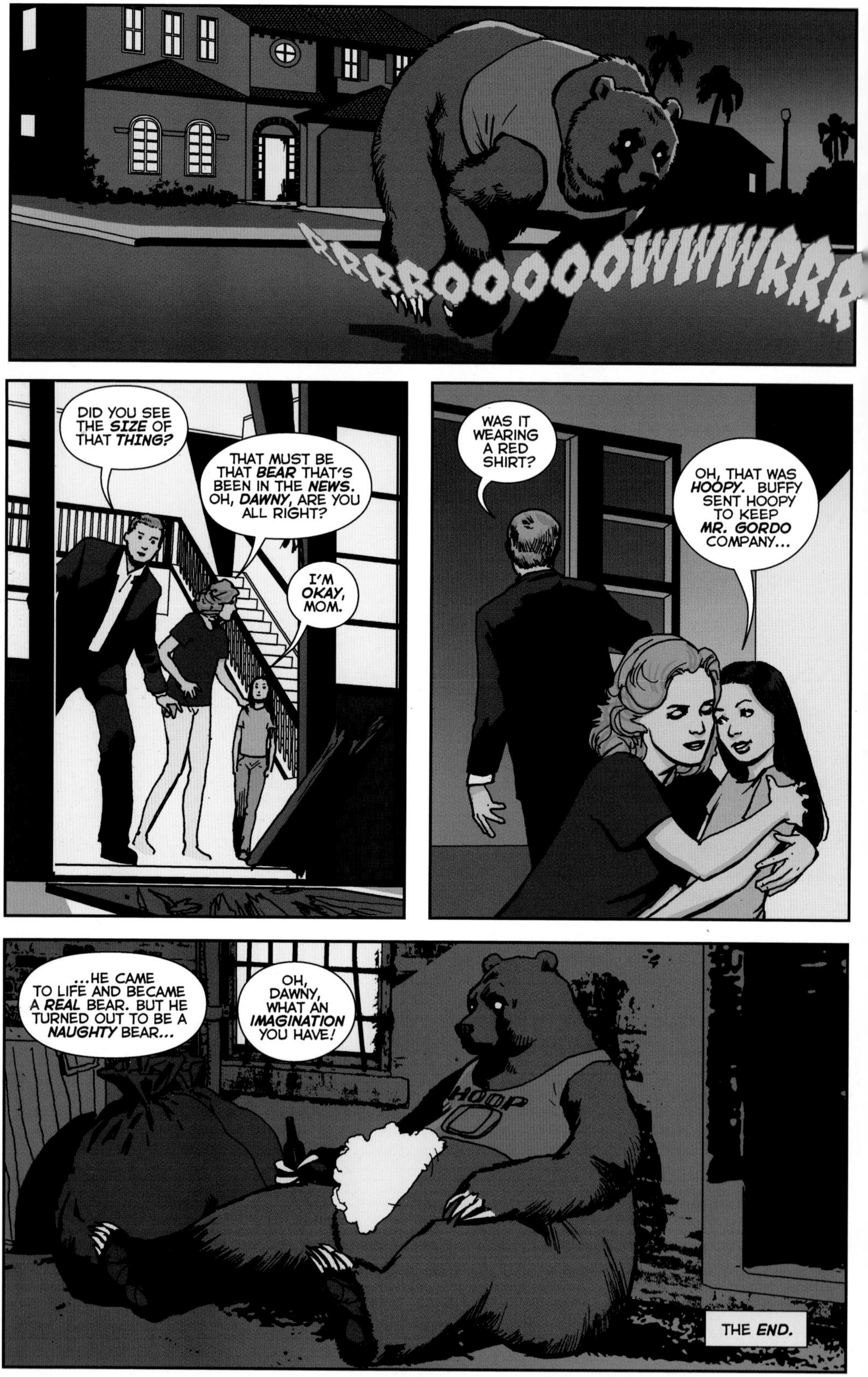
RRRROOOOOOWWWRRR
DID YOU SEE THE *SIZE* OF THAT *THING?*
THAT MUST BE THAT *BEAR* THAT'S BEEN IN THE *NEWS*. OH, *DAWNY*, ARE YOU ALL RIGHT?
I'M *OKAY*, MOM.
WAS IT WEARING A RED SHIRT?
OH, THAT WAS *HOOPY*. BUFFY SENT HOOPY TO KEEP *MR. GORDO* COMPANY...
...HE CAME TO LIFE AND BECAME A *REAL* BEAR. BUT HE TURNED OUT TO BE A *NAUGHTY* BEAR...
OH, DAWNY, WHAT AN *IMAGINATION* YOU HAVE!
HOOP
THE *END.*

SLAYER, INTERRUPTED

CHAPTER I

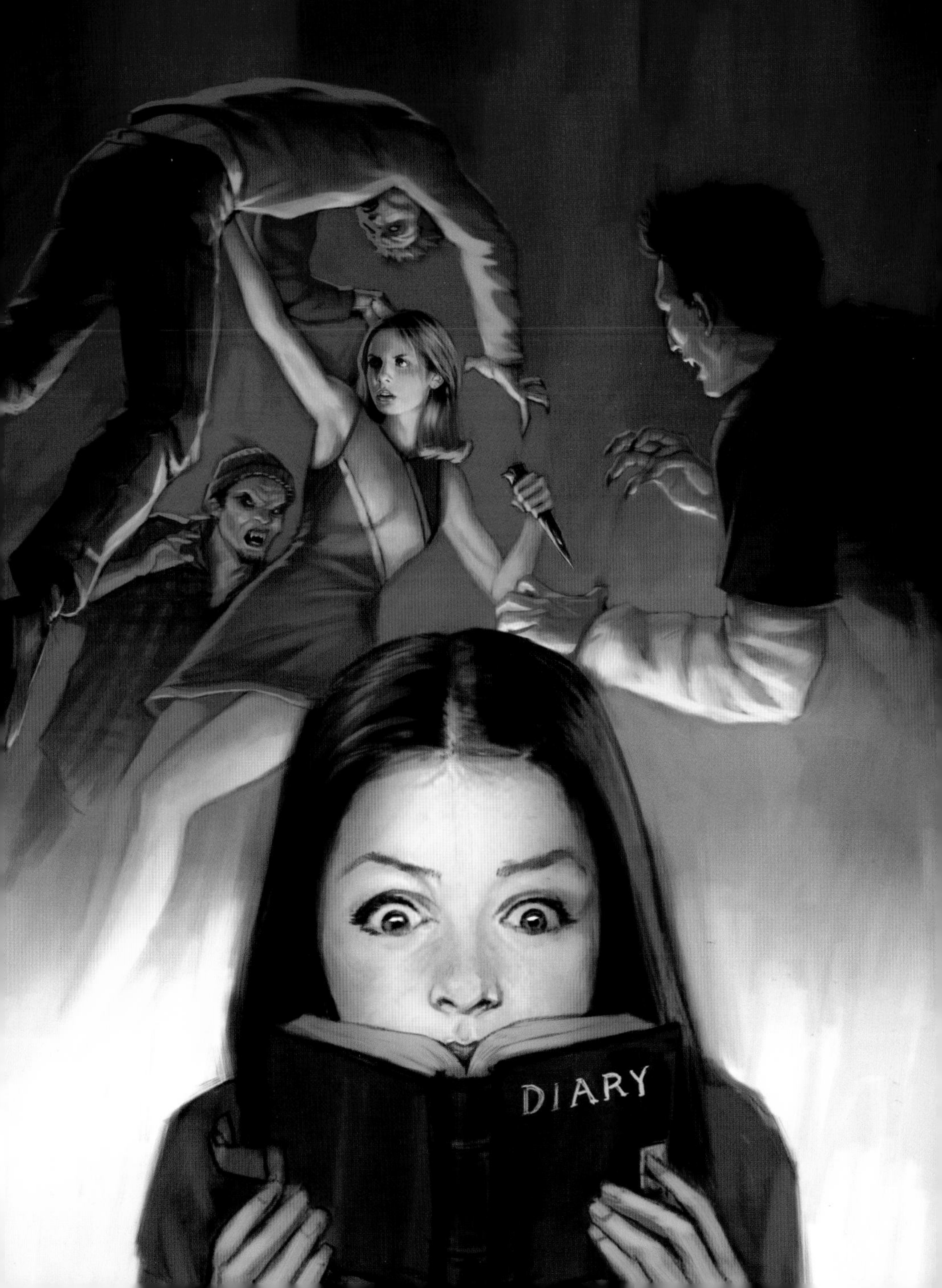
DIARY

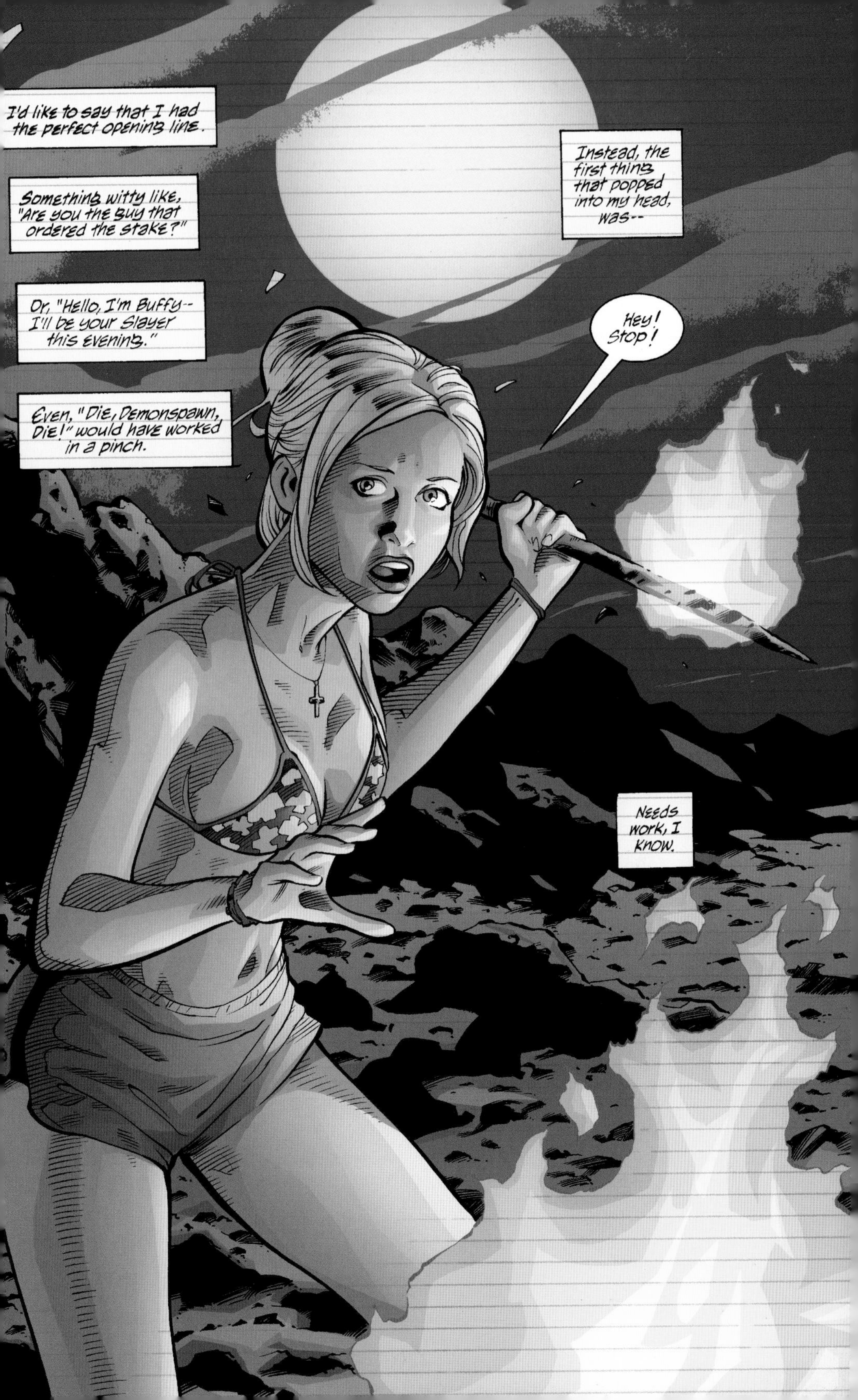
I'd like to say that I had the perfect opening line.
Something witty like, "Are you the guy that ordered the stake?"
Or, "Hello, I'm Buffy-- I'll be your Slayer this evening."
Even, "Die, Demonspawn, Die!" would have worked in a pinch.
Instead, the first thing that popped into my head, was--
Hey! Stop!
Needs work, I know.

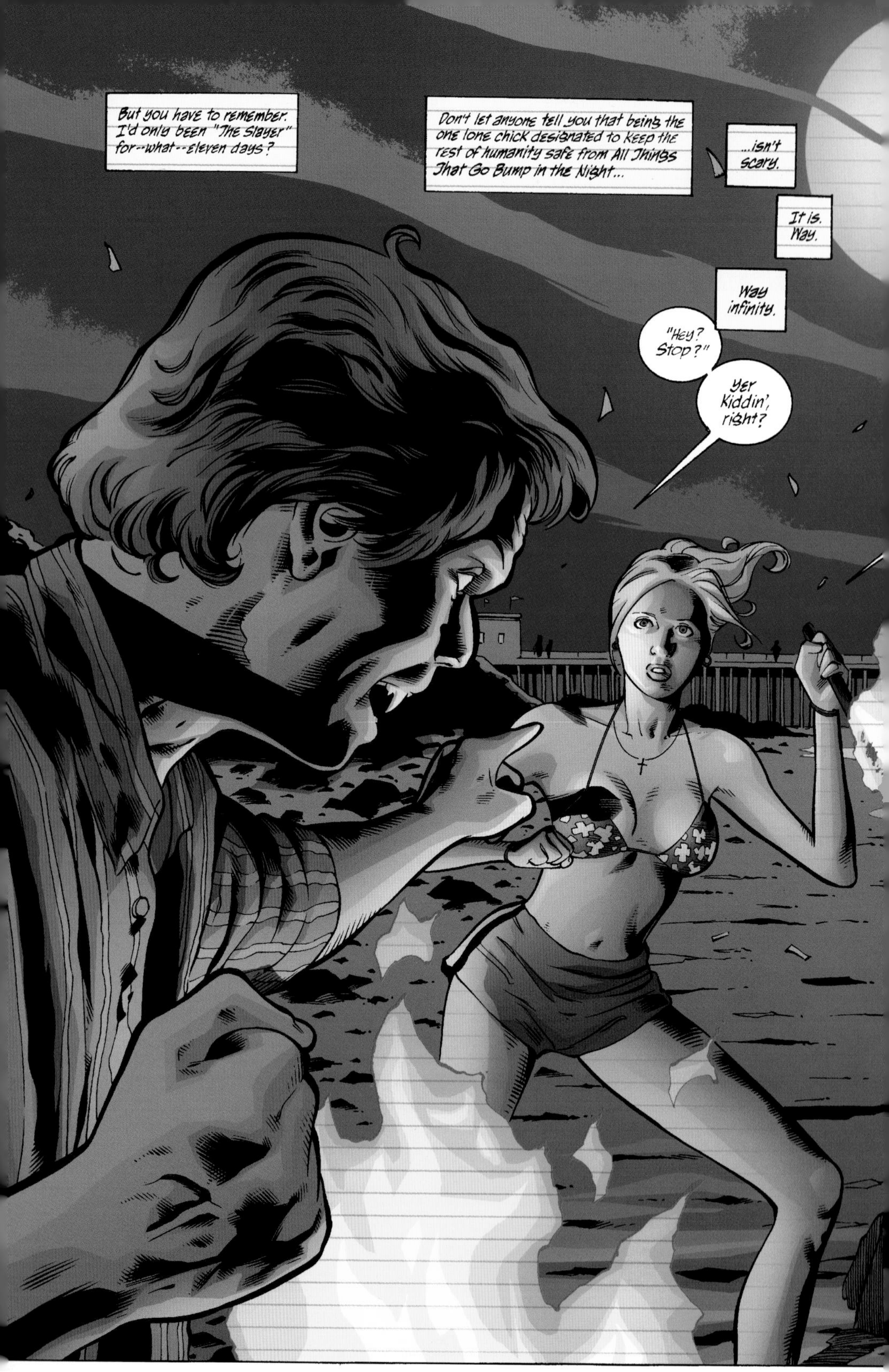
But you have to remember. I'd only been "The Slayer" for--what--eleven days?
Don't let anyone tell you that being the one lone chick designated to keep the rest of humanity safe from All Things That Go Bump in the Night...
...isn't scary.
It is. Way.
Way infinity.
"Hey? Stop?"
Yer Kiddin', right?

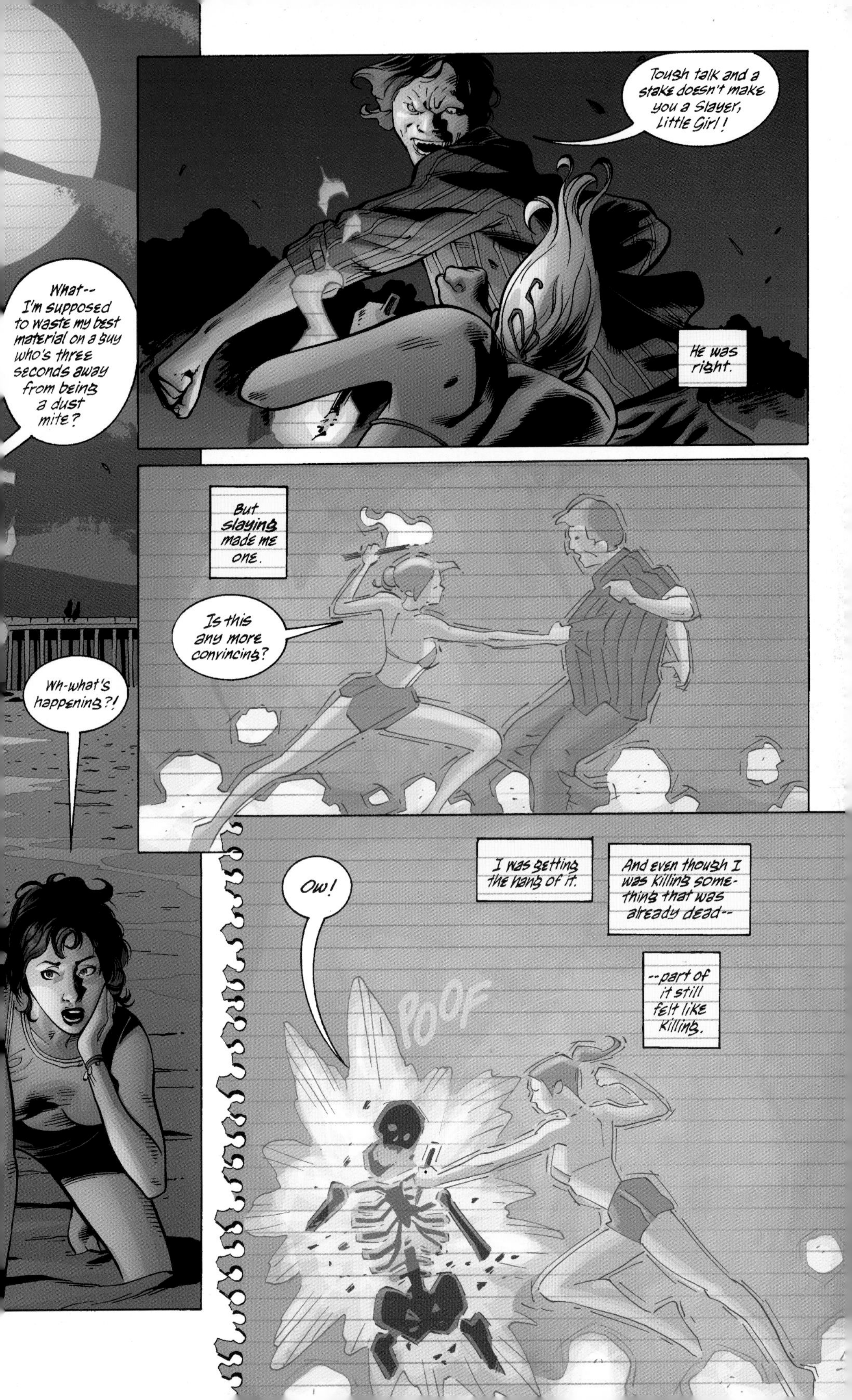
Tough talk and a stake doesn't make you a Slayer, Little Girl!
What-- I'm supposed to waste my best material on a guy who's three seconds away from being a dust mite?
He was right.
But slaying made me one.
Is this any more convincing?
Wh-what's happening?!
I was getting the hang of it.
And even though I was killing something that was already dead--
Ow!
--part of it still felt like killing.
POOF

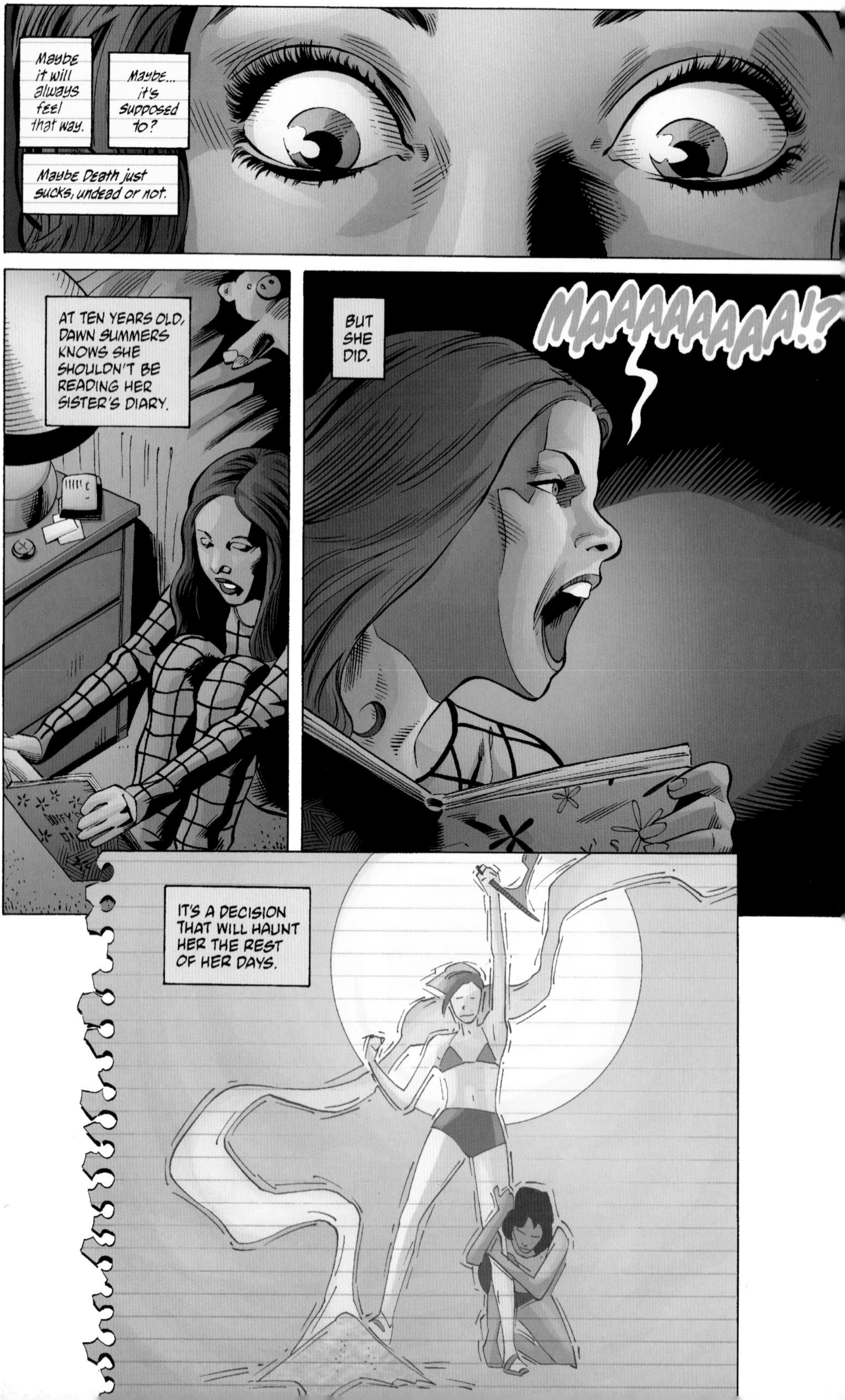

Maybe it will always feel that way.
Maybe... it's supposed to?
Maybe Death just sucks, undead or not.
AT TEN YEARS OLD, DAWN SUMMERS KNOWS SHE SHOULDN'T BE READING HER SISTER'S DIARY.
BUT SHE DID.
MAAAAAAAA!?
IT'S A DECISION THAT WILL HAUNT HER THE REST OF HER DAYS.

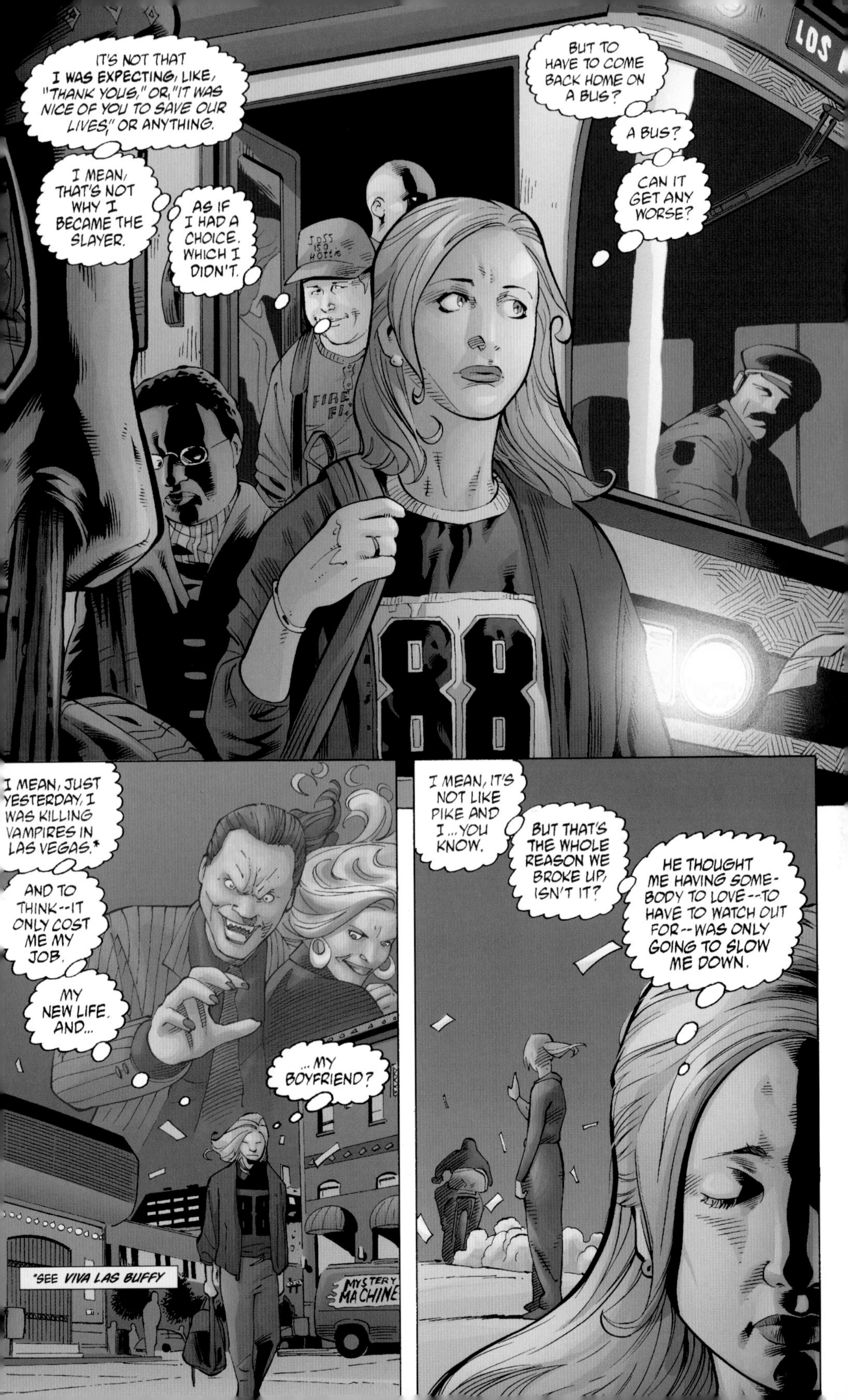

LOS
IT'S NOT THAT I WAS EXPECTING, LIKE, "THANK YOUS," OR, "IT WAS NICE OF YOU TO SAVE OUR LIVES," OR ANYTHING.
I MEAN, THAT'S NOT WHY I BECAME THE SLAYER.
AS IF I HAD A CHOICE. WHICH I DIDN'T.
BUT TO HAVE TO COME BACK HOME ON A BUS?
A BUS?
CAN IT GET ANY WORSE?
I MEAN, JUST YESTERDAY, I WAS KILLING VAMPIRES IN LAS VEGAS.*
AND TO THINK--IT ONLY COST ME MY JOB.
MY NEW LIFE. AND...
...MY BOYFRIEND?
*SEE VIVA LAS BUFFY
MYSTERY MACHINE
I MEAN, IT'S NOT LIKE PIKE AND I...YOU KNOW.
BUT THAT'S THE WHOLE REASON WE BROKE UP, ISN'T IT?
HE THOUGHT ME HAVING SOME-BODY TO LOVE--TO HAVE TO WATCH OUT FOR--WAS ONLY GOING TO SLOW ME DOWN.

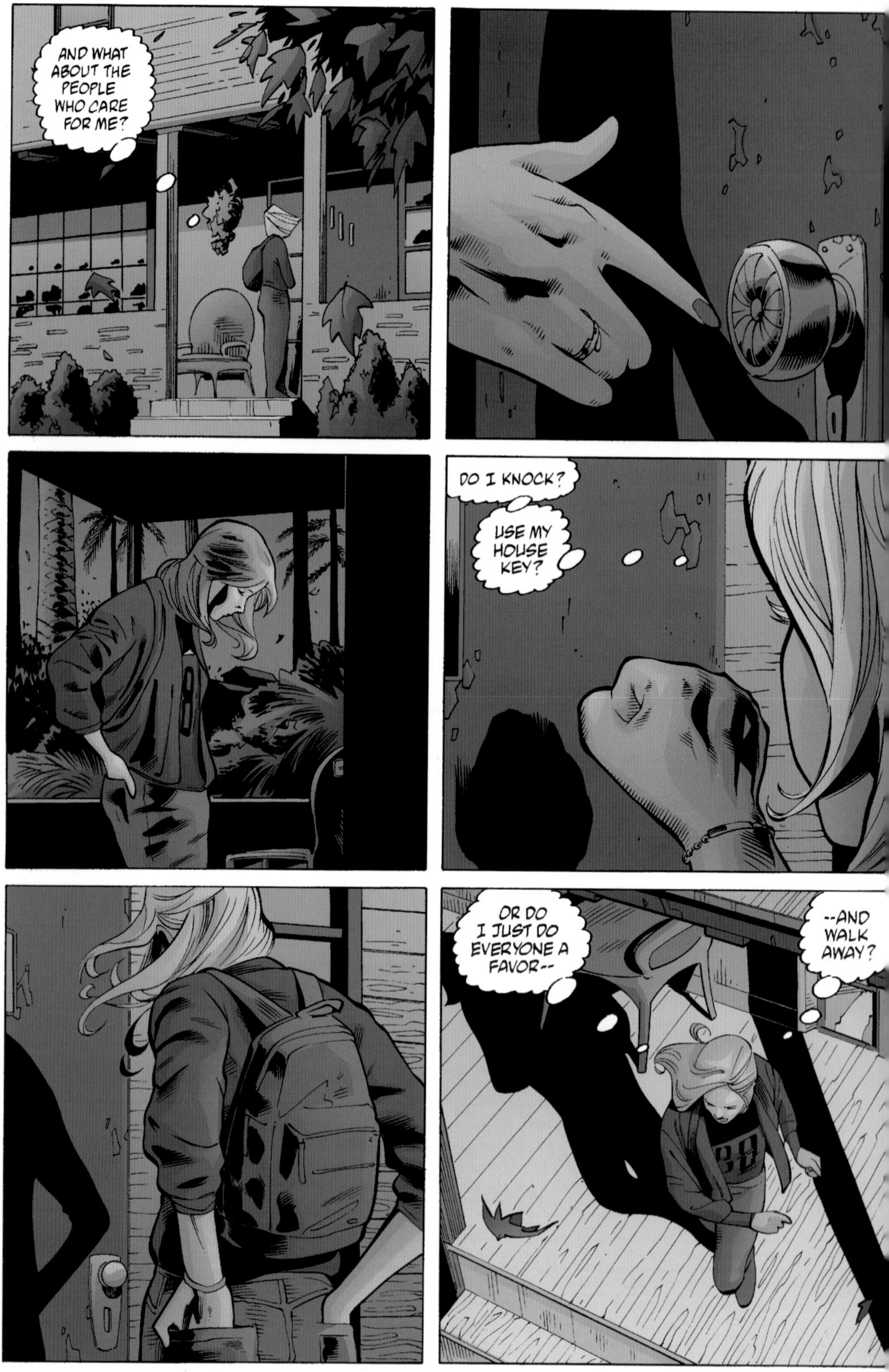
AND WHAT ABOUT THE PEOPLE WHO CARE FOR ME?
DO I KNOCK?
USE MY HOUSE KEY?
OR DO I JUST DO EVERYONE A FAVOR--
--AND WALK AWAY?

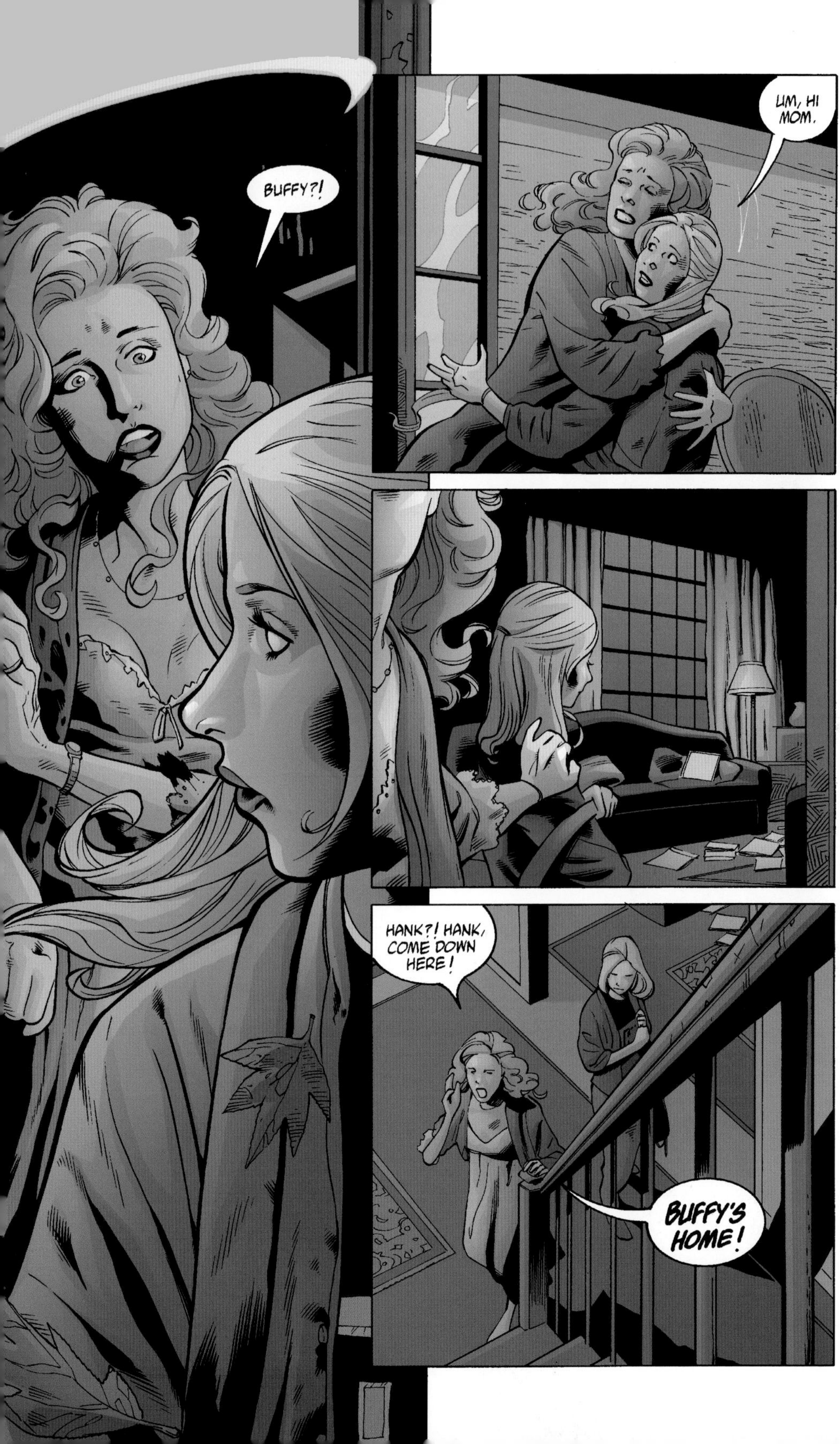
BUFFY?!
UM, HI MOM.
HANK?! HANK, COME DOWN HERE!
BUFFY'S HOME!

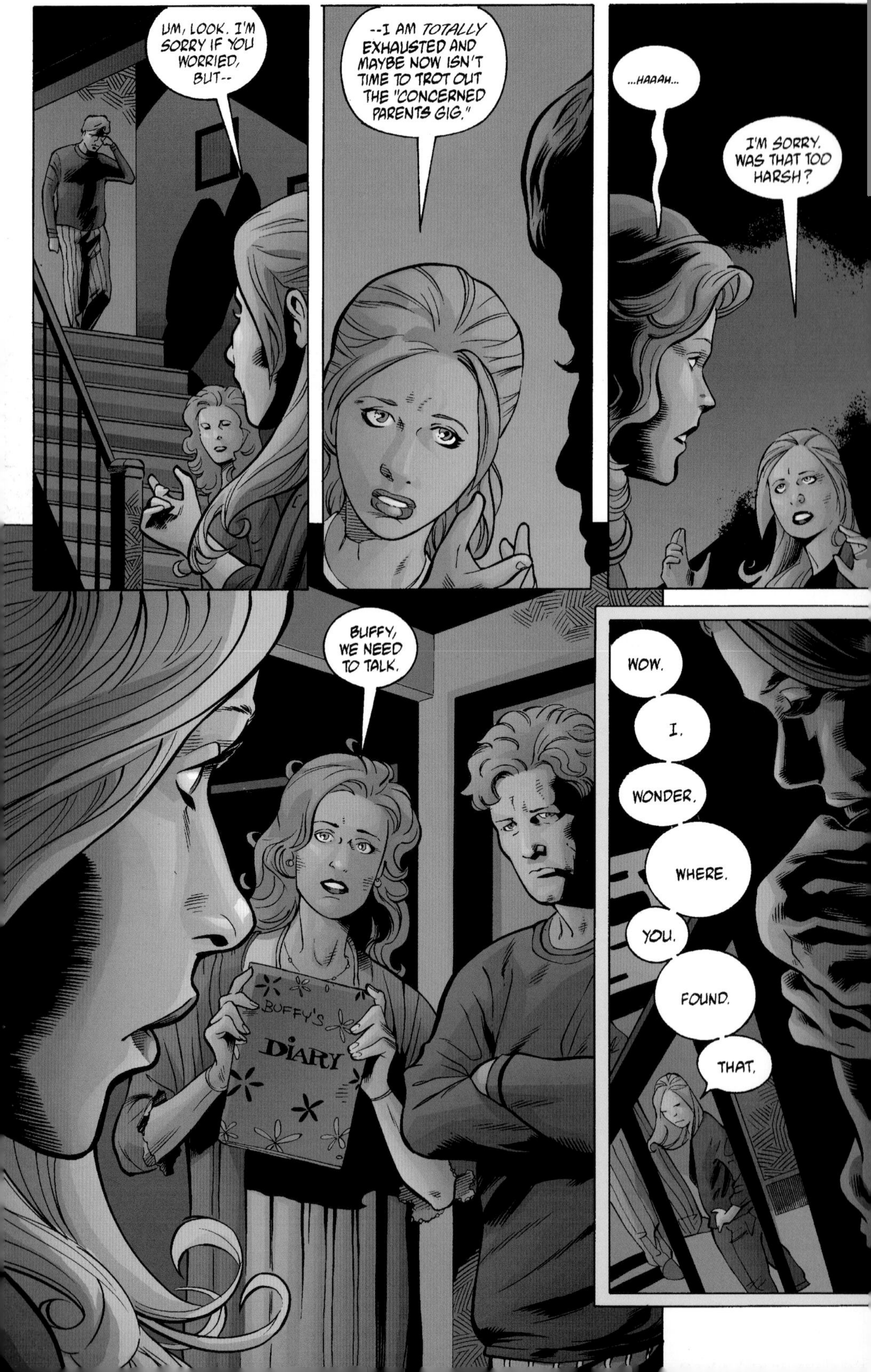
UM, LOOK. I'M SORRY IF YOU WORRIED, BUT--
--I AM TOTALLY EXHAUSTED AND MAYBE NOW ISN'T TIME TO TROT OUT THE "CONCERNED PARENTS GIG."
...HAAAH...
I'M SORRY. WAS THAT TOO HARSH?
BUFFY, WE NEED TO TALK.
BUFFY'S DIARY
WOW.
I.
WONDER.
WHERE.
YOU.
FOUND.
THAT.

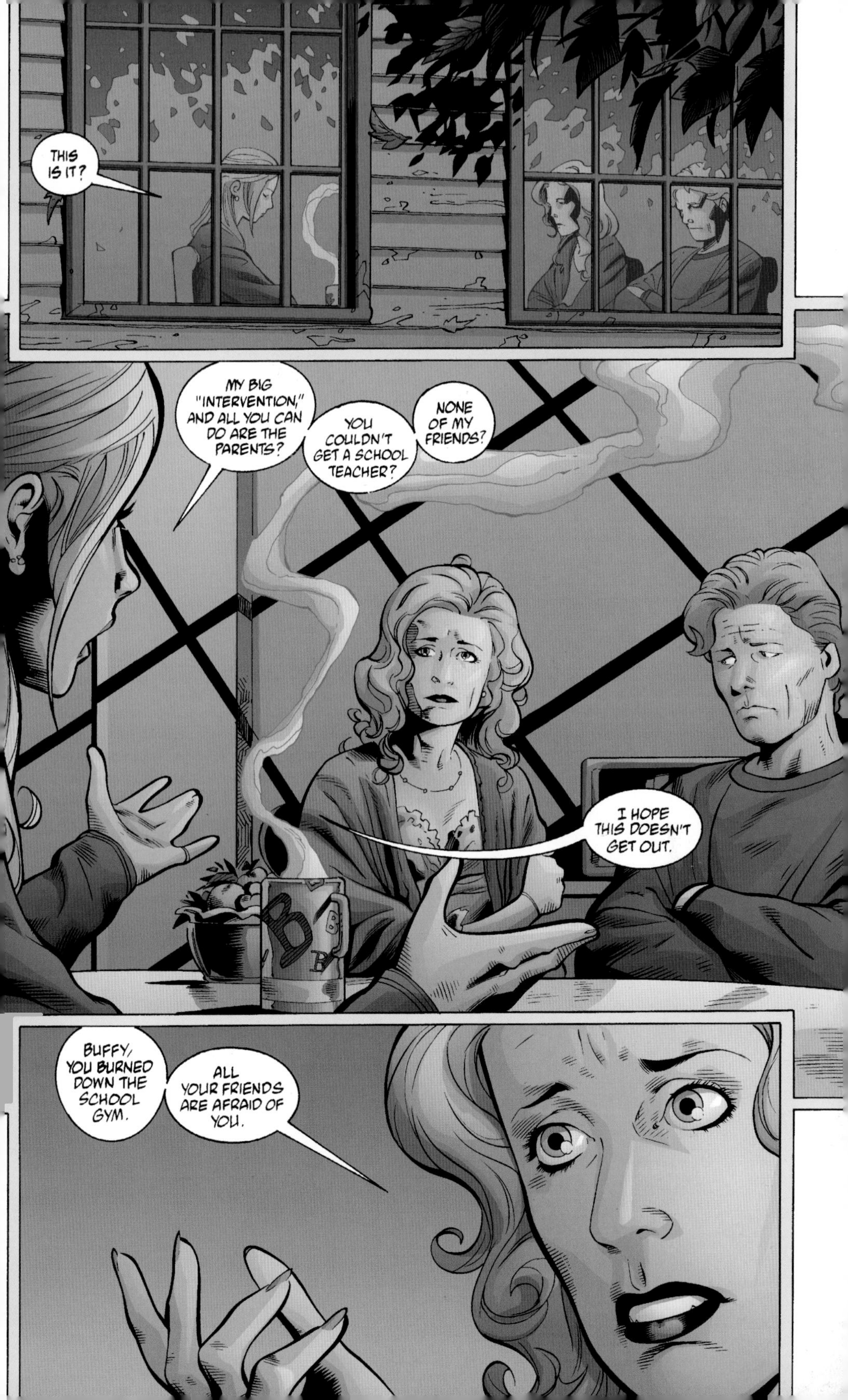
THIS IS IT?
MY BIG "INTERVENTION," AND ALL YOU CAN DO ARE THE PARENTS?
YOU COULDN'T GET A SCHOOL TEACHER?
NONE OF MY FRIENDS?
I HOPE THIS DOESN'T GET OUT.
BUFFY, YOU BURNED DOWN THE SCHOOL GYM.
ALL YOUR FRIENDS ARE AFRAID OF YOU.

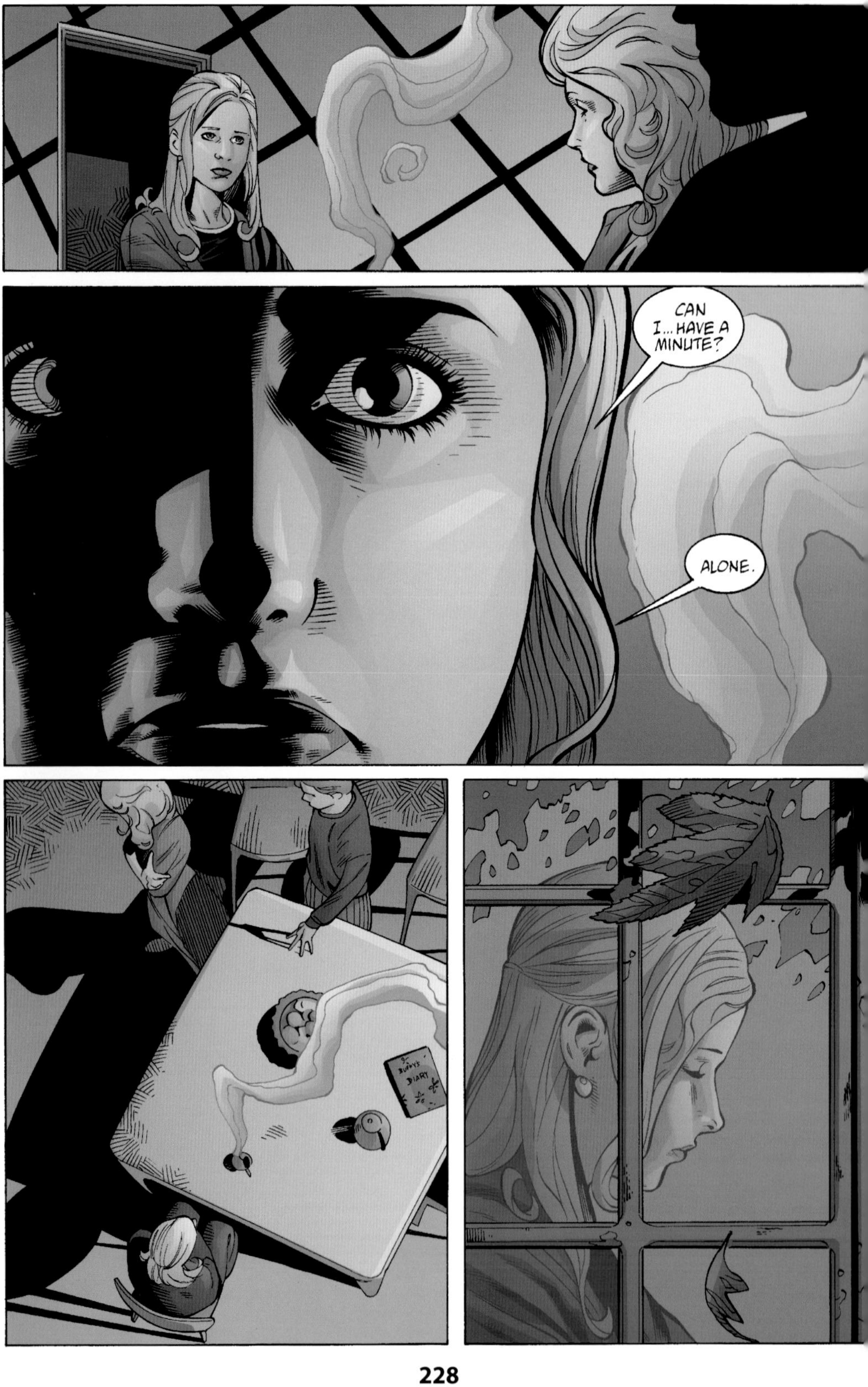
CAN I... HAVE A MINUTE?
ALONE.
BUFFY'S DIARY

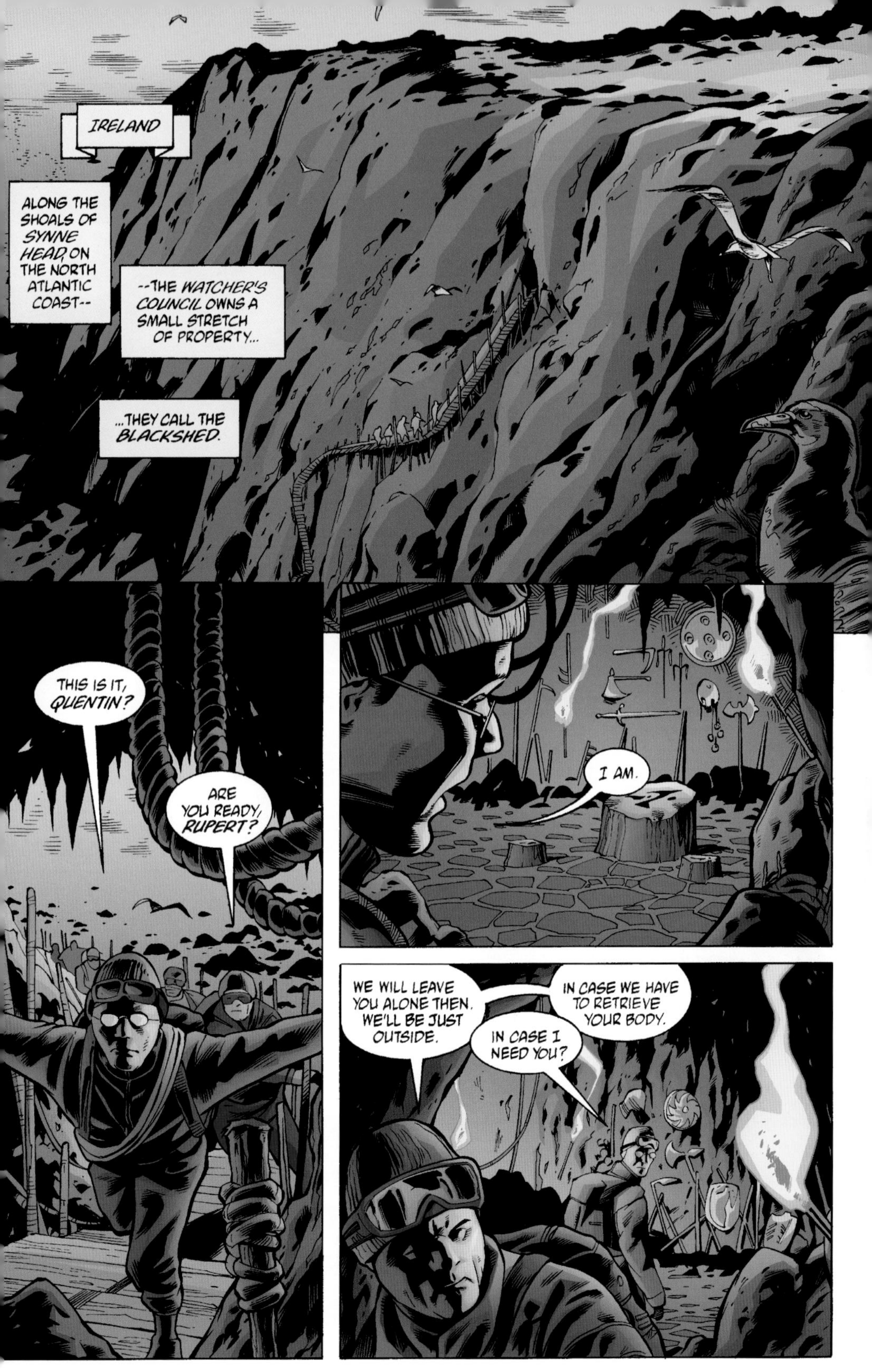
IRELAND
ALONG THE SHOALS OF SYNNE HEAD, ON THE NORTH ATLANTIC COAST--
--THE WATCHER'S COUNCIL OWNS A SMALL STRETCH OF PROPERTY...
...THEY CALL THE BLACKSHED.
THIS IS IT, QUENTIN?
ARE YOU READY, RUPERT?
I AM.
WE WILL LEAVE YOU ALONE THEN. WE'LL BE JUST OUTSIDE.
IN CASE I NEED YOU?
IN CASE WE HAVE TO RETRIEVE YOUR BODY.

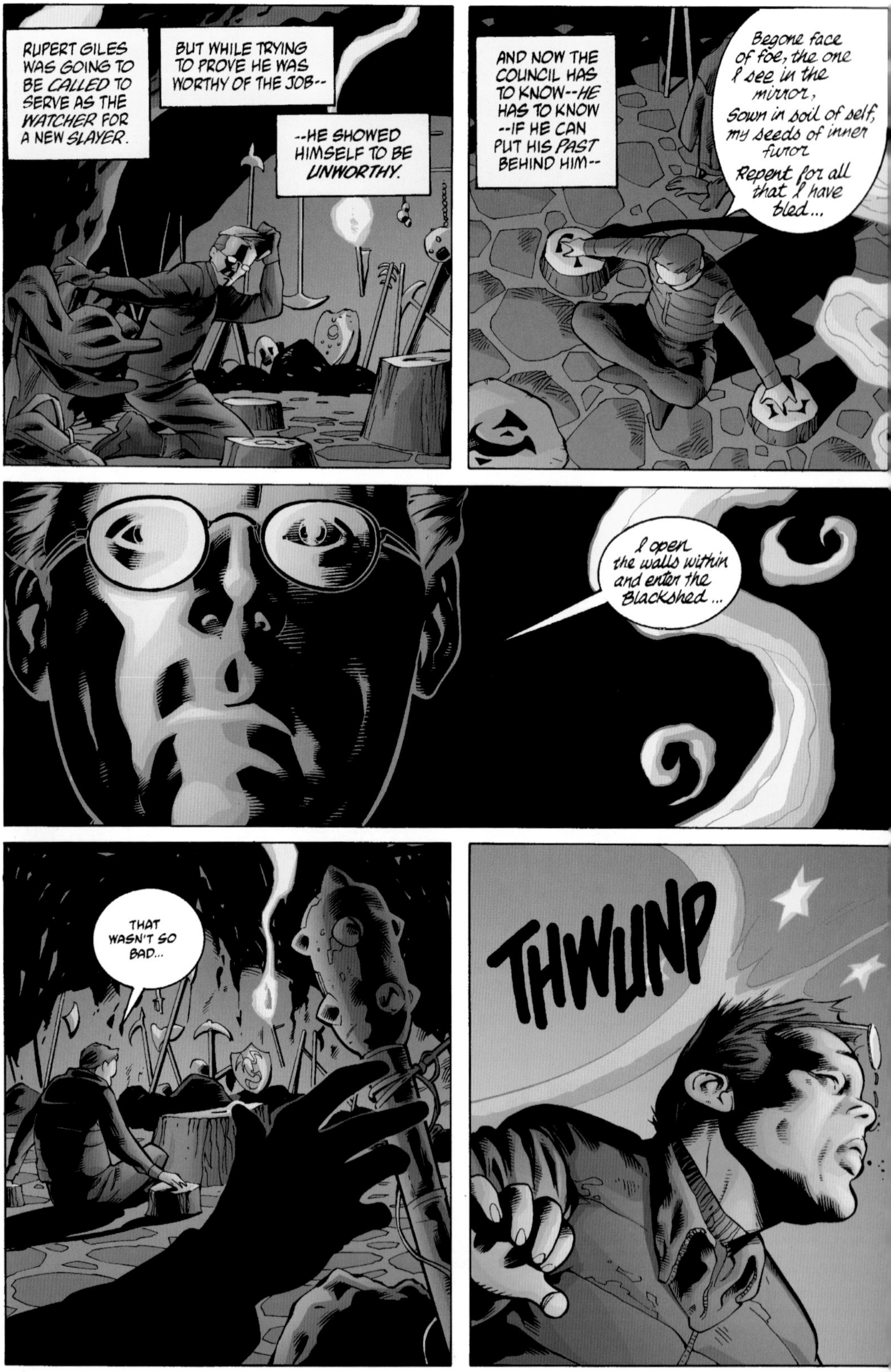
RUPERT GILES WAS GOING TO BE CALLED TO SERVE AS THE WATCHER FOR A NEW SLAYER.
BUT WHILE TRYING TO PROVE HE WAS WORTHY OF THE JOB--
--HE SHOWED HIMSELF TO BE UNWORTHY.
AND NOW THE COUNCIL HAS TO KNOW--HE HAS TO KNOW --IF HE CAN PUT HIS PAST BEHIND HIM--
Begone face of foe, the one I see in the mirror, Sown in soil of self, my seeds of inner furor Repent for all that I have bled...
I open the walls within and enter the Blackshed...
THAT WASN'T SO BAD...
THWUNP

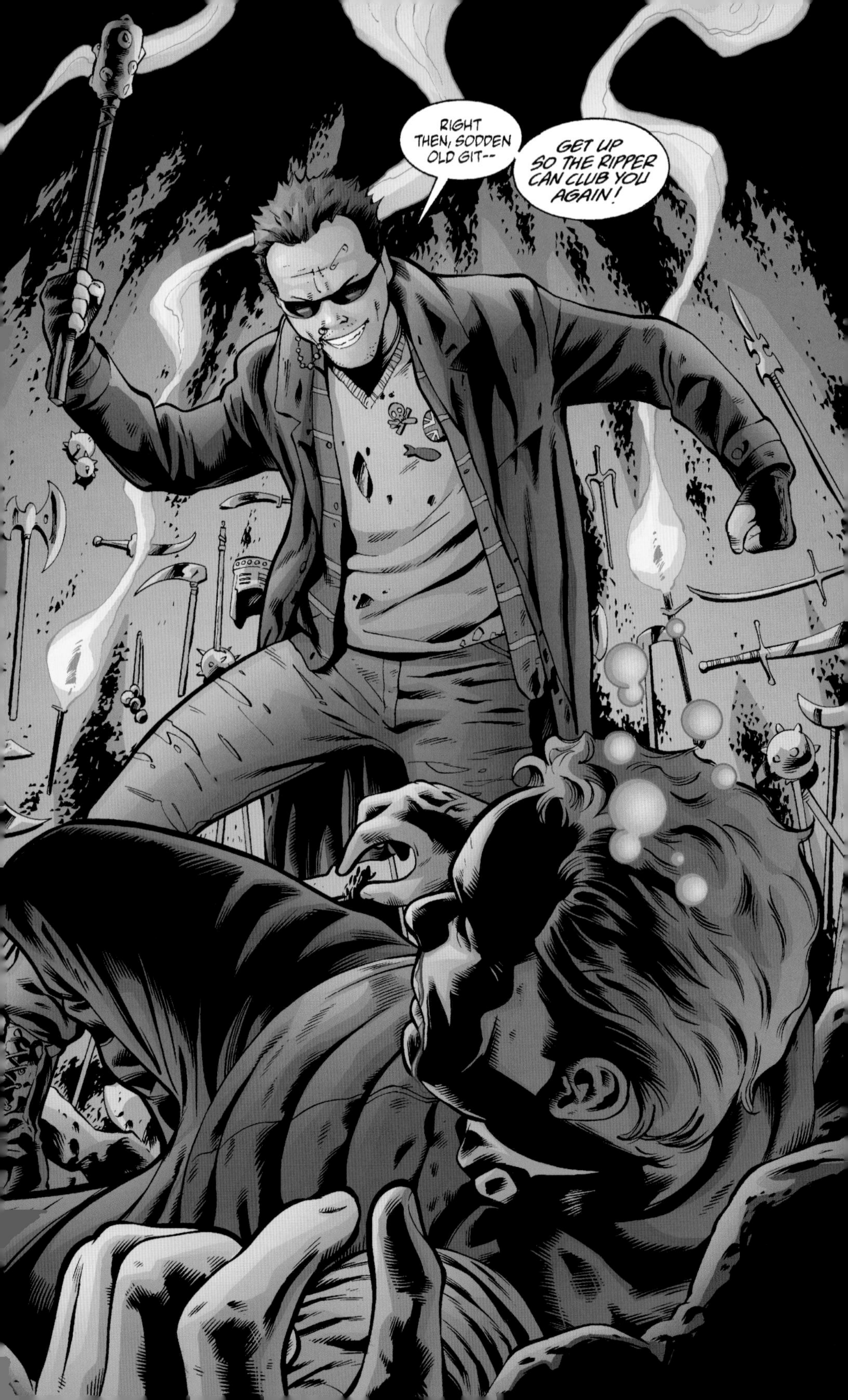
RIGHT THEN, SODDEN OLD GIT--
GET UP SO THE RIPPER CAN CLUB YOU AGAIN!

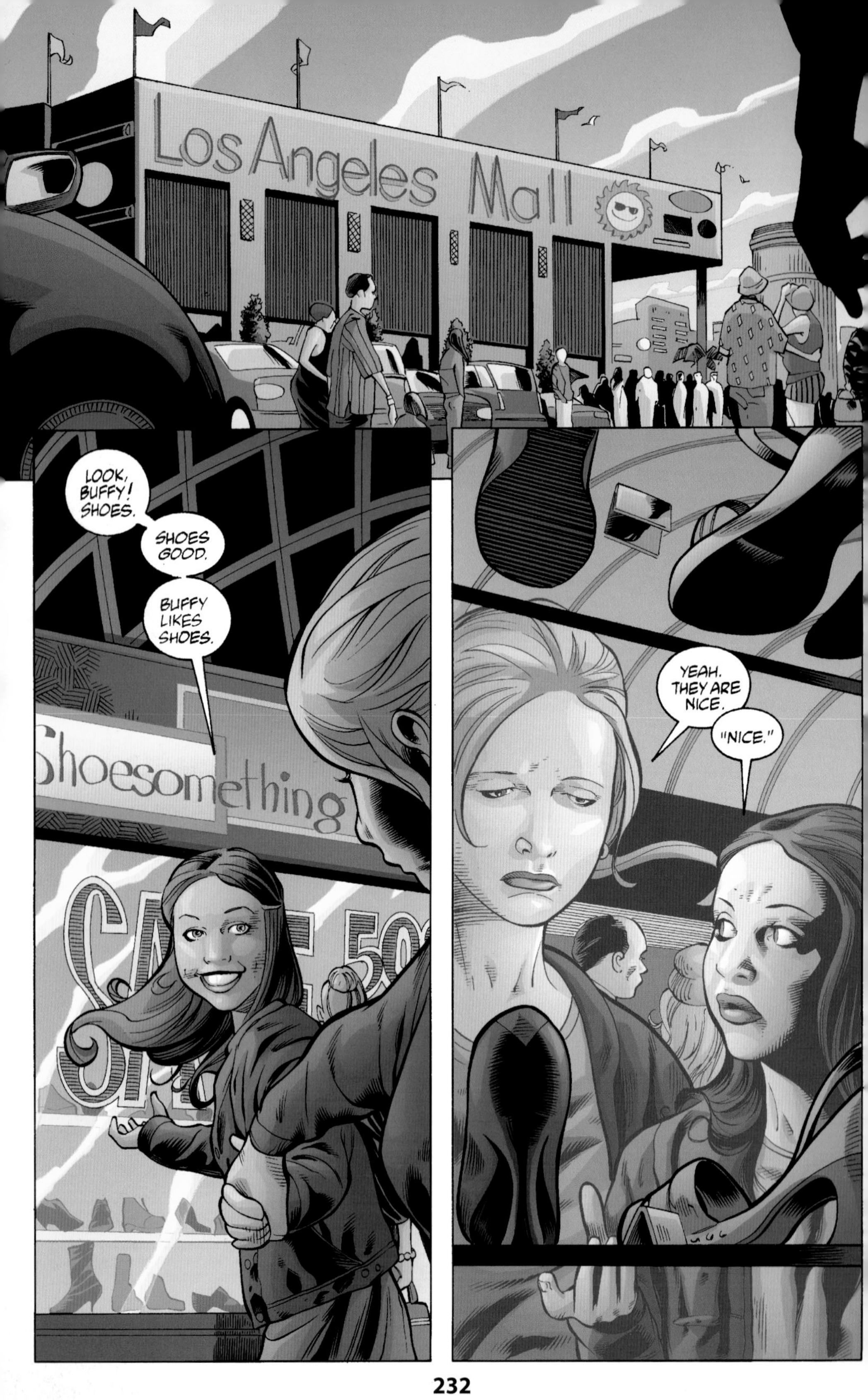

Los Angeles Mall
LOOK, BUFFY! SHOES.
SHOES GOOD.
BUFFY LIKES SHOES.
Shoesomething
YEAH. THEY ARE NICE.
"NICE."

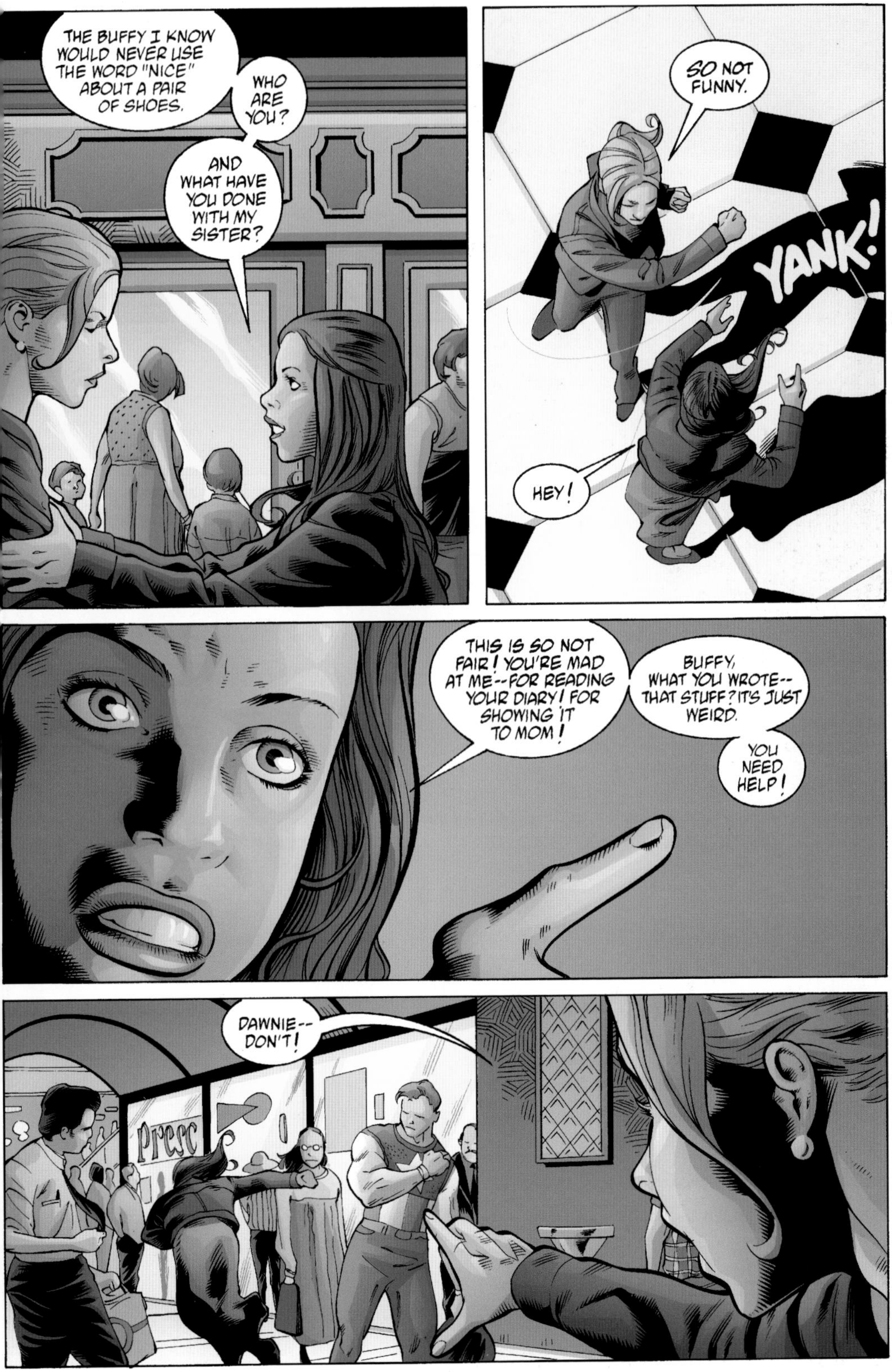
THE BUFFY I KNOW WOULD NEVER USE THE WORD "NICE" ABOUT A PAIR OF SHOES.
WHO ARE YOU?
AND WHAT HAVE YOU DONE WITH MY SISTER?
SO NOT FUNNY.
YANK!
HEY!
THIS IS SO NOT FAIR! YOU'RE MAD AT ME--FOR READING YOUR DIARY! FOR SHOWING IT TO MOM!
BUFFY, WHAT YOU WROTE--THAT STUFF? IT'S JUST WEIRD.
YOU NEED HELP!
DAWNIE--DON'T!
Presc

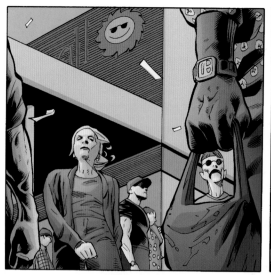

HEY,

HEY.

DO YOU CARE IF, YOU KNOW-- MAYBE--I WALK HOME?

KIND OF DO THE WHOLE CLEARING THE HEAD THING?

THAT WOULD BE FINE. JUST REMEMBER, DINNER'S AT SIX.

DON'T BE LATE.

THANKS, MOM.

YOU KNOW SHE'S GOING TO BE LATE, RIGHT?

SHUSH, DAWN.

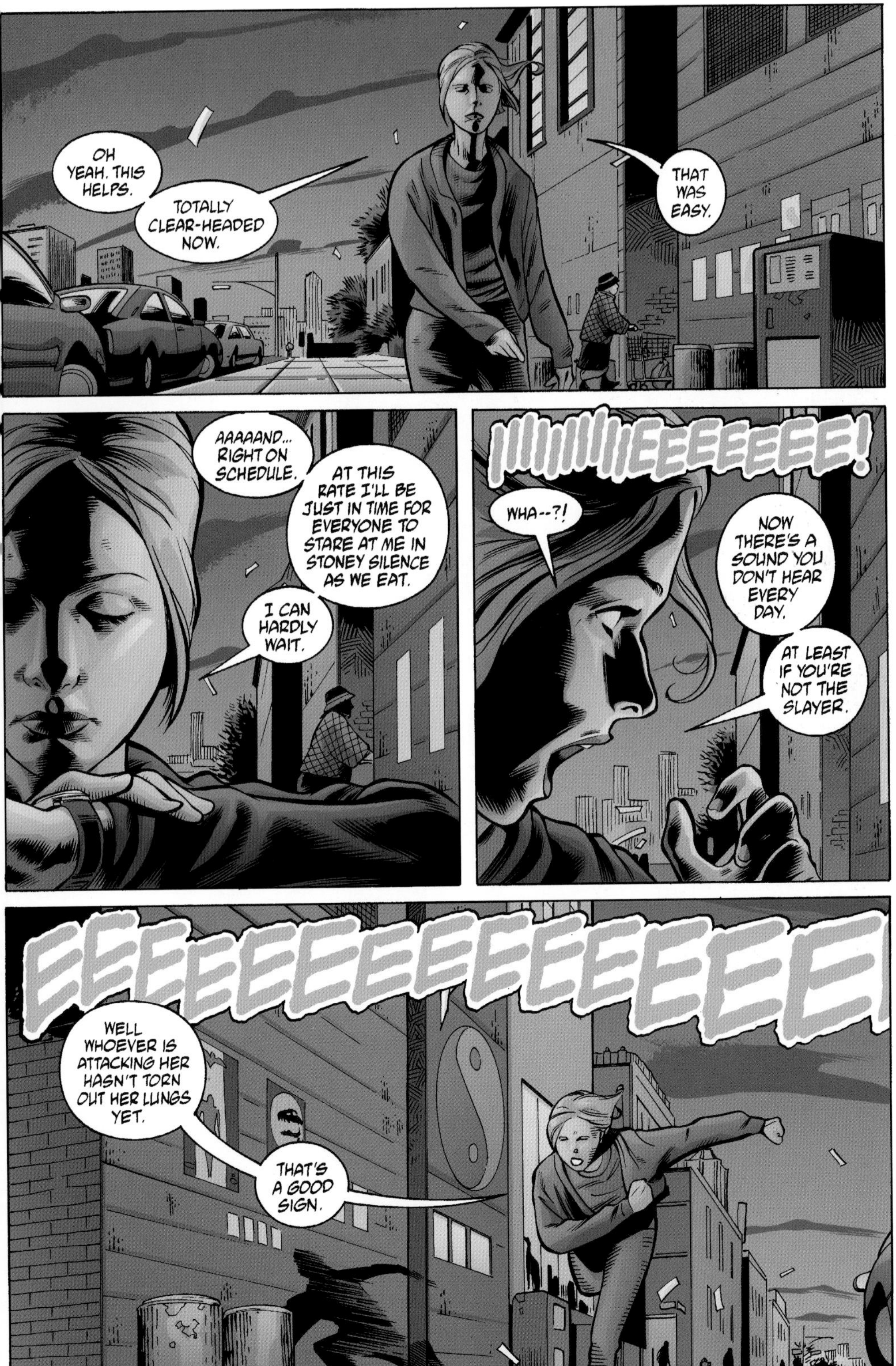
OH YEAH. THIS HELPS.
TOTALLY CLEAR-HEADED NOW.
THAT WAS EASY.
AAAAAND... RIGHT ON SCHEDULE.
AT THIS RATE I'LL BE JUST IN TIME FOR EVERYONE TO STARE AT ME IN STONEY SILENCE AS WE EAT.
I CAN HARDLY WAIT.
IIIIIIIIIEEEEEEEE!
WHA--?!
NOW THERE'S A SOUND YOU DON'T HEAR EVERY DAY.
AT LEAST IF YOU'RE NOT THE SLAYER.
EEEEEEEEEEEEEEEE
WELL WHOEVER IS ATTACKING HER HASN'T TORN OUT HER LUNGS YET.
THAT'S A GOOD SIGN.

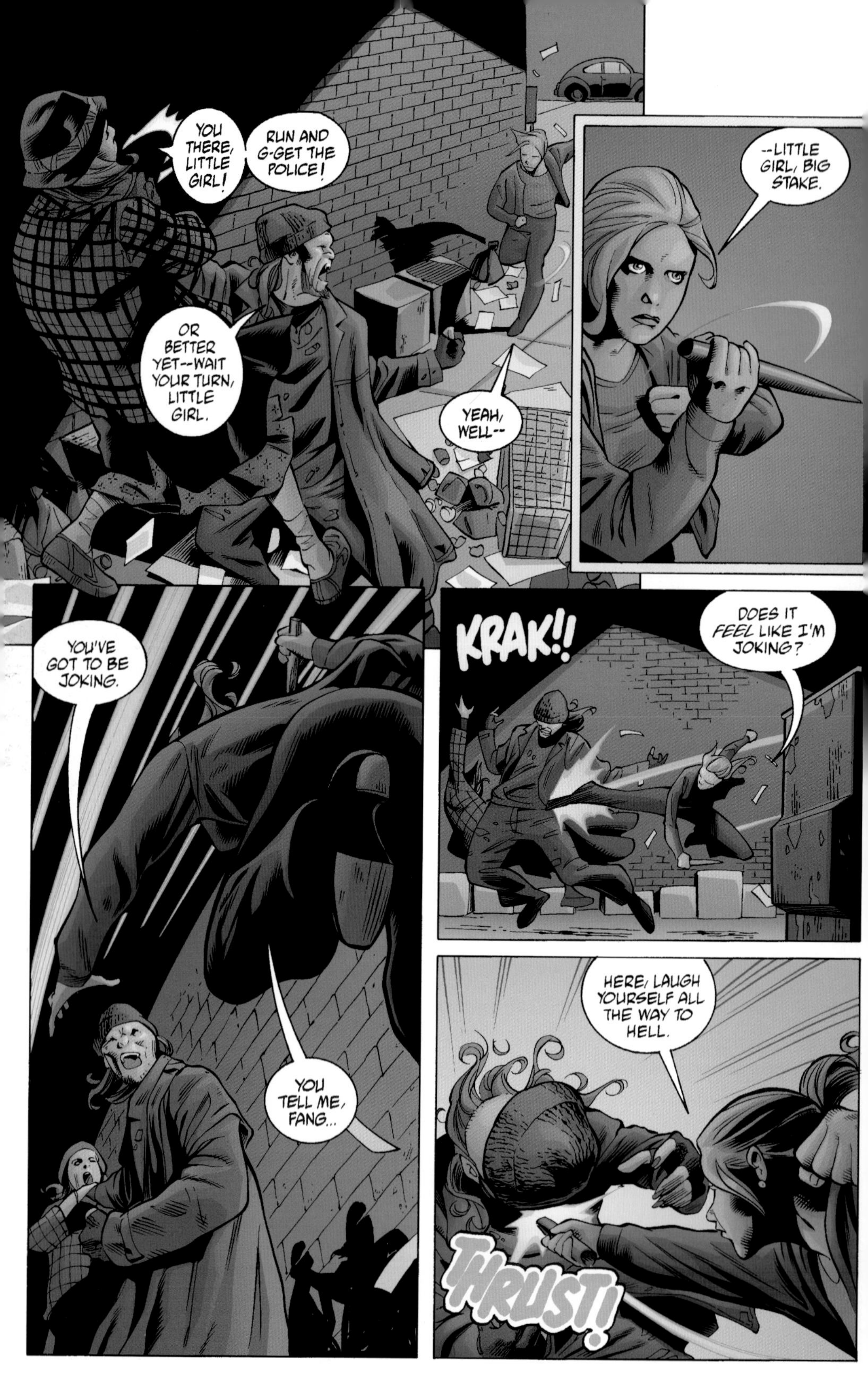
YOU THERE, LITTLE GIRL!
RUN AND G-GET THE POLICE!
OR BETTER YET--WAIT YOUR TURN, LITTLE GIRL.
YEAH, WELL--
--LITTLE GIRL, BIG STAKE.
YOU'VE GOT TO BE JOKING.
YOU TELL ME, FANG...
KRAK!!
DOES IT FEEL LIKE I'M JOKING?
HERE, LAUGH YOURSELF ALL THE WAY TO HELL.
THRUST!

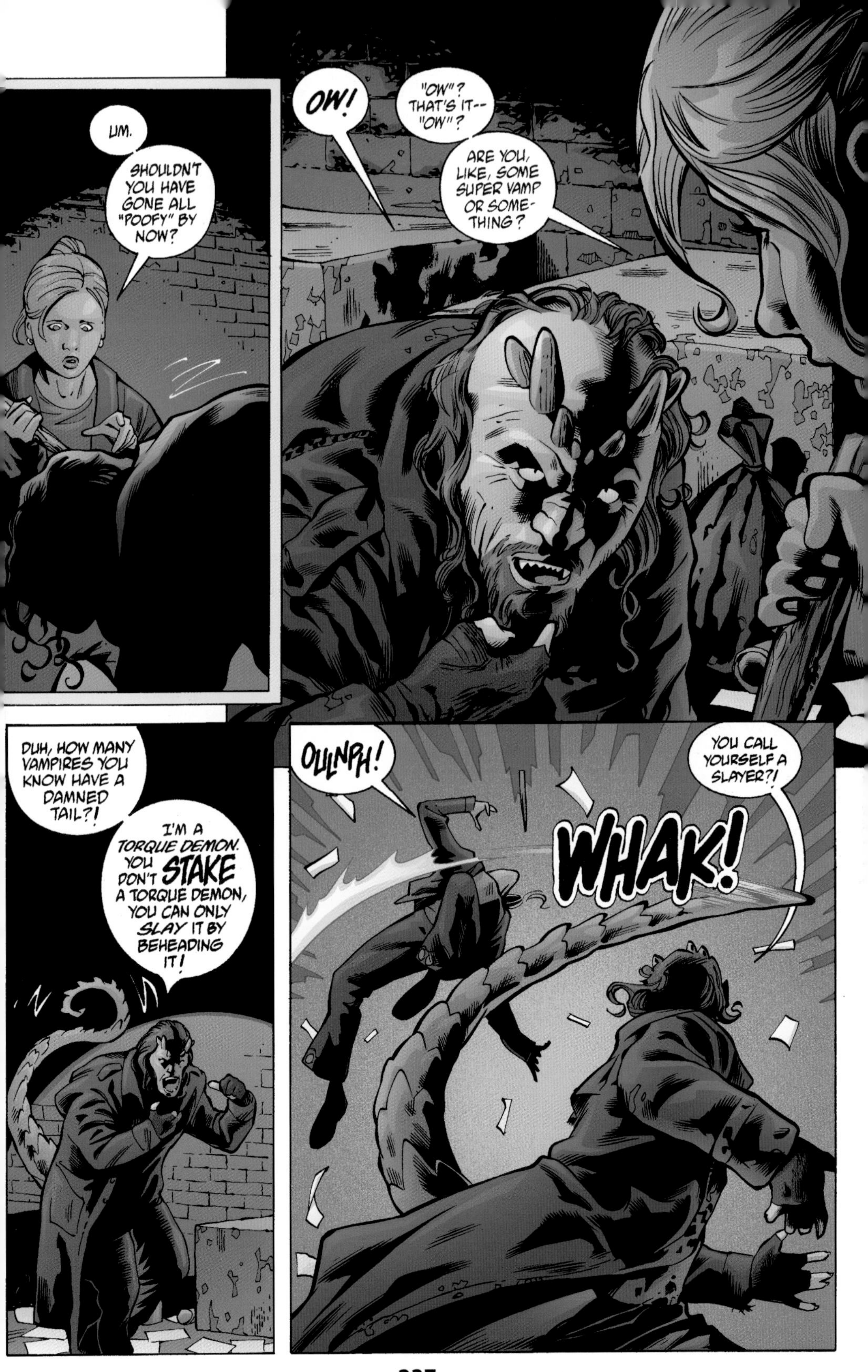
UM.
SHOULDN'T YOU HAVE GONE ALL "POOFY" BY NOW?
OW!
"OW"? THAT'S IT-- "OW"?
ARE YOU, LIKE, SOME SUPER VAMP OR SOME-THING?
DUH, HOW MANY VAMPIRES YOU KNOW HAVE A DAMNED TAIL?!
I'M A TORQUE DEMON. YOU DON'T STAKE A TORQUE DEMON, YOU CAN ONLY SLAY IT BY BEHEADING IT!
OULNPH!
YOU CALL YOURSELF A SLAYER?!
WHAK!

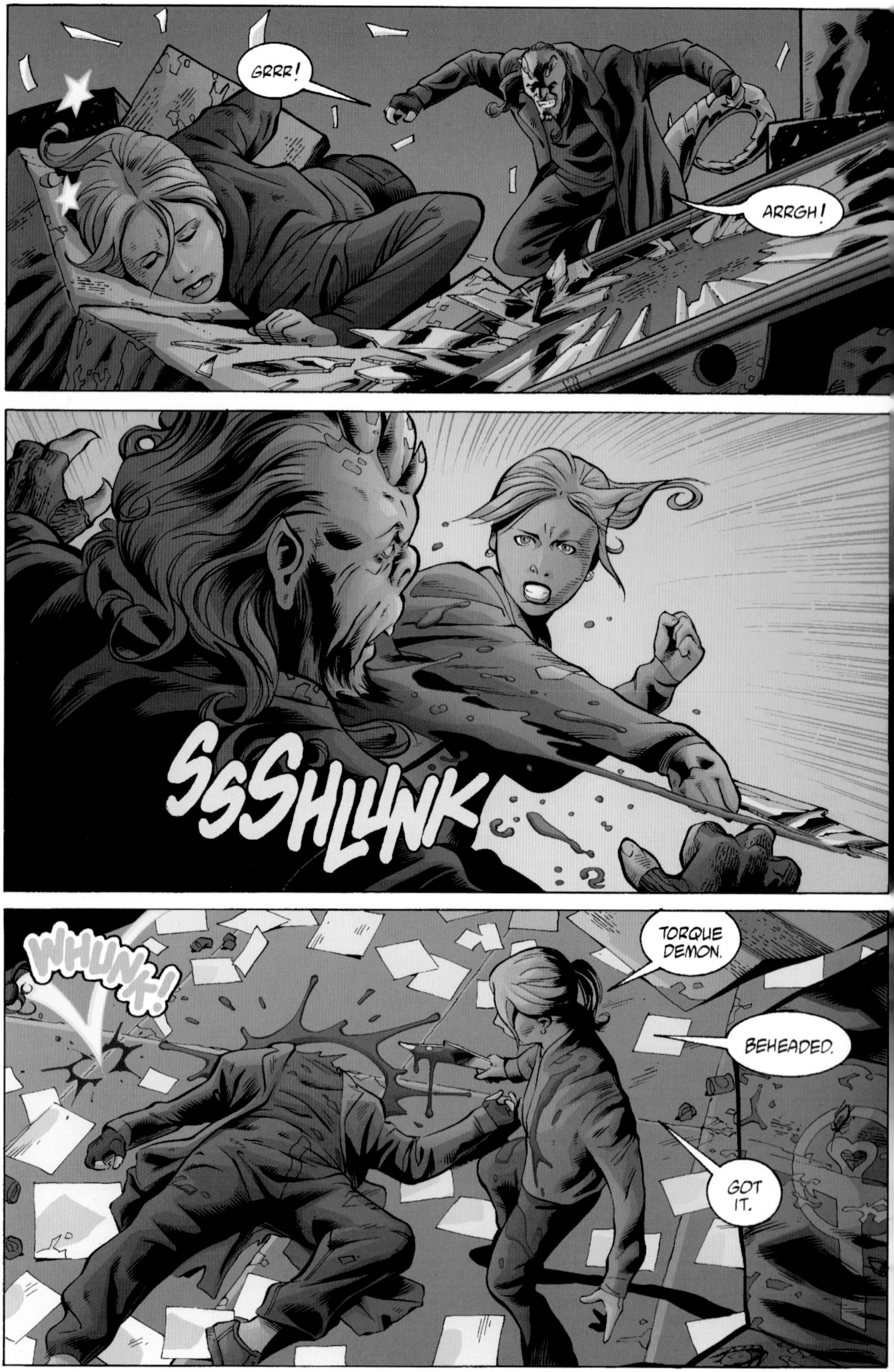
GRRR!
ARRGH!
SSSHLUNK
WHUNK!
TORQUE DEMON.
BEHEADED.
GOT IT.

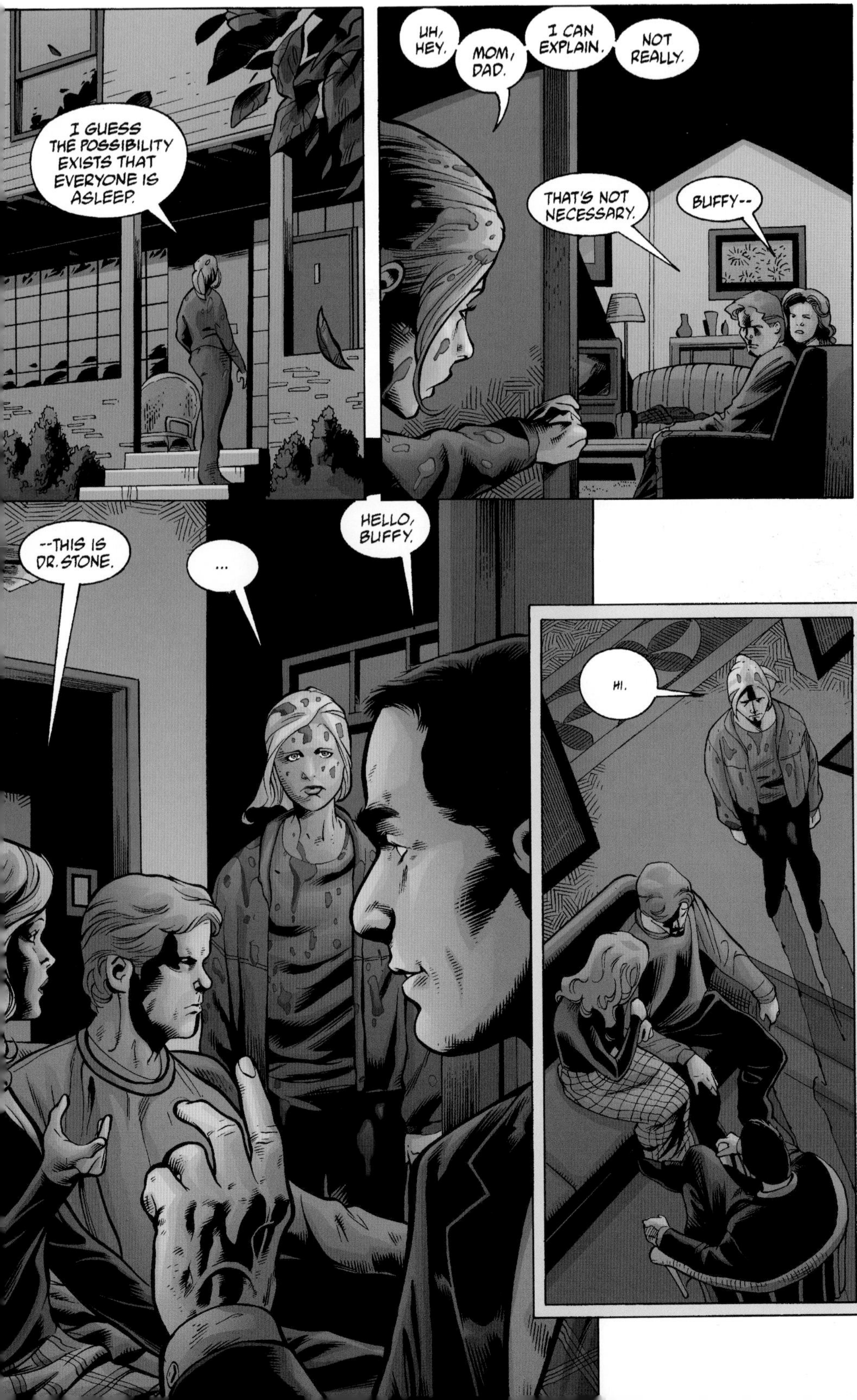
I GUESS THE POSSIBILITY EXISTS THAT EVERYONE IS ASLEEP.
UH, HEY.
MOM, DAD.
I CAN EXPLAIN.
NOT REALLY.
THAT'S NOT NECESSARY.
BUFFY--
--THIS IS DR. STONE.
...
HELLO, BUFFY.
HI.

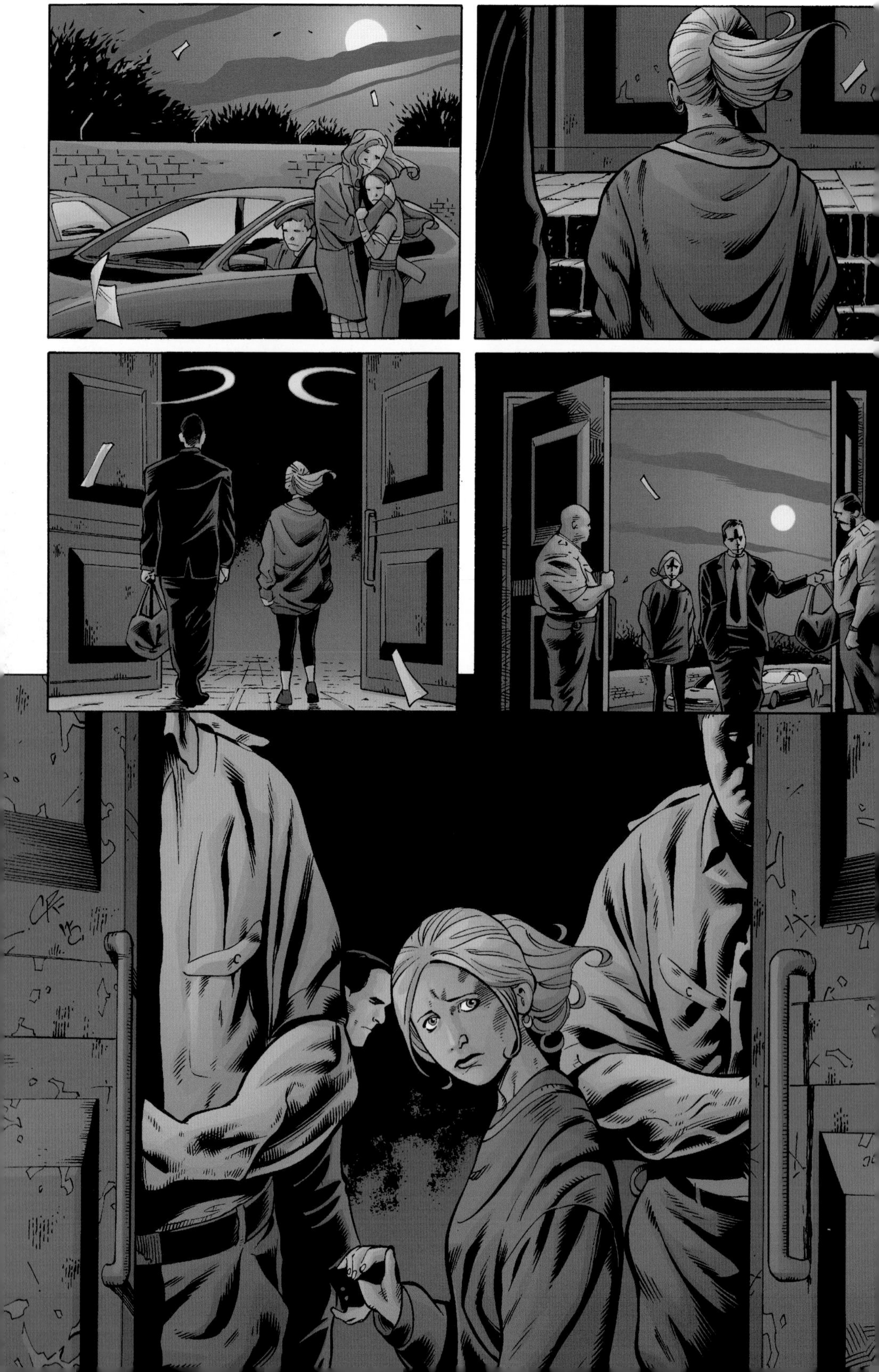

CHAPTER 2

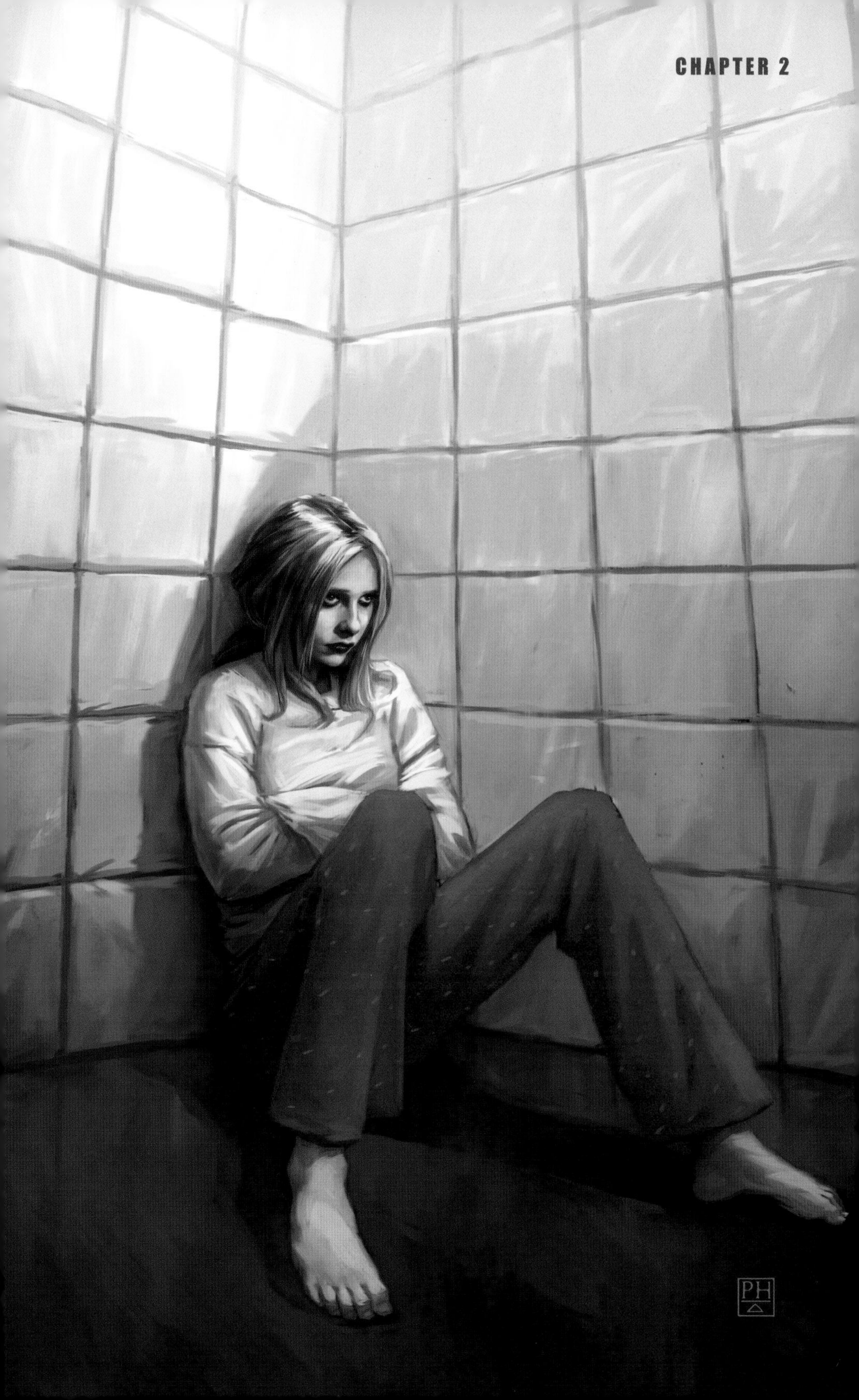

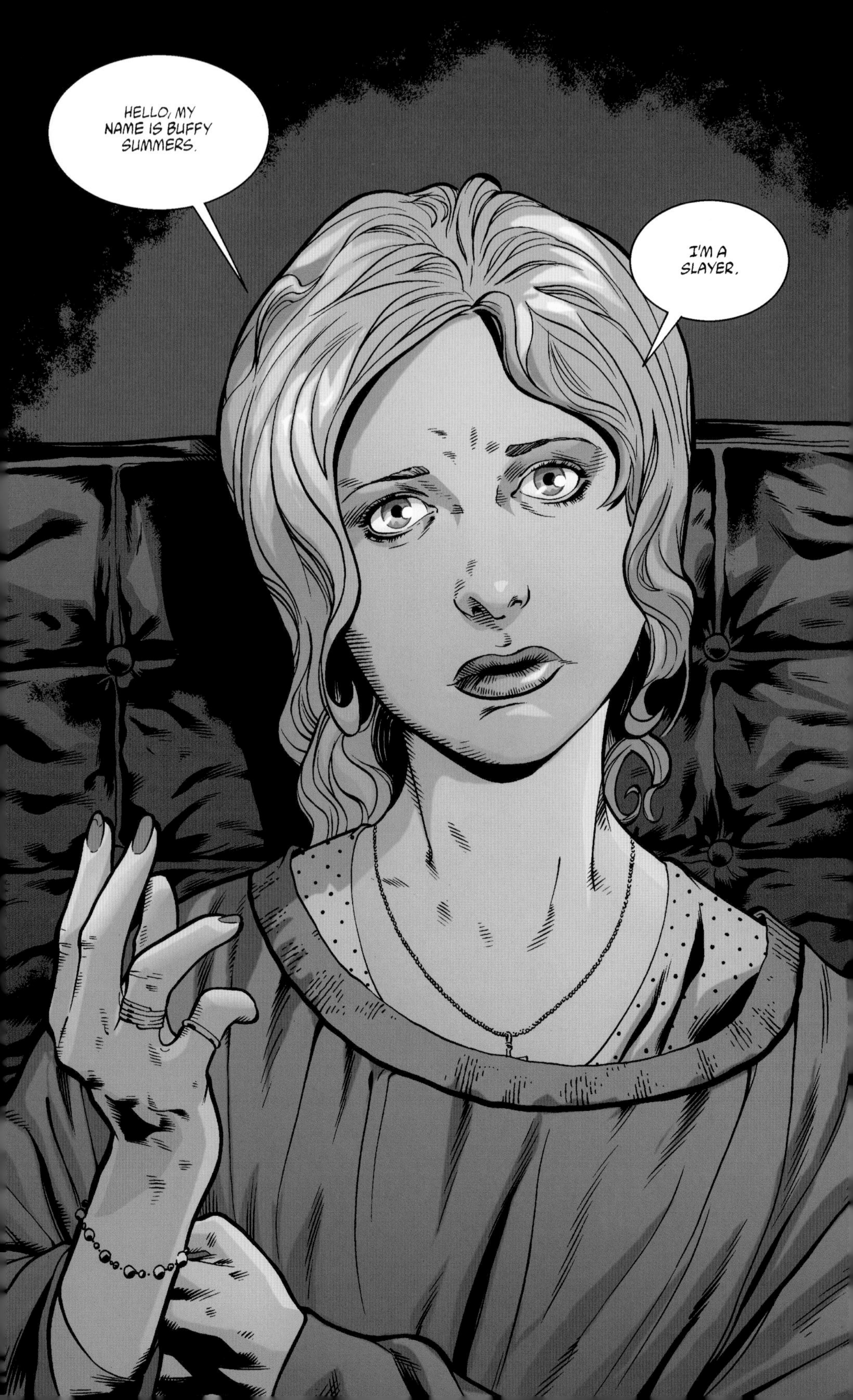
HELLO, MY NAME IS BUFFY SUMMERS.
I'M A SLAYER.

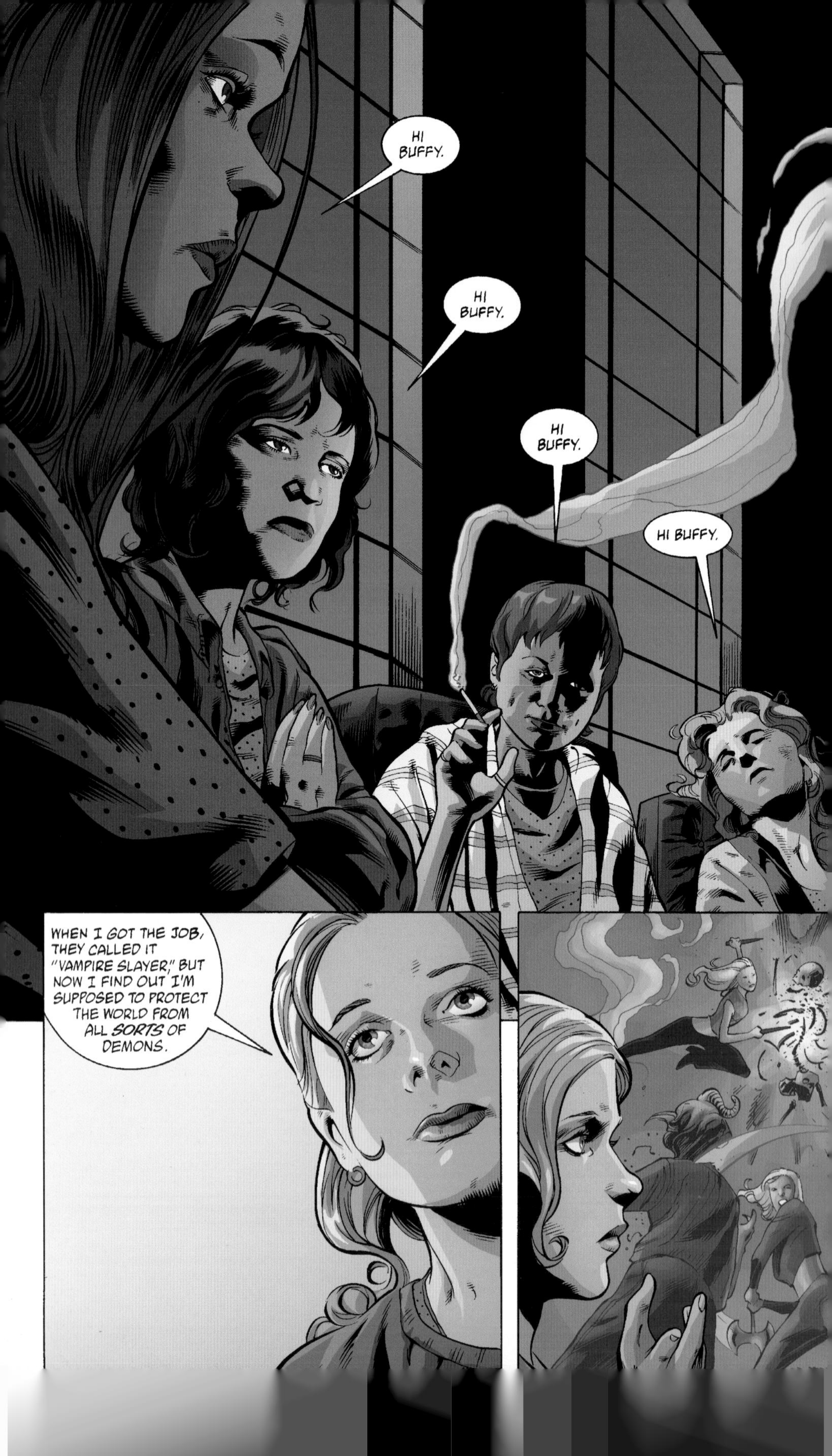
HI BUFFY.
HI BUFFY.
HI BUFFY.
HI BUFFY.
WHEN I GOT THE JOB, THEY CALLED IT "VAMPIRE SLAYER," BUT NOW I FIND OUT I'M SUPPOSED TO PROTECT THE WORLD FROM ALL *SORTS* OF DEMONS.

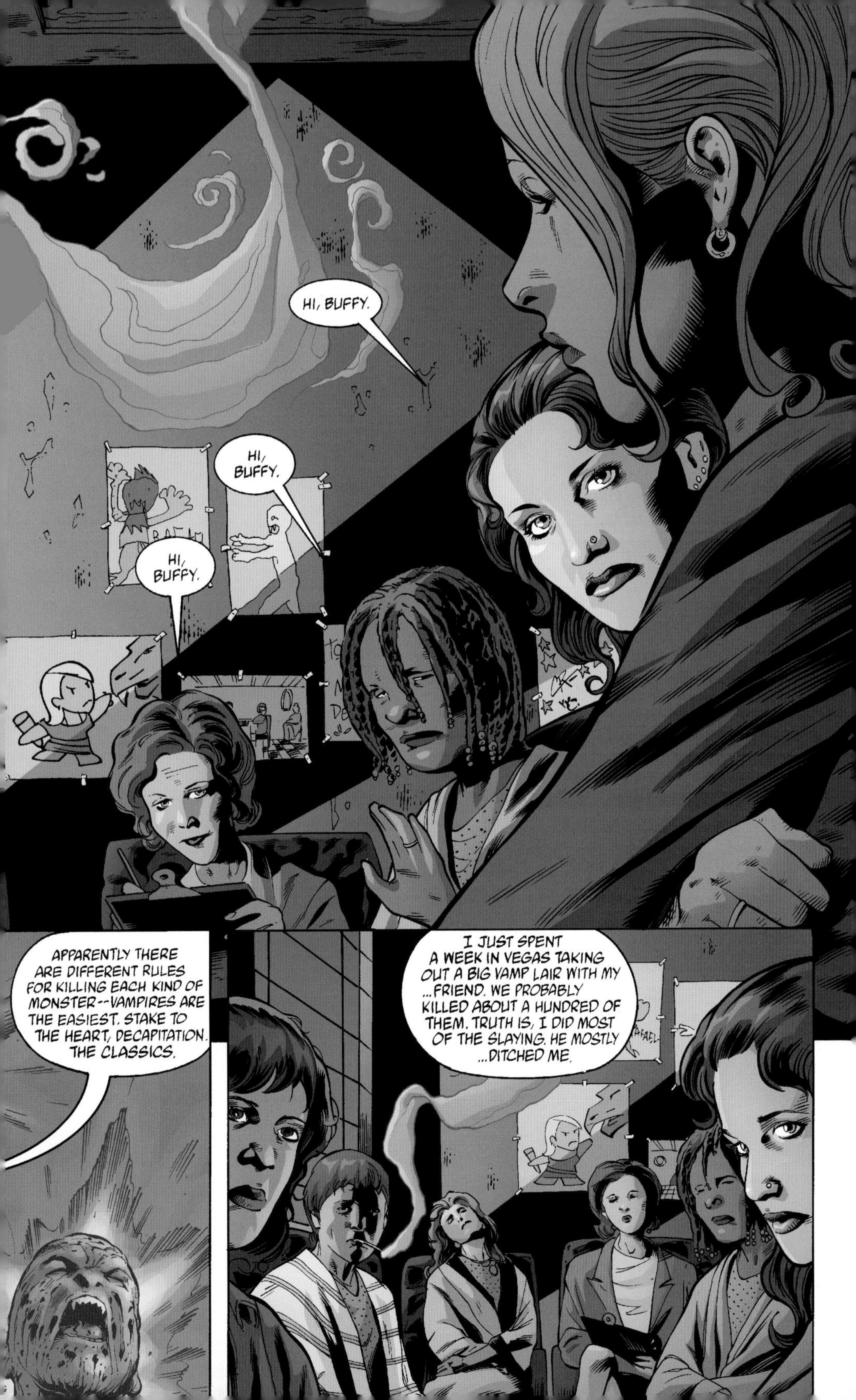
HI, BUFFY.
HI, BUFFY.
HI, BUFFY.
APPARENTLY THERE ARE DIFFERENT RULES FOR KILLING EACH KIND OF MONSTER--VAMPIRES ARE THE EASIEST. STAKE TO THE HEART, DECAPITATION. THE CLASSICS.
I JUST SPENT A WEEK IN VEGAS TAKING OUT A BIG VAMP LAIR WITH MY ...FRIEND. WE PROBABLY KILLED ABOUT A HUNDRED OF THEM. TRUTH IS, I DID MOST OF THE SLAYING. HE MOSTLY ...DITCHED ME.

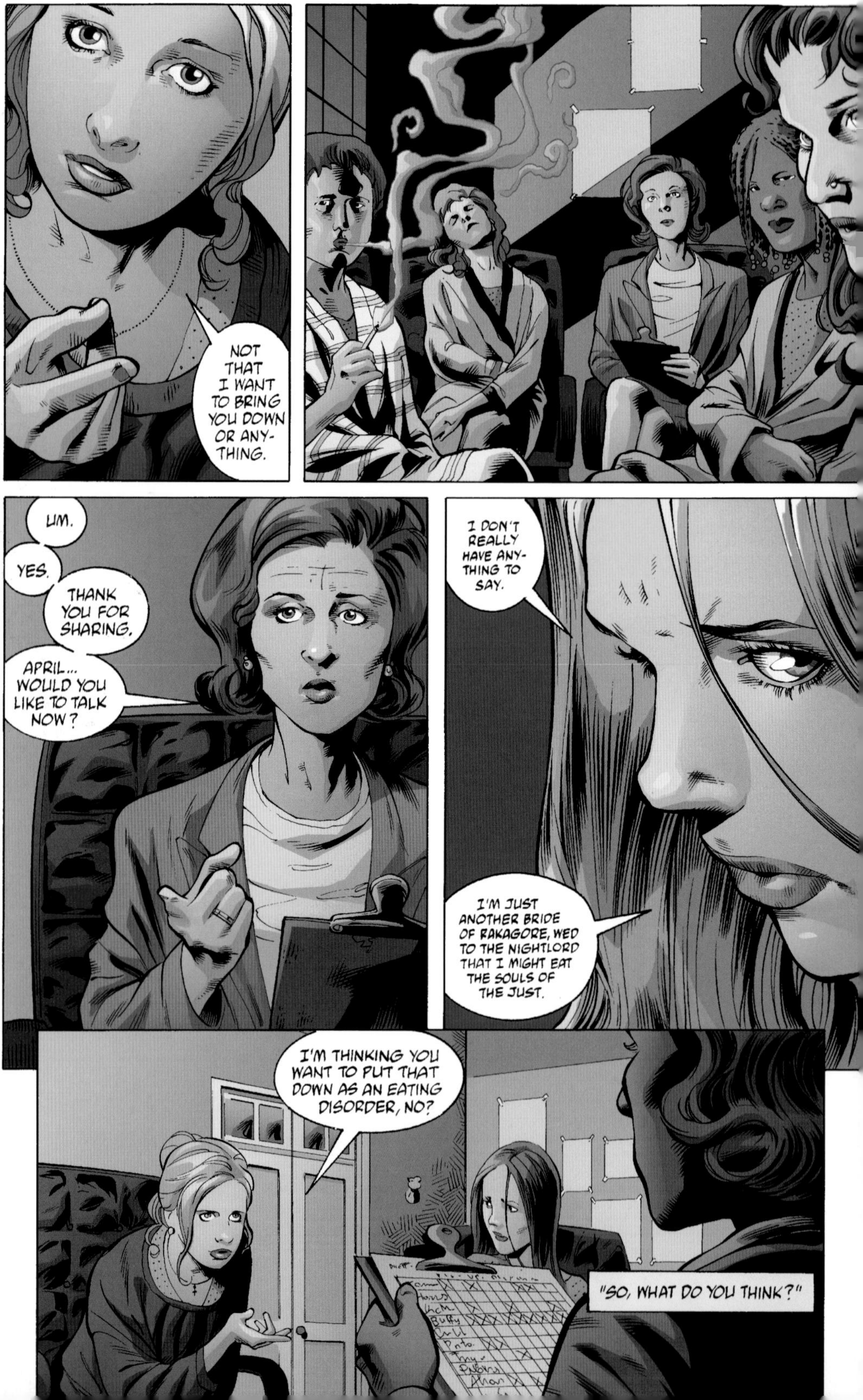
NOT THAT I WANT TO BRING YOU DOWN OR ANY-THING.
UM.
YES.
THANK YOU FOR SHARING.
APRIL... WOULD YOU LIKE TO TALK NOW?
I DON'T REALLY HAVE ANY-THING TO SAY.
I'M JUST ANOTHER BRIDE OF RAKAGORE, WED TO THE NIGHTLORD THAT I MIGHT EAT THE SOULS OF THE JUST.
I'M THINKING YOU WANT TO PUT THAT DOWN AS AN EATING DISORDER, NO?
"SO, WHAT DO YOU THINK?"

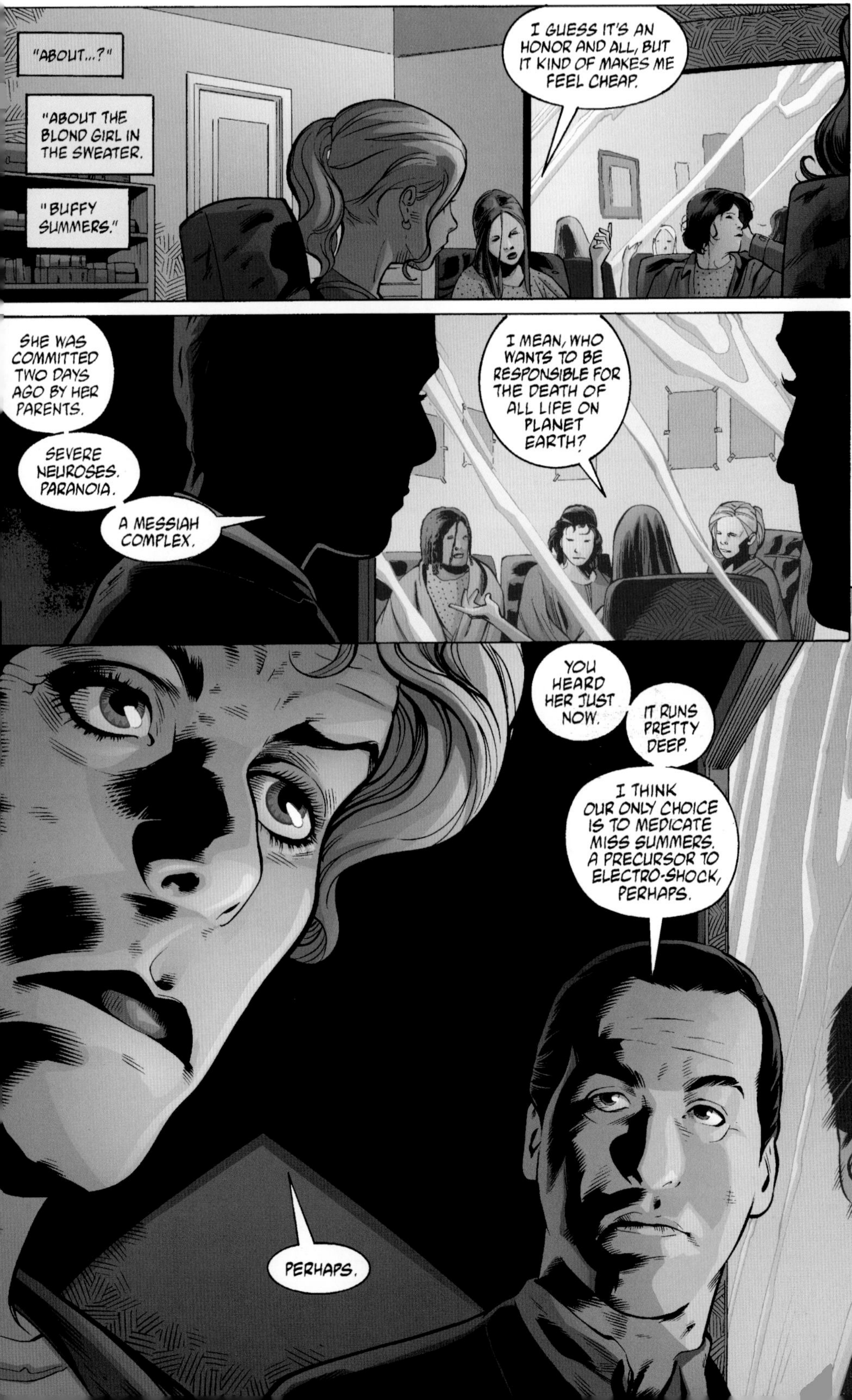
"ABOUT...?"
"ABOUT THE BLOND GIRL IN THE SWEATER.
"BUFFY SUMMERS."
I GUESS IT'S AN HONOR AND ALL, BUT IT KIND OF MAKES ME FEEL CHEAP.
SHE WAS COMMITTED TWO DAYS AGO BY HER PARENTS.
SEVERE NEUROSES. PARANOIA.
A MESSIAH COMPLEX.
I MEAN, WHO WANTS TO BE RESPONSIBLE FOR THE DEATH OF ALL LIFE ON PLANET EARTH?
YOU HEARD HER JUST NOW.
IT RUNS PRETTY DEEP.
I THINK OUR ONLY CHOICE IS TO MEDICATE MISS SUMMERS. A PRECURSOR TO ELECTRO-SHOCK, PERHAPS.
PERHAPS.

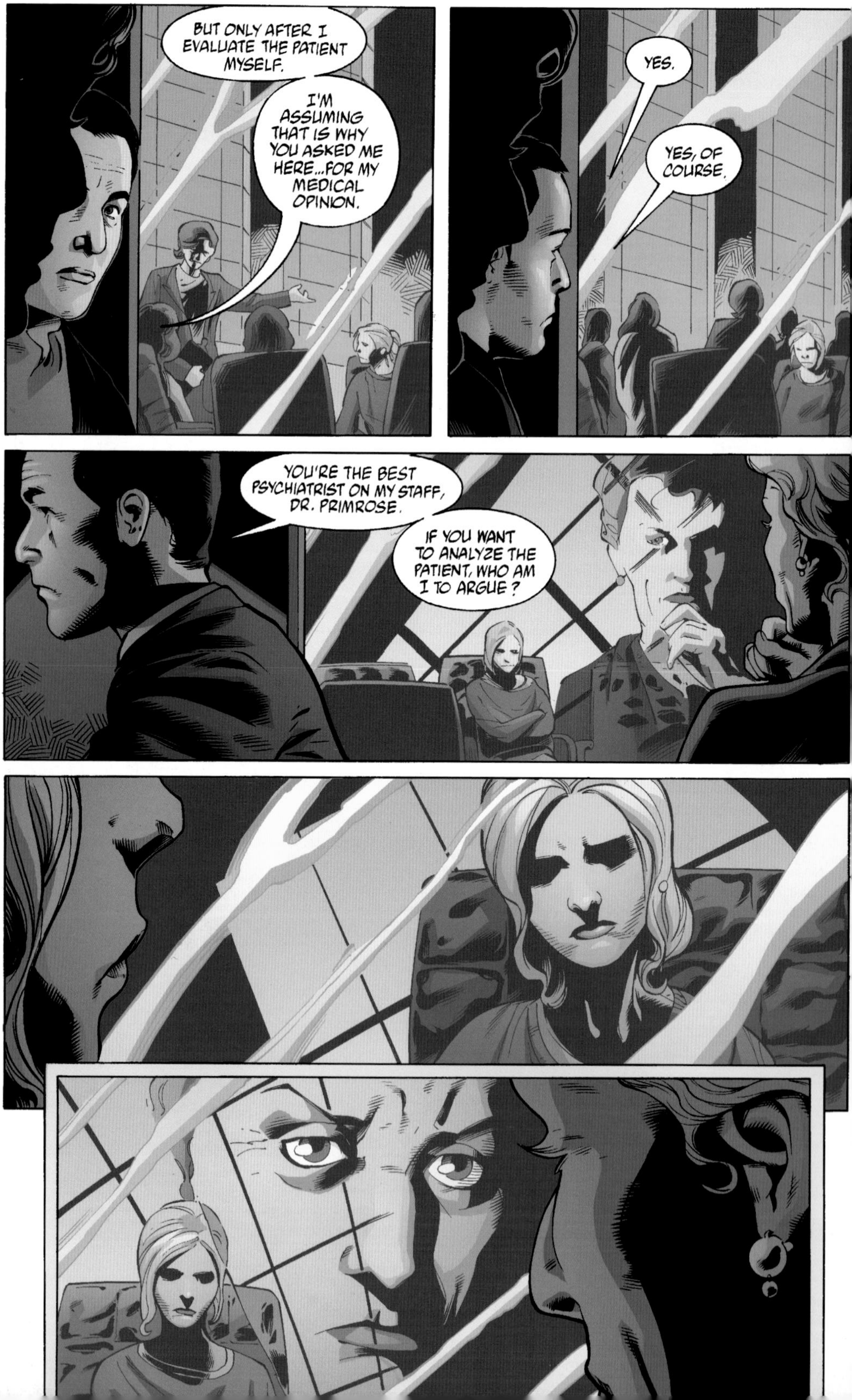
BUT ONLY AFTER I EVALUATE THE PATIENT MYSELF.
I'M ASSUMING THAT IS WHY YOU ASKED ME HERE...FOR MY MEDICAL OPINION.
YES.
YES, OF COURSE.
YOU'RE THE BEST PSYCHIATRIST ON MY STAFF, DR. PRIMROSE.
IF YOU WANT TO ANALYZE THE PATIENT, WHO AM I TO ARGUE?

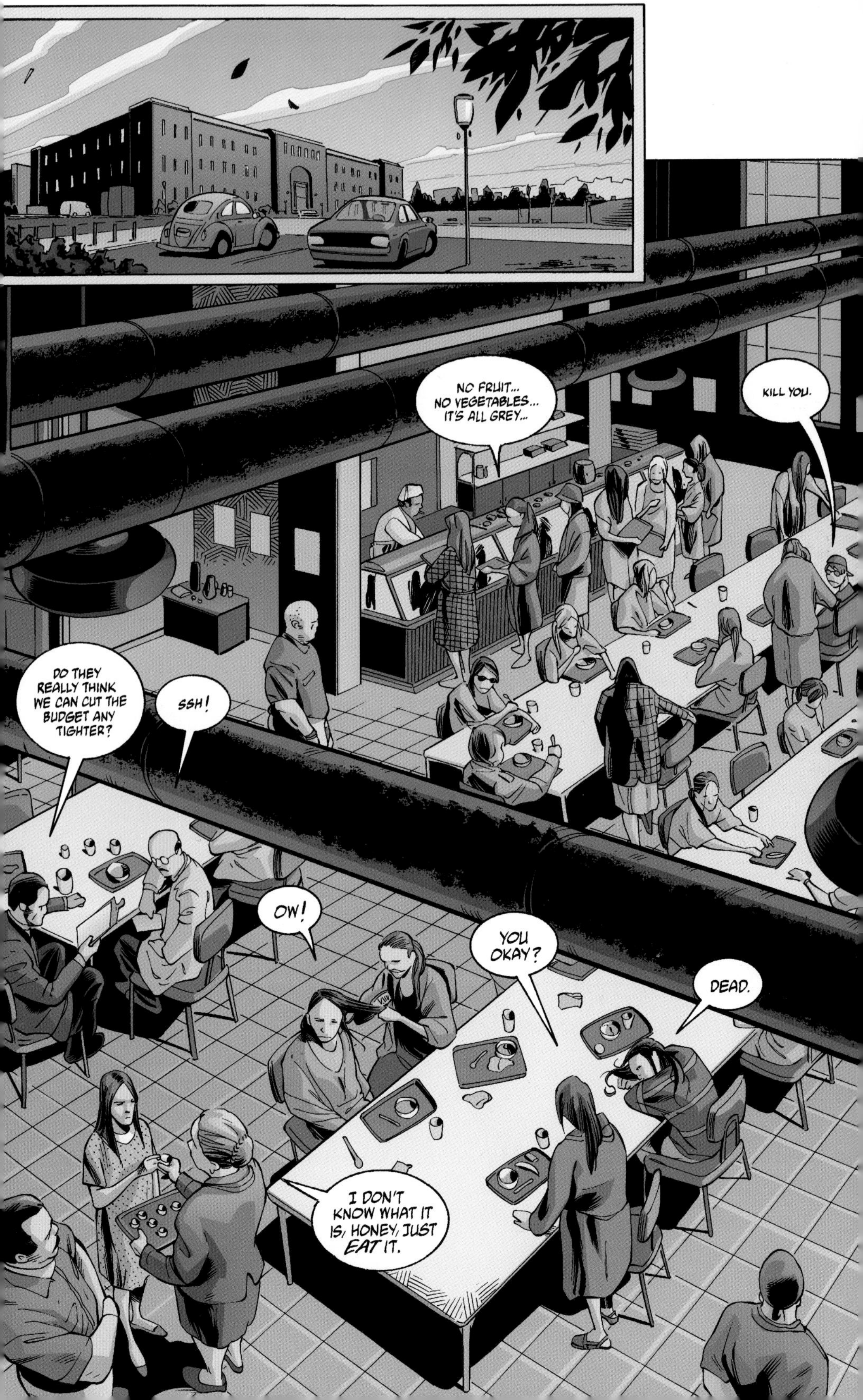
NO FRUIT... NO VEGETABLES... IT'S ALL GREY...
KILL YOU.
DO THEY REALLY THINK WE CAN CUT THE BUDGET ANY TIGHTER?
SSH!
OW!
YOU OKAY?
DEAD.
I DON'T KNOW WHAT IT IS, HONEY, JUST *EAT* IT.

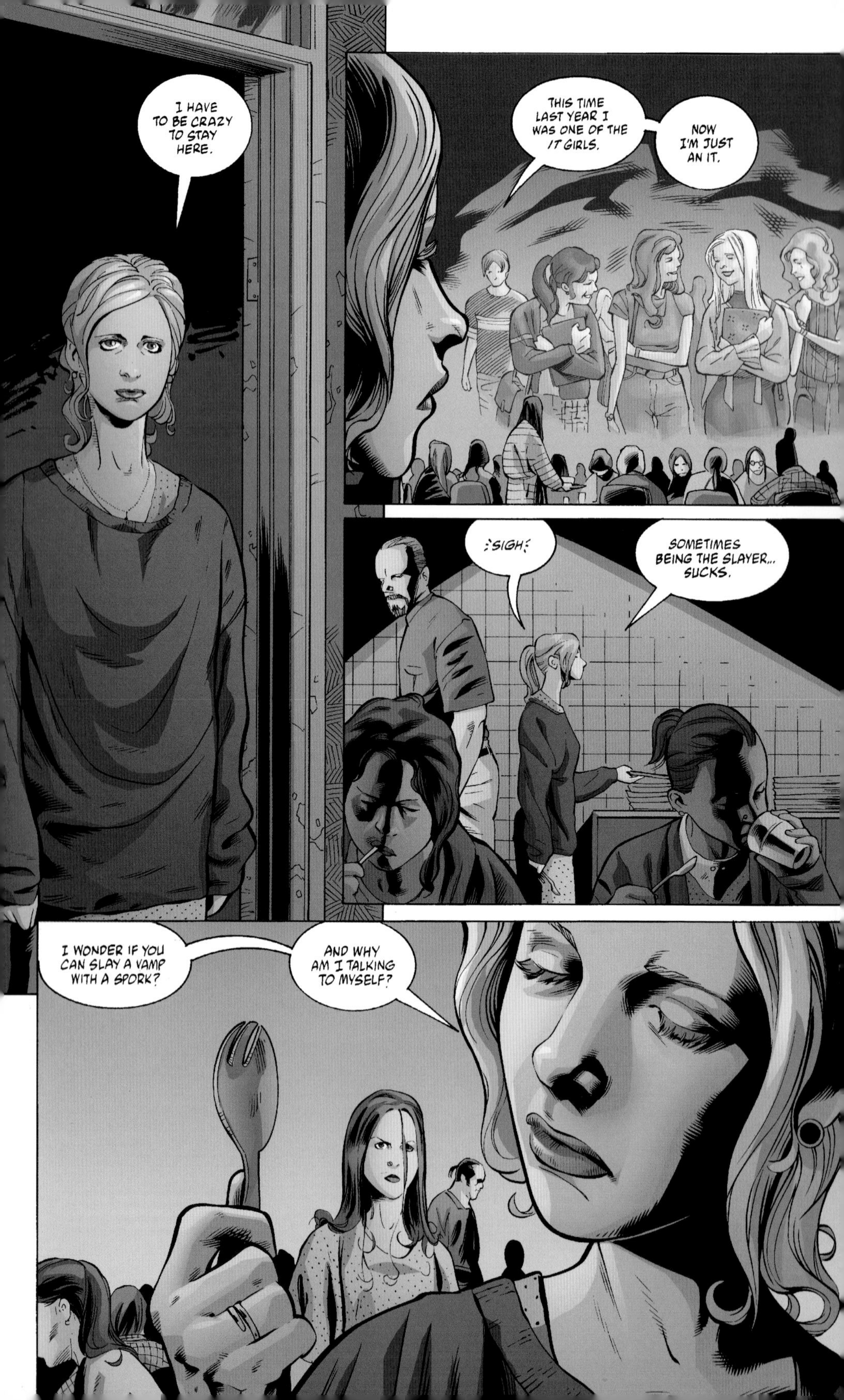
I HAVE TO BE CRAZY TO STAY HERE.
THIS TIME LAST YEAR I WAS ONE OF THE *IT* GIRLS.
NOW I'M JUST AN IT.
SIGH
SOMETIMES BEING THE SLAYER... SUCKS.
I WONDER IF YOU CAN SLAY A VAMP WITH A SPORK?
AND WHY AM I TALKING TO MYSELF?

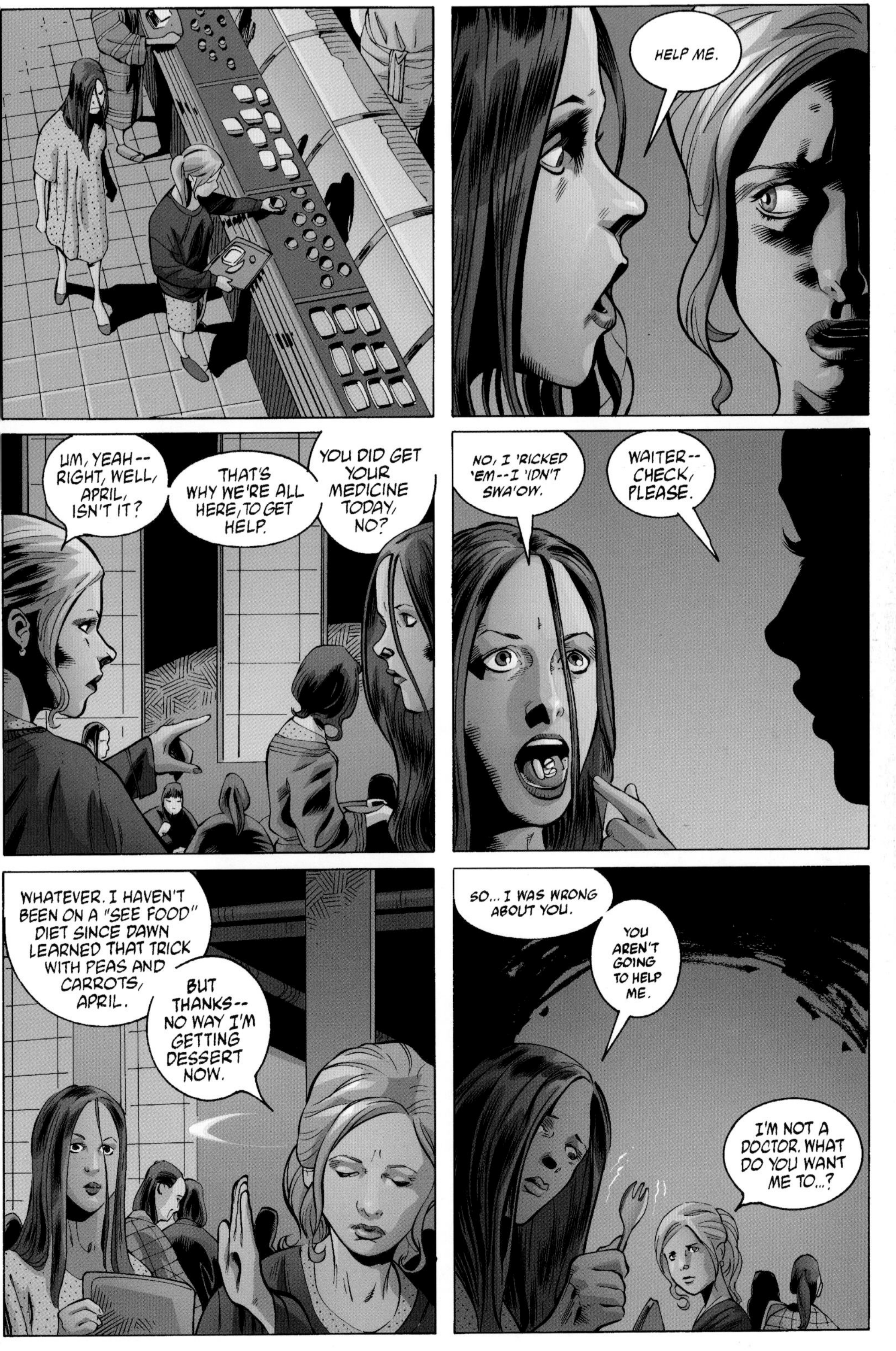
HELP ME.
UM, YEAH-- RIGHT, WELL, APRIL, ISN'T IT?
THAT'S WHY WE'RE ALL HERE, TO GET HELP.
YOU DID GET YOUR MEDICINE TODAY, NO?
NO, I 'RICKED 'EM--I 'IDN'T SWA'OW.
WAITER-- CHECK, PLEASE.
WHATEVER. I HAVEN'T BEEN ON A "SEE FOOD" DIET SINCE DAWN LEARNED THAT TRICK WITH PEAS AND CARROTS, APRIL.
BUT THANKS-- NO WAY I'M GETTING DESSERT NOW.
SO... I WAS WRONG ABOUT YOU.
YOU AREN'T GOING TO HELP ME.
I'M NOT A DOCTOR. WHAT DO YOU WANT ME TO...?

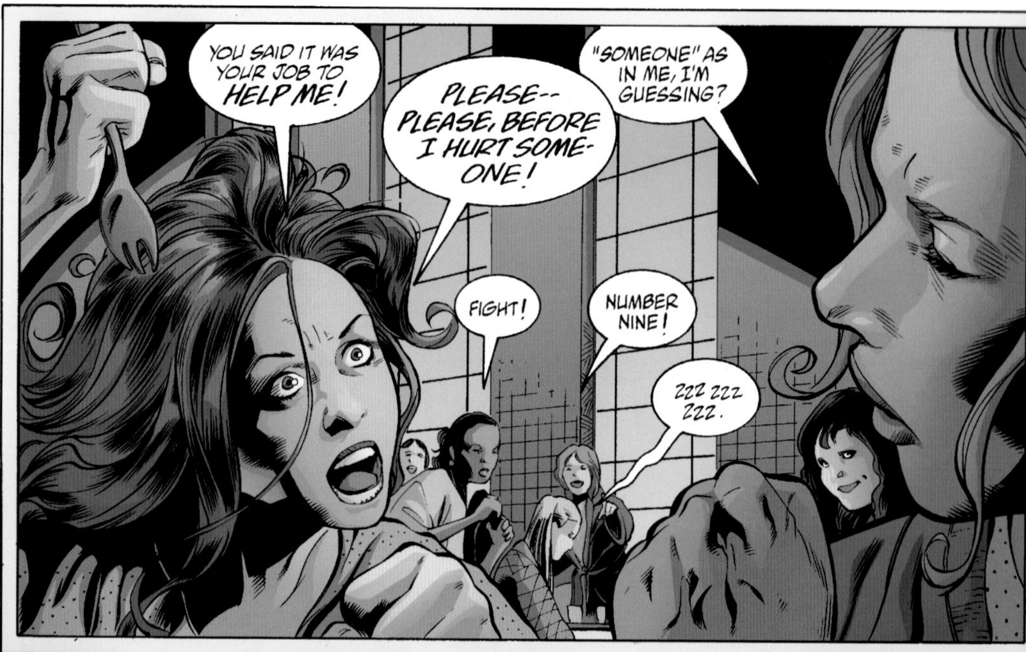
YOU SAID IT WAS YOUR JOB TO HELP ME!
PLEASE-- PLEASE, BEFORE I HURT SOME-ONE!
"SOMEONE" AS IN ME, I'M GUESSING?
FIGHT!
NUMBER NINE!
ZZZ ZZZ ZZZ.

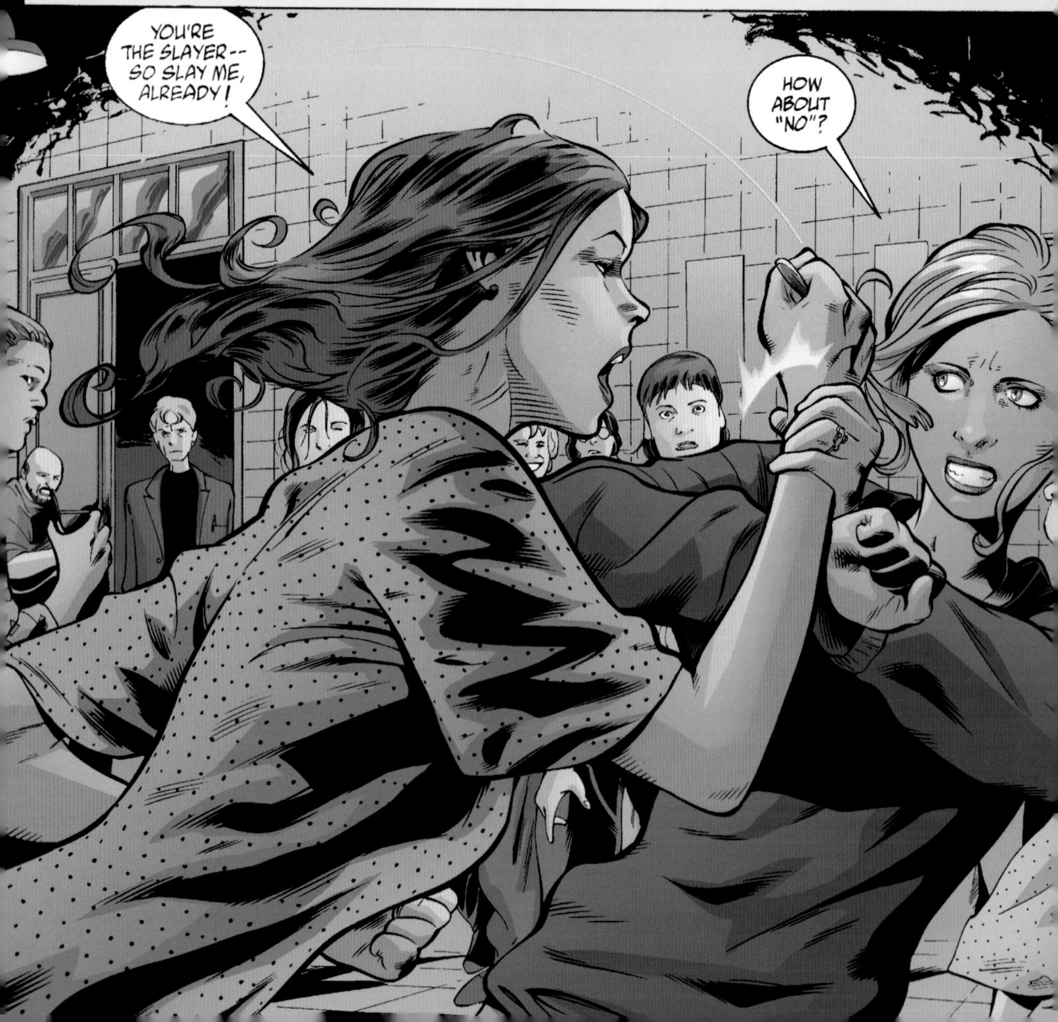
YOU'RE THE SLAYER-- SO SLAY ME, ALREADY!
HOW ABOUT "NO"?

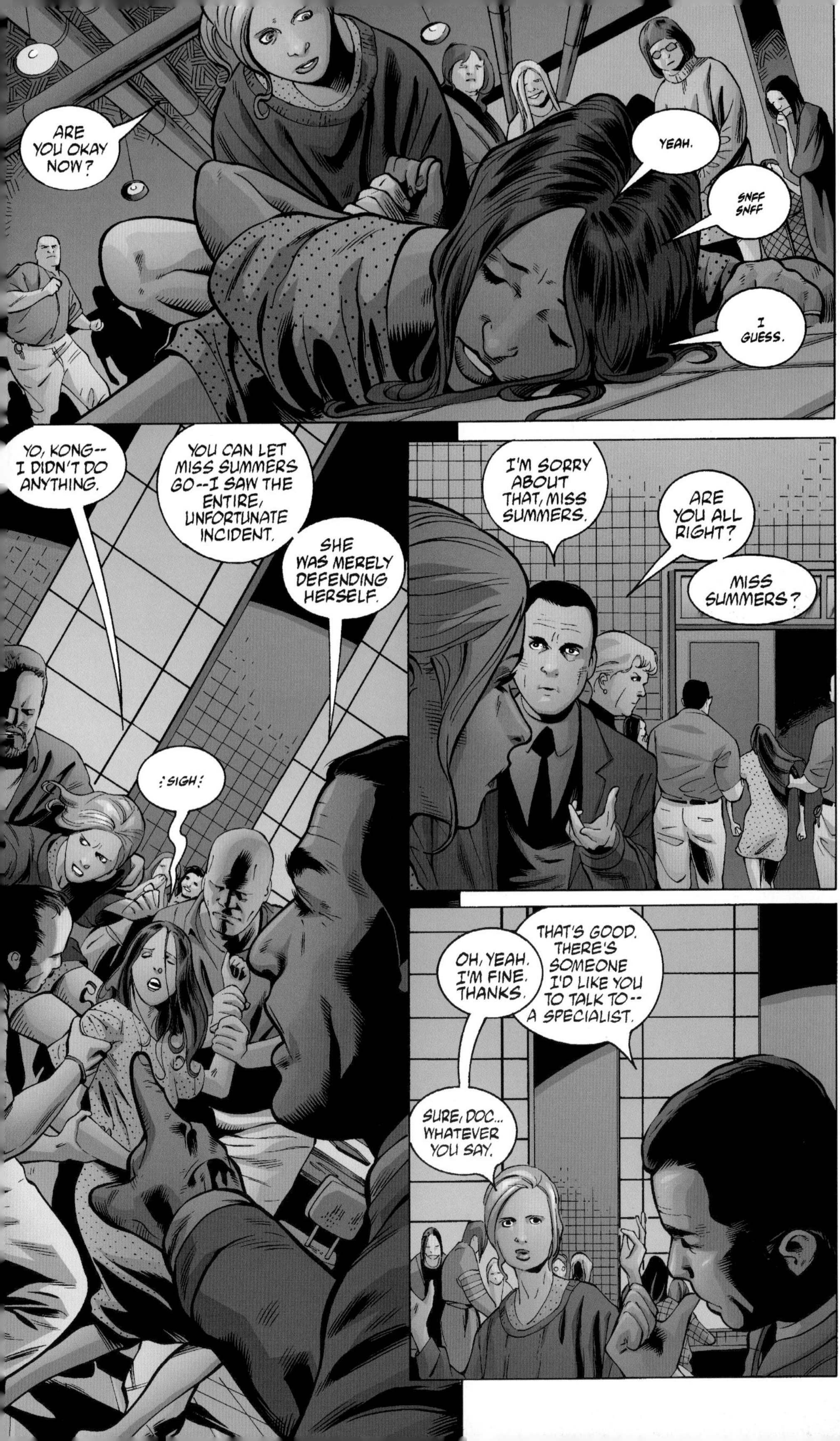
ARE YOU OKAY NOW?
YEAH.
SNFF SNFF
I GUESS.
YO, KONG-- I DIDN'T DO ANYTHING.
YOU CAN LET MISS SUMMERS GO--I SAW THE ENTIRE, UNFORTUNATE INCIDENT.
SHE WAS MERELY DEFENDING HERSELF.
:SIGH:
I'M SORRY ABOUT THAT, MISS SUMMERS.
ARE YOU ALL RIGHT?
MISS SUMMERS?
OH, YEAH. I'M FINE. THANKS.
THAT'S GOOD. THERE'S SOMEONE I'D LIKE YOU TO TALK TO-- A SPECIALIST.
SURE, DOC... WHATEVER YOU SAY.

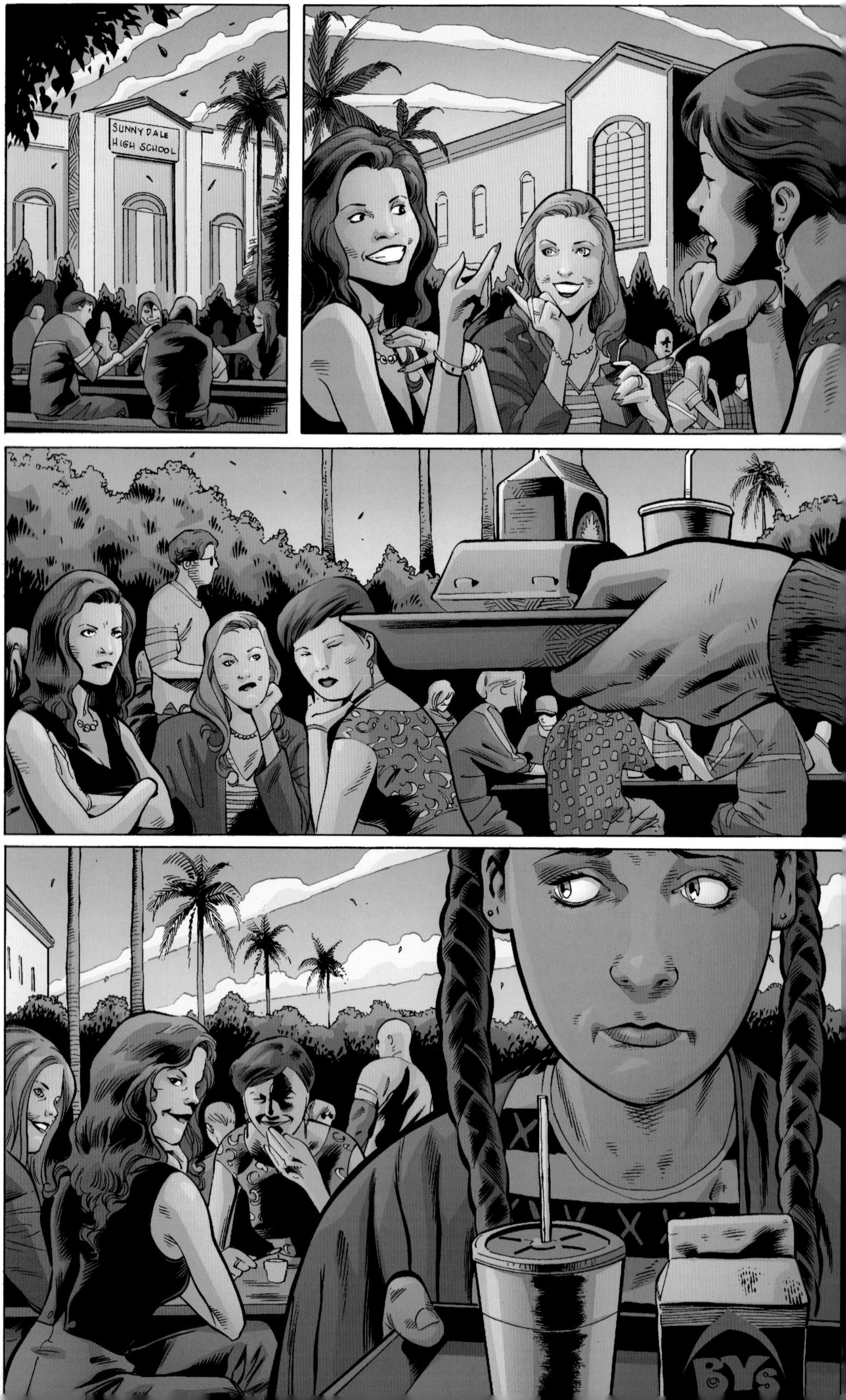
SUNNYDALE
HIGH SCHOOL

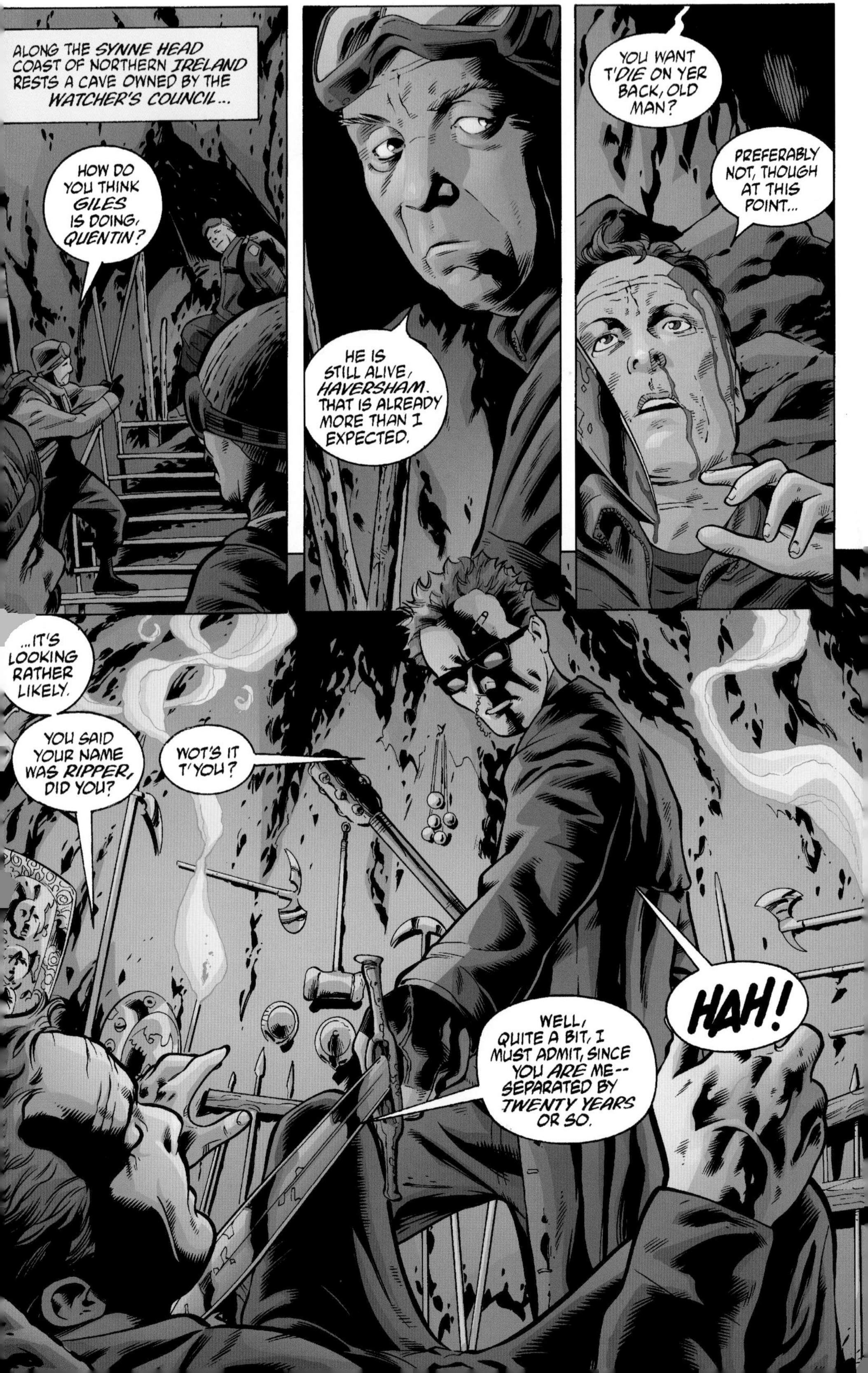
ALONG THE SYNNE HEAD COAST OF NORTHERN IRELAND RESTS A CAVE OWNED BY THE WATCHER'S COUNCIL...
HOW DO YOU THINK GILES IS DOING, QUENTIN?
HE IS STILL ALIVE, HAVERSHAM. THAT IS ALREADY MORE THAN I EXPECTED.
YOU WANT T'DIE ON YER BACK, OLD MAN?
PREFERABLY NOT, THOUGH AT THIS POINT...
...IT'S LOOKING RATHER LIKELY.
YOU SAID YOUR NAME WAS RIPPER, DID YOU?
WOT'S IT T'YOU?
HAH!
WELL, QUITE A BIT, I MUST ADMIT, SINCE YOU ARE ME-- SEPARATED BY TWENTY YEARS OR SO.

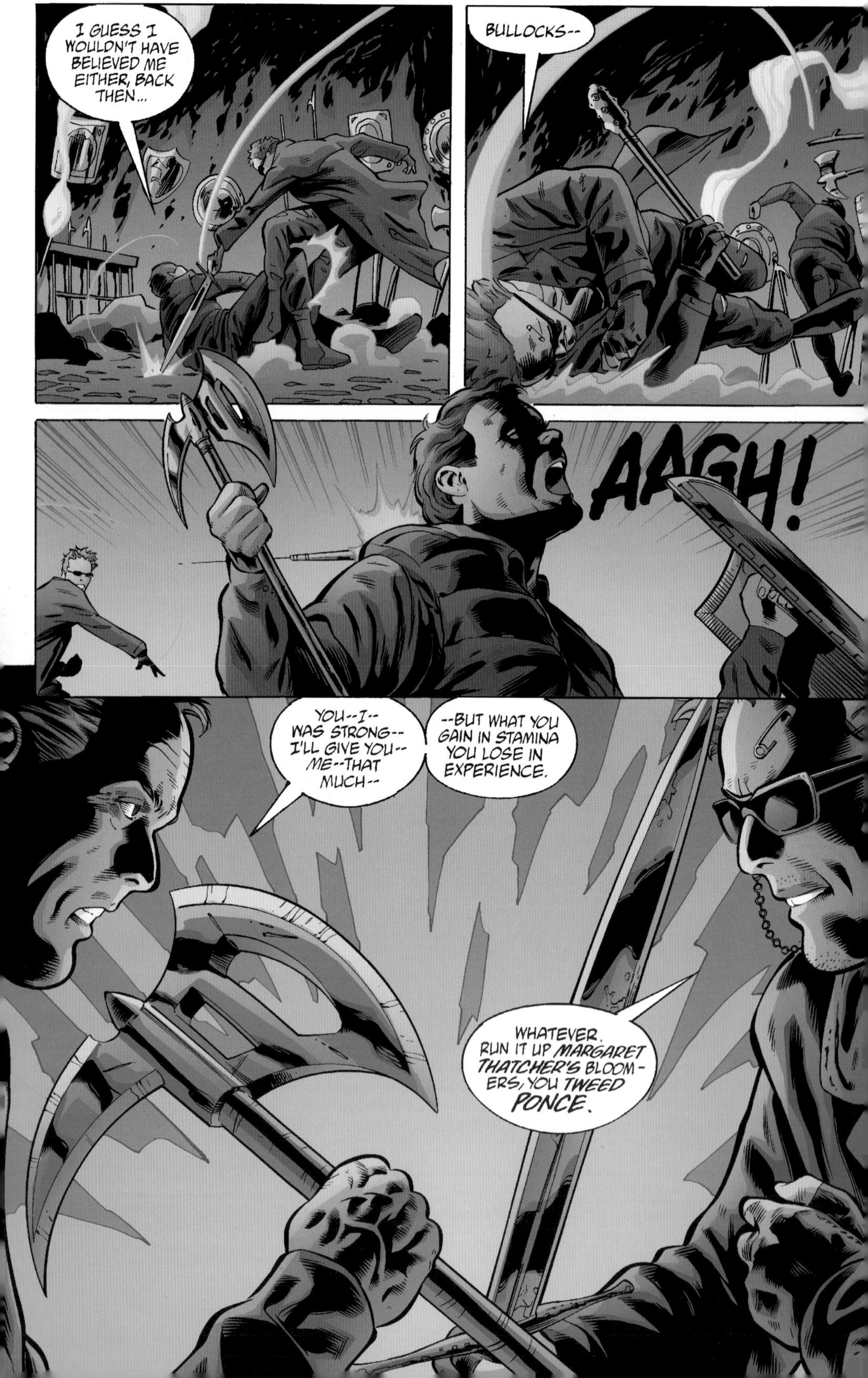
I GUESS I WOULDN'T HAVE BELIEVED ME EITHER, BACK THEN...
BULLOCKS--
AAGH!
YOU--I--WAS STRONG--I'LL GIVE YOU--ME--THAT MUCH--
--BUT WHAT YOU GAIN IN STAMINA YOU LOSE IN EXPERIENCE.
WHATEVER. RUN IT UP MARGARET THATCHER'S BLOOM-ERS, YOU TWEED PONCE.

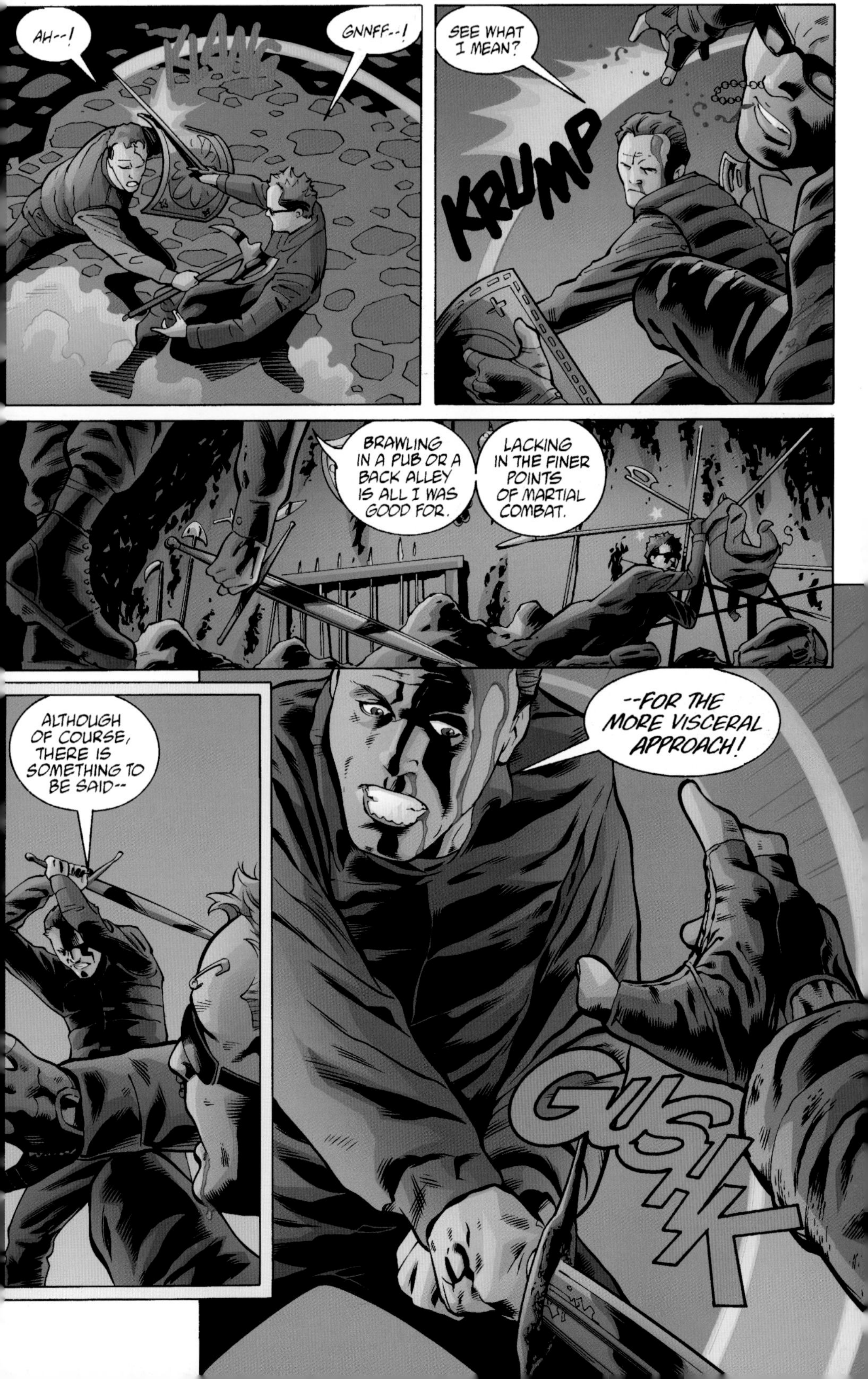
AH--!
KLANG
GNNFF--!
SEE WHAT I MEAN?
KRUMP
BRAWLING IN A PUB OR A BACK ALLEY IS ALL I WAS GOOD FOR.
LACKING IN THE FINER POINTS OF MARTIAL COMBAT.
ALTHOUGH OF COURSE, THERE IS SOMETHING TO BE SAID--
--FOR THE MORE VISCERAL APPROACH!
GUSHK

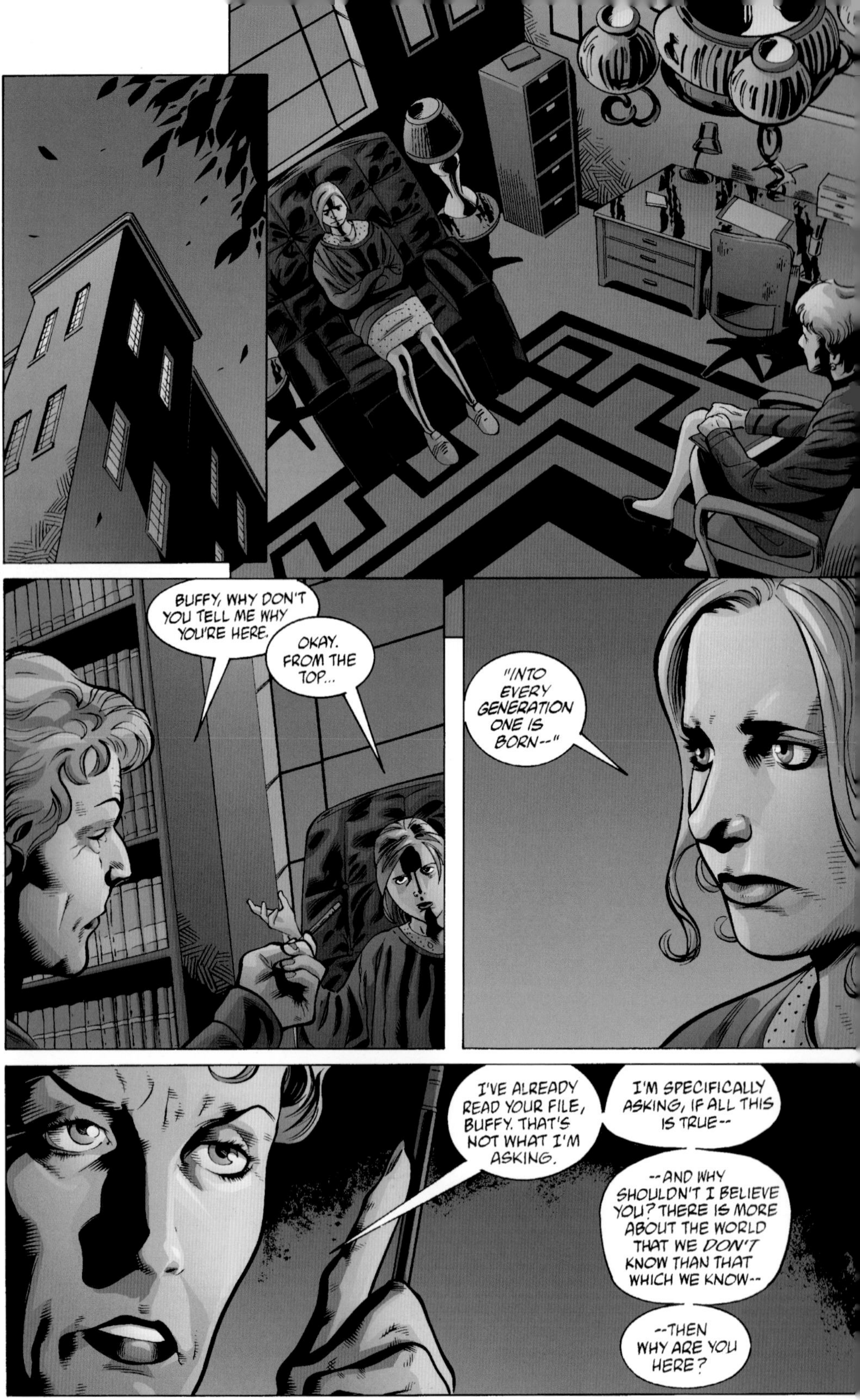
BUFFY, WHY DON'T YOU TELL ME WHY YOU'RE HERE.
OKAY. FROM THE TOP...
"INTO EVERY GENERATION ONE IS BORN--"
I'VE ALREADY READ YOUR FILE, BUFFY. THAT'S NOT WHAT I'M ASKING.
I'M SPECIFICALLY ASKING, IF ALL THIS IS TRUE--
--AND WHY SHOULDN'T I BELIEVE YOU? THERE IS MORE ABOUT THE WORLD THAT WE DON'T KNOW THAN THAT WHICH WE KNOW--
--THEN WHY ARE YOU HERE?

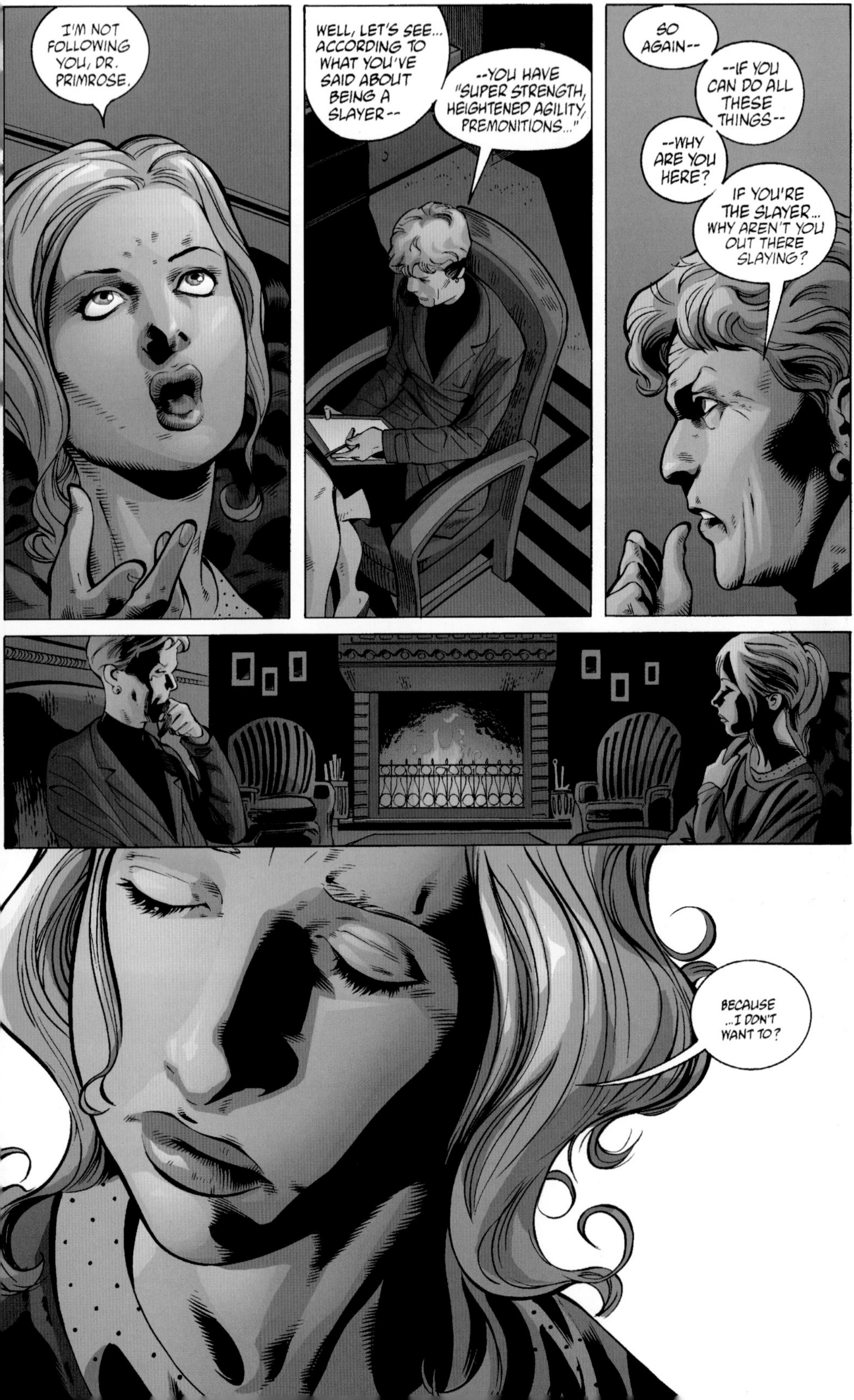
I'M NOT FOLLOWING YOU, DR. PRIMROSE.
WELL, LET'S SEE... ACCORDING TO WHAT YOU'VE SAID ABOUT BEING A SLAYER--
--YOU HAVE "SUPER STRENGTH, HEIGHTENED AGILITY, PREMONITIONS..."
SO AGAIN--
--IF YOU CAN DO ALL THESE THINGS--
--WHY ARE YOU HERE?
IF YOU'RE THE SLAYER... WHY AREN'T YOU OUT THERE SLAYING?
BECAUSE ...I DON'T WANT TO?

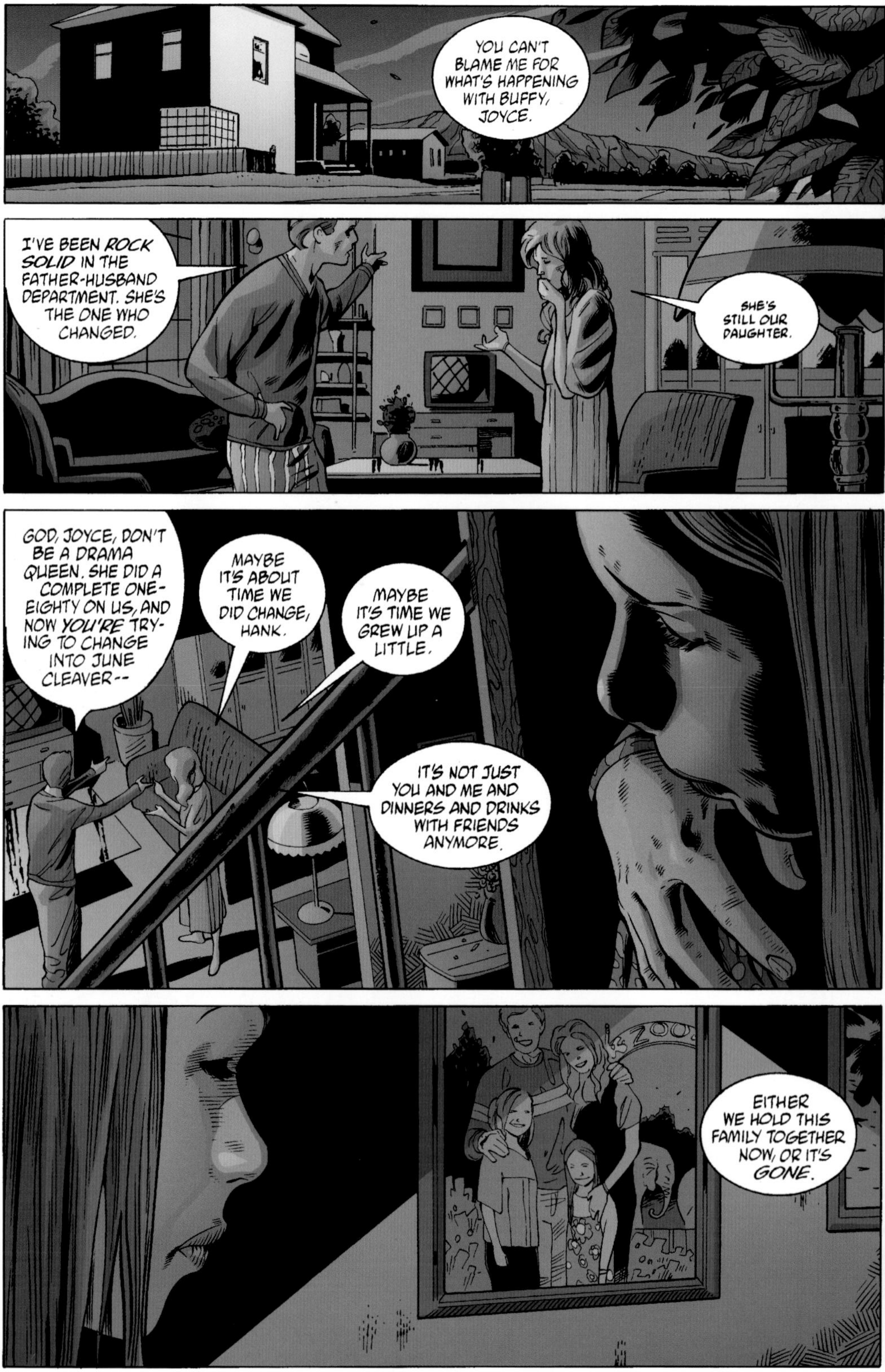
YOU CAN'T BLAME ME FOR WHAT'S HAPPENING WITH BUFFY, JOYCE.
I'VE BEEN ROCK SOLID IN THE FATHER-HUSBAND DEPARTMENT. SHE'S THE ONE WHO CHANGED.
SHE'S STILL OUR DAUGHTER.
GOD, JOYCE, DON'T BE A DRAMA QUEEN. SHE DID A COMPLETE ONE-EIGHTY ON US, AND NOW YOU'RE TRYING TO CHANGE INTO JUNE CLEAVER--
MAYBE IT'S ABOUT TIME WE DID CHANGE, HANK.
MAYBE IT'S TIME WE GREW UP A LITTLE.
IT'S NOT JUST YOU AND ME AND DINNERS AND DRINKS WITH FRIENDS ANYMORE.
EITHER WE HOLD THIS FAMILY TOGETHER NOW, OR IT'S GONE.

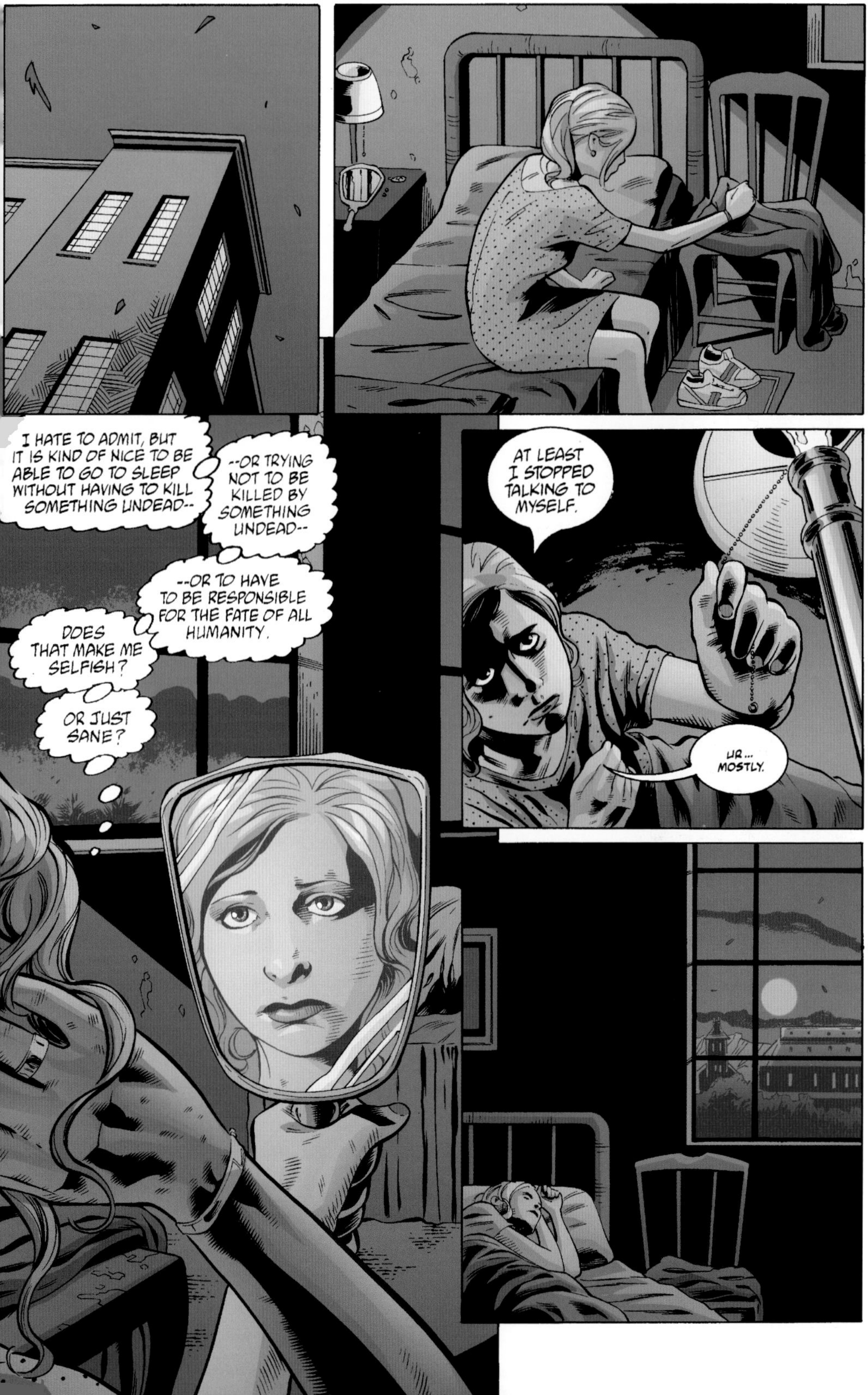
I HATE TO ADMIT, BUT IT IS KIND OF NICE TO BE ABLE TO GO TO SLEEP WITHOUT HAVING TO KILL SOMETHING UNDEAD--
--OR TRYING NOT TO BE KILLED BY SOMETHING UNDEAD--
--OR TO HAVE TO BE RESPONSIBLE FOR THE FATE OF ALL HUMANITY.
DOES THAT MAKE ME SELFISH?
OR JUST SANE?
AT LEAST I STOPPED TALKING TO MYSELF.
UR... MOSTLY.

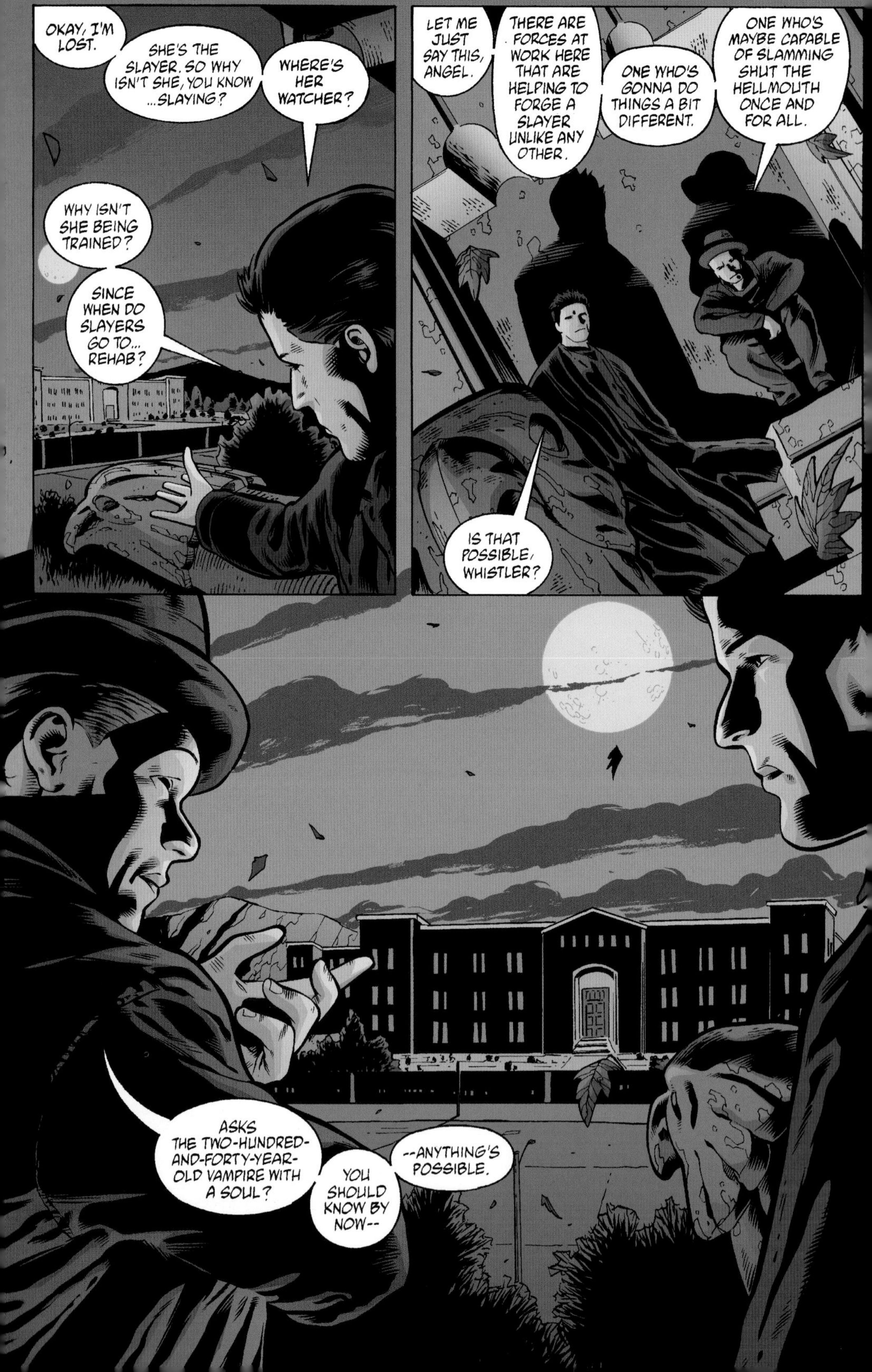
OKAY, I'M LOST.
SHE'S THE SLAYER. SO WHY ISN'T SHE, YOU KNOW ...SLAYING?
WHERE'S HER WATCHER?
WHY ISN'T SHE BEING TRAINED?
SINCE WHEN DO SLAYERS GO TO... REHAB?
LET ME JUST SAY THIS, ANGEL.
THERE ARE FORCES AT WORK HERE THAT ARE HELPING TO FORGE A SLAYER UNLIKE ANY OTHER.
ONE WHO'S GONNA DO THINGS A BIT DIFFERENT.
ONE WHO'S MAYBE CAPABLE OF SLAMMING SHUT THE HELLMOUTH ONCE AND FOR ALL.
IS THAT POSSIBLE, WHISTLER?
ASKS THE TWO-HUNDRED-AND-FORTY-YEAR-OLD VAMPIRE WITH A SOUL?
YOU SHOULD KNOW BY NOW--
--ANYTHING'S POSSIBLE.

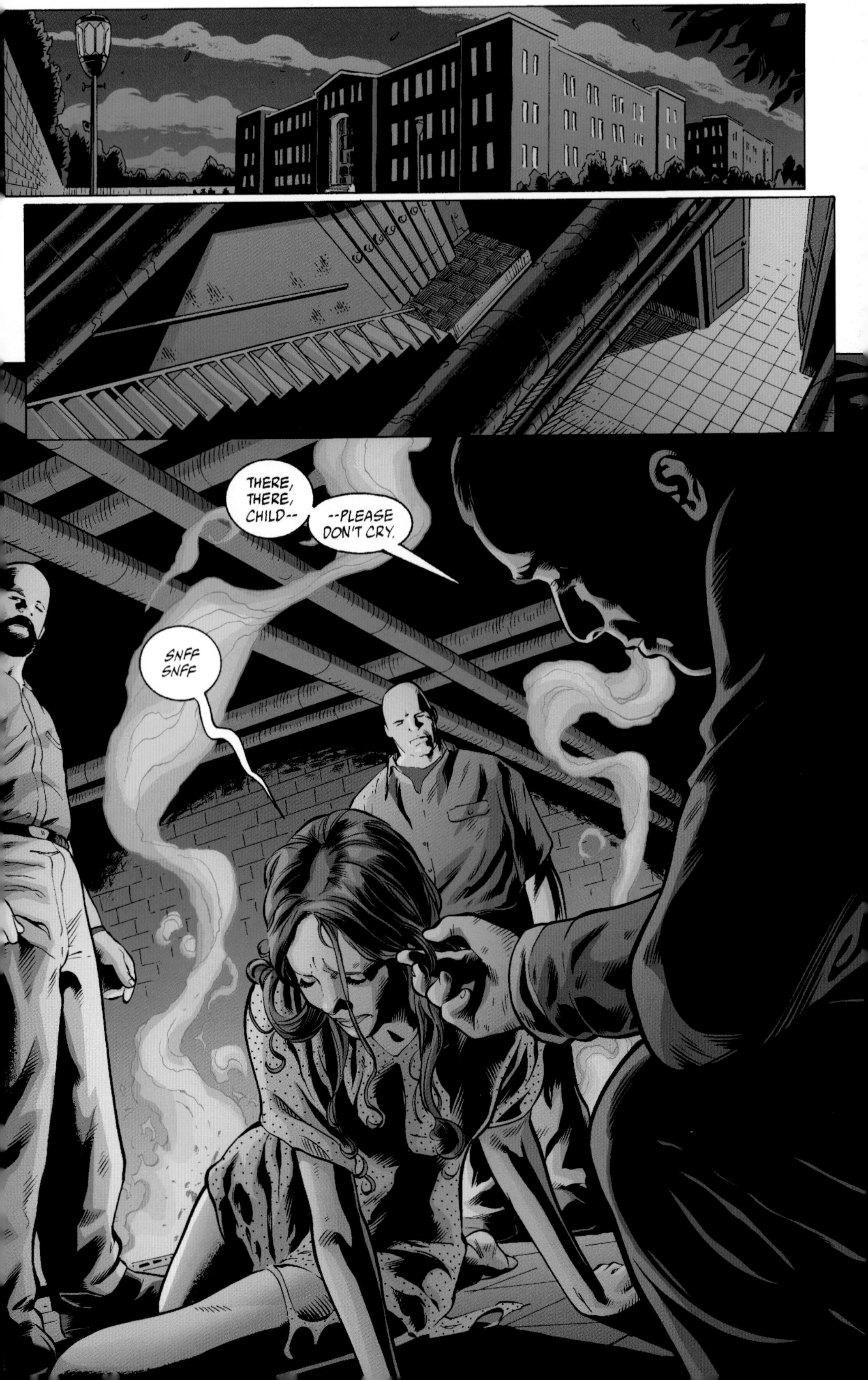
THERE, THERE, CHILD--
--PLEASE DON'T CRY.
SNFF SNFF

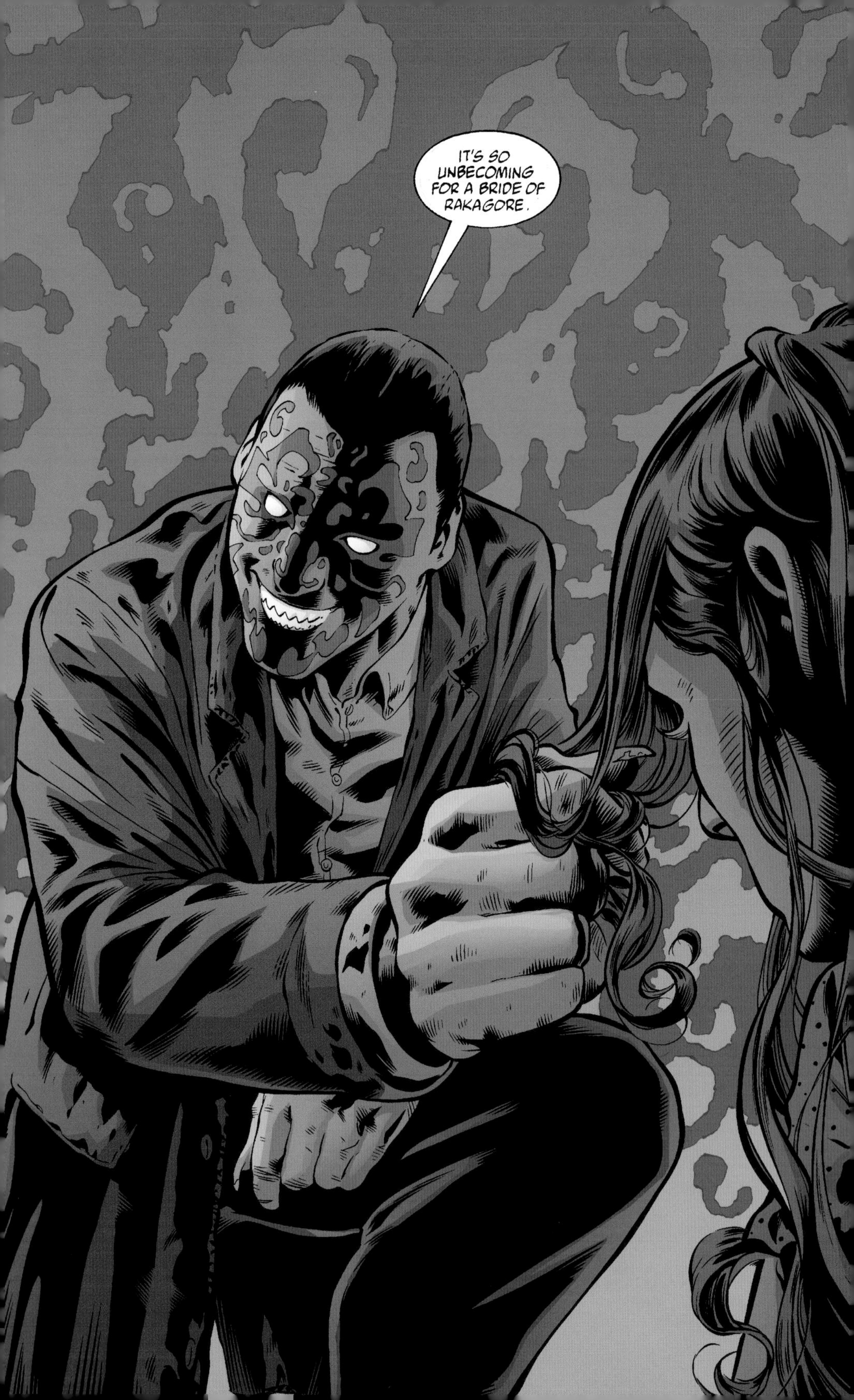
IT'S SO UNBECOMING FOR A BRIDE OF RAKAGORE.

CHAPTER 3

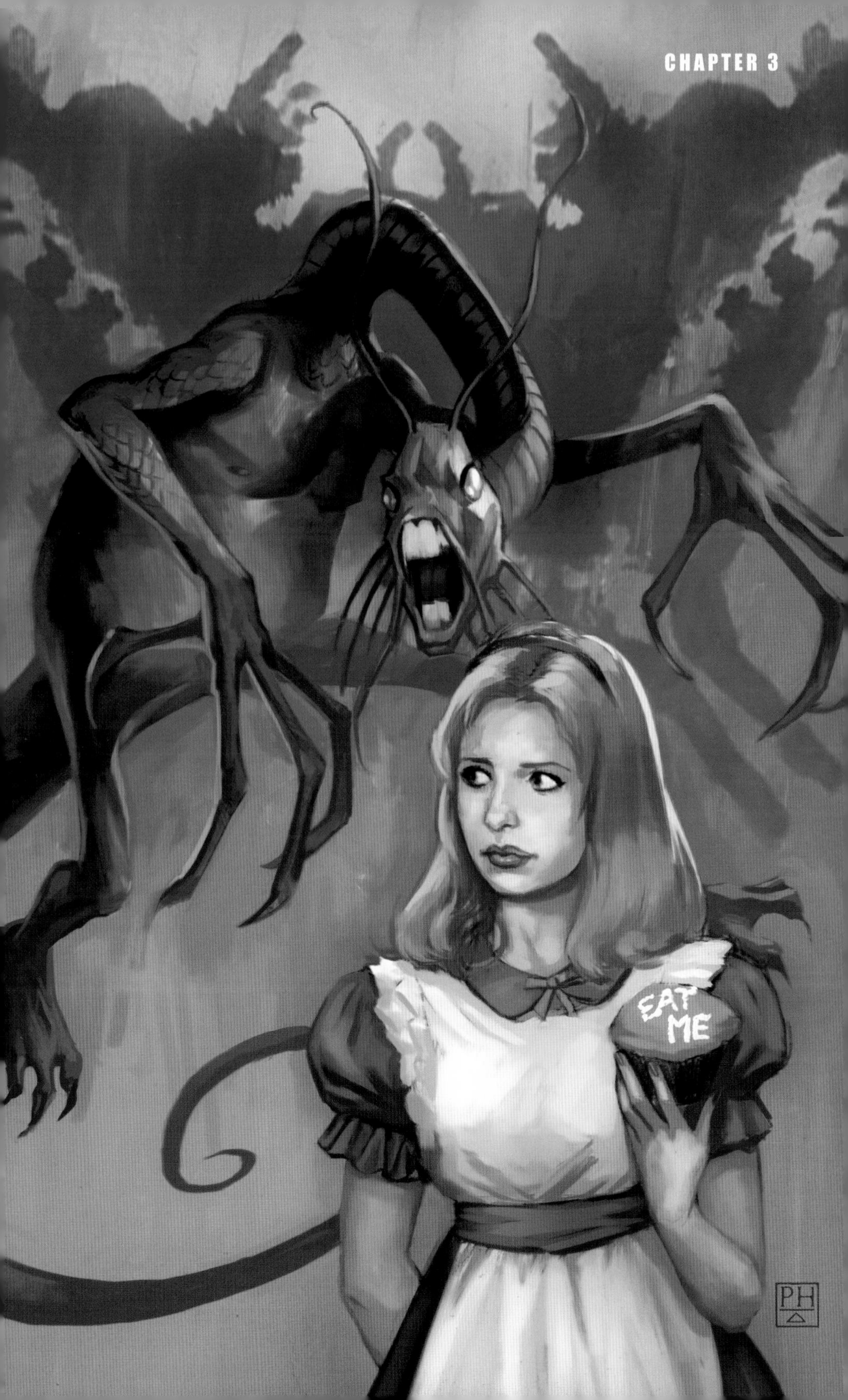
EAT ME

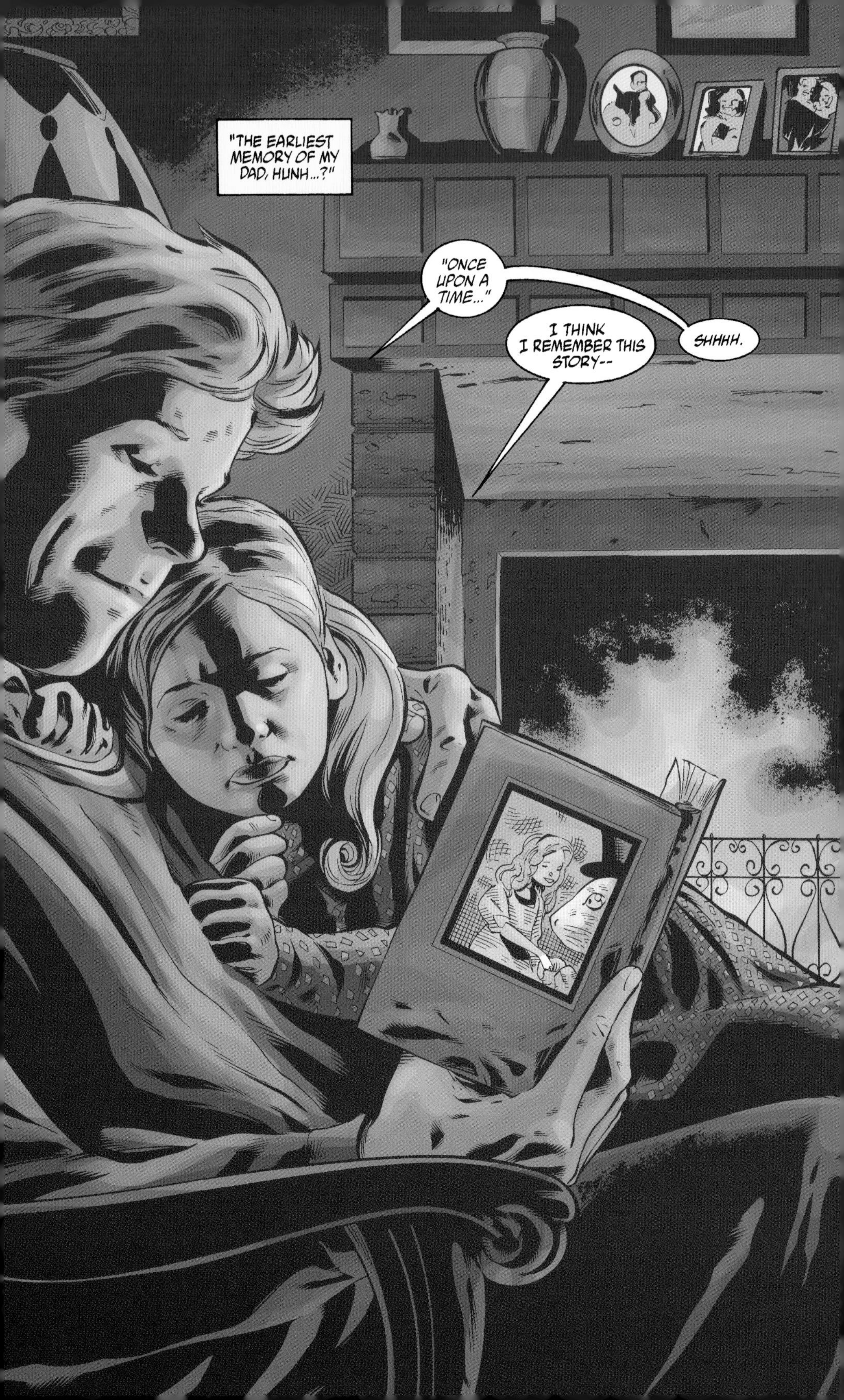
"THE EARLIEST MEMORY OF MY DAD, HUNH...?"
"ONCE UPON A TIME..."
I THINK I REMEMBER THIS STORY--
SHHHH.

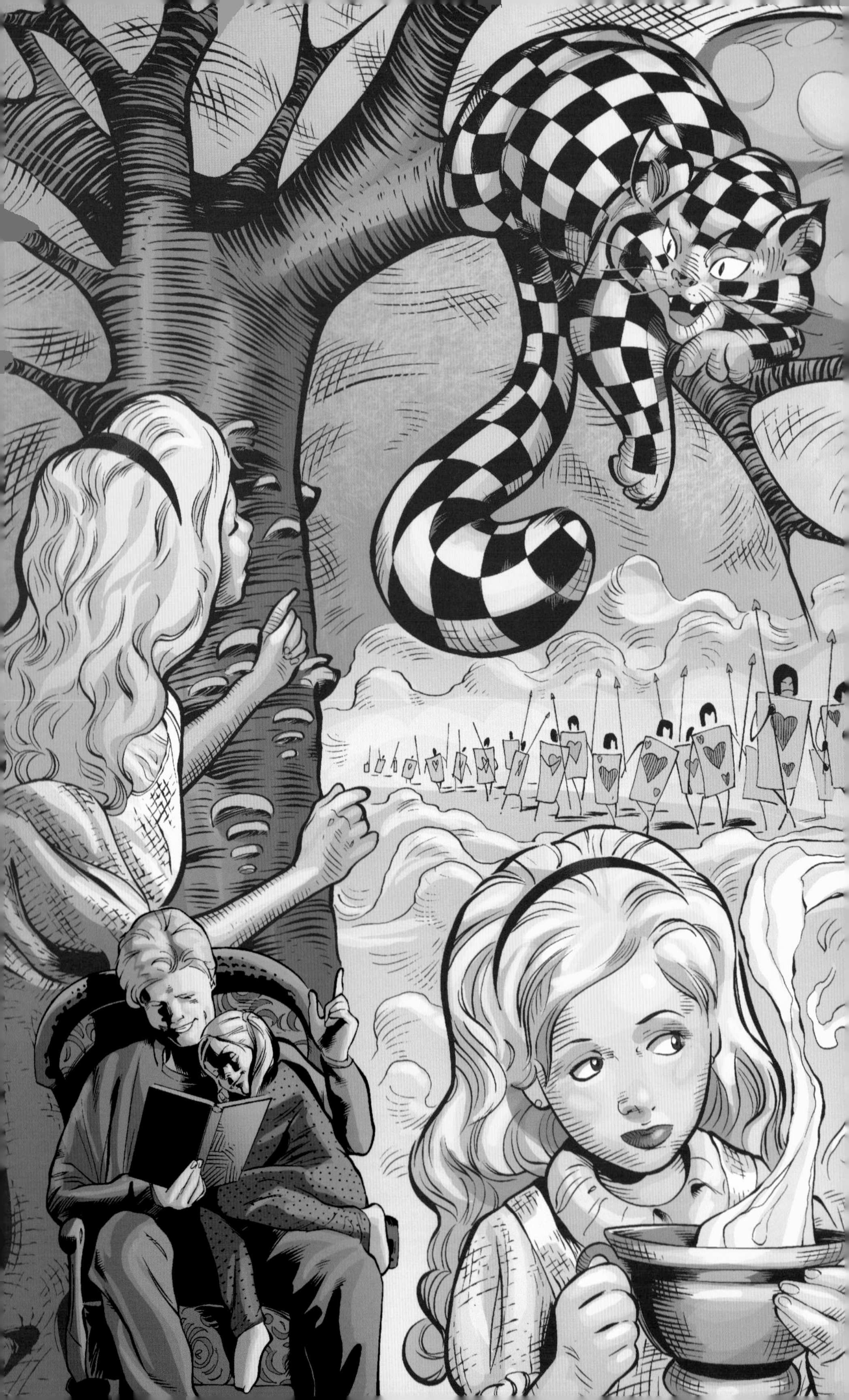

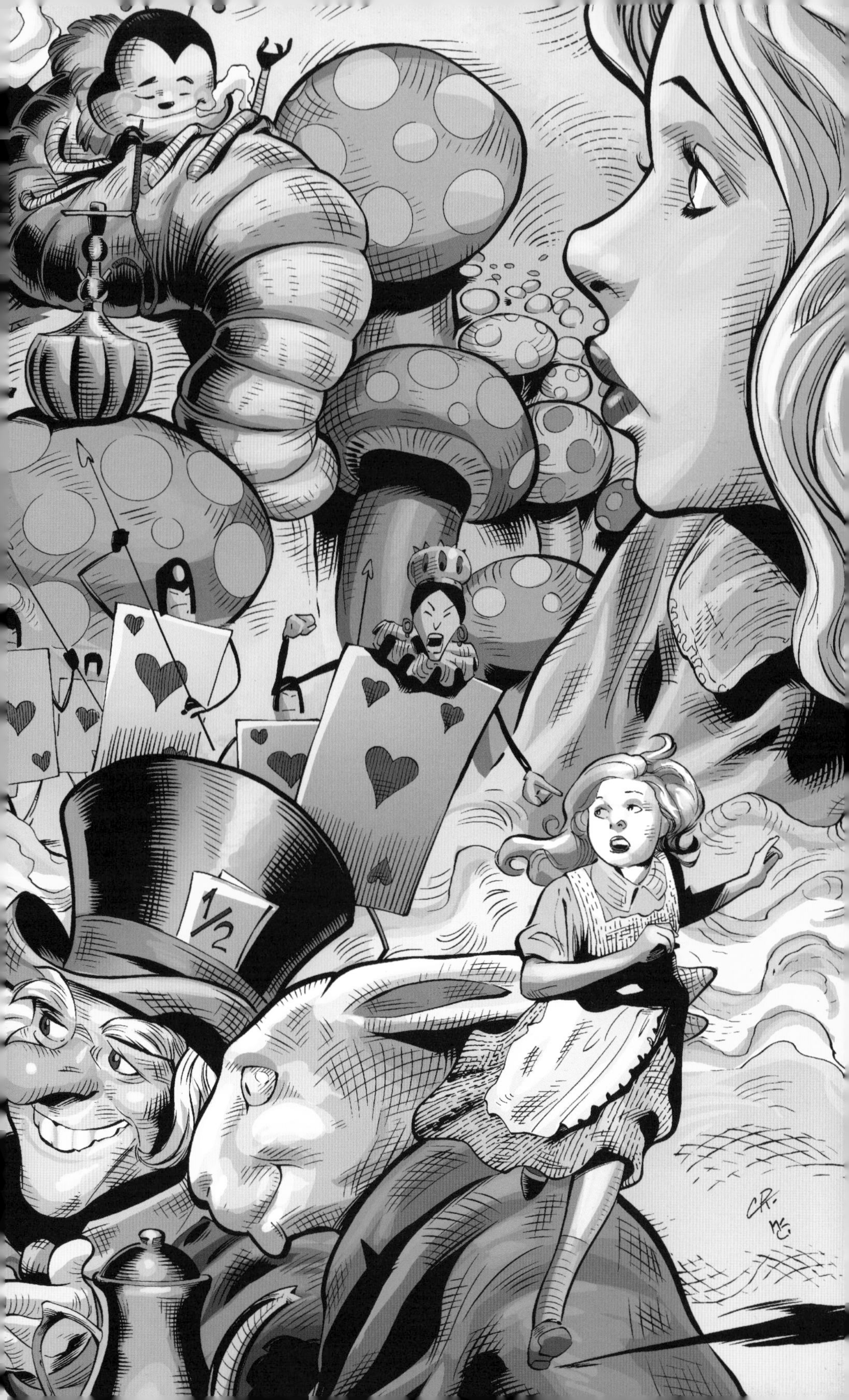
1/2

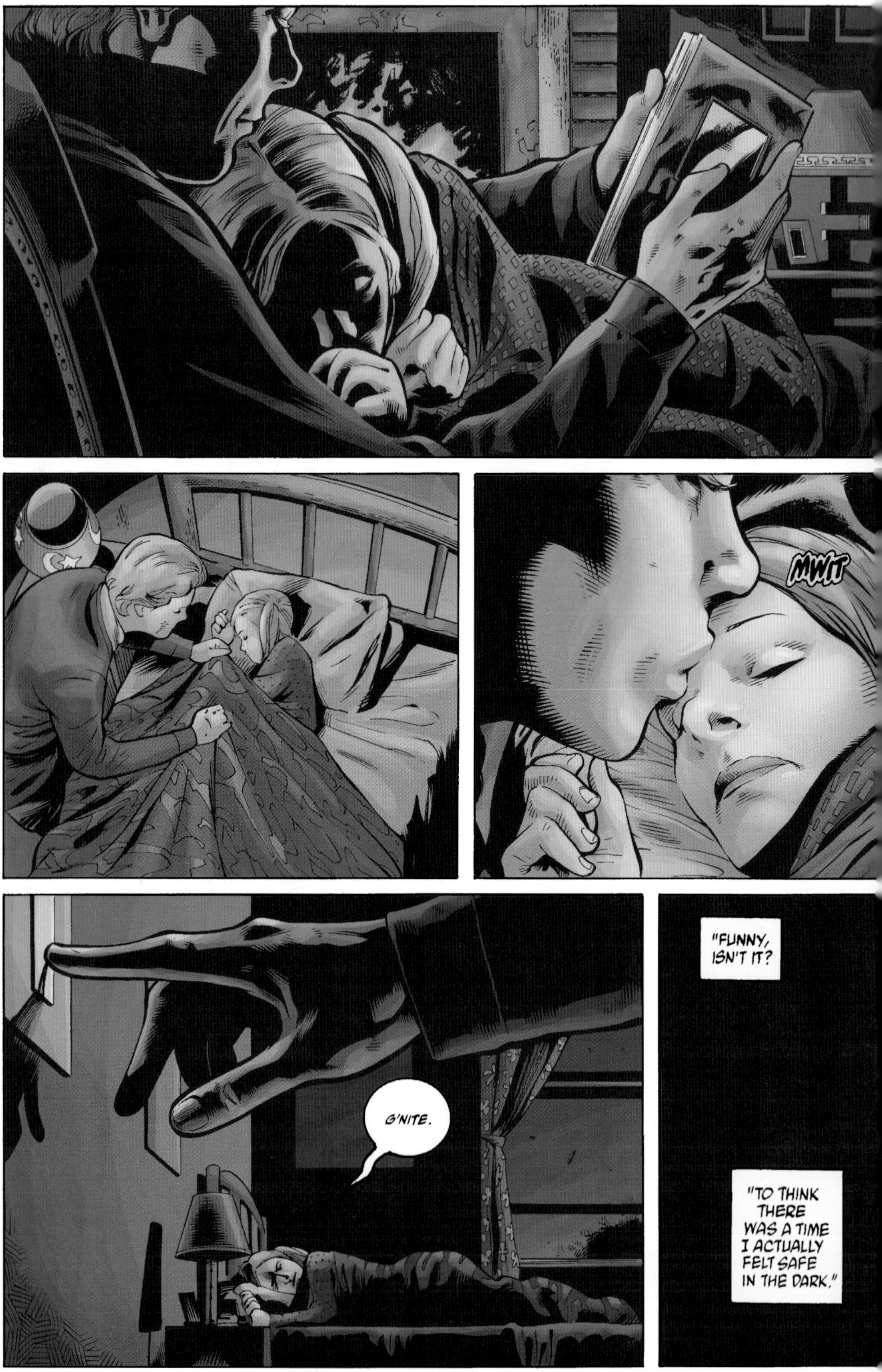
MWIT
G'NITE.
"FUNNY, ISN'T IT?
"TO THINK THERE WAS A TIME I ACTUALLY FELT SAFE IN THE DARK."

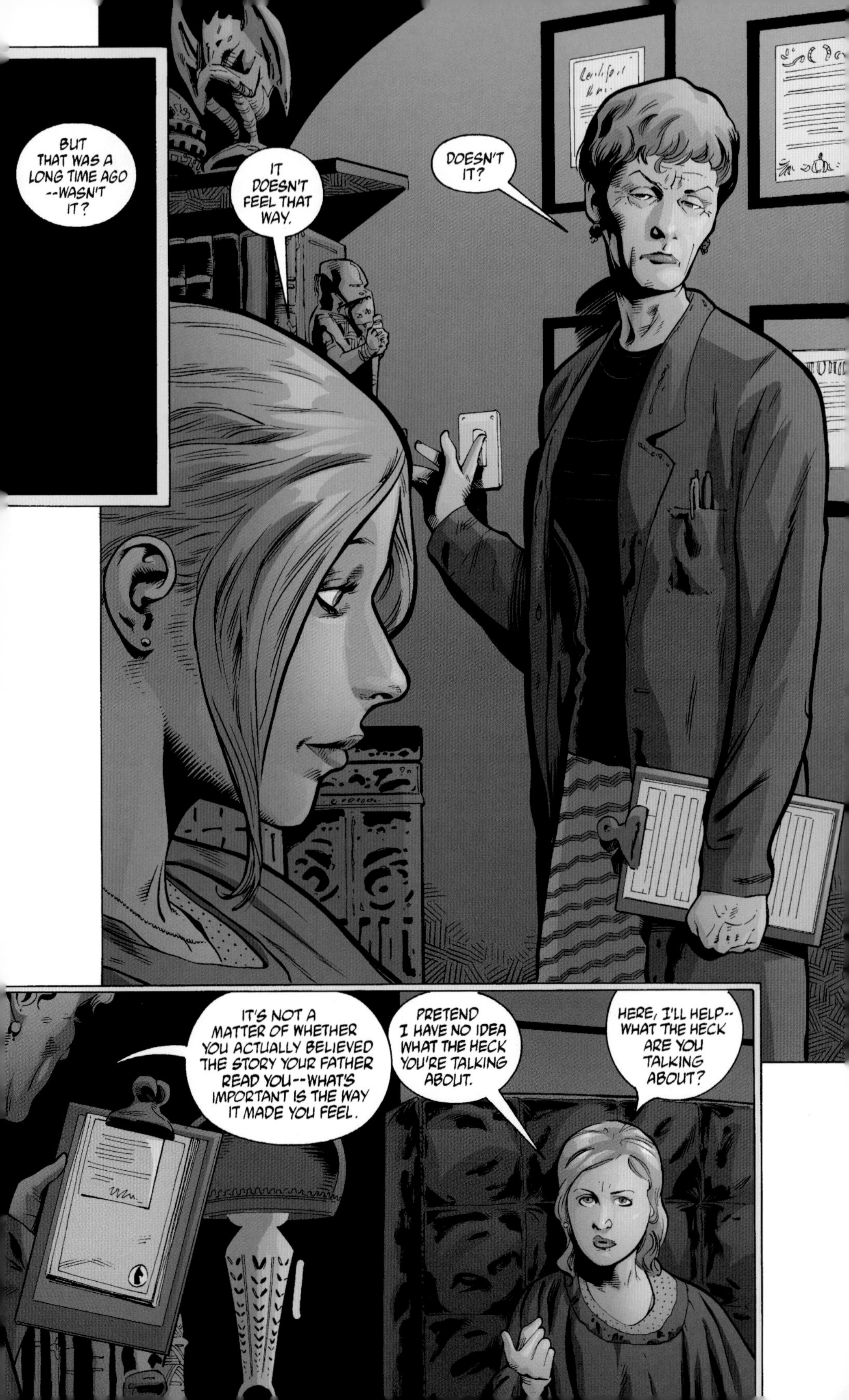
BUT THAT WAS A LONG TIME AGO --WASN'T IT?
IT DOESN'T FEEL THAT WAY.
DOESN'T IT?
IT'S NOT A MATTER OF WHETHER YOU ACTUALLY BELIEVED THE STORY YOUR FATHER READ YOU--WHAT'S IMPORTANT IS THE WAY IT MADE YOU FEEL.
PRETEND I HAVE NO IDEA WHAT THE HECK YOU'RE TALKING ABOUT.
HERE, I'LL HELP-- WHAT THE HECK ARE YOU TALKING ABOUT?

EVERY-THING REPRESENTS SOMETHING. YOU JUST NEED TO THINK ABOUT IT.

AN EXAMPLE-- THE *CHESHIRE CAT* REPRESENTS THAT WHICH CAN NEVER FULLY BE KNOWN.

CREEPY, YES, BUT CUTE.

THE TEA PARTY?

THE CHAOS INHERENT IN MOB RULE.

PORTRAYED HERE AS RELATIVELY HARMLESS.

THE CATEPIL--

LET ME GUESS --LET ME GUESS!

"JUST SAY NO TO DRUGS!"?

A BIT OVERSIMPLISTIC, YES-- BUT YOU GET THE IDEA. AND FINALLY--

--"QUESTION AUTHORITY."

EVEN WHEN IT MEANS, UM-- LOSING YOUR HEAD?

OH, ESPECIALLY THEN.

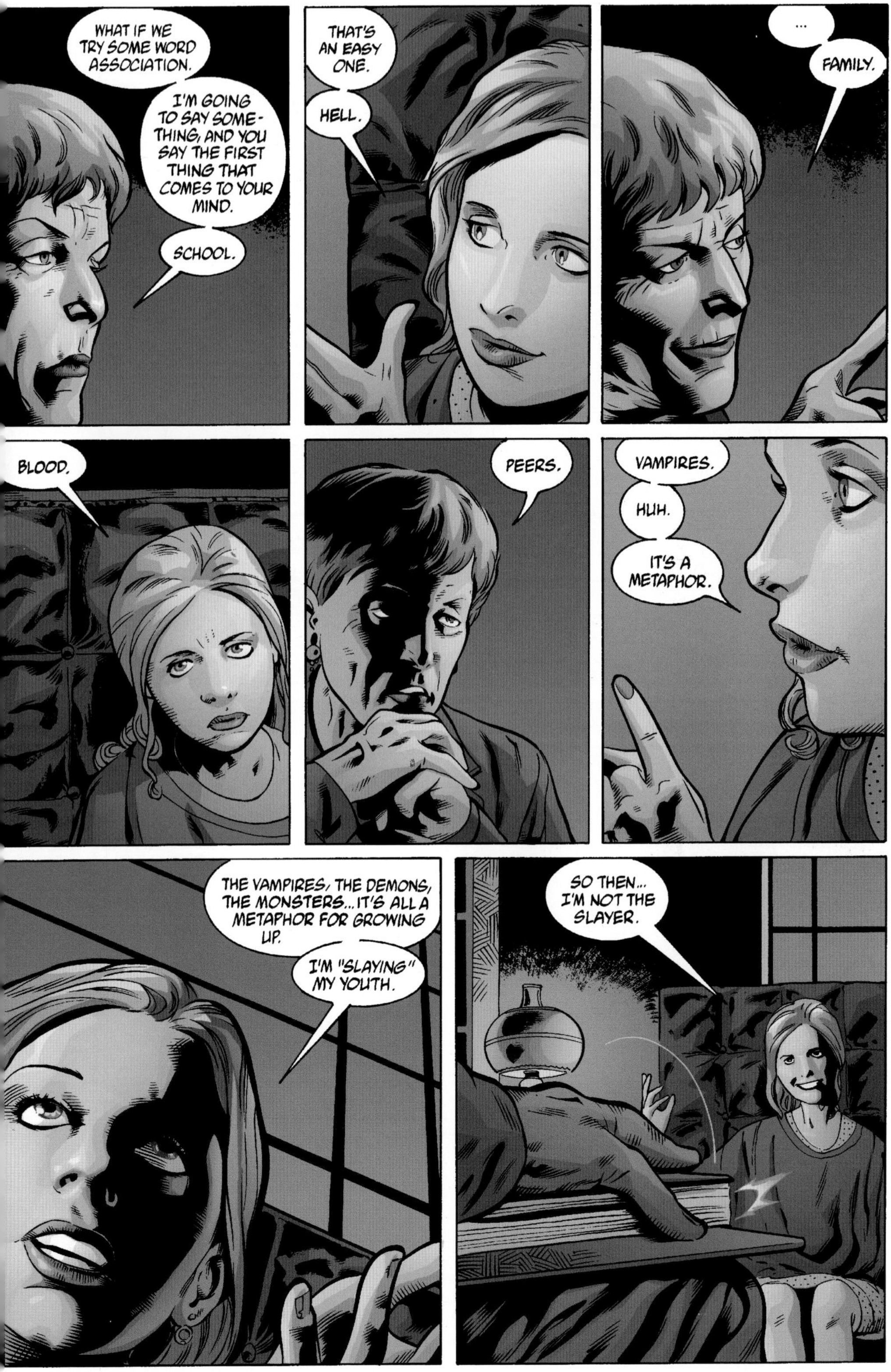
WHAT IF WE TRY SOME WORD ASSOCIATION.
I'M GOING TO SAY SOME-THING, AND YOU SAY THE FIRST THING THAT COMES TO YOUR MIND.
SCHOOL.
THAT'S AN EASY ONE.
HELL.
...
FAMILY.
BLOOD.
PEERS.
VAMPIRES.
HUH.
IT'S A METAPHOR.
THE VAMPIRES, THE DEMONS, THE MONSTERS... IT'S ALL A METAPHOR FOR GROWING UP.
I'M "SLAYING" MY YOUTH.
SO THEN... I'M NOT THE SLAYER.

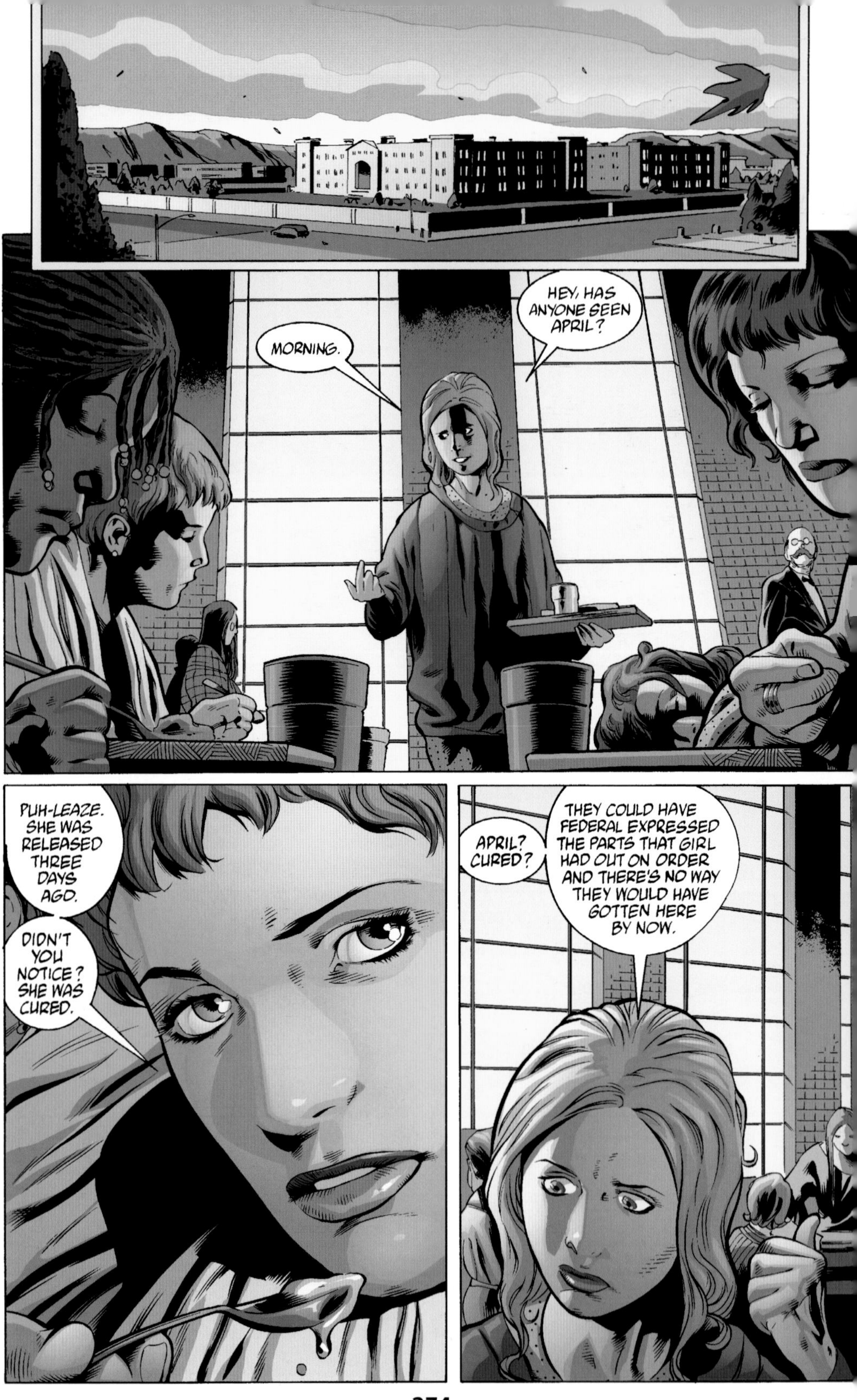
MORNING.
HEY, HAS ANYONE SEEN APRIL?
PUH-LEAZE. SHE WAS RELEASED THREE DAYS AGO.
DIDN'T YOU NOTICE? SHE WAS CURED.
APRIL? CURED?
THEY COULD HAVE FEDERAL EXPRESSED THE PARTS THAT GIRL HAD OUT ON ORDER AND THERE'S NO WAY THEY WOULD HAVE GOTTEN HERE BY NOW.

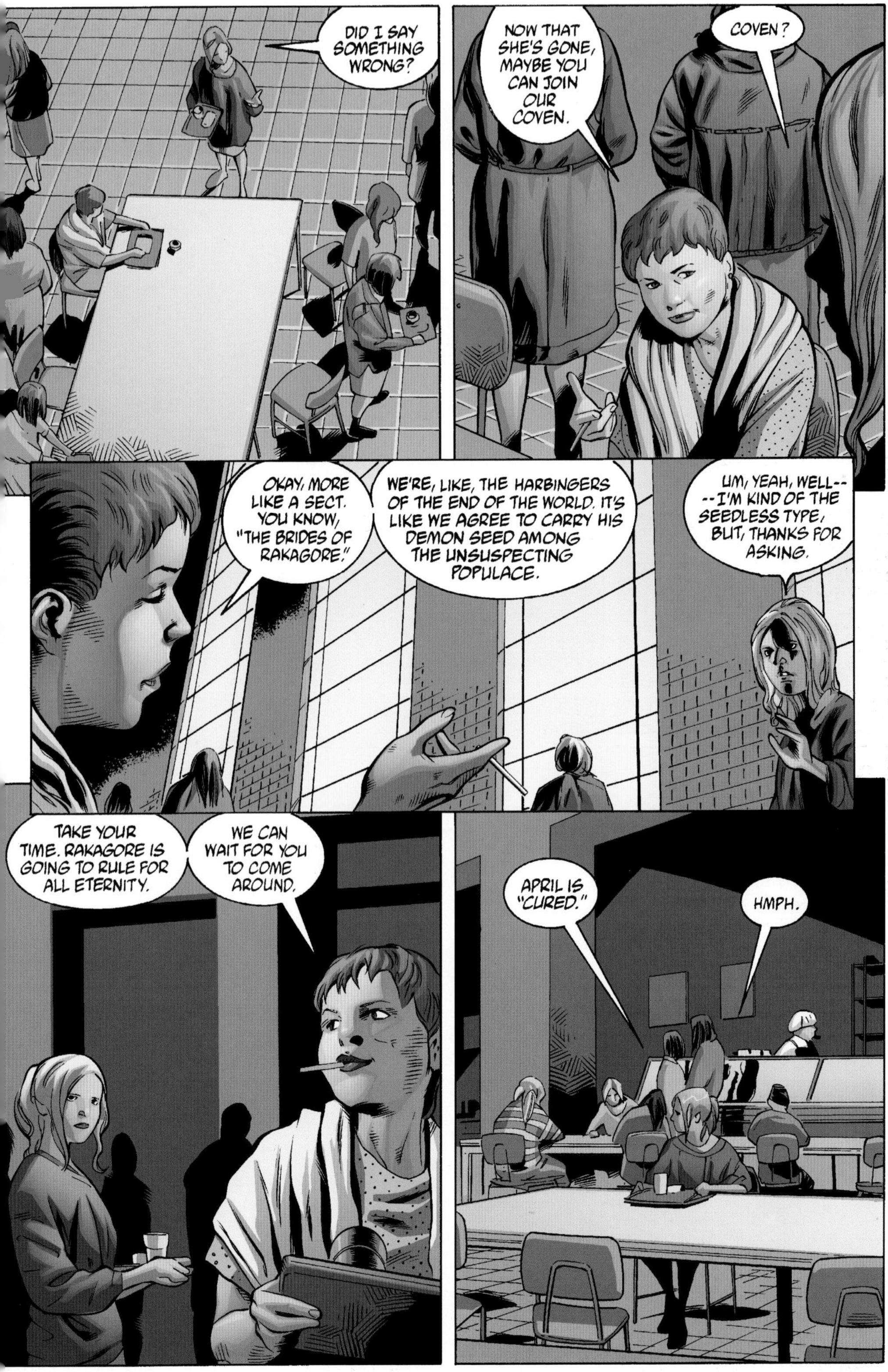
DID I SAY SOMETHING WRONG?
NOW THAT SHE'S GONE, MAYBE YOU CAN JOIN OUR COVEN.
COVEN?
OKAY, MORE LIKE A SECT. YOU KNOW, "THE BRIDES OF RAKAGORE."
WE'RE, LIKE, THE HARBINGERS OF THE END OF THE WORLD. IT'S LIKE WE AGREE TO CARRY HIS DEMON SEED AMONG THE UNSUSPECTING POPULACE.
UM, YEAH, WELL-- --I'M KIND OF THE SEEDLESS TYPE, BUT, THANKS FOR ASKING.
TAKE YOUR TIME. RAKAGORE IS GOING TO RULE FOR ALL ETERNITY.
WE CAN WAIT FOR YOU TO COME AROUND.
APRIL IS "CURED."
HMPH.

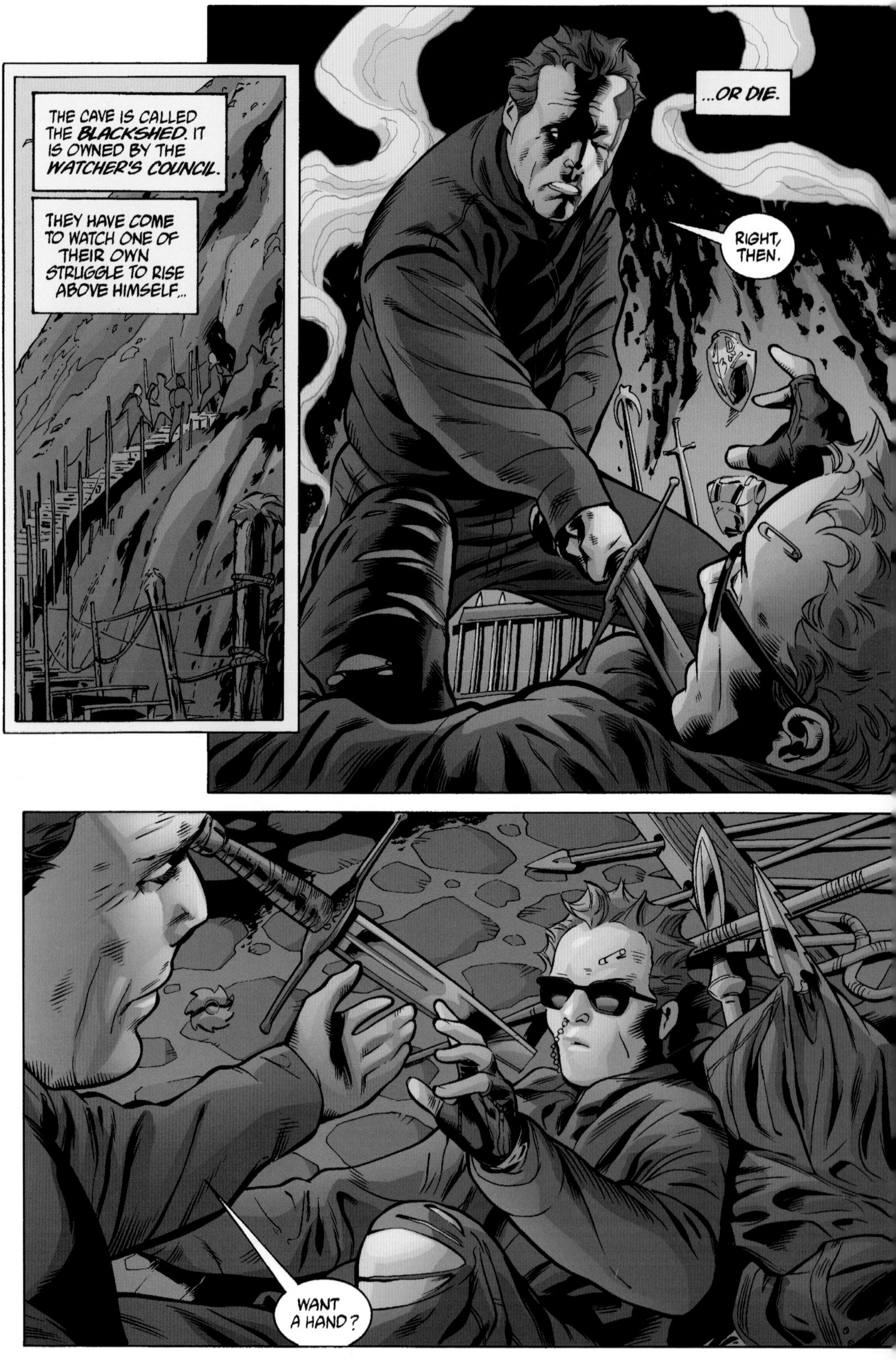
THE CAVE IS CALLED THE BLACKSHED. IT IS OWNED BY THE WATCHER'S COUNCIL.
THEY HAVE COME TO WATCH ONE OF THEIR OWN STRUGGLE TO RISE ABOVE HIMSELF...
...OR DIE.
RIGHT, THEN.
WANT A HAND?

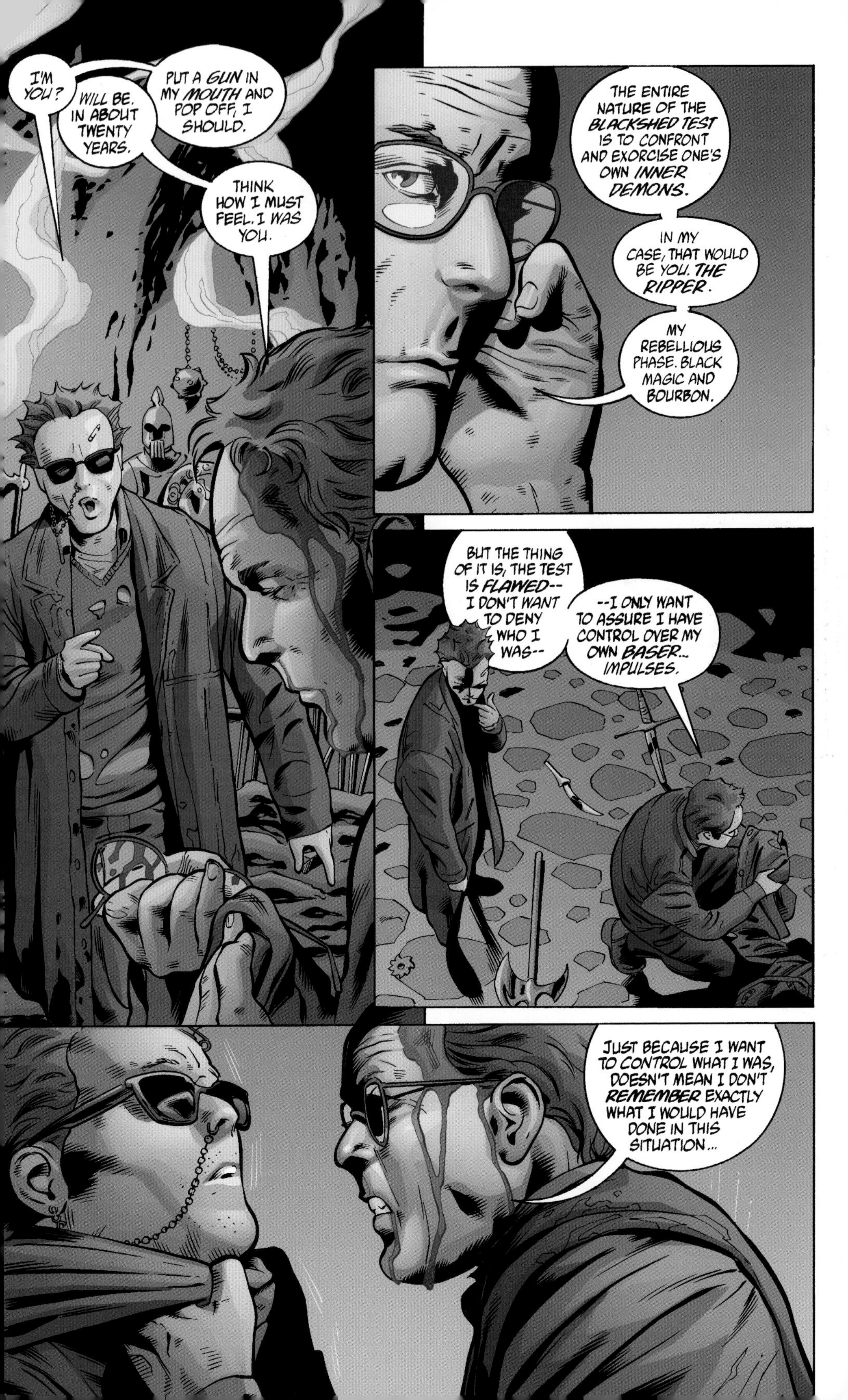
I'M YOU?
WILL BE. IN ABOUT TWENTY YEARS.
PUT A GUN IN MY MOUTH AND POP OFF, I SHOULD.
THINK HOW I MUST FEEL. I WAS YOU.
THE ENTIRE NATURE OF THE BLACKSHED TEST IS TO CONFRONT AND EXORCISE ONE'S OWN INNER DEMONS.
IN MY CASE, THAT WOULD BE YOU. THE RIPPER.
MY REBELLIOUS PHASE. BLACK MAGIC AND BOURBON.
BUT THE THING OF IT IS, THE TEST IS FLAWED-- I DON'T WANT TO DENY WHO I WAS--
--I ONLY WANT TO ASSURE I HAVE CONTROL OVER MY OWN BASER... IMPULSES.
JUST BECAUSE I WANT TO CONTROL WHAT I WAS, DOESN'T MEAN I DON'T REMEMBER EXACTLY WHAT I WOULD HAVE DONE IN THIS SITUATION...

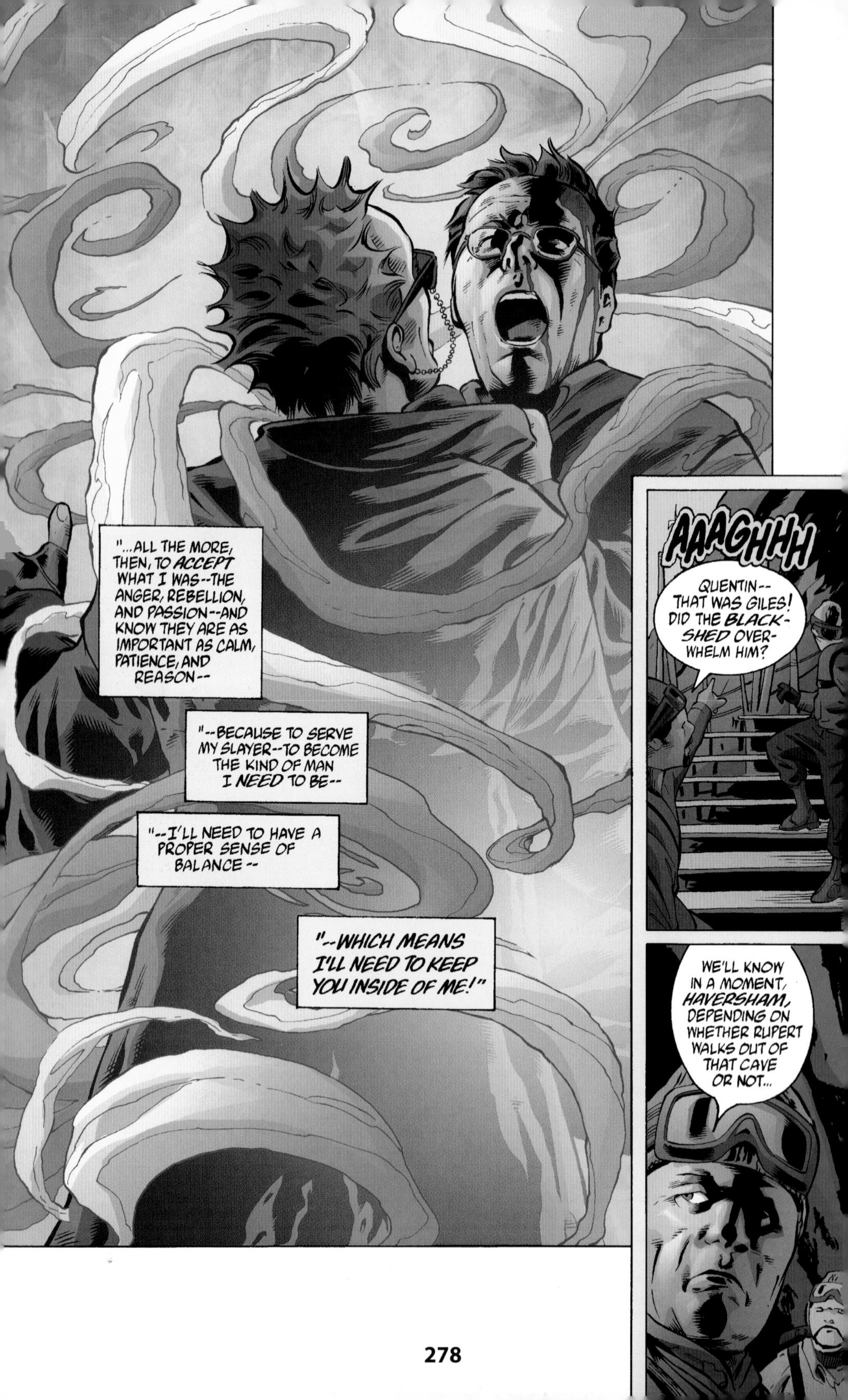
"...ALL THE MORE, THEN, TO ACCEPT WHAT I WAS--THE ANGER, REBELLION, AND PASSION--AND KNOW THEY ARE AS IMPORTANT AS CALM, PATIENCE, AND REASON--
"--BECAUSE TO SERVE MY SLAYER--TO BECOME THE KIND OF MAN I NEED TO BE--
"--I'LL NEED TO HAVE A PROPER SENSE OF BALANCE--
"--WHICH MEANS I'LL NEED TO KEEP YOU INSIDE OF ME!"
AAAGHHH
QUENTIN--THAT WAS GILES! DID THE BLACK-SHED OVER-WHELM HIM?
WE'LL KNOW IN A MOMENT, HAVERSHAM, DEPENDING ON WHETHER RUPERT WALKS OUT OF THAT CAVE OR NOT...

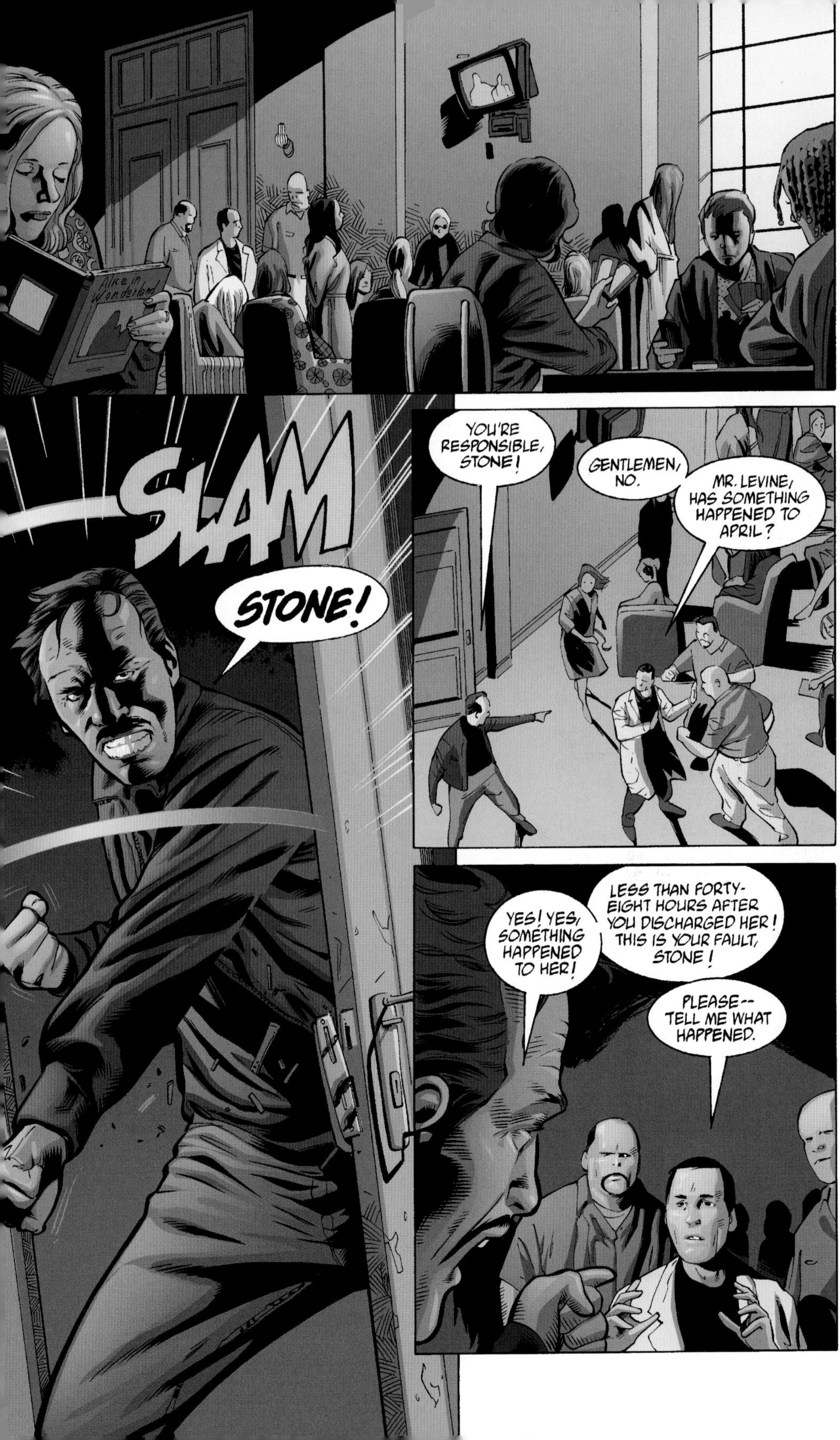
Alice in Wonderland
SLAM
STONE!
YOU'RE RESPONSIBLE, STONE!
GENTLEMEN, NO.
MR. LEVINE, HAS SOMETHING HAPPENED TO APRIL?
YES! YES, SOMETHING HAPPENED TO HER!
LESS THAN FORTY-EIGHT HOURS AFTER YOU DISCHARGED HER! THIS IS YOUR FAULT, STONE!
PLEASE-- TELL ME WHAT HAPPENED.

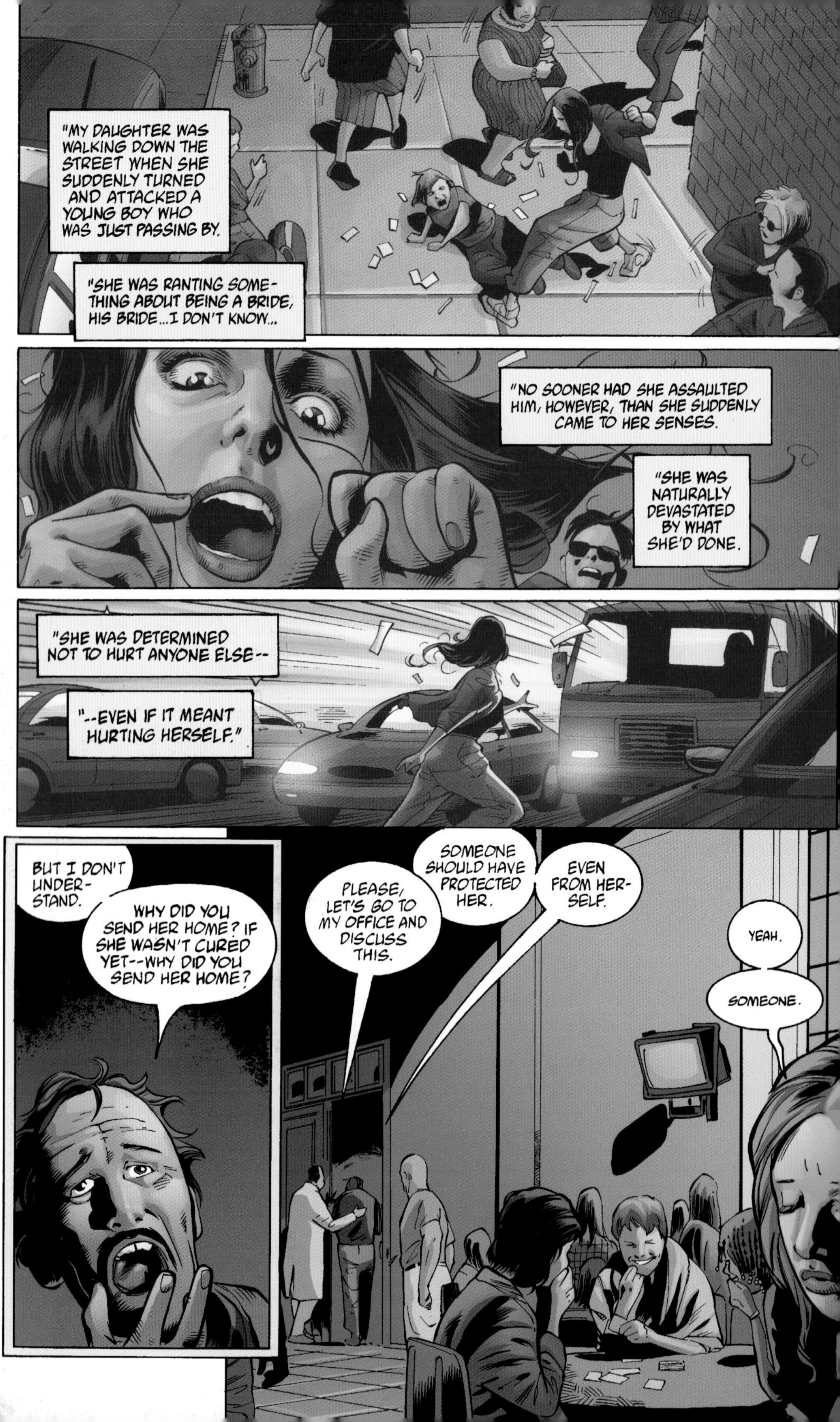
"MY DAUGHTER WAS WALKING DOWN THE STREET WHEN SHE SUDDENLY TURNED AND ATTACKED A YOUNG BOY WHO WAS JUST PASSING BY.
"SHE WAS RANTING SOMETHING ABOUT BEING A BRIDE, HIS BRIDE...I DON'T KNOW...
"NO SOONER HAD SHE ASSAULTED HIM, HOWEVER, THAN SHE SUDDENLY CAME TO HER SENSES.
"SHE WAS NATURALLY DEVASTATED BY WHAT SHE'D DONE.
"SHE WAS DETERMINED NOT TO HURT ANYONE ELSE--
"--EVEN IF IT MEANT HURTING HERSELF."
BUT I DON'T UNDERSTAND.
WHY DID YOU SEND HER HOME? IF SHE WASN'T CURED YET--WHY DID YOU SEND HER HOME?
PLEASE, LET'S GO TO MY OFFICE AND DISCUSS THIS.
SOMEONE SHOULD HAVE PROTECTED HER.
EVEN FROM HERSELF.
YEAH.
SOMEONE.

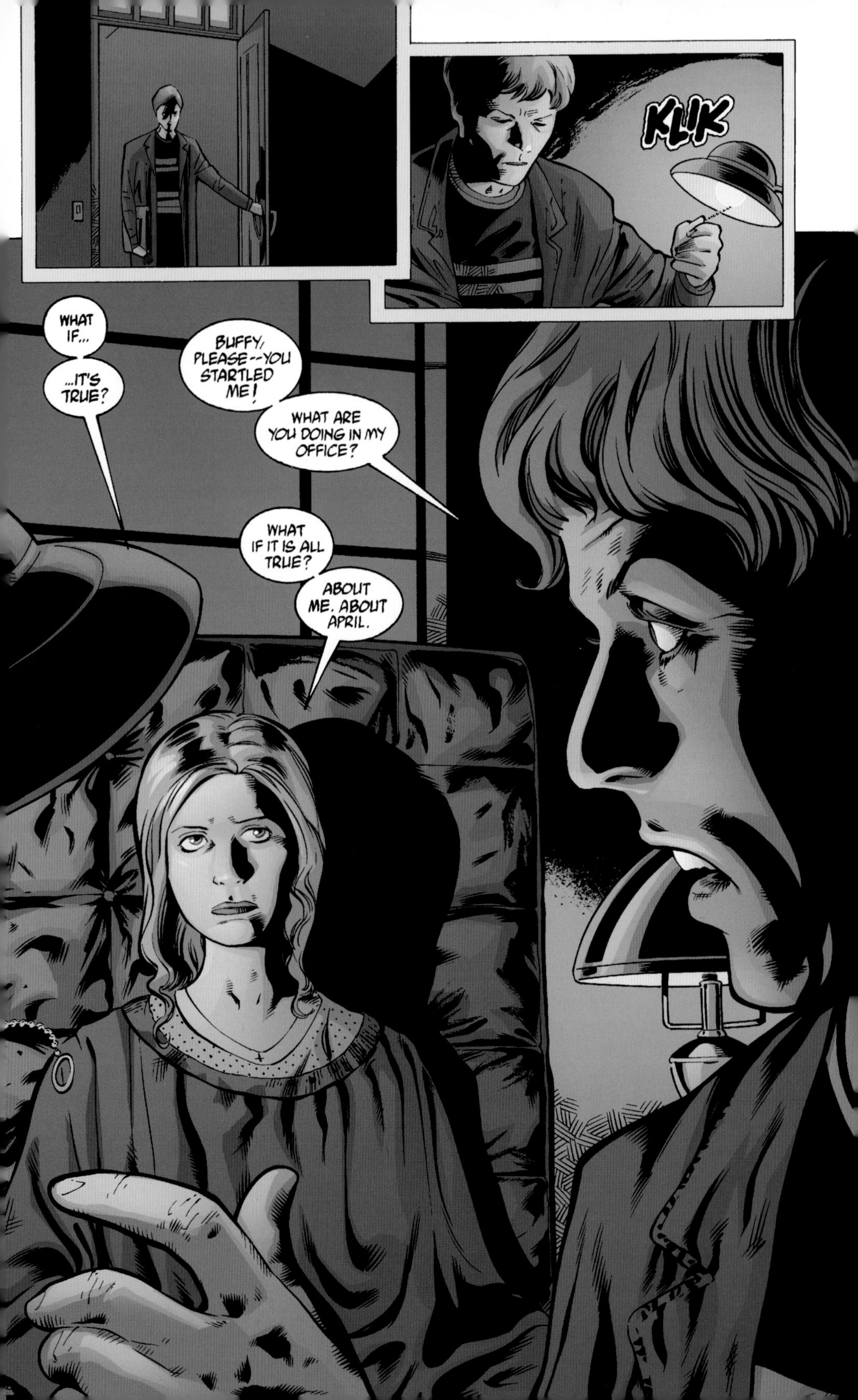
KLIK
WHAT IF...
...IT'S TRUE?
BUFFY, PLEASE--YOU STARTLED ME!
WHAT ARE YOU DOING IN MY OFFICE?
WHAT IF IT IS ALL TRUE?
ABOUT ME. ABOUT APRIL.

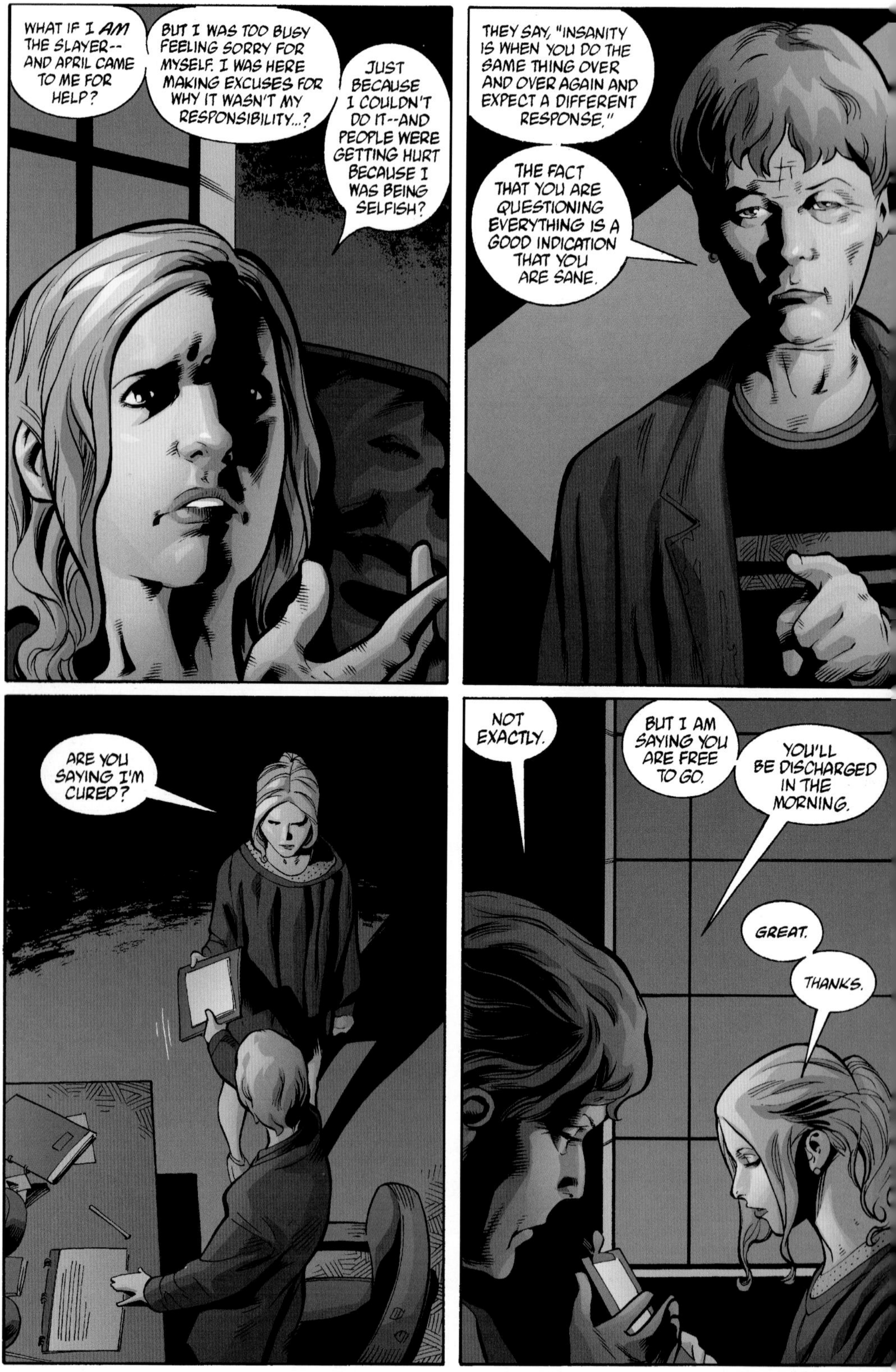

WHAT IF I AM THE SLAYER-- AND APRIL CAME TO ME FOR HELP?
BUT I WAS TOO BUSY FEELING SORRY FOR MYSELF. I WAS HERE MAKING EXCUSES FOR WHY IT WASN'T MY RESPONSIBILITY...?
JUST BECAUSE I COULDN'T DO IT--AND PEOPLE WERE GETTING HURT BECAUSE I WAS BEING SELFISH?
THEY SAY, "INSANITY IS WHEN YOU DO THE SAME THING OVER AND OVER AGAIN AND EXPECT A DIFFERENT RESPONSE."
THE FACT THAT YOU ARE QUESTIONING EVERYTHING IS A GOOD INDICATION THAT YOU ARE SANE.
ARE YOU SAYING I'M CURED?
NOT EXACTLY.
BUT I AM SAYING YOU ARE FREE TO GO.
YOU'LL BE DISCHARGED IN THE MORNING.
GREAT.
THANKS.

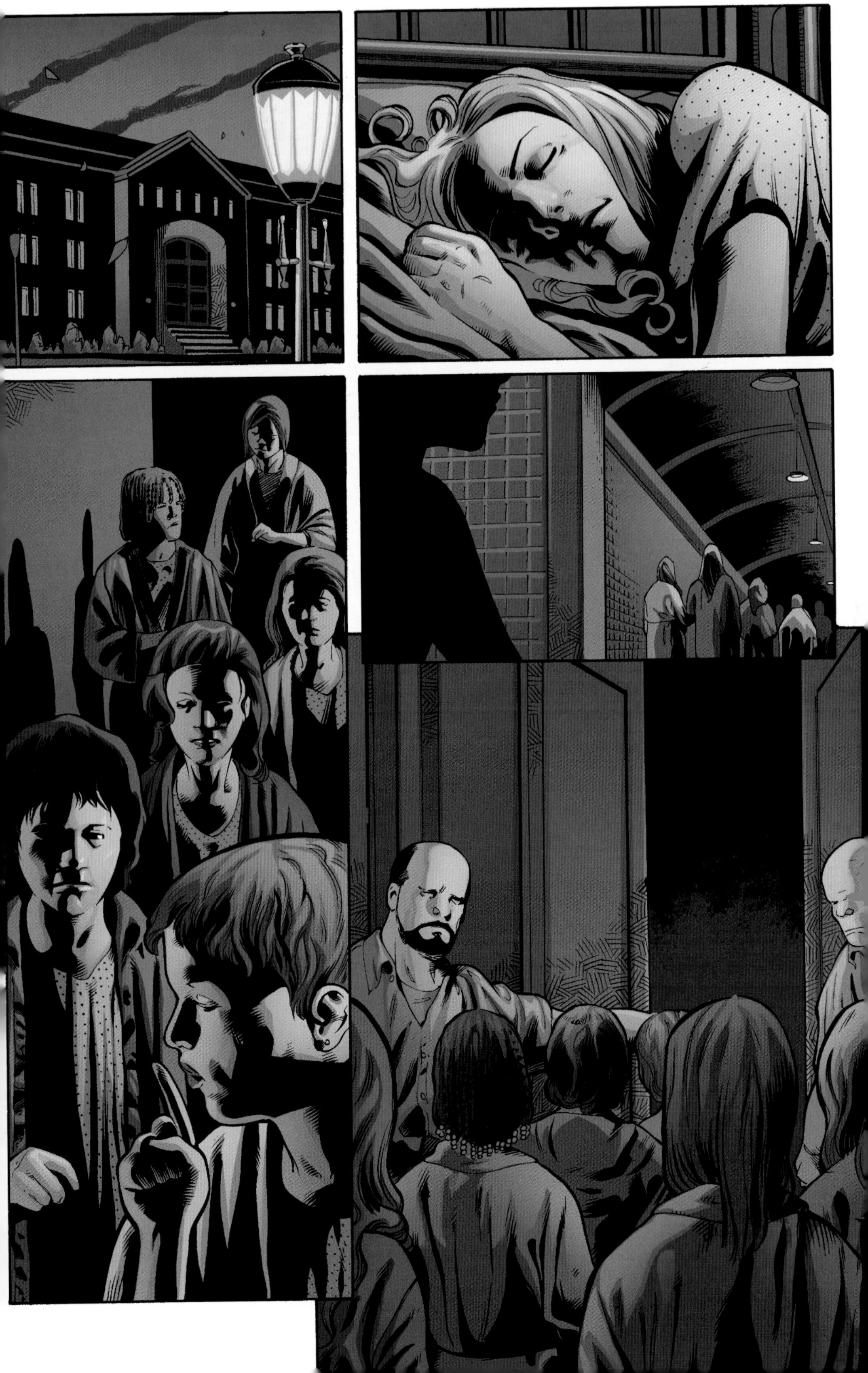

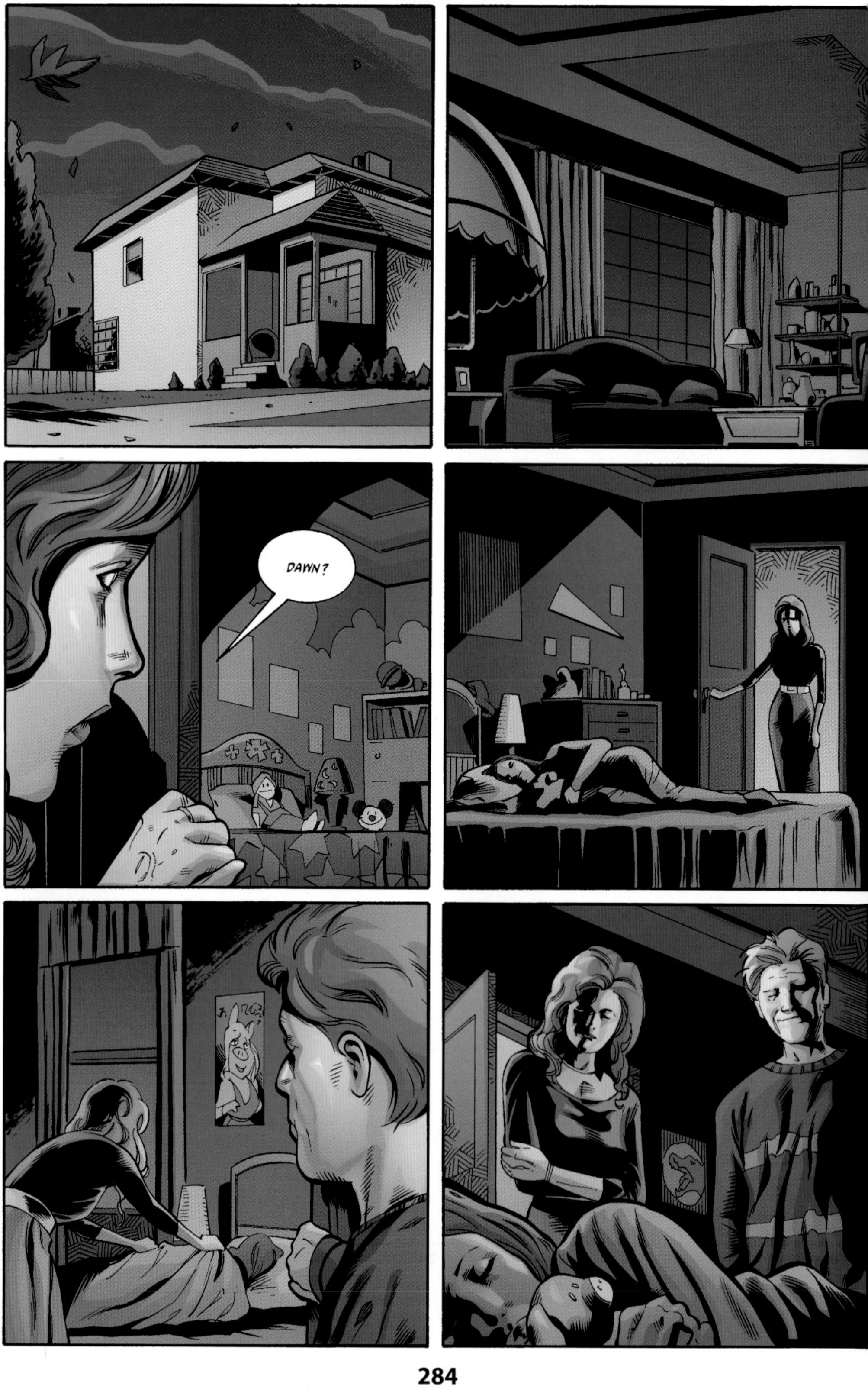
DAWN?

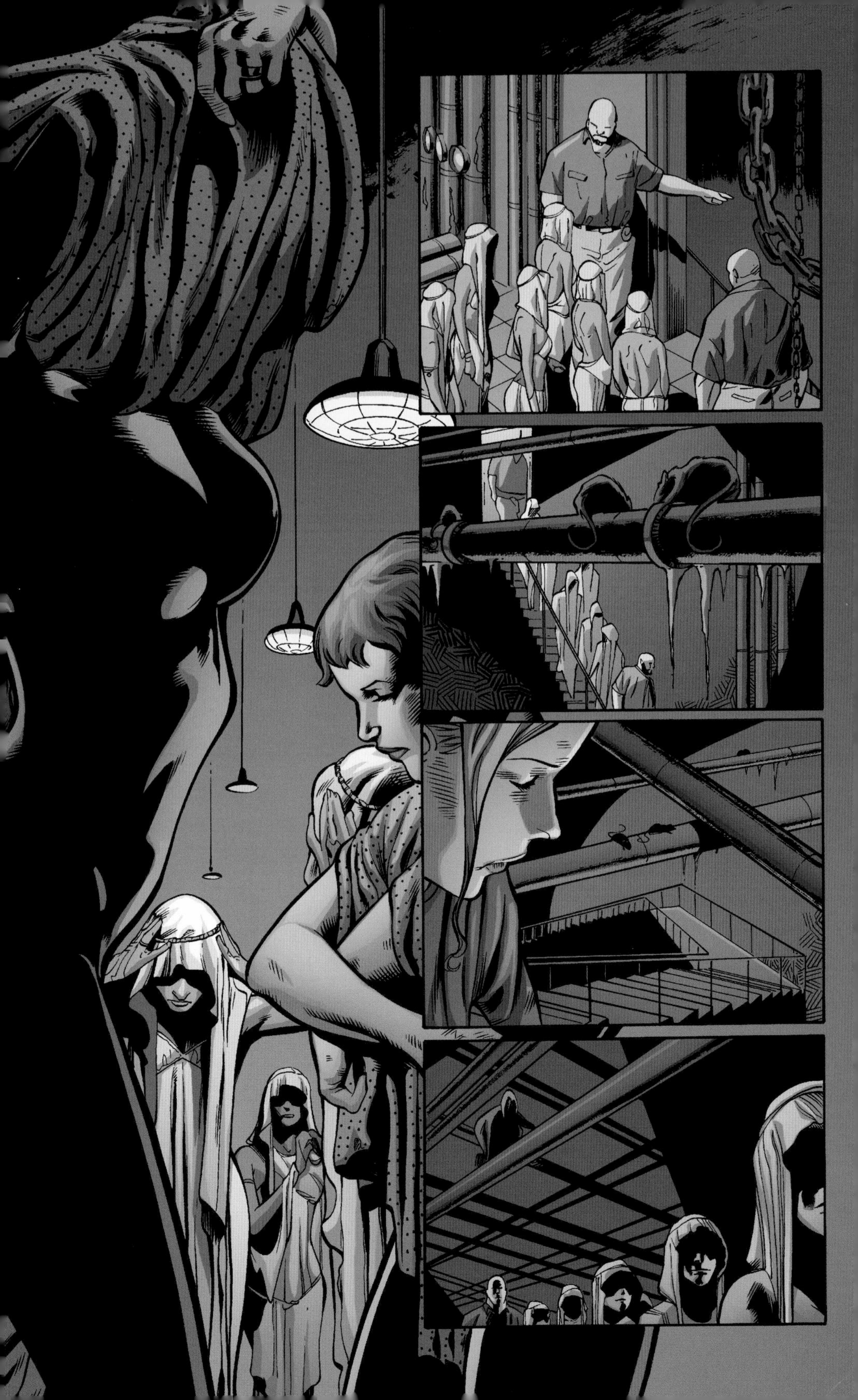

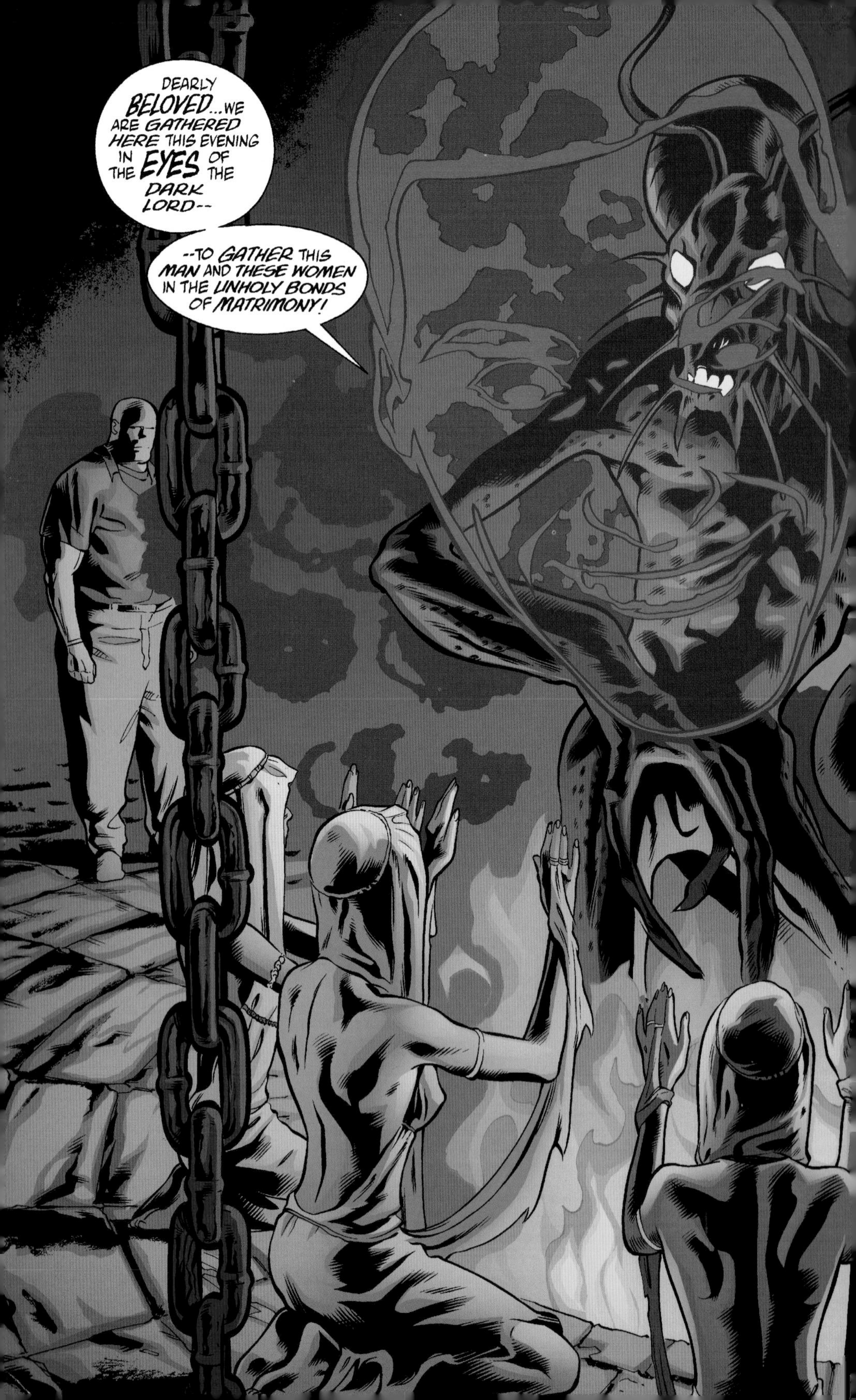
DEARLY BELOVED...WE ARE GATHERED HERE THIS EVENING IN THE EYES OF THE DARK LORD--
--TO GATHER THIS MAN AND THESE WOMEN IN THE UNHOLY BONDS OF MATRIMONY!

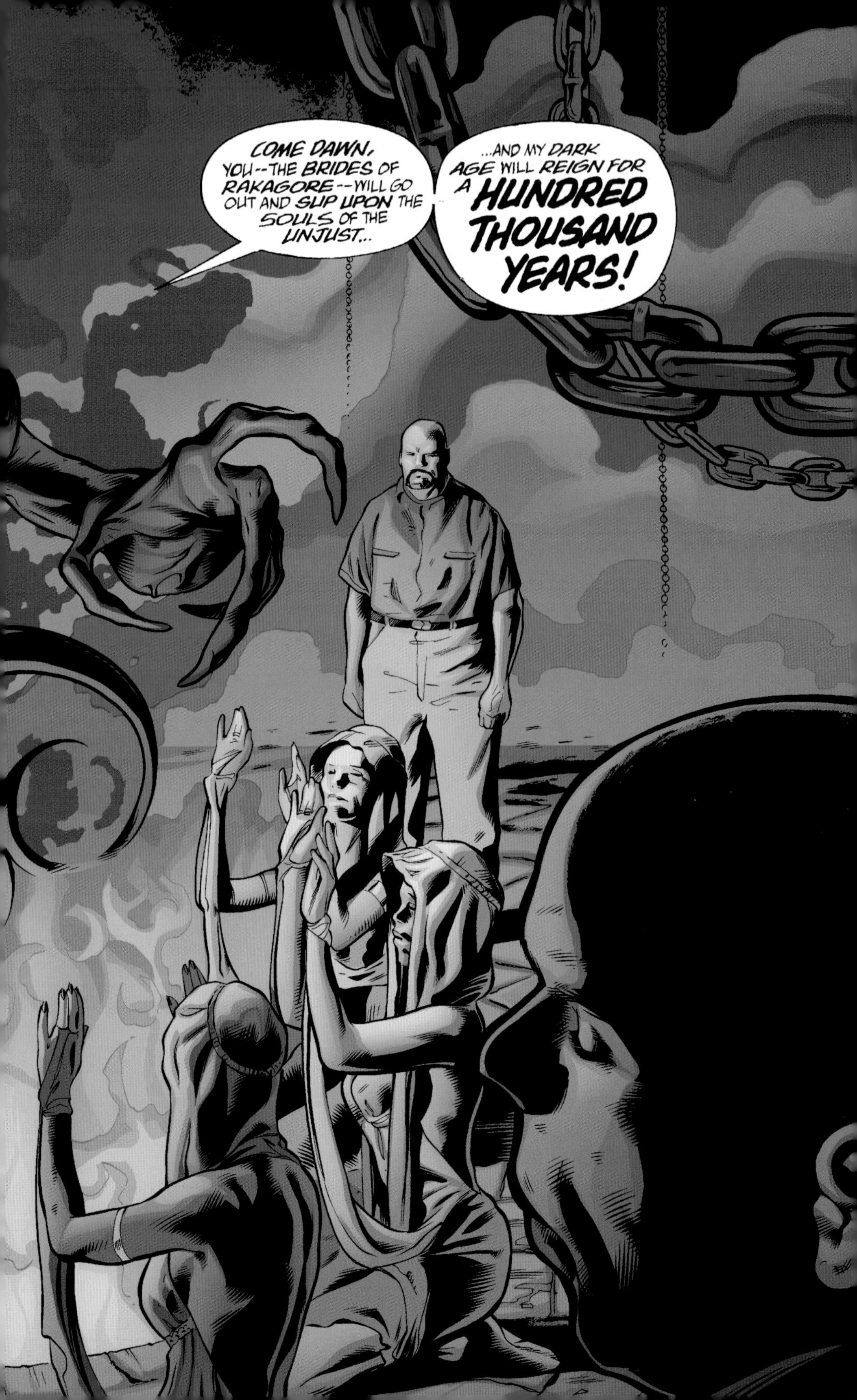
COME DAWN, YOU--THE BRIDES OF RAKAGORE--WILL GO OUT AND SUP UPON THE SOULS OF THE UNJUST...
...AND MY DARK AGE WILL REIGN FOR A HUNDRED THOUSAND YEARS!

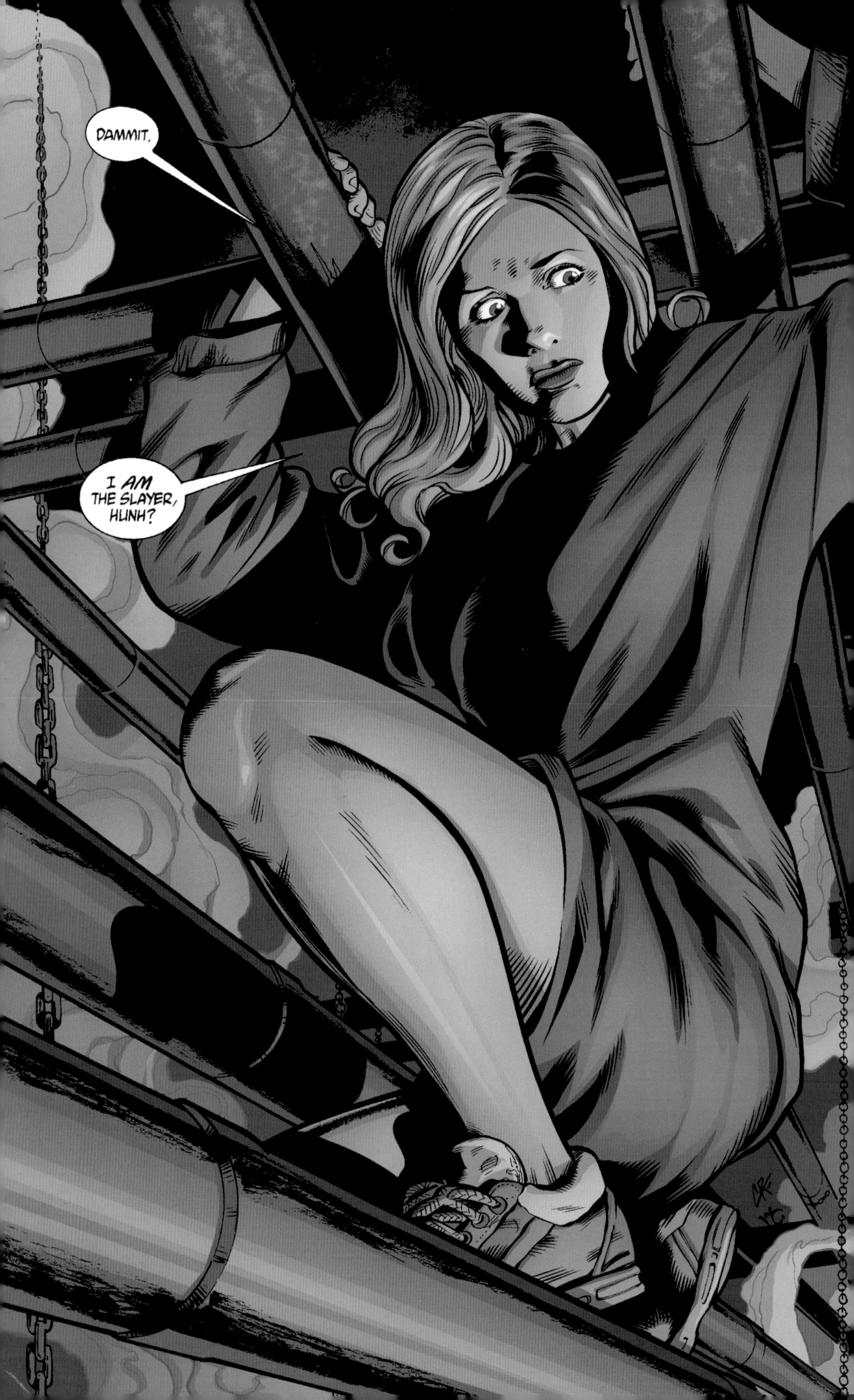
DAMMIT.
I *AM* THE SLAYER, HUNH?

CHAPTER 4

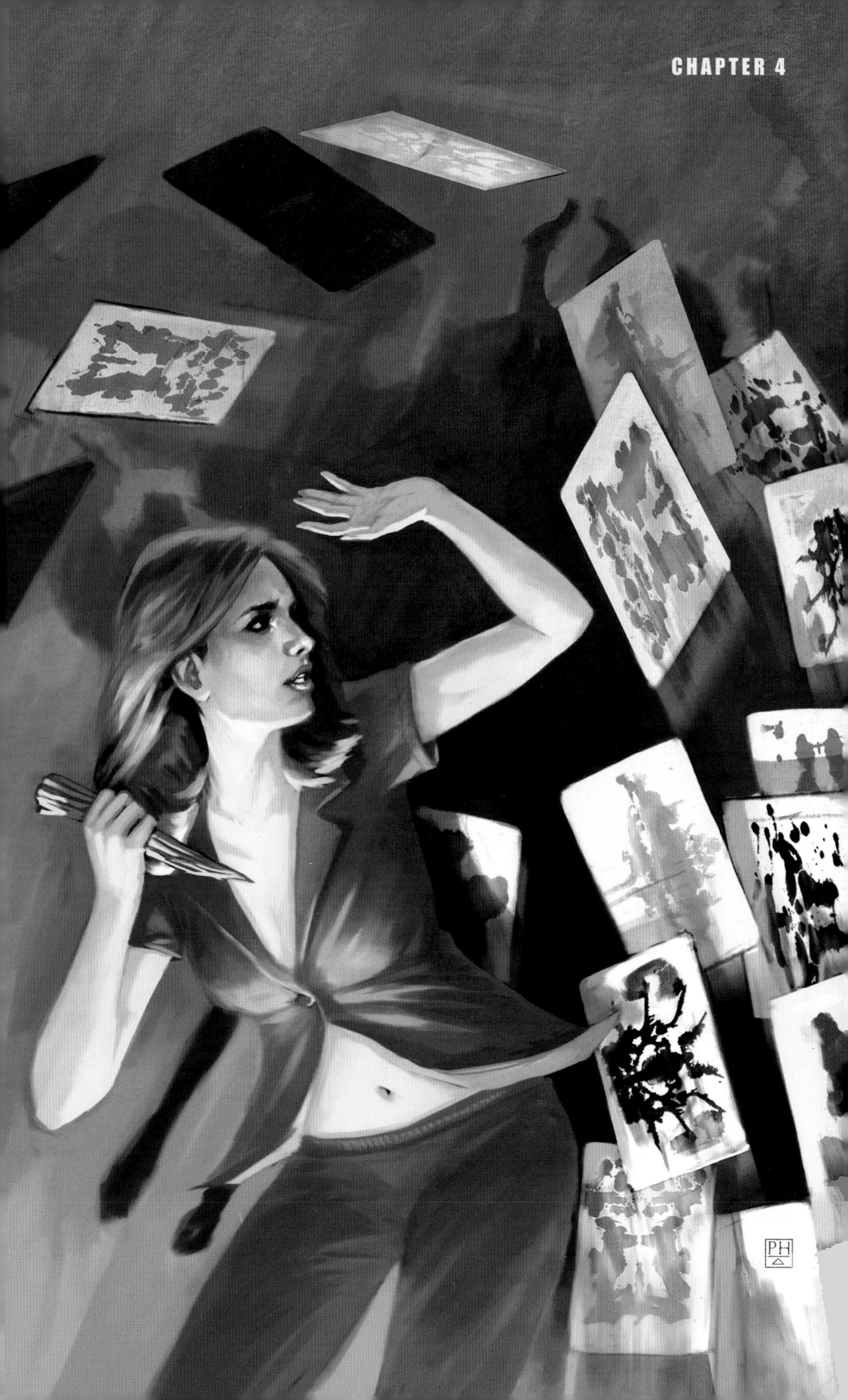

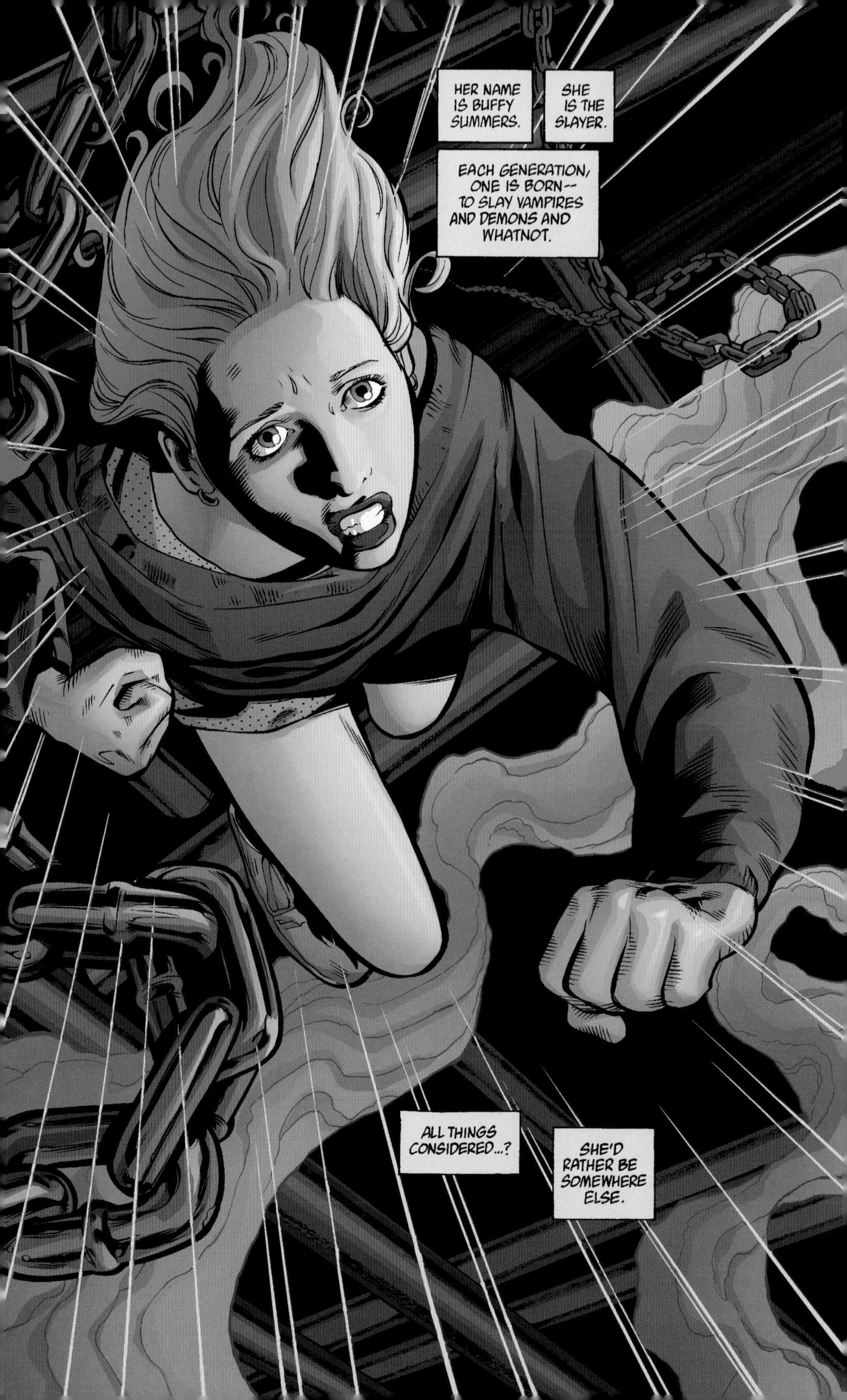
HER NAME IS BUFFY SUMMERS.
SHE IS THE SLAYER.
EACH GENERATION, ONE IS BORN-- TO SLAY VAMPIRES AND DEMONS AND WHATNOT.
ALL THINGS CONSIDERED...?
SHE'D RATHER BE SOMEWHERE ELSE.

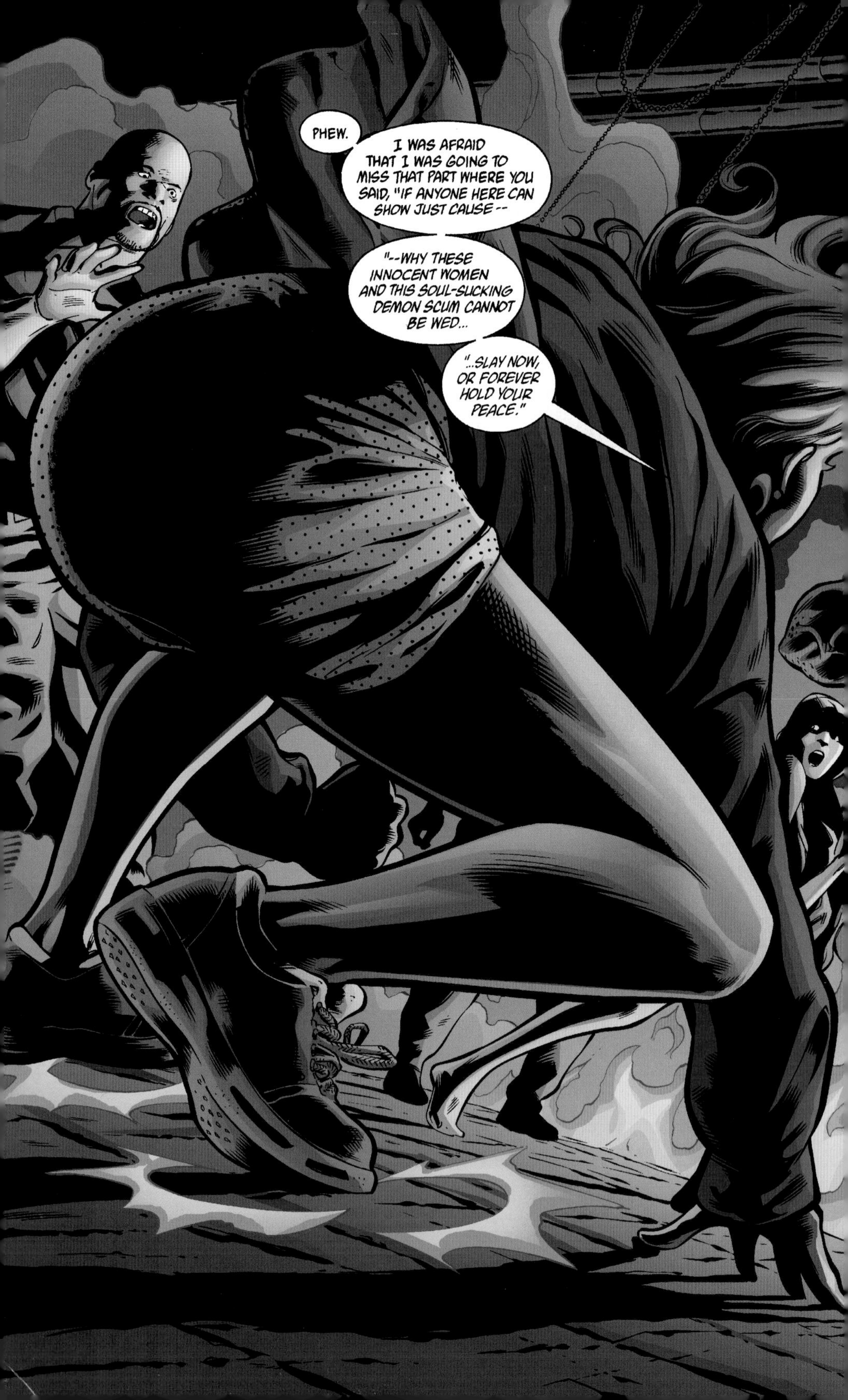
PHEW.
I WAS AFRAID THAT I WAS GOING TO MISS THAT PART WHERE YOU SAID, "IF ANYONE HERE CAN SHOW JUST CAUSE --
"--WHY THESE INNOCENT WOMEN AND THIS SOUL-SUCKING DEMON SCUM CANNOT BE WED...
"...SLAY NOW, OR FOREVER HOLD YOUR PEACE."

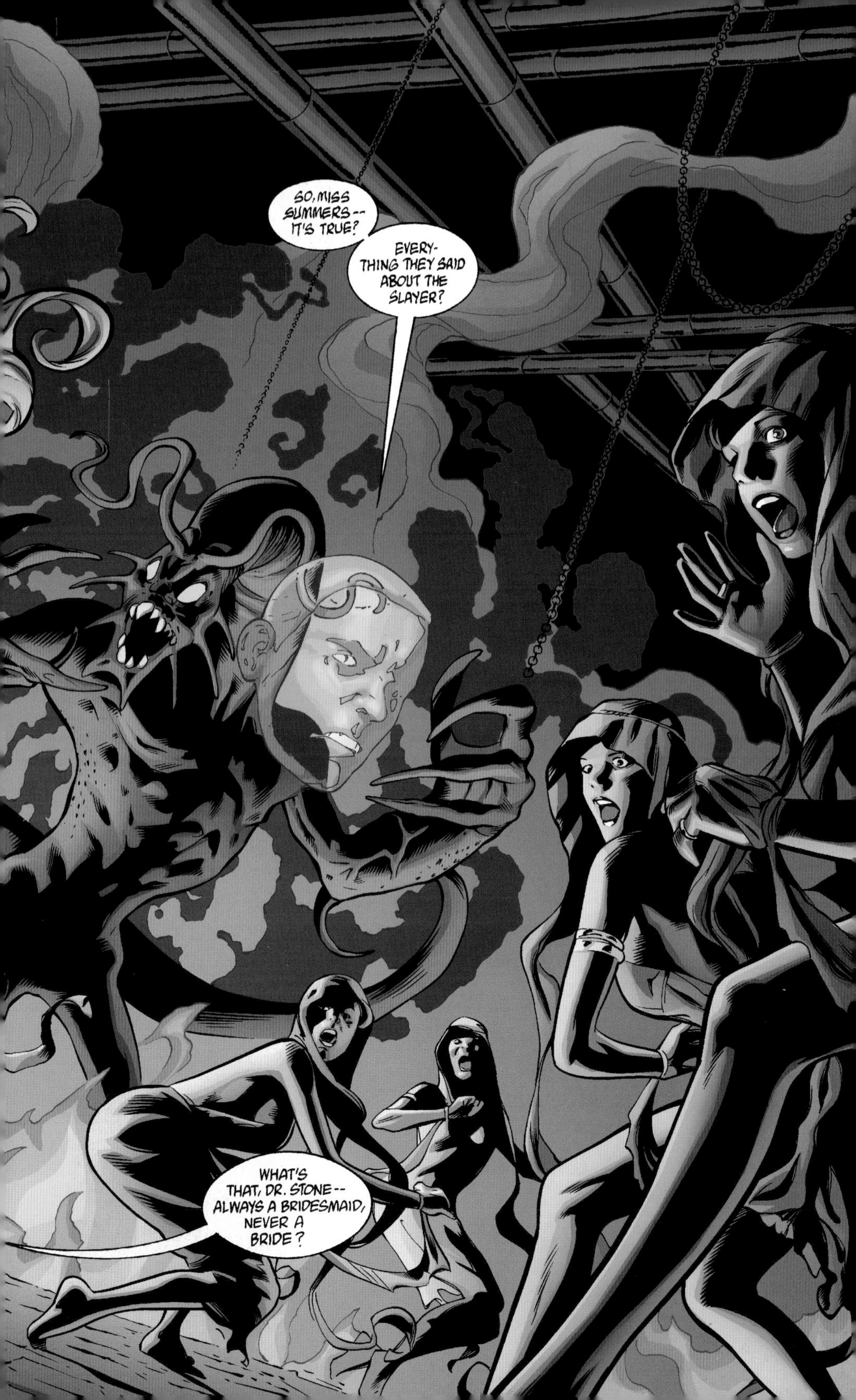
SO, MISS SUMMERS-- IT'S TRUE?
EVERY-THING THEY SAID ABOUT THE SLAYER?
WHAT'S THAT, DR. STONE-- ALWAYS A BRIDESMAID, NEVER A BRIDE?

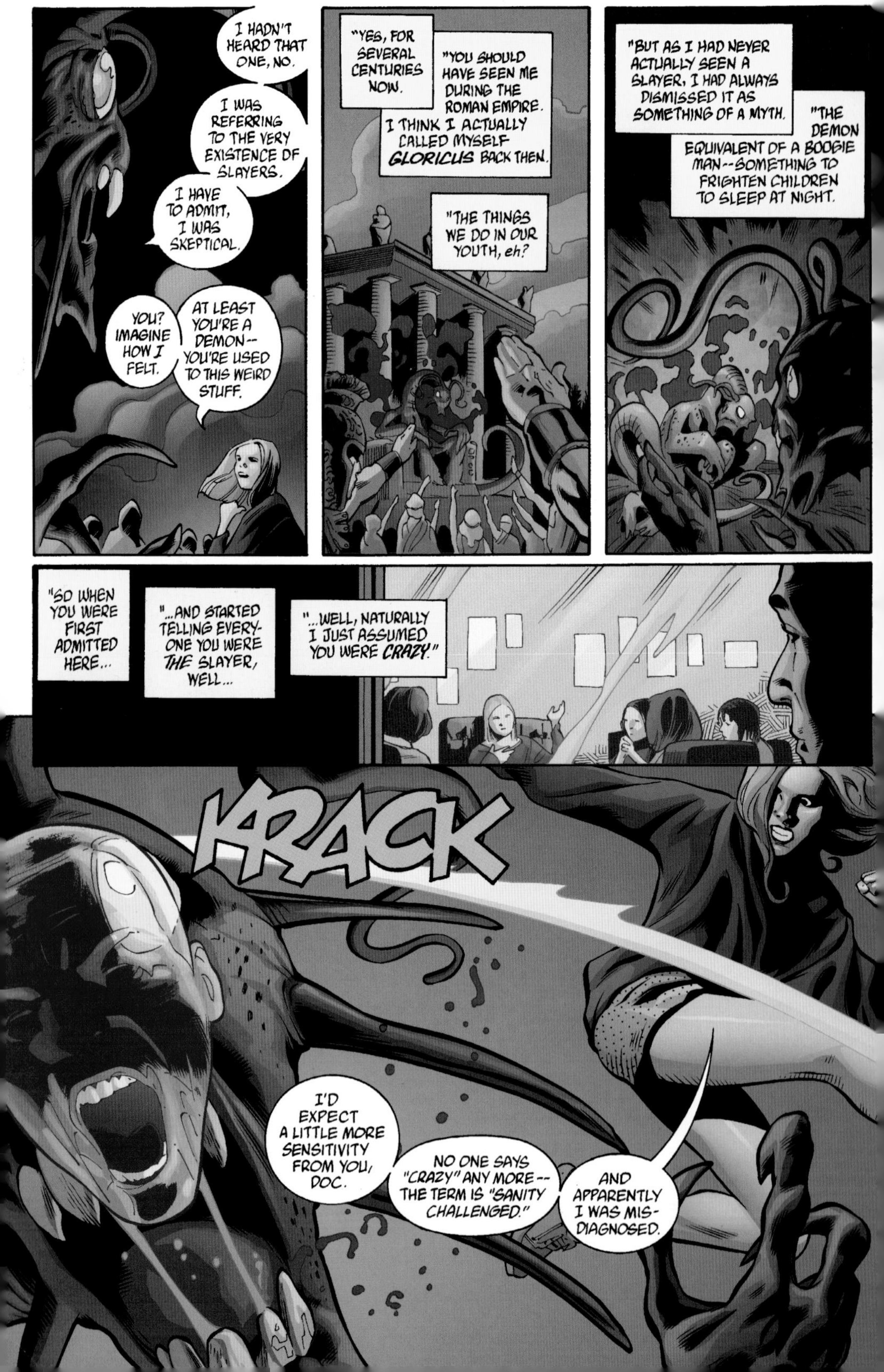
I HADN'T HEARD THAT ONE, NO.
I WAS REFERRING TO THE VERY EXISTENCE OF SLAYERS.
I HAVE TO ADMIT, I WAS SKEPTICAL.
YOU? IMAGINE HOW I FELT.
AT LEAST YOU'RE A DEMON-- YOU'RE USED TO THIS WEIRD STUFF.
"YES, FOR SEVERAL CENTURIES NOW.
"YOU SHOULD HAVE SEEN ME DURING THE ROMAN EMPIRE. I THINK I ACTUALLY CALLED MYSELF GLORICUS BACK THEN.
"THE THINGS WE DO IN OUR YOUTH, eh?
"BUT AS I HAD NEVER ACTUALLY SEEN A SLAYER, I HAD ALWAYS DISMISSED IT AS SOMETHING OF A MYTH.
"THE DEMON EQUIVALENT OF A BOOGIE MAN--SOMETHING TO FRIGHTEN CHILDREN TO SLEEP AT NIGHT.
"SO WHEN YOU WERE FIRST ADMITTED HERE...
"...AND STARTED TELLING EVERY-ONE YOU WERE THE SLAYER, WELL...
"...WELL, NATURALLY I JUST ASSUMED YOU WERE CRAZY."
KRACK
I'D EXPECT A LITTLE MORE SENSITIVITY FROM YOU, DOC.
NO ONE SAYS "CRAZY" ANY MORE -- THE TERM IS "SANITY CHALLENGED."
AND APPARENTLY I WAS MIS-DIAGNOSED.

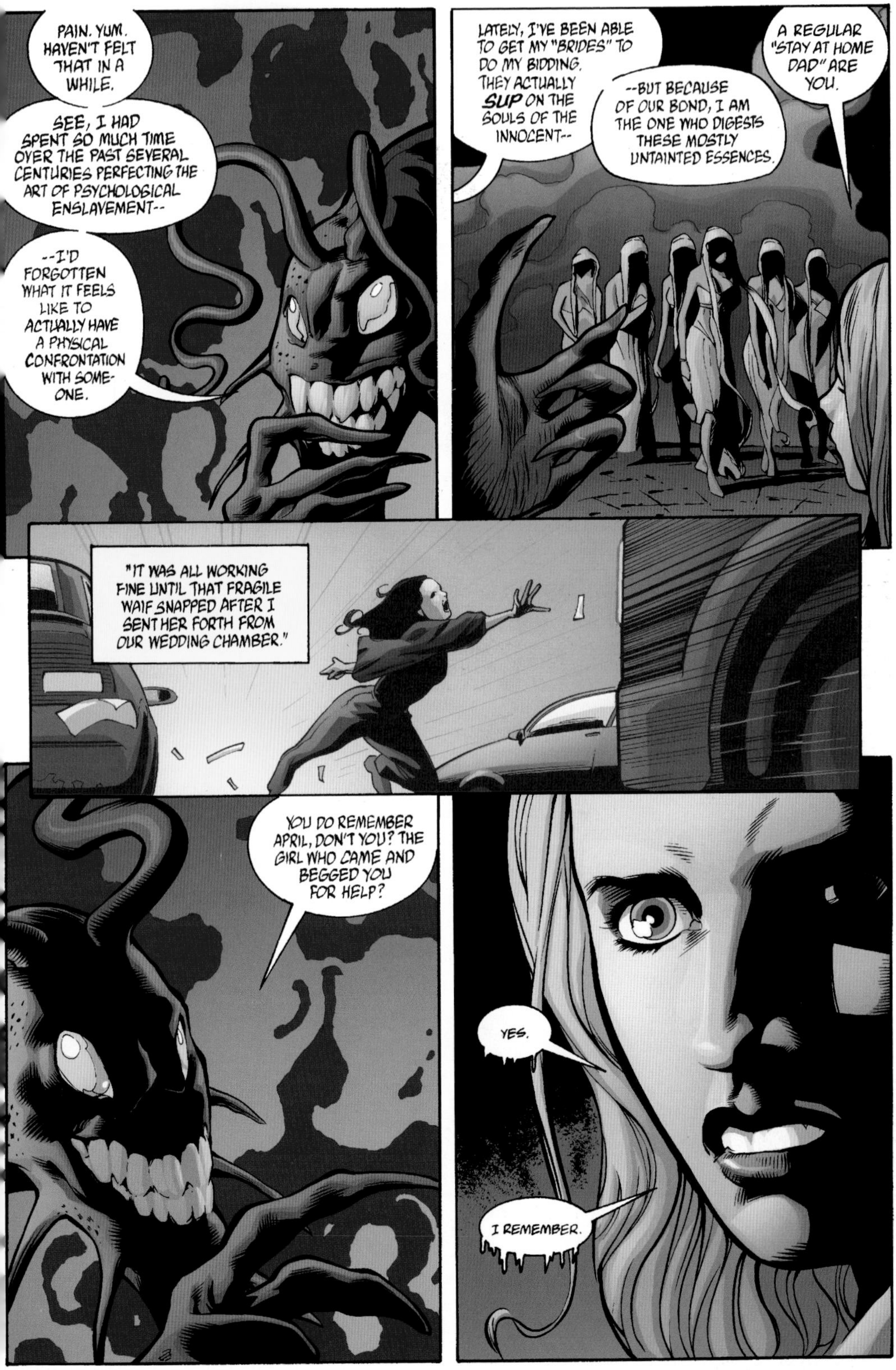
PAIN. YUM. HAVEN'T FELT THAT IN A WHILE.
SEE, I HAD SPENT SO MUCH TIME OVER THE PAST SEVERAL CENTURIES PERFECTING THE ART OF PSYCHOLOGICAL ENSLAVEMENT--
--I'D FORGOTTEN WHAT IT FEELS LIKE TO ACTUALLY HAVE A PHYSICAL CONFRONTATION WITH SOME-ONE.
LATELY, I'VE BEEN ABLE TO GET MY "BRIDES" TO DO MY BIDDING. THEY ACTUALLY SUP ON THE SOULS OF THE INNOCENT--
--BUT BECAUSE OF OUR BOND, I AM THE ONE WHO DIGESTS THESE MOSTLY UNTAINTED ESSENCES.
A REGULAR "STAY AT HOME DAD" ARE YOU.
"IT WAS ALL WORKING FINE UNTIL THAT FRAGILE WAIF SNAPPED AFTER I SENT HER FORTH FROM OUR WEDDING CHAMBER."
YOU DO REMEMBER APRIL, DON'T YOU? THE GIRL WHO CAME AND BEGGED YOU FOR HELP?
YES.
I REMEMBER.

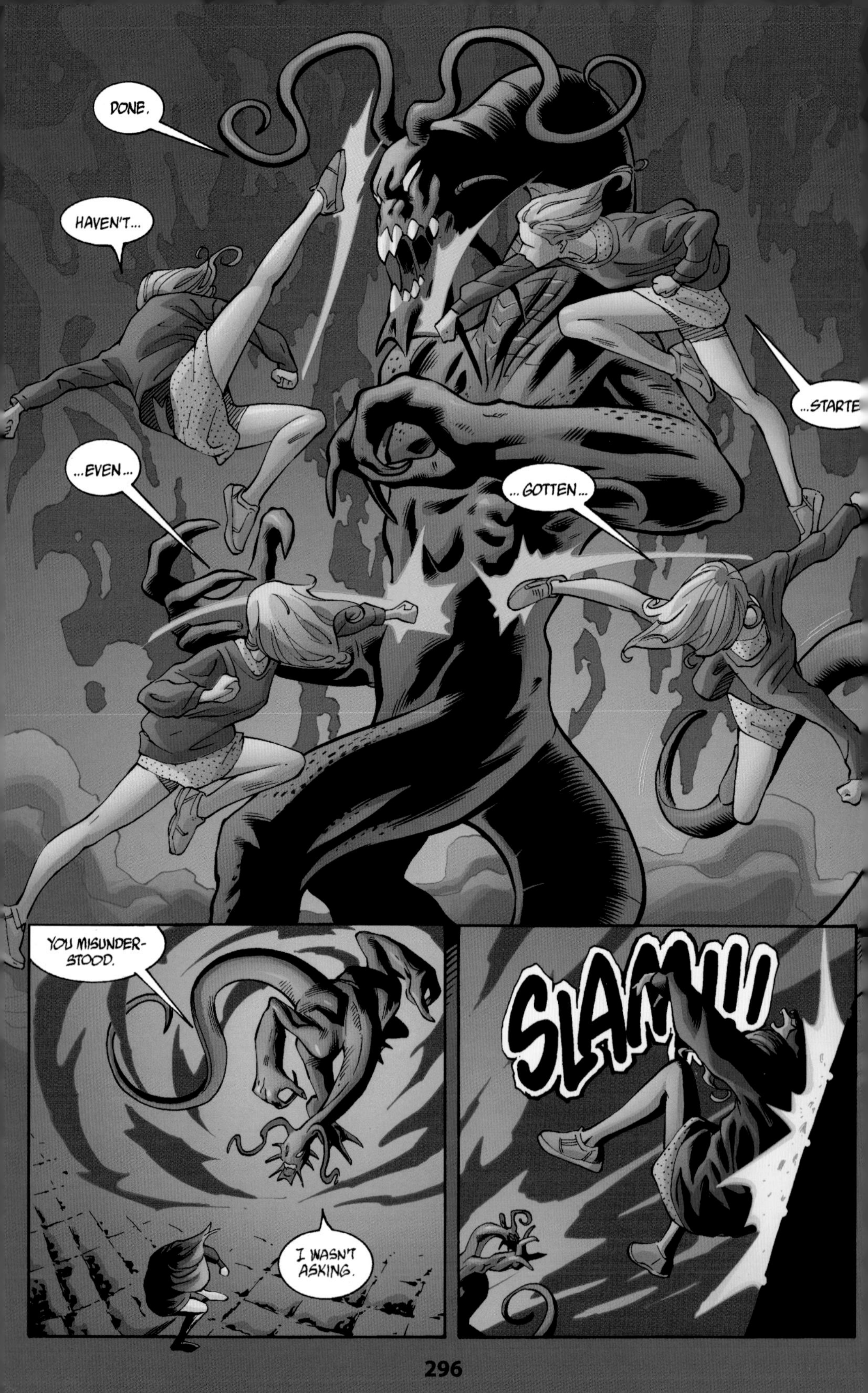

DONE.
HAVEN'T...
...STARTE
...EVEN...
...GOTTEN...
YOU MISUNDER-STOOD.
I WASN'T ASKING.
SLAM!!

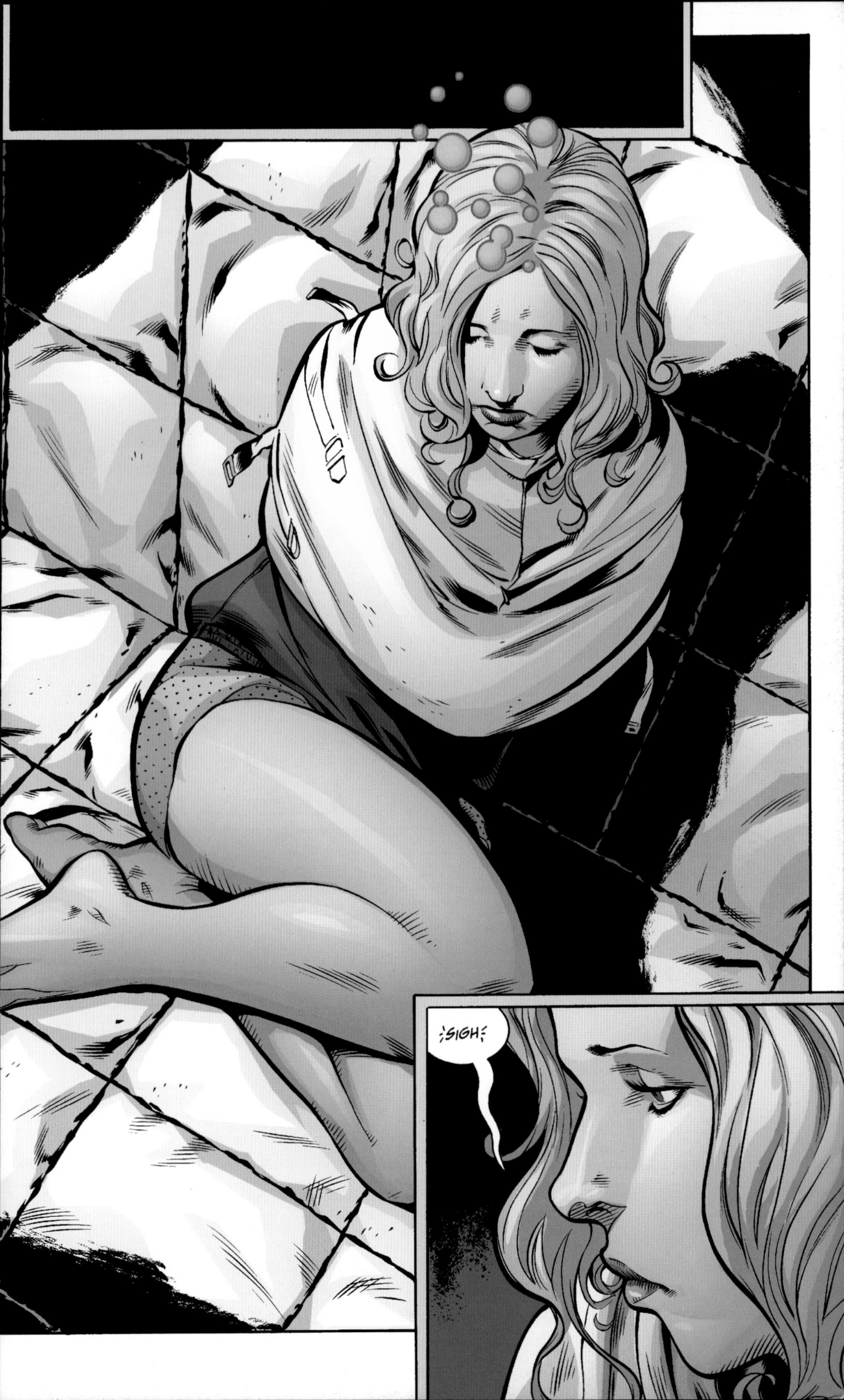
SIGH

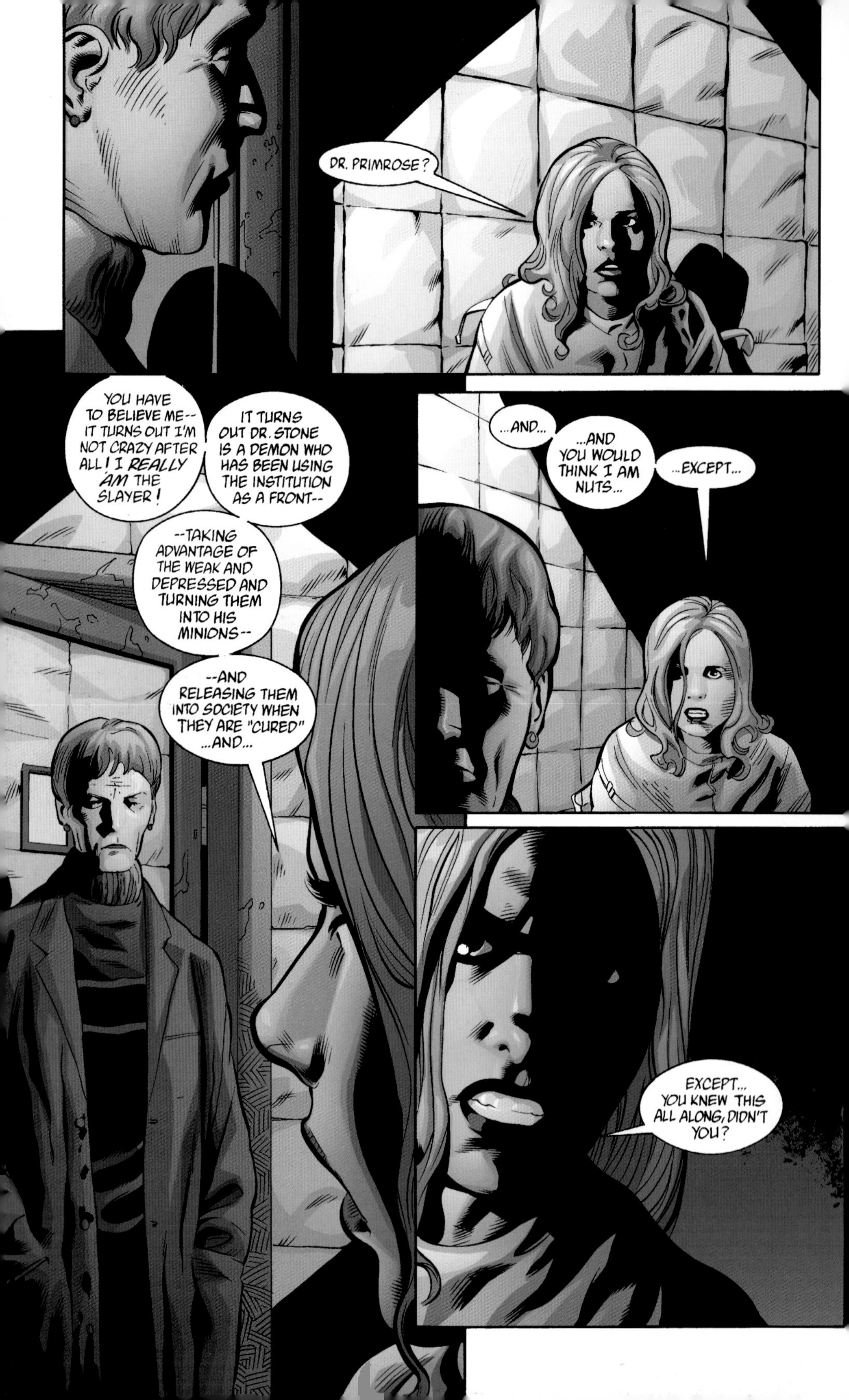
DR. PRIMROSE?
YOU HAVE TO BELIEVE ME-- IT TURNS OUT I'M NOT CRAZY AFTER ALL! I *REALLY AM* THE SLAYER!
IT TURNS OUT DR. STONE IS A DEMON WHO HAS BEEN USING THE INSTITUTION AS A FRONT--
--TAKING ADVANTAGE OF THE WEAK AND DEPRESSED AND TURNING THEM INTO HIS MINIONS--
--AND RELEASING THEM INTO SOCIETY WHEN THEY ARE "CURED" ...AND...
...AND...
...AND YOU WOULD THINK I AM NUTS...
...EXCEPT...
EXCEPT... YOU KNEW THIS ALL ALONG, DIDN'T YOU?

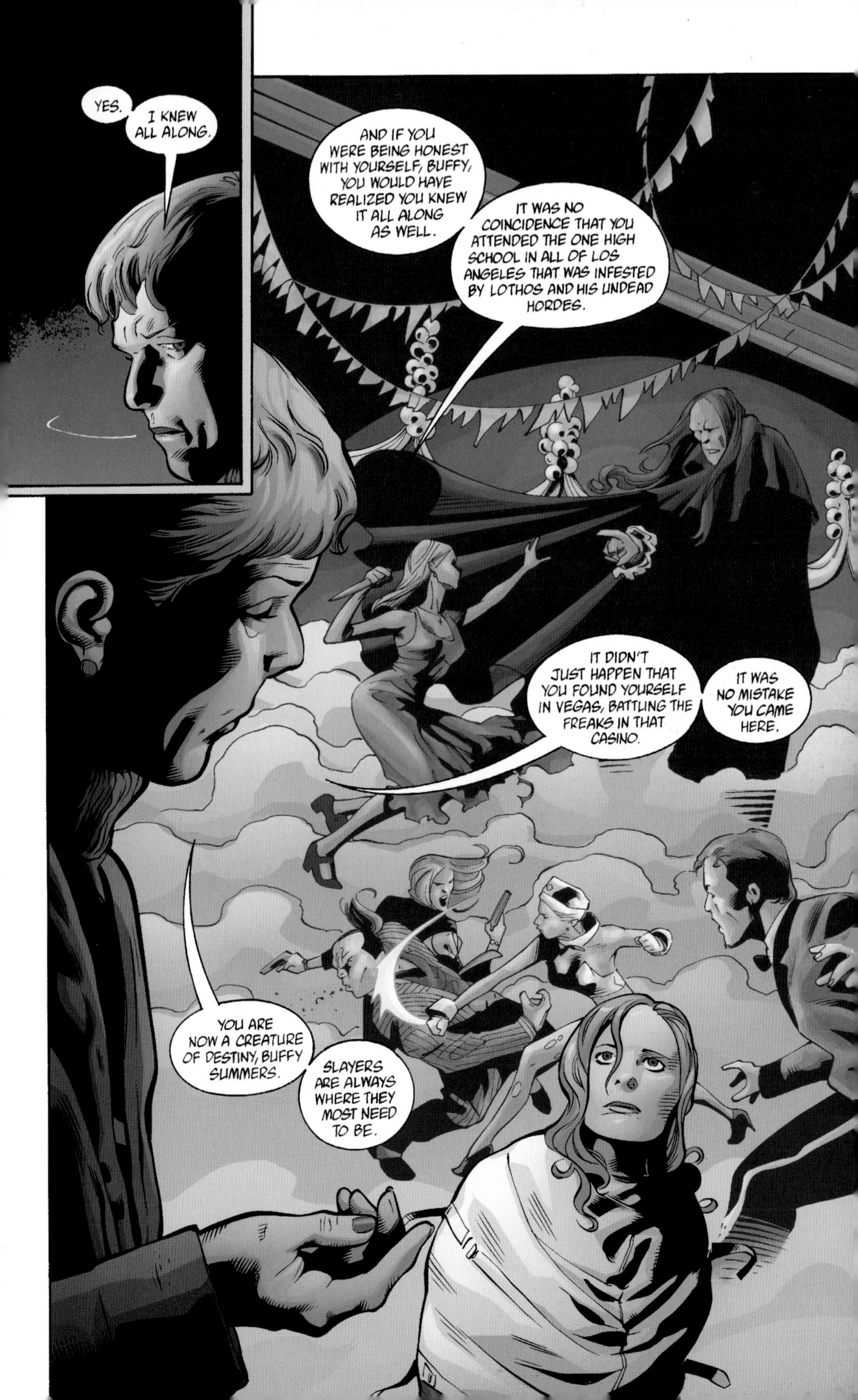
YES.
I KNEW ALL ALONG.
AND IF YOU WERE BEING HONEST WITH YOURSELF, BUFFY, YOU WOULD HAVE REALIZED YOU KNEW IT ALL ALONG AS WELL.
IT WAS NO COINCIDENCE THAT YOU ATTENDED THE ONE HIGH SCHOOL IN ALL OF LOS ANGELES THAT WAS INFESTED BY LOTHOS AND HIS UNDEAD HORDES.
IT DIDN'T JUST HAPPEN THAT YOU FOUND YOURSELF IN VEGAS, BATTLING THE FREAKS IN THAT CASINO.
IT WAS NO MISTAKE YOU CAME HERE.
YOU ARE NOW A CREATURE OF DESTINY, BUFFY SUMMERS.
SLAYERS ARE ALWAYS WHERE THEY MOST NEED TO BE.

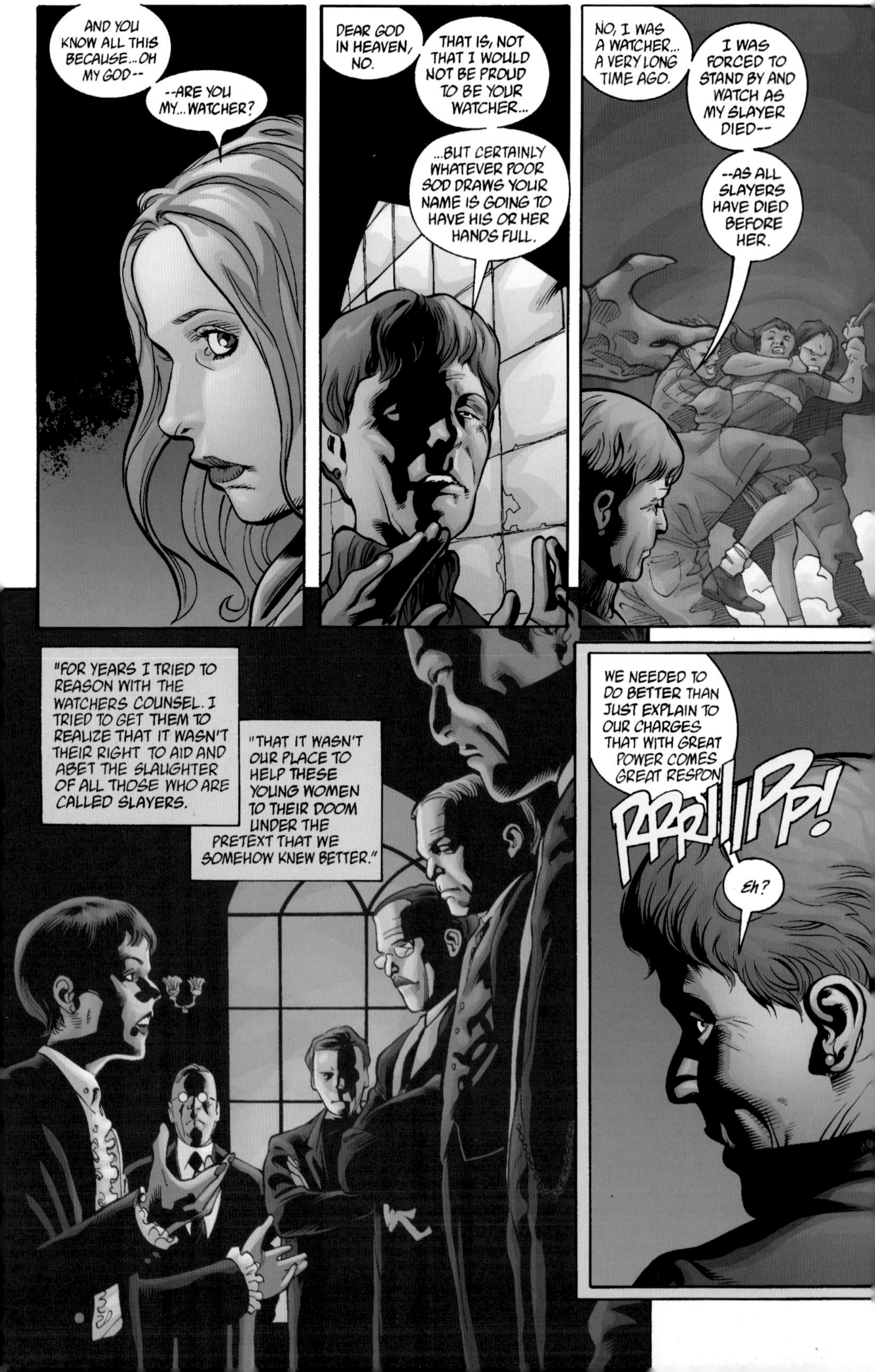
AND YOU KNOW ALL THIS BECAUSE...OH MY GOD--
--ARE YOU MY...WATCHER?
DEAR GOD IN HEAVEN, NO.
THAT IS, NOT THAT I WOULD NOT BE PROUD TO BE YOUR WATCHER...
...BUT CERTAINLY WHATEVER POOR SOD DRAWS YOUR NAME IS GOING TO HAVE HIS OR HER HANDS FULL.
NO, I WAS A WATCHER... A VERY LONG TIME AGO.
I WAS FORCED TO STAND BY AND WATCH AS MY SLAYER DIED--
--AS ALL SLAYERS HAVE DIED BEFORE HER.
"FOR YEARS I TRIED TO REASON WITH THE WATCHERS COUNSEL. I TRIED TO GET THEM TO REALIZE THAT IT WASN'T THEIR RIGHT TO AID AND ABET THE SLAUGHTER OF ALL THOSE WHO ARE CALLED SLAYERS.
"THAT IT WASN'T OUR PLACE TO HELP THESE YOUNG WOMEN TO THEIR DOOM UNDER THE PRETEXT THAT WE SOMEHOW KNEW BETTER."
WE NEEDED TO DO BETTER THAN JUST EXPLAIN TO OUR CHARGES THAT WITH GREAT POWER COMES GREAT RESPON
RRRIIIPP!
Eh?

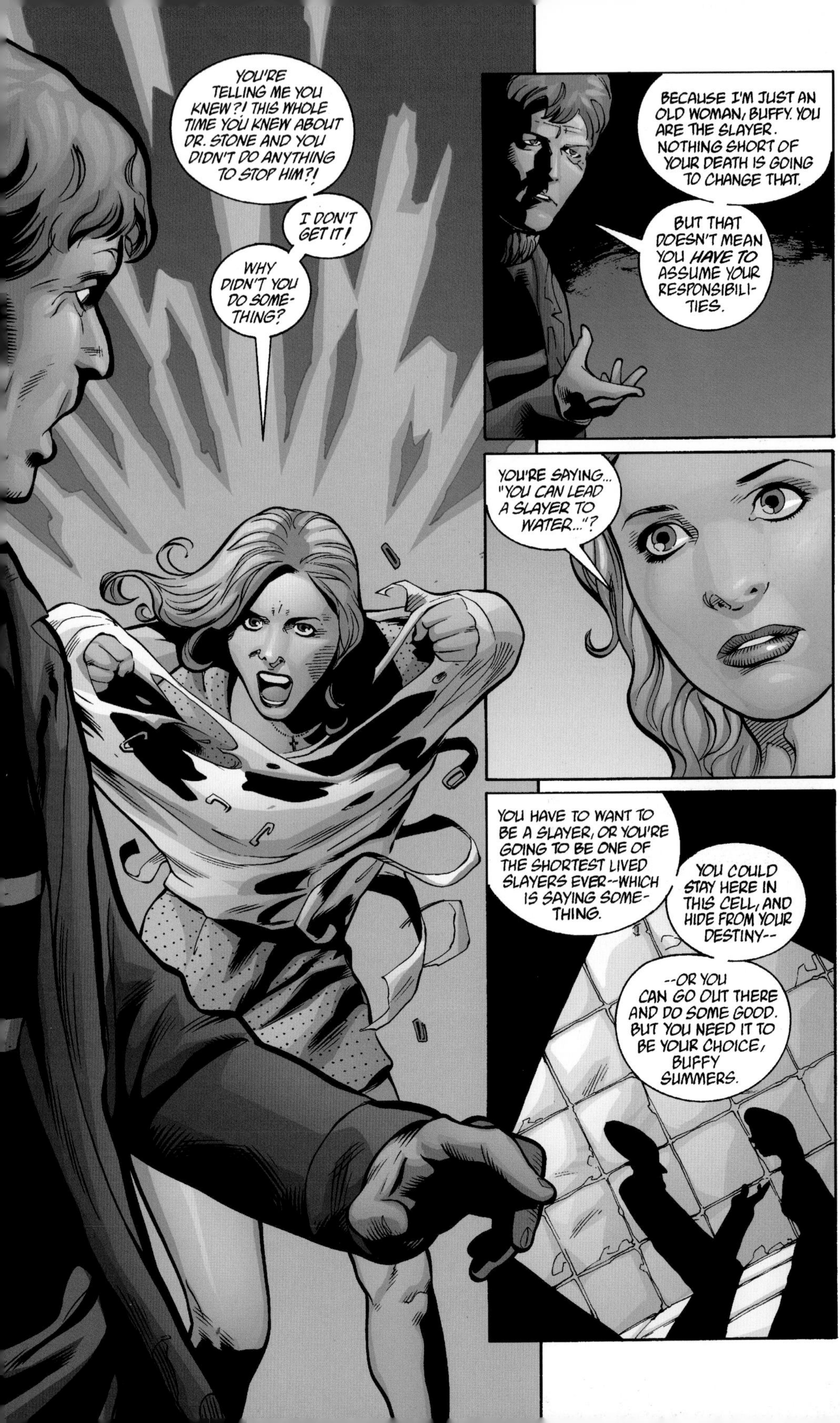
YOU'RE TELLING ME YOU KNEW?! THIS WHOLE TIME YOU KNEW ABOUT DR. STONE AND YOU DIDN'T DO ANYTHING TO STOP HIM?!
I DON'T GET IT!
WHY DIDN'T YOU DO SOME-THING?
BECAUSE I'M JUST AN OLD WOMAN, BUFFY. YOU ARE THE SLAYER. NOTHING SHORT OF YOUR DEATH IS GOING TO CHANGE THAT.
BUT THAT DOESN'T MEAN YOU HAVE TO ASSUME YOUR RESPONSIBILI-TIES.
YOU'RE SAYING... "YOU CAN LEAD A SLAYER TO WATER..."?
YOU HAVE TO WANT TO BE A SLAYER, OR YOU'RE GOING TO BE ONE OF THE SHORTEST LIVED SLAYERS EVER--WHICH IS SAYING SOME-THING.
YOU COULD STAY HERE IN THIS CELL, AND HIDE FROM YOUR DESTINY--
--OR YOU CAN GO OUT THERE AND DO SOME GOOD. BUT YOU NEED IT TO BE YOUR CHOICE, BUFFY SUMMERS.

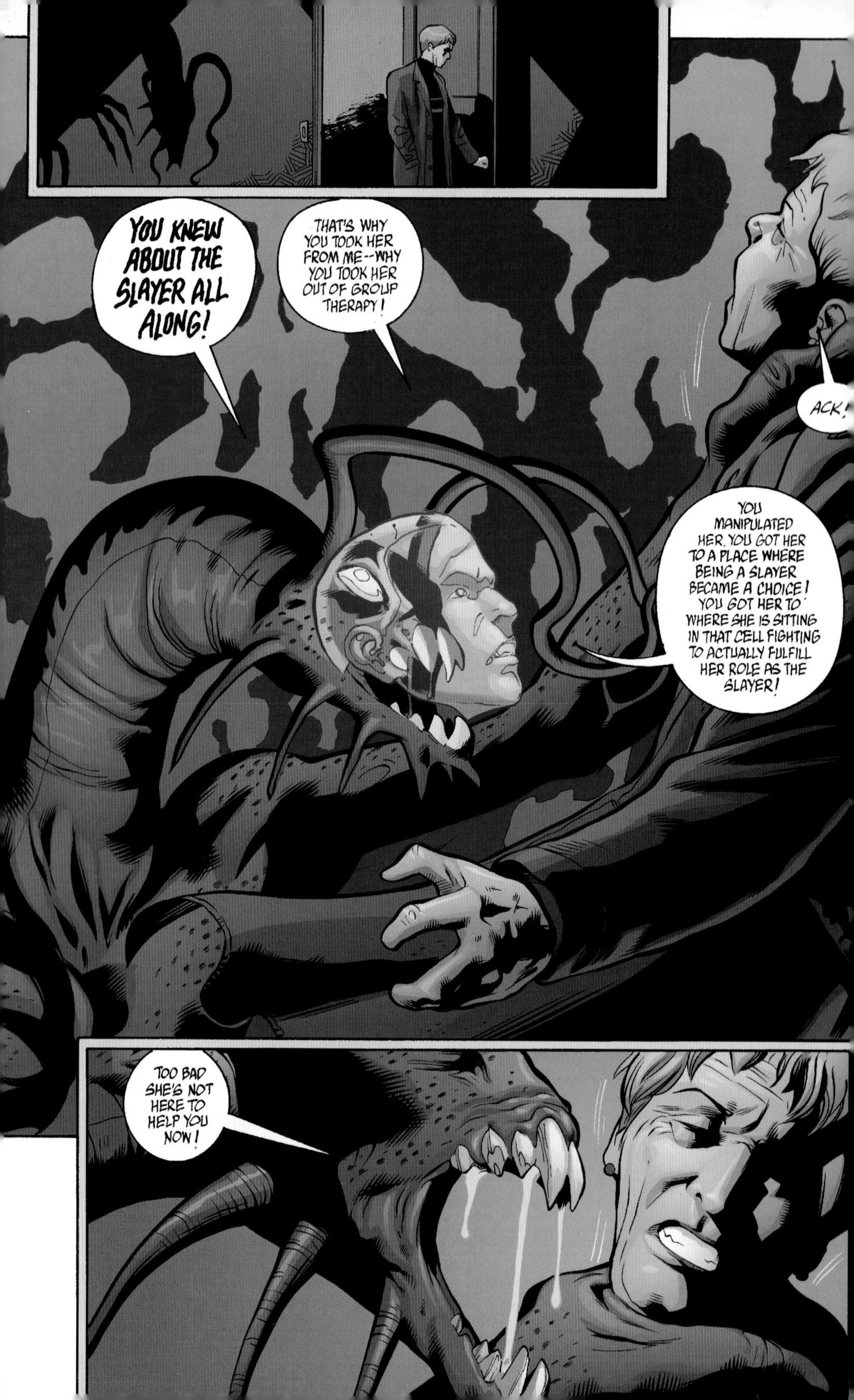
YOU KNEW ABOUT THE SLAYER ALL ALONG!
THAT'S WHY YOU TOOK HER FROM ME--WHY YOU TOOK HER OUT OF GROUP THERAPY!
ACK!
YOU MANIPULATED HER. YOU GOT HER TO A PLACE WHERE BEING A SLAYER BECAME A CHOICE! YOU GOT HER TO WHERE SHE IS SITTING IN THAT CELL FIGHTING TO ACTUALLY FULFILL HER ROLE AS THE SLAYER!
TOO BAD SHE'S NOT HERE TO HELP YOU NOW!

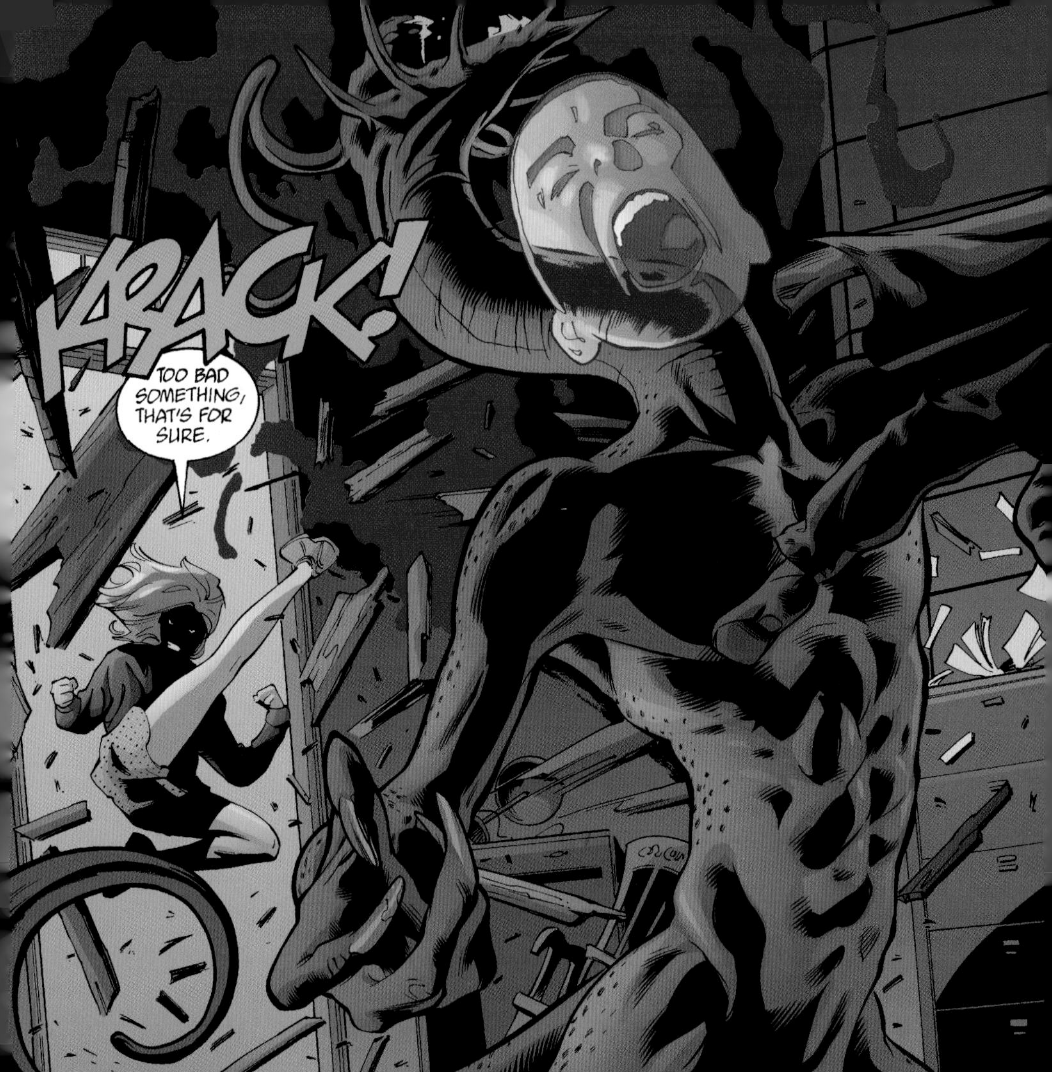
KRACK!
TOO BAD SOMETHING, THAT'S FOR SURE.
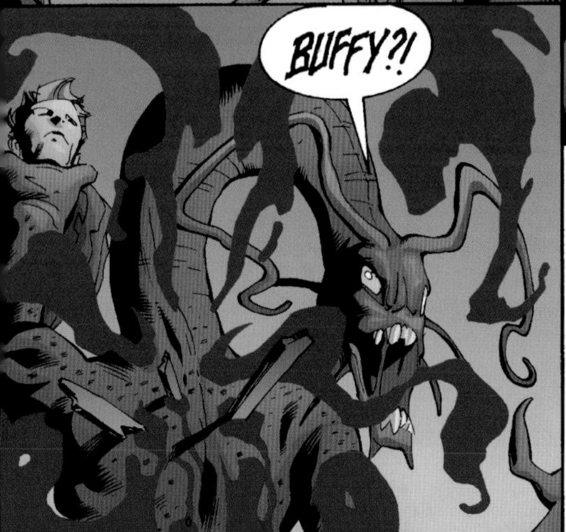
BUFFY?!
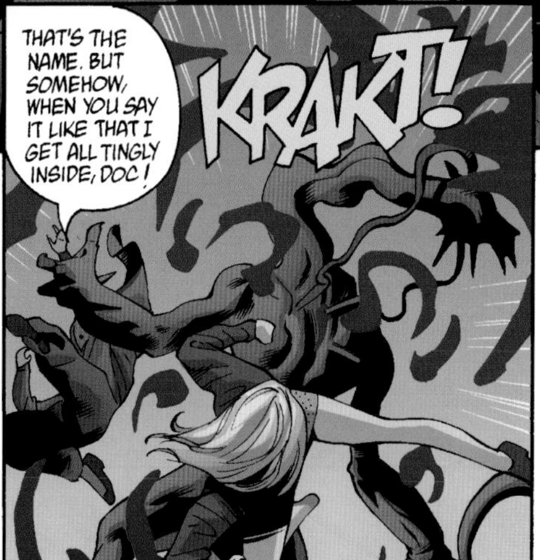
THAT'S THE NAME. BUT SOMEHOW, WHEN YOU SAY IT LIKE THAT I GET ALL TINGLY INSIDE, DOC!
KRAKT!

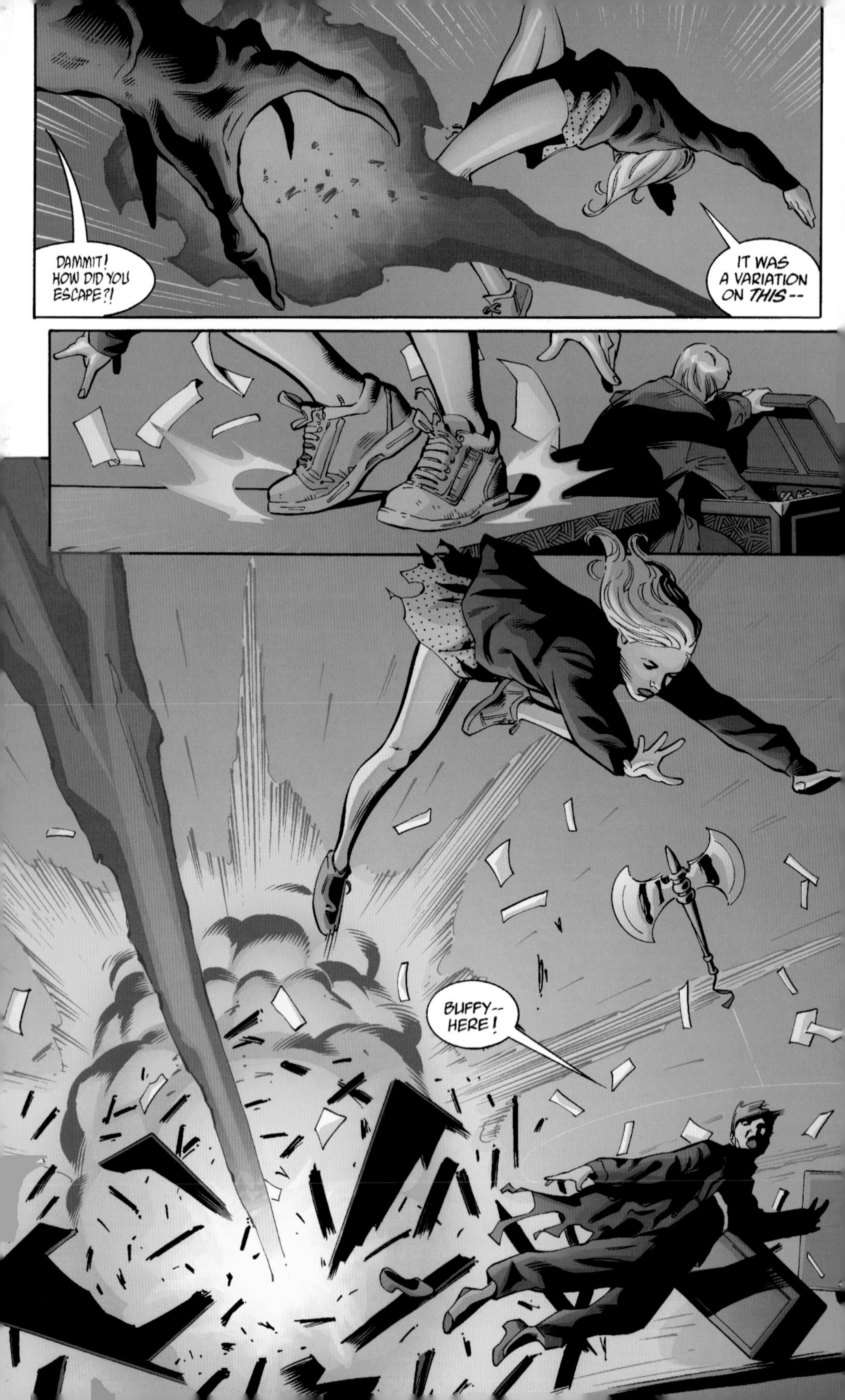
DAMMIT! HOW DID YOU ESCAPE?!
IT WAS A VARIATION ON THIS--
BUFFY-- HERE!

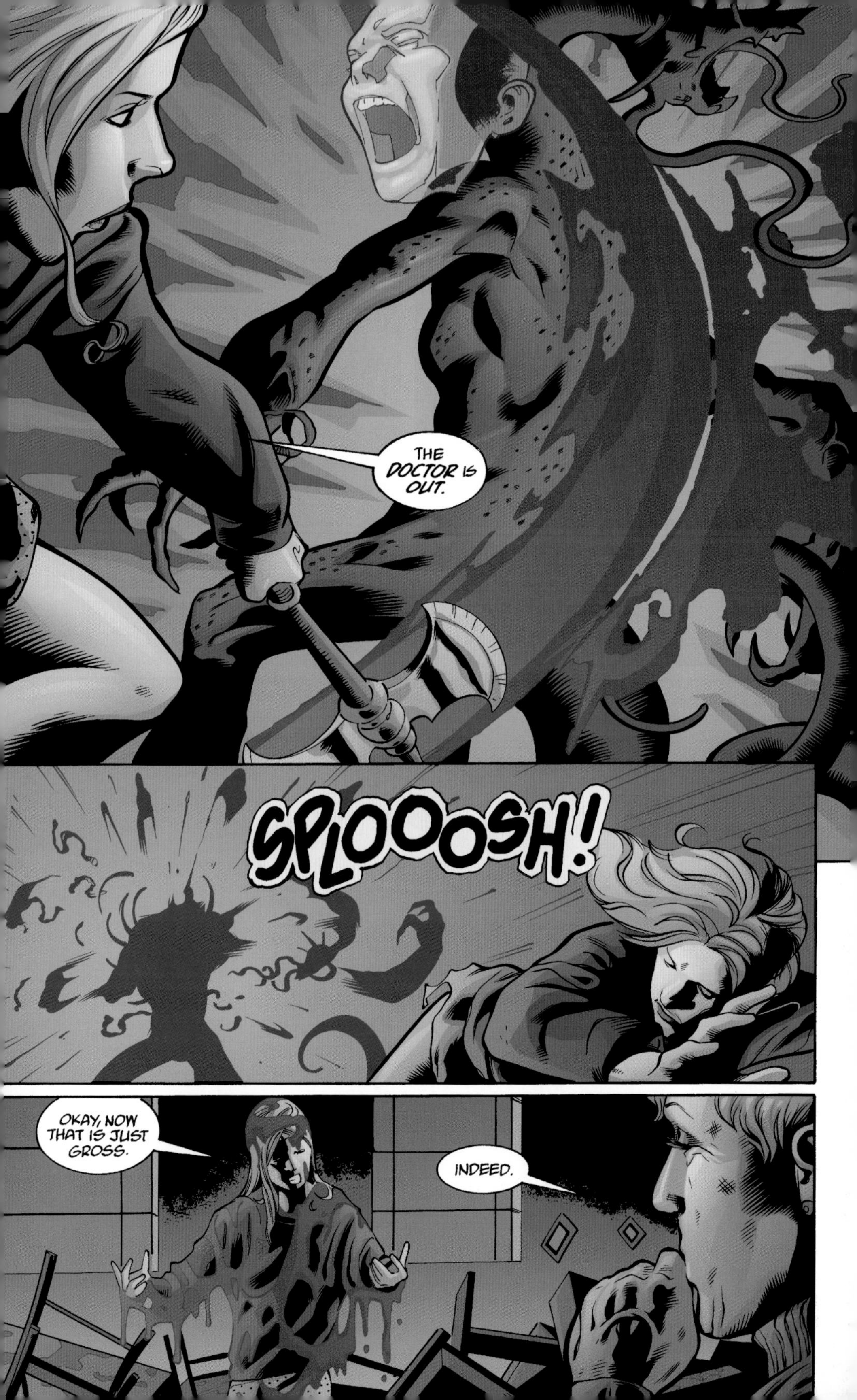
THE DOCTOR IS OUT.
SPLOOOSH!
OKAY, NOW THAT IS JUST GROSS.
INDEED.

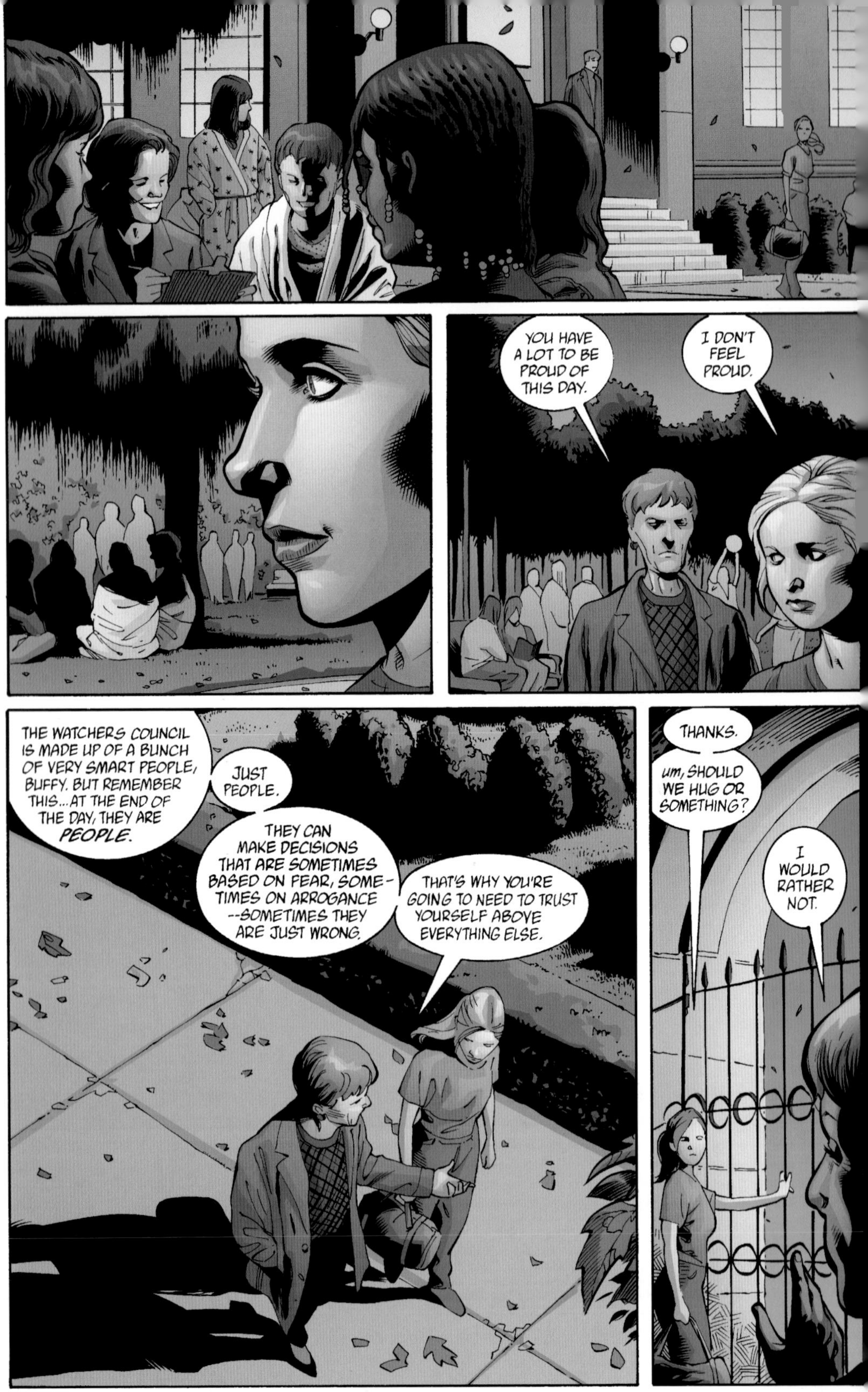
YOU HAVE A LOT TO BE PROUD OF THIS DAY.
I DON'T FEEL PROUD.
THE WATCHERS COUNCIL IS MADE UP OF A BUNCH OF VERY SMART PEOPLE, BUFFY. BUT REMEMBER THIS... AT THE END OF THE DAY, THEY ARE *PEOPLE*.
JUST PEOPLE.
THEY CAN MAKE DECISIONS THAT ARE SOMETIMES BASED ON FEAR, SOME-TIMES ON ARROGANCE --SOMETIMES THEY ARE JUST WRONG.
THAT'S WHY YOU'RE GOING TO NEED TO TRUST YOURSELF ABOVE EVERYTHING ELSE.
THANKS.
UM, SHOULD WE HUG OR SOMETHING?
I WOULD RATHER NOT.

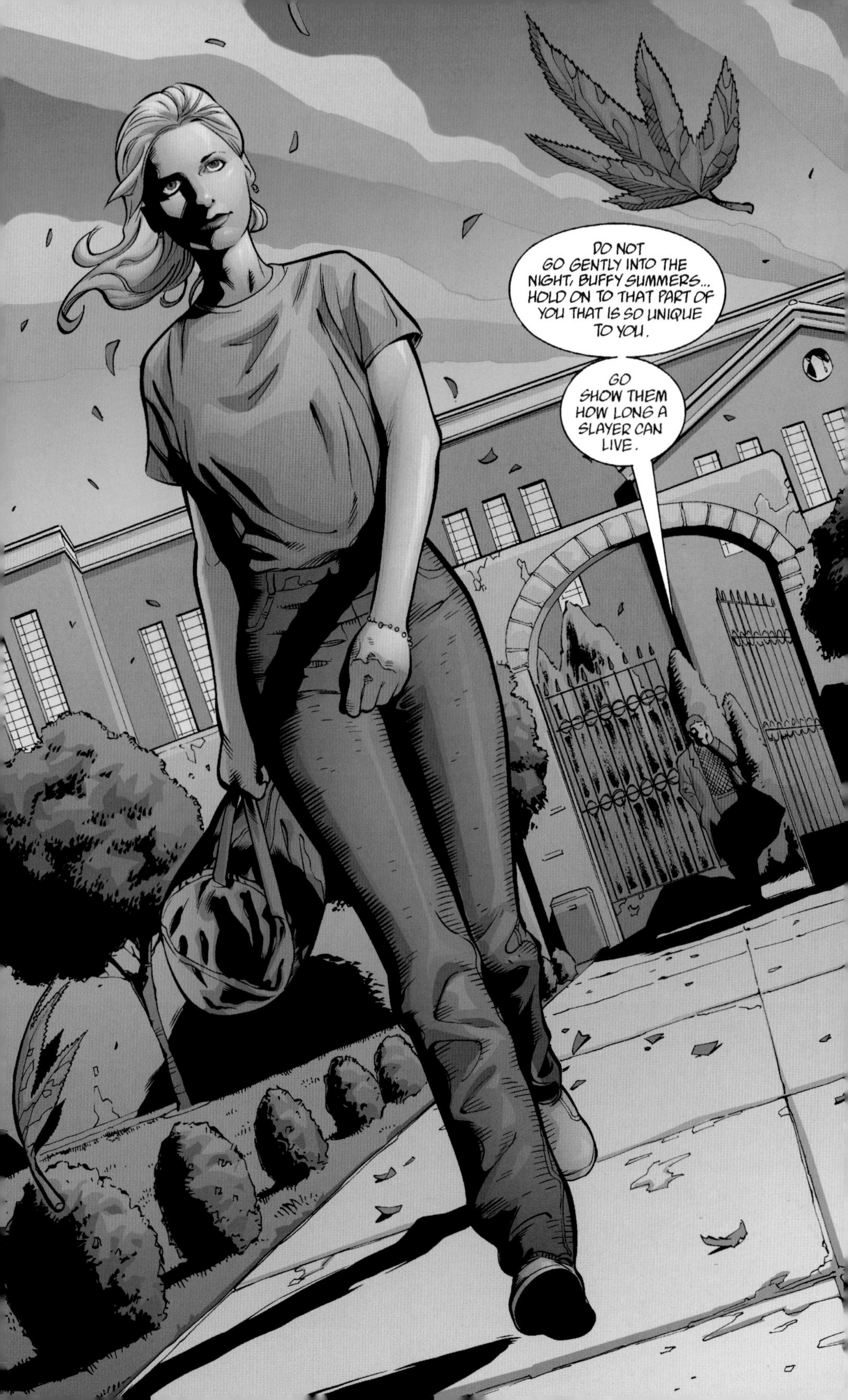
DO NOT GO GENTLY INTO THE NIGHT, BUFFY SUMMERS... HOLD ON TO THAT PART OF YOU THAT IS SO UNIQUE TO YOU.
GO SHOW THEM HOW LONG A SLAYER CAN LIVE.

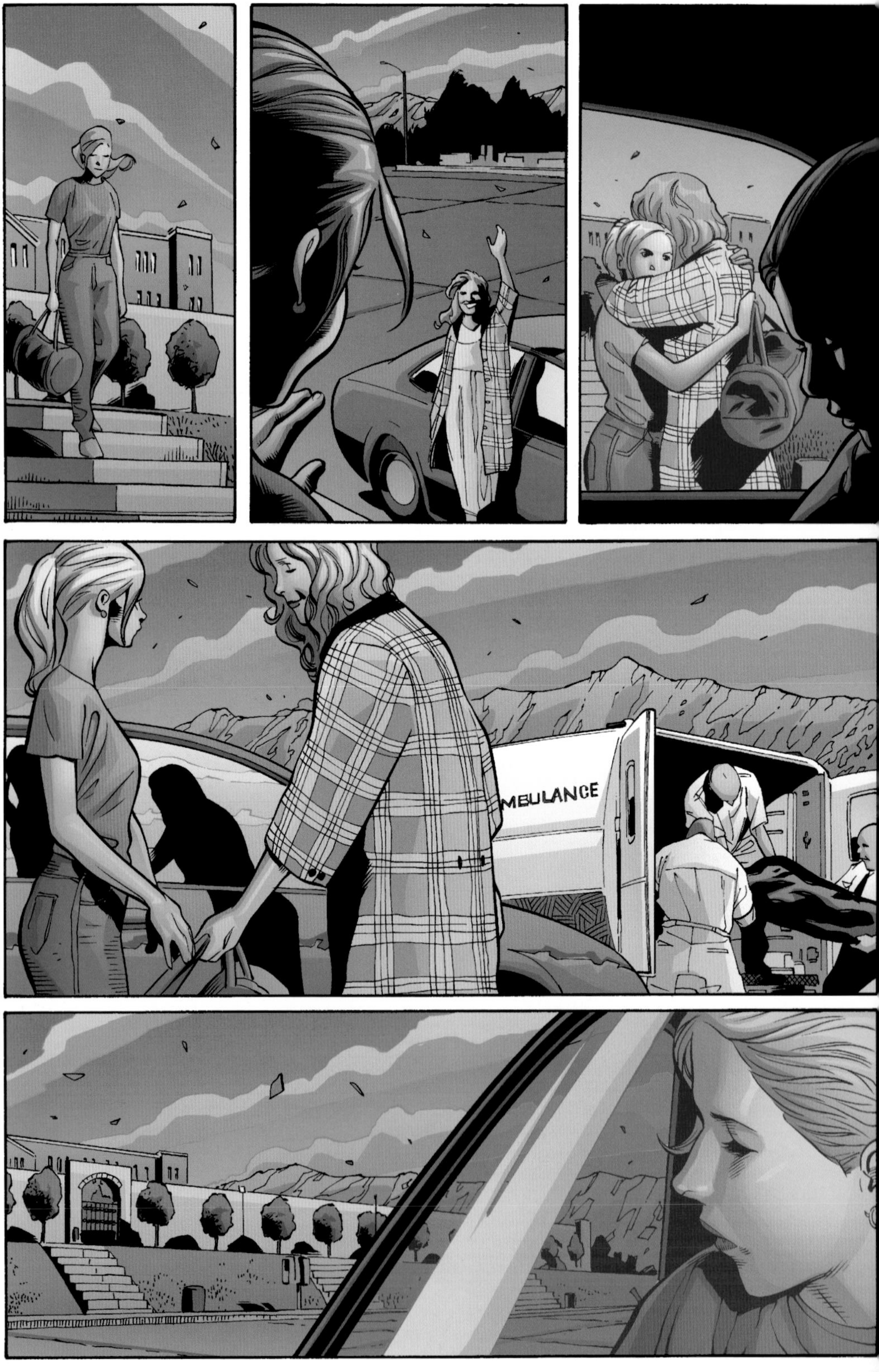
MBULANCE

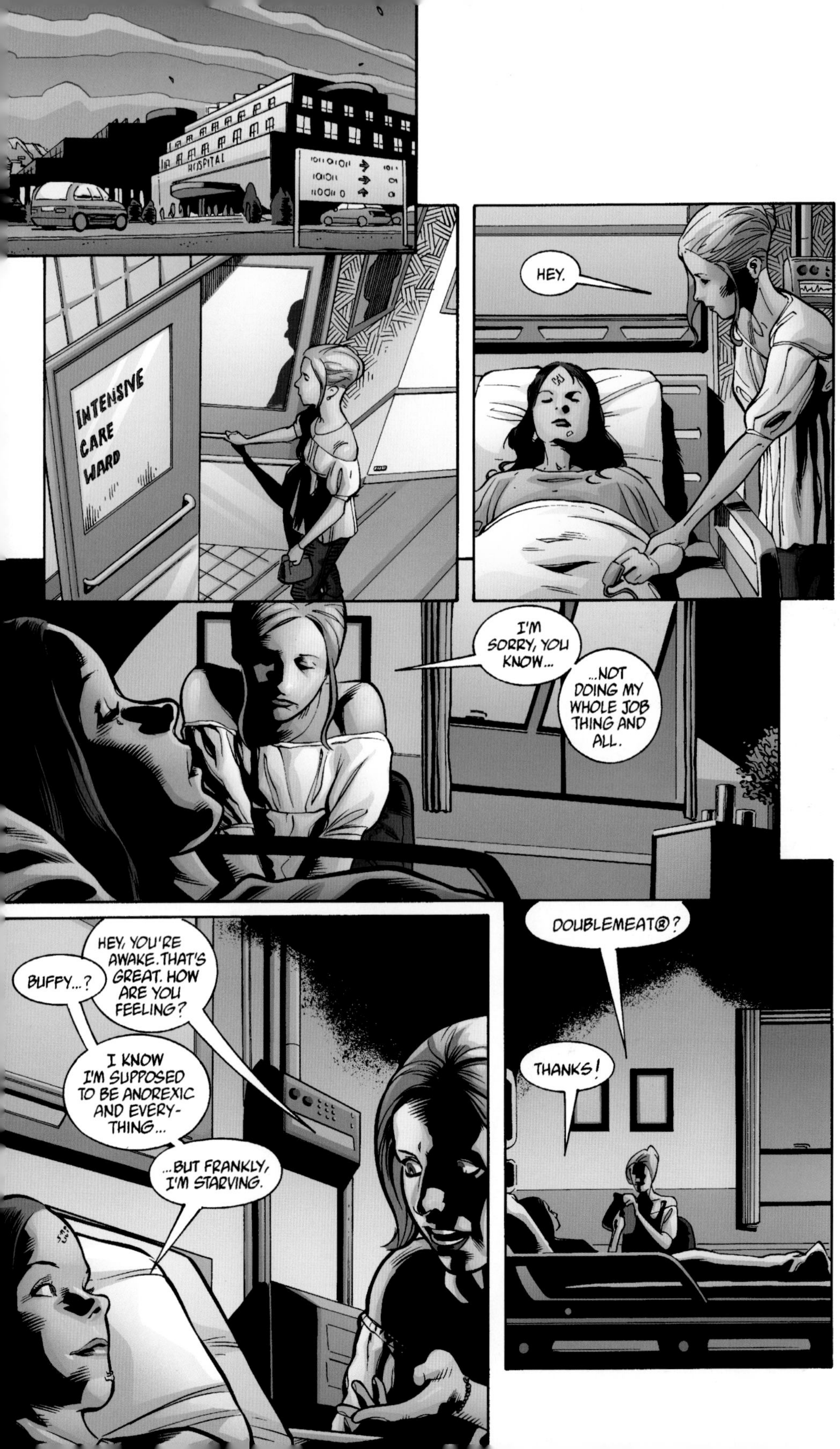
HOSPITAL
INTENSIVE CARE WARD
HEY.
I'M SORRY, YOU KNOW...
...NOT DOING MY WHOLE JOB THING AND ALL.
BUFFY...?
HEY, YOU'RE AWAKE. THAT'S GREAT. HOW ARE YOU FEELING?
I KNOW I'M SUPPOSED TO BE ANOREXIC AND EVERY-THING...
...BUT FRANKLY, I'M STARVING.
DOUBLEMEAT®?
THANKS!

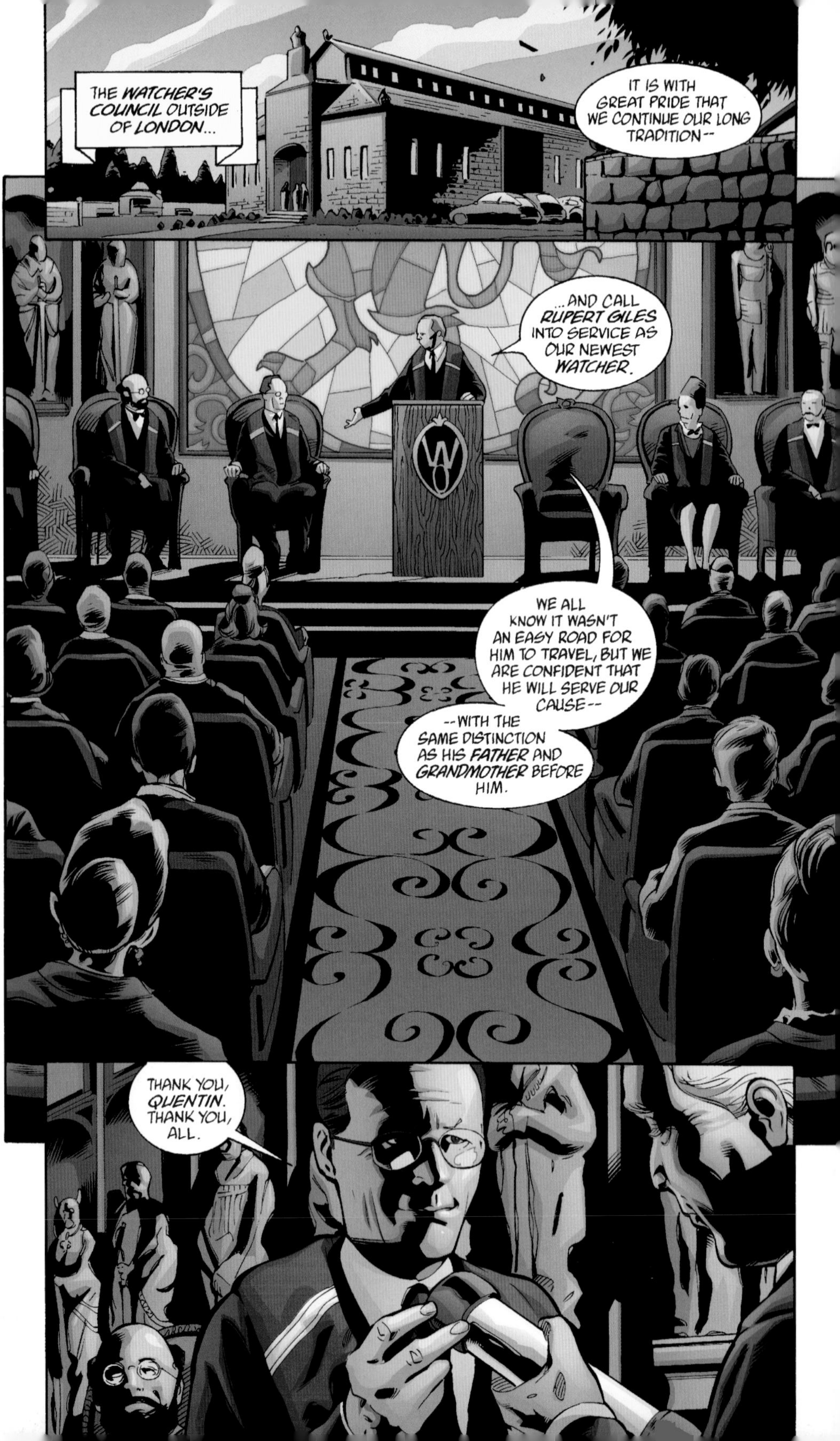
THE WATCHER'S COUNCIL OUTSIDE OF LONDON...
IT IS WITH GREAT PRIDE THAT WE CONTINUE OUR LONG TRADITION--
...AND CALL RUPERT GILES INTO SERVICE AS OUR NEWEST WATCHER.
WE ALL KNOW IT WASN'T AN EASY ROAD FOR HIM TO TRAVEL, BUT WE ARE CONFIDENT THAT HE WILL SERVE OUR CAUSE--
--WITH THE SAME DISTINCTION AS HIS FATHER AND GRANDMOTHER BEFORE HIM.
THANK YOU, QUENTIN. THANK YOU, ALL.

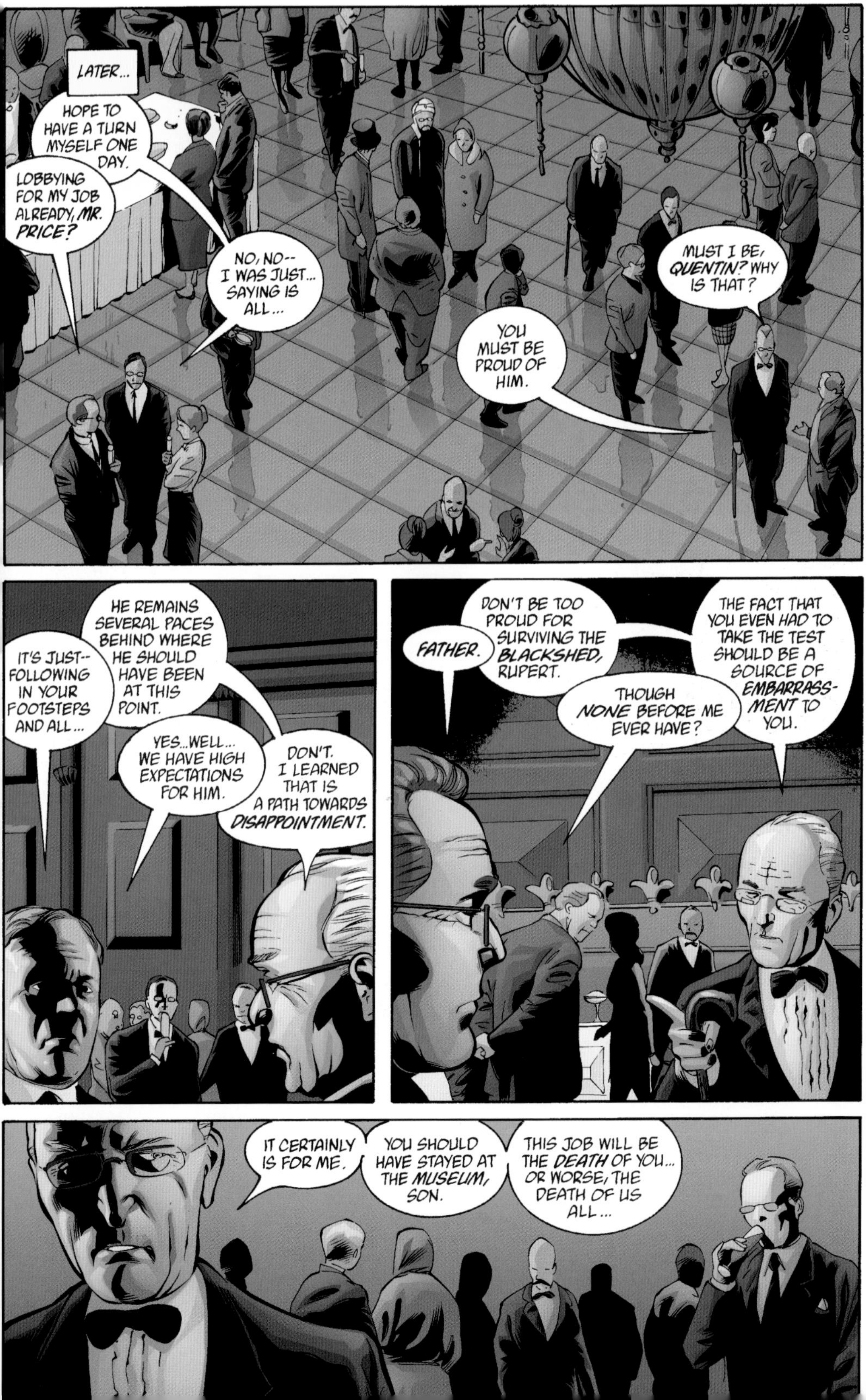
LATER...
HOPE TO HAVE A TURN MYSELF ONE DAY.
LOBBYING FOR MY JOB ALREADY, MR. PRICE?
NO, NO-- I WAS JUST... SAYING IS ALL...
MUST I BE, QUENTIN? WHY IS THAT?
YOU MUST BE PROUD OF HIM.
HE REMAINS SEVERAL PACES BEHIND WHERE HE SHOULD HAVE BEEN AT THIS POINT.
IT'S JUST-- FOLLOWING IN YOUR FOOTSTEPS AND ALL...
YES...WELL... WE HAVE HIGH EXPECTATIONS FOR HIM.
DON'T. I LEARNED THAT IS A PATH TOWARDS DISAPPOINTMENT.
FATHER.
DON'T BE TOO PROUD FOR SURVIVING THE BLACKSHED, RUPERT.
THE FACT THAT YOU EVEN HAD TO TAKE THE TEST SHOULD BE A SOURCE OF EMBARRASSMENT TO YOU.
THOUGH NONE BEFORE ME EVER HAVE?
IT CERTAINLY IS FOR ME.
YOU SHOULD HAVE STAYED AT THE MUSEUM, SON.
THIS JOB WILL BE THE DEATH OF YOU... OR WORSE, THE DEATH OF US ALL...

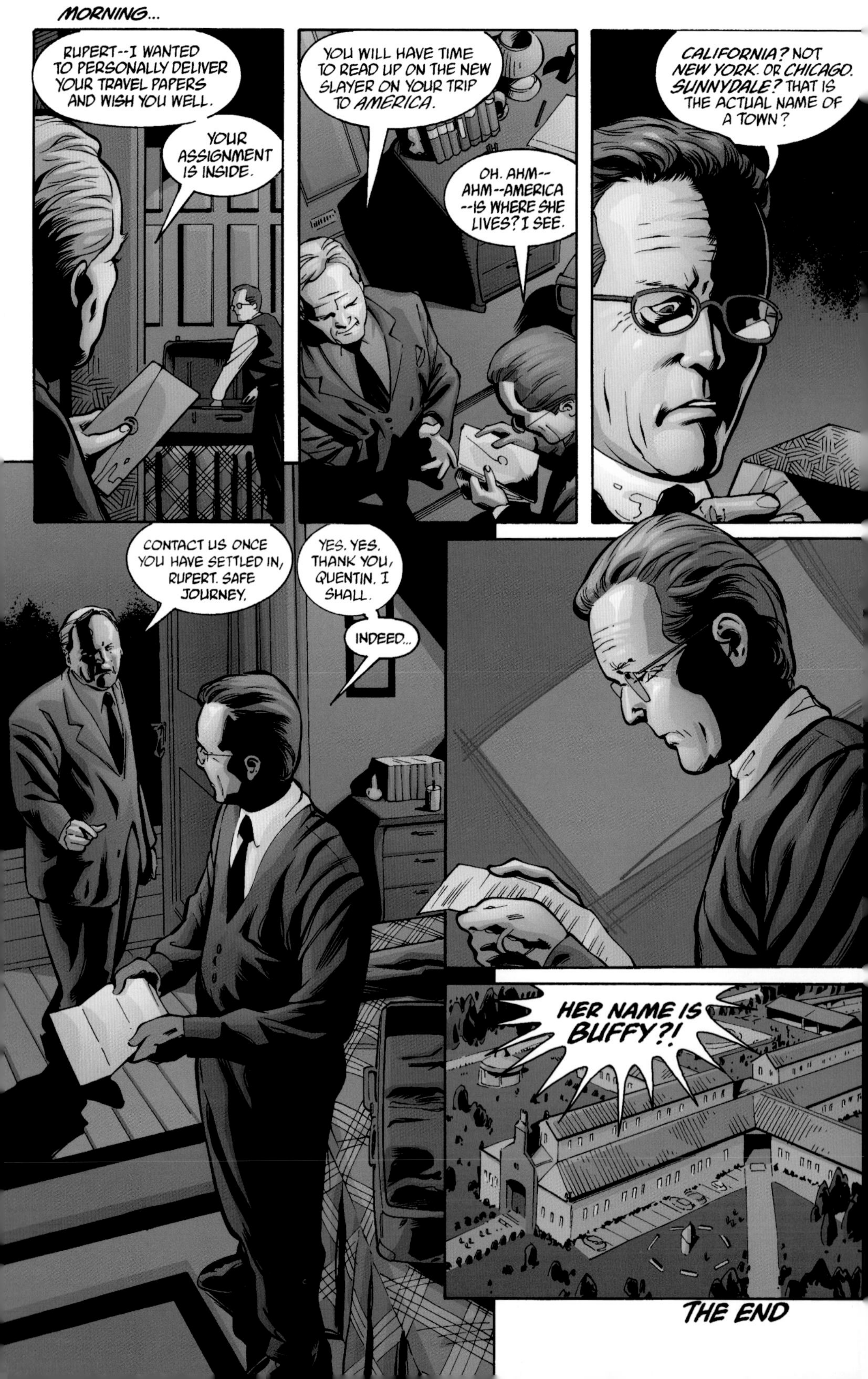
MORNING...
RUPERT--I WANTED TO PERSONALLY DELIVER YOUR TRAVEL PAPERS AND WISH YOU WELL.
YOUR ASSIGNMENT IS INSIDE.
YOU WILL HAVE TIME TO READ UP ON THE NEW SLAYER ON YOUR TRIP TO AMERICA.
OH. AHM-- AHM--AMERICA --IS WHERE SHE LIVES? I SEE.
CALIFORNIA? NOT NEW YORK. OR CHICAGO. SUNNYDALE? THAT IS THE ACTUAL NAME OF A TOWN?
CONTACT US ONCE YOU HAVE SETTLED IN, RUPERT. SAFE JOURNEY.
YES. YES. THANK YOU, QUENTIN. I SHALL.
INDEED...
HER NAME IS BUFFY?!
THE END

COVER GALLERY

BUFFY: THE ORIGIN #1 & #2
by Joe Bennett with J. Jadsen and René Micheletti,
and with Jeromy Cox and Guy Major

BUFFY THE VAMPIRE SLAYER #51–53
by Paul Lee and Brian Horton

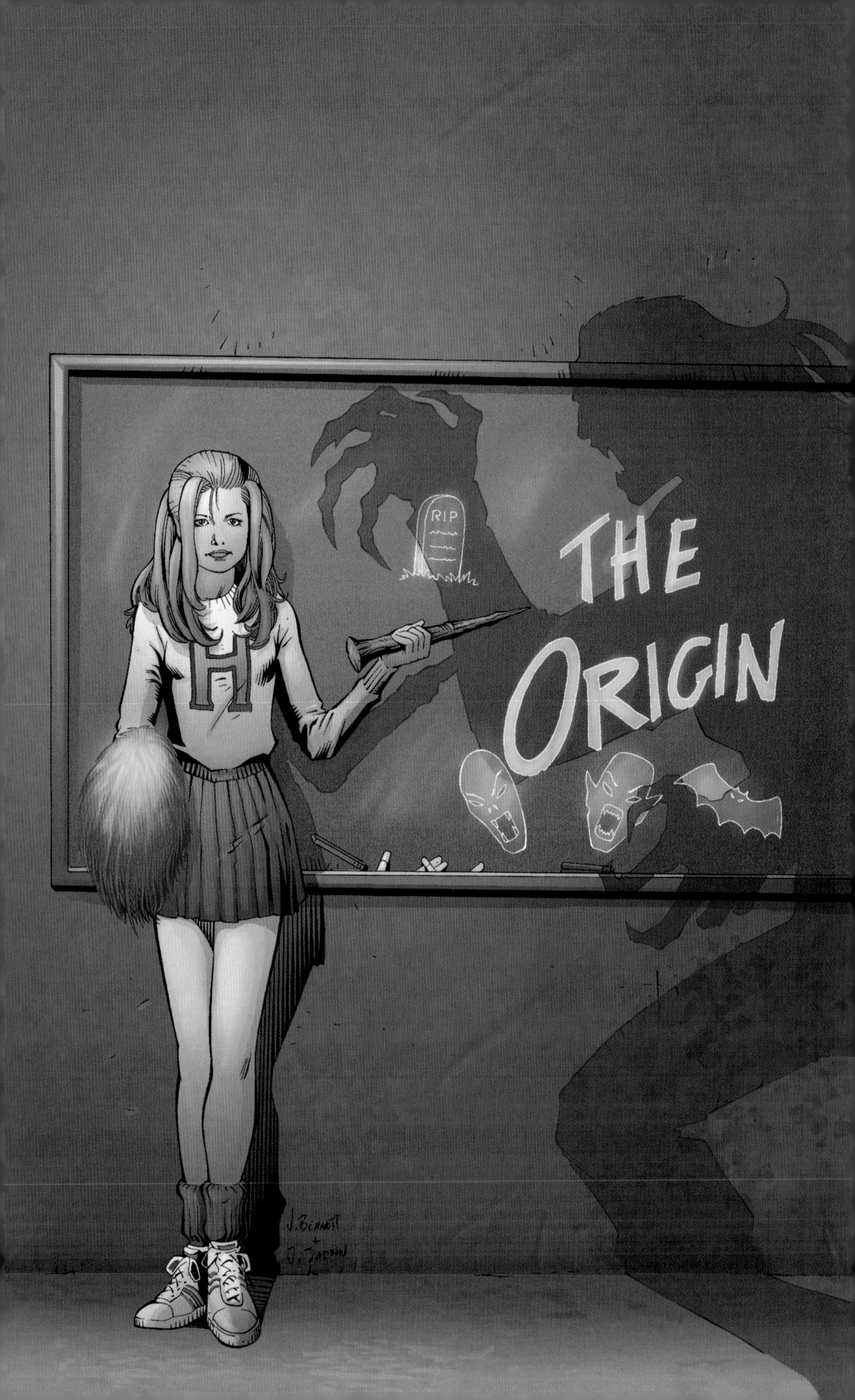
RIP
THE ORIGIN
H
J. Byrne + J. Jadson

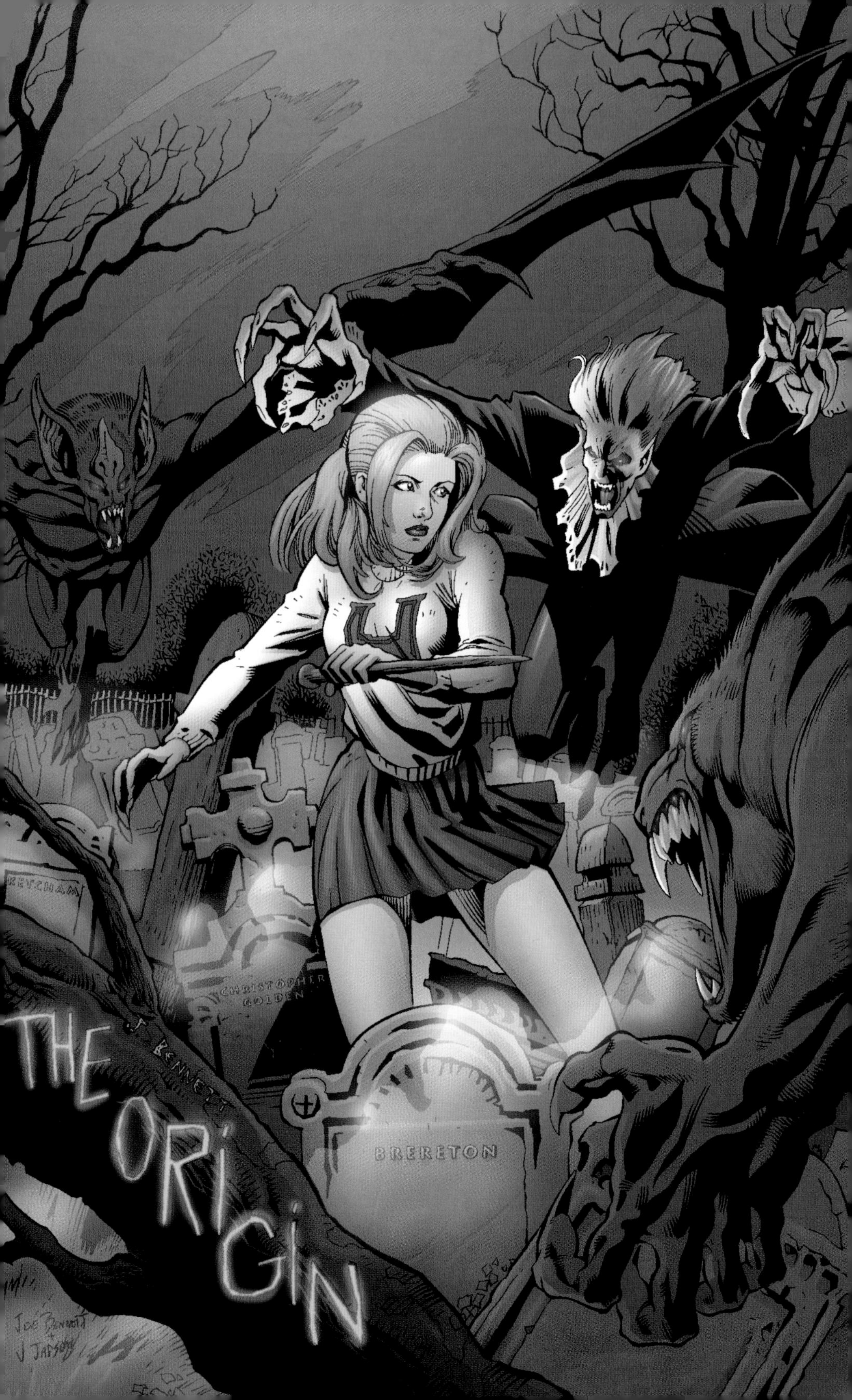
THE ORIGIN
CHRISTOPHER GOLDEN
J. BENNETT
BRERETON

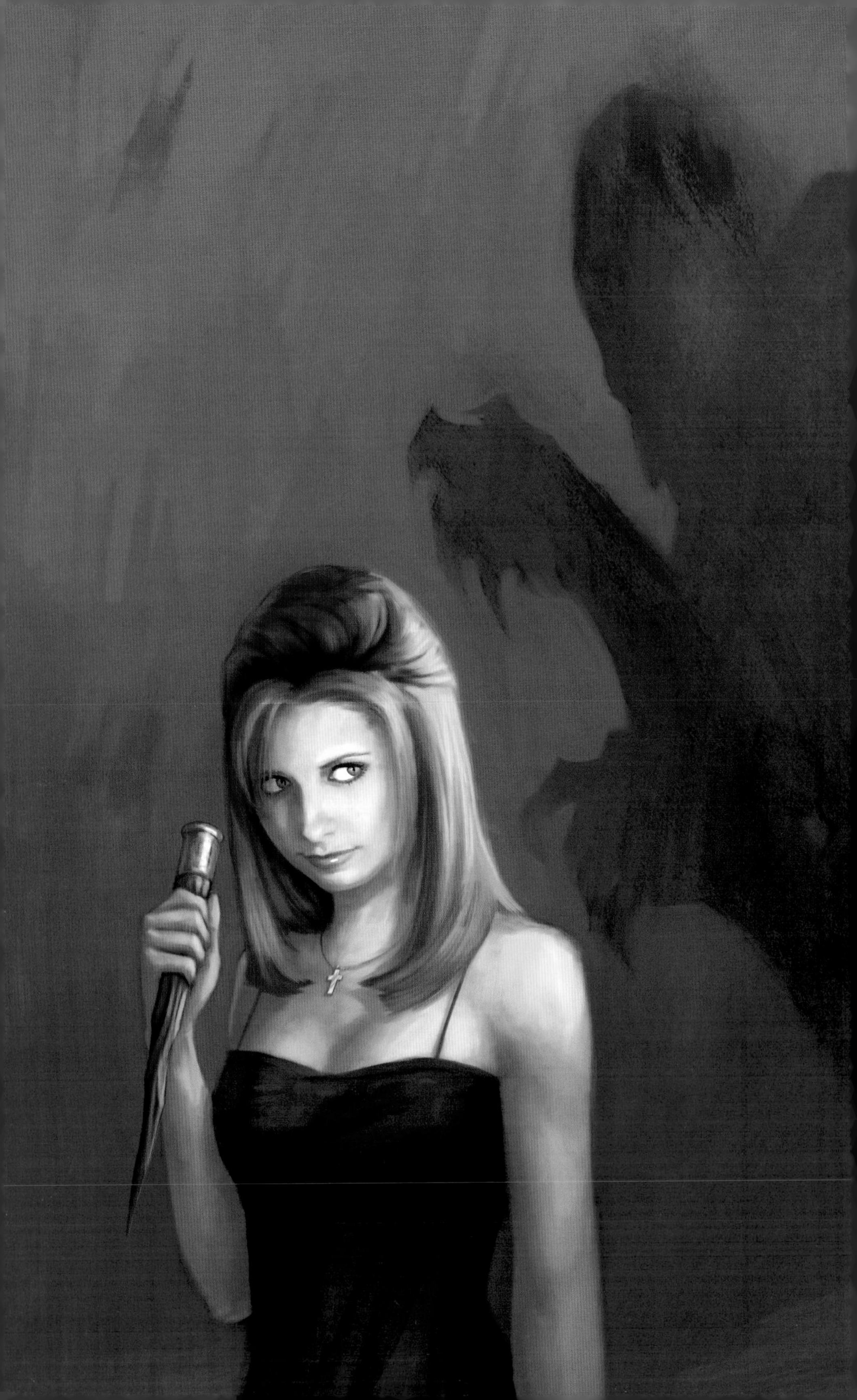

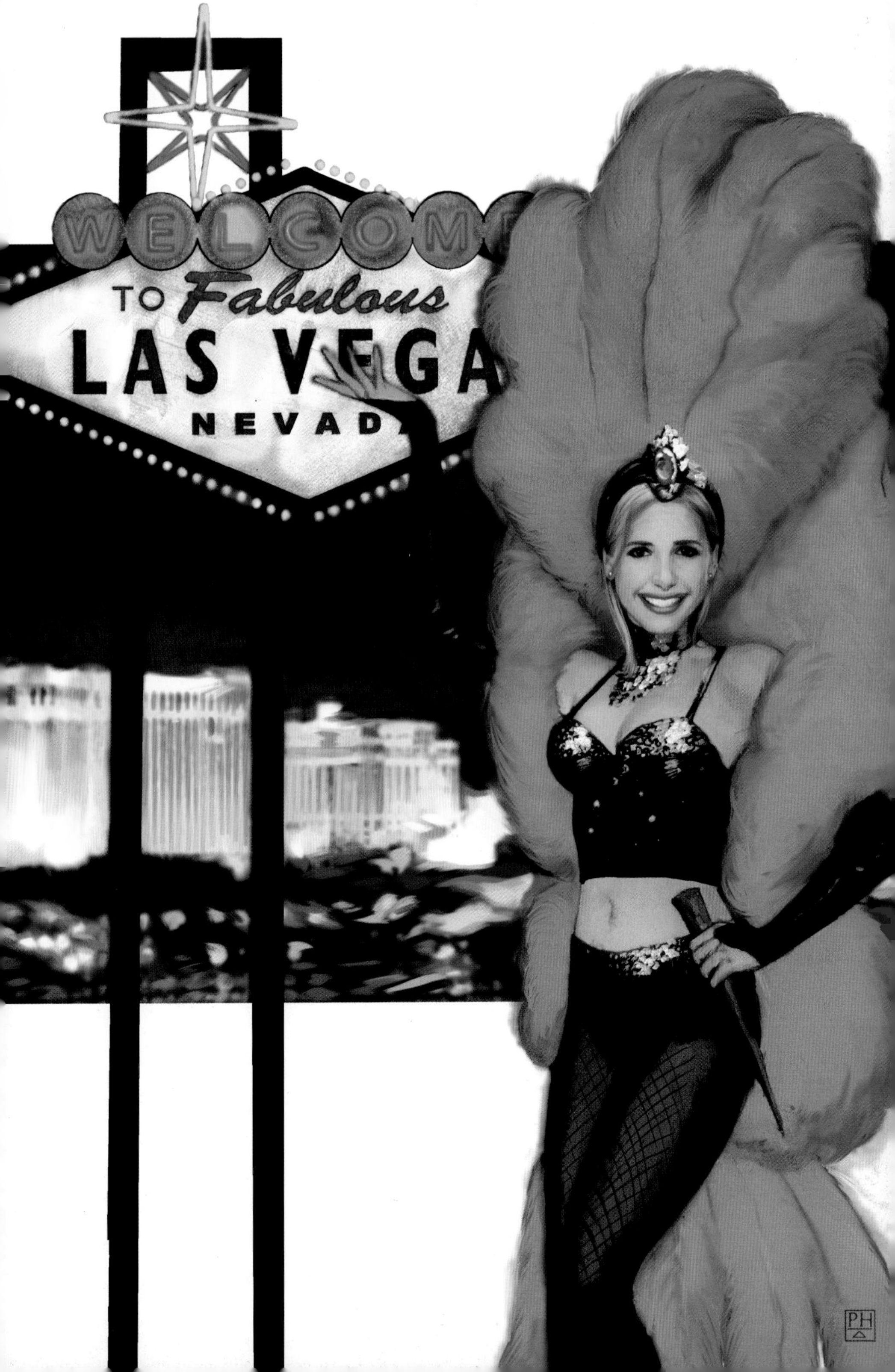
WELCOM
TO Fabulous
LAS VEGA
NEVAD

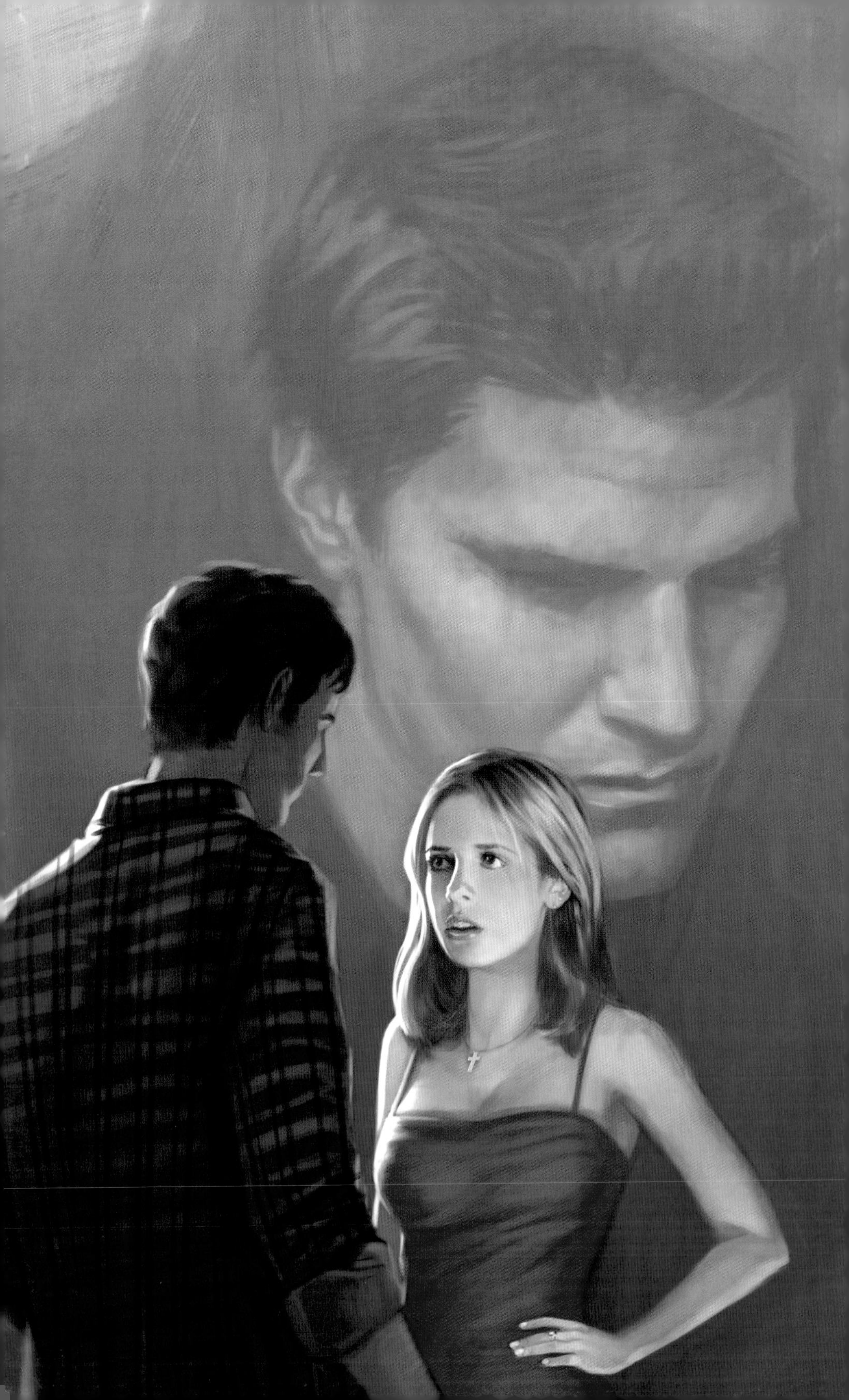

ALSO FROM JOSS WHEDON!

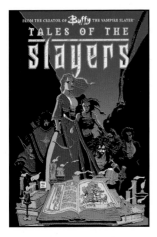

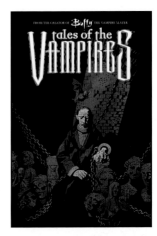

FROM THE CREATOR OF Buffy THE VAMPIRE SLAYER
TALES OF THE
slayers

BUFFY THE VAMPIRE SLAYER: TALES OF THE SLAYERS

Joss Whedon, Leinil Francis Yu, Tim Sale, Brett Matthews, and others

Buffy Summers is only the latest in a long line of women who have battled vampires, demons, and other forces of evil as the Slayer. Now, hear the stories behind other Slayers, past and future, told by the writers of the hit television show and illustrated by some of the most acclaimed artists in comics.

ISBN-10: 1-56971-605-6 / ISBN-13: 978-1-56971-605-2

$14.95

FROM THE CREATOR OF Buffy THE VAMPIRE SLAYER
tales of the
VAMPIRES

BUFFY THE VAMPIRE SLAYER: TALES OF THE VAMPIRES

Joss Whedon, Brett Matthews, Cameron Stewart, Tim Sale, and others

The creator of Buffy the Vampire Slayer reunites with the writers from his hit TV show for a frightening look into the history of vampires. Illustrated by some of comics' greatest artists, the stories span medieval times to today, including Buffy's rematch with Dracula, and Angel's ongoing battle with his own demons.

ISBN-10: 1-56971-749-4 / ISBN-13: 978-1-56971-749-3

$15.95

Buffy
the vampire slayer
creatures of habit
TOM FASSBENDER & JIM PASCOE
and BRIAN HORTON & PAUL LEE

BUFFY THE VAMPIRE SLAYER: CREATURES OF HABIT

Tom Fassbender, Jim Pascoe, Paul Lee, and Brian Horton

An old friend of Spike's is in town, and he's getting every teenager in Sunnydale to trip the light fantastic at some very special underground raves. Buffy and the Scooby gang are going out and getting down to put an end to what's become a euphoric feeding frenzy for some of the baddest baddies in town.

ISBN-10: 1-56971-563-7 / ISBN-13: 978-1-56971-563-5

$17.95

SERENITY
THOSE LEFT BEHIND
JOSS WHEDON BRETT MATTHEWS WILL CONRAD

SERENITY: THOSE LEFT BEHIND

Joss Whedon, Brett Matthews, Will Conrad, and Adam Hughes

Joss Whedon, creator of Buffy the Vampire Slayer and scribe of Marvel's *Astonishing X-Men*, unveils a previously unknown chapter in the lives of his favorite band of space brigands in this comics prequel of the *Serenity* feature film, bridging the gap from Whedon's cult-hit TV show *Firefly*.

ISBN-10: 1-59307-449-2 / ISBN-13: 978-1-59307-449-4

$9.95

AVAILABLE AT YOUR LOCAL COMICS SHOP OR BOOKSTORE! • To find a comics shop in your area, call 1-888-266-4226. For more information or to order direct visit darkhorse.com or call 1-800-862-0052 Mon.-Fri. 9 A.M. to 5 P.M. Pacific Time *Prices and availability subject to change without notice

DARK HORSE COMICS® *drawing on your nightmares*
darkhorse.com

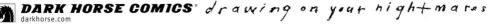

ALSO FROM DARK HORSE BOOKS!

THE GOON
NOTHIN' BUT MISERY
by Eric Powell

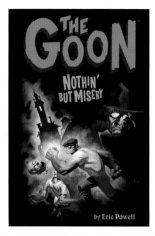

THE GOON VOLUME 1: NOTHIN' BUT MISERY
Eric Powell
The Goon is a laugh-out-loud, action-packed romp through the streets of a town infested with zombies. An insane priest is building himself an army of the undead, and there's only one man who can put them in their place: the man they call Goon.
ISBN-10: 1-56971-998-5 / ISBN-13: 978-1-56971-998-5
$15.95

BUREAU FOR PARANORMAL RESEARCH AND DEFENSE
B.P.R.D.
HOLLOW EARTH & OTHER STORIES
MIKE MIGNOLA
CHRISTOPHER GOLDEN
TOM SNIEGOSKI
RYAN SOOK
CURTIS ARNOLD
BRIAN McDONALD
DEREK THOMPSON
MATT SMITH

B.P.R.D.: HOLLOW EARTH & OTHER STORIES
Mike Mignola, Chris Golden, Tom Sniegoski, and Ryan Sook
From the pages of Mike Mignola's award-winning *Hellboy* come the further adventures of the Bureau for Paranormal Research and Defense. This volume also contains the first solo Abe Sapien comic, *Drums of the Dead* and two previously uncollected short stories.
ISBN-10: 1-56971-862-8 / ISBN-13: 978-1-56971-862-9
$17.95

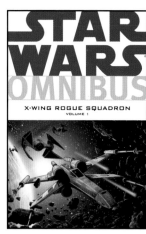

the
BLACKBURNE
COVENANT
fabian
NICIEZA
stefano
RAFFAELE

THE BLACKBURNE COVENANT
Fabian Nicieza and Stefano Raffaele
Someone is following popular fantasy novelist Richard Kaine. Not a demented fan, not a jilted lover, but someone interested in finding out how Richard came up with his runaway bestselling novel. Because, unbeknownst to Richard, his "fantasy" novel was non-fiction.
ISBN-10: 1-56971-889-X / ISBN-13: 978-1-56971-889-6
$12.95

STAR
WARS
OMNIBUS
X-WING ROGUE SQUADRON
VOLUME 1

STAR WARS: OMNIBUS X-WING SQUADRON VOLUME 1
Meet the Rogues for the first time and learn the fate of the galaxy immediately after the events of *Return of the Jedi* as the Rebellion's best pilots battle remnants of the Empire wherever its ugly agenda of fear and domination appears. Along with the critically acclaimed *X-Wing Rogue Squadron: The Phantom Affair* this jam-packed volume contains tons of material never before collected!
ISBN-10: 1-59307-572-3 / ISBN-13: 978-1-59307-572-9
$24.95

AVAILABLE AT YOUR LOCAL COMICS SHOP OR BOOKSTORE! • To find a comics shop in your area, call 1-888-266-4226. For more information or to order direct visit darkhorse.com or call 1-800-862-0052 Mon.-Fri. 9 A.M. to 5 P.M. Pacific Time *Prices and availability subject to change without notice

DARK HORSE COMICS® *drawing on your nightmares*
darkhorse.com